# THE LYLE OFFICIAL ANTIQUES REVIEW 1992

# THE LYLE OFFICIAL ANTIQUES REVIEW 1992

A PERIGEE BOOK

Perigee Books
are published by
The Putnam Publishing Group
200 Madison Avenue
New York, NY 10016

Copyright © 1991 by Lyle Publications
All rights reserved. This book, or parts thereof,
may not be reproduced in any form without permission.
Published simultaneously in Canada

ISBN 0-399-51694-8
LC 74-640592

Cover design by Jack Ribik

Printed in the United States of America
2 3 4 5 6 7 8 9 10

This book is printed on acid-free paper.

# Introduction

This year over 100,000 Antique Dealers and Collectors will make full and profitable use of their Lyle Official Antiques Review. They know that only in this one volume will they find the widest possible variety of goods – illustrated, described and given a current market value to assist them to BUY RIGHT AND SELL RIGHT throughout the year of issue.

They know, too, that by building a collection of these immensely valuable volumes year by year, they will equip themselves with an unparalleled reference library of facts, figures and illustrations which, properly used, cannot fail to help them keep one step ahead of the market.

In its twenty two years of publication, Lyle has gone from strength to strength and has become without doubt the pre-eminent book of reference for the antique trade throughout the world. Each of its fact filled pages are packed with precisely the kind of profitable information the professional Dealer needs – including descriptions, illustrations and values of thousands and thousands of individual items carefully selected to give a representative picture of the current market in antiques and collectibles – and remember all values are prices actually paid, based on accurate sales records in the twelve months prior to publication from the best established and most highly respected auction houses and retail outlets in Europe and America.

This is THE book for the Professional Antiques Dealer. 'The Lyle Book' – we've even heard it called 'The Dealer's Bible'.

Compiled and published afresh each year, the Lyle Official Antiques Review is the most comprehensive up-to-date antiques price guide available. THIS COULD BE YOUR WISEST INVESTMENT OF THE YEAR!

**ANTHONY CURTIS**

The publishers wish to express their sincere thanks to the following for their involvement and assistance in the production of this volume:

EELIN McIVOR (Sub Editor)
NICKY FAIRBURN (Art Director)
ANNETTE CURTIS (Editorial)
CATRIONA DAY (Art Production)
KATE SMITH (Art Production)
FRANK BURRELL (Graphics)
DONNA BONAR
JACQUELINE LEDDY
JAMES BROWN
EILEEN BURRELL
FIONA RUNCIMAN
RICHARD SCOTT
DONNA CRUIKSHANK

While every care has been taken in the compiling of information contained in this volume, the publishers cannot accept any liability for loss, financial or otherwise, incurred by reliance placed on the information herein.

All prices quoted in this book are obtained from a variety of auctions in various countries during the twelve months prior to publication and are converted to dollars at the rate of exchange prevalent at the time of sale.

# CONTENTS


Antiques Review ..... 15
Advertising ..... 16
Aeronautical Items ..... 20
American Comics ..... 22
Amusement Machines ..... 24
Antiquities ..... 26
Architectural Fittings ..... 28
Arms & Armor ..... 30
- Cased Sets ..... 32
- Daggers ..... 34
- Helmets ..... 36
- Pistols ..... 40
- Powder Flasks ..... 42
- Rifles & Guns ..... 44
- Swords ..... 46
- Tsubas ..... 48

Autographed Documents ..... 50
Autographs ..... 54
Automatons ..... 60
Barometers ..... 62
Books ..... 64
Bronze ..... 68
Buckets ..... 76
Caddies & Boxes ..... 77
Cameras ..... 84
Cane Handles ..... 90
Car Mascots ..... 92
Carousel Figures ..... 94
Chandeliers ..... 96
China ..... 98
- American ..... 98
- Arita ..... 102
- Belleek ..... 103
- Berlin ..... 103
- Bow ..... 105
- British ..... 106
- Chelsea ..... 111
- Chinese ..... 114
- Clarice Cliff ..... 118
- Commemorative ..... 120
- Coper ..... 123
- Creamware ..... 124
- Delft ..... 124
- Derby ..... 130
- Doucai ..... 132
- Doulton ..... 133
- European ..... 137
- Famille Rose ..... 140
- Foley ..... 141
- French ..... 142
- German ..... 146
- Goldscheider ..... 149
- Hamada ..... 150
- Henderson ..... 150
- Hispano Moresque ..... 151
- Höchst ..... 151
- Imari ..... 152
- Italian ..... 154
- Kakiemon ..... 158
- Kangxi ..... 159
- Kutani ..... 160
- Korean ..... 160
- Leach ..... 161
- Leeds Creamware ..... 162
- Lenci ..... 162
- Linthorpe ..... 162
- Liverpool Creamware ..... 164
- Lowestoft ..... 164
- Longton Hall ..... 165
- Lucie Rie ..... 166
- Luster ..... 167
- Martinware ..... 167
- Meissen ..... 169
- Minton ..... 174
- Moorcroft ..... 176
- Nantgarw ..... 178
- Nymphenburg ..... 178
- Pearlware ..... 178
- Poole ..... 180
- Prattware ..... 182
- Rockingham ..... 182
- Rookwood ..... 183
- Royal Dux ..... 184
- Ruskin ..... 185
- Satsuma ..... 186
- Sevres ..... 188
- Spode ..... 191
- Staffordshire ..... 192
- Venice ..... 196
- Vincennes ..... 196
- Vienna ..... 197
- Wedgwood ..... 198
- Wemyss ..... 201
- Westerwald ..... 202
- Whieldon ..... 203
- Wood ..... 203
- Worcester ..... 204

Clock & Watches ..... 208

Bracket Clocks ..... 208
Carriage Clocks ..... 210
Clock Sets ..... 212
Lantern Clocks ..... 215
Longcase Clocks ..... 216
Mantel Clocks ..... 220
Skeleton Clocks ..... 228
Wall Clocks ..... 230
Watches ..... 232
Wrist Watches ..... 234
Cloisonne ..... 236
Copper & Brass ..... 238
Corkscrews ..... 242
Costume ..... 243
Disneyana ..... 246
Dolls ..... 248
Domestic Equipment ..... 254
Enamel ..... 256
Fans ..... 258
Film Memorabilia ..... 260
Film Star Photographs ..... 261
Firegrates ..... 266
Fireplace Furniture ..... 267
Fireplaces ..... 268
Fountain Pens ..... 270
Furniture ..... 272
Beds & Cradles ..... 272
Bookcases ..... 274
Bureau Bookcases ..... 276
Bureaux ..... 278
Cabinets ..... 282
Canterburys ..... 286
Chairs, Dining ..... 287
Easy Chairs ..... 292
Elbow Chairs ..... 298
Chests of Drawers ..... 302
Chests on Chests ..... 306
Chests on Stands ..... 308
Chiffoniers ..... 309
Commodes & Pot Cupboards ..... 310
Commode Chests ..... 311
Corner Cupboards ..... 314
Cupboards ..... 316
Davenports ..... 318
Display Cabinets ..... 320
Dressers ..... 322
Kneehole Desks ..... 324
Linen Presses ..... 326
Lowboys ..... 327
Screens ..... 328
Secretaire Bookcases ..... 330
Secretaires ..... 332
Settees & Couches ..... 334
Sideboards ..... 338
Stands ..... 340
Stools ..... 342
Suites ..... 346
Tables ..... 350
Card & Tea Tables ..... 350
Center Tables ..... 354
Console Tables ..... 356
Dining Tables ..... 358
Dressing Tables ..... 360
Drop Leaf Tables ..... 362
Gateleg Tables ..... 364
Large Tables ..... 366
Occasional Tables ..... 368
Pembroke Tables ..... 372
Side Tables ..... 374
Sofa Tables ..... 376
Workboxes & Games Tables ..... 378
Writing Tables & Desks ..... 382
Trunks & Coffers ..... 386
Wardrobes & Armoires ..... 390
Washstands ..... 392
Whatnots ..... 393
Wine Coolers ..... 394
Garden Statuary & Furniture ..... 396
Glass ..... 400
Beakers ..... 400
Bottles ..... 401
Bowls ..... 405
Candlesticks ..... 410
Candy Containers ..... 411
Decanters ..... 412
Dishes ..... 414
Drinking Sets ..... 415
Figures ..... 416
Flasks ..... 417
Goblets ..... 418
Jars ..... 420
Jugs & Pitchers ..... 421
Miscellaneous Glass ..... 422
Paperweights ..... 424
Scent Bottles ..... 426
Shades ..... 428
Tankards ..... 429
Tantalus ..... 429
Vases ..... 430
Wine Glasses ..... 435

Gold ..... 438
Golfing Items ..... 440
Hollywood Posters ..... 444
Icons ..... 448
Inros ..... 450
Instruments ..... 452
Iron & Steel ..... 458
Ivory ..... 462
Jade ..... 466
Jewelry ..... 468
Lacquer ..... 472
Lamps ..... 474
Marble & Alabaster ..... 478
Mechanical Music ..... 482
Mirrors ..... 486
Model Ships ..... 490
Model Trains ..... 492
Models ..... 494
Motor Vehicles ..... 496
Motoring Items ..... 502
Musical Instruments ..... 506
Netsuke ..... 510
Optical Instruments ..... 512
Paper Money ..... 514
Papier Mâché ..... 520
Pewter ..... 522
Photographs ..... 524
Pianos ..... 530
Picture Frames ..... 532
Pipes ..... 534
Portrait Miniatures ..... 536
Prints ..... 540
Quilts ..... 544
Radios ..... 548
Robots ..... 549
Rock 'n' Roll ..... 550
Rugs ..... 556
Samplers ..... 560
Sewing Machines ..... 562
Share Certificates ..... 563
Shibayama ..... 566
Signed Photographs ..... 567
Silhouettes ..... 572
Silver ..... 573
- Argyles ..... 573
- Basins ..... 573
- Baskets ..... 573
- Beakers ..... 576
- Bowls ..... 577
- Boxes ..... 580
- Candelabra ..... 581
- Candlesticks ..... 582
- Casters ..... 584
- Centerpieces ..... 585
- Chambersticks ..... 586
- Chocolate Pots ..... 587
- Cigarette Cases ..... 587
- Claret Jugs ..... 588
- Coasters ..... 590
- Coffee Pots ..... 591
- Cream Jugs ..... 594
- Cruets ..... 595
- Cups ..... 596
- Dishes ..... 598
- Flatware ..... 600
- Frames ..... 602
- Goblets ..... 603
- Inkstands ..... 604
- Jugs ..... 605
- Miscellaneous Silver ..... 607
- Mugs ..... 612
- Mustards ..... 614
- Pitchers & Ewers ..... 616
- Porringers ..... 617
- Salts & Peppers ..... 618
- Sauceboats ..... 619
- Tankards ..... 620
- Tea & Coffee Sets ..... 621
- Tea Caddies ..... 622
- Tea Kettles ..... 623
- Teapots ..... 624
- Toast Racks ..... 627
- Trays & Salvers ..... 628
- Tureens ..... 629
- Urns ..... 630
- Vases ..... 631
- Vesta Cases ..... 632
- Vinaigrettes ..... 632
- Warmers ..... 634
- Wine Coolers ..... 634
- Wine Funnels ..... 634

Snuff Bottles ..... 635
Snuff Boxes ..... 636
Tapestries ..... 638
Teddy Bears ..... 640
Textiles ..... 642
Toys ..... 644
Travel Requisites ..... 654
Weathervanes ..... 656
Wood ..... 658

# Acknowledgements

AB Stockholms Auktionsverk, Box 16256, 103 25 Stockholm, Sweden
Abbots Auction Rooms, The Auction Rooms, Campsea Ash, Woodbridge, Suffolk
Abridge Auction Rooms, Market Place, Abridge, Essex RM4 1UA
Allen & Harris, St Johns Place, Whiteladies Road, Clifton, Bristol BS8 2ST
Jean Claude Anaf, Lyon Brotteaux, 13 bis place Jules Ferry, 69456 Lyon, France
Anderson & Garland, Marlborough House, Marlborough Crescent, Newcastle upon Tyne NE1 4EE
Antique Collectors Club & Co. Ltd, 5 Church Street, Woodbridge, Suffolk IP 12 1DS
Auction Team Köln, Postfach 50 11 68, D-5000 Köln 50 Germany
Auktionshause Arnold, Bleichstr. 42, 6000 Frankfurt a/M, Germany
Barber's Auctions, Woking, Surrey
Bearnes, Rainbow, Avenue Road, Torquay TQ2 5TG
Biddle & Webb, Ladywood Middleway, Birmingham B16 0PP
Bigwood, The Old School, Tiddington, Stratford upon Avon
Black Horse Agencies, Locke & England, 18 Guy Street, Leamington Spa
Boardman Fine Art Auctioneers, Station Road Corner, Haverhill, Suffolk CB9 0EY
Bonhams, Montpelier Street, Knightsbridge, London SW7 1HH
Bonhams Chelsea, 65–69 Lots Road, London SW10 0RN
Bonhams West Country, Dowell Street, Honiton, Devon
British Antique Exporters, School Close, Queen Elizabeth Avenue, Burgess Hill, Sussex
William H Brown, The Warner Auction Rooms, 16–18, Halford Street, Leicester LE1 1JB
Butterfield & Butterfield, 220 San Bruno Avenue, San Francisco CA 94103, USA
Butterfield & Butterfield, 7601 Sunset Boulevard, Los Angeles CA 90046, USA
Central Motor Auctions, Barfield House, Britannia Road, Morley, Leeds, LS27 0HN
H.C. Chapman & Son, The Auction Mart, North Street, Scarborough.
Christie's (International) SA, 8 place de la Taconnerie, 1204 Genève, Switzerland
Christie's Monaco, S.A.M, Park Palace 98000 Monte Carlo, Monaco
Christie's Scotland, 164–166 Bath Street Glasgow G2 4TG
Christie's South Kensington Ltd., 85 Old Brompton Road, London SW7 3LD
Christie's, 8 King Street, London SW1Y 6QT
Christie's East, 219 East 67th Street, New York, NY 10021, USA
Christie's, 502 Park Avenue, New York, NY 10022, USA
Christie's, Cornelis Schuytstraat 57, 1071 JG Amsterdam, Netherlands
Christie's SA Roma, 114 Piazza Navona, 00186 Rome, Italy
Christie's Swire, 1202 Alexandra House, 16–20 Chater Road, Hong Kong
Christie's Australia Pty Ltd., 1 Darling Street, South Yarra, Melbourne, Victoria 3141, Australia
A J Cobern, The Grosvenor Sales Rooms, 93b Eastbank Street, Southport PR8 1DG
Cooper Hirst Auctions, The Granary Saleroom, Victoria Road, Chelmsford, Essex CM2 6LH
Nic Costa/Brian Bates, 10 Madely Street, Tunstall
The Crested China Co., Station House, Driffield, E. Yorks YO25 7PY
Clifford Dann, 20/21 High Street, Lewes, Sussex
Julian Dawson, Lewes Auction Rooms, 56 High Street, Lewes BN7 1XE
Dee & Atkinson, The Exchange Saleroom, Driffield, Nth Humberside YO25 7LJ
Diamond Mills & Co., 117 Hamilton Road, Felixstowe, Suffolk
Dowell Lloyd & Co. Ltd, 118 Putney Bridge Road, London SW15 2NQ
Downer Ross, Charter House, 42 Avebury Boulevard, Central Milton Keynes MK9 2HS
Hy. Duke & Son, 40 South Street, Dorchester, Dorset
Du Mouchelles Art Galleries Co., 409 E. Jefferson Avenue, Detroit, Michigan 48226, USA
Duncan Vincent, 105 London Street, Reading RG1 4LF
Sala de Artes y Subastas Durán, Serrano 12, 28001 Madrid, Spain
Eldred's, Box 796, E. Dennis, MA 02641, USA
Ewbanks, Welbeck House, High Street, Guildford, Surrey, GU1 3JF
Fellows & Son, Augusta House, 19 Augusta Street, Hockley, Birmingham
Finarte, 20121 Milano, Piazzetta Bossi 4, Italy
John D Fleming & Co., 8 Fore Street, Dulverton, Somerset
G A Property Services, Canterbury Auction Galleries, Canterbury, Kent
Galerie Koller, Rämistr. 8, CH 8024 Zürich, Switzerland
Galerie Moderne, 3 rue du Parnasse, 1040 Bruxelles, Belgium
Geering & Colyer (Black Horse Agencies) Highgate, Hawkhurst, Kent
Glerum Auctioneers, Westeinde 12, 2512 HD's Gravenhage, Netherlands
The Goss and Crested China Co., 62 Murray Road, Horndean, Hants PO8 9JL
Graves Son & Pilcher, 71 Church Road, Hove, East Sussex, BN3 2GL
W R J Greenslade & Co., 13 Hammet Street, Taunton, Somerset, TA1 1RN
Peter Günnemann, Ehrenberg Str. 57, 2000 Hamburg 50, Germany
Halifax Property Services, 53 High Street, Tenterden, Kent
Halifax Property Services, 15 Cattle Market, Sandwich, Kent CT13 9AW
Hampton's Fine Art, 93 High Street, Godalming, Surrey
Hanseatisches Auktionshaus für Historica, Neuer Wall 57, 2000 Hamburg 36, Germany
Andrew Hartley Fine Arts, Victoria Hall, Little Lane, Ilkely

Hauswedell & Nolte, D-2000 Hamburg 13, Pöseldorfer Weg 1, Germany
Giles Haywood, The Auction House, St John's Road, Stourbridge, West Midlands, DY8 1EW
Heatheringtons Nationwide Anglia, The Amersham Auction Rooms, 125 Station Road, Amersham, Bucks
Muir Hewitt, Halifax Antiques Centre, Queens Road/Gibbet Street, Halifax HX1 4LR
Hobbs & Chambers, 'At the Sign of the Bell', Market Place, Cirencester, Glos
Hobbs Parker, Romney House, Ashford, Ashford, Kent
Hotel de Ventes Horta, 390 Chaussée de Waterloo (Ma Campagne), 1060 Bruxelles, Belgium
Jacobs & Hunt, Lavant Street, Petersfield, Hants. GU33 3EF
James of Norwich, 33 Timberhill, Norwich NR1 3LA
P Herholdt Jensens Auktioner, Rundforbivej 188, 2850 Nerum, Denmark
G A Key, Aylsham Saleroom, Palmers Lane, Aylsham, Norfolk, NR11 6EH
Kunsthaus am Museum, Drususgasse 1–5, 5000 Köln 1, Germany
Kunsthaus Lempertz, Neumarkt 3, 5000 Köln 1, Germany
Lambert & Foster (County Group), The Auction Sales Room, 102 High Street, Tenterden, Kent
W.H. Lane & Son, 64 Morrab Road, Penzance, Cornwall, TR18 2QT
Langlois Ltd., Westway Rooms, Don Street, St Helier, Channel Islands
Lawrence Butler Fine Art Salerooms, Marine Walk, Hythe, Kent, CT21 5AJ
Lawrence Fine Art, South Street, Crewkerne, Somerset TA18 8AB
Lawrence's Fine Art Auctioneers, Norfolk House, 80 High Street, Bletchingley, Surrey
David Lay, The Penzance Auction House, Alverton, Penzance, Cornwall TA18 4KE
Brian Loomes, Calf Haugh Farm, Pateley Bridge, North Yorks
Lots Road Chelsea Auction Galleries, 71 Lots Road, Chelsea, London SW10 0RN
R K Lucas & Son, Tithe Exchange, 9 Victoria Place, Haverfordwest, SA61 2JX
Duncan McAlpine, Stateside Comics plc, 125 East Barnet Road, London EN4 8RF
John Maxwell, 75 Hawthorn Street, Wilmslow, Cheshire
May & Son, 18 Bridge Street, Andover, Hants
Morphets, 4–6 Albert Street, Harrogate, North Yorks HG1 1JL
D M Nesbit & Co, 7 Clarendon Road, Southsea, Hants PO5 2ED
Onslow's, Metrostore, Townmead Road, London SW6 2RZ
Outhwaite & Litherland, Kingsley Galleries, Fontenoy Street, Liverpool, Merseyside L3 2BE
J R Parkinson Son & Hamer Auctions, The Auction Rooms, Rochdale, Bury, Lancs
Phillips Manchester, Trinity House, 114 Northenden Road, Sale, Manchester M33 3HD
Phillips Son & Neale SA, 10 rue des Chaudronniers, 1204 Genève, Switzerland
Phillips West Two, 10 Salem Road, London W2 4BL
Phillips, 11 Bayle Parade, Folkestone, Kent CT20 1SQ
Phillips, 49 London Road, Sevenoaks, Kent TN13 1UU
Phillips, 65 George Street, Edinburgh EH2 2JL
Phillips, Blenstock House, 7 Blenheim Street, New Bond Street, London W1Y 0AS
Phillips Marylebone, Hayes Place, Lisson Grove, London NW1 6UA
Phillips, New House, 150 Christleton Road, Chester CH3 5TD
Pinney's, 5627 Ferrier, Montreal, Quebec, Canada H4P 2M4
Pooley & Rogers, Regent Auction Rooms, Abbey Street, Penzance
Rennie's, 1 Agincourt Street, Monmouth
Riddetts, Richmond Hill, Bournemouth
Ritchie's, 429 Richmond Street East, Toronto, Canada M5A 1R1
Derek Roberts Antiques, 24–25 Shipbourne Road, Tonbridge, Kent TN10 3DN
Rogers de Rin, 79 Royal Hospital Road, London SW3 4HN
Russell, Baldwin & Bright, The Fine Art Saleroom, Ryelands Road, Leominster HR6 8JG
Sandoes Nationwide Anglia, Tabernacle Road, Wotton under Edge, Glos GL12 7EB
Schrager Auction Galleries, 2915 North Sherman Boulevard, Milwaukee, WI 53210, USA.
Selkirk's, 4166 Olive Street, St Louis, Missouri 63108, USA
Skinner Inc., Bolton Gallery, Route 117, Bolton MA, USA
Southgate Auction Rooms, Munro House, Cline Road, New Southgate, London N11.
Henry Spencer, 40 The Square, Retford, Notts. DN22 6DJ
G E Sworder & Son, Northgate End Salerooms, 15 Northgate End, Bishop Stortford, Herts
Taviner's of Bristol, Prewett Street, Redcliffe, Bristol BS1 6PB
Tennants, 27 Market Place, Leyburn, Yorkshire
Thomson Roddick & Laurie, 24 Lowther Street, Carlisle
Thomson Roddick & Laurie, 60 Whitesands, Dumfries
Venator & Hanstein, Cäcilienstr. 48, 5000 Köln 1, Germany
T Vennett Smith, 11 Nottingham Road, Gotham, Nottingham NG11 0HE
Duncan Vincent, 105 London Road, Reading RG1 4LF
Wallis & Wallis, West Street Auction Galleries, West Street, Lewes, E. Sussex BN7 2NJ
Ward & Morris, Stuart House, 18 Gloucester Road, Ross on Wye HR9 5BN
Warren & Wignall Ltd, The Mill, Earnshaw Bridge, Leyland Lane, Leyland PR5 3PH
Dominique Watine-Arnault, 11 rue François 1er, 75008 Paris, France
Wells Cundall Nationwide Anglia, Staffordshire House, 27 Flowergate, Whitby YO21 3AX
Woltons, 6 Whiting Street, Bury St Edmunds, Suffolk IP33 1PB
Woolley & Wallis, The Castle Auction Mart, Salisbury, Wilts SP1 3SU
Austin Wyatt Nationwide Anglia, Emsworth Road, Lymington, Hants SO41 9BL
Yesterday Child, 118 Islington High Street, London N11 8EG

# ANTIQUES REVIEW 1992

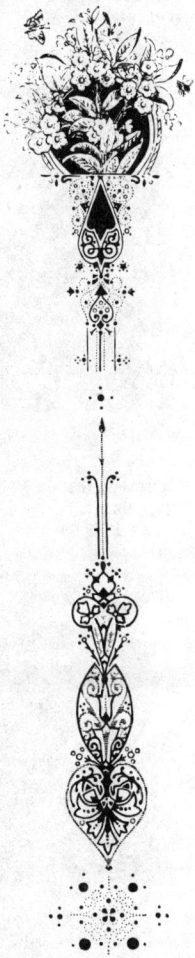

THE Lyle Official Antiques Review is compiled and published with completely fresh information annually, enabling you to begin each new year with an up-to-date knowledge of the current trends, together with the verified values of antiques of all descriptions.

We have endeavoured to obtain a balance between the more expensive collector's items and those which, although not in their true sense antiques, are handled daily by the antiques trade.

The illustrations and prices in the following sections have been arranged to make it easy for the reader to assess the period and value of all items with speed.

You will find illustrations for almost every category of antique and curio, together with a corresponding price collated during the last twelve months, from the auction rooms and retail outlets of the major trading countries.

When dealing with the more popular trade pieces, in some instances, a calculation of an average price has been estimated from the varying accounts researched.

As regards prices, when 'one of a pair' is given in the description the price quoted is for a pair and so that we can make maximum use of the available space it is generally considered that one illustration is sufficient.

It will be noted that in some descriptions taken directly from sales catalogues originating from many different countries, terms such as bureau, secretary and davenport are used in a broader sense than is customary, but in all cases the term used is self explanatory.

Lovely Day For A Guinness by John Gilroy.
(Onslow's) $155

A Foley rectangular pottery advertising plaque, the central reserve depicting a potter and a classical maiden carrying a pitcher of water, 10in. wide.
(Christie's S. Ken) $1,399

Elastic Sportszalag, published by Athenaeum, double royal.
(Onslow's) $82

Drink Taylors', Hop Bitters & Stout, It is the best, 30 x 20in.
(Street Jewellery) $350

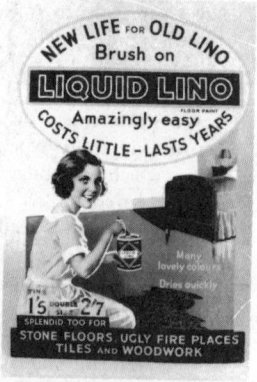


1930's Liquid Lino counter display card with folding stand, 15in. x 25in.
(Bermondsey) $40

There's no tea like Phillips's, 40 x 30in.
(Street Jewellery) $600

A rare plaque by T.J. and J. Mayer, Longport, bearing: Huntley and Palmer, A view of the Factory and inscribed *Huntley and Palmers, Superior Reading Biscuits.*
(Phillips) $3,000

An opaque blue glass petrol pump head, lettered *Super Shell*, 17in. high.
(Christie's) $425

An enamel 'Mitchell's "Maid of Honour"' sign, 25½ x 19in.
(Christie's S. Ken) $1,027

Goodyear, double sided shaped pictorial enamel sign, 87 x 56cm.
(Onslow's) $323

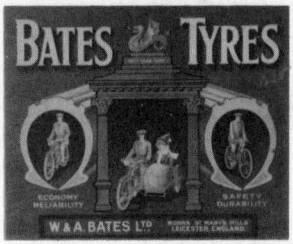


Bates Tyres Leicester, showcard, 48 x 61cm., framed.
(Onslow's) $606

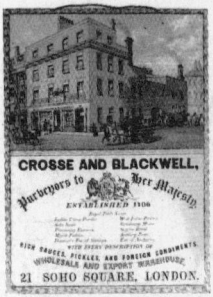


Crosse and Blackwell's advertising plaque, 24.5 x 33cm., blue and white foliate border, restoration to one corner.
(Phillips) $2,200

Wakefield Castrol XXL Revels In Revs, printed tin advertisement, 48 x 34cm.
(Onslow's) $849

Matchless Metal Polish enamel sign, 30 x 24in.
(Street Jewellery) $500

Marfia Kalap Minden Minosegben poster, published by Athenaeum, double royal.
(Onslow's) $164

Will's Star Cigarettes, laminated showcard of Raymond Mays at Brooklands, 48 x 37cm.
(Onslow's) $1,408

Chivers' Jellies 'They always turn out well', a standing cardboard cutout, height 19in.
(David Lay) $460

1930's Valspar enamels and varnish hanging display card, 14in. x 19in.
(Bermondsey) $40

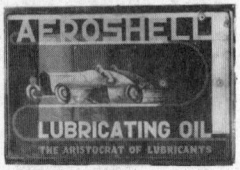


Aero Shell Lubricating Oil The Aristocrat of Lubricants, by E McKnight Kauffer, printed tin advertisement, 1932, 48 x 74cm.
(Onslow's) $1,292

'Shell Lubricating Oils', shaped double sided pictorial enamel, 52 x 61cm.
(Onslow's) $352

A novel late Victorian vesta case designed as an advertisement, of rounded oblong form, decorated in polychrome enamel with an oval cartouche, maker's mark *WJD*, Birmingham, 1894.
(Phillips) $563

Ex-Lax, Chocolate Laxative enamel sign, 34 x 8in.
(Street Jewellery) $150

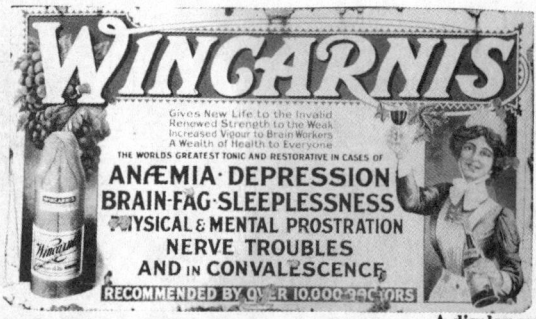


Wincarnis, Recommended by over 10,000 Doctors, 36 x 60in.
(Street Jewellery) $500

A display case containing various boiler and other fittings, formerly offered by Steam Age, including main stop and bypass valves, 39½ x 19½in.
(Christie's S. Ken) $576

Walnut cabinet used for the display and storage of fabric dyes, the polychrome decorated door inscribed *It's easy to dye with Diamond Dyes*, 23in. wide.
(Eldred's) $385

Fry's Homoeopathic Cocoa, a large cardboard simulated tin, 20in. high.
(David Lay) $336

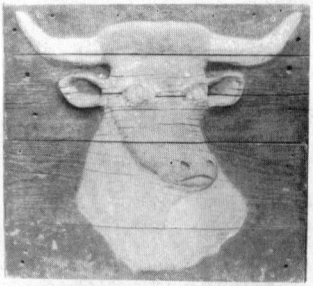

Important carved wood trade sign, in the form of a bull's head with antique swirl glass marble eyes, carved by John Bent, Edgartown, Massachusetts, 35¾in. x 40in.
(Eldred's) $4,675

Carr & Co's Carlisle Biscuits, an Edwardian shop window display box, 9in. long.
(David Lay) $115

A rare enamel advertising sign for Fremlins Ale, in the shape of an elephant, 18 x 23in.
(Christie's S. Ken) $471

Coca Cola advertising poster, cardboard, 25 x 55in., depicting woman with soldier.
(Du Mouchelles) $250

Oxo, The Great Beef Beverage, a three dimensional cardboard cut out of a seated girl, 17in. high.
(David Lay) $460

Two Fry's Chocolate advertising display stands, each of tin, shaped as three imitation Crunchie bars on a plate, 9in. high.
(Christie's S. Ken) $364

Antique advertising sign in the form of a boot, painted black and inscribed *J.W. Bilodeau*, 27in. high.
(Eldred's) $66

Crown, American petrol pump globe, made of glass.
(Onslow's) $700

'Dr. Harter's little liver pills' advertising pitcher, silver plate, 13in. high, *Dr. Harter's Iron Tonic* on reverse.
(Skinner Inc.) $270

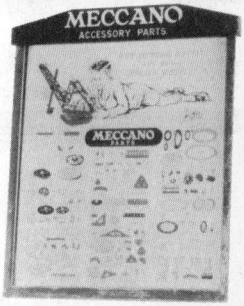


A Meccano No. 1 dealer's display cabinet, circa 1929, with six drawers, made up to 1938 specifications.
(Christie's S. Ken) $1,436

# AERONAUTICAL ITEMS

**A well detailed 1/8th scale flying model of the Hawker Typhoon 1B Serial letters RB222, built by D. Banham, 65in.**
**(Christie's) $1,424**

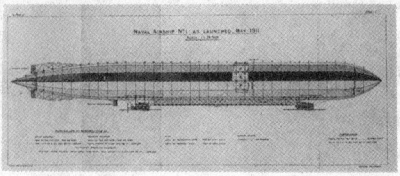

**Handbook on Rigid Airship No. 1, Parts I and II, and Appendix 1913, issued by Admiralty, S. Branch, November 1913.**
**(Christie's) $448**

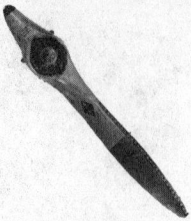

**A rare single blade 'Everill' laminated varnished wooden propeller, with brass leading edge and fabric covered tip, by Everill Propeller Corp, Lancaster, P.A., U.S.A., 38 1/4in. radius.**
**(Christie's) $153**

**A bronze medallion, the obverse embossed with a pilot's head, embossed *'Lindbergh Medal of the Congress United States of America'*, signed *'Lavra Gardin Fraser Sculptor'* and further embossed *'Act May 4 1928'*, 2 3/4in. diameter.**
**(Christie's) $305**

**A brown flying-jacket of the Irvin thermally-insulated type (the zip fasteners at the wrists possibly replaced).**
**(Christie's S. Ken) $676**

**A gong formed from a Monosopape rotary engine, cylinder suspended above a mahogany mount, carved from a propeller boss, 20in.**
**(Christie's) $224**

**A chromium-plated and enameled Brooklands Aero Club badge, the reverse stamped 223, 9.5cm. high.**
**(Onslow's) $1,384**

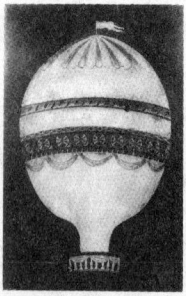

**Montgolfier Balloons, oil on brass sheet, one inscribed and dated *'Mr. Adorne 1784'*; the other *'Mr. Green 1845'*, 26 3/8 x 18in.**
**(Christie's) $2,238**

**A rare model 5-cylinder radial spark-ignition aluminium aero engine, with air-cooled cylinders, push-rod operated valves, carburettor, inlet pipes and exhaust stubs, 5in.**
**(Christie's) $1,119**

# AERONAUTICAL ITEMS

A pre-war Frog de Havilland 80A 'Puss Moth' in original box with winding key, accessories.
(Christie's) $509

A Simplex alarm clock, by The Ansonia Clock Co., U.S.A. with white dial and roman numerals, mounted as the center of two carved mahogany feathered wings, 50in. wide.
(Christie's) $366

A modern painted tinplate Fairey Swordfish torpedo bomber, by Tin Pot Toy Co., 14in. long.
(Christie's) $366

A handpainted pottery mug, decorated with an F-86 Sabre, the crest of 18 Fighter Bomber Wing and lettered *'N.C.O. Open Mess'*, 4in. high.
(Christie's) $81

A control column handgrip from a Bf-109 with armament at ptt switches, with plaque embossed *'Bauart: Argus Motoren G.M.B.H. Hersteller: Original Bruhn'*, 10¼in. high.
(Christie's) $651

A bronze medallion, the obverse with Statue of Liberty, Eiffel Tower, Maiden in flowing robes, embossed *'Commemorating the First New York-Paris Flight by Capt. Charles A. Lindbergh "Spirit of St Louis" New York May 20th Paris May 21st 1927'*, 3¼in. diameter.
(Christie's) $326

A plated mascot in the form of the Short Mayo S20/S21 Composite 'Mercury/Maia', aircraft, mounted on wood plinth, wingspan, 9⅝in.
(Christie's) $448

An extremely rare Anzani full-sized V-twin aero engine, crankcase No. 5435, with starting handle and chain drive.
(Christie's) $3,052

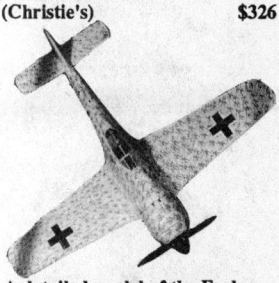

A detailed model of the Focke-Wulf FW 190-A6 single-seater fighter, serial No. 1-5 with considerable external detailing, finished in camouflage, 6 x 15½in.
(Christie's) $407

The Incredible Hulk, 5th Jan.
$250

Batman No 2, Summer Issue.
$8,000

Superboy No 1.
$1,500

Detective Comic No 27, May 1939, first appearance of The Batman.
$40,000

The Amazing Spider-man, No 1, 2 Great Feature-length Spider-man Thrillers!
$2,000

Journey into Mystery No 83, first appearance of The Mighty Thor.
$1,000

Tales of Suspense No 39, first appearance of Iron Man.
$800

Amazing Fantasy, first appearance of Spiderman.
$5,000

Detective Comics No 31, September 1939.
$4,500

(Duncan McAlpine – Stateside Comics plc)

Flaming Carrot Comics No 15.
$55

The Avengers No 1, Earth's Mightiest Super-Heroes!
$700

Batman No 1, Spring Issue 1940.
$14,000

Eastman and Laird's, Teenage Mutant Ninja Turtles.
$325

Lois Lane, Superman's Girl Friend.
$900

Detective Comic No 38, Robin The Boy Wonder.
$20,000

Green Lantern No 1, featuring Menace of the Giant Puppet.
$800

Action Comic No 1, June 1938, first appearance of Superman.
$35,000

Justice League of America, No 28, first appearance.
$1,300

(Duncan McAlpine – Stateside Comics plc)

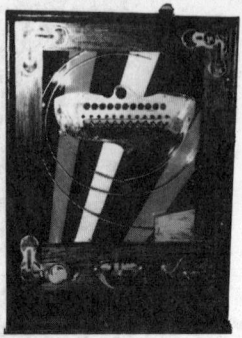

Elevenses, circa 1955, U.K. $450

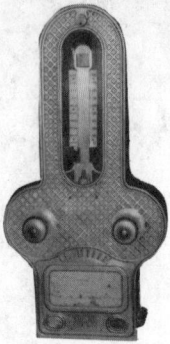

Le Mille, circa 1935, France. $720

Circle Skill, circa 1928, Made in Saxony. $540

Beromat, circa 1959, Germany. $405

Gretna Green, The Smithy, circa 1930, U.K. $630

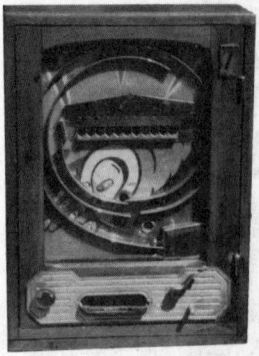

Plentywin, circa 1955, U.K. $450

Bullion, circa 1960, Bryans of Kegworth. $325

Columbus, Ball Chewing Gum Vendor, circa 1932, U.S.A. $180

Dutchboy, circa 1930, U.S.A. $900

(Nic Costa/Brian Bates)

# AMUSEMENT MACHINES

Grip Tester, circa 1930, U.K. $315

Like A Flash, Cigarette Vendor, circa 1935, U.K. $225

Super Steer-A-Ball, circa 1950, U.K. $720

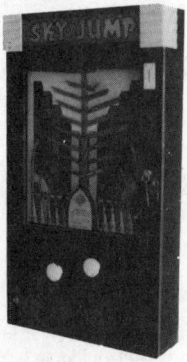


Sky Jump, circa 1948, U.K. $400

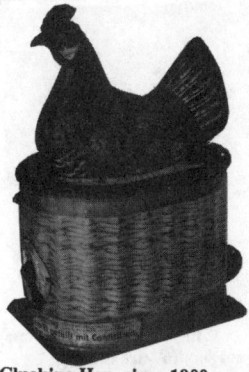

Clucking Hen, circa 1900, Germany. $5,400

Dr. Bone's X-Ray machine, circa 1950, U.K. $360

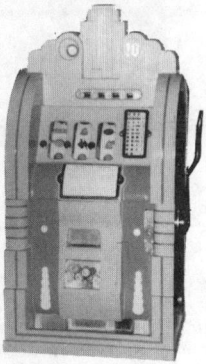

Extraordinary, circa 1933, U.S.A. $900

Mystery, Chinese Crystal Gazer, circa 1930, U.K. $3,600

Three Gun Bomb Dropper, circa 1914, U.K. $1,800

(Nic Costa/Brian Bates)

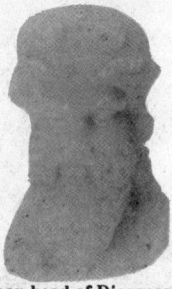

A Roman head of Dionysos, carved in high relief in light pink stone, his long hair swept back from a central parting with a single tress falling to his left shoulder, 17cm. high, probably 2nd century A.D.
(Phillips) $2,035

A bronze bird staff finial, modeled to resemble a pigeon with a rounded head, short curved beak and plump chest, Han Dynasty, 9.6cm. long.
(Christie's) $5,548

A Roman bronze figure of Athena wearing a crested helmet and double-tiered gown, her left hand raised to hold a spear, 8.5cm. high, 2nd–3rd century A.D.
(Phillips) $704

A Roman bronze statue of Diana, the young huntress running in sandals with her knee-length robe flowing behind her, her hair combed back to a bun, 7cm. high, 2nd–3rd century A.D.
(Phillips) $1,056

A Babylonian clay tablet recording the amount of money paid for the hire of three hundred and thirty four female slaves for one day, second year of the reign of Shu-Sin, 2036 B.C.
(Phillips) $740

A Roman amber glass tear bottle with flared rim and knop base, 20.5cm. high, 1st century A.D.
(Phillips) $176

An archaic bronze bell, cast to each side with three bands of raised knops above scrollwork, Western Zhou Dynasty, 39cm. high.
(Christie's) $2,134

An archaic bronze wine vessel and cover, the shoulder cast with a continuous band of spiral scrolls with twelve raised eyes centered at either side, early Western Zhou Dynasty, 33cm. high.
(Christie's) $55,484

A neo-Syrian chalcedony cylinder seal depicting a god standing on the back of a bull, a worshipper before him and a third figure standing behind, 4.1cm. high, first half of the 8th century B.C.
(Phillips) $4,224

A Roman bronze head of a young boy with plump features and full lips, his hair arranged in a middle parting falling in layers of loose curls, 5.8cm. high, 1st–2nd century A.D.
(Phillips) $1,408

A bronze figure of a prancing horse with head held high and mane flying back, 6.3cm. high, 1st–2nd century A.D.
(Phillips) $563

A Romano Egyptian terracotta figure of Baubo, the rotund naked woman seated on the floor with hands raised in adoration, 16cm. high, 2nd–3rd century A.D.
(Phillips) $555

A Roman limestone miniature altar from the Eastern provinces, the deep square-rimmed bowl supported on a plinth which has been carved in high relief with a lion on either side, 14.5cm. high, 1st–2nd century A.D.
(Phillips) $2,288

A fragment of a Roman fresco depicting a young maenad, a wreath of vine leaves in her curly auburn hair, her face turned slightly to the left, cracked and repaired, 19.5cm. high, 1st century B.C.
(Phillips) $13,728

A Sumerian cuneiform cone, the inscription recording the building of the palace of Sin-Kashid of Ur, 6.6cm. high, 1860–1830 B.C.
(Phillips) $810

A Korean gilt bronze seal, the square base surmounted by a tortoise standing foursquare with head raised and cast with a bulbous snout and incised with fangs, Yi Dynasty, 15th/16th century, 9.6cm. square.
(Christie's) $20,273

An Egyptian pale blue falence ushabti, a column of hieroglyphs inscribed down the front of the body identifying it with Semast whose mother was Renpet Nefret, 12.3cm. high, Dynasty XXVI.
(Phillips) $968

A Roman fresco fragment depicting a doe walking on long slender legs with neck stretched forwards and ears pricked, 14.6 x 19.7cm., 1st century B.C.
(Phillips) $3,520

An Adam period demi-lune overdoor, of sectional design, the panels glazed and decorated with lead lambrequin ornament, late 18th century, 19in. high.
(Christie's) $462

A quantity of oak paneling with a carved oak and stone fireplace, each section of paneling with a molded top rail, the paneling: 50ft. long; 42in. high approximately.
(Christie's) $2,950

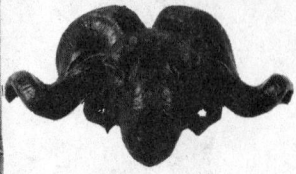

One of a set of ten cast-iron ram's masks, each well modeled with impressive horns, 28in. wide.
(Christie's)
(Ten) $3,140

One of a pair of brown glazed terracotta chimney pots, the 'crown' tops above octagonal shafts and square spreading bases, 37½in. high.
(Christie's) (Three) $102

A set of six architectural white marble Corinthian columns, the cylindrical tapering bodies with acanthus leaf capitals, on square bases, 97½in.
(Christie's)
(Six) $30,525

One of a pair of reconstituted stone gate pier finials, each sphere of two sections, on circular socle and square base, 40in. high.
(Christie's)(Two) $1,110

One of a set of three stained glass panels, possibly by Morris & Co., the pale yellow glass painted and stained in yellow and black, 18¼in. x 17¾in.
(Christie's) (Three) $702

A quantity of oak paneling, incorporating approximately twenty five Chinese soapstone inlaid panels depicting various domestic scenes, average size of panel 11½ x 23½in.
(Christie's) $2,646

One of a set of three carved sandstone capitals, the octagonal tops above deeply carved foliate and floral middle sections, 23½in. wide.
(Christie's) (Three) $740

A Coade stone rectangular frieze panel, the center with a festive urn and flaming finial, with husk festoons, late 18th/early 19th century, damages, 49½in. wide.
(Christie's) $3,325

A George III statuary and rosso antico marble mantel frieze tablet, carved with a portrait relief of a young woman, 19½in. wide.
(Christie's S. Ken) $2,610

One of a collection of four rectangular Coade stone panels, each centered with a rosette within a circular egg-and-dart border, 22¾in. wide.
(Christie's)
(Four) $3,140

One of a pair of varnished oak fluted columns with Corinthian capitals (one a three-quarter column the other virtually a full column), 110½in. high.
(Christie's)(Two) $1,832

A carved stone royal coat-of-arms, flanked by lion and unicorn, supporting shields with George V monogram, the lion, 60½in. high.
(Christie's) $14,245

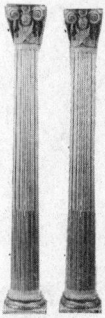

A pair of giltwood and gesso columns, each with an Ionic capital and carved with cherub masks with crossed wings, 101in. high.
(Christie's) $2,600

A carved stone plinth of Baroque design, each side carved with inset panels depicting foliate motifs, 25in. high.
(Christie's) $733

A pair of stone plaques, of trefoil form, one carved with the Fleur de Lys, and the other with the Tudor rose, 21in. high.
(Christie's) $611

A polychrome-painted pine Charles II design pedimented tabernacle frame, supported on fluted Corinthian columns and stepped bases, 135in. high.
(Christie's) $3,663

A miniature armor in the Maximilian style, the helmet with one-piece fluted skull and bellows visor, mounted on a wood stand, 68cm. high, 19th century. (Phillips) $2,375

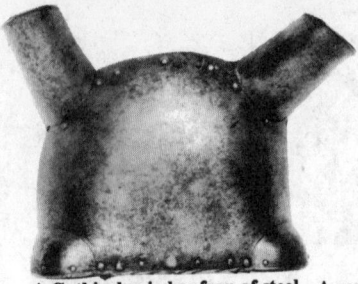

A Gothic demi-chanfron of steel with turned edges, the lower center section roped, circa 1500, lower plate lacking. (Phillips) $760

A rare Swiss pavise shield, of wood covered with gesso, the front painted green with a red border and with shields of arms of the League of St. George and of the town of Winterthur, circa 1460, 42½in. (Christie's) $32,010

A French Carabinier trooper's breast and backplates of heavy steel overlaid in brass, dated 1832 and adapted for the 2nd Empire period with the addition of the imperial eagle. (Phillips) $985

17th century infantryman Nuremburg complete suit of armor, stands 70in. high., includes a halberd, mounted on a wood stand. (Du Mouchelles) $9,000

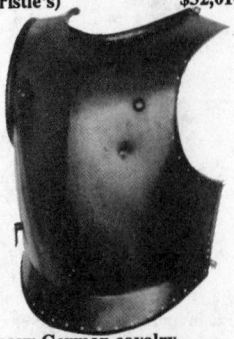

A heavy German cavalry trooper's breastplate circa 1800, musket ball proof mark, lugs for strap fastening, short raised collar, edges pierced with holes for lining attachment. (Wallis & Wallis) $216

An English Commonwealth period breastplate, struck with helmet over A (Commonwealth Armourer's Company mark) and maker's initials E.O. (Wallis & Wallis) $1,040

An unusual German open gauntlet circa 1600, 13in. overall, single plate arm defence with medial ridge retaining buckles for securing. (Wallis & Wallis) $750

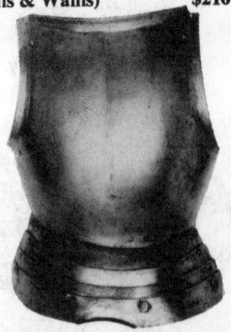

A breast-plate, early 16th century, probably German, 18½in. high. (Christie's S. Ken) $3,238

A very fine pavise shield, covered with gesso painted with a standing figure of St. George in gothic armor, German (perhaps Vienna) or Bohemian, circa 1485, 46in.
(Christie's) $34,144

An iron skull cap or secrete composed of numerous flattened bars riveted together complete with its original leather liner, 17th century.
(Phillips) $1,217

A heavy German cavalry troopers breastplate circa 1800, musket ball proof mark, stamped *Hartkopf*, lugs for strap fastening.
(Wallis & Wallis) $269

A French cuirassier's breastplate, backplate and helmet, steel plates with brass studs, leather backed shoulder chains and buckles, ornamental comb with Medusa head finial.
(Wallis & Wallis) $1,900

An early 17th century suit of armor, the visor with rising peak above fretted eye pieces and fretted front, the breast-plate with period indented test mark, 70in. high.
(Bonhams) $10,000

A well made 19th century miniature copy of a full suit of 16th century Maximilian armor, comprising fluted breast and backplate, helmet with fluted and pierced visor, overall height 23in.
(Wallis & Wallis) $2,059

An Innsbruck breast-plate from an infantry armor (Harnasch), of bright steel and rounded form, circa 1540–50, 17in. high
(Christie's S. Ken) $2,024

A good pair of mid 16th century German mitten gauntlets made for an infantry armor, backs of hand of 11 plates including raised knuckle plate.
(Wallis & Wallis) $716

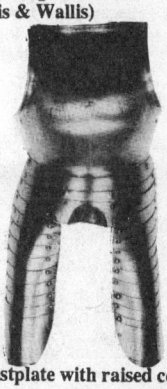

A breastplate with raised central ridge, gussets with turned edges, fauld of three lames and long attached tassets of ten lames, late 16th century.
(Phillips) $3,230

## CASED SETS

**A cased Colt percussion new model Police pistol, single action, 4½in. round barrel signed *address Col. Colt London*, .38 caliber, 5-shot half-fluted cylinder, plain cylinder with London black powder proof marks, plain varnished wooden grips, 10in. overall, in lined and fitted wooden case with accessories.**
**(Bonhams) $960**

**A five-shot 54 bore Beaumont Adams percussion revolver, 14.5cm. sighted octagonal barrel signed Deane & Son, rammer mounted on the left side, plain cylinder engraved with patent number, contained in its baize lined oak case complete with accessories.**
**(Phillips) $1,647**

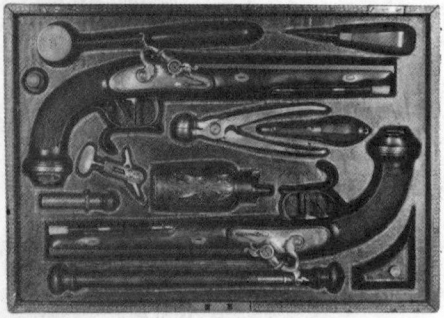

**A rare pair of fulminate primed target or dueling pistols with probable royal connections, 24cm. sighted octagonal damascus barrels with micro-groove rifling, foliate engraved locks signed *Lehanne à Herve*, with tubular vents for the fulminate detonated by plungers in pivoted housings, double set triggers, full stocked, the checkered butts with gold shield shaped escutcheons.**
**(Phillips) $9,925**

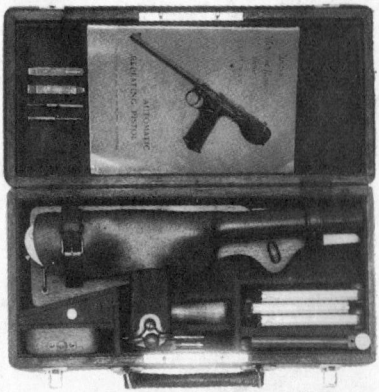

**A rare cased Borchardt 1893 patent 7.65mm. self-loading pistol by Waffenfabrik Loewe, Berlin, retaining virtually all of its original finish, with vertical sliding thumb-safe, V-notched fixed-backsight, pyramidal frontsight, checkered walnut grips, with original 'Patent' magazine, 7½in. barrel, in its original black leather case with white-metal mounts.**
**(Christie's S. Ken) $23,780**

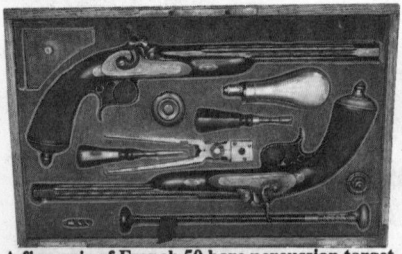

**A fine pair of French 50 bore percussion target pistols by Collombert, Aix-les-Bains 17in. overall, blued fluted barrels 11in., sparsely scroll engraved locks gold inlaid, ebony halfstocks with finely checkered butts.**
**(Wallis & Wallis) $5,031**

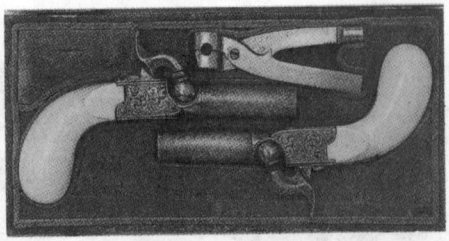

**A pair of small Belgian box-lock percussion pocket pistols with etched twist turn-off barrels, bright actions engraved with scrolling foliage, folding triggers, and swelling ivory butts, Liège proof, mid-19th century, 4¼in.**
**(Christie's S. Ken) $2,024**

## CASED SETS

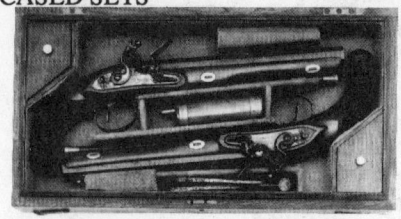

A pair of flintlock holster or dueling pistols, 25cm. sighted octagonal barrels signed H. Nock, London, stepped signed and bolted locks, set triggers, full stocked, the checkered butts with oval silver escutcheons, contained in a baize lined oak case.
(Phillips) $2,685

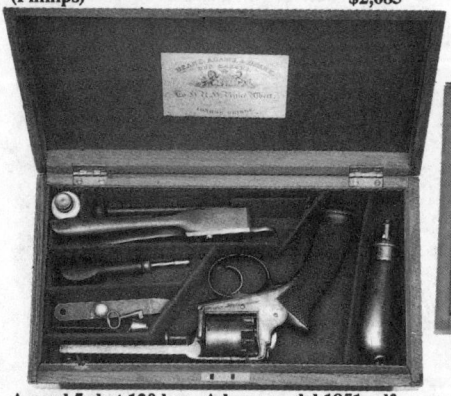

A good 5 shot 120 bore Adams model 1851 self cocking percussion revolver, 9in. overall, barrel 4½in. engraved "Deane, Adams and Deane, 30 King William St, London Bridge," London proved, checkered butt with plain horn cap.
(Wallis & Wallis) $2,516

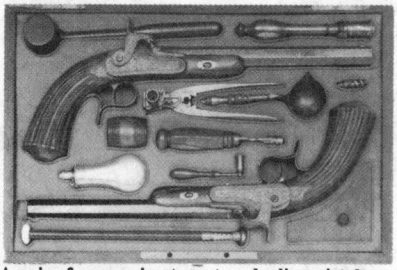

A pair of percussion target or dueling pistols, 26.5cm. octagonal rifled sighted damascus barrels signed in gold on the top flat against a blued ground Lassence-Rongé a Liege, contained in their brass mounted baize lined close fitted mahogany case complete with all accessories.
(Phillips) $6,807

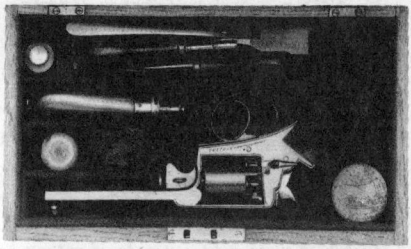

A 120-bore Adams patent double-action five-shot percussion revolver, with blued octagonal sighted rifled barrel, the top strap engraved 'Calderwood & Son, 14, North Earl St, Dublin', in lined and fitted oak case with some accessories including Hawksley flask and bullet mold, 10½in.
(Christie's S. Ken) $1,518

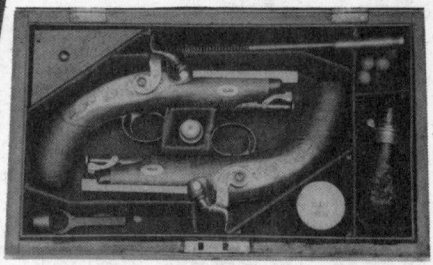

A good pair of 25 bore back action percussion traveling pistols by Wilson & Co Liverpool, circa 1840, 8¼in., octagonal browned twist barrels 4in., silver breech lines and safety plugs, fullstocked, foliate engraved locks and dolphin hammers, rounded checkered butts, in their green felt lined fitted mahogany case.
(Wallis & Wallis) $1,705

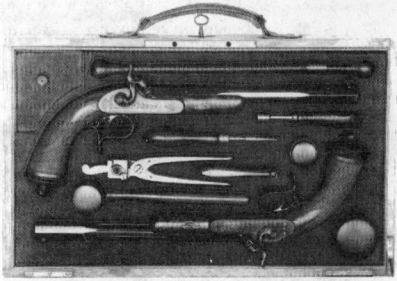

A good pair of percussion target or dueling pistols, 27.5cm. sighted rifled blued octagonal barrels with fluted central sections signed Gastinne Renette à Paris, the finely checkered butts inlaid 1 and 2 in gold, contained in their baize lined close fitted oak case complete with all accessories.
(Phillips) $8,950

## DAGGERS

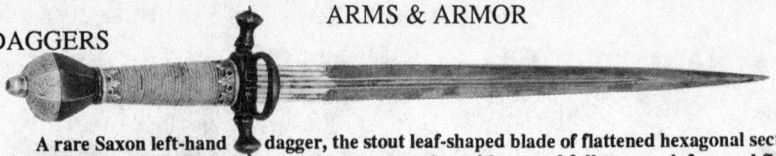

A rare Saxon left-hand dagger, the stout leaf-shaped blade of flattened hexagonal section changing to flattened diamond section at the point, with central fuller on each face and fluted ricasso, the hilt of blackened iron, circa 1570, 16¼in.
(Christie's S. Ken) $22,264

An unusual late 18th century Ottoman Turkish dagger kard, 15½in., slightly T section blade 8½in. of sham damascus watered pattern, foliate chiseled brass ferrule, one piece walrus ivory hilt.
(Wallis & Wallis) $643

A Caucasian kindjal with tapering double-edged blade of flattened diamond section, the hilt and wooden scabbard entirely covered with nielloed silver decorated with scrollwork in low relief, late 19th Century, 19½in.
(Christie's S. Ken) $1,214

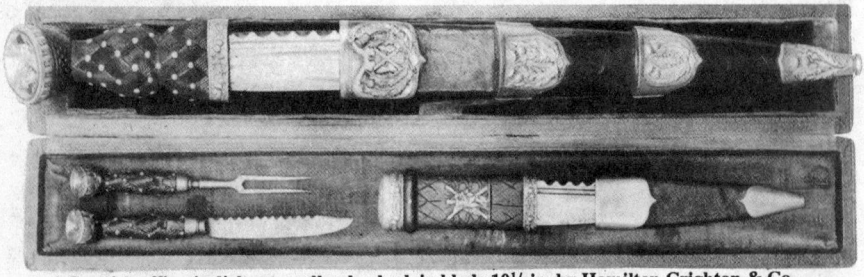

A Scottish officer's dirk set, scallop back plain blade 10½in. by Hamilton Crighton & Co Edinburgh, retaining much original polish, copper gilt mounted hilt, corded wood hilt mounted with gilt studs, thistle decoration to base mount, contained in a leather covered purple velvet lined fitted case.
(Wallis & Wallis) $1,446

A South American silver mounted Gaucho knife, spear point blade 8½in., scallop top edge, etched with mounted huntsmen chasing stag, birds in foliage, South American embossed silver hilt decorated with bull's heads, patterns, Gorgon's head, and engraved with small armorial crest.
(Wallis & Wallis) $62

A good Italian hunting knife, heavy 27.5cm. blade with clip back point deeply chiseled along the back edge with birds amidst scrolling foliage and with classical figures at the forte, circa 1860.
(Phillips) $609

A good Nazi 2nd Pattern Luftwaffe officers dagger, by E Pack & Sohne Siegfried Waffen, gray metal mounts, silver wire bound white grip, in its gray metal sheath with scarce original cardboard makers label attached of "Packis Blanke Waffen".
(Wallis & Wallis) $387

## DAGGERS

A U.S. World War I Mark I brass hilt fighting knife, blade 7in., hilt marked *US 1918 L.F. & C 1918* and pricker engraved with initials, in its metal sheath stamped at throat.
(Wallis & Wallis) $232

A good silver mounted officer's dress dirk of the Argyle and Sutherland Highlanders, 31cm. blade with faceted back edge by Brook & Son, George St., Edinburgh etched with scrolls and regimental badges, hallmarked Edinburgh 1883.
(Phillips) $2,561

A well made 19th century Romantic dagger, 12in., shallow diamond section blade 5in., retaining all its original polish, brass hilt and sheath chiseled with dolphins, grotesques, shells, fruit and foliage.
(Wallis & Wallis) $340

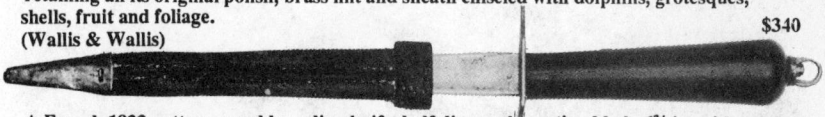

A French 1833 pattern naval boarding knife, half diamond section blade 6¾in. with mark at forte, flat lozenge brass crosspiece stamped with anchor, black round wood hilt, in its leather sheath.
(Wallis & Wallis) $268

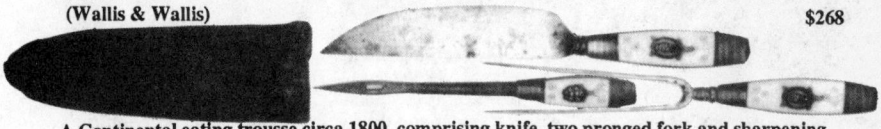

A Continental eating trousse circa 1800, comprising knife, two pronged fork and sharpening steel, knife blade 5¼in. stamped with maker's mark of splayed footed cross.
(Wallis & Wallis) $408

A good nielloed silver mounted dagger kindjal probably from Daghastan dated 1877, broad double edged blade 11¼in., struck twice with maker's mark, geometrically pierced fullers, silver hilt and sheath nielloed and engraved overall with profuse scrolls, foliage and geometric ornament.
(Wallis & Wallis) $1,217

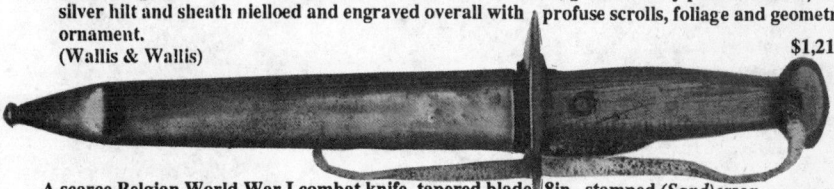

A scarce Belgian World War I combat knife, tapered blade 8in., stamped *(Sand)erson Brothers Newbould* with faint *Sheffield*, oval steel guard, wooden grip, steel sheath with pierced steel belt loop.
(Wallis & Wallis) $185

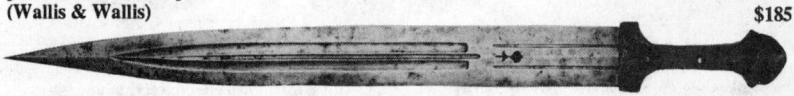

A 19th century Cossack dagger kindjal, 26in., broad tri fullered doubled edged blade 20½in., deeply struck with Arabic maker's inscription within cartouche.
(Wallis & Wallis) $142

## HELMETS

A Cuirassier's close helmet of light construction, the two-piece skull with low comb, the visor with small peak and attached bevor, 17th century.
(Phillips) $1,235

A composite lance-cap (chapka) as for 16th Lancers with Q.V.C. white metal mounted gilt chapka-plate bearing honors to Aliwal and Sobraon.
(Christie's S. Ken) $2,253

A rare officer's helmet of the 1st Loyal Suffolk Troop/West Suffolk Yeomanry Cavalry of black leather with gilt metal mounts including front plate.
(Christie's S. Ken) $1,696

A good Victorian officer's blue cloth spiked helmet of the 4th Volunteer Bn The Royal West Kent Regt, silver plated mounts.
(Wallis & Wallis) $700

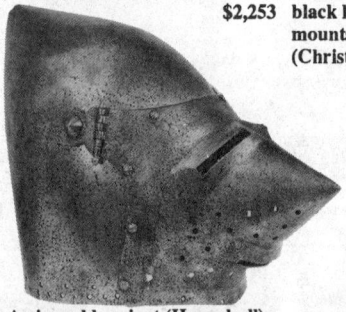

A visored bascinet (Hounskull) in 14th century style, the one-piece skull drawn up to a point to the rear of center and the edges bordered by holes for the lining and vervels for an aventail, 10¹/4in. high.
(Christie's S. Ken) $6,477

A Prussian Cuirassier officer's helmet, the plated steel skull fitted with brass eagle plate, and white metal fluted top spike.
(Phillips) $1,110

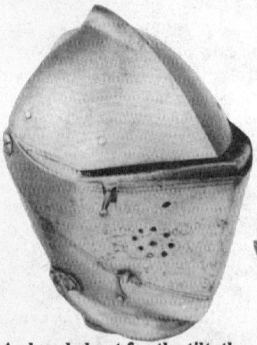

A close helmet for the tilt, the one-piece skull with low roped comb, two-piece visor with single sight aperture, possibly Italian, 16th century.
(Phillips) $6,080

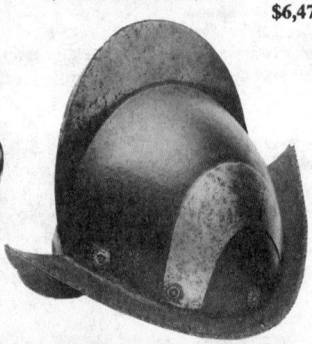

A good German late 16th century Morion, made for a town guard, two piece skull with tall roped comb, turned over ribbed borders.
(Wallis & Wallis) $1,040

A very rare Other Rank's red shako circa 1830 of the 15th Hussars of heavy construction entirely covered in red cloth trimmed with yellow worsted braid around top.
(Christie's S. Ken) $1,690

## HELMETS

A post 1902 officer's blue cloth spiked helmet of The Worcestershire Regt, gilt mounts, velvet backed chinchain with ear rosettes, gilt and silver helmet plate.
(Wallis & Wallis) $500

A French 2nd Empire other ranks leather shako of the 47th Regt, brass eagle helmet plate with stenciled "47" on the ball, red, white and blue tin rosette.
(Wallis & Wallis) $639

A white metal Albert pattern helmet of the 6th (Inniskilling) Dragoons with ornate brass mounts, helmet-plate and wide chin-chain.
(Christie's S. Ken) $1,502

A French 2nd Empire Dragoon trooper's helmet, the brass skull with imitation leopardskin turban, the comb embossed with foliage.
(Phillips) $1,038

An Edward VII officer's lance-cap of The 12th (Prince of Wales's Royal) Lancers black patent leather skull and embroidered peak, gilt lace bands, scarlet cloth sides.
(Wallis & Wallis) $3,870

An Imperial German Infantry officer's Pickelhaube as worn by the 3rd Battalion of the 96th Infantry Regiment, brass helmet plate with German silver Schwarzburg arms.
(Wallis & Wallis) $987

An Imperial German Baden Other Ranks Pickelhaube as worn by the 109th Grenadier Regt., white metal helmet plate, spike and mounts, leather lining and chinstrap.
(Wallis & Wallis) $987

A scarce floppy pill box hat of the Eton Volunteer Rifle Corps, Elcho gray cloth, triple lace headband, leather chinstrap.
(Wallis & Wallis) $166

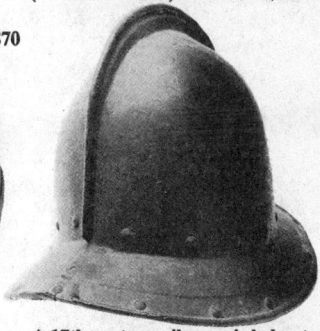

A 17th century pikeman's helmet "pot", two piece skull with shallow raised comb, turned over riveted brim, deeply struck with I.R. armorer's mark.
(Wallis & Wallis) $1,087

## HELMETS

A close-helmet, the rounded skull with low roped comb made in two pieces joined across the back of the neck, the main edges throughout bordered by pairs of engraved lines, English or Flemish, circa 1530–40, 13in. (Christie's S. Ken) $5,262

A rare Saxon Electoral Guard comb-morion of one piece with roped comb and brim, the base of the skull encircled by sixteen gilt-brass lion-masks capping the lining rivets, struck on the brim with the Nuremberg mark, circa 1580, 11½in. high. (Christie's S. Ken) $16,192

An officer's Albert pattern shako of the 90th Regiment, rifle green felt skull with leather top and peaks, dark green ball tuft. (Phillips) $1,195

A rare Imperial German officer's Pickelhaube as worn by the 1st and 2nd Battalion of the 92nd Brunswick Infantry Regiment, enameled cross of the Order of Henry the Lion on breast. (Wallis & Wallis) $1,935

An East European lobster-tailed pot (Zischägge) with one-piece fluted skull studded at the base of the flutes with brass rosettes and fitted at the rear with a brass plume-holder, third quarter of the 17th century, 12in. high. (Christie's S. Ken) $4,453

A scarce Imperial German Saxony General officer's Pickelhaube gilt star helmet plate with superimposed silver star with gilt and enameled center. (Wallis & Wallis) $2,467

A good Morion circa 1580, formed in one piece, roped comb, retaining a few brass rosettes around base, roped edges. (Wallis & Wallis) $1,040

A good officers pillbox hat of The Royal Artillery, gilt lace and braided top ornament, in its tin case. (Wallis & Wallis) $255

A fine officer's Pickelhaube of the Mecklenburg-Schwerin infantry with black parade plume on tall fluted stem, flat gilt chinscales with strap ends. (Christie's S. Ken) $1,878

## HELMETS

An officer's lance-cap (chapka) of the Bedfordshire Yeomanry with patent leather body bearing ornamental gilt metal fittings including rosette with plain gilt half-ball button.
(Christie's S. Ken) $4,882

An extremely rare 1830–55 pattern Russian chapka of an officer of the 18th Serpoukhoff Regiment of Lancers with gilt numerals mounted on the white metal double-headed eagle plate.
(Christie's S. Ken) $7,510

A good officer's fur cap of the 3rd Volunteer Battalion, The Lancashire Fusiliers, with leather backed, graduated link, silver plated chinchain, yellow cut feather plume.
(Wallis & Wallis) $1,113

A scarce Imperial German Wurttemburg General officer's Pickelhaube, gilt helmet plate with superimposed star and enameled center, gilt fluted spike.
(Wallis & Wallis) $1,935

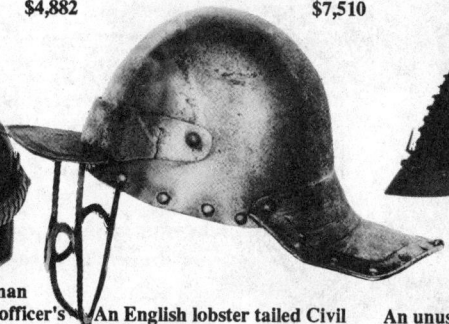

An English lobster tailed Civil War period helmet, two piece siege weight skull, hinged visor with good quality triple bar face guard.
(Wallis & Wallis) $1,742

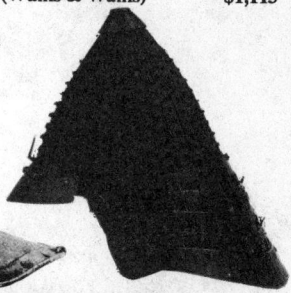

An unusual Hoshi-Bashi kabuto of conical form constructed of thirty-two plates each with ten upstanding rivets, late Momoyama or early Edo Period.
(Phillips) $13,500

An Italian 'Spanish Morion', of one piece, with tall pointed skull, etched throughout in the 'Pisan' manner with bands and borders of trophies, circa 1570, 10¾in. high.
(Christie's S. Ken) $1,619

A scarce Prussian foul weather shako circa 1840, black oil skin covered overall, state metal cockade, black cloth lining.
(Wallis & Wallis) $250

A good officer's 1869 pattern shako of The 76th Regiment, blue cloth, gilt braid trim including 2 lines around the top, gilt mounts.
(Wallis & Wallis) $973

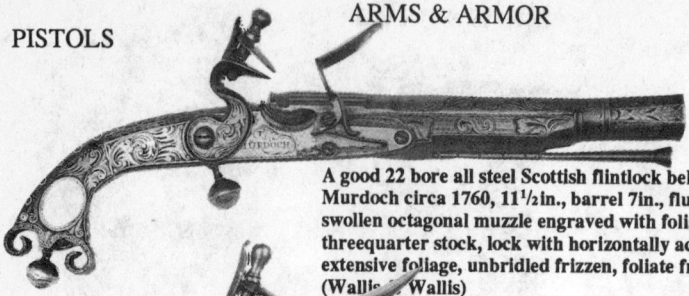

A good 22 bore all steel Scottish flintlock belt pistol by T. Murdoch circa 1760, 11½in., barrel 7in., fluted at breech, swollen octagonal muzzle engraved with foliage, steel threequarter stock, lock with horizontally acting scear with extensive foliage, unbridled frizzen, foliate frizzen spring finial.
(Wallis & Wallis) $5,612

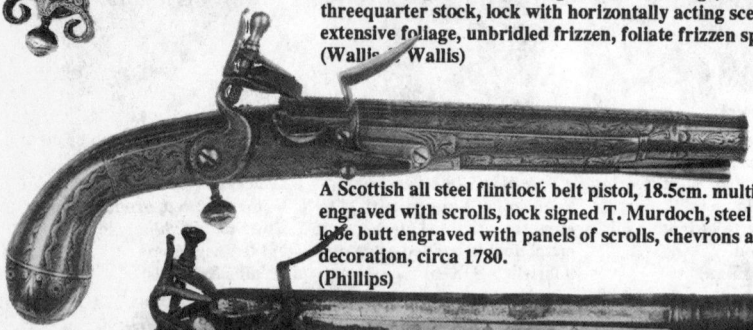

A Scottish all steel flintlock belt pistol, 18.5cm. multi-stage barrel engraved with scrolls, lock signed T. Murdoch, steel stock with lobe butt engraved with panels of scrolls, chevrons and waved decoration, circa 1780.
(Phillips) $3,414

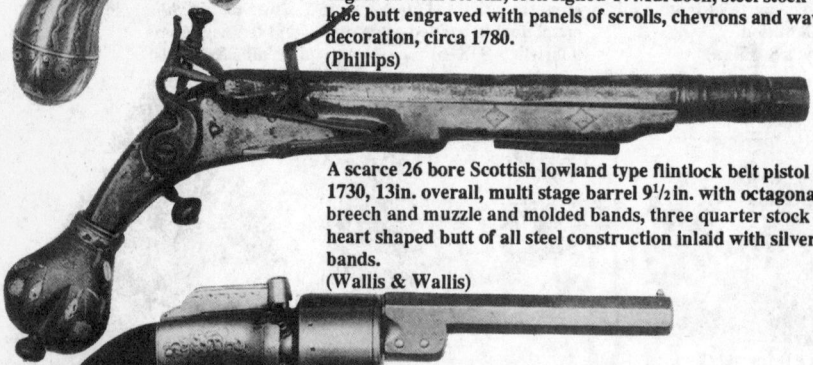

A scarce 26 bore Scottish lowland type flintlock belt pistol circa 1730, 13in. overall, multi stage barrel 9½in. with octagonal breech and muzzle and molded bands, three quarter stock and heart shaped butt of all steel construction inlaid with silver bands.
(Wallis & Wallis) $1,497

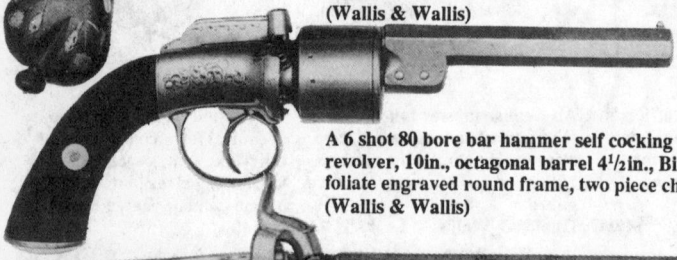

A 6 shot 80 bore bar hammer self cocking percussion transitional revolver, 10in., octagonal barrel 4½in., Birmingham proved, foliate engraved round frame, two piece checkered walnut grips.
(Wallis & Wallis) $365

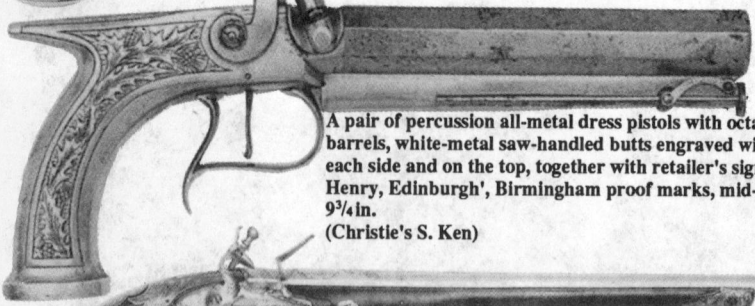

A pair of percussion all-metal dress pistols with octagonal barrels, white-metal saw-handled butts engraved with thistles on each side and on the top, together with retailer's signature 'A. Henry, Edinburgh', Birmingham proof marks, mid-19th century, 9¾in.
(Christie's S. Ken) $2,429

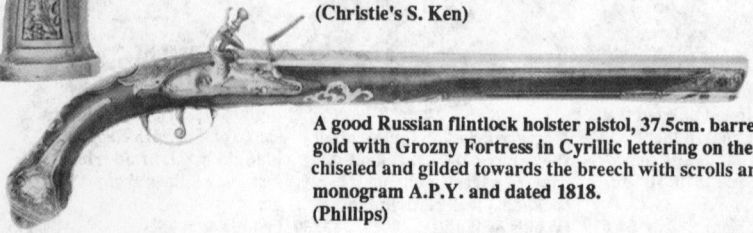

A good Russian flintlock holster pistol, 37.5cm. barrel inlaid in gold with Grozny Fortress in Cyrillic lettering on the top rib and chiseled and gilded towards the breech with scrolls and foliage, a monogram A.P.Y. and dated 1818.
(Phillips) $6,444

## PISTOLS

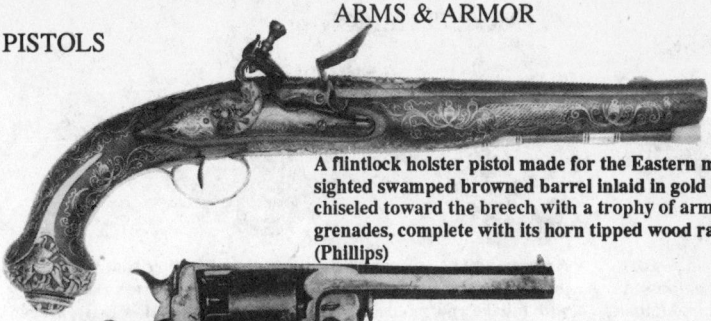

**A flintlock holster pistol made for the Eastern market, 24.5cm. sighted swamped browned barrel inlaid in gold London and chiseled toward the breech with a trophy of arms and flaming grenades, complete with its horn tipped wood ramrod.**
**(Phillips) $2,506**

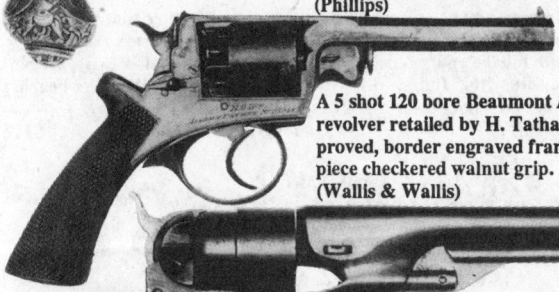

**A 5 shot 120 bore Beaumont Adams double action percussion revolver retailed by H. Tatham, 9¼in., barrel 4¼in., London proved, border engraved frame, sliding cylinder locking bolt, one piece checkered walnut grip.**
**(Wallis & Wallis) $615**

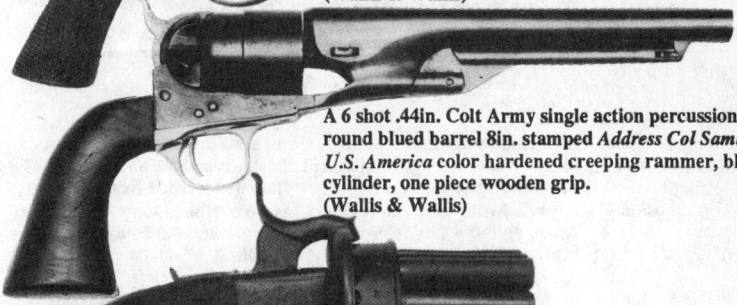

**A 6 shot .44in. Colt Army single action percussion revolver, 14in., round blued barrel 8in. stamped *Address Col Saml Colt New York U.S. America* color hardened creeping rammer, blued rebated cylinder, one piece wooden grip.**
**(Wallis & Wallis) $1,890**

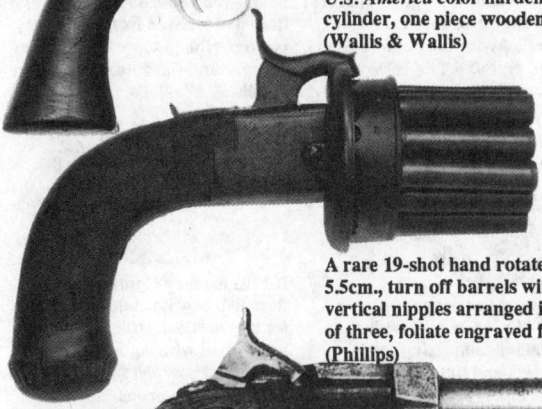

**A rare 19-shot hand rotated percussion pepperbox revolver, 5.5cm., turn off barrels with engraved muzzles, the breech with vertical nipples arranged in two groups of five and three groups of three, foliate engraved frame signed James Richards, Glasgow.**
**(Phillips) $7,220**

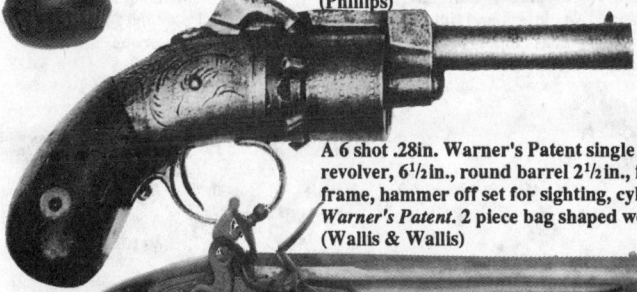

**A 6 shot .28in. Warner's Patent single action percussion pocket revolver, 6½in., round barrel 2½in., foliate engraved rounded frame, hammer off set for sighting, cylinder roll engraved with *Warner's Patent*. 2 piece bag shaped wooden grips.**
**(Wallis & Wallis) $302**

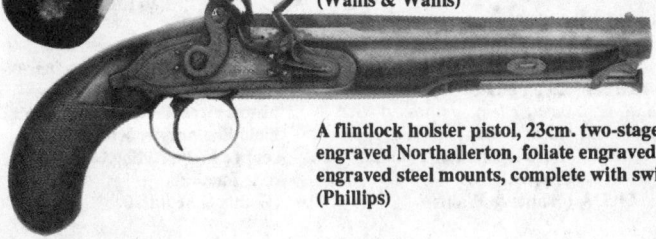

**A flintlock holster pistol, 23cm. two-stage sighted barrel engraved Northallerton, foliate engraved lock signed Spencer, engraved steel mounts, complete with swivel ramrod.**
**(Phillips) $859**

## POWDER FLASKS

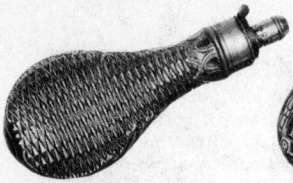

An embossed copper powder flask, 8¼in., body embossed with woven design and foliage, common brass top with adjustable nozzle.
(Wallis & Wallis) $132

A scarce embossed copper powder flask 8¼in., embossed with foliage and geometric devices within flutes, with graduated nozzle.
(Wallis & Wallis) $240

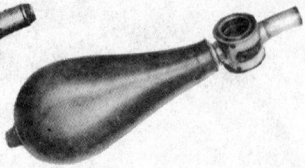

A scarce leather shot bag with variable optic brass charger, 9in., brown leather body, hinged brass charger with roller bearing spring.
(Wallis & Wallis) $117

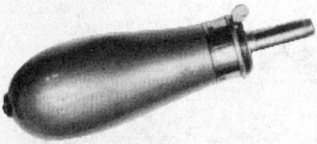

A good bag shaped copper pistol flask, 5¾in., lacquered body and common brass top stamped *James Dixon & Sons*, unusually long nozzle.
(Wallis & Wallis) $321

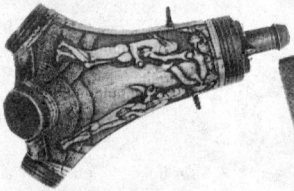

A German staghorn powder-flask with forked body of natural horn, the outer-face carved in low relief with the Temptation of Adam and Eve, late 16th century, 7¾in.
(Christie's S. Ken) $1,316

A rare shaped copper powder flask circa 1800, 6½in., body of flattened waisted form with flat bottom, ribbed top with common charger and fixed nozzle.
(Wallis & Wallis) $165

An embossed copper powder flask, 8¼in., embossed with a design of hanging game above *James Dixon & Sons.*
(Wallis & Wallis) $198

An embossed copper powder flask 8in., embossed with a medallion containing two pointers and hunter, common brass top, graduated nozzle.
(Wallis & Wallis) $165

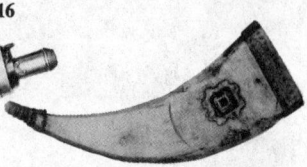

A 17th century Continental flattened cow horn powder flask for a Wheellock rifle, 11¼in., body fitted with squat steel spanner of stepped form with shaped brass aprons.
(Wallis & Wallis) $485

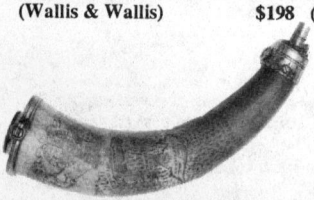

A rare North American cow-horn powder-flask incised with scrimshaw-work depicting in great detail the area of the Great Lakes, and *'Powder and Ball Will Conquer All. Confusion Upon The Foe. A Pox On Them All'*, circa 1812, 12in.
(Christie's S. Ken) $1,518

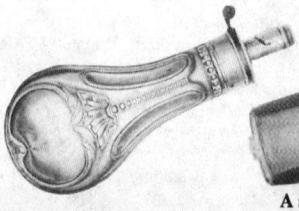

An embossed copper powder flask, 7¾in., embossed with flutes, beads and foliage, patent brass top stamped *James Dixon & Sons.*
(Wallis & Wallis) $116

A scarce 3 way flask for a pair of flintlock holster or dueling pistols circa 1800, 5¾in. overall including nozzle, octagonal copper body, sliding brass box in base for flints.
(Wallis & Wallis) $408

## POWDER FLASKS

A scarce American embossed martial copper powder flask, 8¼in., body embossed with bugle and on one side only *Public Property.*
(Wallis & Wallis) $400

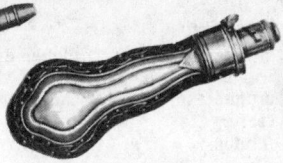

An embossed copper powder flask, 7½in., embossed with laurel, of waisted form, patent top stamped *G&JW Hawksley Sheffield.*
(Wallis & Wallis) $170

An embossed copper powder flask, 8in., embossed with roaring stag, patent top stamped *Improved Patent, James Dixon & Sons Sheffield*, graduated nozzle.
(Wallis & Wallis) $193

An embossed copper powder flask, 8¼in., embossed with swollen fluting, common brass top stamped *G&JW Hawksley Sheffield.*
(Wallis & Wallis) $161

An embossed circular brass powder flask, 6in., body with beaded edge, graduated nozzle stamped *Sykes patent.*
(Wallis & Wallis) $180

An early 19th century gunner's cow horn powder horn, 14in., overall, heavy brass mounts, simple sprung lever charger, twin suspension loops.
(Wallis & Wallis) $622

A late 18th century pressed lant-horn powder flask, 7½in., two piece translucent body with ribbed brass edges.
(Wallis & Wallis) $204

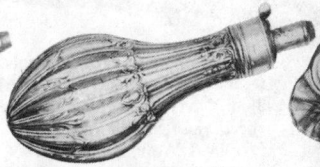

A fluted copper flask, 8¼in., embossed with flutes and foliage, common brass top stamped *G & JW Hawksley.*
(Wallis & Wallis) $174

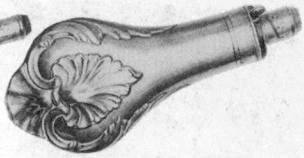

An embossed copper powder flask, 8in., embossed with shell and shaped acanthus foliage, common brass top stamped *G & JW Hawksley.*
(Wallis & Wallis) $116

An embossed gun sized copper powder flask, 8in., body embossed with a pheasant amidst flowering foliage upon shell center.
(Wallis & Wallis) $145

A horn powder flask of flattened form, the body engraved with flowers and geometric patterns, 29.5cm. overall, 17th century.
(Phillips) $573

An embossed copper powder flask, 8¼in., embossed with dog and stag, patent top stamped *G&JW Hawksley Sheffield.*
(Wallis & Wallis) $227

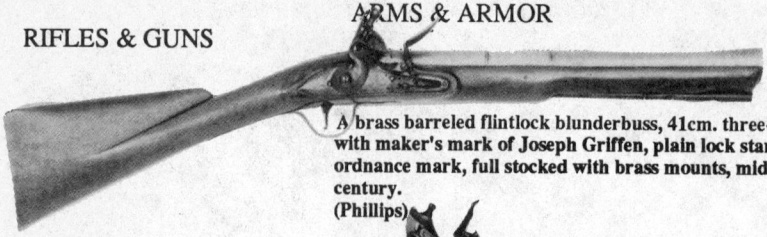

A brass barreled flintlock blunderbuss, 41cm. three-stage barrel with maker's mark of Joseph Griffen, plain lock stamped with ordnance mark, full stocked with brass mounts, mid-18th century.
(Phillips) $1,289

A good .52in. US Hall's Patent model 1819 breech loading flintlock rifle, 52½in., browned barrel 32¾in., sights offset to avoid mechanism, color hardened hinged breech stamped *J.H. Hall H Ferry US 1837* integral with boxlock action.
(Wallis & Wallis) $2,495

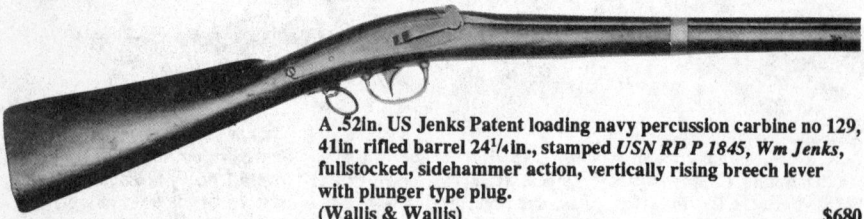

A .52in. US Jenks Patent loading navy percussion carbine no 129, 41in. rifled barrel 24¼in., stamped *USN RP P 1845, Wm Jenks*, fullstocked, sidehammer action, vertically rising breech lever with plunger type plug.
(Wallis & Wallis) $680

A good double barreled 12 bore Westley Richards patent top lever pinfire sporting gun, 46½in. overall, damascus barrels 30in., finely scroll engraved side locks, walnut stock with checkered fore end and wrist.
(Wallis & Wallis) $501

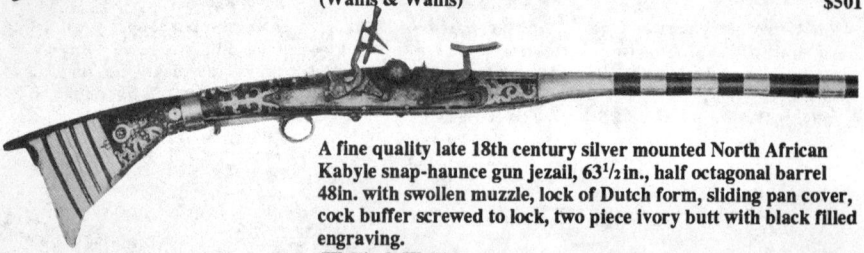

A fine quality late 18th century silver mounted North African Kabyle snap-haunce gun jezail, 63½in., half octagonal barrel 48in. with swollen muzzle, lock of Dutch form, sliding pan cover, cock buffer screwed to lock, two piece ivory butt with black filled engraving.
(Wallis & Wallis) $565

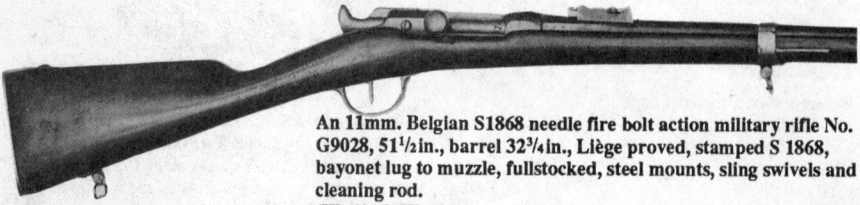

An 11mm. Belgian S1868 needle fire bolt action military rifle No. G9028, 51½in., barrel 32¾in., Liège proved, stamped S 1868, bayonet lug to muzzle, fullstocked, steel mounts, sling swivels and cleaning rod.
(Wallis & Wallis) $370

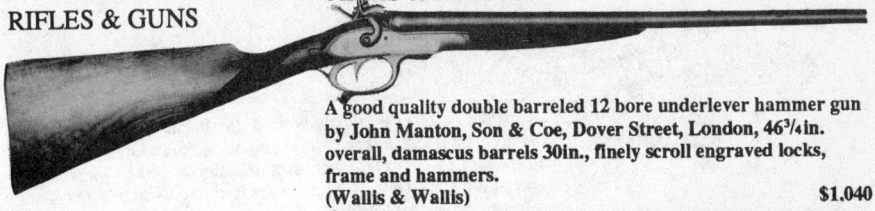

A good quality double barreled 12 bore underlever hammer gun by John Manton, Son & Coe, Dover Street, London, 46¾in. overall, damascus barrels 30in., finely scroll engraved locks, frame and hammers.
(Wallis & Wallis) $1.040

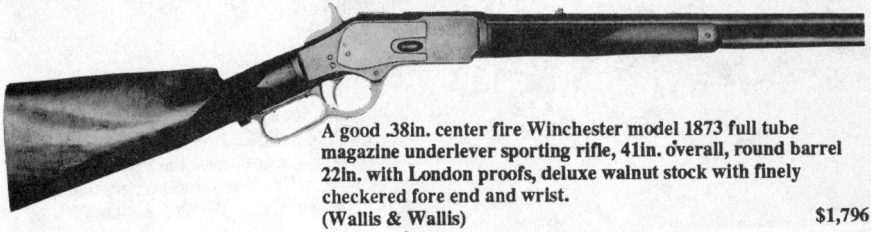

A good .38in. center fire Winchester model 1873 full tube magazine underlever sporting rifle, 41in. overall, round barrel 22in. with London proofs, deluxe walnut stock with finely checkered fore end and wrist.
(Wallis & Wallis) $1,796

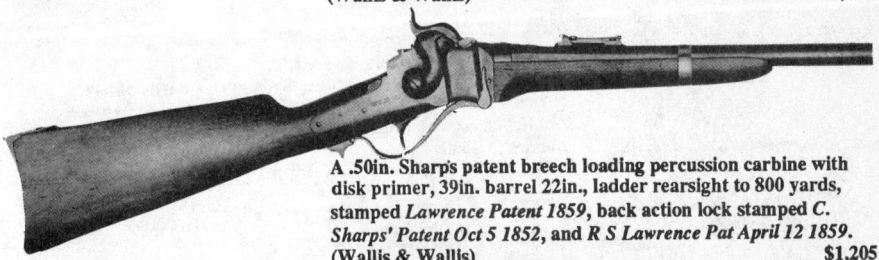

A .50in. Sharp's patent breech loading percussion carbine with disk primer, 39in. barrel 22in., ladder rearsight to 800 yards, stamped *Lawrence Patent 1859*, back action lock stamped *C. Sharps' Patent Oct 5 1852*, and *R S Lawrence Pat April 12 1859*.
(Wallis & Wallis) $1,205

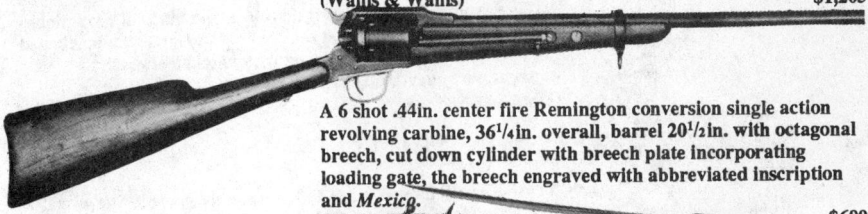

A 6 shot .44in. center fire Remington conversion single action revolving carbine, 36¼in. overall, barrel 20½in. with octagonal breech, cut down cylinder with breech plate incorporating loading gate, the breech engraved with abbreviated inscription and *Mexico*.
(Wallis & Wallis) $699

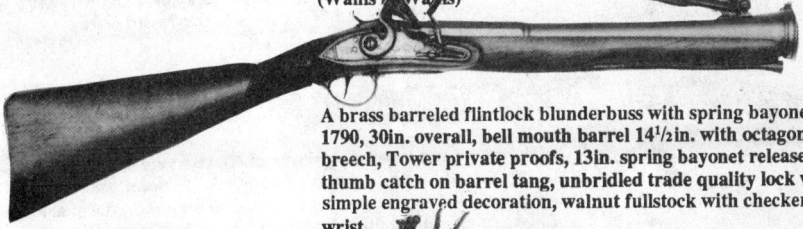

A brass barreled flintlock blunderbuss with spring bayonet circa 1790, 30in. overall, bell mouth barrel 14½in. with octagonal breech, Tower private proofs, 13in. spring bayonet released by thumb catch on barrel tang, unbridled trade quality lock with simple engraved decoration, walnut fullstock with checkered wrist.
(Wallis & Wallis) $1,295

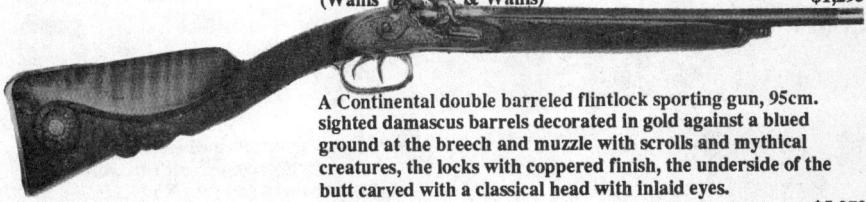

A Continental double barreled flintlock sporting gun, 95cm. sighted damascus barrels decorated in gold against a blued ground at the breech and muzzle with scrolls and mythical creatures, the locks with coppered finish, the underside of the butt carved with a classical head with inlaid eyes.
(Phillips) $5,370

A Scottish basket-hilted broadsword, the broad blade with three fullers on each face at the forte stamped 'Andrea Ferara' and with copper-inlaid orb and cross mark, the iron hilt comprising basket-guard of vertical slender bars framing S-shaped bars, second quarter of the 18th Century, 29½in. blade.
(Christie's S. Ken)

$1,518

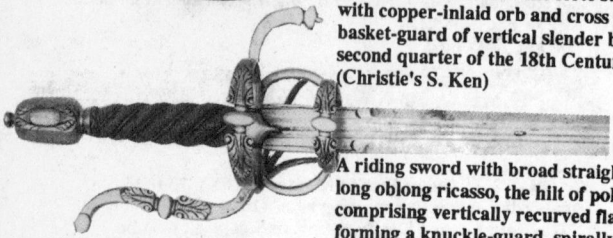

A riding sword with broad straight two-edged fullered blade with long oblong ricasso, the hilt of polished iron with guard comprising vertically recurved flat quillons, the front one forming a knuckle-guard, spirally-ribbed wooden grip bound with brass wire, early 17th Century, probably German, 39½in. blade.
(Christie's S. Ken)

$2,834

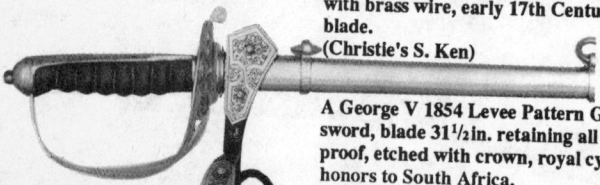

A George V 1854 Levee Pattern Grenadier Guards officer's sword, blade 31½in. retaining all original polish, Wilkinson proof, etched with crown, royal cypher, regimental badge, battle honors to South Africa.
(Wallis & Wallis)

$484

A fine Saxon rapier with stout double-edged blade of hexagonal section with a short fuller on each side at the forte, the blackened hilt overlaid with silver engraved with hatched arabesque patterns, last quarter of the 16th Century, 41½in. blade.
(Christie's S. Ken)

$24,288

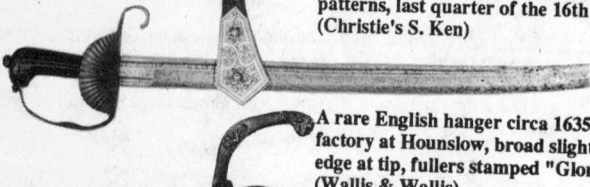

A rare English hanger circa 1635, probably made in the sword factory at Hounslow, broad slightly curved blade 24in., with false edge at tip, fullers stamped "Gloreia Sole Deo" with orbs.
(Wallis & Wallis)

$1,742

A very rare Swiss saber (Schweizersäbel) with long single-edged slightly curved blade double-edged towards the point, and with broad shallow fuller bordering the back on each face, the guard of blackened iron, a saltire-shaped guard of slender round bars, circa 1600, 38¼in.
(Christie's S. Ken)

$50,600

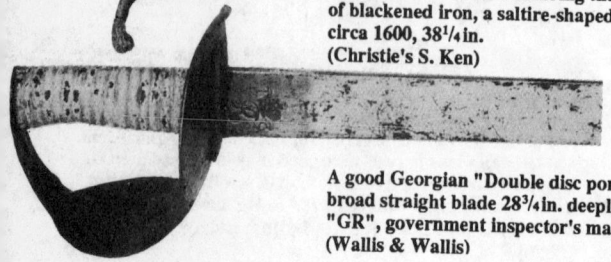

A good Georgian "Double disc pommel" naval boarding cutlass, broad straight blade 28¾in. deeply stamped with crowned "GR", government inspector's mark and rack No 21.
(Wallis & Wallis)

$662

## SWORDS

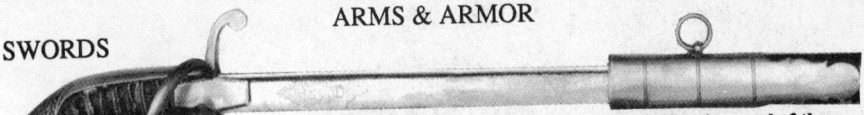

A fine and rare Imperial Russian Naval officer's sword of the reign of Nicholas II, plated, straight, pipeback clipped backed blade 33in., etched with Imperial eagle, crowned royal cypher, fouled anchor, naval trophies and foliage.
(Wallis & Wallis) $1,548

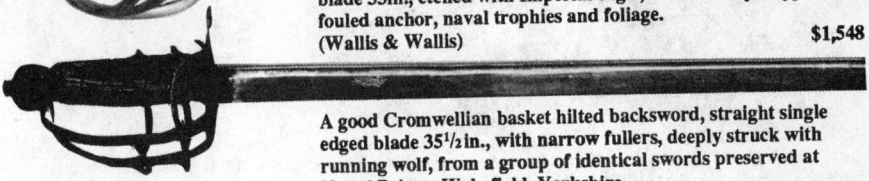

A good Cromwellian basket hilted backsword, straight single edged blade 35½in., with narrow fullers, deeply struck with running wolf, from a group of identical swords preserved at Nostel Priory, Wakefield, Yorkshire
(Wallis & Wallis) $1,596

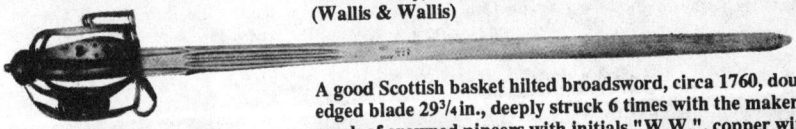

A good Scottish basket hilted broadsword, circa 1760, double edged blade 29¾in., deeply struck 6 times with the maker's mark of crowned pincers with initials "W.W.", copper wire bound sharkskin covered grip with brass ferrules.
(Wallis & Wallis) $1,161

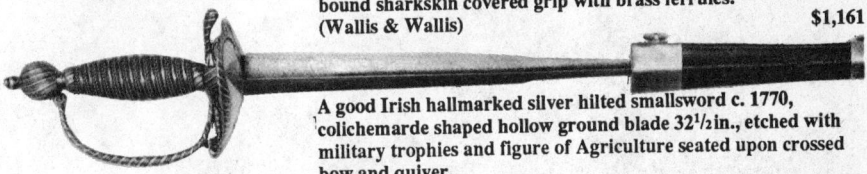

A good Irish hallmarked silver hilted smallsword c. 1770, colichemarde shaped hollow ground blade 32½in., etched with military trophies and figure of Agriculture seated upon crossed bow and quiver.
(Wallis & Wallis) $3,870

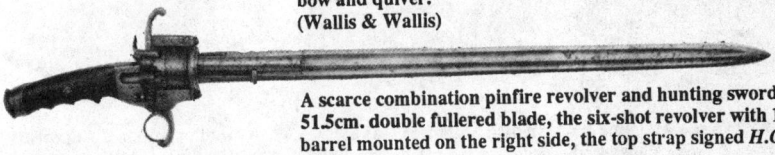

A scarce combination pinfire revolver and hunting sword, 51.5cm. double fullered blade, the six-shot revolver with 10cm. barrel mounted on the right side, the top strap signed *H.G. & F. Brevets.*
(Phillips) $2,417

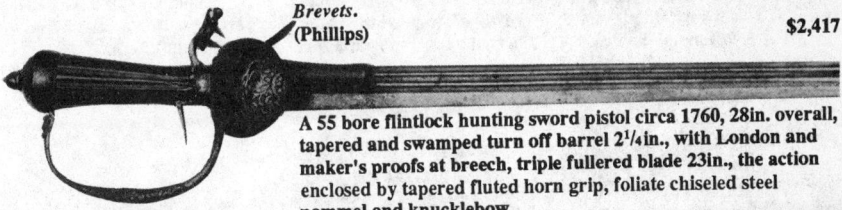

A 55 bore flintlock hunting sword pistol circa 1760, 28in. overall, tapered and swamped turn off barrel 2¼in., with London and maker's proofs at breech, triple fullered blade 23in., the action enclosed by tapered fluted horn grip, foliate chiseled steel pommel and knucklebow.
(Wallis & Wallis) $1,128

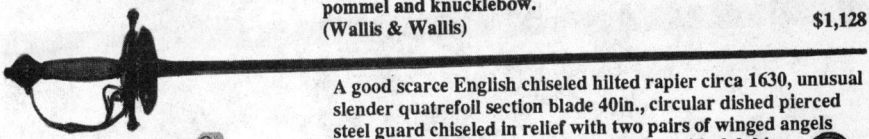

A good scarce English chiseled hilted rapier circa 1630, unusual slender quatrefoil section blade 40in., circular dished pierced steel guard chiseled in relief with two pairs of winged angels supporting crowned busts amidst foliage with dolphins.
(Wallis & Wallis) £1,250 $2,419

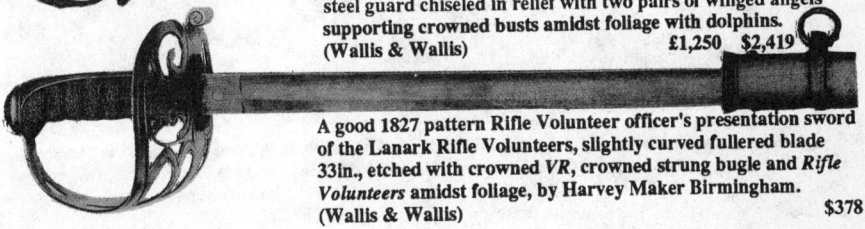

A good 1827 pattern Rifle Volunteer officer's presentation sword of the Lanark Rifle Volunteers, slightly curved fullered blade 33in., etched with crowned *VR*, crowned strung bugle and *Rifle Volunteers* amidst foliage, by Harvey Maker Birmingham.
(Wallis & Wallis) $378

A mokkogata iron hikone-bori tsuba depicting warriors outside a temple among pines, signed *Goshu Hikone ju Soheishi Nyudo Soten sei*, 18th century, 7.8cm.
(Christie's) $1,084

A circular iron tsuchimeji tsuba decorated in iroe takazogan and takabori with a seated Chinese sennin conjuring a dragon and thunderclouds from a small bowl, 18th century, 6.6cm.
(Christie's) $1,084

An oval iron tsuba, a coiled dragon in ikizukashi with gilt detail, signed *Echizen ju Kinai saku*, 18th century, 7.4cm.
(Christie's) $1,192

An iron mokko shaped tsuba carved overall with a figure and various demons within a landscape, soft metal details, 8.4cm.
(Phillips) $228

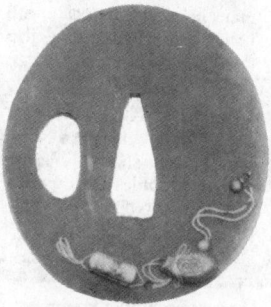

An oval Shibuichi tsuba decorated in soft metals and hardstones, with an inro and pouch, the reverse with a fan, 6.4cm.
(Phillips) $380

A circular iron tsuba decorated with shoki and an oni on the reverse within a raised rim, soft metal detail, 7cm.
(Phillips) $532

A large circular iron Sukashi tsuba carved and pierced with a dragon within a square rim, signed Echizen ju Kanai-saku, 10cm.
(Phillips) $608

An oval iron mokume-ji tsuba with three kosukashi designs representing magical charms, signed *Kihan Masayoshi Namban tetsu o motte kore-o zukuri*, circa 1850, 6.7cm.
(Christie's) $910

A good circular iron tsuba, carved in low relief with horses within a landscape, 8.3cm.
(Phillips) $361

## TSUBAS

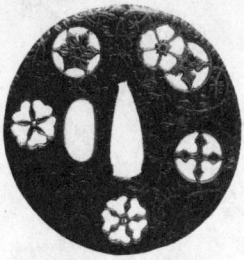

A circular iron tsuba decorated in brass inlay with water-weed fronds and mon-sukashi in yoshiro-zogan style, signed *Saburodaiyu Kore-o Saku*, 18th century, 7.3cm.
(Christie's) $5,634

An oval iron tsuba, a coiled dragon in marubori chasing a flaming tama, unsigned, Echizen Kinai school, 18th century, 7.3cm.
(Christie's) $1,084

A rounded-rectangular iron tsuba decorated with silver sujizogan and gilt nunomezogan in the style of Nakane Heilachiro of Higo, circa 1850, 8.6cm.
(Christie's) $1,192

A good oval iron tsuba carved with a tiger within a stormy landscape, and gold kao, and dated 1866, 7.2cm.
(Phillips) $1330

Japanese inlaid shakudo tsuba, 19th century, of oval form, each hitsu with gold plug, decorated in relief, 3¼ x 3in.
(Du Mouchelles) $275

A rounded shakudo tsuba, 6.4cm., finely katakiri engraved and chiseled with a sage before bamboo.
(Wallis & Wallis) $200

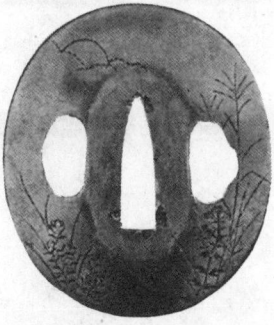

An oval shakudo tsuba, 6.6cm., katakiri engraved with various plants and grasses beneath moon.
(Wallis & Wallis) $166

An oval iron hikone-bori tsuba depicting the Chinese military servant Yojo stabbing the cloak of Prince Cho Bujutsu, signed *Goshu Hikone ju Soheishi Nyudo Soten sei*, 18th century, 7.6cm.
(Christie's) $1,040

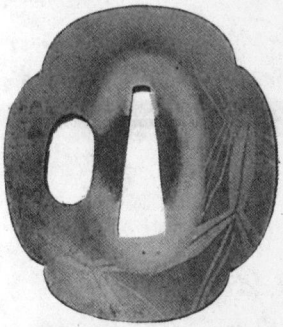

A Mokko sentoku tsuba, 6.2cm., etched with a dragonfly and water plantain leaves, traces of silvered decoration.
(Wallis & Wallis) $150

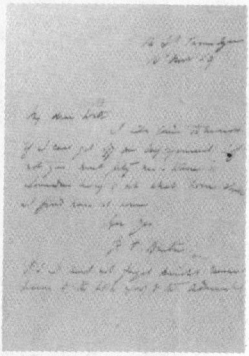

**Sir Richard F. Burton (1829–1890; English Explorer), autograph letter, one page, 10th November 1859, to "My dear Watt', stating that he will try and come tomorrow.**
**(T. Vennett-Smith) $191**

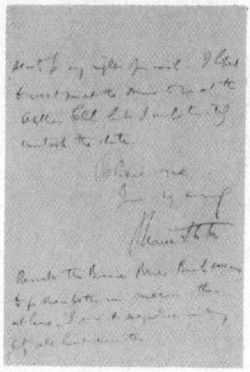

**Bram Stoker, autograph letter, two pages, 3rd June 1891, to Mr. Watson, stating that he should like to meet his correspondent whilst in Liverpool.**
**(T. Vennett-Smith) $401**

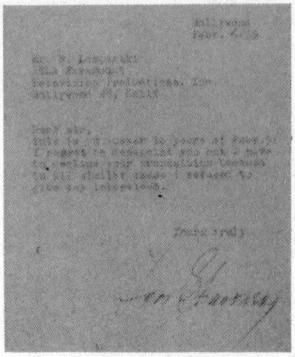

**Igor Stravinsky, typed letter signed, one page, Hollywood, 6th February 1959, to Mr. R. Lamparski of Paramount Television Productions Inc., declining his proposition.**
**(T. Vennett-Smith) $592**

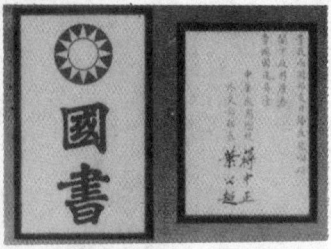

**Chiang Kai-Shek, four pages, 20th September 1957, to the Argentinian President Pedro Eugenio Aramburu, in Chinese, presenting Dr. Shen Shan Hoan as an Ambassador.**
**(T. Vennett-Smith) $201**

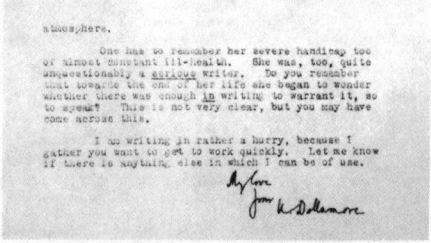

atmosphere.

One has to remember her severe handicap too of almost constant ill-health. She was, too, quite unquestionably a serious writer. Do you remember that towards the end of her life she began to wonder whether there was enough in writing to warrant it, so to speak? This is not very clear, but you may have come across this.

I am writing in rather a hurry, because I gather you want to get to work quickly. Let me know if there is anything else in which I can be of use.

My love
Jon W. Dollamore

**Walter de la Mare and Katherine Mansfield, a 2pp typed letter, signed U[ncle] Dollamore, dated Hill House, Taplow, Buckinghamshire, February 7th, 1933, to Tristram Bersford discussing Katherine Mansfield's work.**
**(Christie's S. Ken) $599**

**King James I(King James VI of Scotland), one page, 18th December 1616, "To the E. Marschall"**
**(T. Vennett-Smith) $1,375**

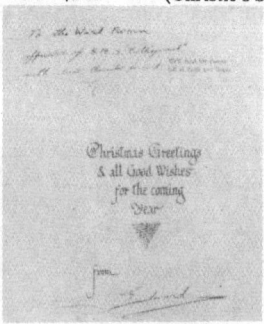

Christmas Greetings
& all Good Wishes
for the coming
Year

**Edward VIII, early signed Christmas card "Edward", inscribed "To the Ward Room officers of H.M.S. "Collingwood" with best thanks for card."**
**(T. Vennett-Smith) $220**

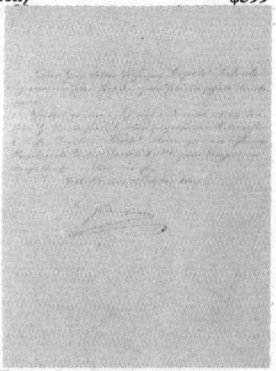

**Franz Josef (1830–1916; Emperor of Austria. Austro-Hungarian Emperor), one page, 26th October 1899, with embossed Royal seal.**
**(T. Vennett-Smith) $286**

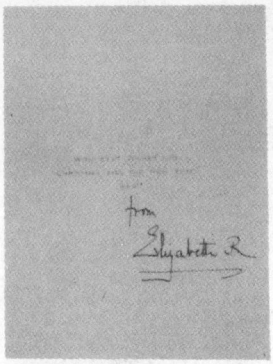

**Elizabeth, The Queen Mother, signed Christmas card for 1959, featuring photograph of Her Majesty.**
**(T. Vennett-Smith) $201**

**Ralph Vaughan Williams, autograph letter, one page, 31st October n.y., to an un-named male correspondent.**
**(T. Vennett-Smith) $124**

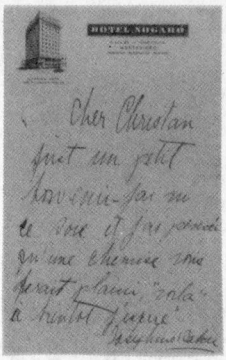


**Josephine Baker, autograph letter, one page, in French, to 'Cher Christian' (her first theatrical hairdresser).**
**(T. Vennett-Smith) $143**

**King George III, St James's, 2nd September 1808, appointing John Glynn to be Assistant Commissary of Stores.**
**(T. Vennett-Smith) $239**

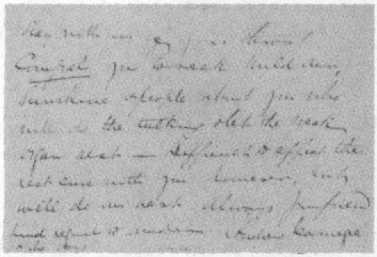

**Andrew Carnegie, autograph letter, four pages, 22nd December 1897, to "My Dear Doctor", inviting him to cruise on the Columba.**
**(T. Vennett-Smith) $286**

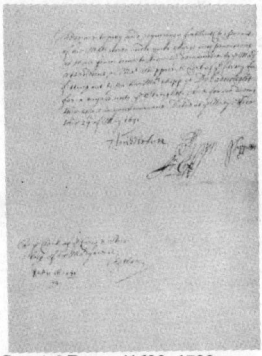

**Samuel Pepys (1633–1703; Diarist and High Naval Officer, Secretary of the Admiralty under Charles II), one page, (London), 27 May 1671, being a warrant to the Clerk of the Stores at Chatham.**
**(T. Vennett-Smith) $1,184**

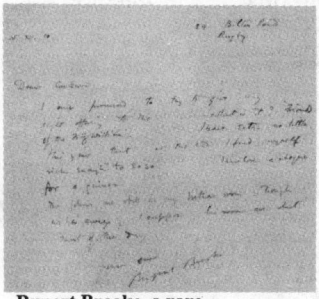

**Rupert Brooke, a rare autograph letter, one page, 15th December 1910, to Sydney Cockerell, Director of the Fitzwilliam Museum at Cambridge, "I once promised to give my slight offering to the –What is it? "Friends of the Fitzwilliam". I enclose a cheque for a guinea."**
**(T. Vennett-Smith) $1,289**

**Gamal Abdel Nasser, one page, 1st May 1958, to Dr. Aturo Froudizi, in Egyptian, regarding the presentation of credentials to the Argentinian President.**
**(T. Vennett-Smith) $145**

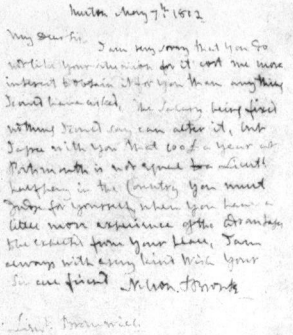

Horatio Nelson, autograph letter, 'Nelson & Bronte', one page, 7th May 1802, to Lieutenant Bromwich, in full "I am very sorry that you do not like your situation for it cost me more interest to obtain it for you than anything I could have asked."
(T. Vennett-Smith) $1,910

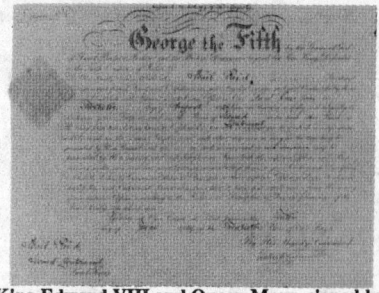


King Edward VIII and Queen Mary, signed by both (Edward as Prince of Wales and Mary as Queen), on behalf of King George V, 10th June 1929, appointing Nevil Reid as Second Lieutenant in the Land Forces.
(T. Vennett-Smith) $315

Sir Winston S. Churchill, early autograph letter, one page, 16th December 1921, on Colonial Office headed notepaper, to the Irish political leader Tim Healy, "My dear Healy", "I am glad to tell you that a vacancy has occurred in the West African Custom Service"
(T. Vennett-Smith) $1,337

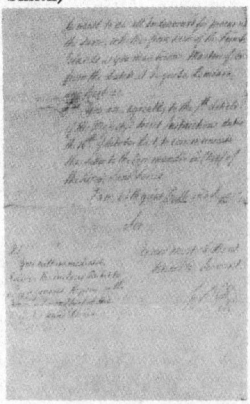

William Pitt, the Elder, interesting signed letter, nine pages, Whitehall, 9th March 1759, to Commodore Moore, marked 'Secret', stating that Captain Tyrrell had arrived with his despatch that had been immediately laid before the King.
(T. Vennett-Smith) $401

Queen Elizabeth II, signed Christmas card, beneath photo showing the Royal Family, accompanied by a Corgi, 1960.
(T. Vennett-Smith) $248

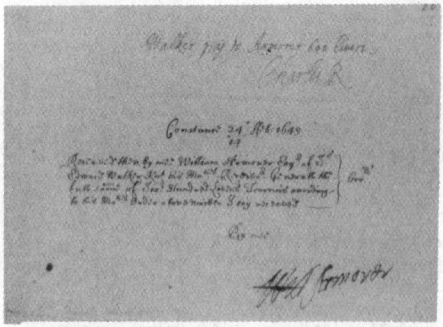

King Charles II, one page, February 1649, being an order of payment of six hundred livers from William Armourer Esq.
(T. Vennett-Smith) $687

**Dwight D. Eisenhower, and Mamie Doud Eisenhower, signed 9.75" x 10" color Christmas Greetings plaque, 1957.**
**(T. Vennett-Smith) $172**

**Prince Charles and Princess Diana, attractive Christmas card signed by both, featuring a color photograph of the Prince and Princess of Wales with their two children.**
**(T. Vennett-Smith) $1,910**

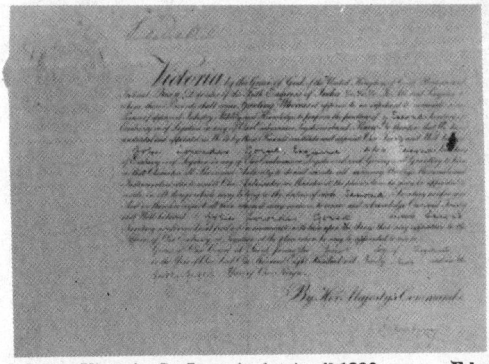

**Queen Victoria, St. James's, 1st April 1892, being a document appointing John Lowndes Gorst a Second Secretary of Embassies or Legations abroad, countersigned by Salisbury.**
**(T. Vennett-Smith) $229**

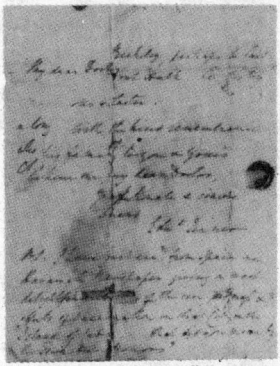

**Edward Jenner, autograph letter, five pages, 'Friday Septr.' (26th added in another hand), to Dr. Worthington, the whole letter stained, torn at folds and generally fragile.**
**(T. Vennett-Smith) $726**

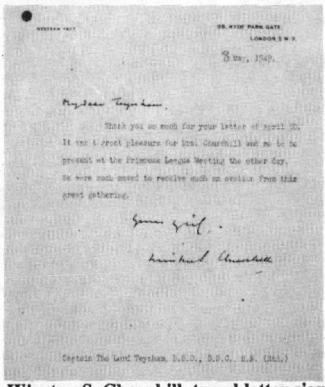

**Sir Winston S. Churchill, typed letter signed, one page, 8th May 1949, to Captain The Lord Teynham, 'My dear Teynham', stating that "It was a great pleasure for Mrs. Churchill and me to be present at the Primrose League Meeting the other day."**
**(T. Vennett-Smith) $936**

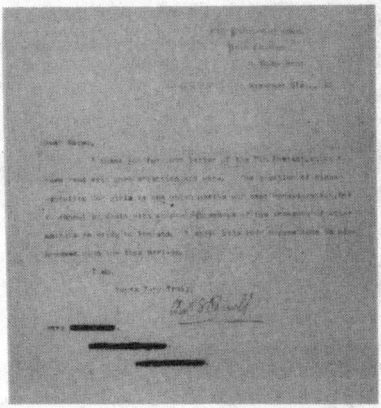

**Charles S. Parnell, typed letter signed, one page, 31st December 1885, to a female correspondent thanking her for her letter.**
**(T. Vennett-Smith) $344**

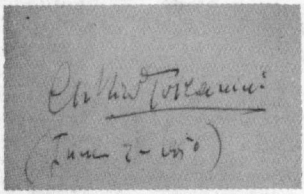

Arturo Toscanini, boldly signed card, in red ink, 2nd June 1950.
(T. Vennett-Smith) $134

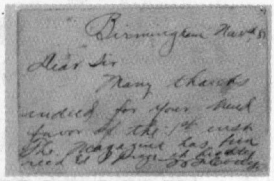

W.F. Cody, 'Buffalo Bill', autograph letter, on one side of a correspondence card, 4th November 1887,, to an unnamed correspondent, thanking him for a magazine which Cody prizes highly.
(T. Vennett-Smith) $649

Woodrow Wilson, signed album page, also signed by E.M. House, 21st June 1919.
(T. Vennett-Smith) $92

King George I, small signed piece, as King, laid down to album page beneath contemporary engraving.
(T. Vennett-Smith) $124

Anna Pavlova, signed piece, overmounted beneath 5.5" x 7.5" reproduction photo.
(T. Vennett-Smith) $86

Gary Cooper, signed cover of Royal Performance Programme, at the Coliseum, Charing Cross, 9th November 1938.
(T. Vennett-Smith) $76

Ernest Hemingway, signed and inscribed edition of Look Magazine, to inside page, 26th January 1954 edition featuring large article about safari in Africa by Hemingway.
(T. Vennett-Smith) $898

Henry Longfellow, good signed piece, 1874, laid down to contemporary album page beneath contemporary sepia photograph.
(T. Vennett-Smith) $117

Cary Grant, signed 7.5" x 10" synopsis sheet for 'Indiscreet', to front cover, featuring caricature of Grant and Bergman.
(T. Vennett-Smith) $86

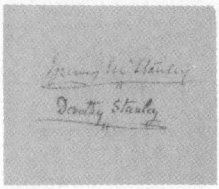

**Henry M. Stanley, signed piece, also signed by his wife Dorothy Stanley, small stain.**
**(T. Vennett-Smith) $143**

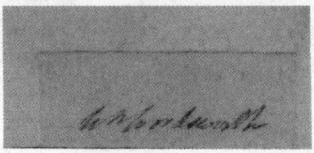

**William Wordsworth, small signed piece, laid down.**
**(T. Vennett-Smith) $118**

**Georges Carpentier, signed album page.**
**(T. Vennett-Smith) $57**

**Neil Armstrong, signed edition of the Tribune for Saturday, 2nd August 1969, featuring picture of Armstrong and captioned 'First to the Moon'.**
**(T. Vennett-Smith) $210**

**Bogart and Bacall, a good pair of individual signed cards, overmounted beneath 8" x 10" reproduction photo.**
**(T. Vennett-Smith) $477**

**Andy Warhol, signed color postcard reproduction of 'Marilyn' from his 'Ten Marilyns'.**
**(T. Vennett-Smith) $325**

**Maria Callas, signed postcard, to lower white border, head and shoulders, photo by Vivienne.**
**(T. Vennett-Smith) $344**

**Leslie Howard, signed and inscribed sheet of Canadian Pacific Cruises headed notepaper, 1935, some creasing.**
**(T. Vennett-Smith) $86**

**Raphael Semmes, Rear-Admiral and famous Confederate Captain of the 'Alabama', which destroyed 82 Union Ships before being sunk itself, signed piece.**
**(T. Vennett-Smith) $191**

**Brigham Young, small signed piece.**
**(T. Vennett-Smith) $220**

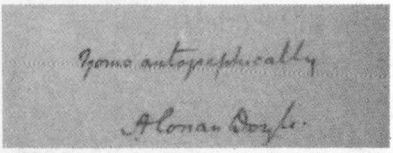

**Sir Arthur Conan Doyle, good signed piece "Yours autographically A. Conan Doyle", very slight smudging.**
**(T. Vennett-Smith) $181**

**Agatha Christie, signed card, with a modern unsigned postcard, crease.**
**(T. Vennett-Smith) $95**

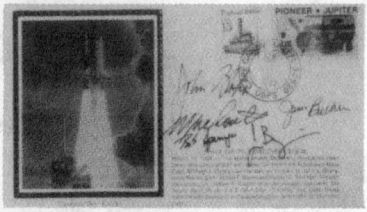

**Astronauts, Space Shuttle Discovery STS-29 crew, signed by Capt. Michael L. Coats, Col. John E. Blaha, Col. James F. Buchli, Col. Robert C. Springer and Dr. James P. Bagian, postally canceled Cape Canaveral, 13th March 1989.**
**(T. Vennett-Smith) $153**

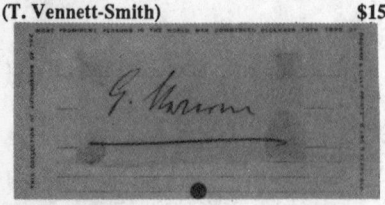

**Guglielmo Marconi, signed piece, laid down to card, some staining to corners, just affecting underline of signature.**
**(T. Vennett-Smith) $67**

**Lon Chaney Snr., small signed piece, cut from official document, rare, slight stain.**
**(T. Vennett-Smith) $420**

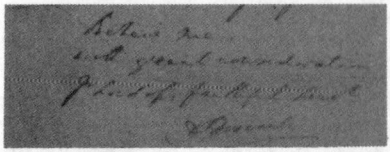

**Benjamin Disraeli, signed piece, cut from end of letter, with nine words of text.**
**(T. Vennett-Smith) $105**

**George B. Brummell, 'Beau Brummell', small signed piece, cut from end of letter.**
**(T. Vennett-Smith) $73**

**Charles Darwin, autograph envelope, unsigned, addressed to Sir J. Paget, Bart, of Hanover Place, Hanover Square, London, postally canceled 4th June 1881.**
**(T. Vennett-Smith) $191**

**King George II, small signed piece, as King, cut from document, lightly laid down to card.**
**(T. Vennett-Smith) $59**

**Robert Stephenson, Builder of the 'Rocket' Railway Engine, signed piece, cut from end of letter.**
**(T. Vennett-Smith) $76**

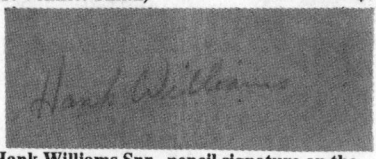

**Hank Williams Snr., pencil signature on the inside of a bar matchbook, 4" x 1.5", rare, some creasing.**
**(T. Vennett-Smith) $382**

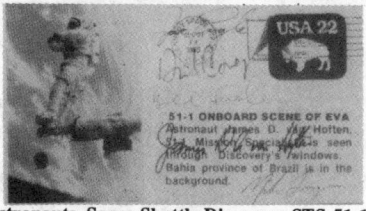


**Astronauts, Space Shuttle Discovery STS-51-1 crew, signed by all five members of the crew, including Joe Engle, James D. van Hoften and three others, postally canceled Kennedy Space Center, 27th August 1985.**
**(T. Vennett-Smith) $134**

**George Stephenson, builder of the 'Rocket' Railway engine, signed piece, alongside modern color postcard.**
**(T. Vennett-Smith) $248**

**Bela Bartok, good boldly signed card, rare.**
**(T. Vennett-Smith) $277**

**John Steinbeck, small signed card.**
**(T. Vennett-Smith) $162**

**Sitting Bull, rare pencil signature on 5.25" x 2" photographers mount board, (the image above removed at some stage of the signature's life).**
**(T. Vennett-Smith) $1,432**

**Louis Bleriot, signed postcard, showing three farm laborers watching Bleriot's aircraft passing above them.**
**(T. Vennett-Smith) $363**

**Louis Bleriot, small signed Savoy Hotel card, in pencil, also signed by Caproni (Italian Aero Designer), 1929.**
**(T. Vennett-Smith) $118**

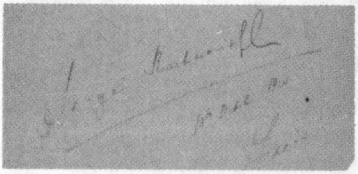

**Sergei Rachmaninoff, signed album page, full signature, Leeds, 13th October 1910.**
**(T. Vennett-Smith) $229**

Peter Lorre, signed piece, with attached newspaper photo.
(T. Vennett-Smith) $95

Spencer Tracy, signed album page, with three attached photos, annotated in another hand 'Died Hollywood'.
(T. Vennett-Smith) $76

Arturo Toscanini, signed bound copy of Beethoven's Symphony No. 6, 29th April 1937.
(T. Vennett-Smith) $143

Montgomery Clift, boldly signed album page, overmounted beneath contemporary postcard, 7.25" x 12" overall.
(T. Vennett-Smith) $134

Errol Flynn, signed and inscribed album page, overmounted beneath 7" x 8" reproduction photo.
(T. Vennett-Smith) $124

Bela Lugosi, large signed album page, in red ink, overmounted beneath 6" x 7.5" photo.
(T. Vennett-Smith) $191

Anna Magnani, signed album page, with attached photo, overmounted beneath 7.5" x 9" reproduction photo.
(T. Vennett-Smith) $134

Judy Garland, irregularly clipped signed piece laid down to modern plain postcard.
(T. Vennett-Smith) $134

Al Jolson, signed and inscribed album page, in pencil, overmounted beneath 7.75" x 8.5" photo.
(T. Vennett-Smith) $86

**Leslie Howard, signed piece, 1933.**
**(T. Vennett-Smith) $80**

**Charles Chaplin, signed album page, annotated in another hand 'London Airport 29-10-52'.**
**(T. Vennett-Smith) $95**

**Louis Armstrong, signed piece.**
**(T. Vennett-Smith) $105**

**John Garfield, signed album page, with small attached photo, overmounted beneath 9.5" x 7.5" reproduction photo.**
**(T. Vennett-Smith) $95**

**Harry Langdon, signed and inscribed album page, overmounted beneath 5" x 9" photo.**
**(T. Vennett-Smith) $73**

**Rita Hayworth, large signed album page, overmounted beneath 7" x 8" reproduction photo.**
**(T. Vennett-Smith) $115**

**Vivien Leigh, signed piece, overmounted beneath color postcard, 6.25" x 11.25" overall.**
**(T. Vennett-Smith) $115**

**Marie Dressler, signed, sheet of notepaper.**
**(T. Vennett-Smith) $95**

**Alfred Hitchcock, signed card, in old age, overmounted beneath 2.5" x 3.5" photo.**
**(T. Vennett-Smith) $86**

A novelty automaton electric-driven watch maker, with illuminated sign to the front and lamp to his desk, 8in. high.
(Christie's S. Ken) $1,181

An electric operated advertising automaton with moving arms, eyes, head and eyebrows, on painted wood base, 30in. high.
(Anderson & Garland) $385

A Chinese automaton, of a nobleman in original silk robes and elaborate saddle cloth and harness, sitting astride a white silk covered horse, 19in. high.
(Christie's S. Ken) $664

A composition-headed standing negro smoking automaton, with moving eyelids and lower jaw and composition hands, in original gray plush top hat, 31in. high, Vichy circa 1890.
(Christie's S. Ken) $9,027

A hand-operated musical automaton, of a cat and dog with composition heads and glass eyes, playing instruments, in original clothes, 12in. wide.
(Christie's S. Ken) $1,192

A very rare early 20th century French electrically-operated life-size black boy magician automaton, in painted papier-mâché, 53½in. high excluding associated top hat, with Cressall speed control.
(Tennants) $9,240

A late 19th century Ives 'Dancing Negroes' automaton, each black painted doll with papier-mâché head, within a wooden box, 10½in. high.
(Phillips) $766

A fine automaton monkey duo comprising a photographer and seated lady, the subject, each with papier-mâché head, glass eyes, articulated kid-covered jaw revealing painted teeth, 26in. base to apex; probably J. Phalibois, late 19th century.
(Phillips) $5,835

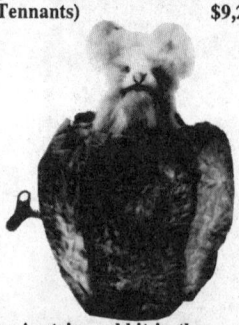

An Austrian rabbit-in-the-lettuce, musical automaton, the rotating white fur-covered rabbit emerging from the painted fabric lettuce, 10in. high.
(Christie's) $927

A fine Leopold Lambert musical automaton 'Clown Playing the Mandolin', the composition heads with painted insects, blue glass eyes, protruding tongue, with white and red mohair wig.
(Phillips) $6,840

'Monkey Cobbler', automaton with papier-mâché head, glass eyes, and articulated jaw, seated on a box.
(Phillips) $1,235

'The Old Nurse', an Excelsior mechanical toy of a seated Negro nurse with ward, when activated, mechanism causes nurse to lean backwards, raising the child in the air.
(Phillips) $1,615

A French Manivelle automaton of a piano player and dancing couple, the pianist seated before a wooden piano, 8½in. high.
(Phillips) $1,098

A Louis XVI ormolu-mounted Paris porcelain musical automaton clock, playing a selection of six tunes through ten organ pipes, cam-and-rod drive through a composition tree to an automaton bird atop flapping its wings, rotating and opening and shutting its beak, 26¼in. high.
(Christie's) $18,422

A German cat picture automaton, depicting a singing master with his choristers, of polychrome painted and lithographed card, framed and glazed, 10½ x 14in., circa 1900.
(Phillips) $1,275

A clockwork musical automaton of a white rabbit in a rose, with brown glass eyes and movements to body, head and ears, 8in. high, by Roullet & Decamps.
(Christie's S. Ken) $1,317

A French musical manivelle of a 'Mouse Tea-Party', each animal having glass eyes and fur covered body.
(Phillips) $1,425

A Roullet et Decamps 'Cat Ironing' musical automaton, the fur covered body with glass eye (one missing), long tail and carved hands.
(Phillips) $760

A mid 19th century mahogany wheel barometer, with 8½in. silvered dial signed *A. Salla.*
(Allen & Harris) $780

A mid 19th century mahogany stick barometer, the exposed tube with silver plate and vernier signed *P. Gally, Cambridge.*
(Allen & Harris) $1,153

A 19th century rosewood and inlaid wheel barometer, with 8in. silvered dial, the level signed *M. Barnasconi*, 3ft. 4in. high.
(Phillips) $740

A 19th century mahogany stick barometer with swan-necked pediment, signed *Bithray, Royal Exchange, London*, 3ft. 2½in. high.
(Phillips) $1,112

A 19th century mahogany marine barometer, the case surmounted by a carved shell decoration, with ivory scales signed *Dennis Bishopsgate St. London*, 40in. high.
(Phillips) $2,204

A late Georgian wheel barometer with silvered scale plates engraved with maker's name *F. Walker, London*, contained in a rosewood banjo case, 38in. high.
(Spencer's) $837

A George III mahogany bow fronted stick barometer, the rectangular silvered dial signed *D. Cohen Newcastle on Tyne*, 3ft. 2in. high.
(Phillips) $2,875

A Regency mahogany wheel barometer signed *A Grego*, on the spirit level disc beneath silvered barometer dial, swan-neck pediment with urn finial, 44in. high.
(Christie's) $1,150

Regency mahogany wheel barometer/clock, Lione & Co., 81 Holborn St. London, early 19th century, with 10-inch dial, 45½in. high. (Skinner Inc.) $1,700

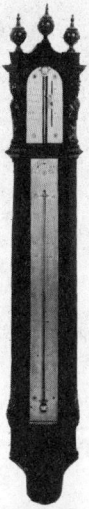

A fine 18th century mahogany barometer in breakarched case, signed *I. Cuff fecit*, 40in. high. (Christie's) $27,527

An early Victorian mahogany wheel barometer, signed *Dollond LONDON*, with thermometer and spirit level, 40in. high. (Christie's) $1,980

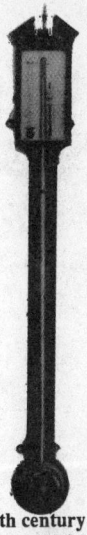

A 19th century mahogany stick barometer, the silvered dial signed *Corti Colchester*, with thermometer and turned cistern cover, 3ft. 2¼in. high. (Phillips) $1,295

A George III mahogany bow-front stick barometer signed *J. Hicks, Maker, London*, glazed thermometer to trunk with molded ebonized cystern cover, 40in. long. (Christie's) $3,344

A large mahogany clock/wheel barometer with swan-neck pediment, signed *D. Fagioli, London*, clock with single chain fusée eight-day movement, 54½in. high. (Christie's S. Ken) $2,877

A 19th century mahogany marine barometer, the ivory dial signed *Henry Frodsham, Castle Street, Liverpool*, 3ft. 1½in. high. (Phillips) $3,330

An early Victorian papier-mâché and mother-of-pearl wheel barometer signed *CICERI & PINI EDINBURGH* on the spirit-level scale, 39in. high. (Christie's) $1,485

Legrain (Pierre, binder), Schmied (François Louis) and Alfred de Vigny: Daphne, number 117 of 140 copies signed by Schmied, large 4to., Paris, F.L. Schmied, 1924.
(Christie's S. Ken) $15,338

[Nelson (Horatio)], The original grant made to Lord Nelson, creating him Duke of Bronte, signed by Ferdinand, King of the Two Sicilies and Infante of Spain ('Ferdinandus P') and bearing his seal.
(Phillips) $54,900

Daniel Defoe 'The Life and Adventures of Robinson Crusoe, embellished with engravings from designs by: Thomas Stothard', two vols, London 1820.
(Du Mouchelles) $2,000

Vanity Fair, 4 albums of 204 colored lithographed plates, 5 folding, of statesmen, judges, men of the day, and sportsmen, 1890, 92, 95–96.
(Phillips) $3,600

Milbert (Jacques Gérard) Itinéraire Pittoresque du Fleuve Hudson et des Parties Latérales de l'Amerique du Nord, 2 vols. of text and atlas vol. of plates with 53 (only, of 54) lithographed views, 1828–29.
(Phillips) $7,030

Voltaire (François Marie Arouet de), La Pucelle d'Orléans, poëme en vingt-un chants, grand papier vélin, 2 vols., engraved portrait by Gaucher and 21 plates, 1799.
(Phillips) $2,960

Linnaeus, Sir Charles, 'An Universal System of Natural History', ed. E. Sibly and others, 14 vols, approx. 420 hand colored plates.
(Lawrence Fine Art) $5,614

THE
Art of Glass,
WHEREIN
Are shown the ways to make and colour Glass, Pebbles, Enamels, [illegible] and other Curiosities.
Written in Latin by Antonio Neri; and Translated into English, with some Observations on the Author.
Whereunto is added an account of the Glass Trade, with some Experiments, Notes, & Medicinal Chap.
LONDON,
Printed by A.W. for Octavian Pulleyn at the Sign of the Rose in St. Paul's Church-yard. MDCLXII.

Neri, A. (Trans. Merrett, C) 'The Art of Glass' small octavo, London, printed by A.W. for Octavian Pulleyn 1662.
(Woolley & Wallis) $1,181

LES
OEUVRES
DE
CLEMENT MAROT
DE CAHORS,
VALET DE CHAMBRE
DU ROY.
TOME I.
A LA HAYE,
Chez ADRIAN MOETJENS,
MDCC.

Marot (Clement), Oeuvres, 2 vols., First edition, first issue with the same printer's mark in both volumes, from Jonathan Swift's library.
(Phillips) $2,960

Harrison (James A.), George Washington: Patriot, Soldier, Statesman, plates, finely bound in full blue crushed morocco, by Riviere, slipcase 1906.
(Phillips) $875

Sinclair (R), Sir Golly de Wogg, Nursery Portrait Gallery, the artist/author's original illustrated manuscript containing ten tipped in watercolor and black ink illustrations of the Golly pursuing various sports.
(Spencer's) $500

Jones (Paul, illustrator), Blunt (Wilfred Jasper Walter): Flora Superba, limited to 406 copies signed by the artist, this an unnumbered presentation copy.
(Christie's S. Ken) $394

Jasper (Theodore, illustrator), Studer (Jacob Henry): The Birds of North America, folio, New York and Columbus, Ohio, 1881.
(Christie's S. Ken) $482

Moore (Thomas): The Ferns of Great Britain and Ireland, new edition, folio, Bradbury and Evans, 1857.
(Christie's S. Ken) $1,532

Wright (Lewis): The Illustrated Book of Poultry, 4to, Cassell & Co., 1890, 50 chromolithographed plates, original cloth, gilt.
(Christie's S. Ken) $1,640

Morris (William), The Well at the World's End, one of 350 copies of an edition of 358, printed in Chaucer type in double columns, Hammersmith, 1896.
(Phillips) $1,830

Selby (Prideaux John), plates to Selby's Illustrations of British Ornithology, hand colored engravings, London 1841.
(Spencer's) $17,500

Wodehouse (P.G.): My Man Jeeves, first edition, George Newnes, [1919], original cloth, Jeeves in the Offing, first edition, first issue, [1960].
(Christie's S. Ken) $657

Wright (John): The Fruit Grower's Guide, 6 vols., 4to, [1891–94], 3 chromolithographed additional titles and 41 plates.
(Christie's S. Ken) $1,423

Hoare (Sir Robert Colt) & others, 'The History of Modern Wiltshire, large paper copy, 7 vols., 135 portraits and plates, including 4 colored aquatints and 10 hand-colored maps, 1822–44–43.
(Phillips) $3,400

Booth (Edward Thomas): Rough Notes on the Birds observed during twenty-five years' shooting and collecting in the British Islands, 3 vols., 114 hand-colored lithographed plates, 1881–87.
(Phillips) $8,080

The Annals of Sporting and Fancy Gazette, vols. 1–13 and a duplicate of vol. 13 containing the June, 1828 issue, 1822–28.
(Christie's S. Ken) $4,816

Fore-edge painting, Frye (Bartholomew, binder), Montgomery (James): The World Before the Flood, third edition, 1814, contemporary blue straight-grained morocco by Bartholomew Frye of Halifax.
(Christie's S. Ken) $986

Daudet (Alphonse): [Works], 24 vols., Champrosay edition, number 1 of 100 copies, Boston, Little Brown, 1899, plates by L. Rossi.
(Christie's S. Ken) $2,410

Founès (Esther, binder), Chimot (Edouard) and Maxime Blum: Pilar d'Algesiras, limited to 103 copies, this number 14 of 20 copies for the artist and his friends, signed by Chimot under the limitation.
(Christie's S. Ken) $1,972

Albin (Eleazar), A Natural History of Spiders and Other Curious Insects, by John Tilly, for R. Montague, 1736.
(Christie's S. Ken) $758

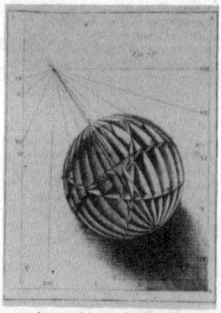

Deparcieux (Antoine): Nouveaux Traités de Trigonometrie Rectiligne et Spherique, 4to, Hippolyte-Louis Guerin & Jacques Guerin, Paris, 1741, 17 folding engraved plates.
(Christie's S. Ken) $438

# BOOKS

Parkinson (John): Theatrum Botanicum, the Theater of Plants, or an universall and complete Herball, First Edition. (Phillips) $323

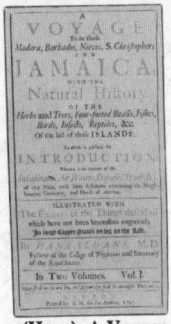


Sloane (Hans), A Voyage to the Islands Madera, Barbados, Nieves, S. Christophers and Jamaica, vol. I only, 1707. (Phillips) $1,119

Günther (Albert C.L.G.): The Gigantic Land-Tortoises (Living and Extinct) in the collection of the British Museum, folio, 1877, 54 lithographed plates. (Christie's S. Ken) $876

Lytton (Edward Bulwer, Lord): The Novels, 26 vols., Edition Magnifique, Dana Estes and Company, Boston, [n.d.], plates in both colored and uncolored states. (Christie's S. Ken) $2,080

Dickens (Charles), a set of the Christmas books, all first editions in original cloth, comprising: A Christmas Carol, The Chimes, The Cricket on the Hearth, The Battle of Life, The Haunted Man and The Ghost's Bargain. (Christie's S. Ken) $14,243

Dickens (Charles): [Works], 'Library edition', 30 vols., Chapman and Hall, engraved plates, contemporary maroon half calf, spines gilt. (Christie's S. Ken) $1,643

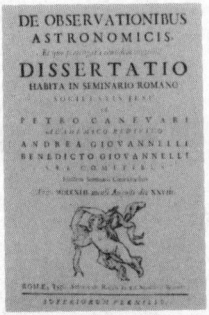


Boscovitch (Roger Joseph): De Observationibus Astronimicis, 4to, Antonii de Rubeis, Rome, 1742, engraved folding title, light spotting to text, early boards. (Christie's S. Ken) $700

Ward (Rowland), Bryden (H.A., editor), Great and Small Game of Africa, number 40 of 500 copies signed by Ward, 1899. (Christie's S. Ken) $910

Churchill (Winston Spencer): London to Ladysmith via Pretoria, 1900, folding map, original pictorial cloth. (Christie's S. Ken) $394

'Sapho', a cold-painted bronze bust cast from a model by E. Villanis, of a young maiden, her hair tied in a bun, green and amber patination, 58cm. high.
(Christie's) $6,138

A 19th century French gilt bronze and plated encrier, modeled with sheep on a rocky promontory, signed *J. Moigniez*, 12in. wide.
(Christie's S. Ken) $602

An English 'New Sculpture' bronze figure of Perseus, cast from a model by Frederick William Pomeroy, the elegant nude hero wearing an elaborate helmet, late 19th century, 20 1/8in. high.
(Christie's) $19,602

A German bronze group of two rearing horses, the two stallions standing adjacent to each other, their forelegs raised and their heads turned down, 19th century, 13in. high.
(Christie's) $4,792

A late 19th century French bronze group of Iris, cast from a model by Henri Honoré Plê, her drapery forming a rainbow, a playful cherub at her side, 30 1/4in. high.
(Christie's S. Ken) $2,660

A 19th century equestrian bronze group of the uniformed Wellington, astride Copenhagen, on a naturalistic rectangular base, 14in. high, overall.
(Christie's S. Ken) $1,104

A Lorenzl bronze figure of a naked dancing girl, standing on one leg, kicking the other, 28cm. high.
(Phillips) $557

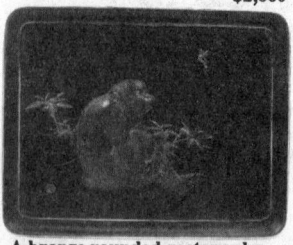

A bronze rounded-rectangular tray decorated in iroe takazogan and hirazogan, depicting a monkey clutching his leg and looking up to a hovering insect, signed *Higashiyama*, with kakihan, silver rims, late 19th century, 26.9 x 20.8cm.
(Christie's) $3,901

A bronze statue of George III, standing on naturalistic ground, a walking stick in his right hand, 28cm.
(Phillips) $4,086

An Italian bronze group of Venus and Cupid, in the style of Pietro Tenerani, Venus reclining against a rock, her head turned and arms raised in surprise, early 19th century, 11½ x 25in.
(Christie's) $4,356

A late 19th century French bronze bust of a bacchante, after C.M. Clodion, her hair garlanded with foliage and fruit, her right breast exposed, 15in. high, overall.
(Christie's S. Ken) $1,064

A French bronze model of a walking bear, cast from a model by Isidore Bonheur, striding forward, on naturalistic ground strewn with the bones of his last meal, 19th century, 5⅛in. high.
(Christie's) $5,227

A late 19th century French bronze figure of the Apollo Belvedere, after the Antique, typically shown naked with his left arm raised, signed *F. BARBEDIENNE. FONDEUR*, 17¾in. high.
(Christie's S. Ken) $2,217

A pair of 19th century French bronze figures of semi-naked infants in the attitude of the dance, in the manner of Clodion.
(Christie's S. Ken) $1,104

'Salammbô', a gilt bronze bust cast from a design by Louis Moreau, of a young female with long flowing hair, wearing an elaborate head-dress, on rock form base, 74.5cm. high.
(Christie's) $8,184

'Peacocks', a cold-painted bronze group cast from a model by A. Kéléty, of two stylized peacocks with polychrome cold-painted decoration, 42.5cm. high.
(Christie's) $2,455

A fine French silvered bronze group of a cockerel and hen, cast from a model by Auguste Nicolas Cain, the cockerel rampant on a basket overflowing with vegetables and straw, signed *CAIN SC* and engraved *CHRISTOPHLE & CIE*, second half 19th century, 8¼in. high.
(Christie's) $2,831

A 19th century bronze and parcel gilt figure of a water goddess, shown seated, her hair tied with a band of bullrushes and foliage, 7in. high.
(Christie's S. Ken) $1,219

A small French bronze group of two stallions, entitled 'l'Accolade', cast from a model by Pierre-Jules Mêne, on naturalistic oval base, 19th century, 7⅞ x 13¼in.
(Christie's) $4,356

A pair of bronze vases decorated in iroe hirazogan and takazogan both depicting birds perched in peony branches, late 19th century, 39.5cm. high.
(Christie's) $7,151

A French bronze group of a mare and dog, cast from a model by Pierre-Jules Mêne, the saddled horse leaning towards the small dog, circa 1860s, 9¾ x 19in.
(Christie's) $2,614

A French bronze group of two bacchantes and a putto, cast from a model by Albert-Ernest Carrier-Belleuse, the two long haired nymphs lightly clad and dancing, 19th century, 35½in. high.
(Christie's) $13,068

A French bronze group of two stallions, cast from a model by Jules Moigniez, on naturalistic oval base, circa 1860, 13⅛ x 16½in.
(Christie's) $6,138

A French spelter figure of a Moorish dancer, cast from a model by Arthur Waagen, the naked maiden with ankle and arm bracelets, necklaces and bejeweled headdress, late 19th century, 29in. high.
(Christie's) $1,432

A French bronze model of a stag, cast from a model by Pierre-Jules Mêne, standing on a rocky outcrop, second half 19th century, 23⅜in. high.
(Christie's) $4,706

A pair of French bronze groups of bacchantes, after Clodion, both female and male bacchante with two putti bearing garlands of flowers, second half of 19th century, 19¾in. high.
(Christie's) $4,706

A French silvered and parcel-gilt bronze figure of Sappho, cast by Victor Paillard from a model by Jean-Jacques Pradier, standing pensively beside a column, mid-19th century, 17¾in. high.
(Christie's) $30,960

A fine English bronze figure of a nymph representing the River Thames, the lightly clad maiden reclining amidst reeds and dispensing water from a ewer, mid-19th century, 10¾ x 17in.
(Christie's) $3,478

A pair of French giltmetal candlesticks, each with everted rim and baluster body cast with acanthus scrolls, third quarter 19th century, 5½in. high.
(Christie's) $777

A French bronze model of a walking lion, cast from a model by Antoine-Louis Barye, his mouth open as he roars, on naturalistic ground and stepped integrally cast base, 19th century, 9¼ x 16in.
(Christie's) $3,920

A French bronze figure of Joan of Arc, cast from a model by Marie d'Orleans, shown standing in full armor, her arms crossed about her sword, with Susse Frères foundry mark and numbered 50, first half 19th century, 19½in. high.
(Christie's) $2,046

Two rare French bronze models of hares, entitled *'Chasse fermée'* and *'Chasse ouverte'*, cast from models by Jules Moigniez, mid 19th century, 11½in. high.
(Christie's) $9,207

A French bronze figure of a nymph, entitled 'Colombe', cast from a model by Mathurin Moreau, shown seated against a rocky column, her veiled drapery billowing behind her, 19th century, 16⅝in. high.
(Christie's) $3,267

A French silvered and parcel-gilt bronze of Penelope, cast from a model by Pierre-Jules Cavelier, seated on a curved chair covered with a tiger skin and cushion, 19th century, 9⅞in. high.
(Christie's) $9,207

A pair of French bronze busts of bacchantes, after Clodion, the female bacchante with a decolleté revealing her breasts, the male wearing a goatskin tunic, 19th century, 10⅝in. high.
(Christie's) $2,046

A French bronze equestrian group of Louis XIV, cast from a model of Baron François-Joseph Bosio, signed *Baron Bosio*, mid 19th century, 17¾in. high.
(Christie's) $3,069

A late 19th century Viennese cold painted bronze figure of a North American buffalo, 7½in. high.
(Christie's S. Ken) $1,441

A Victorian bronze bust of a gentleman, after J.B. Carpeaux, on a square-shaped socle base, 7¼in. high, with a white marble plinth below.
(Christie's S. Ken) $931

A late 19th century bronze figure of the Dying Gaul, after the Antique, shown sitting on his shield with a bow and sword, on an oval base, 14½in. long.
(Christie's S. Ken) $602

'Diana'. A bronze figure, cast from a model by Pierre Le Faguays, modeled as a lithe young woman wearing a short classical tunic, 66.5cm. high.
(Phillips) $2,189

A pair of 19th century French bronzes, cast from a model by Jean Louis Gregoire, each depicting an allegorical maiden, in flowing dress, a cherub at her feet, 16¼in. high. (two)
(Christie's S. Ken) $4,211

A late 19th century French bronze figure of a barefooted young woman playing a violin, cast from a model by A. Boucher, her hair caught in a bun and tied with a ribbon, 25½in. high, overall.
(Christie's S. Ken) $3,325

A bronze group of a Cossack on horseback, shown with his left hand raised to his brow and turning to his rear, a lance to his right hand, indistinctly signed, 10in. high.
(Christie's S. Ken) $887

'Bacchante', a bronze green and brown patinated figure, cast from a model by Pierre Le Faguay, of a nude female kneeling on one leg, the other bent forward, 66.5cm. high.
(Christie's) $11,748

A 19th century Russian bronze group, cast from a model by A. Gratchev, of a soldier on horseback, a lance in his right hand, on a naturalistic base, 11¾in. high.
(Christie's S. Ken) $1,773

**A late 19th century bronze group of a man kneeling at prayer on a rug, cast from a model by M. Bouger, shown with his shoes removed, a saddled and reined horse at his side, 6¾in. wide.**
**(Christie's S. Ken) $1,441**

**A Joë Descomps bronze figure of a naked girl, standing with her arms clasped behind her back, on a pad base supported on a wooden stand, 21.5cm. high.**
**(Phillips) $478**

**A late 18th/early 19th century Italian bronze group of a lion bringing down a stallion, 7in. long, on a marble plinth.**
**(Christie's S. Ken) $4,876**

**Bronze figure of a dancing woman, P. Phillipe, 20th century, costumed figure, marble plinth, signed and titled, 15½in. high.**
**(Skinner Inc.) $1,400**

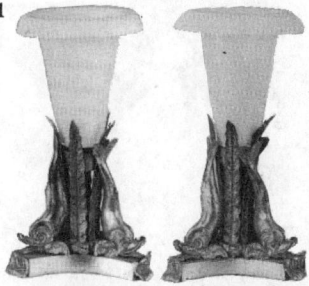

**A pair of William IV gilt bronze epergne stands, each with a later opaline vase, the base formed as three dolphins, 11¼in. high.**
**(Christie's S. Ken) $2,106**

**A mid-19th century French bronze group of Laocoon, after the Antique, raised on a rectangular foot, on a Siena marble base with ormolu plinth, 11¼in. high, overall.**
**(Christie's S. Ken) $2,881**

**A good mid-19th century bronze group of a bloodhound studying the slow traverse of a tortoise, cast from a model by Henri-Alfred-Marie Jaccquemart, 7⅛in. wide.**
**(Christie's S. Ken) $2,106**

**'Dancer', a bronze and ivory figure, cast and carved from a model by Gerdago, of a female dancer poised with arms outstretched, 32.8cm. high.**
**(Christie's) $2,200**

**A late 19th century bronze model of the Farnese Bull, after Giambologna, shown with his left foreleg raised, on a rectangular base, 9in. high.**
**(Christie's S. Ken) $2,217**

A gilt bronze figure of Wei To, wearing intricate chain-mail armor with protective vambraces and leather boots, the sleeves flaring, 17th century, 23cm. high.
(Christie's) $6,829

An unusual Viennese painted bronze group of three carousing foxes, each dressed in similar 19th century style costume, 3½in. high.
(Phillips) $765

Bronze group of medieval figures, after Gustave Doré, 19th century, a knight in full armor leaps over a monk in a hooded cloak, 13¾in. high.
(Skinner Inc.) $4,200

A 19th century Russian bronze group, cast from a model by A. Gratchev, of a Murid tribesman on horseback with a maiden, his horse negotiating a steep incline, 13½in. high.
(Christie's S. Ken) $1,108

A pair of 19th century French bronze groups, after the Antique, of Boreas, the North Wind, carrying off Proserpine; and another of Pluto, God of the Underworld, claiming Ceres's daughter, Oreithyia, inscribed *Girardot*, 18½in. high, overall.
(Christie's S. Ken) $4,432

'Valkyrie', a bronze group cast from a model by Stephan Sinding, a spear maiden astride a stallion, on the naturalistic bronze base, 56cm. high.
(Christie's) $5,320

A late 19th century French bronze group of children playing boules, shown with a boy standing and flanked by two others at his feet, 8¼in. high.
(Christie's S. Ken) $1,330

A pair of French bronze figures of dancing Neapolitan fisherboys, inscribed *Duret and Delafontaine*, on circular slate plinths, 19in. high.
(Lawrence Fine Art) $2,774

A bronze koro modeled as an egret, engraved detail and gilded eyes, the base formed as breaking waves, late 19th century, 12.5cm. high.
(Christie's) $3,678

A 19th century French bronze group, after C.M. Clodion, of two infant bacchanals, their hair garlanded with ivy, playing with an amorino astride a panther, 13in. high.
(Christie's S. Ken) $2,881

A bronze figure of Guanyin seated in rajalilasana on rockwork and a rectangular pedestal, supporting herself by the left arm, Song Dynasty, 22.2cm. high.
(Christie's) $7,469

A bronze group of a horse and dog, cast from a model by Maximilien-Louis Fiot, the horse shown standing, his head bowed looking at the seated dog, signed by the foundry *Susse Frs Edts Paris*, 14 3/4in. high, 23 1/4in. long.
(Christie's S. Ken) $5,541

Pair of bronze figures of Harlequin and Columbine, after Alfred Richard, France, late 19th century, 23in. high.
(Skinner Inc.) $2,500

Art Deco bronze and ivory figure of a young woman, after a model by Johann Philipp Ferdinand "Fritz" Preiss, circa 1930, 8 3/4in. high.
(Skinner Inc.) $4,250

Louis XVI style bronze and ormolu figural candelabra, late 19th century, putto supporting six foliate candlearms, 38in. high.
(Skinner Inc.) $2,000

'Cabaret girl', a bronze and ivory figure, cast and carved from a model by Ferdinand Preiss, wearing a green and silver-patinated costume and skull cap, 38cm. high.
(Christie's) $18,233

A late 19th century French bronze figure of a crouching field mouse, the naturalistic white marble base signed *Valton*, 4 1/2in. high, overall.
(Christie's S. Ken) $429

'Egyptian Dancer', a bronze figure, cast from a model by Cl. J.R. Colinet, of a dancing girl, with flowing skirt and Egyptian headdress, 43cm. high.
(Christie's) $5,577

# BUCKETS

A George III mahogany and brass-bound pail of tapering form, with brass swing handle, 14½in. high.
(Christie's S. Ken) $1,552

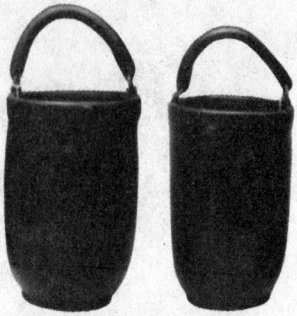

Pair of painted leather fire buckets, Waltham, Massachusetts, 19th century, green painted ground inscribed *Waltham Fire Club H. Hammond 1842.*
(Skinner Inc.) $650

Miniature painted wooden pail, possibly Shaker, 19th century, with green and brown sponge decoration, 4½in. high.
(Skinner Inc.) $650

An Irish George III mahogany and brass bound peat bucket of ribbed construction, with swing carrying handle, 1ft. 4¼in. high.
(Phillips) $2,531

Two Dutch ebony and fruitwood braziers with associated brass liners and carrying handles, 16½in. high, and 18in. high.
(Christie's) $1,287

A Regency brass-bound mahogany bucket of navette shape with brass carrying handle and brass liner, 14¾in. wide.
(Christie's) $2,079

American, 19th century fire bucket, painted green with *City of Boston, Ward No. 11 – Fireman No. 3, 1826* in yellow lettering, 13in. high.
(Eldred's) $880

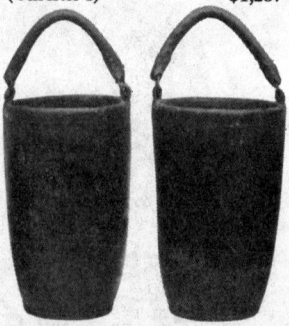

Pair of painted and decorated fire buckets, branded *C. Lincoln*, probably Waltham, Massachusetts, 13in. high.
(Skinner Inc.) $1,000

Painted and decorated leather fire bucket, Waltham, Massachusetts, early 19th century, ground painted green and decorated with scrolling devices, 12½in. high.
(Skinner Inc.) $400

A Louis XIV style ormolu-mounted tortoiseshell veneered jewelry coffer, in the form of a commode à tombeau, 11in. high.
(Christie's East) $3,520

A fine Regency rosewood traveling writing box, the exterior inlaid with foliate cut-brass and with sunken carrying handles, 19in. wide.
(Bearne's) $1,185

An 18th century German marquetry box with hinged, beveled top inset with a mirror to the reverse, the whole inlaid with panels of griffins, birds and mythological animals, 1ft. 8½in.
(Phillips) $1,752

A George III white metal-mounted ivory and tortoiseshell tea-caddy with decagonal hinged top with handle enclosing a well, 4½in. wide.
(Christie's) $1,881

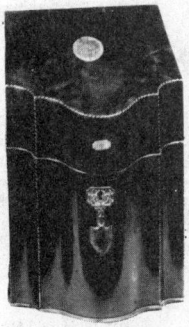

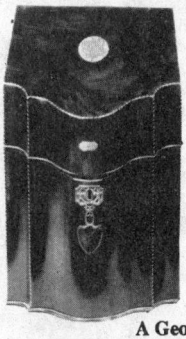

A pair of George III mahogany cutlery boxes inlaid overall with chevron-banding, each with later marquetry oval, 15in. high.
(Christie's) $2,574

A George III fruitwood tea caddy, in the form of a pear, with associate turned ivory knop and steel escutcheon, 7½in. high.
(Bonhams) $2,373

A George III cutlery box of serpentine form, veneered in mahogany, with parquetry stringing and silver handles and lock plate, 14½in. high, 26oz.
(Bearne's) $2,538

Miniature cabinet of cube design with six drawers by Thomas Barton.
(Derek Roberts Antiques) $2,500

A George III mahogany and boxwood strung knife urn, the lid rising to reveal a stepped cutlery matrix, 2ft. 7in. high.
(Phillips) $3,115

A late 18th/early 19th century sycamore workbox in the form of a miniature cottage, with central chimney, the compartmented interior with a thimble, 5½in. wide.
(Christie's S. Ken) $1,662

A Regency horn veneered work box of sarcophagus outline, with ribbed sides and gabled top, 11in. wide.
(Christie's S. Ken) $462

A 19th century pietra dura and ebonized games box, the lid inlaid with a design of a card from each suit and other colored hardstones, 12½ x 9½in.
(Christie's S. Ken) $1,995

An Indo-Portuguese hardwood and ivory inlaid cabinet, geometrically inlaid all-over with a lozenge design, the fall front opening to reveal eight small drawers and a deeper central drawer, 18¼in. wide.
(Christie's S. Ken) $4,433

An early 19th century tortoiseshell veneered, ivory inlaid and pewter strung two-division tea caddy, 4½in. wide.
(Christie's S. Ken) $421

A Momoyama period small rectangular wood coffer and domed cover decorated with panels of mandarin orange trees, magnolia and cherry in gold lacquer, late 16th century, 23 x 13.2 x 15.6cm. high.
(Christie's) $13,002

Queen Anne walnut oyster veneer and brass-bound chest, early 18th century, with fleur-de-lys scroll cut mounts, 12in. wide.
(Skinner Inc.) $1,200

A Victorian miniature oak pillar box, with a hexagonal top, the cylindrical body with a hinged brass aperture for letters, 17¾in. high.
(Christie's S. Ken) $3,413

A Victorian coromandel and foliate-cut brass-mounted traveling writing box, the inset jasperware plaquettes with raised classical figure subjects, the interior compartmented and with fittings, 14in. wide.
(Christie's S. Ken) $1,773

A William IV brass-inlaid red tortoiseshell boulle inkstand inlaid overall with foliate scrolls, the rounded rectangular top with pentray, 10¾in. wide. (Christie's) $2,178

A William IV rosewood book carrier, the rectangular plateau with central division and scroll ends, on fluted bun feet, 16in. high. (Christie's S. Ken) $1,995

A Regency penwork tea caddy, decorated overall with chinoiserie scenes, the coffered hinged lid with Greek-key frieze, the sides with brass lion-mask handles, 12½in. wide. (Christie's) $2,178

A late 18th century fruitwood tea caddy in the form of an apple, 4½in. diameter, 4in. high. (Christie's S. Ken) $798

A Regency leather covered and gilt metal moulded lady's dressing table compendium, the chamfered, reeded top with a gilt metal plaque inscribed *Eliza B. Swayne, March 5th 1817.*, 12in. wide x 13½in. high. (Christie's S. Ken) $1,646

An early 19th century single-division tea caddy, veneered in green stained tortoiseshell, 4½in. wide. (Christie's S. Ken) $399

A Regency amarillo, parquetry and penwork sewing box, the coffered rectangular top inlaid with cube-pattern within a triangular-pattern border. (Christie's) $1,198

A Victorian oak stationery cabinet in the form of a pillar box of octagonal outline with onion dome finial, 14½in. (Christie's S. Ken) $1,305

A Victorian burr walnut and foliate cut brass mounted liqueur casket in the form of a writing slope, with four decanters and a set of twelve cordial glasses, 15in. wide. (Christie's S. Ken) $964

A tortoiseshell tea caddy of serpentine shape inlaid with mother o' pearl, with ivory bun feet and two lidded interior, early 19th century, 7½in. wide. (Lawrence Fine Art) $1,494

Regency rosewood and brass inlaid lap desk, circa 1815, inlaid with star, crescent and leaf design, 21½in. wide. (Skinner Inc.) $1,800

A George III satinwood, tulipwood crossbanded and boxwood outlined rectangular three-division tea caddy, on gilt paw feet, 9in. wide. (Christie's S. Ken) $332

Six graduated oval Shaker boxes, America, 19th century, natural varnish finish, 2¾–5½in. high. (Skinner Inc.) $2,000

A set of three oblong George III tea caddies, each on scrolling base, chased with Chinese figures and buildings, lions' masks and quatrefoils within scroll panels, by Frederick Vonham, 1763, with twelve teaspoons with leaf-shaped bowls and stems, 49oz. (Christie's) $17,820

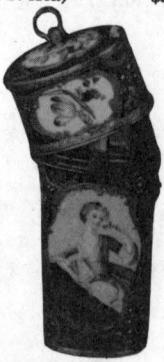

An etui, circa 1760, one side painted with the portrait of a woman, the reverse with a couple out walking, 10cm. (Lawrence Fine Art) $2,703

An enamel tea caddy, late 19th century, on turquoise ground, with fluted cut corners and circular lid, painted with landscape and strolling couple, some repair, 11cm. (Lawrence Fine Art) $1,158

A Guild of Handicraft hammered silver box, the lid with repoussé decoration of tulips, with gilded interior, with London hallmarks for 1905, 19cm. wide, 1040 grams. (Christie's) $2,027

A roironuri box with canted corners and sides decorated in gold and silver hiramakie with hanging wisteria on the top and the sides, late 18th/early 19th century, 18 x 10.8 x 11.5cm. (Christie's) $2,710

A Continental gilt-lined oblong casket on cast and applied dolphin feet, the sides and the hinged cover chased with classical figures, Sheffield 1901, 8¾in., 37.25 oz.
(Christie's S. Ken) $2,023

Round baleen box, America, mid 19th century, sides engraved with patriotic devices, ship at sea, building and leafy vine borders, 8⅜in. diameter.
(Skinner Inc.) $400

George IV rosewood letter box, circa 1825, gilt bronze finial, rectangular form, open turned spindle sides, 7⅜in. high.
(Skinner Inc.) $1,200

A rectangular gold card-case, engraved with figures in a Swiss lake scene within a cartouche of scrolling flowers and foliage, circa 1850, maker's mark *B & Co.*, 3½in. long.
(Christie's) $5,095

A pair of George II oblong tea caddies and matching sugar box, each chased with a band of fruit, scrolls and foliage, by Peter Gillois, 1756, contained in a contemporary silver-mounted shagreen casket, height of sugar box 5¼in., 29oz.
(Christie's) $12,342

A lacquer hi-ire and cover decorated with Genji and Tsurumon on a nashiji ground, concave cover with finial, hirame interior and base, 18th century.
(Christie's) $1,625

A late Georgian green tortoiseshell tea caddy with silver colored metal stringing, the interior with two lidded compartments, 7in. wide.
(Lawrence Fine Art) $1,451

A 19th century Anglo-Indian padouk veneered and ivory inlaid table cabinet, inlaid all-over with a foliate design and checker strung and crossbanded, 12in. wide.
(Christie's S. Ken) $3,103

A Chinese rectangular silver-mounted mother-of-pearl tea-caddy case, the walls and cover carved and engraved with animals, birds and butterflies, the mounts English, circa 1760, 7in. long.
(Christie's) $2,167

A 17th century Italian ebony veneered kingwood and later ivory inlaid table cabinet with ripple moldings, the architectural centre with a balustrade drawer, 3ft. 2½in. wide.
(Phillips) $8,956

A George III amaranth, rosewood and marquetry tea-caddy of rectangular shape with stepped top surmounted by an ormolu Classical urn within a spotted circle of friendship, the interior fitted circa 1820, 13½in. wide.
(Christie's) $32,912

A Regency bronze-mounted mahogany inkstand, two cut-glass inkwells flanking an entwined snake handle, 15½in. wide.
(Christie's) $2,970

A South Indian coromandel workbox with waved hinged rectangular top enclosing a fitted interior with two tiers, 19th century, 17½in. wide.
(Christie's) $5,544

A George III fruitwood tea-caddy in the form of an apple, 4½in. wide.
(Christie's) $5,148

A George III satinwood tea caddy with hinged rectangular lid with white-metal handle enclosing two lidded compartments, 7½in. wide.
(Christie's) $1,287

A George III fruitwood tea-caddy in the form of a Cantaloupe melon, 4½in. wide.
(Christie's) $6,864

A pair of Regency carved mahogany crossbanded and marquetry knife boxes, the domed tops with turned finials concealing fitted graduated interiors for cutlery, 2ft. high.
(Phillips) $6,619

A Regency ivory veneered tea caddy, opening to reveal a single compartment, with rosewood and ivory knopped cover, 4¼in. wide.
(Bonhams) $649

A Regency specimen parquetry tea caddy of sarcophagus form, the hinged domed cover opening to reveal twin, lined compartments, 9in. wide. (Bonhams) $344

A pair of Regency mahogany and ebonized urns each with molded rim and ball finial, possibly Biedermeier, 30in. high. (Christie's) $10,296

An Italian ebony and bone-inlaid table cabinet of canted inverted breakfront outline inlaid overall with scrolling foliage, flowerheads and grotesque masks, 36in. wide, late 19th century, probably Milanese. (Christie's S. Ken) $5,320

A Victorian lace box of plain rectangular form veneered in burr walnut and with elaborate brass hinges and mounts, 21in. wide, mid-19th century. (Bearne's) $1,504

A pair of George III mahogany, kingwood banded and herringbone strung knife boxes, with sloping lid, the front of projecting broken outline. (Phillips) $4,872

A giltmetal-mounted red velvet-covered casket, the fall-flap enclosing two long and four short drawers each mounted with a pierced foliate panel, the sides with carrying handles, early 17th century, 15¾in. wide. (Christie's) $3,432

A George III harewood and marquetry tea-caddy inlaid with end-cut walnut ovals and tea plants, with octagonal hinged lid enclosing two lidded compartments, 7½in. wide. (Christie's) $792

An unusual mid Victorian rosewood and mother of pearl inlaid traveling box, with ring handles to sides and raised on tapering bun feet, 26cm. wide. (Phillips) $660

A Regency tortoiseshell tea caddy, the hinged rectangular cover with chamfered corners, opening to reveal twin covers with ivory finials, 7¼in. wide. (Bonhams) $1,146

A 35mm. Compur Leica camera with a Leitz f/3.5 50mm. lens set into a rim set Compur shutter and a FOFER rangefinder, in maker's box.
(Christie's S. Ken) $7,469

A 35mm. Super Wide Angle Model FVI panoramic camera by Panon Camera Shoko Co. Ltd., Japan with a Lux 26mm. f/2.8 lens, in maker's leather ever ready case.
(Christie's S. Ken) $1,174

A 35mm. black Leica M4-2K camera with delayed action control, featuring a double-wind chrome winding lever and chrome rewind lever.
(Christie's S. Ken) $3,678

A quarter-plate Sibyl De Luxe camera by Newman and Guardia, London with a Carl Zeiss Jena Protarlinse VII 22cm. lens.
(Christie's S. Ken) $445

A 35mm. twin lens Contaflex camera with a Carl Zeiss Jena Sucher-Objectiv f/2.8 8cm. viewing lens.
(Christie's S. Ken) $1,417

A 35mm. Newman and Sinclair cinematographic camera no. 395 with polished duraluminium body, a Ross, London patent Xpres 1½ inch f/1.9 lens.
(Christie's S. Ken) $810

A 5 x 4 inch Artist's Twin lens Reflex camera no. 2 with leather covered wooden body, and a London Stereoscopic Co. Twin Artists Black Band taking lens set into an internally mounted roller blind shutter.
(Christie's S. Ken) $774

A 35mm. Kinarri 35 cinematographic camera by Arnold & Richter, Munich, Germany, with an Arrinar f/2.7 35mm. lens.
(Christie's S. Ken) $5,262

A 35mm. black Leica M6 camera with a black Leitz Summilux-M f/1.4 75mm. lens and instruction booklet.
(Christie's S. Ken) $5,975

A 35mm. Leica M3 camera and instruction sheet, in maker's box; and a Leitz Elmar f/4 9cm. in leather case.
(Christie's S. Ken) $1,518

A 35mm. Leica Ia camera with a Leitz Hektor f/2.5 5cm. lens, in maker's leather ever ready case.
(Christie's S. Ken) $2,226

A 35mm. Leica IIIg camera with a Leitz Elmar 5cm. f/2.8 lens, in leather ever ready case.
(Christie's S. Ken) $1,417

A 118-rollfilm New Ideal Rollfilm Sibyl camera by Newman and Guardia, London with a Ross, London Xpres patent 136mm. f/4.5 lens.
(Christie's S. Ken) $162

A 6 x 6cm. Rolleiflex 2.8F camera by Franke and Heidecke, Braunschweig with a Heidosmat 80mm. f/2.8 viewing lens and a Carl Zeiss Planar 80mm. f/2.8 lens.
(Christie's S. Ken) $1,174

A 4 x 4cm. Taschenbuch camera by Dr. Krügener, Germany with ebonized wood body, leather covered side panels, shutter and internally contained single metal sides.
(Christie's S. Ken) $4,453

A fine half-plate brass and mahogany tailboard camera with red leather bellows, rack and pinion back standard focusing, swing back, rising and cross front by George Hare, London.
(Christie's S. Ken) $810

A 35mm. black Leica R5 camera with a Leitz Vario-Elmar-R f/3.5 35–70mm. lens, in maker's leather ever ready case.
(Christie's S. Ken) $2,988

A 3 x 4cm. Makinette camera with a Plaubel Anticomar f/2.7 5cm. lens set into a Plaubel shutter and a Plaubel-Reflex D.R.G.M. supplementary lens.
(Christie's S. Ken) $1,607

A 35mm. Canon IVSB camera with a Canon Camera Co. Canon 50mm. f/1.8 lens, in maker's leather ever ready case.
(Christie's S. Ken) $607

A very rare 35mm. black Leica M2-R camera no. 1248646.
(Christie's S. Ken) $7,356

A quarterplate The Albemarle Postage Stamp camera with nine single meniscus lenses mounted behind a 9-pinhole mask.
(Christie's S. Ken) $648

A 35mm. Empire No. 3 cinematograph camera with polished mahogany body, brass binding and footage indicator. Manufactured by W. Butcher & Sons Ltd., in maker's fitted leather case.
(Christie's S. Ken) $2,347

A Voigtlander Superb camera with Helomar 1; 3.5 lens and Compur shutter, contained in a brown leather carrying case.
(Henry Spencer) $159

A 127-film blue Kodak Petite camera with cloth covered body, by Eastman Kodak Co., Rochester, NY, U.S.A. with 'flash' pattern baseboard and original blue bellows.
(Christie's S. Ken) $286

A quarter-plate fifteen-lens Royal Mail Copying camera by W. Butcher and Sons, London stamped 15 with polished mahogany body and brass fittings.
(Christie's S. Ken) $1,720

A 35mm. mahogany cased cinematographic camera by Alfred and Darling and Co., with metal binding strips and a Williamson-pattern cinematographic tripod.
(Christie's S. Ken) $567

An L Gaumont et Cie black leather covered Grand Prix 1900 camera, fitted with two Tessar Zeiss 1; 6, 3 F-84E Krauss lenses, contained in a turquoise velvet lined black leather case.
(Henry Spencer) $339

A very rare 2¼ x 3¼ inch-rollfilm No. 2 Cone Pocket Kodak camera with black morocco leather covered body, collapsible optical finder and sighting arm.
(Christie's S. Ken) $6,477

A 5 x 4 inch Alpha hand and stand camera by W. Watson and Sons, London, with a polished mahogany body and a brass bound Watson 5 x 4 R. R. lens.
(Christie's S. Ken) $567

A 35mm. Leica IIIg camera with a Leitz Summarit 5cm. f/1.5 lens, in maker's fitted leather case.
(Christie's S. Ken) $1,619

A 3½ x 2½ inch folding reflex camera with black-leather covered body, metal fittings, lazy-tong bellows extension, and a Carl Zeiss Jena Protarlinse 283mm. lens.
(Christie's S. Ken) $344

A Thornton Pickard brass mounted mahogany cased 'Ruby' camera, with black leather bellows, together with a shutter and spare set of shutter blinds.
(Henry Spencer) $876

A quarter-plate Nydia camera by Newman and Guardia, London with a Ross patent Homocentric f/6.3 lens, with film pack adapter.
(Christie's S. Ken) $911

A 5 x 4 inch Clifford Patent Hand camera by C. Lawrence, London with a brass bound C. P. Goerz, Berlin Doppel-Anastigmat Serie III No. 1 150mm. lens.
(Christie's S. Ken) $850

A 2½ x 2½ inch brass-metal body daguerreotype camera with a brass bound lens with rack and pinion focusing, removable focusing screen, two 2 x 2¼ inch silvered-metal plates and a spirit burner, with blindstamp Manchester Amateur Photographic Society.
(Christie's S. Ken) $4,453

A 2¼ x 2¼ inch The Demon detective camera with lens, flap shutter and removable rear metal cap by American Camera Co., London.
(Christie's S. Ken) $1,214

A 35mm, black Leica M6 camera no. 1702487, in maker's presentation case, with a Leitz, Canada bayonet-fit Summicron-M f/2 35mm. lens.
(Christie's S. Ken) $2,214

A 6.5 x 9cm. Sigriste jumelle camera with polished teak body, leather panels body covering metal fittings, adjustable sportsfinder.
(Christie's S. Ken) $8,200

A rare Hansa Canon camera with pop-up viewfinder, shutter speed dial Z, 20, 30, 40, 60, 100, 200, 500, a Nippon Kogaku Nikkor f/3.5 5cm. lens.
(Christie's S. Ken) $16,400

A 16mm. Cine Kodak A camera no. 4091 with black and polished metal body, hand-crank and a Kodak Anastigmat f/1.8 25mm. lens.
(Christie's S. Ken) $604

A Newman and Guardia quarter plate trellis camera, with Kodak Anastigmat f6.3 170mm. lens, black leather-covered body.
(Christie's) $278

A 35mm. Ensign cinematograph camera no. 128 with black leather covered body, brass fittings, hand-crank and an Aldis-Ensign Anastigmat 2 inch f/3.1 lens.
(Christie's S. Ken) $1,107

A half-plate tropical hand and stand camera with lacquered brass fittings and a brass bound Taylor, Taylor & Hobson Rapid Rectalinear 7.28 inch lens.
(Christie's S. Ken) $1,610

A 35mm. black Leica M4-P camera no. 1649312, instruction book, passport and a Leitz, Canada Summicron-M f/2 50mm. lens.
(Christie's S. Ken) $1,308

A 35mm. hand-cranked, wood-body Superb cine camera with brass fittings, crank and two internal film holders.
(Christie's S. Ken) $615

A 35mm. Canon S-II camera no. 19805 with a Canon Camera Co. Serenar f/3.5 5cm. lens.
(Christie's S. Ken) $362

A cardboard-body novelty Kodak advertising camera with pop-up doll's head and opening drawer marked *Kodak*.
(Christie's S. Ken) $845

A 35mm. Nicnon binocular camera comprising a 7 x 50 pair of binoculars and combined 35mm. camera.
(Christie's S. Ken) $604

A Plaubel Makina quarter plate folding rangefinder camera, with Antloomar f2.9 10cm. lens, Compur shutter, in leather carrying case.
(Christie's) $185

A 5 x 5 inch mahogany sliding box camera with removable focusing screen, wet-plate dark slide, and a brass bound J.B. Payne lens.
(Christie's S. Ken) $2,617

A Sanderson Tropical teak and brass-mounted quarter plate camera, with Ross Xpres f4.5 5½in. lens, Compur shutter.
(Christie's) $593

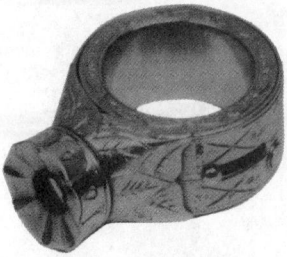

A 5 x 3½mm. decoratively engraved camera disguised as a finger ring with Russian marks on back section.
(Christie's S. Ken) $22,143

A 35mm. Leicaflex SL Olympic camera no. 1335494, special number 722 with a Leitz Summilux-R f/1.4 50mm. lens.
(Christie's S. Ken) $1,509

A 13 x 18mm. Sola subminiature camera with a Schneider Kinoplan f/3 2.5cm. lens, waistlevel finder, sportsfinder and two film cassettes.
(Christie's S. Ken) $2,250

# CANE HANDLES

A hardwood cane, the brass mounted handle incorporating a watch movement with white enamel dial.
(Christie's S. Ken) $261

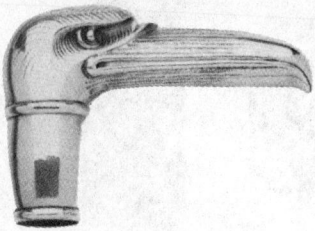

A cane handle by Tiffany & Co., New York, circa 1900, formed as a bird's head above a barrel-shaped collar, 4in. wide, 2oz. 10dwt.
(Christie's) $550

A 19th century French boxwood walking cane, the grip carved with the head and neck of a swan, stamped *BROT PALAIS-ROYAL.*
(Christie's S. Ken) $903

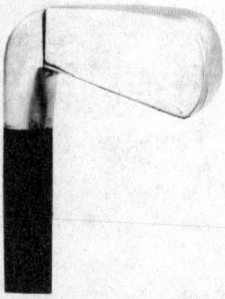

A malacca cane, the silver snuff box handle in the form of a golf club.
(Christie's S. Ken) $1,004

A pair of 19th century walking canes, the carved nut grips modeled with grimacing and smiling infants.
(Christie's S. Ken) $301

A 19th century German malacca cane, the silver and gilt hinged pommel inset with an automaton of an insect with cut and colored glass wings and body.
(Christie's S. Ken) $2,208

A 19th century bamboo walking cane, the carved nut grip modeled in the form of a bulldog's head, collar stamped *BRIGG.*
(Christie's S. Ken) $381

A pair of 19th century Tyrolean walking canes, the ivory pommels carved with the figures of a kneeling boy and girl.
(Christie's S. Ken) $502

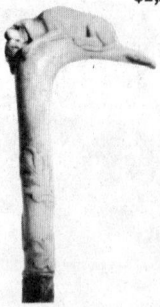

A 19th century sword stick in bamboo scabbard, the horn handle carved with a gun dog.
(Christie's S. Ken) $321

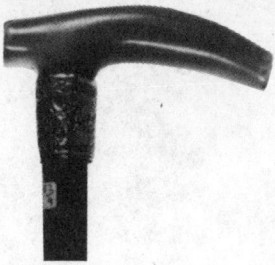

Horn and ebony cane, with gold-plated band engraved *Presented to J. Stables by the British Queen Party, from Drawen to London, 1905*, length 36in.
(Eldred's) $55

A gentleman's malacca cane, the ivory grip with piqué inlay, with initials and dated *I.I. 9 0.*
(Christie's S. Ken) $1,807

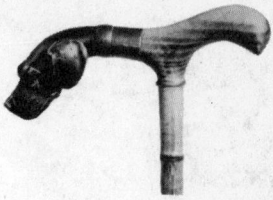

A bamboo walking stick, the handle carved with the head of a gun dog, with overlaid silvered metal and inset glass eyes.
(Christie's S. Ken) $703

A parasol handle of carved ivory, worked with an eagle wrestling with a toothed serpent, probably French, circa 1860.
(Christie's S. Ken) $1,097

An umbrella, the grip carved with a calf's head, and another, the handle in the form of a hare's head with articulated mouth and ears.
(Christie's S. Ken) $1,305

Antique scrimshaw cane, the carved whalebone with a turned whale's tooth handle, length 35½in.
(Eldred's) $935

A malacca military cane, the silver wrythen twist grip, with inscription and Badge of The 3rd V.B. Sherwood Foresters.
(Christie's S. Ken) $361

Two simulated bamboo walking canes, the ivory grips carved in the form of a cat's head.
(Christie's S. Ken) $1,606

A St. Cloud dolphin-shaped cane-handle with an iron-red mouth and eyes and blue, yellow and green head and fins, circa 1740, 8.5cm. high.
(Christie's) $2,988

A white enameled SS Jaguar mascot, the base stamped Gordon Crosby, and mounted on a radiator cap, 8in. long.
(Christie's) $376

A nickel-plated aeroplane radial engine with mobile propeller, 3½in. high.
(Christie's) $263

A brass anvil and hammer, inscribed Bovy, Bruxelles, 3½in. wide.
(Christie's) $470

Archer, a Lalique glass plaque molded *R Lalique* mark, 13cm. high on chromium-plated base fitted to radiator cap.
(Onslow's) $2,020

'Longchamps', a Lalique mascot, the clear and satin-finished glass molded as a stylized horse's head, 12.5cm. high.
(Christie's) $10,769

A nickel-plated Rolls-Royce Spirit of Ecstasy, the base marked *RR Ltd 6.2.11* and signed *Charles Sykes*, 16cm. high on Rolls-Royce radiator cap.
(Onslow's) $1,394

Bright Young Things, a nickel-plated car mascot of a young couple dancing cheek to cheek, the base signed Ruffony, 5in. high.
(Christie's New York) $1,210

Grande Libellule, a Lalique glass amethyst tinted dragonfly molded *R Lalique* and script *R Lalique France* marks, chip to base, 21cm. high.
(Onslow's) $2,020

René Lalique rooster auto mascot, frosted and selectively polished cock with ruffed tail feathers, 8¼in. high.
(Skinner Inc.) $660

A nickel-plated aeroplane radial engine with mobile propeller, the blade signed Robt. Beney & Co., mounted on a radiator cap, 5in. high.
(Christie's New York) $1,100

'Victoire', a good Lalique clear and satin glass 'Spirit of the Wind', car mascot in original Breves Galleries metal mount, 25.80cm. long.
(Phillips) $14,004

A nickel-plated Mickey Mouse car mascot, shaped as Mickey Mouse with his hands on his hips, 5¾in. high, circa 1930's.
(Christie's S. Ken) $379

'Longchamps', a Lalique car mascot, the clear and satin-finished glass molded as a stylized head of a horse, 12cm. high.
(Christie's) $16,088

A nickel-plated Rolls-Royce Spirit of Ecstasy, the underside of the wings inscribed *Trademark Reg Reg US Pat Off*, 12cm. high.
(Onslow's) $525

'Grenouille', a rare Lalique mascot, the clear and satin-finished glass molded as frog poised to jump, 6.1cm. high.
(Christie's) $7,832

A chromium-plated Dodge Ram car mascot, 20cm. long.
(Onslow's) $422

René Lalique falcon auto mascot, molded bird selectively polished and frosted, perched on circular platform base, 6¼in. high.
(Skinner Inc.) $935

'Longchamps', a Lalique satin glass car mascot, molded as the head of a racehorse with spirited expression, 12.70cm. high.
(Phillips) $6,224

**An American carved wood horse, Jumper, the figure with a frightened expression and deeply carved mane, jeweled trappings and saddle with tulips at cantle, 55in. long.**
**(Christie's East) $1,870**

**A carved wood double-sided chariot, with deeply carved depictions of a woman riding a swan adorned with flowers, ribbons and sleeping lion, 54in. long.**
**(Christie's East) $2,860**

**A carved wood pig, Jumper, the figure with a corn cob in its mouth and corn stalk flowing from mouth to rear, 49in. long.**
**(Christie's East) $8,800**

**A carved wood leaping frog, the figure with whimsical expression and carved saddle, vest and bow tie, 38in. high.**
**(Christie's East) $17,600**

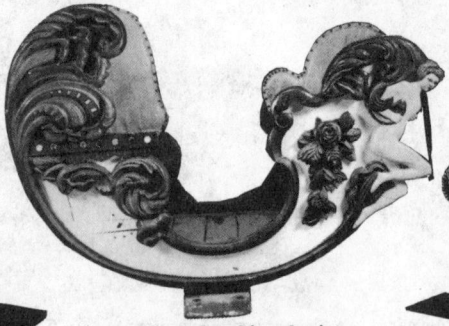

**A carved wood rocking chariot, with a deeply carved depiction of a woman holding onto stylized waves amongst carved flowers and jeweled trappings.**
**(Christie's East) $2,750**

**A carved wood zebra, Jumper, the figure with short carved mane and looped tail, 43in. long.**
**(Christie's East) $11,000**

**An American carved wood horse, Prancer, the figure with expressive face and deeply carved mane, saddle and blanket, 55in. long.**
**(Christie's East) $8,800**

**A French carved wood nodding head donkey, Gustave Bayol of Angers, circa 1885, the figure with carved short mane, saddle and tail, 49in. long.**
**(Christie's East) $6,050**

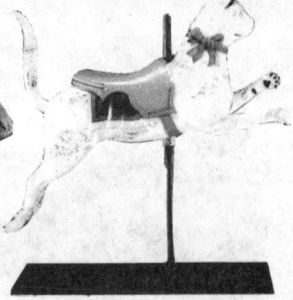

**A carved wood cat, the figure in a leaping pose, with a sweet expressive face and deeply carved bow at the neck, 49in. long.**
**(Christie's East) $19,800**

Light brown ram, Stander, the figure with deeply carved horns and fur, a sweet expressive face and carved saddle, 39in. high.
(Christie's East) $8,800

A carved wood dog, Jumper, the figure with deeply carved fur and sweet expression, carved collar, chains and saddle with tassels, 53in. long.
(Christie's East) $14,300

A carved wood horse, Jumper, the figure with carved mane, saddle and flowing blanket, 49in. long.
(Christie's East) $3,080

A carved wood horse, Prancer, the figure in skygazer pose with deeply carved flowing mane and jeweled tappings, 53in. long.
(Christie's East)
$20,900

A carved wood Uncle Sam chariot, with a deeply carved image of Uncle Sam and an American eagle above an American flag.
(Christie's East) $7,150

A carved wood zebra, Jumper, Stargazer pose, the figure with rearing head and carved cropped mane, 42in. long.
(Christie's East) $8,800

A carved wood stork, the figure in a striding pose with deeply carved feathers, saddle with a baby at cantle and blanket, 67in. high.
(Christie's East) $25300

A German carved wood pig, Jumper, by Friedrich, Heyn, circa 1900, the figure with a sweet expressive face and wagging tongue, 29½in. long.
(Christie's East) $935

Multi colored giraffe, Stander, the figure with carved short cropped mane and sweet expressive face, 59in. high.
(Christie's East) $9,350

A Regency giltmetal and glass hanging lantern, the dished base with Greek-key band mounted with griffin heads and turned candleholder, 22in. high.
(Christie's) $3,485

A late 19th century French ormolu six light chandelier, the scrolling acanthus chased branches emanating from a central bulbous column, 32in. high.
(Christie's S. Ken) $6,105

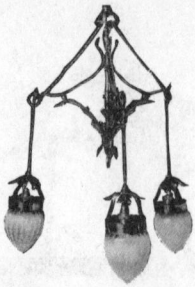

A W.A.S. Benson three-branch electrolier, having ribbed vaseline glass shades of ogee form, approx. 70cm. high.
(Phillips) $2,985

A George IV lacquered brass colza chandelier, the gadrooned dish hung with fruiting finials, the two brasses applied with honeysuckle foliage, 23in. wide.
(Christie's) $2,723

A Dutch style bronze twelve light chandelier, the scrolling branches arranged in two-tiers and intersected by flowerheads, 32in.
(Christie's S. Ken) $1,119

An ormolu and cut-glass eight-light chandelier with foliate corona hung with icicle drops above a cascade of faceted circular drops, basically early 19th century, 33in. high.
(Christie's) $6,098

A late 19th century Murano glass chandelier, with gilt heightened and white enameled tulip shaped sconces and storm shades, 37in. high.
(Christie's S. Ken) $1,628

A late 18th century French style pentagonal hall lantern, the serpentine panes divided by foliate scroll molded glazing bars, 41in. high.
(Christie's S. Ken) $5,088

A William IV ormolu and bronze twenty-one light chandelier with foliate corona hung with later pierced chains, above a pine-cone boss, 44in. high.
(Christie's) $23,958

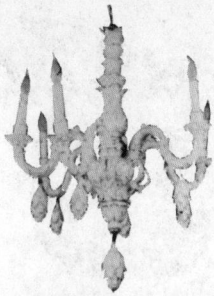

Meissen style porcelain chandelier, white and parcel gilt foliate baluster shelf joined by six candlearms, 2ft. high.
(Skinner Inc.) $225

One of a pair Glenstone Hall hanging shades designed by Sir Edwin Lutyens, with three vaseline glass beads, the entwined supporting vaseline glass disc with three beads, 32.6cm. diameter.
(Christie's)
(Two) $11,097

Carved and painted twelve light chandelier, Continental, 19th century, 38in. diameter.
(Skinner Inc.) $1,000

A late 19th/early 20th century ormolu three light electrolier, the scrolling foliate chased branches emanating from a circular lobed corona, 21in. high.
(Christie's S. Ken) $1,119

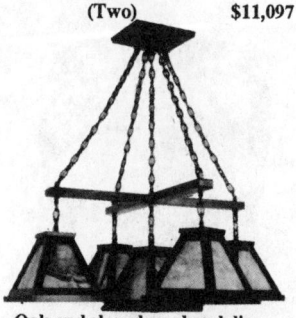

Oak and slag glass chandelier, 20th century, square ceiling plate suspending five chains through oak cross brace with five shades pendant, 36in. diameter.
(Skinner Inc.) $500

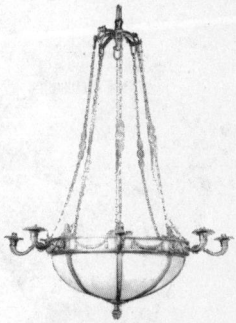

One of a pair of Empire style ormolu eight light chandeliers, the scrolling anthemion chased branches emanating from a circlet interspaced by husk swags, 58in. high.
(Christie's S. Ken)
(Two) $5,088

A pair of Louis XVI style ormolu and cut glass six light electroliers, hung with swags and chains of faceted beads, 48in. high.
(Christie's S. Ken)
(Two) $7,326

One of a pair of large 17th century style Dutch type eight light chandeliers, the scrolling zoomorphically mounted branches radiating from central bulbous knopped columns, 31in. high.
(Christie's S. Ken)
(Two) $4,477

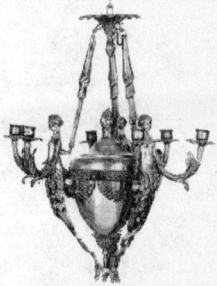

An ormolu six light electrolier, the branches modeled as the arms of caryatid figures, arranged about a vase shaped body, 29in. high.
(Christie's S. Ken) $1,018

## AMERICAN

**Grueby Pottery wide-mouth vase, Boston, circa 1905, with molded leaf decoration, matte oatmeal glaze exterior, 3½in. high.**
**(Skinner Inc.) $375**

**Rockingham glazed mantel ornament, possibly midwestern United States, 19th century, in the form of a recumbent lion, 15in. wide.**
**(Skinner Inc.) $950**

**Important Union porcelain Heathen-Chinee pitcher, Greenpoint, New York, 1876, the relief of Bill Nye, knife in hand, attacking Ah Sin for cheating at cards, 9⅝in. high.**
**(Skinner Inc.) $3,700**

**Fulper Pottery urn, Flemington, New Jersey, circa 1915, cucumber green crystalline glaze, vertical ink mark, 13in. high.**
**(Skinner Inc.) $1,700**

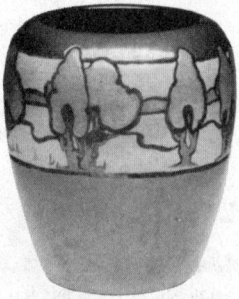

**Paul Revere Pottery decorated vase, Boston, Massachusetts, early 20th century, with incised and painted band of tree design, 8½in. high.**
**(Skinner Inc.) $2,300**

**George E. Ohr Pottery vase, Biloxi, Mississippi, circa 1904, fluted top on cylindrical form, midnight blue over cobalt glossy glaze, 5in. high.**
**(Skinner Inc.) $850**

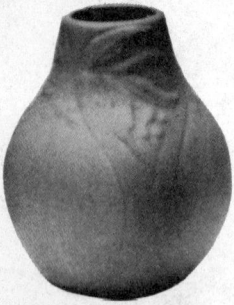

**Van Briggle Pottery vase, Colorado Springs, circa 1904, with molded floral design, yellow and ocher semi-matte glaze, 8½in. high.**
**(Skinner Inc.) $850**

**Saturday Evening Girls Pottery decorated motto pitcher. Boston, Massachusetts, early 20th century, 9¾in. high.**
**(Skinner Inc.) $2,200**

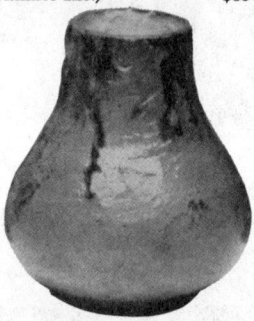

**Dedham Pottery experimental vase, Massachusetts, late 19th/ early 20th century, executed by Hugh C. Robertson, 6in. high.**
**(Skinner Inc.) $350**

## AMERICAN

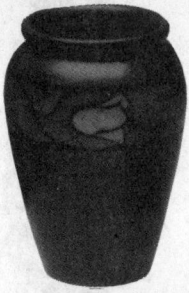

Saturday Evening Girl Pottery vase, Boston, Massachusetts, 1922, with incised and painted band of tulip decoration, 6¾in. high.
(Skinner Inc.) $325

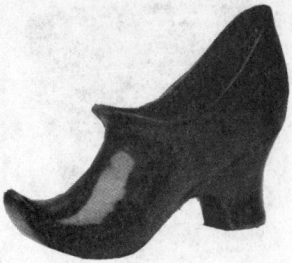

Chelsea Keramic Art Works slipper, Massachusetts, circa 1885, mottled olive green and brown glaze, 6in. long.
(Skinner Inc.) $300

Marblehead Pottery decorated vase, Marblehead, Massachusetts, early 20th century, with incised and painted repeating design of flowers, 3¾in. high.
(Skinner Inc.) $2,000

Dedham Pottery Stein, Massachusetts, early 20th century, rabbit pattern, impressed and ink stamped marks, 5¼in. high.
(Skinner Inc.) $225

Fulper pottery double handled vase, Flemington, New Jersey, circa 1915–25, no. 575, glossy green and eggplant glaze, impressed vertical mark, 6¾in. high.
(Skinner Inc.) $225

Chelsea Keramic Art Works double handled vase, Massachusetts, circa 1885, blue-green and brown glaze, 6¼in. high.
(Skinner Inc.) $200

Dedham Pottery vase, Massachusetts, late 19th/early 20th century, executed by Hugh C. Robertson, 9in. high.
(Skinner Inc.) $250

Paul Revere Pottery decorated tea tile, Boston, Massachusetts, early 20th century, with central decoration of a cottage, 5¾in. diameter.
(Skinner Inc.) $375

Teco pottery vase, Illinois, early 20th century, flared rim, in matte buff color glaze, impressed Teco mark, 12¼in. high.
(Skinner Inc.) $950

Spongeware umbrella stand, late 19th/early 20th century, 21in. high.
(Skinner Inc.) $500

Scheier Pottery bowl, 1941, wide mouth on tapering cylindrical form, relief decorated with repeating figures, flowers, and the sun, 8¾in. diameter.
(Skinner Inc.) $2,500

Walley Pottery vase, Sterling, Massachusetts, early 20th century, in green drip glaze on brown ground, 9½in. high.
(Skinner Inc.) $700

Marblehead Pottery decorated vase, Massachusetts, early 20th century, with design of alternating elongated trees, 6⅜in. high.
(Skinner Inc.) $1,200

A Théodore Deck earthenware vase, with short neck and everted rim, body flanked by a pair of molded mask and ring handles, 28.2cm. high.
(Christie's) $1,860

Marblehead Pottery decorated vase, Massachusetts, early 20th century, with repeating design of parrots on branches, 7in. high.
(Skinner Inc.) $1,600

Grueby Faience Co. vase, Boston, Massachusetts, circa 1902, with bulbous vase molded design, matte green glaze, 7in. high.
(Skinner Inc.) $650

Brown-glazed Redware mantel ornament, America, 19th century, 12in. high.
(Skinner Inc.) $250

Newcomb College Pottery vase, New Orleans, Louisiana, circa 1905, the flaring cylindrical form with incised and painted decoration, 9¾in. high.
(Skinner Inc.) $2,600

## AMERICAN

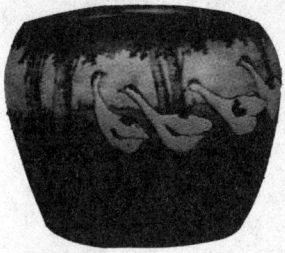

An Amphora oviform earthenware jardinière, painted with geese walking in a wooded landscape, 8½in. high. (Christie's S. Ken) $553

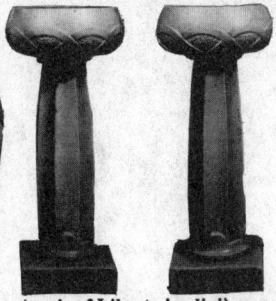

A pair of Liberty jardinières on pedestals, each with shallow hemispherical bowl decorated with entrelac border in relief, 80cm. high. (Christie's) $3,783

Important Union porcelain Liberty cup and saucer, Greenpoint, New York, circa 1880, white molded body with Justice on the one side and Hermes on the other, 4in. high. (Skinner Inc.) $2,600

A sepia Fitzhugh-pattern part dinner service, circa 1800, each piece painted at the center with a flower within radiating panels of animals and trellis pattern and surrounded by four clusters of fruit, flowers and scholar's utensils, all below a band of birds perched in branches and butterflies at the rim, 40 pieces. (Christie's) $9,350

A four-gallon salt-glazed and decorated stoneware crock, 'J. Norton & Co., Bennington, VT,' 1859–1861, with everted neck above applied lug handles, 17in. high. (Christie's) $1,210

A pair of plates from the Dewitt Clinton part dinner service, circa 1805, 8⅞in. diameter. (Christie's) $2,200

A salt-glazed stoneware incised and decorated jug, 'Corlears Hook', New York, 1800–1815, with applied line-incised handle, 17in. high. (Christie's) $1,430

## ARITA

An Arita blue and white ewer with loop handle, the ovoid body decorated with figures in a garden, birds flying overhead, late 17th century, 16.1cm. high.
(Christie's) $2,384

An Arita blue and white rounded octagonal teapot and cover with two shaped panels depicting scenes from O.R. Dapper on a ground of stylized flowers and foliage, circa 1700, 26.7cm. long.
(Christie's) $15,169

An Arita blue and white coffee pot and a cover, decorated with two ho-o birds amongst rockwork, chrysanthemum and peony, late 17th century, 28.2cm. high.
(Christie's) $1,950

A large Arita blue and white octagonal vase decorated in iron-red and green enamels and blue and black enamels in the kakiemon manner, late 17th/ early 18th century, 43.3cm. high.
(Christie's) $11,919

A pair of Arita blue and white foliate-rimmed armorial dishes, the center with a coat-of-arms surrounded by a stylized mantling, 18th century, 22.6cm. wide.
(Christie's) $7,585

An Arita blue and white bottle vase with slightly everted neck, the body with a cherry tree in blossom, the neck with collar and band of lozenge diaper, circa 1700, 21.5cm. high.
(Christie's) $5,418

An Arita blue and shallow dish with a central roundel containing growths of pomegranate and Buddha's finger citron within a band of alternate panels, late 17th century, 42.2cm. diameter.
(Christie's) $2,817

A pair of Arita blue and white baluster tankards with three shaped panels, silver mounts inset with a half-crown of Charles II, circa 1700, 19.7cm. high.
(Christie's) $16,253

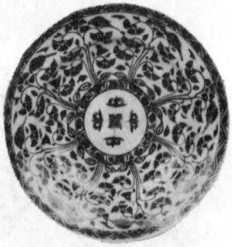

An Arita blue and white charger with a central roundel containing four flowerheads issuing from a single foliate spray, late 17th/early 18th century, 45.6cm. diameter.
(Christie's) $11,919

## BELLEEK

A mid 19th century Belleek porcelain honey pot and cover in the form of a beehive, 14.5cm. high.
(Spencer's) $800

A white Belleek chamber pot, the inside base with black-printed image of Gladstone, 10cm., registration mark for 1877.
(Phillips) $817

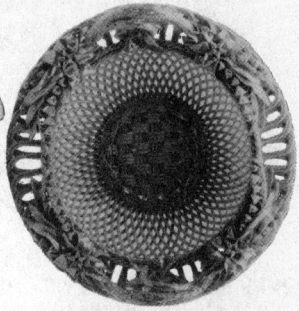

A fine Belleek circular basket, the looped rim applied with opalescent twig handles and sprays of lily-of-the-valley, 23.5cm. diameter.
(Bearne's) $1,146

## BERLIN

A Berlin rectangular plaque painted with a gypsy girl wearing a red scarf, signed *C.S.*, impressed K.P.M., scepter and H marks, circa 1880, 23.5 x 16.5cm.
(Christie's) $5,524

A pair of Berlin armorial oval gold-ground tureens, covers and plinths with linked scroll handles, painted in colors with two putti supporting bronzed swags of fruit hung from satyrs' heads, circa 1820, 45.5cm. wide.
(Christie's) $37,620

A Berlin rectangular plaque of the three Fates, Clotho scantily draped and carding the thread of life, flanked by Lachtsis and Atropos, impressed K.P.M., circa 1880, 40.5 x 26cm.
(Christie's) $11,253

A KPM plaque of Antigone, late 19th century, depicting a fair-haired maiden with an amphora, $9^1/_2$ x $6^1/_2$in.
(Christie's East) $6,600

A Berlin Easter-egg scent-bottle and silver stopper painted with the Warden's dwelling in the Wildpark, after the painting by Carl Daniel Freydanck, circa 1860, 10cm. high overall.
(Christie's) $2,347

A Berlin rectangular plaque of Judith finely painted in half-profile, signed H. Sch., impressed scepter and K.P.M. marks, incised numerals, circa 1880, 53 x 29cm.
(Christie's) $20,460

A Berlin oval plaque painted with a half length portrait of a girl in Greek national dress, impressed K.P.P., scepter and F5 marks, circa 1880, 26.5cm. high.
(Christie's) $5,524

A KPM plaque, late 19th century, depicting Europa and the Bull at the water's edge with attendant maiden and two figures in the distance, 9 x 11in.
(Christie's East) $7,150

A Berlin cabinet plate, the center painted with huntsmen in seventeenth century dress, with their game around a table within a gilt border, incised 16 for 1816, 24.5cm. diameter.
(Christie's) $1,814

An extremely impressive topographical presentation Berlin vase and stand of Franzosische form, the ovoid body finely painted on one side with a panoramic view of the town of Hildesheim, 55.2cm.
(Phillips) $22,440

A finely painted and richly decorated Berlin topographical déjeuner set with pink-mauve ground gilt with a close foliate pattern, the reserved panels painted with views.
(Phillips) $28,798

A Berlin campana-shaped gilt-ground two-handled vase painted with a broad band of garden flowers including roses, carnations, poppies, hydrangeas, delphiniums and nasturtium, circa 1810, 56cm. high.
(Christie's) $14,938

A finely painted Berlin plaque of 'Die Neapolitaner', a head and shoulders portrait of a young girl in pensive mood, 24.5cm. x 18.5cm.
(Phillips) $7,854

A large and finely painted Berlin plaque of the Holy Family after Raphael painted by Otto Wustlich, signed, 48.5cm. x 39cm., impressed *KPM*
(Phillips) $16,830

A Berlin porcelain plaque painted with the head and shoulders of a Neapolitan peasant boy, after the original by Richter, 30.5cm. by 24cm.
(Bearne's) $6,444

## BOW

A Bow figure of a dancer, the boy holding the remains of a garland and standing in pastel clothing with typical opaque sky-blue detail, 5¾in. high, circa 1755–60.
(Tennants) $1,309

A Bow candlestick fountain-group modeled as a gallant and his companion flanking a grotto, 24cm.
(Phillips) $1,683

A Bow figure of a cook wearing a white turban, a pink-lined blue jacket with gilt seams and buttons, white blouse and pale-yellow striped breeches, circa 1756, 17cm. high.
(Christie's) $5,948

A Bow candlestick group of 'Birds in Branches', modeled with two yellow buntings perched in a flower-encrusted tree, 24cm.
(Phillips) $1,496

A Bow model of a squirrel with bushy tail, seated erect nibbling a nut held in its right paw, 1758–60, 20.5cm. high.
(Christie's) $3,346

A Bow figure of the Doctor wearing blue hat, pale-pink cloak, his flowered jacket edged in yellow and blue breeches, standing with his left hand raised, circa 1755, 16cm. high.
(Christie's) $5,790

A Bow figure of Columbine in a dancing pose with her right hand raised to her puce-lined pale-yellow hat and holding a slap-stick in her left hand, circa 1760, 15.5cm. high.
(Christie's) $2,602

A rare Bow fountain chamber-candlestick group with simulated water spouting from a mossy mask and overflowing the basin below, 7¼in. high, circa 1765.
(Tennants) $577

A Bow figure of Harlequin holding his slap-stick beneath his right arm, wearing a black mask and feathered hat, circa 1756, 16cm. high.
(Christie's) $3,346

## BRITISH

An English slipware honey pot, with a combed design in brown under a warm honey colored glaze, 13.5cm.
(Phillips) $1,216

A Burleigh ware character jug of Sir Winston Churchill titled *'Bulldogs'*, 28cm.
(Phillips) $1,062

A Wiltshire inscribed and dated four-handled loving-cup, on a circular spreading foot with a lightly molded geometric pattern, 1706, 23.5cm. diameter.
(Christie's) $1,625

An amusing Newport pottery model of an owl wearing a suit, signed *M. Epworth*, 18.5cm.
(Bearne's) $222

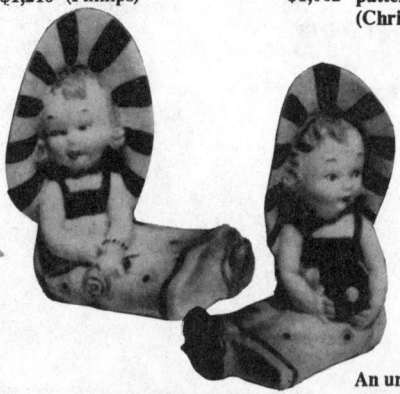

A pair of pottery book-ends in the form of little girls sitting under sunhats, holding a camera and a rose, 5¾in. high, with the William Goebel crown mark.
(Christie's S. Ken) $428

An unusual ceramic covered mug, modeled as a made-up clown, with a tumbling acrobat forming the handle, with a lithophane base showing two gentlemen greeting each other, 18cm. high.
(Phillips) $266

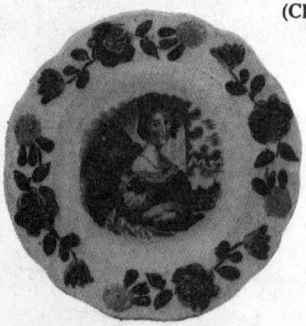

A Dillwyn & Co. pottery plate, painted in bright enamel colors, the center printed in black with the seated figure of the young Queen Victoria, 20.5cm.
(Bearne's) $586

A MacIntyre Moorcroft Aurelian ware biscuit barrel, printed in red and gilt within a cartouche on an agate ground, 10in. high.
(Spencer's) $264

One of a set of twelve Elkin & Co. blue and white pottery plates, each printed with an Irish river landscape, 25.5cm., early 19th century.
(Bearne's)(Twelve) $808

BRITISH

An attractive Derbyshire creamware teapot and cover, painted on both sides with a spray of green flowers in shell shaped panels, 11cm.
(Phillips) $3,179

A Moorcroft 'Macintyre' jar and cover, the stout baluster form with stepped silver cover and ball finial, with shaped handle, 18.5cm. high.
(Christie's) $854

An English porcelain basket, probably Coalbrookdale, applied and painted with flowers, 27.5cm.
(Bearne's) $546

A Wilkinson Ltd. toby jug of Winston Churchill modeled by Clarice Cliff, seated on a bulldog draped with a Union Jack, 30.5cm.
(Phillips) $1,116

A pair of large treacle glazed models of spaniels both wearing collars and name tags around their necks, 43cm.
(Phillips) $2,057

Admiral Beatty dressed in naval uniform, supporting a shell entitled *Dread-nought* between his legs, 26.5cm. high.
(Phillips) $233

'Fantasy', a Charles Vyse pottery group, of a woman seated cross-legged on a grassy base, scantily clad with a turquoise and mauve robe, 21.50cm. high.
(Phillips) $700

A Carter tile, possibly from the Fishing Smacks series designed by Minnie McLeish, in typical colours, molded *Carter 75*, painted *CD2*, 5in. diameter.
(Christie's S. Ken) $82

A Morrisware pottery vase, decorated with peonies in mauve, crimson and olive-green against a sea-green ground, 16.5cm. high.
(Phillips) $557

A West Pans dish with leaf shaped border, painted in colors with a spray of roses, the border with alternating floral sprigs, 22.5cm., mark in blue.
(Phillips) $717

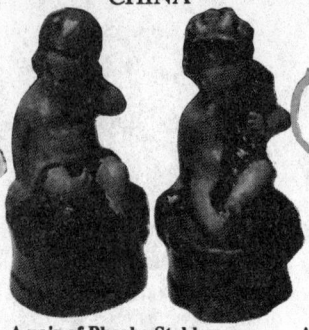

A pair of Pheobe Stabler earthenware figures modeled as a boy and girl, each draped with a garland of flowers, impressed *Hammersmith Bridge* mark, 7in. high.
(Christie's S. Ken) $1,039

A mid 18th century white saltglazed stoneware scratch blue short pedestal loving cup, all-over incised with flower heads and leaves, 19.5cm. high.
(Spencer's) $1,084

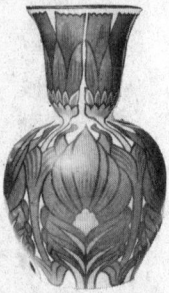

A Maw & Co. pottery vase of bulbous form with extended and flared neck painted with large stylized red floral buds, 33cm. high.
(Phillips) $842

A pair of porcelain figures of 'My Grandmother and My Grandfather', painted in colors and enriched in gilding, 6½in. high, circa 1830.
(Christie's S. Ken) $959

A Charles Vyse group in the form of Pan kneeling on the ground with lambs in his arms, his companion leapfrogging over his shoulders, 33cm.
(Bearne's) $1,110

A tall earthenware baluster shaped slop pail with a spreading foot and shell handles, printed in blue with a version of 'The Gleaners', 30.5cm.
(Phillips) $1,683

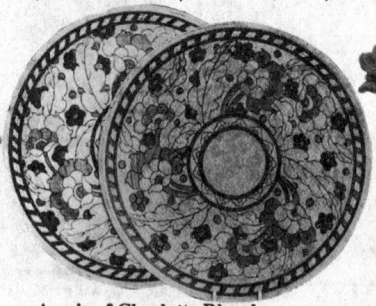

A pair of Charlotte Rhead Crown Ducal pottery wall plaques, tubelined in brown and decorated with orange flowers and scattered blue and red flower heads, 14in. diameter.
(Spencer's) $387

A Davenport caneware wine cooler, molded in relief with a bust of Nelson, the reverse with naval trophies, 25.5cm., impressed mark.
(Phillips) $1,430

A large Rogers meat dish of canted rectangular shape, printed in blue with the 'Camel' pattern, 54cm.
(Phillips) $561

An English porcelain foxhead stirrup cup with gilt collar inscribed *Tallyho*, with bright eyes and pricked ears, 13cm.
(Phillips) $1,459

A Mayer & Newbold shaped oval dessert dish molded with roses and other garden flowers, 23.8cm., circa 1820.
(Bearne's) $364

A buff stoneware 'Gothic Windows' jug, possibly Charles Meigh, 9½in. high.
(Christie's S. Ken) $256

A pair of figures of a rifleman and an archeress, each wearing hats, blue coats, he with yellow breeches and she with a flowered dress, circa 1830, 8in. high.
(Christie's S. Ken) $1,598

A mid 18th century English red stoneware baluster coffee pot, molded and applied with a bird of prey in flight over two figures, 9in. high.
(Spencer's) $278

An extremely rare English salt-glazed coffee pot and cover of silver shape, the tapered cylindrical body with tall straight spout, 20.5cm., circa 1700.
(Phillips) $2,390

A pair of John Ridgway two-handled flared oval vases, covers and stands with gilt scroll handles, painted with loose bouquets and gilt with stylized ornament, circa 1845, 27cm. high.
(Christie's) $3,102

A pottery stick stand, formed as a bear, the naturalistically modeled beast raised upon his hind legs clutching a gnarled branch, 87cm. high.
(Lawrence Fine Art) $633

An important and fine stoneware rose bowl by Michael Cardew, the dark brown glaze with 'basket' pattern through white slip, impressed MC and Wenford Bridge seals, 12in. diameter.
(Bonhams) $1,111

A fine stoneware bowl by Michael Cardew, painted in blue and brown abstract patterns on a gray ground, impressed MC and Wenford Bridge seals, 9¾in. diameter.
(Bonhams) $909

An important and fine stoneware bowl by Michael Cardew, banded with vertical lines alternate with abstracted pattern, impressed MC and Wenford Bridge seals, 12¼in. diameter.
(Bonhams) $3,300

A Glasgow (Delftfield) polychrome slender baluster vase and cover painted in a Fazackerly palette in blue, manganese, yellow and green with flowering foliage issuing from rockwork, circa 1760, 44cm. high.
(Christie's) $17,336

A figure of a child in a plumed hat seated on the back of a deer with iron-red fur markings, 10in. high.
(Christie's S. Ken) $469

A Pilkington's Royal Lancastrian bottle vase decorated by Richard Joyce, the body with a continuous frieze of deer amongst foliage, 1915, 7½in. high. (Christie's S. Ken) $1,143

A terracotta octagonal vase, attributed to John Adams, covered in the 'Chinese Blue' glaze, impressed *CSA Ltd* mark, 8in. high.
(Christie's S. Ken) $287

A Crimean group of an officer and his companion, seated either side of a fire place surmounted by a wall clock, circa 1855.
(Christie's S. Ken) $852

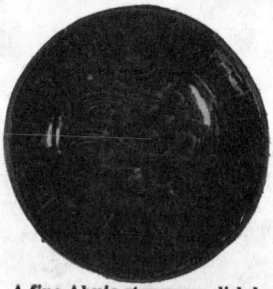

A fine Abuja stoneware dish by Michael Cardew, with river pattern, the flared rim with vertical banding, glazed shiny olive and sage green, impressed twice with MC and Abuja seals, 15¼in. diameter.
(Bonhams) $768

## CHELSEA

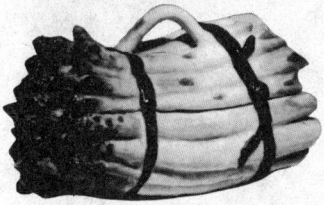

A Chelsea asparagus tureen and a cover, naturally modeled as a bunch of asparagus enriched in puce and green and tied with chocolate-brown ribbon, circa 1755, 18.5cm. wide.
(Christie's) $5,790

A Chelsea lobed beaker painted in a famille rose palette with a bird perched on a trailing branch pendant from blue rockwork, circa 1750, 7cm. high.
(Christie's) $19,070

A Chelsea peach-shaped cream-jug, finely painted in the Meissen style with a river landscape scene showing a figure rowing a boat watched by two travelers, 1749–52, 11.5cm. wide.
(Christie's) $17,578

A Chelsea white Chinaman teapot and cover modeled as a grinning figure of Budai, his loose robe open to reveal his protuberant stomach, 1745–49, 17.5cm. high.
(Christie's) $66,176

A pair of Chelsea figures of the imperial shepherd and shepherdess, he leaning on a staff held in his left hand, his companion holding a basket of flowers under her right arm, circa 1765, 34cm. high.
(Christie's) $8,235

A Chelsea white chinaman and parrot teapot and cover modeled as a grinning figure of Budai, his loose robe open to reveal his protuberant stomach, 1745–49, 17.5cm. high.
(Christie's) $48,334

A Chelsea group of Harlequin and Columbine standing hand-in-hand in a dancing pose before a tree-stump applied with flowers, circa 1760, 17cm. high.
(Christie's) $4,833

A Chelsea fluted baluster cream jug of silver shape, the scroll handle with elaborate foliage-molded scroll terminals, painted with a butterfly, an insect and scattered flowerheads, 1745–49, 12cm. high.
(Christie's) $16,544

A Chelsea model of a little hawk owl, its head turned and with pale-yellow, dark and light-brown and black feather markings, circa 1752, 18cm. high.
(Christie's) $19,646

A Chelsea circular basket with brown twig handles, the interior painted with a variety of whole and sliced fruit, 19cm. (Phillips) $2,431

A Chelsea fable-decorated octagonal teapot painted in the manner of Jefferyes Hammett O'Neale with a wolf barking at a boar, circa 1752, 10cm. high. (Christie's) $4,461

A Chelsea fluted teabowl and saucer painted in colors with flower sprays and scattered sprigs, red anchor mark. (Phillips) $837

A Chelsea figure of a shepherdess wearing pale-lilac hat, pink-lined yellow jacket and a striped green-spotted skirt reserved and gilt with flowerheads, circa 1765, 24cm. high. (Christie's) $2,688

A pair of Chelsea figures of fruit-sellers modeled by Joseph Willems, seated on tree-stumps beside baskets filled with fruit, circa 1756, 22cm. and 24cm. high. (Christie's) $2,974

A rare Girl-in-a-Swing scent bottle as a lady seated on a rocky mound, wearing a low cut yellow bodice, the base inscribed in red *Pour Mon Amour*, 7.5cm. (Phillips) $2,789

A Chelsea figure of a shepherd playing the recorder, wearing pink hat, green jacket and his breeches painted in blue, iron-red and gilt, circa 1765, 21cm. high. (Christie's) $1,758

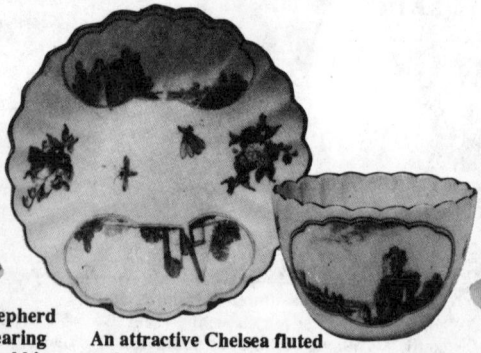

An attractive Chelsea fluted teabowl and saucer painted in Vincennes style with vignettes of figures and buildings in rustic landscapes, red anchor period. (Phillips) $3,586

A Chelsea figure of a monk seated on a stool and reading an open prayer book inscribed *Respice Finem*, 14cm. (Phillips) $2,244

## CHINESE

Chinese export Canton porcelain platter, 19th century, with canted corners, 12½in. wide. (Skinner Inc.) $275

Rose medallion porcelain punchbowl, 19th century, 13½in. diameter. (Skinner Inc.) $850

A Canton chamber candlestick with matching candle snuffer, each piece painted with figures. (Bearne's) $578

A fine and rare Ming yellow and red-glazed jar, painted in reserve on a pale mustard-yellow ground with two five-clawed scaly dragons emitting fire scrolls in a lively motion amongst cloud scrolls, 5 7/16in. high. (Christie's) $130,321

A Ming blue and white pear-shaped vase for the Islamic market, Zhengde, the globular body painted with six roundels containing Islamic script divided by vertical flanges and amidst clouds and a flaming pearl, 10in. high. (Christie's) $16,289

A large Ming blue and white 'Hundred boys' jar, painted to the exterior with a continuous scene of boys at play, with a group acting out the scene of a high official flanked by advisers in audience and a kneeling subject, 15¾in. diameter. (Christie's) $53,313

A Canton famille rose jug and cover, the ovoid body painted with figures in a pavilion, 11¼in. high, 19th century. (Bonhams) $1,746

A pair of Canton vases of hexagonal section, applied at the neck and shoulders with Buddhist lions and dragons, 60.8cm. (Bearne's) $1,597

Canton blue and white teapot and cover, China, mid 19th century, drum shape, coastal village scene with cloud border, 5½in. high. (Skinner Inc.) $150

A large Chinese Export punch bowl, the exterior boldly painted with the coats of arms of four Livery Companies, 40cm. diameter, Qianlong.
(Bearne's) $2,426

A rare large Yuan blue and white bowl, circa 1350–60, the interior with a swimming carp between clumps of waterweeds, 11½in. diameter.
(Christie's) $212,903

A rare late Ming Wucai brushrest, Wanli six-character mark, molded and reticulated with an ascending yellow dragon at the center flanked by four smaller dragons in brown, red, blue and green, 6½in. wide.
(Christie's) $93,677

A fine underglaze-blue and copper-red garlic-head vase, Qianlong seal mark, the compressed globular sides vividly painted with three Buddhistic lion cubs pawing and playing with ribboned brocade balls, 10½in. high.
(Christie's) $63,871

A rare pair of celadon-glazed candlesticks, early Ming Dynasty, formed probably in three parts with small petal-molded sconces, 9¼in high.
(Christie's) $17,031

A Ming blue and white baluster vase, 15th century, painted around the body in inky-blue tones with a foliate lotus-scroll between double lines, 5in. high, box.
(Christie's) $3,690

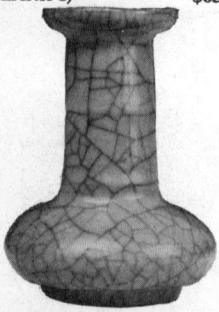

An important Jiaotan Guanyao bottle vase, southern Song Dynasty, with a rich pale gray-blue glaze with irregular light brown crackles, 4⅝in. high.
(Christie's) $354,838

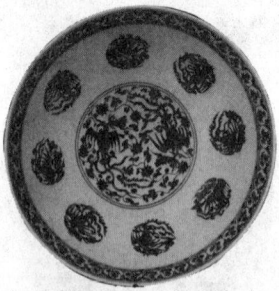

A late Ming blue and white 'phoenix' bowl, the center of the interior painted in bright blue tones with an ascending and a descending phoenix, Wanli six-character mark and of the period, 20cm. diameter.
(Christie's) $6,402

A blue and white stemcup, Qianlong seal mark, the flaring sides of the cup painted to the exterior with lanca characters divided by arches formed by lotus sprays, 3¼in. high.
(Christie's) $5,677

A rare early Ming blue and white baluster vase and cover, guan, painted around the body in inky tones with 'heaping and piling' to depict a continuous lotus meander, Yongle, 27cm. wide.
(Christie's) $96,030

A rare blue-splashed Sancai tripod censer, Tang Dynasty, the body covered with blue, green, orchid and white splashes streaking toward the base, 7½in. diameter.
(Christie's) $15,613

A Cizhou slip-decorated pillow, the concave headrest of ruyi shape, the design of a seated cat with ears erect wearing a floral scarf painted in a brown slip, Northern Song/Jin Dynasty, 32cm. wide.
(Christie's) $149,380

Two rare painted gray pottery zodiac figures, each modeled as a kneeling human figure wearing long robes with broad sleeves, Six Dynasties, 24.5cm. high.
(Christie's) $7,469

A blue, white and famille rose beaker vase, the shaped panels painted with ladies and attendants, 15⅜in. high, Qianlong.
(Bonhams) $532

A pair of turquoise glazed later ormolu mounted brush pots of cylindrical form with pierced sides simulating bamboo and leafy bands, 8½in. high, 18th century.
(Bonhams) $9,139

A rare Yuan blue and white jar, guan, the globular body painted in vivid blue tones with an arching peony scroll comprising six flower-heads, 1350–1360, 46.5cm. high.
(Christie's) $213,400

An amber-glazed shallow bowl, Tang Dynasty, the medallion on the underside with a large flower-head, 3⅞in. diameter.
(Christie's) $3,690

A Sancai pottery figure of a horse, standing foresquare on a rectangular base, well modeled with strongly contoured flanks and facial features, Tang Dynasty, 50.5cm. high.
(Christie's) $21,340

Rose medallion porcelain punchbowl, 19th century, with panels of figures and birds, 13½in. diameter.
(Skinner Inc.) $750

Rose Mandarin footed oval fruit platter, China, circa 1830, central panel of Mandarin figures alternating between precious antique clusters, 15½in. wide.
(Skinner Inc.) $3,100

A Woucai bowl, the exterior painted with dragons in green enamel and iron-red below a border of flowers and Buddhist symbols, 13cm., Qianlong mark.
(Bearne's) $607

Important blue Fitzhugh "Pagoda" decorated footed tray, China, circa 1810, central pagoda design surrounded by four floral panels, 10in. wide.
(Skinner Inc.) $1,500

A pair of large Mandarin palette vases, each painted with panels of officials and ladies on terraces, 18⅞in. high, Qianlong.
(Bonhams) $4,476

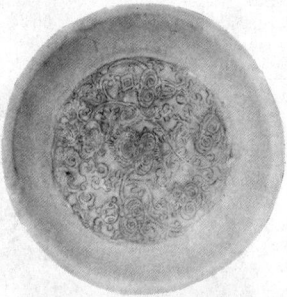

A Ming 'green and yellow' dish, Jiajing six-character mark, the interior with five ruyi connected by a leafy vine, all in olive-green enamel reserved on an ocher-yellow ground, 6¾in. diameter.
(Christie's) $4,968

A Chinese famille rose plate, the center painted with birds and flowers within a border of scrolling foliage, 23cm., Qianlong.
(Bearne's) $412

Rose Mandarin hot water bottle and cover, China, circa 1830, oval panels of figural courtyard scenes surrounded by floral and ornament designs, 14¾in. high.
(Skinner Inc.) $375

A large Chinese blue and white shallow dish, the center painted with deer in a landscape, the rim with a band of insects, 44cm.
(Bearne's) $506

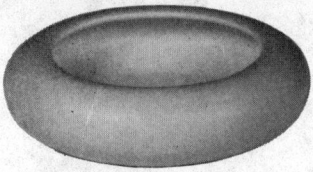

A Clair-de-Lune-glazed brushwasher, Kangxi six-character mark, the well-potted body of compressed globular shape, 4⅝in. diameter.
(Christie's) $2,839

Chinese Export "Blue Fitzhugh" platter, 19th century, 18½in. wide.
(Skinner Inc.) $750

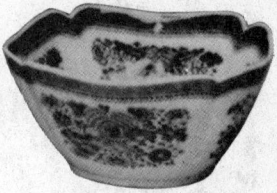

Fitzhugh blue and white salad bowl, China, early 19th century, medallion surrounded by four floral panels, 9½in. wide.
(Skinner Inc.) $800

A blue and white flask, painted with full moons in mountainous river landscapes, the semi domed shoulders with similar scenes, 10¼in. high, 17th century.
(Bonhams) $2,238

A pair of 'egg and spinach' bowls, covered in a lustrous green, yellow, brown and white splashed glaze, 4¾in. diameter, Chenghau nianzhi mark, Kangxi.
(Bonhams) $1,306

A Chinese famille rose jug, the neck with cartouches of landscapes in puce, having gilt dragon handle, Qianlong, 18th century, 9¾in. wide.
(Woolley & Wallis) $1,034

An fine early Ming blue and white dish, the medallion painted with a ribboned bouquet of lotus flowers, leaves, a seed pod, sagittaria and aquatic plants, Yongle, 40.3cm. diameter.
(Christie's) $256,080

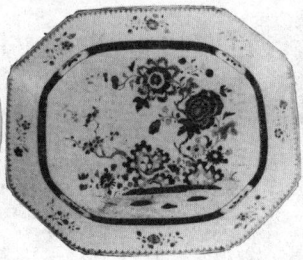

A large famille rose dish, painted with flowering peony, and other flowers amongst rockwork on a grassy bank, 18in., Qianlong.
(Bonhams) $1,679

A blue and white dish, the exterior with dragons chasing the flaming pearl, 7⅞in., Guangxu six character mark and period.
(Bonhams) $187

An 'Appliqué' octagonal plate decorated in the 'Caravan' pattern, painted in colors, 11in. diameter.
(Christie's S. Ken)
$4,426

A 'Bizarre' grotesque mask designed by Ron Birks, covered in a dark blue Inspiration glaze, the features picked out in red.
(Christie's S. Ken)
$2,656

A Clarice Cliff 'Fantasque' ginger jar and cover decorated in the 'Melon' pattern, painted in colors, 8in. high.
(Christie's S. Ken)
$1,081

A Clarice Cliff 'Fantasque' vase, shape No. 358, decorated in the 'Trees and House' pattern, painted in colors, 8in. high.
(Christie's S. Ken)
$935

A pair of Clarice Cliff teddy bear book ends decorated in the 'Red Flower' pattern, painted in colors, 6in. high.
(Christie's S. Ken)
$7,900

A 'Bizarre' Yo-Yo vase decorated in the 'Orange Luxor' pattern, painted in colors, 9in. high.
(Christie's S. Ken)
$4,426

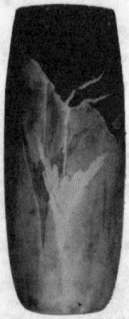

A Clarice Cliff 'Inspiration Bizarre' stick stand, decorated in the 'Caprice' pattern, in shades of pink, lavender and blue on a turquoise ground, 24in. high.
(Christie's S. Ken)
$3,742

A pair of 'Bizarre' bookends, shape No. 406 decorated in the 'Honolulu' pattern, painted in colors, 6in. high.
(Christie's S. Ken)
$996

A 'Bizarre' single-handled Lotus jug decorated in the 'Blue W' pattern, painted in colors between orange borders, 11½in. high.
(Christie's S. Ken)
$4,426

## CLARICE CLIFF

A 'Fantasque Bizarre' Dover jardinière decorated in the 'Trees and House' pattern, rubber stamp mark, 8in. high. (Christie's S. Ken) $2,435

A 'Fantasque Bizarre' ginger jar and cover decorated in the 'Blue Autumn' pattern, painted in colors with contrasting banding, 7¾in. high. (Christie's S. Ken) $1,881

A 'Fantasque' plate decorated in the 'Flora' pattern, painted in orange, yellow, green and black. (Christie's S. Ken) $421

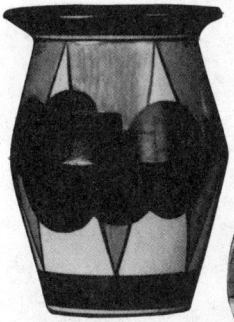

A Clarice Cliff 'Bizarre' vase, shape No. 342, decorated in the 'Sliced Circles' pattern, painted in orange, green and black, 7¾in. high. (Christie's S. Ken) $1,143

A Clarice Cliff 'Fantasque Bizarre' Stamford trio decorated in the 'May Avenue' pattern, painted in colors, height of teapot 4½in. (Christie's S. Ken) $4,573

A 'Bizarre' hexagonal baluster vase decorated in the 'Sunray' pattern, painted in colors between multibanded borders, 15in. high. (Christie's S. Ken) $4,426

A 'Bizarre' single-handled Lotus jug decorated in the 'Lightning' pattern, painted in colors between orange borders, 11½in. high. (Christie's S. Ken) $5,312

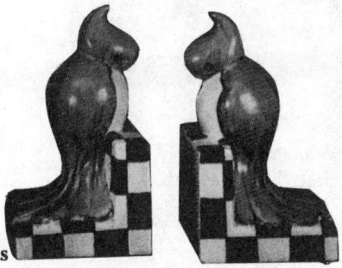

A pair of 'Bizarre' bookends, modeled as a pair of parakeets with green plumage on checkered base, 7in. high. (Christie's S. Ken) $1,771

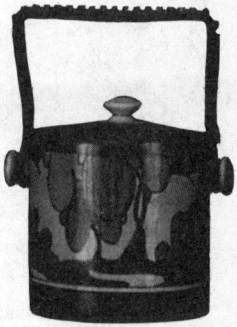

A 'Fantasque Bizarre' cylindrical biscuit barrel and cover decorated in the 'Blue Autumn' pattern, 6¼in. high. (Christie's S. Ken) $620

## COMMEMORATIVE

**An Alnwick election pink luster jug printed in sepia with a portrait, inscribed *Bell For Ever, True Blue*, 12cm.**
**(Phillips) $654**

**A Coalport plate printed in blue in commemoration of Captain Matthew Webb being the first person to swim the English Channel in 1875, 27cm.**
**(Phillips) $266**

**A caricature composition bust of Lloyd George with an extended tongue, inscribed *'Make George Lick the Stamps'*, 8cm.**
**(Phillips) $776**

**A large white Luck and Flaw two-handled caricature loving cup formed as the head of Prince Charles, 20cm.**
**(Phillips) $123**

**A fine quality English biscuit figure of King William IV seated crossed legged on an elegant sofa, 11cm.**
**(Phillips) $572**

**A pearlware spill vase printed in black with a bust after William Beechey of *His Sacred Majesty, King George III*, 12cm.**
**(Phillips) $817**

**An unusual yellow glazed jug, commemorating the death of Lord Nelson in 1805, the reverse with portrait of the Duke of Wellington, 11.5cm.**
**(Phillips) $449**

**A T & R Boote tapering jug commemorating the death of Sir Robert Peel, showing a full-length relief portrait of Peel, on a green ground, 23cm.**
**(Phillips) $776**

**A bulbous porcelain jug, with colored relief-molded portrait busts of Queen Caroline within beaded medallions, inscribed *'Success to Queen Caroline'*, 18.5cm.**
**(Phillips) $245**

## COMMEMORATIVE

**A William Kent bust of John Wesley in clerical attire, on a mottled yellow and green base, 31cm.**
**(Phillips) $245**

**A china plate commemorating the start of the digging of the Channel Tunnel 1987/88, 27cm.**
**(Phillips) $89**

**A rare Crown Staffordshire double caricature of the Kaiser entitled *'Which'll He be'*, 15cm.**
**(Phillips) $654**

**A black printed jug bearing portraits of William IV and Queen Adelaide, probably commemorating the Coronation in 1830, 14cm.**
**(Phillips) $266**

**A pair of Whitman and Roth caricature figures of Gladstone and Disraeli, both standing on mottled turquoise and brown bases, 40cm.**
**(Phillips) $6,538**

**A cylindrical pottery mug printed in colors with flags and inscribed *'G.R. Peace of Europe signed at Paris May 30th, 1814'*, 11 cm.**
**(Phillips) $449**

**A bulbous jug with animal-headed handle, printed in puce with an unusual portrait of the young Queen Victoria, 18cm.**
**(Phillips) $286**

**A pottery jug with three medallions containing profile heads of Victoria and Albert flanking their son Albert Edward dated 1860, 26cm.**
**(Phillips) $306**

**A G.F. Bowers rope handled jug printed in colors with scenes of the Light Cavalry Charge at Balaclava, and the Sebastopol Attack, 20cm.**
**(Phillips) $1,124**

## COMMEMORATIVE

A Continental porcelain bust, modeled as Queen Victoria wearing a crown, veil and sash, height 9in., circa 1880.
(Bonhams) $298

A Staffordshire accession pottery teapot and cover, printed in black on each side with a portrait of the young Queen together with the dates of her birth and proclamation, height 7in., circa 1837.
(Bonhams) $653

An English porcelain flared cylindrical vase, with central rectangular panel painted with a colorful portrait of King George IV wearing ceremonial robes, height 6in., circa 1820.
(Bonhams) $2,424

A Swansea pottery mug, commemorating the coronation of Queen Victoria, the waisted form printed in mauve, height 3¼in., circa 1838.
(Bonhams) $2,238

A Staffordshire equestrian portrait of Queen Victoria wearing full riding habit, and a plumed hat, height 9in., circa 1945.
(Bonhams) $205

A Read and Clementson pottery coronation mug, entitled *Victoria Regina* in bold capitals, together with the inscription *Proclaimed 20 of June 1837 Crowned June 28th 1838*, height 3½in.
(Bonhams) $2,051

A rare Scottish pottery oval plaque, molded in relief with a head and shoulder portrait of King George III, height 9in.
(Bonhams) $3,543

A well colored Staffordshire portrait figure, modeled as King Edward VII, standing bare-headed, in military uniform, height 12¾in., circa 1901.
(Bonhams) $84

A Chinese Export porcelain tankard, enameled with a medallion enclosing a half portrait of the Duke of Cumberland, height 6¼in., Qianlong period.
(Bonhams) $3,170

## COPER

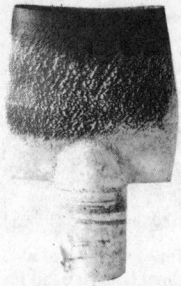

An outstanding stoneware spade pot by Hans Coper, white with a deep manganese band at the rim merging into a textured surface, impressed HC seal, circa 1966, 7¼in. high.
(Bonhams) $16,160

A stoneware shallow bowl by Hans Coper, the interior covered in a matt manganese glaze, the center carved with circular band, impressed *HC* seal, 17.5cm. diameter.
(Christie's) $3,628

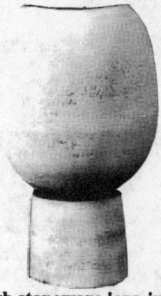

A superb stoneware 'egg-in-cup' form by Hans Coper, white with distinctive brown and bluish shading, impressed HC seal, circa 1975, 7⅜in. high.
(Bonhams) $14,140

A stoneware buff cup form by Hans Coper, on a conical base surmounted by a manganese disc, impressed HC seal, circa 1970, 6¾in. high.
(Bonhams) $2,626

An early stoneware goblet form by Hans Coper, manganese over a 'toffee' glaze, unglazed foot, impressed HC seal, circa 1952, 4¾in. high.
(Bonhams) $4,848

A rare cup form stoneware pot by Hans Coper, distinguished by two dark textured panels and two vertical incised lines, impressed HC seal, circa 1970, 6¼in. high.
(Bonhams) $12,120

A fine stoneware white pot by Hans Coper, the squared form on a drum base, hollowed impressions on both sides, impressed HC seal, circa 1975, 5in. high.
(Bonhams) $10,100

A beautiful stoneware 'hour-glass' vase by Hans Coper, white and brown with distinctive white inlaid lines round the base, impressed HC seal, circa 1963, 12in. high.
(Bonhams) $19,190

An important early stoneware 'thistle' form pot by Hans Coper, with diagonal texturing, impressed HC seal, circa 1958, 12¼in. high.
(Bonhams) $13,130

## CREAMWARE

A rare Wedgwood creamware teapot and cover, depicting on one side the Jeremiah Meyer portrait of George III reversed with the Thomas Frye portrait of Queen Charlotte, height 4½in. (Bonhams) $7,833

A creamware model of a finch with dark-brown beak, brown crest and yellow wing and tail feathers, perhaps Yorkshire, circa 1785, 12cm. high. (Christie's) $1,241

A creamware model of a recumbent lion, its head turned to the front, with pale-green mane and its coat splashed in brown, perhaps Yorkshire, circa 1790, 8.5cm. wide. (Christie's) $496

An English creamware oviform jug with a loop handle, printed in black and colored with a satirical cartoon entitled *British Slavery* after James Gillray, circa 1800, 6½in. high. (Christie's S. Ken) $1,008

A rare pair of creamware cornucopiae vases, modeled as two goats standing before cornucopiae, 20cm. (Phillips) $10,230

A Staffordshire creamware man-on-a-barrel toby-jug of Ralph Wood type holding a jug of frothing ale, wearing black tricorn hat, circa 1780, 25cm. high. (Christie's) $9,101

## DELFT

An English delft plate, painted with the inscription *God Save King George 1716* enclosed by a green garland, diameter 9in., dated 1716. (Bonhams) $2,238

A London polychrome delft Royal portrait footed dish, printed in blue and yellow with half length portraits of King William III and Queen Mary, 8¼in. diameter. circa 1690. (Bonhams) $2,250

A English delft plate, painted in blue with a half portrait of George I wearing coronation robes and crown, diameter 8¾in., circa 1714. (Bonhams) $20,515

## DELFT

An important English delft plate, with a mounted figure on a rearing horse, and inscribed *Duke William for Ever 1746*, 21.5cm.
(Phillips) $7,450

A very rare London delft teapot and cover, painted in blue, iron-red and green with whorl and lozenge-shaped motifs, 9cm.
(Phillips) $39,060

A London Royal portrait delft footed dish, printed in blue with half length portraits of King William III and Queen Mary, 8½in. diameter, circa 1690.
(Bonhams) $1,400

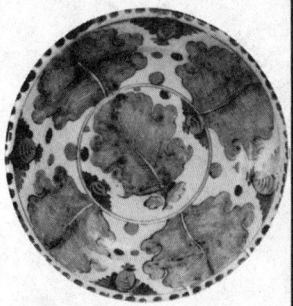

An early 18th century Bristol delft 'oak leaf' charger, the central circular panel painted in blue, green, yellow and brown, 13in. diameter.
(Spencer's) $2,946

A remarkable set of twenty-four Liverpool delft tiles, each painted with a bird in flight, standing or on a stump, each 12.5cm. square.
(Phillips)
(Twenty-four) $5,022

A rare English delft plate, painted in blue with the dispossessed King Charles II hiding in the Boscobel Oak, his visible face encircled by three yellow enamel crowns, diameter 9¼in., circa 1745.
(Bonhams) $16,785

A Bristol delft Royal portrait plate, printed in blue with a half length portrait of Queen Caroline, 8½in. diameter, circa 1727.
(Bonhams) £3,600

An 18th century century English delft puzzle jug with blue printed flower decoration and inscribed *J.J. 1730*, possibly London, 7¼in. high.
(Andrew Hartley) $7,000

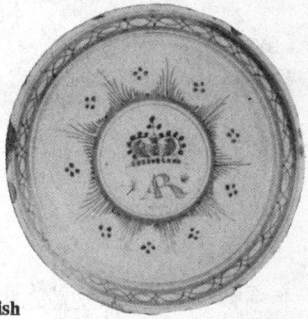

A Lambeth delft plate, painted in blue with a central crown above the initials *A.R.*, diameter 9in., circa 1702 (chips to rim).
(Bonhams) $2,424

## DELFT

A Bristol delft powdered-manganese-ground bowl, reserved with four fish, the interior with flowers and foliage, circa 1750, 10½in. diameter.
(Christie's S. Ken) $3,618

An interesting early English delft mustard pot, possibly Brislington, painted with a Chinese figure amidst trees, shrubs and rocks, 7.5cm. high.
(Phillips) $2,232

English polychrome delft bowl, early 18th century, V-outer border and scrolled inner border in blue, 9in. diameter.
(Skinner Inc.) $950

An English delft polychrome baluster posset-pot and cover, painted in iron-red, blue and green with flowers and insects flanking the spout, London or Bristol, circa 1710, 19cm. high.
(Christie's) $9,306

Liverpool delft wall-pocket of spiral form, lightly molded and painted in a Fazackerly palette with a bird perched on a flowering branch, circa 1760, 20.5cm. long.
(Christie's) $1,654

A good London delft 'Blue Dash' charger, painted with The Fall, Eve with long manganese hair handing an apple to Adam, 35cm.
(Phillips) $4,582

A Liverpool delft blue and white armorial bowl, the center to the interior painted with two figures in a rowing-boat before buildings on an island, circa 1770, 26cm. diameter.
(Christie's) $1,861

A Dutch delft blue and white rococo watch-stand modeled as a scroll-molded watch-case supported by two youths, their clothes enriched in blue, circa 1750, 32.5cm, high.
(Christie's) $1,707

A mid 18th century London delft charger, decorated in blue, red, manganese, green and yellow, 13in. diameter.
(Spencer's) $630

## DELFT

A rare English delft coffee cup, possibly Liverpool, with an everted rim and a blue-dash loop handle, 5.5cm.
(Phillips) $1,793

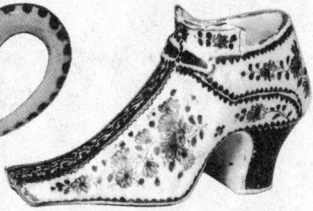

A rare and attractive English delft model of a shoe, with squared-off toe and medium sized heel, painted with sprays of flowers in Oriental style, 16cm.
(Phillips) $1,494

Blue and white Dutch delft charger, Holland, 18th century, with floral bouquet surrounded by a stylized floral border, 15½in. diameter.
(Skinner Inc.) $850

A rare early London delft baluster vase with slightly spreading foot, painted in blue with bold plant motifs and a butterfly, 29cm.
(Phillips) $956

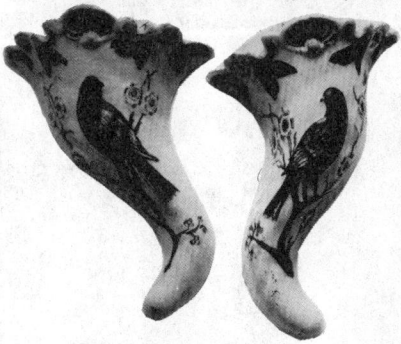

Two Liverpool delft wall-pockets of spirally molded form, lightly molded and painted in a Fazackerly palette with a bird perched on a flowering branch, circa 1760, 22cm. long.
(Christie's) $3,251

One of a pair of Dutch delft tobacco jars, painted in blue with a negro with feathered head-dress and skirt, smoking a pipe, 26cm., 15th century.
(Lawrence Fine Art)
(Two) $6,748

A chinoiserie delft charger, probably London, with a slightly everted rim, painted in yellow and blue with two Chinese figures, 34.5cm.
(Phillips) $2,431

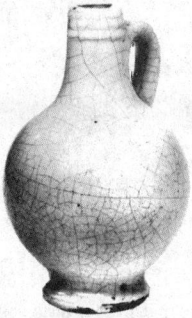

A London delft wine-bottle of globular form with short cylindrical neck and small loop handle, circa 1650, 16cm. high.
(Christie's) $3,034

A Dutch delft lobed dish painted in yellow, blue and green, the center with a man on horseback flanked by trees, circa 1700, 34.5cm. diameter.
(Christie's) $677

## DELFT

A Lambeth delft plate, commemorating the Union of England and Scotland in 1707, with painted polychrome decoration, diameter 8¾in. (Bonhams) $4,662

A London delft 'Royal Portrait' plate, painted in blue with half length portraits of King William III and Queen Mary, diameter 8¾in., circa 1689. (Bonhams) $3.357

A Bristol delft blue dash royal portrait charger, painted predominantly in blue with Queen Anne seated in her coronation robes, diameter 13¼in., circa 1702. (Bonhams) $10,257

A Brislington delft royal portrait charger, painted predominantly in blue with a half portrait of Queen Mary, diameter 9½in., circa 1690. (Bonhams) $20,515

A Bristol blue and white mug with loop handle, painted with pagodas among trees on a rocky island, Benjamin Lund's factory, circa 1750, 12cm. high. (Christie's) $14,476

A London delft plate, painted in manganese and blue, with a half portrait of King George III, diameter 9in. (chips to rim). (Bonhams) $27,975

A Dutch delft royal portrait plate, painted in blue with a bust of King William III wearing a crown, flanked by the initials *K.W.*, diameter 8½in., circa 1689. (Bonhams) $1,399

A London delft blue dash royal equestrian charger, painted with a monarch wearing a crown, and holding a baton, diameter 13½in., circa 1690. (Bonhams) $31,705

A Lambeth delft charger, painted in green, orange, red and blue with a head and shoulder portrait of King George I, diameter 13in., circa 1714. (Bonhams) $31,705

## DERBY

A Derby plate, probably painted by William Billingsley, with three naturalistic floral sprays and a single rose in the center circa 1790.
(Phillips) $3,400

Late 18th century puce marked Derby porcelain bough/crocus pot with twin ram's head handles, 5¼in. high.
(Bigwood) $8,000

A Derby plate, painted in the center, probably by Zachariah Boreman, with a river landscape panel within a blue circle, 1785-90.
(Phillips) $1,160

A Derby coffee can and saucer, the can painted, possibly by George Complin, with two finches perched on a still life of fruit, 7.5cm. high, 1789-95.
(Phillips) $25,300

A pair of Derby candlestick figures of seated putto in loosely draped robes and crowned with flowers, circa 1760, 7in. high.
(Christie's S. Ken) $700

A Derby figure of Apollo crowned with laurels in a green and pink cloak, circa 1765, 7½in. high.
(Christie's S. Ken) $800

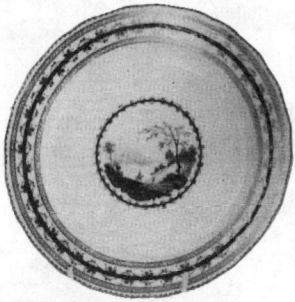

A Derby plate, painted in the center probably by Thomas Steel, with a still life of a vase and fruit, including peaches, grapes, cherries and blackberries, 20,7cm. diameter.
(Phillips) $975

A Derby figure of a reaper in a black hat, turquoise jacket and yellow apron with a scythe on his shoulder, circa 1760, 11¼in. high.
(Christie's S. Ken) $900

A Derby botanical plate, painted in the center, possibly by John Brewer, with a deep border of roses, probably by William Billingsley, 22.5cm. diameter, circa 1795.
(Phillips) $4,080

## DERBY

A Derby sauceboat modeled as a swimming duck with an orange beak and feet, and a gilt dentil rim, 10.5cm.
(Phillips) $1,295

A Derby figure of a youth emblematic of Winter, in ermine trimmed red jacket and lemon breeches, 22.5cm.
(Phillips) $842

A Derby group of two lovers and a jester after the model by J.J. Kändler, the lovers seated before white flowering bocage, Wm. Duesbury & Co., circa 1765, 29cm. high.
(Christie's) $6,501

A pair of Derby turquoise-ground two-handled vases, covers and plinths, the oviform bodies painted in the manner of Richard Askew with putti at play with a dolphin, Wm. Duesbury & Co., circa 1775, 34cm. high.
(Christie's) $6,204

A pair of Derby dishes of kidney shape, painted with panels of birds in landscapes, by Richard Dodson, 25.5cm.
(Phillips) $1,594

Two Derby figures emblematic of Europe and America, one in crown and flowing robes, the other dressed in colored feathers and carrying a quiver of arrows, 24cm. $2,805
(Phillips)

A Derby figure group of a gallant and his companion walking with their arms entwined, he in a pink jacket, she with a lacy mob cap, 16.5cm.
(Phillips) $2,431

A pair of Derby arbor musicians, he playing the bagpipes and his companion the mandolin, Wm. Duesbury & Co., circa 1775, 35.5cm. high.
(Christie's) $11,994

A Derby trout's head stirrup-cup naturally modeled and painted in shades of green, puce and pale-pink, the rim inscribed in gilt *THE ANGLERS DELIGHT*, circa 1825, 13.5cm. high.
(Christie's) $2,482

## DERBY

A Derby vase in the form of a basket with a diaper molded globular body applied with florettes, pierced everted rim and rope handles, 13.5cm.
(Phillips) $2,244

A Derby porcelain standish, the pen wells painted with landscapes, reserved on a blue ground, 29.5cm. long.
(Bearne's) $404

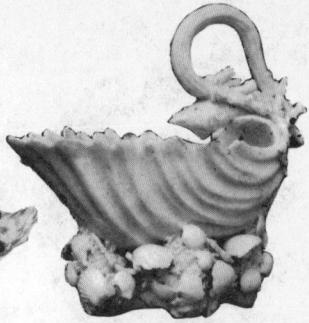

A Derby white crayfish sauceboat modeled as a fluted shell, the handle formed as a looped coral branch resting on the back of a crayfish, Andrew Planché's period, circa 1750, 15.5cm. wide.
(Christie's) $12,408

A Derby turquoise-ground fountain vase of urn shape, the handles formed as putti riding on dolphins alternating with seated putti holding garlands, Wm. Duesbury & Co., circa 1775, 42cm. high.
(Christie's) $11,374

A Bloor Derby jar with foliate handles, applied with a panel of flowers, together with a pair of similar flower encrusted vases.
(Bearne's) $1,810

A Derby figure of a sailor's lass in yellow and claret hat, sprigged dress and black apron, 25cm.
(Phillips) $1,122

A Derby porcelain plate, the center painted with a castle by a lake within a blue border, inscribed *View in Wales*, 23cm.
(Bearne's) $344

A Derby figure of a flower seller in lemon coat, turquoise sprigged breeches and pink shoes, holding a posy of flowers in one hand, 24.5cm.
(Phillips) $1,216

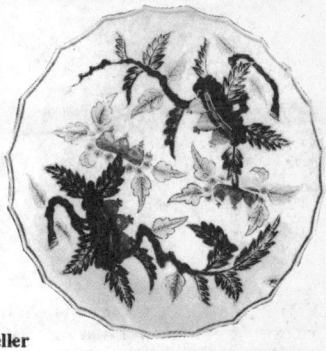

A pair of Derby dishes after the Arita originals, of fluted shell shape decorated in blue, red, green and gold, 22cm.
(Phillips) $673

## DOUCAI

A fine Doucai bowl, encircled Yongzheng six-character mark, painted delicately around the sides with hongbao, the eight Daoist emblems, between a band of linked ruyi-heads, $5^{1}/_{4}$in. diameter. (Christie's) $25,548

A fine large Doucai jardiniere, Qianlong seal mark, finely painted to the side with five medallions filled with lotus flowers and feathery foliate, 13in. diameter. (Christie's) $283,871

A very fine Doucai 'dragon' saucer-dish, encircled Yongzheng six-character mark, the center of the interior enameled with a ferocious five-clawed dragon chasing a flaming pearl amidst clouds, $6^{3}/_{4}$in. diameter. (Christie's) $63,871

A fine Doucai and famille rose moonflask, Qianlong seal mark, elaborately painted to each circular face with the 'three abundances', pomegranate, peach and finger citrus, $12^{1}/_{4}$in. high. (Christie's) $539,355

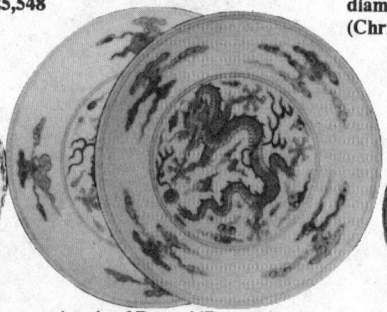

A pair of Doucai 'Dragon' saucer-dishes, the interior with a five-clawed dragon chasing a flaming pearl amidst cloud scrolls below four stylized clouds, $5^{3}/_{4}$in. diameter. (Christie's) $7,405

A Doucai Zhadou, the globular body painted with a lotus scroll, the flower-heads alternating with peaches, Qianlong seal mark, 7.9cm. diameter. (Christie's) $13,871

A Doucai bowl, finely painted to the exterior with six iron-red lotus blossoms framed within elaborate scrollwork, all between a double line below the rim, $5^{3}/_{4}$in. diameter. (Christie's) $6,220

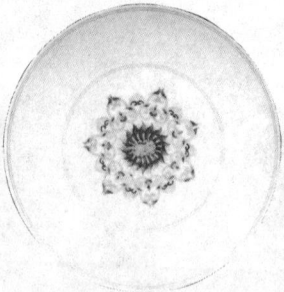

A fine Doucai dish, the interior painted with a double-centered lotus flower-head encircled by stylized ruyi-head scrolls and leaves below double blue lines, $8^{1}/_{4}$in. diameter. (Christie's) $25,176

A pair of Doucai saucer-dishes, encircled Kangxi six-character marks, the central medallion painted with a crane in flight reserved on a shou character, $8^{5}/_{8}$in. diameter. (Christie's) $17,742

## DOULTON

A Royal Doulton figure entitled 'Fortune Teller', H.N.2159, withdrawn 1967.
(Bearne's) $263

A Royal Doulton figure entitled 'Sweet and Twenty', H.N.1298, withdrawn 1969.
(Bearne's) $303

A Royal Doulton figure entitled 'Carpet Seller', H.N.1464.
(Bearne's) $172

A Doulton Lambeth circular pottery plaque, painted in colors with a portrait of young man in antique dress, 13½in. diameter.
(Christie's S. Ken) $374

A large Royal Doulton figure entitled 'Mantilla', H.N.2712, withdrawn 1977.
(Bearne's) $303

A fine Royal Doulton 'Chang' vase by Harry Nixon, Charles Noke and Fred Allen, 22.5cm., painted mark in black.
(Bearne's) $3,670

A Royal Doulton figure entitled 'Kate Hardcastle', H.N.1719, withdrawn 1949.
(Bearne's) $465

A pair of Doulton Lambeth tiles painted by Margaret Armstrong, in the pre-Raphaelite style, painted in colors, each in original frame, 7 x 18½in.
(Christie's S. Ken) $997

A Royal Doulton figure entitled 'The Balloon Seller', H.N.583, withdrawn 1949.
(Bearne's) $182

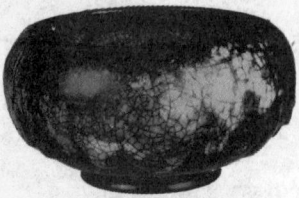

A Royal Doulton Chang bowl by Noke, decorated with green, red, yellow, white and blue glazes on a blue ground, 7in. diameter.
(Spencer's) $1,085

A Royal Doulton inkpot modeled as a baby in brown dress, inscribed *'Bill • Votes For Women'*, 9cm.
(Phillips) $613

A Royal Doulton figure of an English Setter carrying a pheasant in its mouth, HN2529, 30cm. wide.
(Spencer's) $259

A large Royal Doulton pottery vase, decorated with an extensive fox hunting scene between bands of flowers, 57.5cm.
(Bearne's) $344

A pair of Doulton Lambeth stoneware vases by Hannah Barlow, each incised with a broad band depicting stags and deer in landscapes, 19in. high.
(Spencer's) $1,320

A Doulton Lambeth stoneware three-handled loving cup by Mary Aitken, with an inscription commemorating the success of six Liberal candidates in West Riding, 16cm., 1881.
(Phillips) $735

A Royal Doulton stoneware flagon molded with stylized poppies decorated in shades of green, blue, and brown, 24cm. high.
(Spencer's) $197

A pair of Royal Doulton flambé models of penguins, set on an alabaster ashtray with silver mounts, total height 17cm.
(Bearne's) $430

A Doulton Lambeth stoneware jug, the central medallion with a crown above the entwined letters G and M, and below the date 1893, 17cm.
(Phillips) $327

## DOULTON

**A Doulton Lambeth Slaters china stoneware teapot and cover slip trailed in white and incised with blossoming apple boughs.**
**(Spencer's) $137**

**A rare Doulton Lambeth stoneware jug, the bulbous body with three reserve panels depicting golfing scenes, 22cm. tall.**
**(Phillips) $985**

**A Royal Doulton brown and white model of a standing bulldog, H.N.1045.**
**(Bearne's) $627**

**A Royal Doulton group entitled 'The Perfect Pair', H.N.581, withdrawn 1938.**
**(Bearne's) $481**

**A pair of Doulton stoneware bottle vases decorated by Eliza Simmance with foliage and a scrolling beaded design, 23cm.**
**(Bearne's) $616**

**A Royal Doulton figure entitled 'Prudence', H.N.1883, withdrawn 1949.**
**(Bearne's) $520**

**A Doulton Lambeth stoneware jug commemorating Victoria's Diamond Jubilee, inscribed *'She brought her people lasting good'*, 24cm.**
**(Phillips) $388**

**A large Royal Doulton loving cup, produced to commemorate the Silver Jubilee of King George V and Queen Mary, No. 980 of an edition limited to 1000.**
**(Bearne's) $485**

**A Royal Doulton stoneware jug molded with portrait of Field Marshal Haig and swags, inscribed *'Peace with Victory'*, 18.5cm.**
**(Phillips) $388**

## DOULTON

'Ugly Duchess', D.6599, a large Royal Doulton character jug, printed marks, 7in. high
(Christie's S. Ken) $336

A Royal Doulton figure entitled 'Millicent', H.N.1714, withdrawn 1949.
(Bearne's) $627

'Old King Cole' (yellow crown), D6014, a Royal Doulton character jug designed by H. Fenton, printed marks, 5¾in. high.
(Christie's S. Ken)
$2,051

'A Yeoman of the Guard' HN688, a Royal Doulton porcelain figure, printed and painted marks, 6in. high.
(Christie's S. Ken) $746

Doulton Lambeth stoneware jardinière, ovoid and embossed with classical profile heads and flowers within geometric borders, 8in. high.
(Hobbs & Chambers)
$194

A Royal Doulton figure entitled 'The Paisley Shawl', H.N.1460, withdrawn 1949.
(Bearne's) $364

'White-haired Clown'. a large Royal Doulton character jug, printed marks, 6¼in. high.
(Christie's S. Ken) $839

'George Washington Bicentenary', a Royal Doulton limited edition jug designed by C.J. Noke and H. Fenton, 10½in. high.
(Christie's S. Ken)
$4,849

'Mephistopheles', a large Royal Doulton character jug designed by H. Fenton, printed marks, 5½in. high.
(Christie's S. Ken) $1,212

## EUROPEAN

'Allegro Pasto', a Manna polychrome painted ceramic group modeled as a young girl in gingham dress, 11¼in. high.
(Christie's S. Ken) $516

A Baltic faience rectangular tray painted in puce monochrome with ships at sail by a harbour with a town in the distance, circa 1790, the tray 89cm. by 61cm.
(Christie's) $38,412

A Portuguese faience blue and white tile-picture in the form of a gallant painted in bright-blue wearing a peruke, and long frock-coat with wide buttoned cuffs, late 17th/early 18th century, 173.5cm. high.
(Christie's) $18,139

A slipware dish decorated with a black-coated hussar riding a cream-slip horse with brown spots, upper Austria, circa 1790, 31cm. diameter.
(Christie's) $2,534

A Naples (Real Fabbrica Ferdinandea) group of a gallant and companion, he in a black top hat, she in a black shawl over a purple patterned skirt and yellow shoes, circa 1790, 18.5cm. high.
(Christie's) $16,896

A slipware dated dish decorated with a sgraffiato merhorse flanked by the initials *G.S.T.* and *M.S.T.*, probably upper Austria, 1790, 28.5cm. diameter.
(Christie's) $2,323

An Austrian terracotta twin-handled vase in Egyptianesque style, flanked by dragon handles, gilded and cold-painted in colors, impressed *Wsss*, 10½in. high.
(Christie's S. Ken) $37

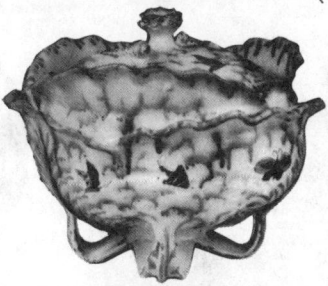

A Brussels cabbage-tureen and cover, the naturally modeled overlapping leaves with waved everted edges and raised midribs, circa 1770, 30.5cm. wide.
(Christie's) $4,647

A Katshutte Thuringia ceramic figure of a dancing girl, standing in profile with arms held aloft, printed factory mark (restored), 12¼in. high.
(Christie's S. Ken) $516

## EUROPEAN

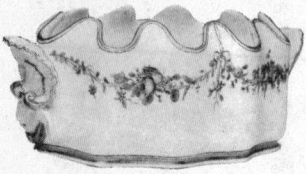

A Buen Retiro two-handled seau crenelé painted with two continuous garlands of flowers hung from blue bows, the shell-shaped handles enriched with blue and gilt lines, circa 1765.
(Christie's) $6,207

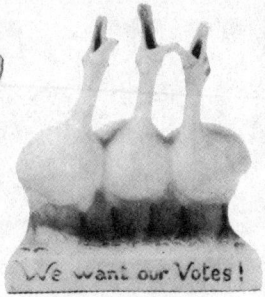


A Continental matchholder modeled as three geese squawking *'We want our votes'*, 12cm.
(Phillips) $409

Majolica footed centerpiece, Czechoslovakia, late 19th century, female-head handles, W. Schiller and Sons, 12½in. wide.
(Skinner Inc.) $175

Pair of large good quality 19th century Continental porcelain figures of a lady and gallant, on circular naturalistic bases each bearing a pseudo Meissen mark, 18in. high.
(Lawrences) $1,222

A Copenhagen oblong octagonal tray painted with two garlands of flowers tied with a purple bow flanked by two oval medallions painted in sepia, circa 1780, 42.5cm. diameter.
(Christie's) $2,821

A fine pair of Pirkenhammer porcelain vases and covers, each decorated in gold with birds on boughs of blossom, 43.5cm.
(Bearne's) $1,496

A Holics plate, the center boldly painted with a pear within a shaped border painted with manganese and blue flower-sprays, circa 1775, 23.5cm. diameter.
(Christie's) $171

A Royal Copenhagen porcelain figure of the Gronland girl, dressed in national costume, holding two bunches of flowers, 6in. high.
(Spencer's) $697

An Austrian plate, the center finely painted with Venus, a musician and Cupid in attendance, 23cm.
(Bearne's) $1,504

## EUROPEAN

A Continental figure of a protesting suffragette holding a flag inscribed *'I want a vote'*, the base also inscribed *'Give me a vote and see what I'll do'*, 12.5cm.
(Phillips) $1,185

One of a pair of Nyon coffee cans and saucers painted in colors with sprays and garlands of flowers, fish marks.
(Phillips) $1,122

A Gardener figure of a Finn in traditional costume, standing before a tree stump, in brown hat, gray jacket and breeches, 26cm., red printed mark.
(Phillips) $598

An Essevi polychrome painted ceramic figure of a naked young boy dressed in drummer's outfit, 12½in. high.
(Christie's S. Ken) $368

A pair of Spanish blue and white oviform drug-jars named for *Flo. Ros. alec.* and *Fol. U inca.* on diagonal ribbons flanked by a double-headed eagle, a bust portrait, a winged angel's head and with stylized shrubs, early 18th century, 27cm. high.
(Christie's) $2,633

A Zsolnay Pecs green luster jug, the handle modeled as a nude maiden gazing over rim, 16in. high.
(Christie's S. Ken) $1,200

A Rozenburg pottery vase decorated in mauve, brown, green, blue and yellow, with an elaborate pattern of fleshy flowers, 30cm. high.
(Phillips) $597

A Spanish maiolica dish painted in blue, yellow and ocher with a portrait of the Virgin in profile to the left within two bands of flowerheads, 18th century, 30.5cm. diameter.
(Christie's) $1,693

A pair of Helena Wolfsohn porcelain vases, each baluster body painted in the Meissen manner with harbor scenes, 36.8cm., 19th century.
(Bearne's) $2,310

An unusual relief-decorated famille rose teapot and cover of pear shape, brightly enameled on either side with a butterfly, 4½in. high, Yongzheng/early Qianlong.
(Tennants) $1,059

A famille rose baluster vase, iron-red Qianlong seal mark, the turquoise body enameled in white with scrolling lotus, applied round the shoulders and base with six Chinese boys, 12¼in. high.
(Christie's) $5,394

One of a rare pair of 19th century Canton famille rose lotus-petal jardinières and stands, each piece molded on the exterior with overlapping petals detailed in bright enamels, 6¾in. high.
(Tennants)
(Two) $4,620

A very fine famille rose charger, Yongzheng, brilliantly enameled in all the colors of the early Qing palette at the center with two black and white birds perched on a long curling branch of leafy blossoming tree peony, 20¾in. diameter.
(Christie's) $21,290

A rare famille rose watch stand and cover, the body with a circular aperture surrounded by insects and butterflies amongst molded scrolling floral sprays, 8¼in. high, Qianlong.
(Bonhams) $1,679

A fine famille rose rubyback eggshell deep plate, Yongzheng, the center with a multi-robed elegant seated lady with two playing children flanking her, 8¼in. diameter.
(Christie's) $21,290

A famille rose seated Buddha, Qianlong/Jiaqing, seated on a detachable double-lotus base, wearing a polychrome tiara above a serene expression, 11¼in. high.
(Christie's) $9,935

One of a pair of brilliant famille rose lotus-flower teapots and covers, each molded with petals and applied with flowering stems, 4¾in. high, Qianlong.
(Tennants)
(Two) $2,887

A large famille rose bottle vase, enameled with nine peaches issuing from gnarled, flowering branches, Qianlong seal mark, 19th century, 47cm. high.
(Christie's) $12,804

## FOLEY

A Foley Intarsio baluster vase printed and painted in colors with kingfishers perched on branches above a band of carp, 9in. high.
(Christie's S. Ken) $522

A Foley Intarsio teapot and cover modeled as Kruger wearing green jacket, blue waistcoat and brown pants, 4½in. high.
(Christie's S. Ken) $839

A Foley Intarsio cylindrical biscuit barrel with electroplate mount and cover, printed and painted in colors with panels of drinking scenes and flowers, 7¼in. high.
(Christie's S. Ken) $1,399

A Foley Intarsio three-handled vase and cover, printed and painted in typical colors with panels depicting the Queen of Hearts, 8in. high.
(Christie's S. Ken) $932

A Foley Intarsio single-handled spherical vase, printed and painted in colors with a band of buttercups and flowerheads on the shoulders, 6in. high.
(Christie's S. Ken) $354

A Foley Intarsio miniature grandfather clock printed and painted in colors with Father Time and bearing the inscription *Time and Tide wait for no man*, 10in. high.
(Christie's S. Ken) $932

A Foley Intarsio vase, printed and painted in colors with panels of seagulls in fiords, above a band of entrelac foliate motifs, 8½in. high.
(Christie's S. Ken) $224

A Foley Intarsio small oviform jardinière printed and painted in colors with a band of carp amongst waves, 4½in. high.
(Christie's S. Ken) $410

A Foley Intarsio twin-handled baluster vase, printed and painted in colors with band of lavender and yellow flowers, 9¼in high.
(Christie's S. Ken) $168

FRENCH

A Paris pink-ground barrel-shaped coffee-cup and saucer painted with a chinoiserie figure smoking a pipe, fabulous trees and plants, circa 1810.
(Christie's) $640

One of a pair of St. Cloud blue and white spice-boxes and covers, each with four compartments and standing on three paw feet, circa 1710, 14cm. wide.
(Christie's)
(Two) $2,974

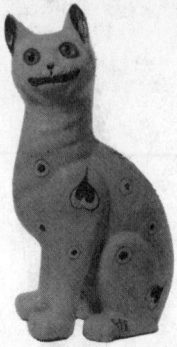

A Gallé faience model of a cat, the creature sitting back on its haunches and gazing with glass eyes and whiskered grin, 34cm. high.
(Phillips) $1,751

A French 'Empire' cabinet cup decorated at the Feuillet workshop in Paris, painted with a colonnaded country house, 12cm. (Phillips) $598

A pair of Jacob Petit vases of ogee shape with flared rims, painted in colors with bouquets on both sides, 18cm.
(Phillips) $748

One of a pair of Paris vases, painted with a landscape and a river scene, with figures and buildings, 34cm., signed Feuillet.
(Lawrence Fine Art)
(Two) $2,952

A Chantilly teabowl painted in kakiemon style with a panel of flowering prunus issuing from rockwork, 4.5cm., red horn mark.
(Phillips) $935

'Reverie', a bisque and gilt-bronze bust of a lady cast from a model by Théophile François Somme, French, late 19th century, 10¼in. high.
(Christie's East) $935

A Paris biscuit roundel of Napoleon, the head of the Emperor molded with a laurel wreath, pierced for hanging, circa 1810, 15.5cm. diameter.
(Christie's) $715

## FRENCH

A 1870s Chantilly dish with gros bleu ground and a central gilt cartouche depicting, in puce, a chateau by a lakeside, 24cm. across.
(Phillips) $456

Twelve Saint Cloud blue and white knife handles, painted with bands of lambrequin and scrolls, circa 1715, the handles 8cm. long.
(Christie's) $1,223

Paris porcelain American historical pitcher, France, circa 1862, enamel decorated portraits of Grant and Farragut in military dress, 8³/₈in. high.
(Skinner Inc.) $21,000

A pair of Samson white figures of Saints Andrew and John, the former standing before his cross, the latter holding the Book of Revelation, circa 1880, 15¹/₂in. high.
(Christie's) $2,257

A Clément Massier earthenware jardinière with a pedestal, decorated in relief with irises, the pedestal naturalistically molded with a heron among bulrushes, 38cm. diameter of jardinière.
(Christie's) $3,584

Two French soft-paste figures of a man playing a guitar and his companion dressed as a huntress holding a rifle, he with incised *R*, circa 1750, 19cm. and 20cm. high.
(Christie's) $3,201

An ormolu-mounted Samson porcelain vase, decorated overall with foliage, flowers and birds, late 19th century, 17¹/₂in. high.
(Christie's) $1,411

A Jacob Petit garniture of a clock and a pair of candlesticks all molded with rococo scrolls, shells and leaf motifs, 39.5cm.
(Phillips) $1,683

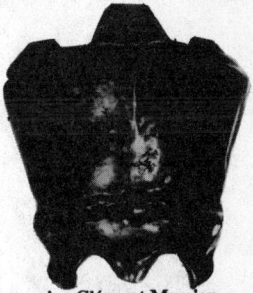

A massive Clément Massier jardinière, of irregular tapering form, decorated in an overall lustre glaze of green, yellow, amethyst and amber, 56cm. high.
(Christie's) $1,394

A French Art Deco pottery group modeled as a nude woman leaning back into the embrace of a man in cape, 12½in. high.
(Christie's S. Ken) $332

A pair of faience bucket-shaped jardinières, the sides painted in yellow, green, iron-red and underglaze blue with an Oriental by shrubs in a garden, probably Nevers, circa 1680, 13.5cm. high.
(Christie's) $5,643

A Vincennes blue lapis teacup and saucer (gobelet calabre) with indented loop handle painted in puce camaleu with Cupid holding a torch and a putto with a bunch of grapes and a spear, date letter A for 1753.
(Christie's) $5,122

A Lallemant polychrome painted earthenware vase, painted with scenes of Chopin playing the piano to a couple standing behind, 11in. high.
(Christie's S. Ken) $461

A pair of ormolu-mounted Paris pale blue-ground campana-shaped vases, one painted with a stag-hunt, the other with a boar-hunt, circa 1810–20, 38in. high.
(Christie's) $9,100

A French oval porcelain plaque painted with a young girl wearing 18th century-style dress, late 19th century, plaque 6in. long.
(Christie's S. Ken) $588

An earthenware plate decorated to a design by Marcel Goupy, painted in red, black and blue, 12½in. diameter.
(Christie's S. Ken) $184

A large French ceramic jardinière and stand, the stand decorated in mottled browns and pinks flanked by bulrushes and foliage and a large naturalistic heron, total height 1.28m., signed *Jerome Massier fils, Vallauris A.M.* (Phillips) $5,252

A Tournai fable teacup and saucer painted in the manner of Duvivier with 'The Fox and The Crane', gilt castle marks, circa 1765.
(Christie's) $1,881

## FRENCH

A Continental plaque, depicting a monk beside a reclining nude nymph by the water, 8½ x 11in. (Christie's East) $3,080

An Amphora polychrome painted porcelain group, modeled as a young woman, being presented with a casket from a small boy, 13in. high. (Christie's S. Ken) $276

A massive Nevers bleu persan bucket-shaped jardinière, the strapwork and foliage handles with bearded mask terminals, circa 1680, 47cm. high. (Christie's) $4,268

A pair of 19th century ormolu mounted porcelain candlesticks, decorated in the Louis XVI Sèvres style, French, 19th century, 31.5cm. high. (Duran, Madrid) $1,819

A Paris gold-ground baluster coffee-pot and cover painted at Naples each side with figures watching a puppet-show and spaghetti vendors, circa 1800, 18.5cm. high. (Christie's) $3,386

Two figures of jazz musicians, one with trumpet and the other with saxophone, painted in silver lustre, painted factory mark, 11½in. maximum. (Christie's S. Ken) $829

A Paris (Stone, Coquerel et le Gros) plate transfer-printed in sepia with a view of Chateau de Houghton, Comté de Norfolk, circa 1820, 23.5cm. diameter. (Christie's) $836

An Amphora polychrome-painted pottery group modeled as a Bedouin tribesman astride a camel, 19in. high. (Christie's S. Ken) $350

A Tournai spirally-molded plate painted by Michel Joseph Duvivier in puce camaieu with a coastal scene, a man on horseback urging his cattle towards a boat, circa 1765, 23cm. diameter. (Christie's) $2,821

A Limbach figure of a fisherman leaning against a tree-stump, one bare foot raised, holding a large fish in his arms, circa 1770, 14cm. high.
(Christie's) $1,280

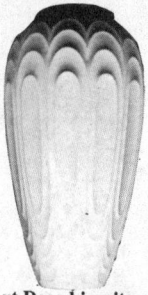

Large Art Deco biscuit porcelain vase, circa 1930, Heinrich and Co., Selb, Bavaria, wide mouth on flaring cylindrical form sculpted and paneled sides, 23½in. high.
(Skinner Inc.) $700

A Limbach figure of a girl emblematic of Summer in a yellow hat, orange bodice and puce skirt under a yellow-flowered apron filled with a sheaf of corn, circa 1770, 13cm. high. (Christie's) $640

A German fayence lobed dish painted in blue with birds in an extensive stylized landscape, 35cm.
(Phillips) $299

A pair of Potschappel pierced two-handled vases, painted in colors with Classical figures in landscape within borders, 22½in. high.
(Christie's S. Ken) $2,781

A Carl Thieme Potschappel pierced centerpiece applied with flowers, the base with four figures, 12½in. high.
(Christie's S. Ken) $718

A Gmundner Keramik covered box, designed by Dagobert Peche for the Wiener Werkstaette in 1912, of octagonal section with domed lid, 16cm. high.
(Phillips) $584

A pair of German porcelain figures of Cupid-like figures, each with a bow and quiver, standing on a foliate base, 37.5cm.
(Bearne's) $485

A rare and attractive Bottger polished stoneware tea canister, the vertical panels molded in relief and gilt with birds in flight and perched in trees, 12.5cm.
(Phillips) $15,936

A Wallendorf figure of a fruit vendor in a black hat, gray jacket, iron-red patterned waistcoat, puce breeches and black shoes, circa 1770, 13cm. high. (Christie's) $1,601

An amusing Goebels ceramic decanter set, comprising: a decanter and stopper modeled as a young man dressed in black, red and white and a set of six liqueur goblets, each painted in colors with the head of a girl. (Phillips) $696

A Frankenthal figure of a lady emblematic of Spring modeled by J.W. Lanz, stepping forward and holding her flower-laden apron before her, circa 1760, 14cm. high. (Christie's) $2,347

A German fayence cylindrical tankard with pewter hinged cover, painted in colors with an cathedral, dated 1848, 10¾in. high. (Christie's S. Ken) $426

Four Ludwigsburg putti emblematic of the Senses, after models by Johann Heinrich Schmid, Taste eating fruit, Smell with a basket of flowers, Hearing listening to a watch and Touch holding fruit, circa 1780, 24cm. high overall. (Christie's) $4,055

An Annaberg stoneware baluster jug molded and colored with a crowned king on horseback and holding his orb, with a coat-of-arms and the date 1689, 25.5cm. high. (Christie's) $1,505

A Rosenthal porcelain figure of Autumn, modeled by Gerhard Schliepstein, design as a kneeling, attenuated barely clad maiden holding a basket of fruit, 18cm. high. (Phillips) $1,011

KPM porcelain plaque of young woman: Rebecca, late 19th century, painted after C.E.H. Lecomte-Vernet, 9¼ x 6¼in. (Skinner Inc.) $5,250

A colored Wurzberg figure of a putto, after the Nymphenburg models by Bustelli, standing and leaning against a yellow lyre, 10cm. (Phillips) $1,096

A Böttger Hausmalerei saucer painted in iron-red with an equestrian figure in full dress, holding a banner, his horse dressed with plumes, circa 1720, 12.5cm. diameter.
(Christie's) $2,069

A Frankenthal baluster ewer and cover probably painted by Jakob Osterspey with Bacchus and Venus reclining beside him scantily clad in brown and pink drapes, circa 1758, 23.5cm. high.
(Christie's) $17,072

A massive German fayence armorial dish, the central Arms in yellow and underglaze blue surrounded by meandering flowers flanked by martial trophies, early 18th century, 50cm. diameter.
(Christie's) $6,019

A Hutschenreuther Hohenburg rectangular plaque painted by Wagner with the Duchess of Devonshire, late 19th century, plaque 7in. x 4¾in.
(Christie's S. Ken) $1,050

A rare pair of bisque busts of children, the boy cradling a dog, the girl with a cat, 11in. high, probably early Heubach.
(Christie's S. Ken) $3,901

An Ansbach arched rectangular tea-caddy and cover painted with men fishing from a rock and in a boat before a village and distant mountains, circa 1775, 12.5cm. high.
(Christie's) $2,561

A Ludwigsburg group of Bacchus and a Bacchante modeled by Johann Christian Wilhelm Beyer, the naked figures embracing and she squeezing a bunch of grapes into his bowl, circa 1765, 24cm. high.
(Christie's) $5,335

A German porcelain massive garniture, the central pierced flared bowl supported by three bound slaves of three continents, 28in. high.
(Christie's S. Ken) $18,909

An Ansbach baluster coffee-pot and a cover, painted with two birds perched in branches flanked by scattered sprigs of puce flowers, circa 1770, 18.5cm. high overall.
(Christie's) $1,814

A Goldscheider terracotta wallmask modeled as the head of a young woman with turquoise ringlets and a yellow tulip at the neck, 10in. long.
(Christie's S. Ken) $774

An unusual Goldscheider pottery wallmask modeled as Shirley Temple, painted in colors, 10in. long.
(Christie's S. Ken) $774

A Goldscheider terracotta wallmask modeled as an exotic woman partially concealed behind a mask, 14in. long.
(Christie's S. Ken) $440

A Goldscheider polychrome-painted pottery figure of a dancer, modeled by Dakon, wearing blue spotted bodice and floral divided skirt, 10½in. high.
(Christie's S. Ken) $884

A Goldscheider terracotta wall mask of a female profile painted with turquoise ringlets, orange-banded black hat and yellow scarf, 10in. long.
(Christie's S. Ken) $484

A Goldscheider Art Nouveau pottery figure of a naked maiden supporting a circular mirror on her thigh, 30in. high.
(Christie's S. Ken) $1,842

A Goldscheider terracotta wallmask modeled as the profile of a young woman with orange hair and lips, and green eyes, 11in. long.
(Christie's S. Ken) $553

A Goldscheider terracotta wall hanging, modeled as a female bather standing amongst rushes, with towel draped over right forearm, 15in. long.
(Christie's S. Ken) $1,105

A Goldscheider terracotta wallmask, modeled as the stylized head of a woman with pierced eyes, orange hair and lips, 12in. long.
(Christie's S. Ken) $737

## HAMADA

A two handled white pot by Shoji Hamada, with a brown rim, 5 3/4in. high.
(Bonhams) $1,111

A fine stoneware bottle vase by Shoji Hamada, tenmoku with wax resist floral decoration, in a fitted wooden box with Japanese characters, 8in. high.
(Bonhams) $9,696

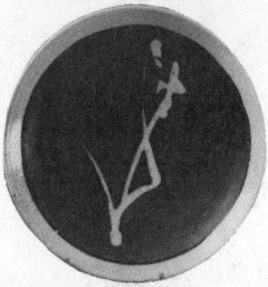

A stoneware wax resist decorated dish by Shoji Hamada, with a floral motif, rust, buff rim and motif, 11in. diameter.
(Bonhams) $3,434

A tenmoku stoneware teabowl by Shoji Hamada, with central ridge, decorated with rust colored splashes, 4 1/4in. high.
(Bonhams) $3,636

An outstanding curved stoneware vase by Shoji Hamada, speckled gray with white vertical lines and brown foliate decoration, in fitted wooden box with Japanese characters, 10in. high.
(Bonhams) $15,150

A stoneware teabowl by Shoji Hamada, with brushed pale gray hakeme band below rim over sage green, 4in. high.
(Bonhams) $1,111

## HENDERSON

A stoneware sculptural form by Ewen Henderson, handbuilt, highly pitted areas of beige, pink and gray, 19in. high.
(Bonhams) $3,232

A fine pink stoneware vessel by Ewen Henderson, with laminated porcelain areas, highly pitted purple areas, 15 3/4in. high.
(Bonhams) $3,232

A massive stoneware vase by Ewen Henderson, of flattened and bended form, laminated and highly pitted pale green and brown areas, 25 1/2in. high.
(Bonhams) $3,232

## HISPANO MORESQUE

An Hispano-Moresque copper-luster large dish of pale color and large size, the raised central boss with a swan surrounded by a band of stylized script century, 41cm. diameter. (Christie's) $4,268

An Hispano-Moresque tapering waisted albarello decorated in blue and copper-luster with two bands of stylized bunches of grapes, late 15th century, 18cm. high. (Christie's) $4,514

An Hispano-Moresque gold-luster armorial dish, the raised central boss with the Arms of a rampant lion within a spirally gadrooned surround, late 15th century, 48cm. diameter. (Christie's) $14,107

Hispano-Moresque charger decorated in luster with plant motifs, Valencian, md 16th century. (Christie's Rome) $2,799

An Hispano-Moresque copper-lustre oviform jar, the short cylindrical neck with four grooved loop handles divided by waisted panels of flowers and loop-pattern, 17th century, 22cm. high. (Christie's) $7,469

An Hispano-Moresque blue and copper-luster large dish with a raised central boss with a quatrefoil surrounded by a band of radiating fronds, 16th century, 41cm. diameter. (Christie's) $4,695

## HÖCHST

One of a pair of Höchst teacups and saucers painted with pastoral scenes after engravings by J.E. Nilson, circa 1765. (Christie's) $6,830

One of a pair of Höchst pot-pourri vases painted in the manner of Andreas Philipp Oettner, circa 1765, 25cm. high. (Christie's) $26,675

A Höchst copper-gilt mounted oval snuff-box painted with scenes of lovers in landscape vignettes beside sheep and a masked figure, circa 1775, 9.5cm. wide. (Christie's) $8,913

## IMARI

An Imari charger, the central roundel depicting a bijin walking up stairs leading to a porch behind which stands a blossoming cherry tree, circa 1700, 54.3cm. diameter.
(Christie's) $6,501

A pair of Imari baluster vases and covers decorated in iron-red enamel and gilt on underglaze blue, the domed covers surmounted by karashishi finials, late 17th/early 18th century, 47.0cm. high.
(Christie's) $11,919

Japanese Imari porcelain Jardinière, mid 19th century, flat rim with fluted body, decorated in blue, rust and gilt, 6¼in. high.
(Skinner Inc.) $475

An Imari charger decorated in typical colored enamels and gilt on underglaze blue, circa 1700, mounted as a Victorian giltwood and composition occasional table on column supports, 58.5cm. diameter.
(Christie's) $14,086

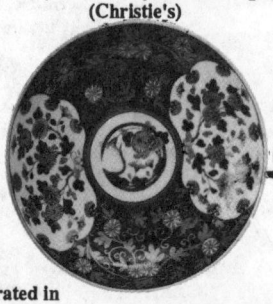

An Imari circular tureen, cover and stand decorated in iron-red, green and aubergine enamels and gilt on underglaze blue, lappet handles, kiku mon, circa 1700, dish 27.7cm. diameter, tureen 19.8cm. high.
(Christie's) $17,336

An Imari gin-cask modeled as a bijin seated on a stylized cart, her kimono decorated with stylized flowerheads and foliage including paulownia, late 17th-early 18th century, 38.5cm. high.
(Christie's) $30,338

An Imari polychrome bottle vase, painted with peonies and chrysanthemums amongst scrolling foliage with birds flying above, 30.5cm., late 17th century.
(Bearne's) $3,134

An unusual Imari comport, the interior painted with landscapes, the cavetto painted with vases of flowers andd boughs of blossom, 23.3cm. high.
(Bearne's) $647

A Chinese Imari tankard of cylindrical form, painted in underglaze blue, iron-red and gilding, 5¼in. high, Kangxi.
(Bonhams) $333

## IMARI

A large Imari bowl for a tureen, the body with four lappet panels containing birds among trees, reserved on a ground of various grasses and flowers, late 17th-early 18th century, 37.8cm. diameter, 26.3cm. high.
(Christie's) $6,501

A pair of Imari bottle vases decorated in iron-red enamel and gilt on underglaze blue, the globular body with plants set in roundels and birds on a ground of cloud pattern, late 17th century, 25cm. high.
(Christie's) $4,452

An Imari pierced box decorated in iron-red, black, yellow, green and aubergine enamels and gilt on underglaze blue, late 17th/early 18th century, 9cm. high, approx. 14.6cm. square.
(Christie's) $3,901

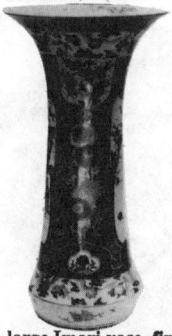

A large Imari vase, finely painted on either side with two ladies strolling in a garden with a cat on a lead, 76.8cm., early 19th century.
(Bearne's) $8,492

A pair of Imari jars of square section, each facet painted with a jardinière of chrysanthemums, 24.5cm.
(Bearne's) $2,022

An ormolu-mounted Imari coffee urn and cover, the fluted sides with a continuous design of ho-o birds among flowering and fruiting boughs, the cover similarly decorated, late 17th century, overall height 30.5cm.
(Christie's) $23,232

An Imari model of a bijin decorated in iron-red, green and black enamels and gilt, her robes decorated with chrysanthemum and other flowers on a bamboo frame, late 17th century, 39.3cm. high.
(Christie's) $1,936

A pair of Imari jars and covers decorated in iron-red, green, yellow, black and aubergine enamels and gilt on underglaze blue, late 17th century, 40.5cm. high.
(Christie's) $8,712

An Imari model of an actor, his kimono decorated with chrysanthemum and cherry blossom flowers and foliage amongst brocaded ribbons, circa 1700, 39cm. high.
(Christie's) $5,634

A very spirited Urbino Istoriato plate painted by Francesco Durantino, showing the victorious Scipio, 29cm.
(Phillips) $24,900

A Capodimonte group of a youth riding a mastiff modeled by Guiseppe Gricci, the youth in peaked pale-pink cap with gilt bow, 1755–1759, 17cm. high.
(Christie's) $7,148

A Cantagalli charger, possibly by Farini, the central roundel depicting two putti rowing a galleon across choppy waters, 51cm. diameter.
(Phillips) $1,556

A Castel Durante wet-drug jar with short yellow spout and wide strap handle, named for *S. ABSINTII* on a yellow rectangular cartouche, circa 1570, 21cm. high.
(Christie's) $5,335

A pair of Naples armorial waisted albarelli, the central quartered Arms in ocher, yellow and blue within a beaded cartouche, mid-16th century, 23cm. high.
(Christie's) $14,938

A finely painted Venetian large oviform jar painted with the forefront of a galloping horse, amongst military and musical trophies, 32.5cm., mid-16th century.
(Phillips) $47,808

A Castel Durante tondino with a central yellow and ocher foliage mask inscribed *PACIFICAB* on a ribbon above reserved on a blue ground, circa 1525, 22cm. diameter.
(Christie's) $8,109

A Siena wall-plaque painted in blue with buildings in a rocky wooded landscape, within an ocher and brown marbled pierced frame molded with putti, circa 1740, 46.5cm. high.
(Christie's) $3,841

A Castel Durante Armorial saucer dish with a coat of arms above a hilly landscape, within a wide blue border, 22.5cm., circa 1570.
(Phillips) $9,562

An Urbino istoriato tazza painted with Marcus Curtius leaping into the abyss on a white stallion surrounded by soldiers before a tree, circa 1545, 25.5cm. diameter.
(Christie's) $13,871

A Savona dated figure of Winter modeled as a bearded man clasping a fur-lined yellow cloak about his shoulders, incised with the date 1779, 33.5cm. high.
(Christie's) $3,841

A Castelli armorial small dish painted in the Grue workshop and lightly enriched in gilding, the center with Venus scantily draped and combing Cupid's hair, late 17th/early 18th century, 24.5cm. diameter.
(Christie's) $8,963

A Castel Durante portrait dish boldly painted with an almost full face portrait of 'Faustina Bella', her hair coiled and braided with a white bandeau, 23cm., circa 1540.
(Phillips) $21,912

A pair of Siena massive campana-shaped ewers with molded gilt-winged caryatid handles and an applied gilt foliate mask beneath the lip, the bodies painted with Bacchic fauns, circa 1730, 63cm. high.
(Christie's) $32,010

A Montelupo crespina boldly painted in ocher, yellow, blue and green with a central circular medallion of a fox surrounded by radiating panels of sylized foliage, mid-17th century, 25cm. diameter. (Christie's) $2,347

A Castelli armorial plate painted in the Grue workshop with a traveler and companion riding a horse and a donkey, circa 1720, 24cm. diameter.
(Christie's) $4,695

A Tuscan wet-drug jar with short waisted neck, the oviform body decorated in blue and ocher with the sacred *YHS* monogram, circa 1460, 25cm. high.
(Christie's) $8,109

A Montelupo crespina, the center with the bust portrait of a girl draped in a green shawl and inscribed *VESTRO* within a border of radiating panels, early 17th century, 23.5cm. diameter.
(Christie's) $3,414

## ITALIAN

A Doccia baluster coffee-pot and cover painted with scattered sprays of flowers, the reeded dragon's head spout and scroll handle enriched in yellow, blue and puce, circa 1760, 20cm. high. (Christie's) $1,494

A Naples (Real Fabbrica Ferdinandea) Royal portrait medallion with the heads of King Ferdinando IV and Queen Maria Caroline, circa 1790, 6.5cm. diameter. (Christie's) $3,414

An extremely rare and finely painted Capodimonte candlestick base of triangular shape, modeled by Gaetano Fumo and Giuseppe Gricci, 18.5cm. high. (Phillips) $2,988

An attractive Venice albarello of cylindrical form, painted in colors with bands of convolvulus on a scrolling blue ground, 14.5cm. (Phillips) $2,057

Two Talavera blue and white waisted albarelli boldly painted in a gray-blue and manganese with a figure standing by an urn and tree in a rocky landscape, circa 1780, 20.5cm. and 21.5cm. high. (Christie's) $2,445

A Ligurian wet drug jar of globular form with short spout and strap handle, inscribed in manganese with *Syr*Rosar Firr*, 20cm. (Phillips) $1,216

A large Savona charger painted in blue with a figure of Neptune in a shell-shaped chariot, 46cm., shield mark. (Phillips) $3,179

An Italian maiolica armorial two-handled vase, painted with a milkmaid, a shepherd and a cow, 15¼in. high. (Christie's S. Ken) $384

A Deruta Armorial dish painted in the center with a shield with a wide band in ocher on a dark blue ground, 38cm. (Phillips) $6,175

## ITALIAN

A Montelupo à Quatieri crespina painted in blue, ocher, yellow and green with a putto in a landscape, 27cm.
(Phillips) $2,057

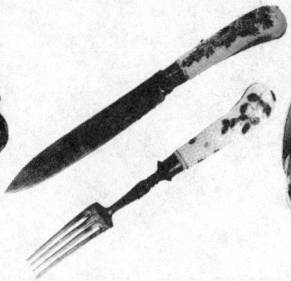

Two Nove pistol-shaped handles painted with fruit and flowers, fitted with a steel four-pronged fork and a blade, 19th century, 7.5cm. and 8cm. long.
(Christie's) $341

An Urbino Istoriato dish painted with a figure of a bearded man, possibly intended for Hercules, 26cm.
(Phillips) $3,179

A Caltagirone albarello of waisted cylindrical form, painted in ocher and pale green with scrolling foliage on a pale blue ground, 23cm.
(Phillips) $711

A North Italian cruet painted with birds perched among scrolling red and yellow flowers with blue berries beneath blue scroll borders, probably Turin, circa 1750.
(Christie's) $2,347

A Doccia coffee pot and cover of baluster shape and loop handle and bird's head spout, 25cm.
(Phillips) $446

A Faenza crespina with fluted rim, and on a low foot, painted in the center with a standing figure of a warrior, 30cm., late 16th century.
(Phillips) $2,992

A Palermo wet drug jar with pointed ovoid body painted with flowerheads and leaves in yellow and green, on a blue ground, 20cm., 17th century.
(Phillips) $1,295

An Urbino maiolica accouchement bowl painted inside the deep bowl with an expectant mother and child, 15.5cm. diameter, Patanazzi workshop, last quarter 16th century. (Phillips) $2,805

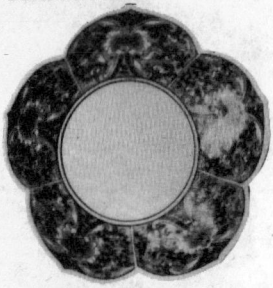

A kakiemon style blue and white six-lobed dish, the plain central roundel bordered by six panels, each containing a flower blossom, late 17th/early 18th century, 13.1cm. diameter.
(Christie's) $1,842

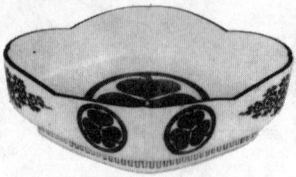

A kakiemon blue and white four-lobed dish, the central decoration a large Tokugawa mon, the exterior with smaller versions of the same, circa 1700, 15.2cm. long.
(Christie's) $11,919

A kakiemon blue and white foliate-rimmed dish decorated with a goose among reeds on a riverbank, another hovering above, circa 1700, 25cm. wide.
(Christie's) $5,418

A kakiemon blue and white shallow dish with a central roundel containing a pavilion in a lakeside landscape perched on a rocky precipice, fuku mark, seven spur marks, late 17th century, 25.8cm. diameter.
(Christie's) $8,235

A kakiemon style celadon kendi decorated in iron-red, blue, green and black enamels, late 17th century, 19.6cm. high.
(Christie's) $3,684

A kakiemon blue and white shallow dish with a pair of quail pecking amongst autumn grasses, late 17th century, 15cm. diameter.
(Christie's) $13,002

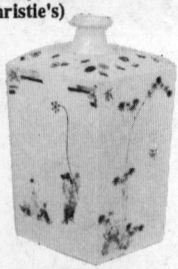

A kakiemon rectangular sake bottle decorated with children playing and flying a kite among plum blossom, bamboo, birds and rockwork, late 17th century, 15cm. high.
(Christie's) $8,235

An early enameled kakiemon style teapot decorated in iron-red, blue, green, yellow and black enamels, with two shaped panels depicting ho-o birds, late 17th century, 15cm. long.
(Christie's) $43,340

A fine early enameled kakiemon vase with boats in a lakeside landscape, beneath willows and other trees among rocks, late 17th century, 19cm. high.
(Christie's) $47,674

A blue and white ginger jar of ovoid form, painted with cartouches enclosing precious objects, wood stand and cover, 10in. high, Kangxi.
(Bonhams) $499

A peachbloom-glazed beehive waterpot, taibo zun, Kangxi six-character mark, the well-potted domed sides rising to a narrow waisted neck, 5in. diameter.
(Christie's) $42,581

A blue and white silver mounted jar and cover, painted with panels of Long Eliza and prunus blossom below a band of cloud scrolls, 5¼in., Kangxi.
(Bonhams) $410

An aubergine and green yellow-ground incised 'dragon' dish, encircled Kangxi six-character mark, the center of the interior with an aubergine and a green incised five-clawed dragon, 5½in. diameter.
(Christie's) $1,845

A famille verte pear-shaped vase, Kangxi, brightly enameled in iron-red, green, turquoise, aubergine and gilt, 9in. high.
(Christie's) $4,968

A fine 'green dragon' dish, Kangxi six-character mark, painted to the center of the interior with a circular panel of a scaly dragon reaching for a flaming pearl, 7¾in. diameter.
(Christie's) $14,194

A blue and red square brushpot, Kangxi six-character mark, painted in underglaze-blue and copper-red on the waisted body, 6½in. square.
(Christie's) $3,974

A famille verte 'magpie and prunus' rouleau vase, Kangxi, decorated to the cylindrical body with two magpies perched on a blossoming prunus tree amongst bamboo, 17¾in. high.
(Christie's) $11,355

A blue and white jardinière, Kangxi, painted to the exterior with The Three Friends, pine, prunus and bamboo below a band of key pattern, 17in. diameter.
(Christie's) $1,419

## KUTANI

A Kutani Koro, painted in predominantly iron-red and gilt with panels of ladies playing musical instruments and dancing, 10½in. diameter, Meiji period.
(Bonhams) $665

One of a pair of Kutani vases, painted in iron-red and gilt with cockerels amongst peony between ho-o, 14in. high, Meiji period.
(Bonhams) $1,119

## CHINA

A Kutani koro and cover of typical form, painted all over in iron-red and gilt with Shishi and cash symbols, 11¾in., Meiji period.
(Bonhams) $1,000

A Kutani style shallow dish, depicting a farmstead, the upper section with lozenge diaper design, the reverse with cherry blossom sprays, fuku mark, circa 1700, 14.5cm. diameter.
(Christie's) $6,934

A garniture of three Kutani vases, the central covered jar with Buddist lion knop, each painted on one side with a woman and children in a garden, 30cm.
(Bearne's) $1,335

A Kutani vase of lobed ovoid form, painted in colored enamels, iron-red and gilt with two rabbits, 8¼in. high, Meiji period.
(Bonhams) $249

## KOREAN

A Korean blue and white pear-shaped vase, painted to the sides in grayish-blue tones with two leafy stalks of fruiting finger-citrus, Yi Dynasty, 19th century, 33.5cm. high.
(Christie's) $17,107

An unusual Korean blue-glazed jar of squat globular shape, incised with a net pattern, the rim with a lappet band, the interior covered with a thick creamy white glaze, 18cm. diameter, Yi Dynasty, 19th century.
(Christie's) $5,402

A Korean underglaze blue and copper-red kendi modeled in the form of a tortoise on a lotus-leaf-shaped body with the four legs protruding below the shell, Yi Dynasty, circa 1800, 17cm. high.
(Christie's) $110,968

A tall stoneware jug by Bernard Leach, covered in green running glaze, the body decorated with a series of indented studs, impressed BL and St. Ives seals, circa 1961, 12¼in. high.
(Bonhams) $2,222

A fine stoneware slab bottle by Bernard Leach, covered in a pitted mushroom colored glaze, the front and back faces quartered, 19.5cm. high.
(Christie's) $3,841

An important tall vase by Bernard Leach, light greenish speckled glaze with incised and combed willow tree decoration, impressed BL and St. Ives seals, circa 1955, 14½in. high.
(Bonhams) $5,454

A stoneware vase by Bernard Leach, decorated with brush strokes and spots, in brown and blue, impressed St. Ives, circa 1938, 4¾in. high.
(Bonhams) $808

A rare stoneware plate by Bernard Leach, decorated with a painted mountain goat, impressed BL and St. Ives seals, circa 1955, 9¾in. diameter.
(Bonhams) $3,030

A stoneware vase by Bernard Leach, a celadon glaze with tenmoku raised rim, impressed BL and St. Ives seals, circa 1930, 7¼in. high.
(Bonhams) $889

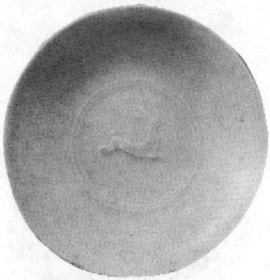

A fine porcelain dish by Bernard Leach, pale celadon, with an embossed deer surrounded by two circles, impressed BL and St. Ives seals, circa 1967, 7½in. diameter.
(Bonhams) $2,424

An outstanding stoneware vase by Bernard Leach, glazed in tenmoku, this 'bottle form' would have been thrown on the wheel then beaten and shaved to a square section, impressed BL and St. Ives seals, circa 1963, 14in. high.
(Bonhams) $7,676

A magnificent stoneware Pilgrim dish by Bernard Leach, with the figure of a pilgrim, rust, khaki and black tenmoku, impressed BL and St. Ives seals, circa 1970, 13in. diameter.
(Bonhams) $10,504

## LEEDS CREAMWARE

A Leeds creamware teapot and cover with 'beaded' edges, brightly painted with Chinese figures in a garden, 17cm., late 18th century.
(Bearne's) $412

A Leeds creamware plate, the center painted with the portraits of the Prince and Princess William V of Orange, 24.7cm.
(Bearne's) $304

A Leeds creamware baluster jug, boldly painted below the spout with a portrait of the Princess of Orange, 14cm., late 18th century.
(Bearne's) $206

## LENCI

A Lenci ceramic figure, of a nude girl wearing a checkered cap kneeling on the top of a globe, with a book in one hand and a dog by her side, with painted signature *Lenci, Made in Italy, Torino*, 48cm. high.
(Christie's) $7,049

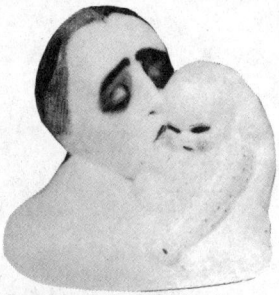

A Lenci bust of a father and baby, the sleekly groomed, dark-haired man clasping and kissing a rosy-cheeked, fair-haired and somewhat reluctant baby, 18cm. high.
(Phillips) $1,244

A Lenci figure group, of a bare-breasted native woman wearing an abstract patterned wrap-around skirt in yellow, green and black, 44cm. high.
(Phillips) $1,751

## LINTHORPE

A Linthorpe vase, designed by Dr. Christopher Dresser, the streaky glaze in tones of green and brown, with incised decoration of a single fern encircling the gourd, 19cm. high.
(Christie's) $1,944

A Linthorpe pottery jug, designed by Dr. Christopher Dresser, with everted rim continuing to form an angled handle, terminating in a rippled design, covered in a streaky caramel, green and crimson glaze, 21cm. high.
(Christie's) $3,841

A Linthorpe vase, designed by Dr. Christopher Dresser, the gourd-shaped body with double angular spout and curved carrying-bar, streaked glaze of green and brown.
(Christie's) $2,046

## LINTHORPE

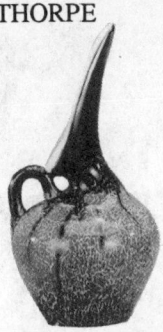

A Linthorpe vase, designed by Dr. Christopher Dresser, glazed in streaky pale and dark brown with a white crackelé effect, 25cm. high
(Christie's) $921

A Linthorpe vase, designed by Dr. Christopher Dresser, formed as a cluster of five pointed gourd shapes encircling a central funnel-shaped neck, 11cm. high.
(Christie's) $2,660

A Linthorpe pottery vase, designed by Dr. Christopher Dresser, the center decorated with pierced flower bud design, 20cm. high.
(Christie's) $1,387

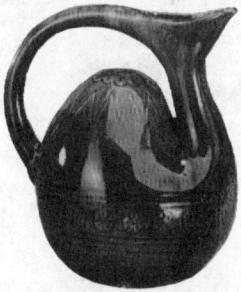

A Linthorpe jug, designed by Dr. Christopher Dresser, humped shape with vertical spout and carved handle, incised geometric pattern, 18cm. high.
(Christie's) $1,125

A Linthorpe face vase, designed by Dr. Christopher Dresser, domed cylindrical shape with double angular spout, decorated with a stylized face on one side, 15.5cm. high.
(Christie's) $1,228

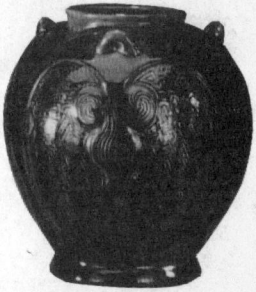

A Linthorpe vase, designed by Dr. Christopher Dresser, glazed in streaky pale and dark green, with molded maze patterns and linear designs, 22.5cm. high.
(Christie's) $982

A Linthorpe goat's-head vase, designed by Dr. Christopher Dresser, double gourd shape, decorated with four goats' heads, 28cm. high.
(Christie's) $5,933

A Linthorpe vase, designed by Dr. Christopher Dresser, with frilled lug handles and incised decoration of a bearded face on one side, 22cm. high.
(Christie's) $5,320

A Linthorpe vase, designed by Dr Christopher Dresser, decorated with four grotesque heads, each forming a handle, covered in a streaky green glaze, 22.5cm. high.
(Christie's) $1,931

## LIVERPOOL CREAMWARE

**Liverpool creamware presentation pitcher, early 19th century, black transfer decorated with portrait of Benjamin Franklin, 9½in. high. (Skinner Inc.) $4,600**

**Liverpool creamware pitcher, England, circa 1800, black transfer printed three-masted ship flying the American flag, 10in. high. (Skinner Inc.) $1,900**

**Liverpool creamware pottery pitcher, England, 1807–09, transfer printed cartoon depicting cow pulled by Bunopart and John Bull and milked by Jefferson, 8¼in. high. (Skinner Inc.) $8,500**

## LOWESTOFT

**A Lowestoft feeding cup, painted in blue with a five petalled flower with two sprays and a moth, 7.5cm. (Phillips) $1,116**

**A Lowestoft oviform punch-pot and cover painted in a famille rose palette with Oriental figures at various pursuits, circa 1780, 22cm. high. (Christie's) $4,963**

**A Lowestoft miniature teapot and cover of globular shape, printed in blue with a version of the 'Three Flowers' pattern, 8.5cm. (Phillips) $893**

**A rare Lowestoft custard cup painted in colors with a 'Redgrave' pattern beneath an egg and flower border, 6cm. (Phillips) $595**

**A rare Lowestoft model of a pug dog with a green collar and a brown coat, seated on a green rectangular base, 9cm. (Phillips) $2,790**

**A late 18th century Lowestoft porcelain sparrow beak jug of baluster form, painted with Long Elizas, 9cm. high. (Spencer's) $720**

## LONGTON HALL

A Longton Hall figure emblematic of Winter in a brown overcoat and lime green lining and buttoned cuffs, circa 1755, 4½in. high.
(Christie's S. Ken) $800

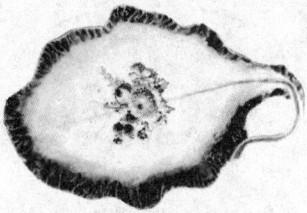

A Longton Hall leaf-dish, the center painted with a loose bouquet and with puce veining, circa 1755, 24cm. long.
(Christie's) $1,300

A Longton Hall candlestick-group modeled as a seated figure of a nymph scantily clad in a tunic painted with loose bouquets and with flowing yellow drapery, circa 1760, 28cm. high overall.
(Christie's) $1,448

A Longton Hall figure emblematic of Plenty, seated on a mound in a plumed hat blue pink lined coat and pink dress, circa 1755, 5¼in. high.
(Christie's S. Ken) $1,000

A pair of Longton Hall pigeon-tureens and covers, the naturally modeled birds to left and right with purple feather markings, circa 1755, 22cm. long.
(Christie's) $13,002

A Longton Hall figure of a flower seller, seated on a tall scroll-molded base, wearing a yellow coat with fan collar, 4⅝in. high, circa 1755.
(Tennants) $1,251

A Longton Hall mug of cylindrical shape with a spurred handle, painted in blue with an Oriental style landscape, 6.5cm.
(Phillips) $1,302

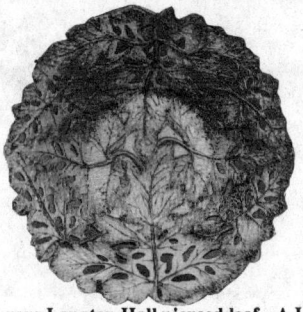

A rare Longton Hall pierced leaf basket of deep circular shape, the overlapping leaves with light puce ribs, 25.5cm. wide.
(Phillips) $6,700

A Longton Hall vase of inverted baluster form with spreading neck and fluted base, the body painted in colors, 4¾in. high.
(Christie's S. Ken) $430

## LUCIE RIE

A porcelain inlaid sgraffito bowl by Lucie Rie, covered in a pink glaze between two bands of turquoise, the rim and foot covered in a lustrous bronze glaze, circa 1980, 18.2cm. diameter.
(Christie's) $5,548

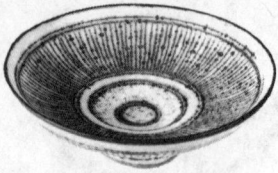

A fine stoneware 'knitted' bowl by Lucie Rie, inlaid with concentric dark circles from the well, impressed LR seal, circa 1982, 9in. diameter.
(Bonhams) $6,060

A porcelain footed bowl by Lucie Rie, 'American' yellow glaze, impressed LR seal, circa 1970, 6 1/8 in. diameter.
(Bonhams) $2,626

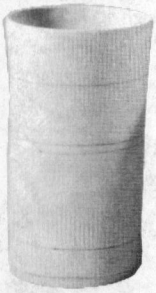

A porcelain beaker by Lucie Rie, with four inlaid circular lines, impressed LR seal, circa 1975, 4 3/4 in. high.
(Bonhams) $1,212

A rare stoneware bowl by Lucie Rie, covered in a translucent white glaze with a bronze rim running into the white body, impressed LR seal, circa 1955, 4 1/4 in. high.
(Bonhams) $1,515

A stoneware coffee pot by Lucie Rie, brown with cane handle, impressed LR seal, circa 1952, 7 1/4 in. high.
(Bonhams) $222

A rare stoneware vase by Lucie Rie, dolomite glaze, the body slightly flattened, impressed LR seal, circa 1965, 8 1/4 in. high.
(Bonhams) $1,717

A superb porcelain bowl by Lucie Rie, uranium yellow with deep bronze running band at rim, impressed seal, circa 1975, 7in. diameter.
(Bonhams) $12,120

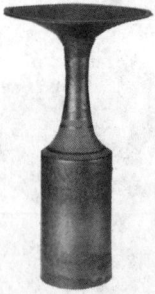

A superb porcelain vase by Lucie Rie, cylindrical with slender neck and widely flaring rim, impressed LR seal, circa 1978, 9 1/2 in. high.
(Bonhams) $21,210

## LUSTER

A William de Morgan red luster vase and cover, the white ground decorated in red, with three bands of stylized birds and beasts, with scolloped borders at rim and base, 33.6cm. high.
(Christie's) $4,695

A Sunderland luster jug decorated in colors with scenes and insignia relating to the Alliance of England and France, 17cm.
(Phillips) $735

A Sunderland pink luster jug printed in black with a portrait bust of Earl Grey and inscribed *'The Choice of the People and England's Glory'*, 19cm.
(Phillips) $1,124

## MARTINWARE

A Martin Brothers stoneware model of a bird, his removable head wears a slightly forlorn expression, 28cm. high.
(Phillips) $4,279

A Martin Brothers stoneware vase, incised with a pattern of wild roses in a cream glaze with briers and leaves in green on an oatmeal ground, 25.50cm. high.
(Phillips) $1,206

A Martin Brothers jug, with incised decoration of a stork-like creature with a long pelican bill on two of the three sides, 1898, 24cm. high.
(Christie's) $1,921

A Martin Brothers stoneware cylindrical spill vase, incised and painted with birds on the branches of a fruit tree, 19cm.
(Bearne's) $303

A Martin Bros. stoneware jug, molded and painted with a 'knobbled' design in blue and brown enamels, 23.3cm., inscribed *Martin Bros, London & Southall, 10–1895.*
(Bearne's) $752

A Martin Brothers grotesque bird, the head incised *Martin Bros., 3–1902, London & Southall*, mounted on circular ebonized wooden base, 25cm. high.
(Christie's) $7,256

A Martin Brothers vase, the writhen globular body with four handles modeled as snakes biting the rim of the vase, 1899, 27.5cm. high.
(Christie's) $4,695

A Martin Brothers vase, the body glazed in dark green with an incised cellular pattern, incised *Martin Bros., London & Southall*, 18.5cm. high.
(Christie's) $896

A Martin Brothers character jug, modeled as a grotesque seal-like creature holding its sides, its gaping mouth forming the spout, greeny-blue body glaze, 24.5cm. high.
(Christie's) $896

A Martin Brothers stoneware vase, decorated with magnolia blooms and insects nearby, against a textured ground glazed in brown and white, 23.60cm. high.
(Phillips) $700

An amusing Martin Brothers stoneware model of a baby owl, the creature has a pale brown round body resting on a circular base above ebonized stand, 27.50cm. high, signed *Martin Bros. London & Southall* and dated *10–1895*.
(Phillips) $5,835

An unusual Martin Brothers stoneware timepiece, formed as a tower with domed and floral decorated top, foliate and beaded decoration flanking the face and panels of birds, London 1875.
(Phillips) $1,206

A Martin Brothers stoneware jug, covered in a brown and mottled green-blue glaze, decorated with incised grotesque sea creatures and lines of verse, dated 12–1888, 23.5cm. high.
(Christie's) $2,561

A large Martin Brothers jardinière, the swollen form with everted pie-crust rim, on short ridged foot, incised decoration of scrolling plants and foliage, 1888, 50cm. high.
(Christie's) $4,695

An amusing Martin Brothers stoneware bird, having a removable head with bushy brows and a broad brown beak, 33cm. high, signed on head and base *R.W. Martin & Bros. London & Southall*, dated 1892.
(Phillips) $5,057

## MEISSEN

Meissen porcelain bust of a child, Germany, late 19th century, enamel decorated with gilt trim, raised floral corsage, 6in. high.
(Skinner Inc.) $450

A Meissen group of two men in 18th century costume with tricorn hats, a globe and navigational instruments between them.
(Bearne's) $2,021

A Meissen group of a shepherdess and companion, she wearing a yellow cloak and flowered dress and he in striped jacket and turquoise breeches, circa 1770, 15cm. high.
(Christie's) $3,414

A Meissen Hausmalerei tapering hexagonal tea-caddy painted by Ignaz Bottengruber with a raven, a long-eared owl and a fabulous bird in black and brown, circa 1725, 9.5cm. high.
(Christie's) $3,201

A Meissen Purpurmalerei écuelle, a cover and a stand, painted with estuary and landscape scenes, buildings, figures and ships, circa 1740, the stand 23.5cm. diameter.
(Christie's) $9,816

A Meissen chinoiserie cylindrical tankard painted in the manner of J.G. Höroldt with figures around a table playing mandolins and drinking tea before a palm tree, circa 1730, Belgian imports marks for 1831–69, 18cm. high.
(Christie's) $21,340

A Meissen group of musicians, a gentleman holding a violin and offering a lady a beaker of wine, below a girl playing a guitar and a boy trying to embrace her, circa 1770, 36cm. high.
(Christie's) $8,963

A Continental porcelain pagoda figure in the Meissen style, in the form of a laughing seated Chinaman with nodding head, 28cm.
(Bearne's) $385

A late Meissen group of Harlequin and Columbine modeled by Paul Scheurich, on oval base, 27cm.
(Phillips) $2,805

## MEISSEN

Meissen porcelain cherub figure, Germany, late 19th century, seated on a brick oven-like stand, holding a pot in one hand, 5¾in. high.
(Skinner Inc.) $650

A pair of Meissen Imari tureens and covers, each freely painted in the typical palette enriched with gilding, with two exotic cockerels among flowering peony and chrysanthemum, circa 1735, 34cm. high.
(Christie's) $60,192

A finely painted Meissen needle case of cylindrical shape, painted with scattered flower sprays, mushrooms and walnuts, 10.5cm.
(Phillips) $2,805

A Meissen porcelain group of two semi-naked children, the girl with a bird and a cage, her companion with a large mask, 15cm. high.
(Bearne's) $768

An academic Meissen hen and chicks tureen and cover modeled as a seated hen with seven chicks around her, 20cm.
(Phillips) $4,675

A Meissen group of two maidens and Cupid, one standing wearing a flowered turquoise robe, the other seated on clouds, circa 1880, 8in. high.
(Christie's S. Ken) $2,521

A Meissen figure of Harlequin as a sailor standing against a tree trunk, holding a short oar over his shoulder, wearing a puce waistcoat, 18.5cm.
(Phillips) $2,191

A pair of Meissen kakiemon baluster oil and vinegar ewers and covers, with dragon and mask-head spouts and terminal, Dreher's marks Z, circa 1735, 16.5cm. and 15.5cm. high.
(Christie's) $5,548

A Meissen group of the rape of Proserpine modeled by J.J. Kändler, Proserpine scantily draped in a white dress with gilt flowers holding a nosegay, held aloft by Pluto draped in a blue cloak, circa 1755, 19cm. high.
(Christie's) $940

A Meissen porcelain covered cup and saucer finely painted with deer hunting scenes, late 18th/ early 19th century.
(Bearne's) $770

Meissen porcelain group of children working a wine press, Germany, late 19th century, crossed swords mark, 13in. high.
(Skinner Inc.) $2,500

A Meissen Hausmalerei goldchinesen two-handled beaker and a saucer, gilt at Augsburg in the Seuter workshop with figures at various pursuits, circa 1725.
(Christie's) $1,707

A Meissen group of the hand kiss modeled by J.J. Kändler, the gallant wearing a gilt flower and black foliage gray waistcoat over black breeches and yellow shoes with red rosettes, circa 1740, 18cm. high.
(Christie's) $7,148

A Meissen baluster pot-pourri vase and a pierced cover, the green branch handles with applied trailing fruit and flower terminals, the side of the vase with Cupid, blue crossed swords mark, circa 1870, 59.5cm. overall.
(Christie's) $7,775

A Meissen group of Europa and the bull draped in pink and white, on an oval mound base molded with gilt scrolls, blue crossed swords mark, circa 1880, 24cm. high.
(Christie's) $1,023

A Meissen porcelain group in the form of Jupiter on the back of an eagle in flight, 26.5cm.
(Bearne's) $770

A pair of Meissen may-blossom campana-shaped vases, each applied with a woodpecker and a bullfinch perched on trailing flowering branches, circa 1880, 35cm. high.
(Christie's) $4,501

Meissen porcelain figure of a lady, Germany, late 19th century, enamel decorated and modeled standing wearing winter clothing, 8in. high.
(Skinner Inc.) $1,300

## MEISSEN

A Meissen cream pot and domed cover, of circular form with scroll molded spout and handle on three claw feet, 11cm.
(Phillips) $2,057

An attractive Meissen dessert tureen, pierced cover, stand and sifter spoon, of oval shape, painted in colors with panels of various animals, 17cm.
(Phillips) $4,382

A Meissen écuelle and cover of circular shape with double loop handles and flower finial, painted with vignettes of hunting scenes, 19cm. overall diameter.
(Phillips) $1,892

A Meissen kakiemon baluster sugar-castor and pierced artichoke cover painted with a winged kylin, a bird in flight and indianische Blumen, circa 1735, 16cm. high.
(Christie's) $6,829

A pair of Meissen models of quail by J.J. Kändler, on circular mound bases applied with corn and water weeds, circa 1745, 14cm. high.
(Christie's) $12,804

A Meissen baluster coffee-pot and domed cover molded with gadroons enriched alternately with gilding and Böttgerluster, painted in colors with figures chopping wood, circa 1735, 22cm. high.
(Christie's) $16,005

A Meissen group of Harlequin and Columbine after the model by J.J. Kändler, Harlequin wearing a mask and a tunic half checkered and half with playing cards, circa 1740, 15.5cm. high.
(Christie's) $11,737

Two Meissen porcelain scent bottles and stoppers, each in the form of a begging dog, each enhanced in gold, 7.2cm.
(Bearne's) $768

A Meissen equestrian group emblematic of Europe from the series of the Continents modeled by J.J. Kändler, the female figure, sitting on a rearing white horse, wearing a gilt crown, circa 1745, 19cm. high.
(Christie's) $3,841

## MEISSEN

A Meissen chinoiserie teapot and cover of depressed pear shape with curved spout, painted in the manner of Höroldt with Orientals among furniture, shrubs and vases of flowers, circa 1725, 10.5cm. high.
(Christie's) $10,670

A Meissen cabinet cup and saucer, the cup painted with a view of the city of Dresden, crossed swords marks.
(Phillips) $1,309

A Meissen Fläschenhalter from the Swan service modeled by J.J. Kändler and J.F. Eberlein for Count Brühl, of compressed oval shape with a gilt undulating rim, 1737–41, 24cm. wide.
(Christie's) $25,608

A Meissen blue-ground campana-shaped vase painted with a lover and companion in a wooded landscape, blue crossed swords marks, circa 1880, 48cm. high.
(Christie's) $7,161

A pair of Meissen cylindrical tobacco-jars and covers painted with soldiers in encampments and with landscape scenes within quatrefoil panels linked by gilt trellis, circa 1740, later French gilt-metal mounts. 14.5cm. high.
(Christie's) $14,938

A Meissen powdered-purple-ground cream-pot, cover and stand of squat baluster form, painted in the manner of J.G. Höroldt with harbor scenes, circa 1730, the stand 17.5cm. diameter.
(Christie's) $23,474

A Meissen group of a nurse and two children modeled by J.F. Eberlein, the nurse seated on a rococo-scroll chair, wearing a puce bodice and yellow skirt with indianische Blumen, circa 1755, 16.5cm. high.
(Christie's) $4,268

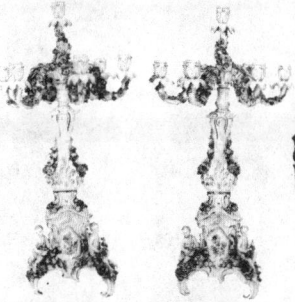

A pair of late Meissen tall six branch candelabra on triangular bases painted and encrusted with flowers in colors and with three seated figures of putti holding garlands, overall height 64cm.
(Phillips) $6,732

An extremely large late Meissen group of Count Bruhl's tailor riding on a goat, the tailor dressed as a courtier, 43cm. high, incised numeral.
(Phillips) $6,545

## MINTON

A fine pair of Minton porcelain pedestal jars and covers in the Sèvres manner, 41cm., circa 1860.
(Bearne's) $6,086

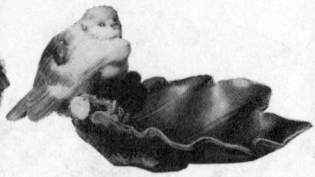

A Minton majolica ware oak leaf dish, in bright green resting on a brown branch with acorns and a blue tit perched on the end, 20cm., date code for 1867.
(Phillips) $717

A pair of Minton style porcelain candlesticks brightly painted with flowers on a gold decorated green and white foliate ground, 24.4cm., late 19th century.
(Bearne's) $2,730

A Minton slipware jardinière, the inscription commemorating the 1911 Coronation, 16cm.
(Phillips) $368

Two Minton parian groups of putti riding on sea horses, with wings and curling fish tails, 34cm., impressed date symbols possibly for 1851 or 1855.
(Phillips) $1,295

A Minton style majolica jardinière, decorated with basket weave molding and colorful bands of flower heads, 37cm.
(Bearne's) $644

A Mintons porcelain rectangular plaque painted with a young woman sitting in an arbor, 35.5cm. x 21cm.
(Bearne's) $809

A pair of Minton candle-snuffers modeled as ladies wearing brightly colored and gilt eighteenth century dress, circa 1830, 9.5cm. high.
(Christie's) $1,758

A Minton majolica lavender-ground garden seat, molded in relief with stylized honeysuckle alternating with passion-flowers, date code for 1869, 18½in. high.
(Christie's S. Ken) $1,786

## MINTON

A Minton biscuit figure of Hannah Moore seated in an armchair on scrolling base, 17cm.
(Phillips) $409

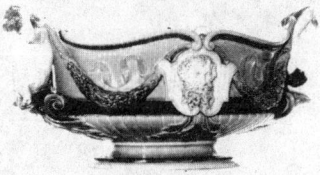

A Minton majolica oval jardinière, the two handles modeled as a scantily clad cherub kneeling on a scroll, 1868, 18in. wide.
(Christie's S. Ken) $1,873

A Minton blue-ground vase and cover in the Art Nouveau style, the body and stem painted with swags of pink roses, date code for 1919, 10½in. high.
(Christie's S. Ken) $745

A Minton style majolica jardinière and stand, the rims molded with petal-like designs, painted in typical green, brown and cream enamels, total height 25cm.
(Bearne's) $578

A pair of Minton majolica cornucopia vases, circa 1872, modeled as putti astride cornucopiae issuing from dolphins, 27in. high.
(Christie's East) $5,280

A Mintons majolica jardinière, the blue ground molded in relief with vertical flat ribs, terminating in paw feet, circa 1870's, 10¾in. high.
(Christie's S. Ken) $639

A pair of finely painted Minton vases and covers, the pointed ovoid bodies painted within oval panels with shipping scenes, 38cm.
(Phillips) $2,431

A Minton majolica garden-seat in the form of a seated monkey eating fruit and wearing a lugubrious expression, date code for 1867, 19½in. high.
(Christie's S. Ken) $1,809

A pair of Minton candleholders modeled as a youth and companion wearing broad-brimmed hats and striped and flowered dress, circa 1835–36, 9in. high.
(Christie's S. Ken) $1,786

## MOORCROFT

A Moorcroft pottery 'Claremont' pattern jardinière decorated with mushrooms and colored in streaked red, blue and yellow glaze against a green ground, 12.5cm. high.
(Phillips) $995

A large Moorcroft Pomegranate pattern vase, white piped decoration of fruit and berries, covered in a puce, green, red and blue glaze, 31.6cm. high.
(Christie's) $3,628

A Moorcroft pottery bowl in the 'Pomegranate' pattern, centered with a band of large red fruit with leaves and purple berries, 21cm. diameter.
(Phillips) $439

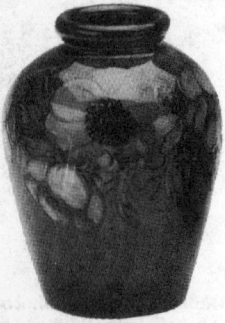

A Moorcroft pottery vase, the ovoid body painted with the anemone pattern on a red ground, 16.5cm.
(Bearne's) $485

A Moorcroft pottery fruit bowl of circular form, painted with fish, seaweed and sea anemones in shades of red, blue, yellow and green, 24.5cm. diameter.
(Spencer's) $835

Moorcroft potpourri and cover, England, circa 1905, pomegranate and pansy design in green, blue, red, yellow and blue, 5in. high.
(Skinner Inc.) $1,000

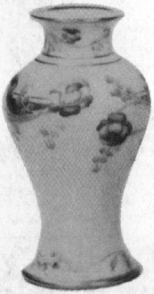

A pair of Moorcroft vases, designed for James Macintyre & Co., circa 1904–1913, the white ground decorated with a rose garland design, 20cm. high.
(Christie's) $3,186

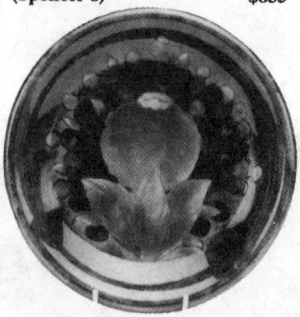

A Moorcroft plate, the cavetto decorated with the pomegranate and grape pattern, 22.3cm.
(Bearne's) $263

A Moorcroft 'Florian Ware' vase, designed for Liberty & Co., circa 1903–1913, the olive green ground decorated with a dark green and blue poppy design, stamped mark *Made for Liberty & Co.*, 31cm. high.
(Christie's) $4,181

## MOORCROFT

A Moorcroft twin-handled vase decorated with the 'Pomegranate' pattern against a dark blue ground, 13cm.
(Phillips) $478

A Moorcroft pottery bowl with broad everted rim on footed base, decorated to the inside with a band of red, mauve and purple pansies, 23cm. diameter.
(Phillips) $293

Moorcroft pottery box and cover, England, circa 1945, cylindrical form, berry and leaves in deep tones of red, yellow, green and blue, 3¾in. high.
(Skinner Inc.) $400

A Moorcroft 'Florian Ware' two-handled vase designed for James Macintyre & Co., 1898–circa 1905, with two small lug handles at the neck, the white ground decorated in green and blue with the poppy design, 25.2cm. high.
(Christie's) $1,891

A three-piece Moorcroft 'Florian Ware' tea-service, designed for James Macintyre & Co., decorated in a white slip and dark blue floral design, with silver mounts, 12.5cm. high.
(Christie's) $2,389

A Moorcroft 'Florian Ware' vase, made for Liberty & Co., the blue-green ground decorated in slip and various shades of green with poppies, 25.5cm. high.
(Christie's) $3,584

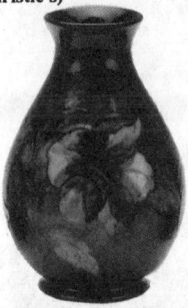

A Moorcroft pottery vase of ovoid form painted with the hibiscus design on a deep red ground, 21.4cm.
(Bearne's) $526

A Moorcroft pottery globular vase decorated with the 'Big poppy' design on a thin blue wash ground, 16.3cm.
(Bearne's) $866

Moorcroft pomegranate and pansy footed vase, England, circa 1915, design in red, yellow, green and blue, 8¼in. high.
(Skinner Inc.) $900

## NANTGARW

A Nantgarw plate painted by Thomas Pardoe, the center with two pheasants perched on a tree in a landscape vignette, circa 1820, 22cm. diameter.
(Christie's) $2,895

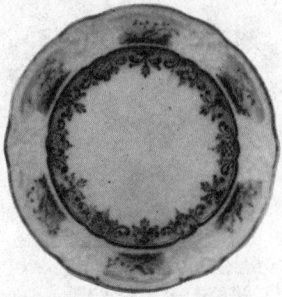

A Nantgarw plate painted by Thomas Pardoe, the border with exotic birds perched on trees in landscape vignettes within molded foliage-scroll cartouches, circa 1820, 21.5cm. diameter. (Christie's) $931

A Nantgarw (London-decorated) ornithological soup-plate, the center painted with Black Grouse, named on the reverse, circa 1820, 24cm. diameter.
(Christie's) $3,346

## NYMPHENBURG

A well-painted Nymphenburg topographical cup, and a saucer, the cup with a view of Marsbach.
(Phillips) $785

A Nymphenburg shaped circular dish from the Hof service painted with a large spray of roses, chrysanthemum and tulips, further flowers and a butterfly, circa 1762, 23.5cm. diameter.
(Christie's) $5,335

A Nymphenburg figure of a parrot modeled by Dominicus Auliczek, its plumage painted naturalistically in green, yellow, iron-red and blue, circa 1765, 15.5cm. high.
(Christie's) $7,682

## PEARLWARE

A pearlware toby jug and cover, probably Yorkshire, the seated man with a pipe by his side and a foaming jug of ale on his knee, 26.5cm.
(Bearne's) $1,294

A pearlware figure of a hound seated erect with a dead bird at its feet, on a shaped base, Staffordshire or Yorkshire, circa 1785, 10.5cm. wide.
(Christie's) $951

A pearlware group depicting the marriage of John Macdonald, he and his companion flanking an anvil with a priest attending, circa 1810, 8½in. high.
(Christie's S. Ken) $1,065

## PEARLWARE

A pearlware toby-jug holding a frothing jug of ale, in blue, yellow and manganese jacket, circa 1790, 10in. high.
(Christie's S. Ken) $2,131

A Lakin & Poole pearlware group of the assassination of Marat, Charlotte Cordé standing holding a metal knife in her right hand, her bonnet embellished with a green bow, impressed mark, circa 1794, 35cm. high.
(Christie's) $4,117

A Hall pearlware group of a ewe and lamb, their coats splashed in iron-red, the ewe standing before a flowering bocage, circa 1820, 15.5cm. high.
(Christie's) $786

A 19th century pearlware slops jar and cover, of baluster form with grotesque animal mask handles, 11in. high.
(Spencer's) $1,705

A Staffordshire pearlware figure of Ceres of Pratt type, holding a sickle and sheaf of corn, circa 1800, 21.5cm. high.
(Christie's) $620

A John Meir blue and white pearlware plate, the center printed with a portrait of Queen Caroline wearing a coat and feathered hat, 21.5cm.
(Bearne's) $728

A Staffordshire pearlware figure of the Prophet Jeremiah, his robe painted in iron-red with flower-sprays and wearing a pale-lilac-lined mottled blue cloak, circa 1820, 28cm. high.
(Christie's) $2,275

A Staffordshire pearlware shaped rectangular plaque, molded in relief with a bust portrait of Queen Victoria, circa 1845, 8¾in. high.
(Christie's S. Ken) $362

A pearlware figure of Amphitrite and the dolphin, in red robes on a green base, perhaps Scottish circa 1800, 6in. high.
(Christie's S. Ken) $277

## POOLE POTTERY

A pottery wall decoration modeled as a yacht in full sail, glazed in yellow on gray base, impressed *Poole England* mark, 4in. high.
(Christie's S. Ken) $73

A pottery vase, shape No. 334, decorated with a leaping stag amongst flowers and foliage, impressed *Poole England* mark, 5in. high.
(Christie's S. Ken) $308

'Buster Boy', a pottery figure by Phoebe Stabler of a putto seated on a rock with floral garland draped around his body, incised *Stabler Hammersmith London 1916*, 7in. high.
(Christie's S. Ken) $369

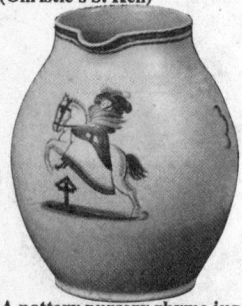

A pottery nursery rhyme jug, designed by Dora Batty and painted by Ruth Pavely, depicting a scene from 'Ride a Cock Horse to Banbury Cross', impressed *Poole England* mark, 7½in. high.
(Christie's S. Ken) $164

A collection of Poole pottery tiles painted in colors with fishing and pastoral scenes, comprising sixteen pictorial tiles, 5in. square.
(Christie's S. Ken) $727

A pottery twin-handled vase, decorated by Eileen Prangnell with a leaping stag amongst foliage, impressed *Poole England*, painted insignia and *TZ*, 5in. high.
(Christie's S. Ken) $349

'The Bathrobe', a pottery figure modeled by Phoebe Stabler of a standing young girl with a large bathrobe wrapped round her, impressed *CSA* mark, 7in. high.
(Christie's S. Ken) $226

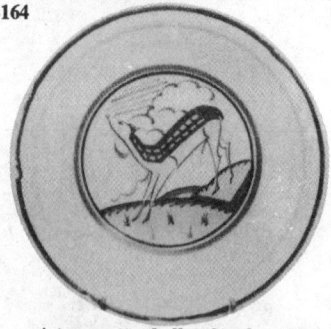

A terracotta shallow bowl, decorated by Anne Hatchard painted with a deer in an open landscape, impressed *CSA* mark, painted insignia and *RG*, 9½in. diameter.
(Christie's S. Ken) $451

A terracotta vase, painted with flowers and foliage in shades of green, yellow, blue and black on a white ground, 5½in. high.
(Christie's S. Ken) $196

## POOLE POTTERY

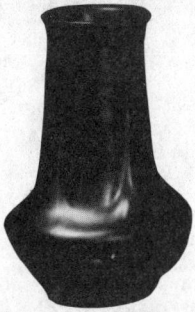

A Carter red luster flambé vase, with compressed base and lobed cylindrical neck, incised *Carter Poole 1905*, 11in. high.
(Christie's S. Ken) $205

A terracotta sculpture of a fully rigged galleon modeled by Harry Stabler, glazed in shades of blue, green, yellow and white, 20½in. high.
(Christie's S. Ken) $1,436

A Free Form Ware vase, shape No. 691, designed by A.B.Read, decorated with vertical lines of stylized foliage, printed *Poole Dolphin* mark, 11½in. high.
(Christie's S. Ken) $451

A pottery vase, shape No. 466, painted by Rene Hayes with a band of geometric pattern in typical colors on a white ground, impressed *CSA Ltd* mark and painted insignia, 5½in. high.
(Christie's S. Ken) $175

A pair of pottery bookends each modeled in full relief as leaping gazelles, impressed *Poole* and incised *831*, 8in. high.
(Christie's S. Ken) $821

A pottery candelabra, molded with fruit and foliage and covered in a light blue glaze, impressed *Poole England* mark, 8½in. high.
(Christie's S. Ken) $123

A pottery vase, decorated with scrolling flowers and foliage, in typical colors on a white ground, impressed *CSA Ltd.* mark, 7in. high.
(Christie's S. Ken) $226

A pair of pottery doves designed by John Adams and modeled by Harry Brown, impressed *Poole England*, 8¼in. high.
(Christie's S. Ken) $512

A terracotta two-handled oviform vase shape No. 973, painted with flowers and foliage below geometric border, impressed *CSA Ltd.* mark, 7in. high.
(Christie's S. Ken) $821

## PRATTWARE

A Prattware relief-molded jug decorated in colors, depicting Admiral Duncan in profile flanked by two ships, 17cm.
(Phillips) $735

A Pratt pottery sauce boat molded in the form of a dolphin, painted in green, brown and ocher enamels, 15.5cm. long.
(Bearne's) $607

A Prattware watch holder of a longcase clock decorated in Pratt colors and molded in relief with various Classical figures, 27cm.
(Phillips) $1,403

A Prattware group of Saint George slaying a dragon, flanked by two female figures in ocher dress, 25cm.
(Phillips) $1,085

A Prattware model of a young woman wearing a deep-ocher bodice and green skirt, circa 1790, 8in. high.
(Christie's S. Ken) $746

A Prattware George IV commemorative plate with a profile head of the King wearing a laurel wreath and naval uniform, 22cm.
(Phillips) $711

## ROCKINGHAM

One of a pair of Rockingham plates, the centers printed in pale-green with a bird in flight with a twig in its beak and painted with scattered loose bouquets, circa 1835, 25.5cm. diameter.
(Christie's) (Two) $662

A Rockingham porcelain neo rococo style teapot and sucrier and covers, painted in colors probably by John Randall with exotic birds.
(Spencer's) $1,675

One of a pair of early Rockingham primrose leaf molded plates, painted with flowers in vases on marble tables, probably by Edwin Steele, 24.5cm.
(Phillips) $1,892

## ROOKWOOD

Rookwood Pottery Vellum vase, Cincinnati, Ohio, 1907, executed by Elizabeth Neave Lingenfelter Lincoln (1892-1931), 8in. high. (Skinner Inc.) $225

Rookwood Pottery vase, Cincinnati, Ohio, 1887, executed by Kataro Shirayamadani in his first year with the pottery, 12in. long. (Skinner Inc.) $1,500

Rookwood Pottery vase, Cincinnati, Ohio, circa 1883, with silver glaze neck, three impressed gold bands over body, 10½in. high. (Skinner Inc.) $2,000

Rookwood decorated vellum vase, Cincinnati, Ohio, 1910, executed by Edward Diers (1896–1931), 8¾in. high. (Skinner Inc.) $425

Rookwood Pottery scenic vellum plaque, Cincinnati, Ohio, 1914, executed by Edward George Diers, (1896–1931), 10¾in. high. (Skinner Inc.) $1,600

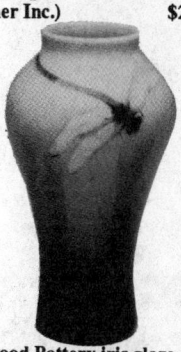

Rookwood Pottery iris glaze vase, Cincinnati, Ohio, 1906, executed by Charles Schmidt (1896–1927), 9⅝in. high. (Skinner Inc.) $4,400

Rookwood Pottery wax resist vase, Cincinnati, Ohio, 1928, executed by Elizabeth Neave Lingenfelter Lincoln (1892–1931), 11in. high. (Skinner Inc.) $300

Two rookwood Pottery tiger eye vases, Kataro Shirayamadani, Cincinnati, Ohio, (1887–1915 and 1925–1948), 14½in. high. (Skinner Inc.) $3,000

Rookwood Pottery porcelain vase, Cincinnati, Ohio, 1925, executed by Kataro Shirayamadani (1865–1948), 8in. high. (Skinner Inc.) $1,200

## ROYAL DUX

A Royal Dux group in the form of Pierrot kissing the hand of a young woman wearing a flowing ball gown, after a design by Schaff, 28.5cm.
(Bearne's) $1,002

A pair of Royal Dux bisque porcelain figures of a rustic boy and girl, the young boy wearing a green hat, the girl wearing a décolleté pink blouse, 17in. high.
(Spencer's) $888

A Royal Dux porcelain figural posy holder, in the form of a young girl in Kate Greenaway type dress, 25cm. high.
(Spencer's) $687

A Royal Dux bisque porcelain figure group of a traveler on a camel, the traveler wearing flowing robes, an attendant at the camel's feet, 17in. high.
(Spencer's) $1,162

A Royal Dux bisque porcelain figure of a bathing belle, seated wearing a green head scarf, and brown bathing costume, 16in. high.
(Spencer's) $1,453

A Royal Dux bisque porcelain Art Nouveau style flower holder, as a maiden draped in a brown robe seated upon a rocky outcrop, 27cm. high.
(Spencer's) $856

A pair of Royal Dux figures, one of a goat-herd wearing a bear skin over his tunic, his companion feeding a lamb from flowers, 52cm.
(Bearne's) $1,733

A Royal Dux bisque porcelain figure group, of a young boy wearing a hat, open shirt and rolled-up trousers leading a pair of harnessed oxen, 15in. long.
(Spencer's) $880

A pair of Royal Dux bisque porcelain figures of harvesters after F. Otto, the young boy wearing a sou'wester, the young girl wearing a white blouse and purple bodice, 21in. high.
(Spencer's) $1,110

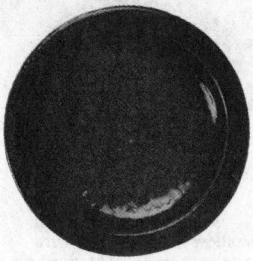

A Ruskin high-fired stoneware dish, covered in a rich mottled purple and green over deep red, circa 1920, 24.3cm. diameter. (Christie's) $1,387

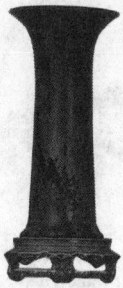

A Ruskin high-fired stoneware vase, the even purple-red glaze irregularly flecked in green, incised *W Howson Taylor, 1932*, 34.2cm. high. (Christie's) $3,841

A Ruskin high-fired stoneware bowl, the exterior glazed in deep red clouding over gray, the interior red speckled with purple and green, 1933, 24.5cm. diameter. (Christie's) $1,707

A Ruskin high-fired stoneware vase, the oatmeal ground clouded with green and speckled with irregular areas of purple and blue, 1915, 21.cm. high. (Christie's) $2,134

A Ruskin high-fired stoneware bowl, the oatmeal ground mottled overall in dove-gray overlaid with red and purple clouding, with green speckling, 31cm. diameter. (Christie's) $3,84

A Ruskin high-fired stoneware vase, pale ground mottled overall in purples and greens fragmented with random 'snake-skin' patterning, 1914, 32.3cm. high. (Christie's) $3,201

A Ruskin high-fired stoneware vase, the liver-red glaze clouding in areas over a mottled dove-gray ground, impressed *Ruskin, England, 1926*, 37.5cm. high. (Christie's) $2,561

A Ruskin high-fired egg-shell stoneware bowl, with dark mottled red glaze clouding to green and purple towards tne foot, 21cm. diameter. (Christie's) $2,134

A Ruskin high-fired stoneware vase, the mottled gray ground overlaid with a cloudy red, purple and grey, breaking into grey speckling, 1926, 31.5cm. high. Christie's) $2,561

## SATSUMA

A Satsuma beaker, the exterior with a continuous decoration of three levels from the heavenly to the terrestial, with Kannon, birds, students and bijin, signed *Inkinzan zo*, late 19th century, 8.6cm. high.
(Christie's) $2,600

A Satsuma teapot and cover, the upper surface with two rectangular panels depicting children playing by a lakeside, and a marriage procession crossing a river, signed *Kizan*, late 19th century, 7.1cm. high.
(Christie's) $1,734

A shallow Satsuma dish with foliate rim decorated in various colored enamels and gilt the well depicting a cockerel and hen, signed *Kizan*, late 19th century, 15.9cm. diameter.
(Christie's) $1,517

A Satsuma model of Kannon, the standing goddess wearing an elaborate headdress and holding a lotus leaf, her robes embroidered with the swastika, signed *Stasuma yaki Nangakurei ga*, late 19th century, 37.2cm. high.
(Christie's) $5,418

Two Satsuma eggcups decorated in various colored enamels and gilt with scenes of threshing, harvesting and other activities, signed *Kinkozan zo*, Meiji Period (1868–1912), 6.5cm. high.
(Christie's) $3,034

A Satsuma vase of tapering square form, the sides with boldly painted irises before clouds, the shoulder and neck richly decorated with key-pattern, signed *Nanbe Seizo*, late 19th century, 30.8cm. high.
(Christie's) $2,167

A large Satsuma vase decorated in various colored enamels and gilt with a profusion of chrysanthemums and other flowers and foliage, late 19th century, 46cm. high.
(Christie's) $11,919

A Satsuma shallow dish, the interior depicting figures among household ornaments holding various objects, signed *Renmiken zo*, late 19th century, 23.6cm. diameter.
(Christie's) $1,300

A Satsuma figure of Kannon, the seated divinity wearing an elaborate necklace and robes decorated with swirling cloud, mon and lozenge design, signed *Yasukyo saku*, late 19th century, 61.5cm. high.
(Christie's) $8,668

A Satsuma koro and cover decorated in various colored enamels and gilt, the body with two rectangular panels depicting a daimyo's procession and a misty wooded landscape, signed *Kinkozan zo*, late 19th century, 6.4cm. diameter.
(Christie's) $1,084

A pair of Satsuma oviform vases decorated in various colored enamels and gilt with a profusion of mixed flowers issuing from brushwood and wooden fences, signed *Satsuma yaki cho Shuzan sei*, Meiji Period (1868–1912), 18.3cm. high.
(Christie's) $2,600

A Satsuma rectangular box and cover decorated in various colored enamels with a shaped panel depicting ladies and children in a lakeside landscape in Spring, signed *Ryozan*, late 19th century, 14cm. long.
(Christie's) $7,585

A Satsuma koro and cover in the shape of a basket tied in a large bag decorated in various colored enamels and gilt, signed *Kinkozan*, late 19th century, 9.9cm. high.
(Christie's) $5,634

A Satsuma shallow dish decorated with a scene of courtiers marvelling at the beauty of a lady's kimono within a circle of stylized fungus pattern, signed *Kinkozan zo*, Meiji period (1868–1912), 30.6cm. diameter.
(Christie's) $4,117

A fine and large Satsuma oviform jar and cover with three shaped panels depicting flowering shoots of peony and chrysanthemum, signed *Nihon Satsuma, Kinran Toki, Tokozan zo*, late 19th century, 52.5cm. high.
(Christie's) $69,344

A Satsuma miniature teapot decorated in various colored enamels and gilt with a continuous decoration of bijin and children walking in an extensive hilly landscape, signed *Seikozan*, late 19th century, 6.2cm. long.
(Christie's) $1,517

A pair of Satsuma vases decorated in various colored enamels and gilt, the tapering cylindrical bodies with a continuous decoration of bijin and children strolling in an extensive landscape, signed *Seikozan zo*, late 19th century, 11.8cm. high.
(Christie's) $3,467

A Satsuma tripod koro, the body with three irregularly shaped panels depicting civic and military scenes on a ground of massed chrysanthemum heads and other flowers, signed *Hotado*, late 19th century, approx. 7.8cm. high.
(Christie's) $4,334

## SEVRES

A pair of Sèvres-pattern cylindrical jars and covers painted with narrow blue and gilt vertical stripes entwined with pink ribbon and gilt foliage divided by loose bouquets of flowers, late 19th century, 13.5cm. high.
(Christie's) $777

A Sèvres pink oeil-de-perdrix ground coffee-can and saucer painted with musical instruments and trophies in reserves, date letter R for 1770.
(Christie's) $2,988

A pair of Sèvres-pattern gilt-metal mounted blue-ground oviform vases and covers with cast rope-twist, scroll and mask handles, painted by L. Bertion, circa 1900, 51.5cm. high.
(Christie's) $3,069

A Sèvres Empire cabinet-cup and saucer painted with a portrait medallion of Darnalt on a silver ground with foliage swags, circa 1820.
(Christie's) $1,881

Massive Sèvres porcelain urn, late 19th century, painted with a scene of the marriage of Napoleon, 61in. high.
(Skinner Inc.) $15,000

A Sèvres style cabinet cup, cover and stand painted with a courting couple and river landscapes, total height 14.5cm.
(Bearne's) $693

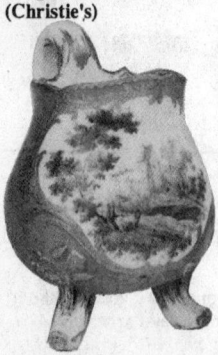

A Sevres green-ground milk-jug (pot à lait à trois pieds), the gilt branch handle and three feet with gilt flower and foliage terminals, circa 1758, 8cm. high.
(Christie's) $1,387

A pair of Sèvres-pattern turquoise-ground ormolu-mounted jardinieres painted with a gallant and two female companions in wooded landscapes, circa 1880, 30cm. high overall.
(Christie's) $3,274

A large Sèvres porcelain vase, designed by Emile Decoeur, decorated by P. Gaucher, with a narrative frieze of mermaids, nereids and sea creatures in tones of blue and green, 50cm. high.
(Christie's) $10,950

A Sèvres bleu celeste two-handled seau à crenelé painted with birds in wooded landscapes within oval gilt line reserves, date letter V for 1774, 30cm. wide.
(Christie's) $4,695

Sèvres bisque allegorical bust of La Republique Francaise, after Jean-Antoine Injalbert, circa 1891, 21in. high.
(Skinner Inc.) $700

A Sèvres oval tureen and cover with blue and gilt feuilles-de-choux decoration and sprays of flowers, the entwined handles and rims enriched with gilding, circa 1760, 15.5cm. wide.
(Christie's) $1,067

A pair of Sèvres-pattern blue-ground ormolu-mounted vases and covers, the egg-shaped bodies enriched in gilding with a caillouté pattern, mid-19th century, 7¾in. high.
(Christie's S. Ken) $1,050

One of a pair of Sèvres-pattern dark-blue-ground slender oviform vases and covers with two gilt entwined double-serpent handles, mid-19th century, 15½in. high.
(Christie's S. Ken)
(Two) $1,680

A pair of Sèvres green-ground pots à fard painted with figures by buildings, strolling and fishing in wooded river landscapes within gilt scroll, date letter E for 1757, 9cm. high.
(Christie's) $18,139

A Sèvres green and blue-ground square tray (plateau carré) with flared sides, the center painted with a bouquet within a circular gilt cartouche, date letter F for 1758, 11cm. wide.
(Christie's) $3,414

A Sèvres coffee-can and saucer painted in blue camaieu with pink flesh tints with a boy playing with a bird and a girl playing the pipes in landscape vignettes, 1766.
(Christie's) $1,208

A Sèvres bleu lapis orange-tub with gilt vermiculé decoration, painted with bouquets of garden flowers within reserves, date letter H for 1760, painter's mark for Thévenet, 9cm. high.
(Christie's) $1,129

## SEVRES

A Sèvres saucer painted by Falot and gilded by Prevost, the center painted with doves, date mark for 1781.
(Bearne's) $424

A Sèvres white porcelain group of Diana the huntress and two other figures on a rocky outcrop, 33cm. total height.
(Bearne's) $895

A fine Sèvres plate, the bleu lapis ground border with gilt bell-flower motifs, barbs and leaves, 23.5cm., painter's mark W. probably for Joseph-Leopold Weydinger.
(Phillips) $1,870

A pair of Sèvres style turquoise ground vases with pointed oviform bodies painted with figures of a lady and gentleman in 18th century costume, 29.5cm.
(Phillips) $935

A 19th century French giltwood occasional table set with a 'Sèvres' porcelain dish, the central oval panel painted with two lovers and a goat resting in a landscape signed *Boucher*, 1ft. 5in. wide.
(Spencer's) $704

An important pair of Sèvres Royal portrait vases of 'vase etrusque carafe' shape with double leaf scroll handles, 33cm.
(Phillips) $5,610

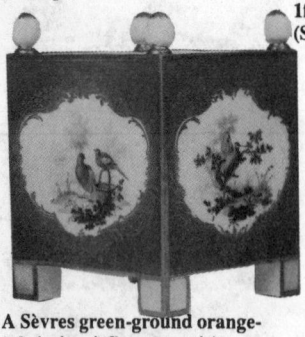

A Sèvres green-ground orange-tub (caisse à fleurs carrée) painted with birds among trees, shrubs and plants within shaped gilt quatrefoil scroll, date letter D for 1756, 14.5cm. high.
(Christie's) $17,072

Sèvres porcelain covered urn, late 19th century, retailed by Bailey, Banks and Biddle, signed *"G. Poiterin"*, 22in. high.
(Skinner Inc.) $1,600

A Sèvres green-trellis-ground small sugar-bowl and cover (pot à sucre calabre) the gilt-edged green trellis ribbons joined by flowerheads, circa 1765, 6.5cm. diameter.
(Christie's) $2,774

## SPODE

A Spode ironstone celadon-ground two-handled flared cylindrical bowl and cover painted in the famille rose palette, 8in. high, circa 1815.
(Christie's S. Ken) $600

A Spode dog trough, printed in blue with the 'Queen Charlotte' pattern showing a chinoiserie landscape with two figures, 18cm.
(Phillips) $561

An unusual ice pail, attributed to Spode, with two upright loop handles, printed in blue with the 'Greek' pattern, 23.5cm.
(Phillips) $785

A Spode blue-ground two-handled oviform vase, painted with loose bouquets of luxuriant flowers and scattered flower-sprays on a dark-blue ground, circa 1820, 15.5cm. high.
(Christie's) $2,059

A Spode Felspar porcelain part tea and coffee service, each piece painted in gold with sprays of barley and garlands of flowers, early 19th century.
(Bearne's) $1,038

A Spode blue-ground two-handled oviform vase with waisted neck and on a spreading circular foot, circa 1820, 15.5cm. high.
(Christie's) $867

A pair of Spode two-handled pot-pourri vases, pierced covers and stands painted with loose bouquets of luxuriant flowers on dark-blue grounds, circa 1820, the stands 11cm. diameter.
(Christie's) $3,722

A Spode flared spill-vase with white bead and gilt band borders, pattern no. 1166, 11cm. high.
(Christie's) $724

A pair of Spode pedestal sauce tureens and covers, each piece brightly decorated with the 'Peacock' pattern within a spearhead border, 15cm. high, early 19th century.
(Bearne's) $849

## STAFFORDSHIRE

A Staffordshire character jug of Stanley Baldwin, shown seated with pipe in hand, 16.5cm.
(Phillips) $695

A Staffordshire pottery octagonal plate printed in black with a bust portrait of Charles Stuart Parnell, 24cm.
(Phillips) $654

A Staffordshire figure of Sir Robert Peel mounted on horseback, in black top hat, yellow waistcoat and brown jacket, 27cm.
(Phillips) $1,430

A rare Staffordshire arbor group of two musicians, the lady and gentleman seated on green stools and the lady playing a mandoline, the man a pipe, 16.5cm.
(Phillips) $3.386

A Staffordshire pearlware cow creamer and stopper with a pink lustered border, a milkmaid seated to one side, 14cm.
(Phillips) $898

A Staffordshire oval relief molded plaque with a bust portrait of a woman within a molded frame, perhaps depicting Charlotte Corday, circa 1795, 10½in. high.
(Christie's S. Ken) $405

A Staffordshire saltglaze small mug of cylindrical form with loop handle, painted in colors with a trailing flower spray, 7cm.
(Phillips) $636

A Staffordshire pottery character jug formed as the head of Lord Kitchener, 18cm.
(Phillips) $225

A Staffordshire pottery Victorian coronation mug, printed in underglaze purple with the Swansea transfer of the young Queen and her dates, 9cm. high.
(Spencer's) $1,773

## STAFFORDSHIRE

A figure of a standing camel before a tree stump applied with foliage, painted in colors on a shaped oval base, 6½in. high.
(Christie's S. Ken) $1,491

Staffordshire pottery "Boxing" pitcher, England, circa 1825, titled below *Spring and Langan*, and with floral decorated rim and handle, 8½in. high.
(Skinner Inc.) $375

A colorful Staffordshire pottery group, the Prince of Wales and Princess Alexandra of Denmark, 26cm.
(Bearne's) $404

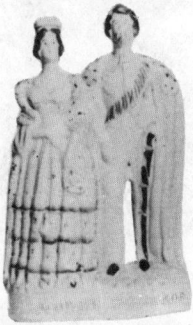

A group of the Queen and Emperor, painted in colors on a shaped oval base, named in raised capitals and enriched in gilding, 11½in. high.
(Christie's S. Ken) $469

A Staffordshire pottery savings bank, in the form of a two chimneyed building, with three arched windows, 6in. high.
(Spencer's) $800

An early Staffordshire pottery group of a shepherd sitting on a rocky outcrop, playing a flute, his companion standing at his side, 25cm.
(Bearne's) $687

A Staffordshire octagonal plate with a portrait of Fred Archer, detailing various horse races which he won, 24cm.
(Phillips) $449

A Staffordshire figure of Wellington, seated in a large high-backed chair, with colored face, 31cm.
(Phillips) $695

A 19th century Staffordshire pottery jug made to commemorate the Coronation of Queen Victoria, 17cm. high.
(Spencer's) $697

## STAFFORDSHIRE

A bull-baiting group modeled as a bull with black-sponged markings and with a hound snapping at its lower head, circa 1800, 5in. high.
(Christie's S. Ken) $639

A pair of Staffordshire pottery figures of a young man and woman, he with a monkey, she with a tambourine, 18cm.
(Bearne's) $192

A Staffordshire large blue printed meat dish, with a farmer's wife, surrounded by her children, offering food to a blind and lame traveler, 52cm.
(Phillips) $956

A large brown salt glazed stoneware spirit flask modeled as a standing figure of Sir Robert Peel, holding a scroll inscribed *'Bread for the Millions'*, 36cm.
(Phillips) $1,839

A pair of Staffordshire pottery groups each in the form of a cow by a stream with the farmer or the milkmaid, 21cm. high.
(Bearne's) $465

A Staffordshire figure of Gladstone shown standing, his hand resting on two books, well colored, 30cm.
(Phillips) $572

A figure of Eliza Cook in brown jacket and green and pink dress, named in gilt indented capitals, circa 1849, 10in. high.
(Christie's S. Ken) $298

A pair of Salt pottery bocage figures, one inscribed *Sportsman*, his lady companion entitled *Archer*, 17.3cm.
(Bearne's) $1,040

A Staffordshire pottery group in the form of a young Welshman and woman, supporting a bucket on a milestone inscribed *Langolen 1 Mile*, 27cm.
(Bearne's) $578

## STAFFORDSHIRE

Staffordshire creamware coffeepot and cover, England, circa 1780, black transfer decoration of "The Tea Party" to one side, 10in. high.
(Skinner Inc.) $225

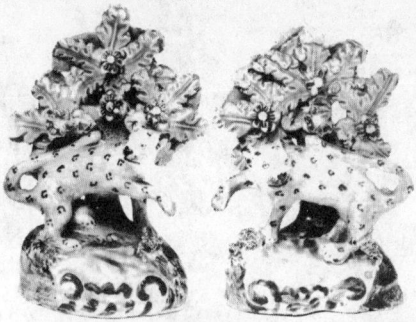

A pair of early Staffordshire models of pumas with brown spotted coats, their tails arched over their backs, 9.5cm.
(Phillips) $2,244

A Staffordshire figure of R. Cobden, shown seated and well colored, 18cm.
(Phillips) $367

A brightly colored Staffordshire porcelain figure of Nelson in dress uniform, 16.5cm.
(Bearne's) $172

A pair of models of grayhounds their fur with shaped black patches and with curled forelocks, one with a rabbit in its jaws, circa 1860, 10¼in. high.
(Christie's S. Ken) $1,598

A pastille-burner modeled as a gothic gazebo with pierced windows and doors, circa 1840, 11½in. high.
(Christie's S. Ken) $426

A Victorian Staffordshire group of Napoleon III and Albert shaking hands before crossed flags.
(Phillips) $233

An equestrian figure of Marshal Arnaud, 7½in. high, and an equestrian figure of the Sultan in similar colors, circa 1854.
(Christie's S. Ken) $639

A figure of a batsman at the wicket, probably Julius Caesar, painted in colors and enriched in gilding, circa 1865, 14¼in. high.
(Christie's S. Ken) $1,385

## VENICE

A Venice istoriato dish of shallow cardinal's hat form, painted with the story of Jacob and the Angel, workshop of Domenico da Venezia, circa 1560, 30cm. diameter. (Christie's) $10,670

A Venice (Vezzi) teapot and a cover with colored chinoiserie figures in panels at various pursuits including swinging on a rope, playing a horn and carrying a snail, incised Z mark circa 1725, 16.5cm. wide. (Christie's) $19,750

A Venice (Vezzi) blue and white teabowl painted in a gray-blue with two birds in flight among plants and flowering shrubs flanked by buildings between blue line rims, circa 1725, 7.3cm. diameter. (Christie's) $11,737

## VINCENNES

A Vincennes miniature campana vase, painted in colors with sprays of heartsease, gilt rims, 6cm., interlaced L's marks. (Phillips) $837

A Vincennes bleu celeste teacup and saucer (gobelet Hébert) with gilt entwined branch handle, painted with trailing flowers from cornucopia-shaped bleu celeste borders, date letter B for 1754. (Christie's) $5,122

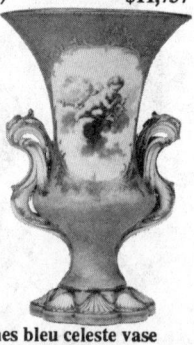

A Vincennes bleu celeste vase duplessis of flared trumpet shape, painted in puce camaieu with Cupid among clouds within gilt scroll and flower cartouches beneath a gilt dentil rim, date letter C for 1755, 19.5cm. high. (Christie's) $12,804

A Vincennes bleu celeste sugar-bowl and cover (pot à sucre du roy) painted with figures walking by buildings in wooded landscapes, date letter B for 1754, 8.5cm. diameter. (Christie's) $6,829

A Vincennes bleu lapis coffee-cup and saucer (gobelet à la reine) with loop handle, each side of the cup and the center of the saucer painted with two birds. (Christie's) $3,414

A Vincennes circular baluster sugar-bowl and cover painted with sprays of flowers including pink roses, date letter for 1754, 8cm. diameter. (Christie's) $836

## VIENNA

A Vienna style silver-mounted snuff box of canted rectangular form, painted in colors with a hunting scene, 8.5cm.
(Phillips) $972

A Vienna purple-ground coffee-can and saucer, the saucer painted with scantily clad maidens with fruit and flowers and the cup painted with a nymph being helped onto the back of a satyr.
(Christie's) $896

A Vienna cabaret painted in purple camaïeu with peasants at various pursuits in wooded landscape vignettes within lime-green borders, circa 1775, the tray 31.5cm. wide.
(Christie's) $2,134

A Vienna porcelain cabinet plate, of dished circular form, the central circular panel painted by F. Pauli with 'Theseus'.
(Spencer's) $355

A pair of Vienna vases and covers, painted with nymphs, satyrs and putti in landscapes, 21cm.
(Lawrence Fine Art) $5,272

A Vienna porcelain cabinet plate, the central circular panel painted by Wagner with 'Psyche Am Wasserspiegel', within a gilt and blue border.
(Spencer's) $1,182

A Vienna powdered-claret-ground baluster mug and stepped domed cover, with entwined branch handle and dahlia finial, circa 1780, 8cm. high.
(Christie's) $384

An attractively painted Vienna style plate with a portrait of Amalie von Shintling after the portrait by F. Stieler, signed indistinctly, 24cm.
(Phillips) $2,057

A Vienna dated gold-ground urn-shaped vase and cover with ormolu entwined serpent handles, the sides painted with Julius Caesar standing on a pedestal addressing five soldiers, date code for 1817, 81cm. high.
(Christie's) $28,215

## WEDGWOOD

Wedgwood caneware game pie dish, England, early 19th century, oval shape with insert dish and cover, 10½in. wide.
(Skinner Inc.) $475

'Zodiac Bull', a Wedgwood porcelain bull, designed by Arnold Machin, the cream-glazed body with brown-painted features, stars and signs of the Zodiac, circa 1945, 40.5cm. long.
(Christie's) $854

A Wedgwood caneware rectangular bough-pot on scroll feet, the shaped front applied with Classical figures at various pursuits in a landscape on a blue ground, circa 1790, 19.5cm. wide.
(Christie's) $1,137

A Wedgwood black basalt encaustic-decorated oviform vase and cover, the shoulder with upright loop handles, painted with Classical figures at various pursuits, circa 1820, 24cm. high.
(Christie's) $1,344

A pair of Wedgwood pearlware snake-handled vases, the oviform bodies painted by John Holloway with continuous seascapes depicting figures on a quay attempting to rescue a ship, circa 1876, 37.5cm. high.
(Christie's) $3,722

A Wedgwood Fairyland luster ovoid vase decorated in purple, green, black, yellow and gilt, with the 'Candlemas' pattern, 18.5cm.
(Phillips) $3,179

A Wedgwood baluster jug, painted on the front with the Arms of the Company in blue, the supporters bearing banners with red crosses, 21.5cm.
(Lawrence Fine Art) $2,169

A Wedgwood blue and white jasper 'ruined column' vase, the white fluted columns molded with lichen supported on a solid-blue rectangular base, circa 1795, 21cm. wide.
(Christie's) $10,340

A large Wedgwood blue jasperware dip two-handled campana-shaped pot-pourri jar, 41.5cm.
(Bearne's) $680

## WEDGWOOD

A blue and white pottery supper set, probably by Ralph Wedgwood, each piece printed with a Chinese landscape featuring an elephant with a howdah, 60cm. wide.
(Bearne's) $890

A Wedgwood rosso antico teapot and cover of boat shape with crabstock handle, spout and finial, 12cm.
(Phillips) $673

Wedgwood dark blue jasper Stilton cheese dish and cover, England, late 19th century, with continuous classical scene, 11⅝in. diameter.
(Skinner Inc.) $375

A Wedgwood Fairyland luster vase decorated with the 'Imps on a Bridge' pattern, with the brown boy and blue Rock bird, 23cm.
(Bearne's) $2,696

A pair of Wedgwood Fairyland luster square vases decorated with panels of the 'Dana' pattern, 19.5cm.
(Phillips) $5,049

A Wedgwood 'Argus Pheasant' luster vase, decorated in red and gold with two long tailed birds on a blue mottled ground, 23cm.
(Phillips) $2,431

A Wedgwood Fairyland luster punch bowl, the interior decorated with The Woodland Bridge pattern, 28.5cm. diameter.
(Bearne's) $3,437

Rare Wedgwood and Company Prattware "Faces" pitcher, England, circa 1795, central band with four molded faces showing various emotional expressions, 12¾in. high.
(Skinner Inc.) $950

A rare Wedgwood drabware coffee biggin, the olive body with a blue sprigged band of fruiting vines, 18.5cm.
(Phillips) $411

A Wedgwood creamware globular teapot and cover, $5^{3}/_{4}$in. high, circa 1770.
(Dreweatt Neate) $3,510

Wedgwood Queensware gilt and bronzed vase, England, late 19th century, molded floral and leafy decorations surrounded by fields of hand painted dot and floral designs, $5^{1}/_{2}$in. high.
(Skinner Inc.) $650

A Wedgwood creamware teapot and cover of globular form, printed in black, by Sadler, with 'La Bonne Aventure', 15cm.
(Phillips) $1,195

A Wedgwood Fairyland luster vase decorated with the 'Imps on a Bridge' pattern, this version with the brown boy and green Rock bird, 26.3cm.
(Bearne's) $4,246

A Wedgwood Fairyland luster footed bowl decorated inside with a 'Picnic by a River' around a central panel of a mermaid, 27.5cm.
(Phillips) $2,191

A Wedgwood Fairyland luster vase decorated with the Ghostly Wood pattern, 35cm.
(Bearne's) $17,187

A Wedgwood pottery mug, designed by Keith Murray, the rim inscribed *Edward VIII Coronation 1937*, height $4^{3}/_{4}$in.
(Bonhams) $336

An encaustic basalt vase, probably Wedgwood, of baluster shape, decorated with rosso antico anthemion and key fret bands, 15cm.
(Phillips) $243

A Wedgwood Fairyland luster plate decorated with 'Boys on a Bridge', with a green bat above a boy in a boat below the bridge, 27cm.
(Phillips) $2,490

## WEMYSS

A Wemyss 1902 Coronation twin handled cup, the lid with thistle finial, the exterior with all-over decoration, 8¾in. high.
(David Lay) $1,095

A Wemyss dog's bowl, impressed mark, 6¾in. diameter.
(Dreweatt Neate) $702

An attractive Wemyss (Bovey Tracey) model of a pig in the usual squatting pose, with ears pricked, painted all over the back and ears with sprays of flowering clover, 46cm.
(Phillips) $3,785

Wemyss ware plant pot decorated with branches of cherries, green borders, spiral fluted body, 8½in. x 7in.
(Barbers Auctions) $722

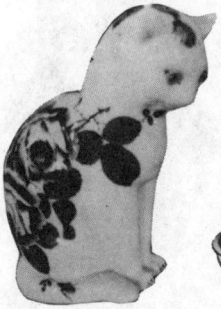

A Wemyss Plichta cat signed *Nekola.*
(R.K. Lucas) $1,060

An unusual Wemyss pottery part toilet set, painted in colors with pink carnations within typical sea green borders.
(Spencer's) $1,369

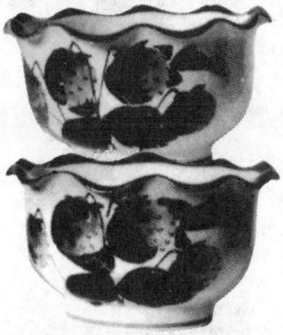

Pair of Wemyss fruit bowls, decorated with strawberry pattern, green borders, 5in. diameter.
(G.A. Key) $250

A Wemyss (Bovey Tracey) large pig, made for Jan Plicta, painted with pink and green thistles, 41.5cm. long.
(Phillips) $850

A Wemyss pottery preserve jar and cover painted with strawberries.
(Bearne's) $289

Westerwald stoneware flagon, with portrait mask, 18th century.
(Auktionshaus Arnold) $715

A Westerwald stoneware cylindrical mug with loop handle, incised with four interlocking oval cartouches of prancing horses, early 18th century, 22.5cm. high.
(Christie's) $414

A Westerwald stoneware jug with loop handle and short flared neck applied with a mask, the shoulder with alternating panels of rouletting and fleurs-de-lys, late 17th century, 18.5cm. high. (Christie's) $854

A German Westerwald gray stoneware globular jug, enriched in blue and manganese and molded in relief with three oblong-octagonal medallions of the Crucifixion, early 18th century, 7¼in. high.
(Christie's S. Ken) $252

A Westerwald stoneware globular jug with loop handle, applied with an octagonal portrait medallion of William III flanked by scrolling flowers enriched in manganese and with incised stems, on a blue ground beneath a ribbed manganese neck, late 17th century, 13.5cm. high. (Christie's) $960

An unusual Westerwald William III Krug with ovoid body, cylindrical neck molded with horizontal ribbing and a ribbed loop handle, 18.55cm., end 17th century.
(Phillips) $823

A German Westerwald grey stoneware globular jug, the body enriched in blue and stamped with bands of flowerheads enriched in manganese, late 17th century, 10½in. high.
(Christie's S. Ken) $336

Westerwald-type stoneware jug, Northern Europe, 18th century, globular shape underglazed blue scrolls and highlighting, 8½in. high.
(Skinner Inc.) $275

A German Westerwald stoneware globular GR jug, enriched in blue and incised with five horizontal bands of interlaced scrolls, 18th century, 13in. high.
(Christie's S. Ken) $525

## WHIELDON

A Whieldon cauliflower molded teapot and cover with green scrolling handle, the oviform body naturalistically modeled with green glazed leaves, 11cm.
(Phillips) $1,767

A Whieldon style teapot and cover, the portrait of Flora molded on either side with flowing hair, 14cm. high.
(Bearne's) $8,085

A Whieldon solid agate pecten shell teapot and cover molded in the form of a shell and marbled in gray, brown and cream below a clear lead glaze, 13.5cm.
(Phillips) $3,386

A creamware cauliflower-molded baluster coffee-pot and cover of Whieldon type, the upper part with cream florettes and the lower part with crisply molded overlapping green leaves, circa 1765, 24.5cm. high.
(Christie's) $8,272

A creamware arbor group of Whieldon type, modeled as a garden shelter of semi-circular form, a woman in a crinoline sitting on either side of the curved seat, 14.5cm. high.
(Bearne's) $64,704

An important Whieldon figure of a bagpiper, the gentleman dressed in short coat, buttoned waistcoat and striped breeches, 19cm.
(Phillips) $17,670

## WOOD

A Staffordshire pearlware figure of a gentleman of Ralph Wood type, wearing a black hat, his gray-lined pale-green cloak tied with a blue ribbon, circa 1785, 25cm. high.
(Christie's) $2,688

An Enoch Wood bust of Reverend John Wesley of typical form, on a socle base, circa 1820, 12¾in. high.
(Christie's S. Ken) $810

A Ralph Wood pearlware figure of St. Peter standing holding a crucifix and a Bible under his right arm, wearing puce-lined green robe and turquoise trousers, circa 1800, 36cm. high.
(Christie's) $1,344

A Worcester pierced basket, the interior painted in colors with a spray of summer flowers and scattered sprigs, 23cm.
(Phillips) $1,346

A rare Worcester eye bath of boat shape on a slender stem with a spreading foot, painted in blue, 4.5cm.
(Phillips) $3,179

A Chaffers teapot and cover of globular shape, painted in blue with an Oriental style fence landscape, 14cm.
(Phillips) $781

A tall tear-shaped vase and cover with a ribbed neck, the body painted with pink and yellow roses, signed *Hood*, 24.5cm.
(Phillips) $860

A pair of Royal Worcester figures of seated musicians, he playing a pipe, his companion playing a guitar, 4in. high.
(Christie's S. Ken) $400

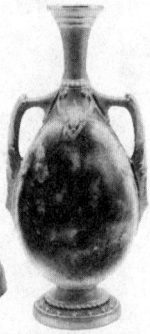

A rare Royal Worcester vase painted with rabbits by C.H.C. Baldwyn, signed, the handles in pale metallic green, cream and gold, 10¾in. high.
(Tennants) $3,657

A globular pot-pourri vase and cover, painted on a matt sky-blue ground with a flock of four swans emerging from raised gold plants, signed *G. Johnson*, 15cm.
(Phillips) $2,992

A fine early Worcester cylindrical mug, painted in deep mauve monochrome with overgrown Classical ruins in a gentle landscape, 8.5cm.
(Phillips) $8,041

An attractive Worcester sucrier and cover, richly decorated in the Sèvres style with rococo shaped turquoise panels edged in gold, 12.5cm.
(Phillips) $4,862

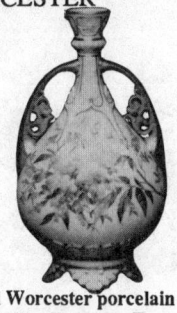

Royal Worcester porcelain double-handled vase, England, late 19th century, matte ivory enamel decorated flowers surrounded by gilt leaves, 13in. high.
(Skinner Inc.) $925

A Royal Worcester cabaret set molded in relief with scrolls and foliage in green and flutes in ivory and peach, printed mark for 1886.
(Christie's S. Ken) $1,000

A good James Hadley & Sons Worcester earthenware bottle vase painted with three japanesque cranes, circa 1896–97, 10in. high.
(Tennants) $289

A very fine large Worcester mug of bell shape with a plain handle, painted in bright Chinese style enamels with the 'Beckoning Chinaman' pattern, 14cm., circa 1754–56.
(Phillips) $7,854

A pair of Royal Worcester porcelain 'Miniature Cairo' water carriers, both standing wearing robes and carrying amphoras, 1913 and 1916, 9 and 10in. high.
(Spencer's) $985

An unrecorded Worcester plate painted in blue with a high handled basket containing prunus, chrysanthemums and paeonies, 21cm.
(Phillips) $972

A Royal Worcester figure of a woman on a swing, entitled 'Alice', from the series of Victorian figures by Ronald Van Ruyckevelt.
(Bearne's) $465

A Worcester finger bowl stand, painted in colors with sprays of flowers, 14.5cm., and a saucer en suite, 13cm.
(Phillips) (Two) $1,085

A Worcester Flight & Barr oviform jug, with central medallion painted by John Pennington in grisaille with a portrait of King George III, height 6½in., circa 1790.
(Bonhams) $3,170

## WORCESTER

A Worcester partridge-tureen and cover, the bird on an oval nest to the right, its plumage enriched in shades of brown, the edge of the cover with stylized entwined straw, circa 1765, 17.5cm. long.
(Christie's) $15,169

Pair of Royal Worcester Cairo water carriers, England, 1883, enamel and gilt accenting over an ivory body, modeled by James Hadley, 21in. high.
(Skinner Inc.) $1,500

A Barr, Flight & Barr inkstand with two ear-shaped holders at the side flanking a loop handle with gilt mask, 14cm.
(Phillips) $1,309

James Stinton, a tall cylindrical vase with flared rim and foot shaded in bright gold, painted with a brace of pheasant, 22.5cm., date code for 1923.
(Phillips) $1,029

A pair of pot-pourri vases, covers and inner covers of spreading baluster shape with foliate scroll handles, 25.5cm.
(Phillips) $1,870

Singing Monk, a very rare Kerr and Binns extinguisher in unglazed Parian, 11.5cm.
(Phillips) $1,403

An early Worcester baluster tankard with a spurred loop handle and scroll terminal, the body painted in colors with Oriental flowering peony, 9.5cm.
(Phillips) $5,976

A wide trophy-shaped vase, on a fluted circular base, the body painted with yellow and white roses, signed *J. Lander*, 19cm., date code for 1909.
(Phillips) $1,029

A Barr, Flight & Barr inkwell painted with a shell attributed to Samuel Smith, painted with a whelk-type shell and seaweed, 7cm.
(Phillips) $5,797

## WORCESTER

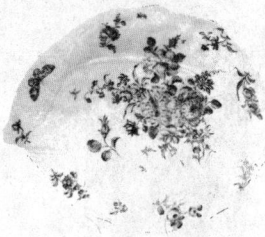

A large Worcester leaf dish molded as overlapping lettuce leaves with crossed stalk handle, 35cm.
(Phillips) $1,683

James Hadley, set of five figures of the Down and Out Menu Men, fully colored, and standing on gray brick bases, approx. 15cm.
(Phillips) $2,390

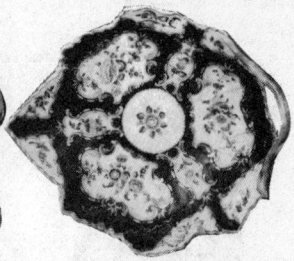

A Worcester leaf shaped dish with gilt serrated rim and green twig handle, painted in colors with festoons of flowers, 22cm.
(Phillips) $1,590

A large Chamberlain jug, finely gilt with bands of hops and foliage on alternating blue and white grounds, 19.5cm.
(Phillips) $1,590

An early Flight and Barr yellow ground bough pot and cover, the central panel painted with convolvulus, roses, poppies and stocks.
(Phillips) $4,382

A rare Royal Worcester porcelain 'Persian' pierced vase modeled by James Hadley, with gilded decoration by Samuel Ranford, of birds amongst scrolling foliage, 7in. high.
(Spencer's) $1,970

An early Worcester fluted coffee cup with scrolling handle, painted in famille-rose palette with trailing flower sprays, 5cm.
(Phillips) $2,805

A very rare Worcester wine funnel, painted in famille-rose enamels with flowering paeony branches, 9.8cm., 1753–1755.
(Phillips) $22,320

A remarkable globular pot-pourri vase and cover with scroll handles, painted with brilliant specimens of Easter cacti, signed *W Hale*, 20.5cm., date code for 1905. (Phillips) $3,386

## BRACKET CLOCKS

An ebonized bracket clock, the five pillar repeating fusée movement with anchor escapement, signed *Geor. Yonge, Strand, London*, 16¼in. high.
(Lawrence Fine Art)
$2,988

A mahogany bracket clock, the two train chain fusée repeating movement with anchor escapement, blued steel moon hands and signed *Cooper*, 15in. high.
(Lawrence Fine Art)
$3,414

A small Regency mahogany bracket clock, the five pillar fusée movement with anchor escapement, signed *Dwerrihouse, Carter & Son, Berkeley Square*, 13in. high.
(Lawrence Fine Art)
$4,268

A Victorian mahogany striking bracket clock, the glazed circular cream painted dial signed *Jas. McInnes Dunbarton* with concentric calendar ring, blued steel moon hands, 18¼in. high.
(Christie's)
$1,045

A Regency mahogany bracket clock in rectangular-shaped case, with stepped chamfered top, ring handles and pierced scalloped side frets, twin-chain fusée movement, 16½in. high.
(Christie's S. Ken)
$2,213

An Austrian ebonized grande sonnerie bracket clock, the bell top case with crowned cherub carrying handle and winged paw feet, mid 18th century, 23½in. high.
(Christie's New York)
$3,520

A mahogany bracket clock, the eight inch dial with Roman numerals, moon hands and signed *Scott, Dublin*, contained in a domed case, 17in. high.
(Lawrence Fine Art)
$1,024

An early Victorian mahogany quarter chiming bracket clock, signed *Cradock King Street, Covent Garden, London*, the massive five pillar triple chain fusée movement with anchor escapement, 37in. high overall.
(Christie's)
$1,714

A George III mahogany bracket clock, with caryatid and floral mounts to the corners, on bracket feet, the arched silvered dial signed *Thos Oldmeadon Lynn*, 1ft. 10in. high.
(Phillips)
$2,960

## BRACKET CLOCKS

An ormolu mounted George III Turkish market musical small bracket clock by Markwick Markham Perigal, London, the scroll engraved backplate enclosing signature, mid 18th century, 17in. high. (Christie's New York) $27,500

A good George III mahogany bracket clock, the arched case surmounted by a spire and urn finial, the circular enamel dial signed *Grant, Fleet Street, London*, 1ft. 7in. high. (Phillips) $7,160

An ebonised quarter chiming bracket clock, the arched brass dial with silvered chapter ring and subsidiaries for pendulum regulation, the triple fusée movement with anchor escapement, 2ft. 3¼in. high. (Phillips) $1,758

A George III mahogany musical bracket clock, the arched silvered dial signed *Sam^l Whatson*, the twin fusée movement now converted to anchor escapement, 1ft. 6in. high. (Phillips) $3,580

A Charles II silver-mounted ebony striking bracket clock of Phase II type, the velvet-covered dial signed *Joseph Knibb Londini Fecit* on a pierced foliate silver disk to the center, 12in. high. (Christie's) $82,346

An 18th century ebonized bracket clock, the case with inverted bell top and carrying handle, the arched brass dial with silvered chapter ring signed *Jn° Watts, Canterbury*, 1ft. 7in. high. (Phillips) $2,685

A George III mahogany bracket clock, the arched case surmounted by a carrying handle, the twin fusée movement with verge escapement, 1ft. 4in. high. (Phillips) $2,685

A 19th century mahogany and brass inlaid bracket clock, with brass mounted canted angles on ball feet, the circular painted dial signed *E. Handscomb Woburn*, 1ft. 9¾in. high. (Phillips) $925

An unusual 18th century ebonized quarter chiming bracket clock, the arched brass dial with silvered chapter ring signed *Jos Kirk*, 1ft. 7½in. high. (Phillips) $3,938

## CARRIAGE CLOCKS

A 19th century French brass and enamel carriage clock, the lever movement striking on a gong with push repeat, 18cm. high. (Phillips) $2,327

A 19th century French oval miniature brass carriage timepiece, with replaced lever platform bearing the *Henri Jacot* trademark, 10cm. high. (Phillips) $1,432

A gilt brass and porcelain paneled carriage timepiece with alarm, in corniche case, the porcelain panels to the sides depicting figures and landscape scenes, 5in. high. (Christie's S. Ken) $1,589

A miniature tortoiseshell silver-gilt carriage timepiece, the backplate stamped *French made*, Roman and Arabic enamel dial signed *Drew & Sons Picc. Circus London. W.*, 3 1/8 in. high. (Christie's) $836

A gilt brass quarter chiming giant carriage clock, the triple chain fusée movement with platform lever escapement, bimetallic balance, striking the hours on bell, bearing the signature *Smith & Sons, Clerkenwell, London*, third quarter 19th century, 13in. diameter. (Christie's New York) $22,000

A brass grande sonnerie/alarm carriage clock in gorge case, eight-day repeating movement with platform lever escapement striking the hours and quarters with two gongs, 5 1/2 in. high. (Christie's S. Ken) $1,992

A fine and rare brass grande sonnerie and minute repeating/alarm carriage clock in oval Corinthian case, signed by the retailer *Bailey, Banks & Biddle Co., Philadelphia*, 4 3/4 in. high. (Christie's S. Ken) $8,410

A French brass carriage clock, the circular enamel dial within a floral champlevé mask in a pillared case, 20cm. high. (Phillips) $1,253

A 19th century French oval gilt brass carriage clock, the enamel dial signed for *Mercier & Fils, Genève*, in an oval case, 17cm. high. (Phillips) $1,432

## CARRIAGE CLOCKS

A chased gilt petite sonnerie carriage clock with calendar, the gilt platform with counterpoised right angle lever escapement, French, circa 1860, 5¼in. high. (Christie's New York) $2,860

A gilt brass striking carriage clock with uncut bimetallic balance to silvered lever platform, white enamel Roman dial with blued moon hands, 5½in. high. (Christie's) $940

A French miniature brass carriage timepiece, the cylinder movement with enamel dial in a corniche case, 9.5cm. high. (Phillips) $501

A French gilt brass and enamel paneled strike/repeat carriage clock, the eight-day movement with platform lever escapement striking on a gong, signed in the base *L. Contreau, 36 Bld des Italiens, Paris*, 4in. high. (Christie's S. Ken) $4,807

A Liberty & Co. pewter carriage clock, the copper dial with black enamel chapters, on a mottled blue and green enameled ground, stamped *English Pewter, Made by Liberty & Co.*, 12.2cm. high. (Christie's) $1,174

A fine chased gilt grande sonnerie carriage clock with moon phase, calendar, thermometer and winding indicator, the movement stamped *H.L.* in lozenge punch, circa 1860, 8in. high. (Christie's New York) $22,000

A gilt brass quarter striking carriage clock with cut bimetallic balance to lever platform, dial signed in Cyrillic *Pavel Buhre*, blued spade hands, within gilt mask, 6¼in. high. (Christie's) $1,359

A silver miniature carriage timepiece with cut bimetallic balance to lever platform, the base stamped *Aspreys London* (London 1913); blue leather traveling case, 2⅞in. high. (Christie's) (Two) $940

A French gilt brass carriage clock, the lever movement striking on a gong with push repeat numbered *7936*, 18.5cm. high. (Phillips) $1,038

## CLOCK SETS

A 19th century French ormolu and porcelain clock garniture, with the figures of a couple, the lady selling flowers, on a scroll base, 1ft. 1½in. high, together with the matching pair of two-branch candelabra.
(Phillips) $2,685

Egyptian Revival marble and onyx three-piece clock garniture, circa 1880, the black marble mantel clock applied with bronze Egyptian figures and surmounted by a bronze sphinx, time and strike movement, impressed *R & C/ Paris*, 18½in. high.
(Skinner Inc.) $1,000

An ormolu and white marble clock garniture comprising: a pair of brules parfums, each with a domed top cast with foliage, and a mantel clock with circular enamel dial inscribed *TIFFANY & CO.* and twin going barrel striking on gong movement, the brules parfums 13½in. high, the clock 14in. high.
(Christie's) $7,161

An ormolu and Paris porcelain clock garniture comprising: a pair of cassolettes, each with a lid with a pineapple finial, and a mantel clock, the rectangular dial indistinctly inscribed *ROB^T. H. HALFORD*, the bell-striking going barrel movement similarly signed, late 19th century, the clock 18in. high, the cassolettes 15in. high.
(Christie's) $4,501

A French porcelain clock-set comprising a clock-case and two nine-light candelabra, the clock-case formed as a circular drum flanked by two putti, circa 1880, the clock-case 47cm. wide, the candelabra 69cm. high.
(Christie's) $7,161

A 19th century French ormolu clock garniture, the shaped case of scroll and floral design with circular enamel dial, the movement striking on a bell, 25cm. high, together with a matching pair of two-armed candelabra.
(Phillips) $1,164

## CLOCK SETS

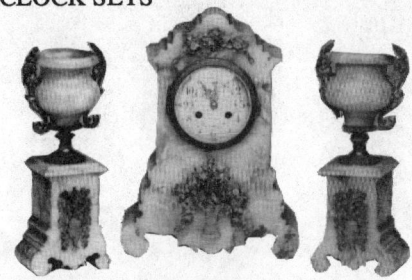

**Tiffany & Co. onyx and gilt bronze three-piece clock garniture, second-half 19th century, with bronze foliate mounts, 13½in. high.**
**(Skinner Inc.) $550**

**A French ormolu and white marble clock garniture, in rectangular-shaped case, surmounted by a motif of birds, wreath bow and arrow, the eight-day movement striking on a bell, 11in. high; with a matching pair of ormolu and white marble two-light candelabra.**
**(Christie's S. Ken) $2,213**

**A French gilt brass and porcelain mounted striking clock garniture, the balustraded case with foliage fruiting finials, detached acanthus and Corinthian capped columns, the two similarly painted urns en suite on similar bases, 16½in. high.**
**(Christie's) $2,090**

**Renaissance Revival three-piece brass clock garniture, France, late 19th century, with foliate-pierced urn and pedestal base, by Japy Frères, clock 20in. high.**
**(Skinner Inc.) $700**

**A 19th century French ormolu and porcelain clock garniture, the shaped case surmounted by two putti and a tortoise flanked by two flaming urns, with inset panels, 1ft. 4in. high, together with an associated pair of vases.**
**(Phillips) $1,432**

**A 19th century French ormolu clock garniture, the shaped case of scroll design, the circular enamel dial with pierced gilt hands, 13¾in. high, together with a matching pair of two armed candelabra.**
**(Phillips) $2,960**

## CLOCK SETS

An Egyptian Revival red and black marble garniture, comprising two obelisks on molded plinths, the clock, en suite, surmounted by sphinx, the white enamel dial, signed *Savage, Lyman & Co., Montreal*, French, circa 1875, 16in. high.
(Christie's New York) $6,600

A French 19th century ormolu and porcelain mounted clock garniture, the eight-day movement striking on a bell, bearing the maker's stamp *Hy. Marc, Paris*, 13in. high; with a matching pair of porcelain and ormolu urn shaped sidepieces, 8in. high.
(Christie's S. Ken) $1,672

A 19th century French ormolu and porcelain mounted clock garniture, the clock case surmounted by a twin-handled urn flanked by mask heads, 1ft. 2½in. high, together with a pair of associated vases.
(Phillips) $2,396

A French ormolu mantel timepiece garniture in drum-shaped case with foliage decoration supported by two putti on scrolled base, 8¼in. high; with a matching pair of single-light candelabra, 7¾in. high.
(Christie's S. Ken) $2,656

A 19th century ormolu clock garniture, the shaped case surmounted by three winged cherubs and floral swags, the movement stamped Japy Freres, 1ft. 3¾in. high, together with a matching pair of two arm candelabra.
(Phillips) $2,492

A 19th century gilt brass and champlevé enamel mantel timepiece garniture, the rectangular case surmounted by a pineapple finial, 8¼in. high, together with a matching pair of candlesticks.
(Phillips) $1,438

## LANTERN CLOCKS

English lantern clock, signed R T Evans, Halstead with 8-day Vicentini movement, short pendulum, striking on a bell, late 19th century, 40cm. high.
(Duran, Madrid) $1,750

18th century brass lantern clock, with engraved decoration, probably English, 14in. high.
(Eldred's) $1,100

Italian lantern clock, the brass dial with Roman and Arabic numerals, circa 1700, 27cm. high.
(Galerie Koller) $3,270

Brass lantern clock, on an oak bracket, the clock inscribed *Roger Moore, Ipswich.*
(G.A. Key) $1,271

18th century lantern clock with painted enclosed iron casing, striking on two bells, German, possibly Simmental, 33cm. high.
(Galerie Koller) $10,626

A rare quarter chiming lantern clock, the going train with verge escapement and later pendulum suspension, signed *D. Lesturgeon, London*, circa 1700, 7in. wide.
(Christie's New York) $2,860

Pierced and engraved brass lantern clock, circa 1700, possibly western Switzerland, 26cm. high.
(Galerie Koller) $2,289

A brass lantern clock, the dial with brass chapter and engraved center signed *Tho Muddle, Rotherfield*, 1ft 3½in. high.
(Phillips) $1,250

Late gothic lantern clock with wrought iron dial painted with Mary and Christ in heaven, Roman numerals, striking on two bells, circa 1580, 40cm. high.
(Galerie Koller) $10,218

## LONGCASE CLOCKS

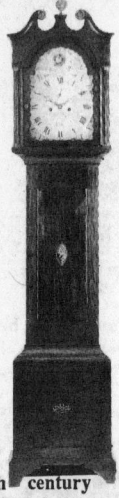

A 19th century mahogany longcase clock, the 12in. arched painted dial with subsidiary seconds and date aperture, signed *Lawley & Co.*, 7ft. 2in. high. (Phillips)

$2,685

Carved maple tall case clock, Stonington/Westerly, Connecticut area, circa 1800, the polychrome brass dial with niche in the arch enclosing a carved figure, 85½in. high. (Skinner Inc.)

$15,000

American mahogany tall case clock with chimes, circa 1880, leaf carved swan's neck pediment over arched dial with painted moon phase, silvered chapter ring, 9ft. 5in. high. (Skinner Inc.)

$4,250

A Victorian mahogany longcase clock, the painted dial signed *Simcock Warrington* with subsidiary dials for seconds and calendar aperture, 7ft ½in. high. (Christie's)

$2,926

An 18th century oak longcase clock, the 12in. arched brass dial with brass chapter, subsidiary seconds and date aperture, signed *Robert Cox, Christchurch*, 7ft. 5in. high. (Phillips)

$1,850

A mahogany, boxwood and fruitwood inlay longcase clock, signed *Jas. Cawfon*, with lunar calendar, eight-day movement striking on a bell, with pendulum and two weights, 93in. high. (Christie's S. Ken)

$3,984

A George III mahogany longcase clock, the arched hood with three ball and spire finials flanked by fluted columns, signed *Tho' Smart, Ryder Street, St. James*, 7ft. 6½in. high. (Phillips)

$4,440

A rare and impressive mid 18th century month going astronomical quarter chiming longcase clock by Thomas Ogden, Halifax, the hood with swan-neck pediment, 107in. high. (Christie's S. Ken)

$18,700

## LONGCASE CLOCKS

An unusual 18th century Continental walnut longcase clock, inscribed on a cartouche in the arch *William Jordain, London*, 7ft. 4in. high. (Phillips) $8,592

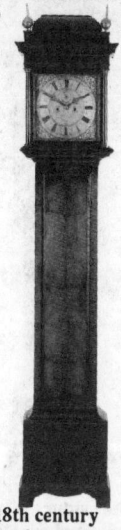

An 18th century walnut longcase clock, signed *Peter King, Longacre*, with subsidiary seconds and date aperture, 7ft. 6in. high. (Phillips) $3,222

A mahogany long case clock, the eight day five pillar movement rack striking, signed in the low arch *Willm. Dutton & Sons*, 79in. high. (Lawrence Fine Art) $26,675

A George III mahogany and inlaid longcase clock, signed on a cartouche *Benjn Heeley, Deptford*, and with strike silent subsidiary, 7ft. 2in. high. (Phillips) $6,265

An early 19th century American cherrywood longcase clock, the 11½in. arched painted wood dial signed *L. Watson, Cincinnati*, with subsidiaries for seconds and date, 7ft. 6in. high. (Phillips) $3,700

A 19th century mahogany longcase clock, the 12in. circular painted dial now signed *John Grant*, the five pillar movement with anchor escapement, 6ft. 9in. high. (Phillips) $4,070

A walnut longcase clock with automaton by Nicholas Weilandt, Amsterdam, the movement with anchor escapement, Dutch striking on two bells, third quarter 18th century, 98½in. high. (Christie's New York) $9,900

A William III floral marquetry longcase clock signed *John Motley, Londini Fecit*, the movement with five ringed pillars, later dead beat escapement with V-anchor, circa 1695, 78in. high. (Christie's New York) $7,700

## LONGCASE CLOCKS

An Edwardian carved mahogany and inlaid nine tube chiming longcase clock, with decorative carved pediment, 108in. high. (Christie's S. Ken) $5,016

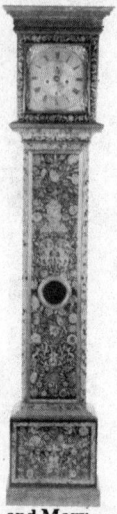

William and Mary marquetry tall case clock, William Tomlinson, London, late 17th century, rectangular cornice above a waisted case, 83in. high. (Skinner Inc.) $6,000

A fine third quarter of the 18th century automata and quarter-striking inlaid burr-walnut longcase clock by Jan Henkels, Amsterdam, 100in. high. (Christie's S. Ken) $15,492

Federal mahogany inlaid tall case clock with alarm mechanism, David Williams, Newport, Rhode Island, circa 1800, 91¾in. high. (Skinner Inc.) $11,000

A 19th century oak and mahogany longcase clock, the 12in. arch painted dial, with subsidiary seconds and date aperture signed, *Garrat, Peterborough*, with moonphase in the arch, 6ft. 7½in. high. (Phillips) $1,943

A George III mahogany longcase clock, the silvered center with subsidiaries for seconds and date signed *Joseph Hatton, Tooley Street, Southwark*, 8ft. 1in. high. (Phillips) $4,625

A nine-bell chiming mahogany and boxwood inlay longcase clock, signed *J.L. Bath*, the three-train movement striking the quarters on eight bells and the hours on a ninth, 95in. high. (Christie's S. Ken) $4,426

A Scottish Regency mahogany longcase clock in the gothic taste, the 12in. circular engraved silvered dial signed *W. Young Dundee* with subsidiary seconds and calendar rings, 7ft. 1in. high. (Christie's) $3,901

## LONGCASE CLOCKS

Dutch baroque walnut tall case clock, 18th century, pagoda top with carved frieze, arched dial with painted moon phase, 97in. high. (Skinner Inc.) $4,750

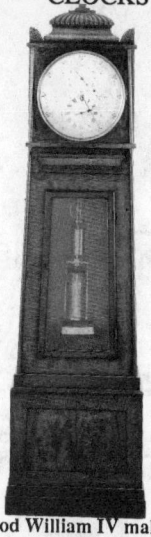

A good William IV mahogany and ebony strung regulator, the tapering case surmounted by a gadrooned caddy, signed *James Condliff*, 7ft. high. (Phillips) $12,799

George III bleached oak tall case clock, Thos. Gordon, Edinburgh, late 18th century, 93in. high. (Skinner Inc.) $1,300

A mahogany long case clock with rack striking eight day movement, signed *Abrm. Larnill, Frome*, 93in. high. (Lawrence Fine Art) $2,988

A George III oak grandmother longcase clock, the case on bracket feet, signed *Thos. Grimes London*, the four pillar rack striking movement with anchor escapement, 5ft. 9in. high. (Christie's) $1,045

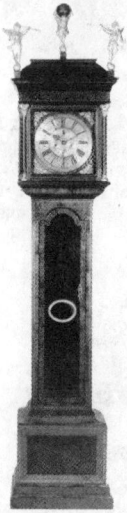

A George I burr walnut longcase clock, the 13½in. square dial signed *Jas. Booth, Dublin* on the broad silvered chapter ring, four pillar movement with inside countwheel strike and anchor escapement, 8ft. high. (Christie's) $6,270

A month-going longcase regulator with equation of time, the dial signed *George Graham, London*, the dial and movement circa 1750, the pendulum and case early 19th century, 75in. high. (Christie's New York) $33,000

A Charles II longcase clock movement signed *John Williamson Londini fecit* on the 10in. square dial, in purpose-made walnut and olivewood parquetry convex molded case, 7ft. high. (Christie's) $8,360

## MANTEL CLOCKS

Empire ormolu mantel clock, 19th century, circular dial inscribed *Manneville Rue St. Honore a Paris*, 18½in. high. (Skinner Inc.) $3,000

A gilt brass combination timepiece aneroid barometer and thermometer, the timepiece with platform lever escapement, 11in. high. (Lawrence Fine Art) $854

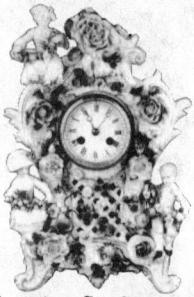

Meissen type floral encrusted porcelain mantel clock, 19th century, three figures seated among floral scrollwork, 13in. high. (Skinner Inc.) $1,000

An interesting English fruitwood four-glass chronometer mantel timepiece by Viner, London, the unusual eight-day chain fusée movement with three plates and four screwed pillars, 7¼in. high. (Christie's S. Ken) $5,610

An unusual astronomical clock movement by Matthias Ernst, Lindau, the gilt dial with 60-minute ring enclosing seconds and anti-clockwise hour rings, circa 1700, 10in. wide. (Christie's New York) $7,700

A 19th century rosewood mantel timepiece, the square silvered dial signed *Muston & Garth, Bristol*, the fusée movement with anchor escapement, 11¼in. high. (Phillips) $1,018

An unusual gilt bronze nautical mantel clock in drum-shaped case, the silvered dial with Roman numerals, inscribed *J.W. Benson, London*, 19¼in. high. (Christie's S. Ken) $1,683

A Liberty & Co. pewter and enamel clock of domed rectangular outline, the circular dial centered in blue and turquoise enamels, 18cm. high, factory marks and *'01156'* to base. (Phillips) $988

A French ormolu mantel clock, inscribed on the dial *J.B. Baillon, a Paris*, eight-day movement with platform escapement, striking on a bell, 8½in. high. (Christie's S. Ken) $3,098

A rare American globe calendar clock, signed *Patent 1860 improved by Leonard Thorn*, on molded circular base engraved with year calendar, 13½in. high. (Christie's New York) $11,000

A 19th century Viennese enamel and silver-mounted timepiece of lyre shape, painted with scenes of Omphale, Queen of Lydia, with Hercules spinning yarn, 11½in. high, overall. (Christie's S. Ken) $5,541

A 19th century bronze and ormolu mantel clock, the circular case surmounted by the figure of Cupid and raised on the back of an elephant, signed *Thuret à Paris*, 1ft. 5¼in. high. (Phillips) $4,475

A French gilt brass four glass mantel clock, with decorated enamel dial and twin glass mercury pendulum, 10¼in. high. (Phillips) $931

An attractive strut timepiece with square agate surround, the frosted gilt movement with bimetallic balance and lever escapement, engraved to the dust cover *Cartier*, 3¾in. square. (Christie's S. Ken) $2,213

A French ormolu and rouge marble mantel clock in drum-shaped case, with ribbon-tie cresting, eight-day movement striking on a bell, 15¼in. high. (Christie's S. Ken) $3,098

A 19th century French porcelain and gilt metal mantel timepiece, the shaped case flanked by lion masks on a shaped base, 11in. high. (Phillips) $627

An Empire ormolu striking mantel clock, the circular Roman dial signed *Caillard à Paris* with blued moon hands, twin going barrel movement with anchor escapement and silk suspended pendulum, 21in. high. (Christie's) $2,508

French brass and champlevé enamel mantel clock, retailed by A. Stowell, Boston, 19th century, domed top over a glazed case, 16in. high. (Skinner Inc.) $1,900

## MANTEL CLOCKS

A fin-de siècle ormolu and porcelain mounted mantel clock, white enamel Roman and Arabic dial signed *Jas. Muirhead Glasgow* with pierced gilt hands, the twin going barrel movement with anchor escapement and strike on bell, 17¾in. high.
(Christie's) $4,807

A fine silver/gilt and enamel minute repeating timepiece by European Watch & Clock Co., for Cartier, in red leather traveling case, 2 13/16in. high.
(Christie's S. Ken) $11,066

An early 19th century ormolu and white mantel timepiece, surmounted by an ormolu figure of a boy and swan, the single fusée movement lacking pendulum, 11½in. high.
(Christie's S. Ken) $2,057

A French late 19th century red tortoiseshell and gilt metal mounted mantel clock, signed on a white enamel plaque *Thuret a Paris*, the eight-day movement striking on a gong, 13in. high.
(Christie's S. Ken) $984

A brass desk timepiece with barometer and thermometer, the rectangular case surmounted by a handle with compass below, 8in. high.
(Phillips) $777

A 19th century French ormolu and porcelain mantel clock, the shaped case surmounted by two seated putti on a naturalised ground, the circular enamel dial signed for *Bennett*, 1ft. 7in. high.
(Phillips) $4,117

A French 19th century ormolu and white marble mantel clock, the globe case surmounted by putti, bands and signs of the Zodiac, signed *E. Vittoz, Paris*, 25½in. high.
(Christie's S. Ken) $2,299

A burr-walnut and bronze mounted mantel clock in rectangular case with decorative bronze frieze, signed below the six *Frodsham, Gracechurch Street, London*, twin chain fusée movement striking on a gong, 15¼in. high.
(Christie's S. Ken) $1,672

A Louis XVI ormolu bronze and rouge marble striking mantel clock, the glazed circular enamel Arabic dial signed *Schmit à Paris*, the movement with outside countwheel strike and later Brocot escapement, 12¼in. high.
(Christie's) $2,090

## MANTEL CLOCKS

A French ormolu and porcelain paneled mantel clock, signed on the dial *Le Roy & Fils, Palais Royal, a Paris, Rue Montpellier*, the eight-day movement with outside countwheel strike on a bell, 12in. high.
(Christie's S. Ken) $984

A fin-de-siècle pink marble and ormolu small mantel timepiece, signed *Le Roy & Fils 57 New Bond Strt. Made in France Palais Royal Paris* with pierced gilt hands, the going barrel movement with lever escapement, 6¼in. high.
(Christie's) $1,463

A 19th century English ormolu and bronze mantel timepiece, the fusée movement with anchor escapement, signed on a cartouche *Baetens, 23 Gerrard Street, Soho, London*, 11¾in. high.
(Phillips) $3,222

A 19th century ormolu and white marble mantel clock, the circular case decorated to the side with a winged putto reading and with foliage and a globe, signed *Mannheim à Paris*, 12½in. high.
(Phillips) $1,253

A Eureka electric clock with large vertical balance wheel, the movement supported on two brass pillars, on circular brass base with glass dome, 9½in. high.
(Christie's S. Ken) $1,083

A French ormolu mounted gray and white marble mantel clock, the white enamel dial with Roman numerals, pierced gilt hands and signed *Chopin a Paris*, 24½in. high.
(Lawrence Fine Art) $1,174

A 19th century French tortoiseshell and cut-brass bracket clock, the shaped case surmounted by a galleried fret and four finials, 2ft. 2in. high.
(Phillips) $1,522

A Second Empire porcelain mounted ormolu mantel clock, the Sèvres style dial with Roman chapters, backplate with the stamp of *Brocot*, set with a further porcelain panel of Cupid, 13in. high.
(Christie's) $1,150

A 19th century walnut mantel timepiece, the rectangular case, with engraved silvered dial, signed *Fred^k Bryant, London*, the fusée movement with anchor escapement, 10½in. high.
(Phillips) $1,164

## MANTEL CLOCKS

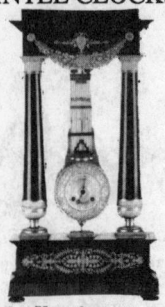

Charles X mahogany and ormolu mantel clock, circa 1830, with enameled numbers suspended between columnar supports on a stepped base, 22in. high.
(Skinner Inc.) $7,500

A lythalin and gilt metal mantel timpiece, the case supported by two columns with gilt capitals, on rectangular base, ivorine dial with Arabic numerals, 5½in. high.
(Christie's S. Ken) $627

A 19th century French ormolu mantel clock, the case surmounted by a twin-handled urn decorated with fruit and swags, the circular enamel dial signed *Denigre Paris*, 1ft. 5¾in. high.
(Phillips) $962

A black japanned pendule Neuchateloise and wall bracket en suite, the twin going barrel movement with spring suspended verge escapement, signed *Henri Ducommun à la Chaux de fonds*, 36in. high.
(Christie's) $2,508

An interesting late 19th century industrial mantel timepiece in the form of a watermill, the large paddle wheel driven by a separate movement rotating in a simulated waterway, inscribed *M. Grumberg, Bombay & Paris*, 15in. high.
(Christie's S. Ken) $11,066

A fine silver gilt and enamel timepiece, the rectangular case with chamfered angles, floral gilt decoration and swags in high relief, on mother-of-pearl base with bun feet, 2¾in. high.
(Christie's S. Ken) $3,984

An unusual French marine clock, modeled in the form of a shell with propellor fuse, inscribed *DUGHS CASTELNAUDARY*, 22in. high.
(Christie's S. Ken) $811

'Inseparables', a Lalique opalescent clock, the clear and opalescent glass molded with two pairs of budgerigars among prunus blossom, 11.2cm. high.
(Christie's) $3,861

A 19th century French ormolu mantel clock with automaton, the circular case raised above a glazed base housing a singing bird, 1ft. 4½in.
(Phillips) $4,117

## MANTEL CLOCKS

A late 19th century South German automaton quarter striking bracket clock, the stained wooden case in the style of a church with onion spire finial and belfry, 30in. high.
(Christie's S. Ken) $2,166

A small French vari-coloured marble and gilt mantel timepiece, in drum-shaped case surmounted by a marble stylized urn finial, with timepiece movement, 8in. high.
(Christie's S. Ken) $551

A 19th century French ormolu mantel clock, the circular case surmounted by an urn and raised on the back of a stallion, 1ft. 1in. high.
(Phillips) $680

An unusual industrial steam engine incorporating a timepiece and barometer with thermometer, the horizontal boiler surmounted by the horizontal single cylinder steam engine with governor and flywheel driven by a separate spring barrel, 11in. high.
(Christie's S. Ken) $4,922

A French mahogany portico clock, the gilt dial with Roman numerals and engine-turned centerfield signed *Bernard et fils, Bordeaux*, the eight-day movement with outside countwheel strike on a bell, 18½in. high.
(Christie's S. Ken) $945

A Japanese gilt brass spring clock engraved with stylized flowering peony with going barrel for the outside Japanese countwheel strike on bell above the spring balance of the verge escapement to the chain fusée going, 4½in. high.
(Christie's) $2,384

Federal mahogany pillar and scroll clock, Riley Whiting, Winchester, Connecticut, circa 1820, 30in. high.
(Skinner Inc.) $800

A 19th century French red tortoiseshell and cut-brass inlaid mantel clock, the shaped case with gilt mounts, signed *Rollin à Paris*, 1ft. 4in. high.
(Phillips) $680

A 19th century French gilt brass and champlevé enamel four glass mantel clock, 38cm. high.
(Henry Spencer) $1,564

## MANTEL CLOCKS

A gilt-brass mantel timepiece with alarm, the rectangular dial signed *Cartier 8 days alarm Swiss* with raised blued Arabic chapters, the movement signed *Concord Watch Co.*, 3½in. high.
(Christie's) $2,508

A gilt quarter striking table clock with alarm by *Johann Gottlieb Thÿm à Thorn*, on four silvered lion feet, the sides with conforming glazed panels, early 18th century, 5½in. wide.
(Christie's New York) $8,800

A Victorian mahogany eight-bell chiming mantel clock, the drum-shaped case flanked by carved scrolls, on rectangular base, 28in. wide x 18in. high.
(Christie's S. Ken) $1,496

A thuya wood brass inlaid 8-day Hertfordshire Mercer mantel chronometer, brass bezel to glazed circular silvered engraved dial signed *George Makin & Sons, Ltd. Manchester. 669 Auxillary Compensation*, winding key, 11½in. high.
(Christie's) $9,752

A gilt and patinated bronze industrial clock, signed *Japy Frères*, in the form of a trip hammer on oblong base, the hammer serving as the pendulum, circa 1880, 17¼in. high.
(Christie's New York) $3,080

An early Victorian four-glass mantel timepiece, engraved silvered dial signed *W. Davis & Sons*, the four pillar single chain fusée movement with anchor escapement, 8¾in. high.
(Christie's) $1,630

A 19th century French ormolu and porcelain mantel clock, the case surmounted by an urn flanked by lion mask mounts, 17in. high, together with a gilt wood base.
(Phillips) $1,850

An interesting 19th century Japanese table clock in pierced cast gilt brass drum case glazed to the top, the white enamel chapter-ring with Japanese numerals, 4¾in. high.
(Christie's S. Ken) $4,869

A 19th century brass double-dialled barometer and timepiece in the form of a ship's wheel surmounted by a gimballed compass, signed *La Fontaine Opticien*, 11½in. high.
(Christie's S. Ken) $2,213

## MANTEL CLOCKS

A good black marble and bronze mounted mantel timepiece in Egyptian style, single fusée movement signed on the backplate *Vulliamy, London*, 9in. high.
(Christie's S. Ken) $53,117

A 19th century Continental porcelain mantel clock, the Meissen case decorated with four putti representing the seasons, the associated movement stamped *Hy Marc Paris*, 1ft. 6in. high.
(Phillips) $5,920

A modern brass Congreve clock, on four column supports, surmounted by five ball and spike finials, on ball feet, minute dial flanked by two subsidiary dials for hours and seconds, 16in. high.
(Christie's S. Ken) $1,992

A Louis XIV tortoiseshell and ormolu striking pendule religieuse with flambeau urn finials, signed *Rabby à Paris*, the five-baluster pillar twin going barrel movement now with tic-tac escapement, 20¼in. high.
(Christie's) $3,034

An unusual Continental fruitwood and enamel mantel timepiece, the verge fusée watch movement with bridge cock, signed *Pre. Rigaud, Geneve*, 8½in. high.
(Christie's S. Ken) $1,496

A mahogany striking mantel clock with engraved silvered dial now signed *Brockbank & Atkins London*, the four pillar twin chain fusée movement with anchor escapement and strike on gong, 10¼in. high.
(Christie's) $1,045

An Empire ormolu striking mantel clock, the glazed engine-turned Roman dial with blued moon hands and foliate bezel, the twin going barrel movement with anchor escapement and silk suspended pendulum, 22½in. high.
(Christie's) $2,299

An early Victorian rosewood four-glass striking mantel clock, the engraved silvered dial with foliate engraved spandrels and silvered bezel, the five pillar twin chain fusée movement with anchor escapement, 13in. high.
(Christie's) $2,090

A Louis XVI gray marble and ormolu striking mantel clock, the white enamel Roman dial signed *Durand* with pierced gilt hands, twin going barrel movement with anchor escapement and sunburst pendulum, 21¾in. high.
(Christie's) $3,762

## SKELETON CLOCKS

A 19th century brass skeleton timepiece, the scroll plates with silvered chapter ring signed *Thos Bunyan*, on a marble base, 42cm. high. (Phillips) $895

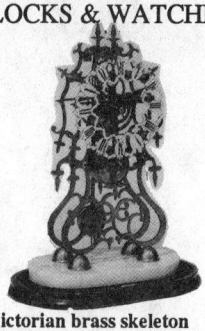

A Victorian brass skeleton timepiece, the single fusée movement with four-armed wheels and anchor escapement, on oval white marble and ebonized wood base, 16in. high. (Christie's) $794

English skeleton clock, with pierced and silvered dial and Graham escapement, 19th century, 40cm. high. (Duran, Madrid) $1,400

A brass two-train cathedral skeleton clock with gothic numerals, eight-day fuseé movement with six-spoke wheel work striking the half-hours on a bell and the hours on a gong, 19½in. high. (Christie's S. Ken) $3,201

A small brass skeleton timepiece in rafter framė, the brass chapter-ring with Roman numerals, signed on a brass strip *Salmon, Pimlico, 1841*, the single chain fusée movement with four-spoke wheel work, 7½in. high. (Christie's S. Ken) $984

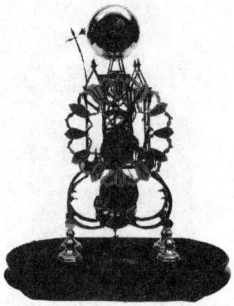

Victorian skeleton clock signed by John Neal, on wooden pedestal base, lacking glass casing, late 19th century. (Duran, Madrid) $850

A 19th century brass skeleton timepiece, the fusée movement with five spoke wheels and anchor escapement with passing strike, signed on an applied swag W. Gibbs, 18½in. high. (Phillips) $863

A 19th century skeleton timepiece, with skeletonized dial and Roman numerals, the scroll plates surmounted by a bell with eight-day fuseé movement, 14in. high. (Christie's S. Ken) $1,174

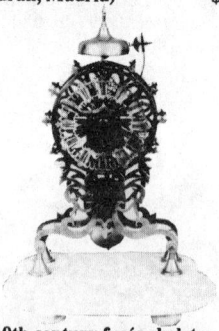

A 19th century fusée skeleton clock by Louis B Twells of Ashbourne, the circular framework supporting a bell with hammer on shaped supporting brackets, 17½in. high. (Michael Newman) $1,015

## SKELETON CLOCKS

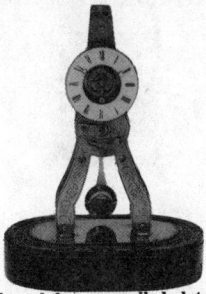

A French brass small skeleton timepiece, the going-barrel movement with four-armed wheels, anchor escapement and silk suspended foliate engraved pendulum, on oval ebonized wood base, 8¾in. high.
(Christie's) $941

A Victorian striking skeleton clock by *Jas. Condliff Liverpool* signed to the front of the block base with going barrel, six-arm greatwheel of large diameter, five-arm wheels thereafter to anchor escapement, 15in. high.
(Christie's) $7,585

A brass skeleton timepiece, with stylised gothic plates, turned feet on white marble base, the single chain fusée movement with six-spoke wheelwork, with pendulum, 11¼in. high.
(Christie's S. Ken) $945

A brass two-train Westminster Abbey skeleton clock on veined white marble base, the chapter-ring with gothic numerals, 23in. high.
(Christie's S. Ken) $4,114

An unusual gilt great wheel skeleton clock within wirework case, the arched openwork case flanked on either side by half column surmounted by urn linked with chain to central urn finial, French, circa 1825, 15½in. high.
(Christie's New York) $7,700

A quarter chiming skeleton clock and vitrine, W.F. Evans & Sons, Handsworth, retailed by Bell Bros., Doncaster, the brass quadruple frame pierced to represent Westminster Abbey, third quarter 19th century, 21½in. high.
(Christie's New York) $7,700

An unusual miniature brass skeleton clock, the circular silvered dial with black Roman numerals, maker's name *Whaley, Lambeth*, 13cm. high.
(Henry Spencer) $1,155

A 19th century brass 'Cathedral' skeleton clock, 64cm. high overall.
(Henry Spencer) $2,807

An interesting brass skeleton timepiece with detent escapement in scroll frame, on ball feet, by Brotherston & Son, Dalkeith, 8½in. high.
(Christie's S. Ken) $2,805

## WALL CLOCKS

A 19th century mahogany and brass inlaid bracket timepiece, the circular case surmounted by a flame finial, 2ft. 1/2in. high.
(Phillips) $859

An interesting mid 18th century alarm verge traveling wall clock, the weight-driven rectangular verge movement with alarm train to the side and short bob pendulum, 8 1/4in. high.
(Christie's S. Ken) $2,877

A late 19th century mahogany bracket clock, the circular painted dial signed *Camerer Cuss & Co., London*, the twin fusée movement with anchor escapement, 1ft. 6in. high.
(Phillips) $1,164

A Dutch oak alarm staartklok, arched hood surmounted by three giltwood figures, in typical case, painted dial with typical Dutch scene in the arch, gilt repoussé spandrels, 48in. high.
(Christie's S. Ken) $1,280

A German framed automaton windmill novelty timepiece, the printed landscape depicting a windmill with automaton sails, dated *1892* above the doorway, 20 1/4in. high.
(Christie's) $2,299

A 19th century Austrian rosewood Vienna wall timepiece, the circular enamel dial with subsidiary seconds signed *Franz Möhslinger in Wien*, the weight driven movement with dead beat escapement, 3ft. 3 1/2in. high.
(Phillips) $2,035

Rosewood double dial calendar timepiece, Seth Thomas Clock Co., Thomaston, Connecticut, mid 19th century, eight-day movement, 27 1/2in. high.
(Skinner Inc.) $700

A unique wall clock, designed and executed by Margaret Gilmour, the square tin body decorated in repoussé with Celtic entrelac designs on a hammered ground, 45.7cm. square.
(Christie's) $23,474

A Black Forest carved wood striking cuckoo clock of standard form, the dial with Roman chapter ring, pierced bone hands, a cuckoo and seated boy appearing on the hour behind shutters, 30in. high.
(Christie's) $1,714

## WALL CLOCKS

An 18th century South German verge 'Telleruhr' timepiece, signed below the six *Martin Heigl*, the circular brass movement with four turned brass baluster pillars, 15in. high.
(Christie's S. Ken) $1,772

A wall clock by André Dubreuil, the green-tinted domed glass clock with copper face of repoussé decoration, mounted in a black iron scrolling frame, 77.5cm. long.
(Christie's) $4,695

An ebonized 'Zaanseklok', the brass 30-hour straight line movement with vertical verge escapement, signed *Claus Van Rossen op de Koog*, basically circa 1700, 28½in. high.
(Christie's) $6,068

Presentation banjo timepiece, Waltham Clock Co., Waltham, Massachusetts, 20th century, eagle finial, brass bezel, 43in. high.
(Skinner Inc.) $2,100

A Viennese picture clock depicting sportsmen and their dogs, twin going barrel movement stamped *Villenense* with recoil escapement and strike on gong, 28¼ x 23in.
(Christie's) $3,135

An 18th century Japanese mahogany pillar clock, the brass front plate shaped and engraved as a basket of flowers flanked by two baluster turned brass pillars, 39.5cm. high.
(Henry Spencer) $598

An Edwardian ebonized and gilt metal mounted quarter-chiming bracket clock with stepped flat top surmounted by flame finials, the massive three-chain movement chiming on eight bells and four gongs, 22in. high.
(Christie's S. Ken)
$2,090

A mid-Georgian black japanned Act of Parliament clock signed *Willm. Calvert, Bury* on the shaped 28in. dial with Roman and Arabic gold painted chapters, 6in. high.
(Christie's) $2,926

An unusual mid 19th century American rosewood hanging wall timepiece, the 7in. circular white painted dial signed *E. Howard & Co. BOSTON*, 28½in. high.
(Christie's S. Ken) $522

## WATCHES

An 18th century gold quarter repeating watch, the movement with pierced cock and diamond endstone signed *James Tregent*, marked *London 1766*, 45mm. diameter.
(Phillips) $2,035

A late 18th century gold dumb quarter-repeating cylinder pocket watch by Just. Vulliamy, London, in engine-turned and engraved consular case, 54mm. diameter.
(Christie's S. Ken) $9,295

An early 18th century quarter repeating verge watch movement, signed *Tho Tompion, London, 136*, with pierced tulip pillars and engraved cock, 56mm. diameter.
(Phillips) $3,700

A Continental gold and enamel verge open-face pocket watch in chased and engraved case, the reverse with enamel portrait of a lady in paste set of reserve, 43mm. diameter.
(Christie's S. Ken) $752

A Swiss 18 carat gold keyless lever split second chronograph, the enamel dial with subsidiaries for seconds and for minutes elapsed, 52mm. diameter.
(Phillips) $2,775

A Continental gilt and enamel open-face verge pocket watch in decorative case, the reverse with enamel plaque depicting a couple in a garden scene, 45mm. diameter.
(Christie's S. Ken) $1,254

A rare verge automata pocket watch, with aperture above the twelve revealing painted figures revolving past a landscape, signed *Roux Roman Bordier & Compe*, 52mm. diameter.
(Christie's S. Ken) $2,090

A Continental silver gilt and translucent red enamel form watch in the shape of an umbrella, with painted gilt Arabic numerals and outer twenty-four hour ring, 4in. diameter.
(Christie's S. Ken) $1,359

A keyless pink gold open-face pocket watch by A. Langer & Sohne, Glashutte b/Dresden in plain case with engraved monogram to the reverse, the white enamel dial with Arabic numerals, 49mm. diameter.
(Christie's S. Ken) $1,254

## WATCHES

An unusual gold keyless open-faced double dialled pocket watch in plain case, the white enamel dial inscribed *The Royal Astronomer*, 54mm. diameter. (Christie's S. Ken) $7,746

An unusual gold duplex hunter pocket watch in plain case, the white enamel dial with eccentric chapter-ring with Roman numerals, 47mm. diameter. (Christie's S. Ken) $1,045

A white metal keyless open-face Mickey Mouse pocket watch by Ingersoll in plain case, the white dial with Arabic numerals, 49mm. diameter. (Christie's S. Ken) $885

A fine and rare 18ct. gold keyless open-face split-second chronograph carousel by J.W. Benson, in plain case, the white enamel dial with Willis to the back, with chain fusée, London 1906, 59mm. diameter. (Christie's S. Ken) $50,160

A rare quarter repeating watch incorporating an automaton of Moses, Fleury l'Ainé, signed in the watchmaker's hand *Fait par A. Fleury à la Chaux de Fonds en Suisse, Vendu à Berbiee 1807*, within a plain 18ct. gold case, 64.5mm. diameter. (Christie's New York) $165,000

A Continental gilt enamel and paste set open-face verge pocket watch, the white enamel dial with paste set bezel, Arabic numerals and signed *Reimirol & Cie*, 55mm. diameter. (Christie's S. Ken) $1,463

An unusual gold keyless open-face double sided full calendar and moonphase pocket watch, inscribed *Avertisseur Electrique et Calendrier*, 48mm. diameter. (Christie's S. Ken) $3,098

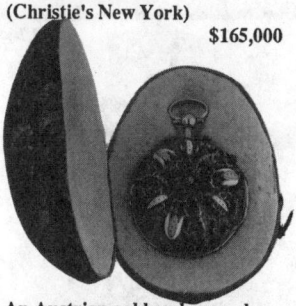

An Austrian gold and enamel verge pendant watch of small size, the frosted gilt fusée movement with bridge cock inscribed with the initials *J.S. Wien*, 29mm. diameter. (Christie's S. Ken) $5,312

A silver keyless open-face eight-day calendar pocket watch by Hebdomas in engine-turned case, the white enamel dial with eccentric chapter-ring, 47mm. diameter. (Christie's S. Ken) $1,328

## WRIST WATCHES

A steel Rolex Oyster Perpetual date submariner wristwatch with black revolving bezel, the matt black dial with dot and baton numerals, 40mm. diameter.
(Christie's S. Ken) $1,881

A 9ct. gold Rolex Prince wristwatch in rectangular case, the matt silvered dial with Arabic numerals and large subsidiary seconds, 39 x 21mm.
(Christie's S. Ken) $5,852

A steel Breitling, Geneve, Navitimer chronograph wristwatch with rotating bezel, the black dial with outer tachymetric and telemetric scales, 40mm. diameter.
(Christie's S. Ken) $1,045

A gold steel Rolex Oyster Perpetual chronometer bubble-back wristwatch with gold bezel, the pink dial with Arabic quarter-hour marks, 30mm. diameter.
(Christie's S. Ken) $1,568

A rare early 1950's Patek Philippe & Co, Geneve, Calatrava wristwatch made for Gubelin in typical case with white enamel dial and Breguet numerals, 31mm. diameter.
(Christie's S. Ken) $44,264

An 18 carat gold gentleman's wristwatch by Patek Philippe, with chronograph, the signed movement with twenty-three jewels, London 1938, 33mm. diameter.
(Phillips) $28,640

A battery-operated advertising display in the form of a wristwatch in gilt case with milled bezel, with leather strap and gilt buckle, 115mm. diameter.
(Christie's S. Ken) $221

A Swiss steel and gilt metal circular gentleman's wristwatch by Rolex, the signed circular movement marked *'patented super balance'*, 35mm. diameter.
(Phillips) $501

A gentleman's large gold full calendar and moonphase chronograph wristwatch by Onsa, the movement jeweled to the centre with seventeen jewels, 37mm. diameter.
(Christie's S. Ken) $1,881

## WRIST WATCHES

A 9ct. gold Rolex Oyster Speedking wristwatch, the silvered dial with raised dagger numerals and subsidiary seconds, the case with screw-down winder, 28mm. diameter.
(Christie's S. Ken) $1,463

A Swiss gold rectangular gentleman's wristwatch by Omega, the signed silvered dial with subsidiary seconds and Arabic numerals, 34 x 21mm.
(Phillips) $680

An 18ct. gold Rolex Cosmograph Daytona chronograph wristwatch, so-called Paul Newman model, the gold bezel with tachymetric scale, 36mm. diameter.
(Christie's S. Ken) $38,730

A Swiss gilt metal circular gentleman's Futurematic wristwatch by Le Coultre, the signed silvered dial with subsidiaries for seconds, 35mm. diameter.
(Phillips) $269

A Swiss steel Oyster Perpetual cosmograph Daytona wristwatch, by Rolex, the signed white dial with subsidiaries for seconds, minutes and for hours elapsed, 38mm. diameter.
(Phillips) $5,920

A Swiss gold circular gentleman's self-winding wristwatch by Patek Philippe, the movement with signed gold rotor, 34mm. diameter.
(Phillips) $4,440

A Swiss 9 carat gold wristwatch by Rolex, the signed quartered silvered dial with subsidiary seconds, 1935, 27mm. diameter.
(Phillips) $1,400

A gold Movado calendar wristwatch made for Tiffany & Co., in circular case, the polished and matt silvered dial with outer date ring and central date hand, 31mm. diameter.
(Christie's S. Ken) $1,881

A Swiss 18 carat gold gentleman's dress wristwatch by Baume & Mercier, with signed circular movement, 34 x 25mm.
(Phillips) $985

A cloisonné vase decorated in various colored enamel and thicknesses of silver wire, on an apricot ground with sprays of purple and white flowers, signed *Komoru*, late 19th century, 18.9cm. high.
(Christie's) $2,384

A pair of cloisonné vases of shouldered square form decorated with four shaped panels depicting growths of wisteria, iris and other flowers, late 19th century, 12.6cm. high.
(Christie's) $3,034

A cloisonné enamel and gilt-bronze pear-shaped vase, decorated with flowering and fruiting sprays of finger citrus, pomegranate and peach, 17th century, 38cm. high.
(Christie's) $5,762

Large red basse-taille cloisonné vase, 20th century, either side decorated with flowering chrysanthemums and other blossoms in multicolored opaque enamels, 12in. high.
(Butterfield & Butterfield)
$1,540

One of two massive cloisonné enamel vases, each decorated in bright pink, light green, gray, blue, yellow, orange and black enamels, 56¾in. high.
(Butterfield & Butterfield)
(Two) $4,950

Large cloisonné enamel charger, Meiji period, decorated in polychrome enamels with a large writhing dragon on a blue ground, 17⅞in. diameter.
(Butterfield & Butterfield)
$440

One of a pair of cloisonné and gilt-bronze horses and riders, the riders seated on saddle cloths, wearing long cloaks and wide brimmed hats, 12½in. high, 19th century.
(Bonhams)
(Two) $7,460

One of a pair of very large cloisonné dishes decorated in various colored enamels, depicting seven storks preening before a meandering stream near a bamboo grove, late 19th century, 105.7cm. diameter.
(Christie's) $13,002

A cloisonné enamel vase with a shouldered cylindrical body worked in Musen enamels and lilies, 30cm. high.
(Hy. Duke & Son) $2,975

A gin-bari shallow cloisonné bowl, the interior decorated in translucent enamels with mauve clematis over a punched silver foil ground, Meiji period (1868–1912), 19cm. diameter. (Christie's) $975

A large Sino-Tibetan cloisonné enamel qilin, standing boldly foursquare on a draped waisted rectangular base decorated with shou characters, swastikas, floral scrolls and lotus panels, Qianlong, 61.8cm. high. (Christie's) $13,871

A cloisonné spherical tripod koro and silver cover decorated with the nami-ni-chidori motif, the body with high breaking waves in musen shippo, Meiji period (1868–1912), 8.7cm. high. (Christie's) $3,901

A cloisonné enamel censer, decorated with prunus and petals on a cracked-ice ground above a band of lotus panels above the pedestal foot, incised Qianlong four-character seal mark, 20cm. wide. (Christie's) $8,536

A cloisonné enamel and gilt-bronze baluster vase, enamelled with an arching lotus scroll, the neck with two elephant-mask handles above a band of archaistic dragons at the shoulder, Qianlong, 48.5cm. high. (Christie's) $11,164

A cloisonné enamel box and cover of hexagonal form, the cover decorated with a cockatoo perched on a maple branch, signed 12.5cm. (Hy. Duke & Son) $21,000

A plique -à-jour vase with an ovoid body decorated in polychrome with a sparrow perched on a rocky out-crop, 18cm. high. (Hy. Duke & Son) $735

A pair of cloisonné enamel vases decorated in polychrome with a blossoming prunus tree sprouting from amidst a mass of flowers, 24.5cm. high. (Hy. Duke & Son) $560

A pair of cloisonné enamel vases of shouldered ovoid form decorated with three cranes on a dark indigo ground, 12.5cm. high. (Hy. Duke & Son) $315

A Perry, Son & Co. brass chamber stick, designed by Dr. Christopher Dresser, with curving wooden handle, stamped *C. Dresser's Design*, and with registration lozenge for 1883, 14.5cm. high.
(Christie's) $737

A Guild of Handicraft Ltd. copper and enameled box, the hinged cover set with an enameled landscape panel painted in naturalistic colors, 21cm. long.
(Phillips) $1,751

Near pair of domed base brass candlesticks, probably Spain, late 17th century, 7½in. and 7¾in. high.
(Skinner Inc.) $500

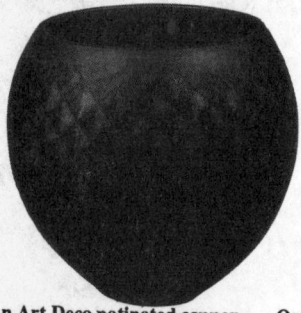

An Art Deco patinated copper globular vase by Claudius Linossier, decorated around the upper body with a band of silver and black patinated lozenges, 17cm. high.
(Phillips) $8,500

One of a handsome pair of gilt metal pedestals, with tapered columns headed by bacchic masks and cast with intricate acanthus scrolls, 45in. high.
(Bonhams) (Two) $5,157

A hammered copper vase by John Pearson, with repoussé decoration of fantastical creatures, base engraved *J.P. 1899*, 20cm. high.
(Christie's) $683

A late 17th century Scandinavian brass candlestick, with repoussé decoration of fruit and flowers, 9in. high.
(Christie's S. Ken) $621

A pair of late Empire gilt brass centerpieces, the pierced flaring basket with hatched and scale decoration beneath, on short spreading foot, 1ft. 3in. high.
(Phillips) $3,134

An unusual Arts and Crafts kettle, by Fred Courthorpe, with domed cover having abalone shell finial and overhead handle with wooden grips, 75cm. total height.
(Phillips) $2,237

A mid 19th century brass tavern tobacco box with central carrying handle flanked by two lidded compartments.
(Phillips) $369

A Flemish brass oval jardinière with beaded rim, the sides with repoussé decoration of a bed of flowerheads, with lion-mask ring-handles, on paw feet, 19th century, 17½in. wide.
(Christie's) $2,789

Chase coffee urn, sugar, creamer and undertray, Chase Brass and Copper Co., Waterbury, Connecticut, circa 1930, 12¼in. wide.
(Skinner Inc.) $350

A brass lantern in the form of a pierced owl, a hinged opening to one side, late 19th/early 20th century, 13in. high.
(Christie's) $5,634

Four brass Standard Measures by DeGrave Short and Fanner London.
(Christie's S. Ken) $1,062

A Gorham & Company red patinated copper and white-metal teapot, stand and burner, with ebonized turned bar handle, the body applied with white-metal flowers, blossom and butterflies, 26.7cm. high.
(Christie's) $2,937

A Hagenauer brass bust of a young woman, lightly beaten textured surface applied with brass strips to form the flowing hair and features, 47cm. high.
(Christie's) $8,593

A large enameled copper wall plaque, the roundel bearing a repoussé galleon and fish on enameled blue and eau-de-nil ground, in square frame, circa 1895, 90cm. diameter.
(Christie's) $1,330

A George III brass samovar with circular ribbed lid and foliate finial, with scrolled bone handles on a plinth base and bun feet, 17in. high.
(Christie's) $792

Pair of signed brass andirons, America, early 19th century, 22in. high.
(Skinner Inc.) $2,000

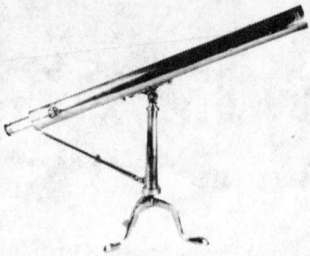

Adie brass telescope with stand, 19th century, length without extension 38in.
(Skinner Inc.) $800

Rare clockmaker's brass tong balance, circa 1830, signed E Berner Gienne.
(Auction Team Köln) $63

Late 19th century copper coal scuttle with swing handle.
(G.A. Key) $191

A pair of George I brass candlesticks, on shaped bases, 6¼in. high.
(Dreweatt Neate) $936

A South German brass alms dish, the well repoussé with Adam and Eve beneath the Tree of Knowledge, 14¾in. diameter.
(Bonhams) $1,045

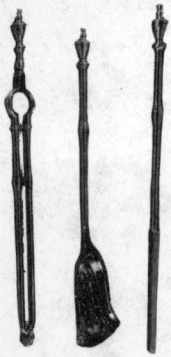

A set of three George III brass fire-irons, each with an urn-finial, restorations, the shovel 25in. long.
(Christie's) $2,904

A Flemish brass jardinière, the circular rim with beaded edge, the sides with lion-mask ring-handles, on paw feet, 19th century, 12in. diameter.
(Christie's) $965

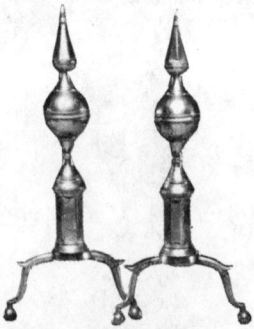

A pair of Federal brass andirons, mid-Atlantic States, 1790–1810, each with a faceted steeple finial over a molded sphere, 24in. high.
(Christie's) $1,320

A George III brass rectangular inkstand, 10in. wide overall.
(Dreweatt Neate) $488

Fine early 20th century copper diving helmet, with original canvas suit, marked *San Francisco, 1915.*
(Eldred's) $2,090

Gilt brass 'fan' fire screen in Regency style with mask mount, scroll base, 23½in. high.
(G.A. Key) $288

Copper and brass kettle, burner and stand, 19th century.
(G.A. Key) $90

A large brass alms dish, the centre repoussé with Adam and Eve under the apple tree, 20½in. diameter.
(Bonhams) $1,425

Early 19th century copper samovar of squat circular form with bone handles, brass tap, stemmed to a rectangular base, 15in. high.
(G.A. Key) $630

A pair of Georgian brass candlesticks, the stepped square bases rising on square tapering fluted stems, 25cm. high.
(Allen & Harris) $121

Large brass helmet shaped coal scuttle, together with shovel, turned wooden handles, 20in. wide.
(G.A. Key) $409

A pair of gilt brass andirons, on conforming scroll bases centered by female masks, 27½in. high.
(Christie's) $7,200

A Charles Hull's 1864 Royal Club corkscrew, with brass tablet fixed, bearing traces of bronze paint.
(Christie's S. Ken) $1,325

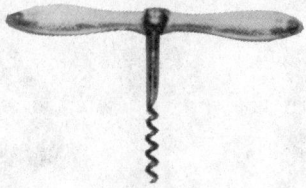

An unusual simple corkscrew, the electroplated handle formed as two opposing fish, bearing Victorian diamond registration marks.
(Christie's S. Ken) $860

A Thomason corkscrew, the brass barrel embossed with vine decoration and with turned bone handle, brush lacking.
(Christie's S. Ken) $720

A brass-barreled King's Screw corkscrew with turned bone handle and side handle, brush deficient.
(Christie's S. Ken) $548

A Thomason patent corkscrew with bone handle, the brass barrel cast with vines, damaged.
(Christie's S. Ken) $358

A Thomason open barrel cork screw with turned bone handle, the barrel top marked: *Edward's Compound, Ne Plus Ultra, Thomason's Patent.*
(Christie's S. Ken) $739

A brass-barreled Dowler patent corkscrew with applied tablet, the turned bone handle with suspension loop.
(Christie's S. Ken) $575

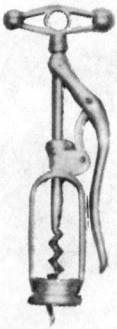

A French nickel-plated Perilles patent 'Le Presto' lever corkscrew.
(Christie's S. Ken) $450

A Thomason brass-barreled corkscrew with royal coat of arms tablet, fixed and turned bone handle, brush lacking.
(Christie's S. Ken) $490

A suit of pink and apple green checked bouclé wool, the jacket weighted with a chain at the hem, labeled *Chanel*, 1960's.
(Christie's S. Ken) $366

A jacket of red cotton woven with a quilted effect and printed with sprays of berries, with pouched hem and wrap over three quarter length sleeves, labeled *Schiapareli*, 1940's.
(Christie's S. Ken) $1,592

An early 20th century young lady's evening gown of magenta plush, the skirt flared, the décolleté bodice having full puffed sleeves, circa 1910's.
(Phillips) $239

A mid 19th century lady's three piece gown of taupe silk, the slightly trained full skirt lavishly trimmed with shades of brown velour and silk fringe, circa 1855.
(Phillips) $1,362

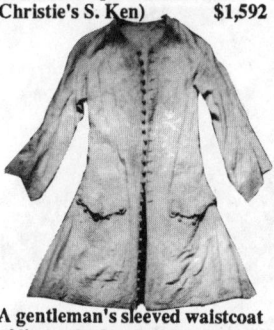

A gentleman's sleeved waistcoat of linen, the borders worked with exotic leaves in corded and knotted work, with small ball-shaped self-embroidered buttons to the hem, circa 1690.
(Christie's S. Ken) $4,246

A dress of charcoal gray wool, the bodice of checked dove gray wool, the jacket lined with matching fabric, all labeled *Christian Dior London*, 1960's.
(Christie's S. Ken) $81

A open robe, with sack back, and petticoat of yellow silk woven with silvery white sprays of honeysuckle and roses, English, circa 1760.
(Christie's S. Ken) $26,598

A redingote of ivory silk taffeta trimmed with piping and rouleaux down the front and at the puffed oversleeves and cuffs, circa 1815.
(Christie's S. Ken) $3,821

An early 20th century lady's evening gown of ivory silk, the black net overlay having bold taffeta and braid appliqué, circa 1910's.
(Phillips) $331

An early 18th century lady's short apron of ivory ribbed silk pleated to the waistband, having bold and elaborate embroidery, English, circa 1720's.
(Phillips) $1,051

A late 19th century Han Chinese lady's padded jacket of red satin silk, bordered in pale yellow to the neck, sides and hem, circa 1890.
(Phillips) $589

A pair of late 19th century lady's shoes of ivory silk in original box *Grands Magazines du Louvre les plus vastes du Monde Paris*, circa 1870.
(Phillips) $156

A fine double-breasted waistcoat of pale blue satin with an overlay of net worked with black velvet dots and sequins, circa 1790.
(Christie's S. Ken) $1,773

A gentleman's linen nightcap, embroidered in coloured silks, gilt and silver gilt threads, with a repeating pattern of Tudor roses and pansies, English, circa 1600.
(Christie's S. Ken) $27,599

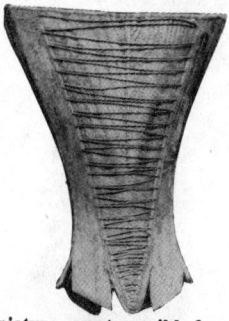

A miniature corset, possibly for a doll but probably an apprentice's masterpiece of linen, the front woven in silk damask with a pattern of berries and trimmed with lacing, 6in. high, circa 1770.
(Christie's S. Ken) $2,335

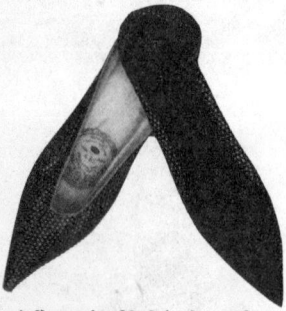

A fine pair of lady's shoes of purple and white spotted kid, one shoe labeled *Edwd. Hogg Ladies Cheap Shoe Warehouse*, circa 1795.
(Christie's S. Ken) $4,876

A late 17th century lady's linen waistcoat, having colorful wool chain stitch embroidered flowers against a natural backstitched meander design, English, circa 1670's.
(Phillips) $382

A rare pair of lady's mules of pale blue satin embroidered in white thread partly wrapped in silver with sunbursts trimmed with sequins, with square toes, circa 1665.
(Christie's S. Ken) $23,353

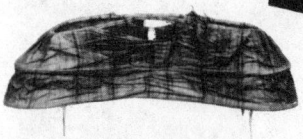

A rare hoop of blue, pink and gray striped cotton with three bamboo hoops, 47in. wide, mid-18th century.
(Christie's S. Ken) $8,067

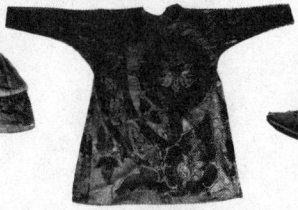

A coat of sage green velvet, stenciled in gold with thistles and roses in a Renaissance style, labeled *Mariano Fortuny Venise*, circa 1915–1920.
(Christie's S. Ken) $3,325

A pair of lady's high heeled shoes of blue damask woven with flowers and leaves, with white kid rands, circa 1740.
(Christie's S. Ken) $5,960

A Sioux buckskin waistcoat, the entire surface sewn with beads, the front panels decorated with representational geometric designs in blue, red, yellow and green.
(Phillips) $2,220

A rare pair lady's shoes of white kid painted in pink and gray with sprigs of flowers, and trimmed with silk rosettes, circa 1700.
(Christie's S. Ken) $18,046

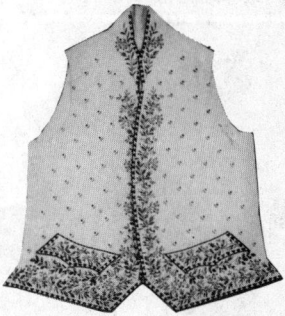

An early 19th century gentleman's waistcoat of ivory satin with fine colored silk embroidery to the high front and pocket flaps.
(Phillips) $350

A pen and ink design for a 'rabat' collar of Venetian Gros Point de Venise lace, executed on vellum, circa 1675.
(Christie's S. Ken) $3,990

Painted and decorated parade fire hat, Philadelphia, circa 1854, decorated with a central medallion depicting William Rush's figure "Water Nymph and Bittern".
(Skinner Inc.) $8,500

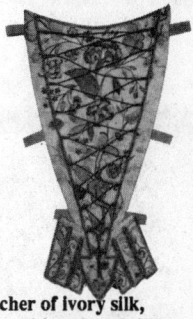

A stomacher of ivory silk, embroidered in colored silks, gilt and silver gilt threads, with a pattern of trailing naturalistic flowers and leaves, early 18th century.
(Christie's S. Ken) $1,592

Der Fuehrer's Face, Disney, 1943, one-sheet, linen backed poster, 41 x 27in.
(Christie's East) $3,300

A Mickey Mouse wicker and colored plastic cane hand bag, 25½in. high.
(David Lay) $336

Silly Symphony, Disney, 1933, one-sheet, linen backed poster, 41 x 27in.
(Christie's East) $6,600

A plush-covered Minnie Mouse with felt-covered cardboard-lined ears, holding a wire and felt flower, 16in. high, 1930's.
(Christie's S. Ken) $379

A set of eight Snow White and the Seven Dwarfs hand-painted porcelain toothbrush holders, 6in. and 4¼in. high.
(Christie's S. Ken) $885

A large felt-covered Mickey Mouse with yellow gloves, green shoes, red shorts, a stitched smile and felt eyes, 16¼in. high.
(Christie's S. Ken) $843

Snow White and the Seven Dwarfs, Disney, 1937, one-sheet, linen backed poster, 41 x 27in.
(Christie's East) $8,800

Mickey Mouse, Two Gun Mickey, 1934 – Mickey With Lasso, a concept drawing, graphite pencil on paper, 9¼ x 12in.
(Christie's S. Ken) $1,159

Fantasia, Disney, 1940, one-sheet, linen backed poster, 41 x 27in.
(Christie's East) $6,820

A Wadeheath pottery Walt Disney teapot, the body molded in relief with Grumpy and various woodland animals, 6½in. high.
(Christie's S. Ken) $379

A Mickey Mouse Ingersoll pocket watch, depicting Mickey Mouse on the face, the animated hour and minute-hands shaped as Mickey's arms and hands, 2½in. high.
(Christie's S. Ken) $843

A Wadeheath pottery Walt Disney series jug, the body molded in relief with Dopey and various woodland animals, 8in. high.
(Christie's S. Ken) $590

A felt-covered Grandmother Duck with wire glasses, wooden broomstick, and original 'Lenci' swing-tag ticket, 20in. high.
(Christie's S. Ken) $2,001

A dralon plush-covered Donald Duck with yellow felt feet and a Daisey Duck with brown felt high-heeled shoes and handbag, with three smaller similarly covered Huey, Duey and Louie toys.
(Christie's S. Ken) $2,317

A Japanese celluloid clockwork Popeye, with original label *Copyright King Syndicate Inc. 1929*, 8in. high.
(Christie's S. Ken) $337

Dumbo, Disney, 1941, one-sheet, linen backed poster, 41 x 27in.
(Christie's East) $4,400

A painted wooden rocking Mickey Mouse swinging on a stand, made by Triang, circa 1938–9, 32¼in. long.
(Christie's S. Ken) $737

Bambi, Disney, 1942, one-sheet, cond. A, linen backed, 41 x 27in.
(Christie's East) $1,980

A bisque headed bébé, with closed mouth, fixed blue eyes, blonde wig, and composition body, 14in. high, stamped in red, *Déposé Tête Jumeau Bte.*
(Christie's S. Ken) $5,201

A bisque-headed child doll , with blue lashed sleeping eyes, pierced ears and blonde mohair wig, 21in. high, marked *Simon & Halbig K*R 53.*
(Christie's S. Ken) $1,231

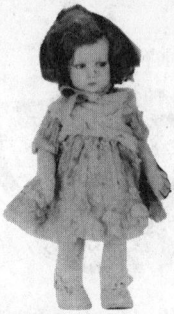

A painted felt doll, wearing original organdie frock decorated with felt flowers, 17½in. high, 300 Series by Lenci.
(Christie's S. Ken) $780

A bisque swivel shoulder-headed doll, with blue yeux fibres, feathered brows, upper and lower teeth, 15in. high, by Jules Nicholas steiner, circa 1880.
(Christie's S. Ken) $2,384

A bisque swivel-headed fashionable doll, with closed smiling mouth, narrow gray eyes and kid body in contemporary cream trained dress and underclothes, 12in. high, impressed *B*, probably by Bru.
(Christie's S. Ken) $2,770

A bisque-headed character doll, with closed mouth, gray painted eyes and jointed composition body, 15½in. high, impressed *K * R 114 43.*
(Christie's S. Ken) $3,282

A brown bisque-headed child doll, with brown sleeping eyes, pierced ears and jointed body, 29in. high.
(Christie's S. Ken) $1,744

Two composition dolls, modeled as Shirley Temple, with green eyes and curly blonde mohair wigs, 24 and 21in. high.
(Christie's S. Ken) $910

A poured wax headed doll, with blonde mohair wig, the stuffed body with wax limbs, dressed in contemporary red frock, 21in. high.
(Christie's S. Ken) $390

A Simon and Halbig bisque head Indian character doll with black mohair wig, feathered brows, fixed brown glass eyes, 13½in., marked *1368*.
(Phillips) $563

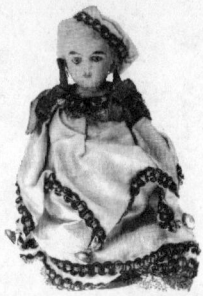

A François Gaultier bisque shoulder head marotte with fixed blue glass eyes, pierced ears and closed mouth, 7in., marked *FIG*.
(Phillips) $362

A bisque headed bébé, with brown yeux fibres, pierced ears, fair mohair wig and jointed wood and composition body, 28in. high, impressed *1907 13*.
(Christie's S. Ken) $1,413

A bisque-headed three-faced doll, the faces crying, sleeping and smiling, wearing tucked frock with lace insertions, 16in. high, stamped *CB* in a circle for Carl Bergner.
(Christie's S. Ken) $2,154

A pair of black composition character china dolls, with brown sleeping flirting eyes, smiling mouths and toddler bodies, 16½in. high, impressed *K & W 134 12/0*, by Konig & Wernicke.
(Christie's S. Ken) $739

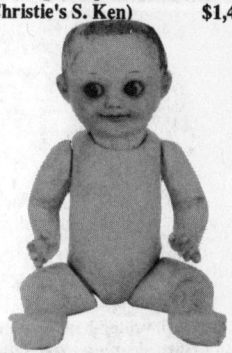

A bisque-headed googlie-eyed doll, with brown sleeping side-glancing eyes, smiling closed mouth and composition baby's body, 8½in. high, impressed *323 A 5/0 M*.
(Christie's S. Ken) $821

A wax swivel-headed doll, with blue eyes, blonde mohair wig, the stuffed body with wax shoulder plate, 19in. high, circa 1870s.
(Christie's S. Ken) $545

A china-headed pedlar doll, dressed in original striped and printed cotton frock, 10in. high, late 19th century, under dome.
(Christie's S. Ken) $967

A bisque flange-necked fashionable doll, with unusual construction allowing the head to turn only 90 degrees, 14½in. high, circa 1870.
(Christie's S. Ken) $1,333

A bisque swivel shoulder-headed Parisienne, with blue eyes, feathered brows, pierced ears, the stuffed body with kid arms and individually stitched fingers, 11in. high, probably by Gaultier. (Christie's S. Ken) $841

A Lenci pressed felt head doll with side glancing brown eyes and 'pursed' lips, 18½in. (Phillips) $602

A poured wax headed doll, with blue sleeping eyes, the stuffed body with wax limbs dressed in original fawn silk frock, 22in. high, damage to leg. (Christie's S. Ken) $2,059

A bisque shoulder-headed doll, with brown sleeping eyes, blonde wig and stuffed body with composition arms, wearing contemporary farm laborer's costume, 23in. high, impressed *370 AM 2½ DEP.*(Christie's S. Ken) $677

A wax over composition headed doll, with fixed blue eyes, long blonde wool wig and stuffed body with waxed limbs, 16in. high, possibly French circa 1865. (Christie's S. Ken) $821

A composition doll, modeled as Shirley Temple, the straight limbed composition body dressed in outfit from the film "Miss Annie Roonie", 15in. high. (Christie's S. Ken) $185

A fine bisque swivel-headed bébé, with closed mouth, fixed brown yeux fibres outlined in black with pink shaded lids, 20in. high, impressed *BRU Jne 7*, circa 1880. (Christie's S. Ken) $22,567

A bisque shoulder-headed doll in the French taste, with solid pate, closed mouth, the stuffed body with bisque arms wearing white lawn frock, 13½in. high, German circa 1880. (Christie's S. Ken) $2,154

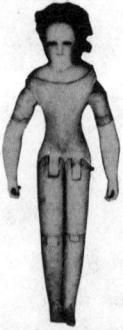

A rare early bisque shoulder-headed Parisienne, with short blonde mohair curls, unpierced ears and kid over wood jointed body, 10½in. high, possibly by Bru, circa 1870. (Christie's S. Ken) $2,872

A painted felt-headed child doll, in original Royal Air Force tunic and flying suit, 28in. high, by Norah Wellings, with original Harry the Hawk R.A.F. comforts fund swing ticket.
(Christie's S. Ken) $1,436

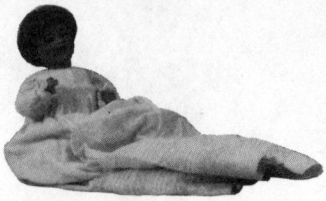

A bisque-headed character doll, modeled as a laughing child, with open/closed mouth, 12½in. high, impressed 4 the Gebruder Heubach sunburst 41.
(Christie's S. Ken) $1,378

Betty Oxo, a cloth doll with painted features, blue side-glancing eyes, smiling mouth and blonde mohair wig, 17in. high, marked with Dean's Rag Book label, especially made for Oxo Ltd. (Christie's S. Ken) $923

A bisque headed bébé, with blue lever-operated sleeping eyes, pierced ears, two rows of teeth, blonde skin wig and jointed wood composition body, 17in. high, marked *STe A 1*, Steiner, circa 1880. (Christie's S. Ken) $5,634

A bisque-headed bébé, with closed mouth, fixed brown eyes, blonde mohair wig and fixed wrist wood and papier mâché body, 12in. high, impressed *DEPOSE E 4 J* and the shoes marked *E. JUMEAU MED. OR 1878 PARIS*. (Christie's S. Ken) $7,796

A wax over composition pumpkin headed doll, with dark inset eyes, molded blonde hair with black band, the stuffed body with squeaker, 12in. high, circa 1860. (Christie's S. Ken) $410

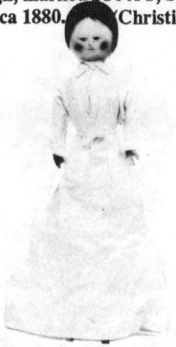

A painted wooden doll, with inset enamel eyes, rouged cheeks, "stitched" eyebrows and eyelashes, 19in. high, English early 19th century.
(Christie's S. Ken) $1,413

A clockwork musical dancing doll, with waxed papier mâché head, wired composition arms and tiered organdie skirt hiding the mechanism, 11in. high, with A. Theroude's stamps, circa 1850.
(Christie's S. Ken) $1,395

A beeswax headed figure of a woman, with bead eyes, cloth body and wax hands, in original embroidered muslin dress decorated with metal braid and blue and white silk tasseled fringe, 11in. high, 1795.
(Christie's S. Ken) $1,846

A china shoulder-headed doll, the molded black hair swept into a loop over each ear and into a plaited bun at the nape, 22in. high, circa 1860. (Christie's S. Ken) $1,528

A bisque-headed character doll, modeled as an Oriental, with sleeping slanting brown eyes, and yellow jointed wood and composition body, 15in. high, impressed *S H 1199 DEP 6½*. (Christie's S. Ken) $2,069

A Gebruder Heubach bisque socket head baby boy doll, with molded hair line, painted features and composition body, 36.5cm. tall. (Spencer's) $950

A Kestner 'Googly' eyed bisque head character doll, with large blue eyes, on a jointed wood and composition toddler body, 17in., marked *Made in Germany*. (Phillips) $5,475

A pair of all-bisque Kewpie dolls, with jointed arms, 5½in. high, impressed *O'Neill* on the feet, in original boxes. (Christie's S. Ken) $1,317

A bisque-headed bébé, with closed mouth, fixed blue eyes, pierced ears and jointed wood and composition body, 23in. high, stamped in red *Déposé Tête Jumeau*. (Christie's S. Ken) $5,643

A bisque-headed bébé, with blue yeux fibres, heavy brows, pierced ears, brown wig and jointed wood and composition body, 18in. high, stamped in red *Tete Jumeau*. (Christie's S. Ken) $2,445

A waxed composition shoulder head doll with white ringleted wig, on a stuffed cloth body with pink kid forearms, 13in., circa 1840. (Phillips) $958

A papier mâché shoulder-headed pedlar doll, with painted features, brown wig and stuffed body, wearing a flower-sprigged dress, red cloak and brown bonnet, circa 1840, 12in. high. (Christie's) $1,390

A German 'Frozen Charlotte', the pink tinted china body with black painted and brushstroked head, 16in.
(Phillips) $498

A bisque swivel-headed child doll, with blonde mohair wig arranged in elaborate plaits, and jointed body in original Hungarian costume, 22in. high, impressed *H 12 129*, by J.D. Kestner.
(Christie's S. Ken) $1,092

A bisque-headed bébé, with closed mouth, fixed brown eyes, pierced ears and jointed wood and composition body, 25in. high, stamped in red *Dépose Tête Jumeau 11*.
(Christie's S. Ken) $3,574

A good Chad Valley 'Princess Elizabeth' character doll with pressed felt head having mohair wig, 17in.
(Phillips) $689

A pair of bisque-headed baby dolls, with open/closed mouths, gray painted eyes and baby's bodies, 15in. high, impressed *36 K * R 100*.
(Christie's S. Ken) $1,599

An Armand Marseille 'Googly'-eyed bisque head character doll with light brown mohair wig, 13½in., marked *Germany 323 AOM*.
(Phillips) $1,245

A bisque-headed character baby doll, with open/closed mouth, blue sleeping eyes and baby's body, 18½in. high, impressed *R S. F.B.J. 236 PARIS 10*.
(Christie's S. Ken) $1,035

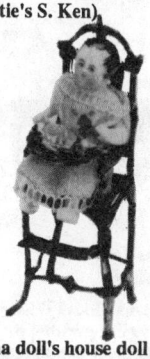

A china doll's house doll with painted features, in seated position, in a dressed metal high-chair, 3in. high.
(Christie's) $389

A bisque-headed child doll, with blue sleeping eyes, and fixed wrist jointed composition body dressed as Little Red Riding Hood, 13in. high, impressed *192 2*, by Kestner.
(Christie's S. Ken) $917

Calor electric heater with light blue Art Nouveau ceramic front and 3 stage bakelite control, 48 x 40cm., circa 1920.
(Auction Team Köln) $141

R F T Super Type 4 U 62 all mains receiver, with UCH11, UBF11 and UCL11, bakelite housing, by Funkwerk Dresden, circa 1950.
(Auction Team Köln) $86

PhiliShave 6 dry electric razor by Philips, Holland, with bakelite case and plug in original box, circa 1938.
(Auction Team Köln) $67

Katalyt 'Sun in Winter' paraffin heater, circa 1930.
(Auction Team Köln) $126

National Model 345 cash register, with extensively decorated nickel housing, prices in English currency, receipt dispenser, marble cover plate, circa 1920.
(Auction Team Köln) $378

Original Miele butter machine, complete wooden barrel construction with original wooden lid, circa 1900.
(Auction Team Köln) $118

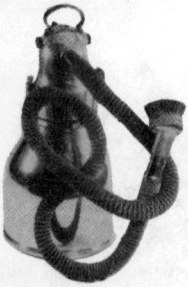

Nilfisk vacuum cleaner, an early industrial cleaner in original box with tools, circa 1935.
(Auction Team Köln) $94

Prometheus Model WRS 4 toaster, 4 slice parallel tip mechanism, adjustable for 2–4 slices with control light and bakelite base, chrome, circa 1955.
(Auction Team Köln) $204

Ericsson Skeleton desk telephone with megohmmeter, circa 1910.
(Auction Team Köln) $630

English line dial, an early ebony desk telephone with separate earpiece, connection rosette and 10 stage switch, by Walker Bros. Birmingham, circa 1900.
(Auction Team Köln) $275

Ox tongue iron, cast brass with pusher and nailed on handle, circa 1860.
(Auction Team Köln) $55

Graeztor electric fire, black enamel with copper housing, 30 x 50cm., circa 1930.
(Auction Team Köln) $189

Coffee percolator, copper, boiler with decorated base complete with sieve equipment, petroleum burner and jug, circa 1880.
(Auction Team Köln) $220

The first ever hot air fan with 2 stroke hot air motor driven by a copper petroleum lamp, on a richly decorated cast metal tripod stand with 2 wooden carrying handles, 113cm. high, only known example, circa 1860.
(Auction Team Köln) $4,173

A Peugeot & Cie coffee mill, cast iron with wooden drawer without front lid, 30cm. high, circa 1900.
(Auction Team Köln) $86

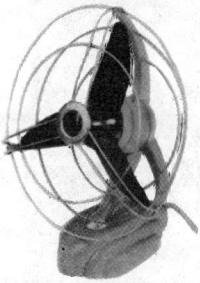

Libelle fan with green hammer finish bakelite propeller, by Schoeller & Co Frankfurt, circa 1955.
(Auction Team Köln) $96

Charcoal eye iron with 2 segment apertures on each side, with lock, handle possibly renewed, circa 1900.
(Auction Team Köln) $86

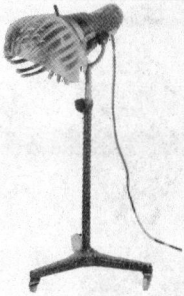

Müholos Trumpf hair drier with stiff heated rods and swing head on movable tripod stand, by Elektro Apparatebau Alfred Müller, circa 1938.
(Auction Team Köln) $300

A 19th century French enamel encrier, the turquoise ground with raised gilt scrolls and painted with pastoral scenes and reserves of flowers, 7in. wide.
(Christie's S. Ken) $815

A gin bari enamel bowl worked in repoussé with goldfish on a punched silver ground, silver mounts, Meiji period (1868–1912), 7.5cm. high.
(Christie's) $823

A South Staffordshire rectangular enamel snuff-box, the cover painted with a couple strolling in a landscape, circa 1765, 3 1/8in. long.
(Christie's) $1,089

A pair of 19th century French enamel and ormolu cassolettes, the pink ground painted with figures and animals in landscapes, 8in. high.
(Christie's S. Ken) $1,030

A Viennese table casket of ivory and enamel, with a central finial of St. George slaying the dragon, the whole set with polychrome enamel plaques of allegorical figures, 19th century, 17cm. high x 15cm. wide.
(Lawrence Fine Art) $4,659

A pair of rare South Staffordshire enamel spirally fluted candlesticks, painted overall with flowers on a white ground, gilt-metal mounts, circa 1760, 10in. high.
(Christie's) $8,316

A South Staffordshire enamel turquoise ground vase painted with a fisherman by a ruined tower, a man on a bridge in the background, circa 1770, 10in. high.
(Christie's) $2,772

A 19th century Viennese enamel bulbous ewer and stand, the ewer with bear's head lid with silver and raised enamel collar, 10in. high; the matching stand of ovoid, lobed outline, 9 3/4in. wide.
(Christie's S. Ken) $10,196

A South Staffordshire enamel pink ground traveling writing case, the cover painted with a shepherd and shepherdess by a river with buildings in the background, circa 1765, 2 3/4in. wide.
(Christie's) $3,960

A rare South Staffordshire enamel rectangular inkstand with two pen trays, one side painted with a gentleman on a horse, the other with two gentlemen, circa 1765, 9in. long.
(Christie's) $4,356

A small plique-à-jour enamel vase decorated in shades of crimson, green, blue and purple enamels and silver wire, signed *Hattori*, late 19th century, 6.8cm. diameter at rim.
(Christie's) $7,585

A Liberty & Co. silver and enameled hair brush designed by Jessie King, of repoussé foliate and swagged decoration with mottled blue and green enameled details.
(Christie's) $384

A pair of South Staffordshire enamel white ground taper sticks each painted on the stem and shaped circular base with animals and figures in landscapes, circa 1765, 6½in. high.
(Christie's) $3,168

A 19th century Viennese enamel bellied spouted jug and cover, painted with reserves of classical figures, insects and flowers within cartouche panels, 9½in. high.
(Christie's S. Ken) $751

A pair of mid-18th century Battersea enamel candlesticks, the blue ground painted en grisaille and reserved with polychrome sprays of birds and flowers, 9½in. high.
(Christie's S. Ken)
(Two) $2,574

A 19th century French enamel and gilt metal mounted box and cover, the pink ground painted with figures in landscapes, 4¾in. wide.
(Christie's S. Ken) $815

A South Staffordshire enamel white ground necessaire of tapering octagonal section, the cover front and back painted with cherubs, circa 1765, 2¾in. high.
(Christie's) $1,188

A bell push in Fabergé style, the white guilloché enamel body with gold and silver gilt mounts and set with a sapphire and demantoid garnets, apparently unmarked, 5cm.
(Lawrence Fine Art) $3,388

A novelty fan in the form of a pistol, as the trigger is pulled the barrel opens to reveal a fan, 10in., circa 1885.
(Christie's S. Ken) $1,863

A fan lacquered in various tones of gold on both sides with pheasant and flowering plants, the guardsticks decorated with shibayama work, 9in., Japanese, late 19th century.
(Christie's S. Ken) $4,382

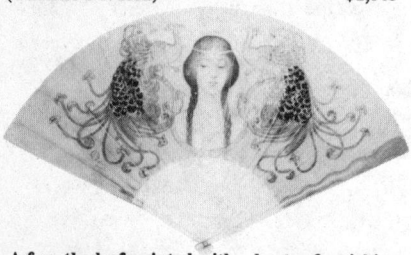

A fan, the leaf painted with a buste of a girl in medieval dress flanked by two peacocks embroidered with blue sequins, signed *G. Darcy*, 10½in., circa 1900.
(Christie's S. Ken) $1,534

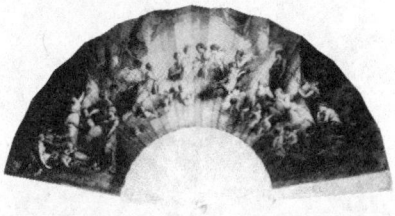

A fine fan, the leaf painted with nymphs and putti, signed in red *J. Calamatta 1870* verso signed *Alexandre*, the mother of pearl sticks finely carved and pierced.
(Christie's S. Ken) $8,906

The Twentieth birthday of Le Grand Dauphin, a rare unmounted fan leaf painted in bodycolor with Louis XIV, seated beside the Queen, Marie Therese, 11in. x 21in., French, circa 1681.
(Christie's S. Ken) $20,240

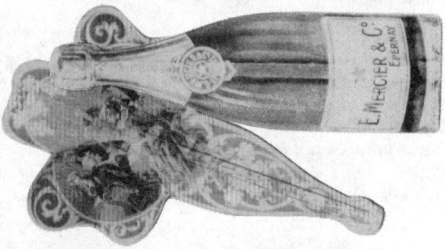


E. Mercier, a chromolithographic menu fan in the shape of a champagne bottle opening twice, first to reveal a menu, secondly to reveal a handscreen, published by Chambrelant, circa 1910.
(Christie's S. Ken) $607

A fan, the silk leaf painted with children in 18th century dress dancing to insect musicians, signed *E. de Beaumont*, 11in., circa 1865.
(Christie's S. Ken) $930

Exposition Universelle 1855, a lithographic fan on paper published by Briade, with wooden sticks, 10½in., 1855.
(Christie's S. Ken) $1,972

**The Royal Family of Great Britain, a lithographic fan on paper for which Duvelleroy won a silver medal in 1849, 11in., in Duvelleroy box.**
**(Christie's S. Ken) $1,271**

**A fine fan, the leaf painted with an elegant lady and putti fishing, signed M. Rodigue, the ivory sticks carved, pierced and painted with putti, 14in., circa 1890.**
**(Christie's S. Ken) $2,429**

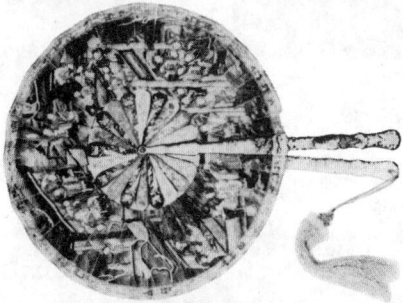

**A Canton cockade fan, the leaf painted with figures, with ivory faces and silk clothes, the verso painted with flowers and birds, 16in. diameter including handle, circa 1840.**
**(Christie's S. Ken) $2,429**

**An early 18th century Flemish fan, portraying the scene of Jupiter appearing in a shower of gold coins to Danae reclining on a cushion, 28cm. long, circa 1720.**
**(Phillips) $1,415**

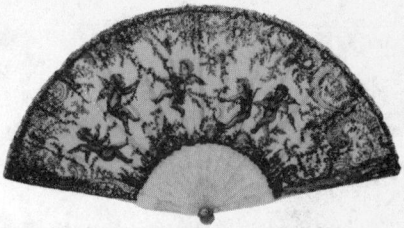

**A lace fan, the Chantilly lace leaf worked with putti and flowers, the blonde tortoiseshell sticks carved and pierced with putti, 13in., circa 1885, in box by Tiffany & Co., London.**
**(Christie's S. Ken) $2,429**

**A fine fan, the leaf painted with The Birth of Venus in bright colors, the verso painted with sprigs of flowers and fruit, with ivory sticks, 10in., Italian, circa 1690.**
**(Christie's S. Ken) $5,060**

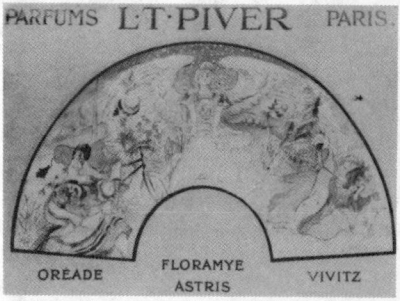


**A design for a fanleaf by A. Willette, with an allegorical scene with France Ancient and other figures, 1906, the mount an advertisement for L.T. Piver.**
**(Christie's S. Ken) $283**

**He shoots the Hippopotamus with bullets made of platinum [Belloc], an unmounted fan leaf painted on silk by John Kettlewell, 10in. x 21in., circa 1918.**
**(Christie's S. Ken) $1,214**

# FILM MEMORABILIA

**An illustrated handbill advertising the Maid of the Mist Steamboat ..., signed *Marilyn Monroe* in blue ink, 1952, 4 x 6in.**
**(Christie's S. Ken) $2,528**

**A pair of leather-soled black suede side-lacing stage-shoes worn by Laurence Olivier in the late 1940's, and worn by him in productions at The Old Vic Theatre.**
**(Christie's S. Ken) $1,159**

**A Ketubbah/Jewish marriage contract, inscribed with the bride and groom's names Arthur Miller and Marilyn Monroe, the secular date July 1, 1956.**
**(Christie's S. Ken) $13,692**

**A shirt of cream silk woven with purple stripes worn by Rudolph Valentino as Ahmed – The Sheik in the early scenes of his last film, The Son of the Sheik, United Artists, 1926.**
**(Christie's S. Ken) $8,426**

**A worn black leather wallet, stamped inside with gilt lettering *James Dean*, made by Rolfs, 7 x 4in., accompanied by an affidavit confirming the provenance.**
**(Christie's S. Ken) $10,533**

**A 1950s bathing outfit comprising a one-piece bathing suit in black cotton decorated with P.V.C. polka dots, with handwritten labels stitched inside, inscribed *M. Monroe*, designed for the film There's No Business Like Show Business, Twentieth Century Fox, 1954.**
**(Christie's) $22,110**

**A black chiffon cocktail dress, made by Chanel accompanied by a still of Delphine Seyrig wearing the dress in the 1961 film Last Year in Marienbad.**
**(Christie's S. Ken) $674**

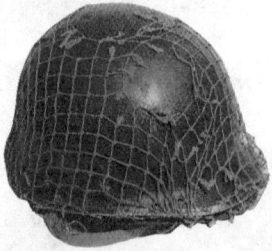

**An American G.I.'s World War II combat helmet initialed inside R.G.; a unit list from the film Yanks, and a still of Richard Gere wearing a similar helmet.**
**(Christie's S. Ken) $674**

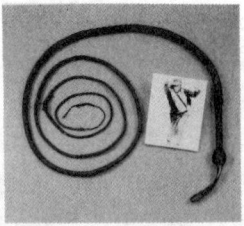

**A hand-made sixteen-plait bull-whip of kangaroo hide with 106in. long lash – used by Harrison Ford as Indiana Jones in all three Stephen Spielberg/ George Lucas adventure films.**
**(Christie's S. Ken) $23,172**

**A head and shoulders publicity photograph, signed and inscribed on margin *Best Always! Stan Laurel and Oliver Hardy*, 8 x 10in.**
**(Christie's S. Ken) $1,011**

**A head and shoulders publicity photograph, circa 1956, signed and inscribed by subject *To Charles, Marilyn Monroe*, 10 x 8in.**
**(Christie's S. Ken) $5,898**

**A publicity photograph of Vivien Leigh as Scarlett O'Hara, signed by subject, and an illustrated Atlanta, première programme for Gone With The Wind, 1939.**
**(Christie's S. Ken) $843**

**A rare full-length photograph on board R.M.S. 'Queen Elizabeth', signed on margin *Stan Laurel and Oliver Hardy*, 4¾ x 3¾in.**
**(Christie's S. Ken) $295**

**A three-quarter length portrait still of subject in the 1941 film Manpower, signed *Marlene Dietrich* in blue ink, 9½ x 7½in.**
**(Christie's S. Ken) $463**

**Cher, signed 8" x 10", three quarter length standing, as Rusty Dennis from 'Mask', apparently obtained in person at a London Hotel.**
**(T. Vennett-Smith) $57**

**Charlie Chaplin, a head and shoulders portrait photograph, signed and inscribed *Yours Sincerely Charlie Chaplin* 19-41, 9¾ x 7¾in.**
**(Christie's S. Ken) $400**

**A film still from Star Trek III, The Search For Spock, signed and inscribed by four members of the production including *Gene Roddenberry, Harve Bennett* and *Leonard Nimoy*, 9 x 12in.**
**(Christie's) $332**

**A head and shoulders publicity photograph, circa 1956, signed and inscribed by subject in white ink, *To Briget Warmest Regards, Marilyn Monroe*, 10 x 8in.**
**(Christie's S. Ken) $4,634**

**Joan Crawford, signed color postcard, three quarter length.**
**(T. Vennett-Smith) $42**

**Shirley Temple, signed 8" x 10", three quarter length with, but not signed by, Victor McLaglen from 'Wee Willie Winkie'.**
**(T. Vennett-Smith) $124**

**Basil Rathbone, signed sepia postcard.**
**(T. Vennett-Smith) $210**

**Charles Boyer, signed color postcard, half length.**
**(T. Vennett-Smith) $38**

**Audrey Hepburn, signed 8" x 10", head and shoulders from 'My Fair Lady'.**
**(T. Vennett-Smith) $86**

**Ingrid Bergman, signed postcard, Picturegoer No. W161.**
**(T. Vennett-Smith) $124**

**Boris Karloff, signed 8" x 10", head and shoulders, slight creasing.**
**(T. Vennett-Smith) $191**

**Ben Turpin, signed 4.5" x 7.75", head and shoulders in characteristic pose wearing bowler hat.**
**(T. Vennett-Smith) $936**

**David Niven, signed 7" x 5", head and shoulders, in later years.**
**(T. Vennett-Smith) $57**

Mae West, signed 8" x 10", head and shoulders, modern reproduction signed in later years.
(T. Vennett-Smith) $76

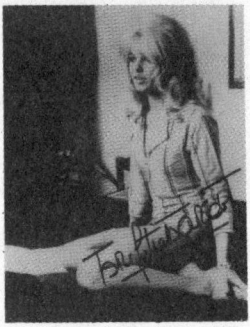

Brigitte Bardot, signed 8" x 10", full length seated wearing shirt.
(T. Vennett-Smith) $90

Montgomery Clift, good signed 8" x 10", head and shoulders, apparently obtained in person at the Connaught Hotel, London.
(T. Vennett-Smith) $477

Mae West, signed postcard, head and shoulders, Picturegoer No. 781, corner crease.
(T. Vennett-Smith) $76

The Three Stooges, signed and inscribed 8" x 10" by Moe, Larry and Shemp, each individually, with first names only, slight corner creasing.
(T. Vennett-Smith) $621

Basil Rathbone, signed postcard, three quarter length holding two small terriers.
(T. Vennett-Smith) $191

Clark Gable, signed and inscribed postcard, head and shoulders.
(T. Vennett-Smith) $344

Rudolph Valentino, signed and inscribed sepia 8" x 10", half length, as Vladimir Dubrovsky from 'The Eagle'.
(T. Vennett-Smith) $859

Vivien Leigh, signed color postcard, half length as Scarlett O'Hara from 'Gone With The Wind'.
(T. Vennett-Smith) $420

**Laurence Olivier, signed postcard, to lower white border, full signature, as Richard III. (T. Vennett-Smith) $107**

**Harold Lloyd, signed and inscribed sepia 3" x 2", head and shoulders. (T. Vennett-Smith) $69**

**Gloria Swanson, signed postcard, Picturegoer No. 128a, early. (T. Vennett-Smith) $46**

**Douglas Fairbanks Snr., signed 6.5" x 8.5", three quarter length standing. (T. Vennett-Smith) $115**

**Laural and Hardy, signed and inscribed sepia 7" x 5", half length, very slight surface crease. (T. Vennett-Smith) $592**

**Anita Ekberg, signed 8" x 10", three quarter length naked, rare in this form. (T. Vennett-Smith) $162**

**Leslie Howard, signed sepia 7" x 5", head and shoulders. (T. Vennett-Smith) $181**

**Gary Cooper, signed 6.5" x 8.5", head and shoulders. (T. Vennett-Smith) $191**

**Betty Grable, signed and inscribed, slight smudging. (T. Vennett-Smith) $82**

**Marlene Dietrich, signed sepia postcard, in green ink, full signature.**
**(T. Vennett-Smith) $105**

**Tyrone Power, signed color postcard.**
**(T. Vennett-Smith) $67**

**Charles Chaplin, signed postcard, to lower white border, head and shoulders, in later years.**
**(T. Vennett-Smith) $181**

**Robert Taylor, signed and inscribed 8" x 10", head and shoulders in military uniform.**
**(T. Vennett-Smith) $115**

**Errol Flynn, signed 7" x 5", half length, slight corner creasing.**
**(T. Vennett-Smith) $325**

**Fred Astaire, signed sepia postcard, head and shoulders in bow tie.**
**(T. Vennett-Smith) $95**

**Edward G. Robinson, good signed and inscribed sepia 8" x 10", head and shoulders smoking pipe, photo by Elmer Fryer of Hollywood.**
**(T. Vennett-Smith) $118**

**William Holden, signed 8" x 10", head and shoulders, four pinholes to white border and corner creasing.**
**(T. Vennett-Smith) $92**

**Ingrid Bergman, signed and inscribed 8" x 10", head and shoulders, modern reproduction signed in later years.**
**(T. Vennett-Smith) $220**

A late 19th century gilt brass and cast iron fire grate, the barred front flanked by square fluted uprights with draped urn surmounts, 37½in. high.
(Christie's S. Ken)
$2,442

A cast iron and steel fire grate, the railed serpentine front above a fret pierced frieze with beaded borders, 32½in. wide
(Christie's S. Ken) $1,730

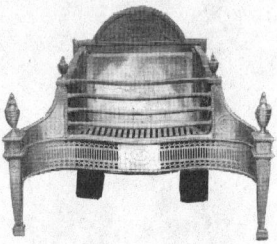

A 19th century engraved brass, steel and cast iron serpentine fronted fire grate, the railed front above a pierced frieze, 36in. wide.
(Christie's S. Ken)
$7,123

A Regency brass-mounted polished steel and cast-iron fire-grate in the style of George Bullock, the basket with turned rails and pyramid finials, 40½in. wide.
(Christie's) $7,128

An Adam style brass and cast iron fire grate, the barred serpentine front above a pierced frieze flanked by square tapering uprights, 28¼in.
(Christie's S. Ken)
$2,035

A Regency cast iron and steel hearth grate, the railed front flanked by scroll jambs, the shaped backplate with raised foliate ornament, 36in. wide.
(Christie's S. Ken)
$1,933

An early George III cast-iron and seamed brass basket grate, with pierced fretwork apron, on turned baluster supports and square bases, 29½in. wide.
(Christie's) $4,792

A Regency cast iron fire grate, with gilt outlined double scroll back, with cable decoration and on paw supports, 96cm. wide.
(Allen & Harris) $3,939

A fine Neo Classical style steel and cast iron serpentine fronted fire grate, the polished and engraved steel façade of waisted outline, surmounted by acanthus chased urns, 43in. wide.
(Christie's S. Ken)
$9,158

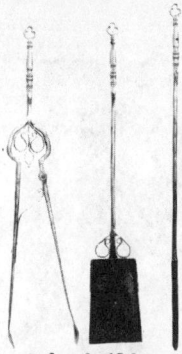

A set of early 18th century English brass and steel fire irons, comprising: poker, shovel and tongs, 62cm. to 66cm. long.
(Phillips) $1,460

A pair of Louis XVI ormolu and bronze chenets with recumbent lions upon draped shaped rectangular plinths with pine-cone finials, 15¾in. wide.
(Christie's) $10,835

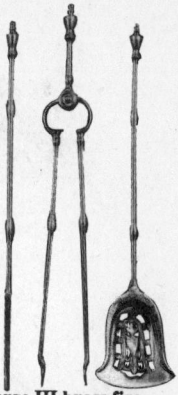

A set of George III brass fire-irons comprising: a pair of tongs, a shovel with engraved pierced pan and a poker, 30in. long.
(Christie's) $7,430

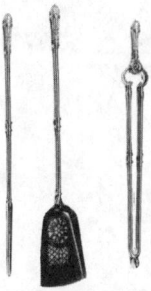

A set of three Regency ormolu and steel fire-irons, comprising: a shovel, a pair of tongs and a poker, 30½in. long.
(Christie's) $2,920

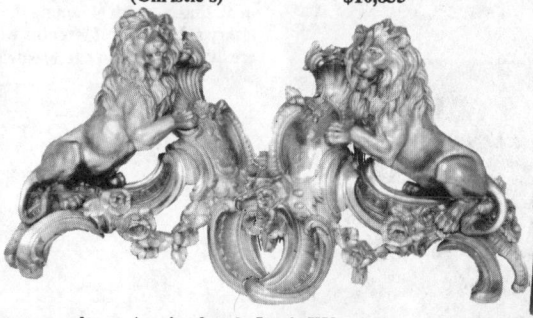

A pair of early Louis XV ormolu chenets of scrolled outline, cast with C- and S-scroll rockwork, supporting a rearing lion, 15in. wide.
(Christie's) $18,700

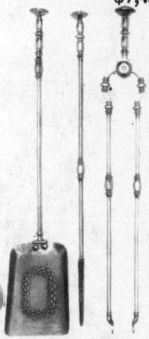

A set of Victorian brass fire-irons each with faceted finial, comprising: tongs, poker and a pierced shovel, 29½in. long.
(Christie's) $2,376

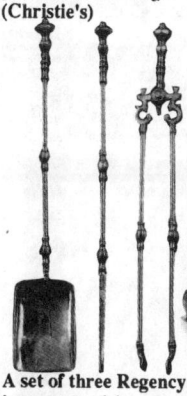

A set of three Regency brass fire-irons comprising: a pair of tongs, a shovel and a poker, each with turned shaft and octagonal finial, 29in. long.
(Christie's) $2,335

A pair of Transitional ormolu chenets, each with a seated dog, probably Iñes and Mimi, the pet dogs of Madame de Pompadour, 9¾in. high.
(Christie's) $8,976

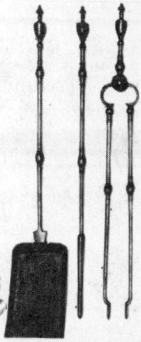

A Harlequin set of George III steel fire-irons, each with engraved vase-shaped finial, comprising: tongs, a poker and a shovel, 30in. long.
(Christie's) $1,386

A George II style pine fire surround, the pedimented shelf above acanthus leaf carved border with plain central tablet, the scrolled jambs carved with flower heads and bell husks, 60in. wide. (Christie's) $814

An 18th century statuary white marble and siena chimney piece, the rectangular breakfront shelf above a plain siena frieze with central tablet carved with an oval medallion depicting a classical female figure, flanked at either side by floral wreaths with ribbon tie crestings, 72in. wide. (Christie's) $40,700

A 19th century variegated white marble fire surround of Louis XVI design, the rectangular breakfront shelf above a frieze carved with foliate arabesques centred by an oval with a monogram of *MA*, 60½in. wide. (Christie's) $6,919

George III siena marble mantle, late 18th century, in Adam style applied with carved white marble urns and swags, 43in. high. (Skinner Inc.) $12,000

A George III jeweled, grained, ebonized and composition chimneypiece, with molded rectangular inverted-breakfront cornice decorated with acanthus above a tablet decorated with an urn flanked by volutes, 78in. x 63in. (Christie's) $3,098

A late Georgian pine and carved walnut mounted chimney piece, the rectangular breakfront shelf above a fluted frieze carved with central tablet supporting a medallion carved with blind Justice flanked by flaming torchères, 68½in. wide. (Christie's) $11,193

An attractive early 19th century cream painted pine and composition fire surround, the shallow overmantel with apex pediment, tongue and groove carved borders, over a frieze with a rectangular panel carved with crossed staffs, 6ft. 10in. wide.(Spencer's) $986

A 19th century pine and gesso fire surround, the rectangular shelf above egg-and-dart and dentiled border with breakfront frieze modeled with foliate scrolls, 73in. wide. (Christie's) $509

A 19th century white marble fire surround, in the French/Grecian style, the rectangular molded shelf above a paneled frieze centered by a medallion of the Goddess Juno hung from bowed ribbons festooned with laurel baguettes and framed by triumphal laurel branches, 76¼in. wide. (Christie's) $6,512

An 18th century white marble chimney piece, the rectangular breakfront shelf above a fluted frieze centered by a tablet carved with an allegory of music, the angles both surmounted by musical figures, above figures and motifs emblematic of Spring, 73¼in. wide. (Christie's) $40,700

A large early 19th century pine and gesso chimney piece, the rectangular breakfront shelf above a central tablet decorated with a figure of Plenty being driven in a chariot, flanked either side by stylized classical urns, 90½in. wide. (Christie's) $1,425

A Regency pine and gesso chimney piece, the rectangular breakfront shelf above an anthemion frieze centered by a tablet depicting Cupid and Psyche, with rosette roundels at the angles above quiver jambs, 70½in. wide. (Christie's) $5,291

**A 14ct. gold engine turned Swan pen with vacumatic filling, inserted ball clip and original No.2 nib, circa 1920.**
**(Christie's S. Ken)** **$880**

**A shagreen Parker desk set with two lapis blue Parker Duofold pens with vulcanite tapers and gold Duofold nibs.**
**(Christie's S. Ken)** **$330**

**A 9ct. engine turned barleycorn design, lever filled Waterman's pen, with ball clip, circa 1920–29.**
**(Christie's S. Ken)** **$770**

**A gold colored Parker 51 with gray nib section, the cap inscribed 18K., in an original retailers box.**
**(Christie's S. Ken)** **$374**

**A lapis blue streamlined Parker Duofold junior pen with two cap bands and ball clip, circa 1927–28.**
**(Christie's S. Ken)** **$198**

**A dark green vacumatic filling Parker 51 with 'Icicle' pink and gold caps inscribed 14K and a matching propeling pencil, circa 1944.**
**(Christie's S. Ken)** **$1,430**

**A mandarin yellow hard rubber Parker Duofold Lucky Curve Senior pen with two narrow cap bands and ball clip, circa 1928–29.**
**(Christie's S. Ken)** **$880**

**A gold filled Hick's 'Detachable' pen, with telescopic barrel fitting into barleycorn decorated casing with ribbon ring, in original box with instructions in the base.**
**(Christie's S. Ken)** **$132**

**Dunhill-Namiki: a Taka Maki-E lacquer pen, decorated with three carp swimming amongst green aquatic plants, signed by the lever, circa 1937.**
**(Bonhams)** **$2,250**

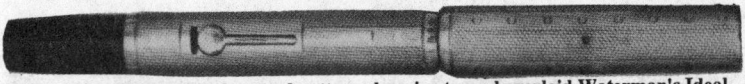

A 9ct. 'barleycorn' panel and spotted patterned engine turned overlaid Waterman's Ideal lever filled pen, circa 1915–29.
(Christie's S. Ken) $704

A sterling silver 'Gothic' design overlaid Waterman's lever filled pen, circa 1926.
(Christie's S. Ken) $286

An emerald pearl Parker vacumatic standard pen and pencil set with three narrow cap bands and original Canadian arrow nib, circa 1933–36.
(Christie's S. Ken) $308

A heavily chased and scrolled sterling silver eyedropper Swan over fed pen, in original presentation box with red velvet lining, circa 1900–1908.
(Christie's S. Ken) $1,210

A sterling silver 'filigree' design overlay eyedropper Waterman's 12 pen, circa 1900–03.
(Christie's S. Ken) $572

A gold filled scrolled and twisted design overlay eyedropper Swan pen with over/under feed nib, circa 1908–12.
(Christie's S. Ken) $1,100

A Pelican self feeding reservoir pen by Thomas de la Rue, hallmarked *London 1897*.
(Bonhams) $10,000

A fine lacquered Dunhill Namiki lever fill pen, with Maki-E design of a Japanese fisherman wearing large hat, carrying rod and bait basket on the barrel, with original Dunhill Namiki no. 20 nib.
(Christie's S. Ken) $4,840

Dunhill Namiki: a gold dust Maki-E lacquer pen, decorated with a small wood surrounding a lake with an erupting volcano in the distance, with 18ct. gold top.
(Bonhams) $1,450

L. & J.G. Stickley davenport bed, circa 1912, no. 285, seat rail slides out opening to a bed, 77in. long.
(Skinner Inc.) $1,600

A rare Napoleon I ormolu-mounted mahogany cradle of slatted boat-shape suspended between two turned uprights, 52in. long.
(Tennants) $13,475

A Biedermeier bird's eye maple and ebony bed with conforming headboard and foot-board each with scrolled top, with boxspring and mattress, the seat-rail with replaced backboard, 86in. wide.
(Christie's) $4,767

A black and gilt-japanned four poster bed decorated overall with chinoiserie scenes, the rectangular canopy pierced with open-fretwork centered by pagodas and hung with black and gilt chinoiserie-pattern silk, 86in. long.
(Christie's) $5,544

An oak tester bed, the canopy with arcaded frieze, the paneled backboard carved with foliage and arcading above foliage-filled lozenges, 17th century and later, 77½in. wide. (Christie's)
$5,792

A mahogany tester bed, the canopy with waved fringe and padded backboard covered in blue floral silk damask with two George III turned stop-fluted front posts, 82in. long.
(Christie's) $2,772

An Arts and Crafts oak crib, the cylindrical barrel type rocking body supported by tall triangular rounded plank ends, 1.27m. high x 1.10m. long.
(Phillips) $545

An Italian baroque giltwood cradle in the form of a shell carved with flowerheads, each end with a putto, one leaning over the edge, the other seated and holding a garland of flowers, probably Roman, early 18th century, 61in. wide.
(Christie's) $17,765

A rare George III oak bed-bureau, the front faced as a sloping fall above four long graduated drawers, with the folding bed enclosed at the back, 27½in. wide.
(Bonhams) $2,470

## BEDS & CRADLES

A Leleu Art Deco three-piece bedroom suite, comprising: a grand lit with arched headboard and two bedside tables, with circular overhanging tops, 191cm. long measurement of bed.
(Christie's) $11,253

A Robert 'Mouseman' Thompson oak double bed, on casters, the paneled adze finished headboard carved with two rosettes and with three grotesque carved terminals, 152cm. wide.
(Christie's) $2,134

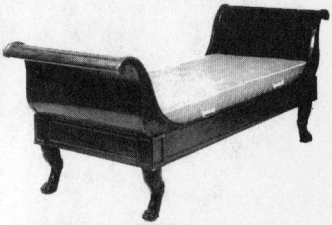

An Empire brass-inlaid mahogany lit-en-bateau banded overall with ebony, the scrolling head and foot-board with paterae, on ebonized lion's paw feet, 103½in. wide.
(Christie's) $10,835

A walnut and parcel-gilt lit en bateau with paneled ends between column angles with bands of foliage and gadrooned ball feet, the shaped concave side edged with ribbon-tied reeding and scrolls carved with laurel foliage, early 19th century, probably German, 82in. long.
(Christie's) $28,050

A grey and blue-painted lit à la polonaise with domed hanging canopy with waved molded rail, centered by flowerheads and foliage and hung with floral chintz, 61in. wide.
(Christie's) $13,090

George III style mahogany tester bed, raised on Marlborough legs, approximate height 94½in.
(Skinner Inc.) $2000

A classical mahogany sleigh bed, New York, 1820–1840, on rectangular molded feet and casters, 60¾in. wide.
(Christie's) $1,870

American maple faux bamboo bed, circa 1880, headboard, footboard, side rails, turned finials, incised details, 72½in. long. (Skinner Inc.) $750

A French mahogany, parquetry and giltmetal mounted bed of Louis XVI design, each end with a pierced laurel floral ribbon-tied cresting, 49in. wide.
(Christie's S. Ken) $3,291

## BOOKCASES

A Regency mahogany breakfront bookcase-on-stand in five sections with molded cornice above four glazed doors, on scroll feet, 111½in. wide. (Christie's S. Ken) $8,866

Renaissance Revival walnut cabinet, third-quarter 19th century, carved broken pediment crest with bust of Shakespeare, 54½in. wide. (Skinner Inc.) $4,500

A mahogany library breakfront bookcase carved with acanthus scrolls and foliate lunette borders, on cabriole legs with claw-and-ball feet, stamped *Gillows*, 91in. wide. (Christie's S. Ken) $9,309

Oak bookcase, 20th century, gallery top, shelf with double keyed tenon over median shelf with single keyed tenons, 28⅛in. wide. (Skinner Inc.) $250

Arts and Crafts bookcase, Jamestown, Ohio, circa 1912, cut out gallery flanked by two cabinet doors, 51½in. wide. (Skinner Inc.) $1,600

A Victorian mahogany bookcase with two glazed doors, two frieze drawers, two paneled doors and on a plinth base, 50in. wide. (Bearne's) $2,452

A Regency mahogany dwarf bookcase, the shaped back above open shelving with two panel doors below, 56½ x 48½in. (Christie's S. Ken) $5,421

An inlaid mahogany bookcase with molded dentil cornice above a pair of astragal glazed doors with inlaid cupboard doors below, late 18th century, 39in. wide. (Christie's S. Ken) $2,130

A mahogany breakfront library bookcase fitment with a molded cornice and enclosed by four glazed doors above four radial paneled doors, 92in. wide, late 18th century and later. (Christie's S. Ken) $9,636

## BOOKCASES

A French green painted pharmacy cupboard, with a pair of cupboard doors painted with book spines between fluted column pilasters, on bun feet, 19th century, 60in. wide.
(Christie's S. Ken) $2,409

A mid-Victorian ormolu-mounted ebony, ebonized, brass and brown tortoiseshell bibliothèque bas inlaid à contre partie, decorated overall with birds and masks, 74in. wide.
(Christie's) $4,702

A George III mahogany bookcase with molded rectangular cornice above two geometrically-glazed doors enclosing three shelves, the lower section with two paneled doors, 49½in. wide.
(Christie's) $10,454

A mahogany breakfront bookcase in six sections with molded cornice above four glazed doors enclosing shelves, each with arched glazing bars, 120in. wide.
(Christie's) $12,870

A Victorian mahogany bookcase, the molded cornice above three pointed arch glazed sliding doors, on a plinth base, 79in. wide.
(Bonhams) $2,483

A late George III mahogany breakfront library bookcase with four astragal-glazed doors, four paneled doors applied with beading and on a plinth base, 105in. wide.
(Bearne's) $5,516

A Victorian walnut and marquetry library bookcase with a cavetto cornice above inverted breakfront with four doors, each inlaid with sprays of flowers, 87in. wide.
(Lawrence Fine Art) $12,360

A George III mahogany breakfront bookcase, the molded cornice decorated with roundels, above six rectilinear astragal glazed doors, 128in. wide.
(Bonhams) $13,370

A fine Victorian burr walnut veneered breakfront library bookcase, the molded cornice above adjustable shelves, 8ft. 4in. wide.
(Woolley & Wallis) $21,257

Federal mahogany veneered inlaid cylinder fall desk, Philadelphia, circa 1800, with six adjustable shelves, 42in. wide. (Skinner Inc.) $3,000

A Regency burr elm-veneered bureau bookcase inlaid with ebonized lines, the triangular pediment applied with gilt brass mounts, 30¼in. wide. (Bearne's) $2,256

Queen Anne walnut double dome secretary bookcase, first quarter 18th century, with carved giltwood finials above a pair of shaped mirrored doors, raised on bun feet, 92½in. high. (Skinner Inc.) $7,250

A Queen Anne walnut bureau bookcase, the fall front enclosing a stepped interior of drawers and pigeonholes around a cupboard door inlaid with a foliate oval, 41in. wide. (Bonhams) $11,863

An unusual Edwardian mahogany inlaid bureau bookcase, the breakfront cornice with checker inlaid frieze. 126cm. wide. (Phillips) $3,298

A walnut bureau cabinet, in three sections, the double dome molded cornice above a pair of arched mirror glazed doors with gilt slips, on bracket feet, 42½in. wide. (Bonhams) $9,168

A walnut bureau bookcase, the double dome upper section with a pair of astragal glazed doors, the fall front enclosing a stepped interior, on bracket feet, 39in. wide. (Bonhams) $5,157

Country Federal grain painted secretary desk, second-quarter 19th century, with faux mahogany grained interior, 39½in. wide. (Skinner Inc.) $6,750

A mid-18th century oak bureau cabinet with two fielded paneled doors enclosing shelves, sloping flap enclosing a cupboard, pigeon holes, drawers and a well, 40in. wide. (Bearne's) $2,554

A small walnut bureau bookcase with a cavetto cornice above a single glazed door enclosing shelves, on bracket feet, 25½ x 74in. high. (Lawrence Fine Art) $18,139

A mahogany bureau cabinet with a twin-arched cavetto molded cornice, twin-candle slides and a pair of fielded doors enclosing pigeon-holes, basically early 18th century, 40½in. wide. (Christie's S. Ken) $15,959

An early 19th century 'plum pudding' mahogany cylinder bureau bookcase, on slender ring-turned legs, 30in. wide. (Bearne's) $9,212

A mid-18th century mahogany bureau cabinet with dentil-molded broken pediment, two paneled doors and a sloping flap enclosing a fitted interior, 44½in. wide. (Bearne's) $5,925

A late 18th/early 19th century Dutch walnut bureau display cabinet of small size with canted sides, the upper part with floral carved platform cresting and fitted with carved laurel gilt serpentine shelves, 4ft. 11in. wide. (Phillips) $7,009

A Finnish oak bureau-cabinet with scrolling broken pediment cresting above a pair of paneled cupboard doors, above two paneled short drawers, the sloping flap enclosing a fitted interior with tiered drawers, mid 18th century, 47in. wide. (Christie's) $12,569

A Queen Anne walnut, crossbanded and feather strung bureau cabinet of small size, the upper part with a molded cornice, fitted with adjustable shelves and enclosed by a pair of arched beveled plates, 3ft. wide. (Phillips) $19,470

Chippendale cherry desk and bookcase, Connecticut, late 18th century, refinished, replaced brasses, 36¼in. wide. (Skinner Inc.) $2,500

An Italian walnut and parcel-gilt bureau-cabinet, the cornice with broken pediment centered by a mirrored cresting, above two mirrored doors enclosing two shelves, 52in. wide. (Christie's) $14,086

## BUREAUX

Chippendale mahogany carved block front desk, North Shore, Massachusetts, 1770–90, old refinish, replaced brasses, 40¾in. wide.
(Skinner Inc.) $14,000

Chippendale carved serpentine mahogany slant lid desk, North Shore Massachusetts, 1785–1800, the prospect door with mirror and fan carving, 42in. wide.
(Skinner Inc.) $13,000

A late George III oak bureau with rectangular top and sloping fall front above four graduated long drawers, on later feet, 36in. wide.
(Christie's S. Ken) $1,548

A George III mahogany bureau, with four long graduated drawers, on ogee bracket feet, 36½in. wide.
(Bonhams) $2,865

An early Georgian walnut bureau inlaid overall with featherbanding with rectangular top and hinged flap with reading ledge enclosing a fitted interior with walnut drawer-linings, 26in. wide.
(Christie's) $11,484

A Japanese Export ebonized and marquetry cylinder bureau, last quarter 19th century, with a rectangular molded cornice above a superstructure fitted with pigeonholes, 45¾in. wide.
(Christie's East) $9,900

A Dutch walnut, burr walnut and marquetry bureau inlaid overall with scrolling foliage and flowerheads, the rectangular top and hinged flap enclosing a fitted interior with slide, the reverse inlaid with dice, a candle and a pipe, 52in. wide.
(Christie's) $20,587

A Louis XV lacquered brass-mounted kingwood bureau, the rectangular top and waved quarter-veneered flap enclosing a fitted interior with slide and secret drawers, 35in. wide.
(Christie's) $4,767

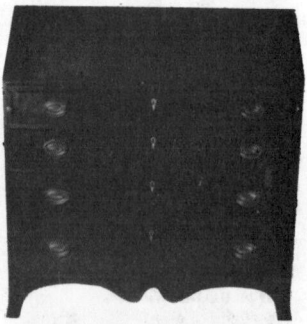

Federal cherry inlaid slant lid desk, New England, circa 1800, the interior of small drawers and valanced compartments, 40in. wide.
(Skinner Inc.) $2,200

A North Italian walnut, ebonized and bone-inlaid bureau, with rectangular top and hinged flap inlaid with an oval of Leda and the Swan, enclosing a fitted interior with slide, 47in. wide. (Christie's) $21,670

A brass-mounted mahogany bureau à cylindre, the rectangular white-marble top with three-quarter gallery above two drawers and fitted interior with slide above one long drawer, 26in. wide. (Christie's) $7,585

A Veneto olivewood and ebonized bureau with rectangular top and hinged flap enclosing a fitted interior with slide, above three bowfronted graduated long drawers, mid-18th century, possibly Friulano, 49in. wide. (Christie's) $39,006

An 18th century Italian walnut crossbanded and strung bureau, the sloping fall opening to reveal a fitted interior with open center part, on scrolled bracket feet, 4ft. wide. (Phillips) $18,496

An 18th century South German walnut crossbanded fruitwood and burr maple veneered bureau cabinet, the projecting concave fronted lower part containing three long drawers, on later bracket feet, 4ft. 4in. wide. (Phillips) $15,576

A William and Mary walnut and seaweed marquetry bureau-on-stand with rectangular top and hinged flap enclosing a fitted interior, 30½in. wide. (Christie's) $16,088

A Milanese walnut bureau, banded overall with tulipwood, with stepped rectangular top with a drawer above a hinged flap enclosing a fitted interior, on shaped bracket feet, 46in. wide. (Christie's) $54,175

A Victorian walnut-veneered and marquetry lady's bureau inlaid throughout with foliate arabesques and applied with gilt brass mounts, 34½in. wide. (Bearne's) $4,801

A South German walnut, fruitwood and marquetry bureau, the rectangular top and waved flap inlaid with rosebuds, enclosing a fitted interior above two graduated long serpentine drawers, mid 18th century, 44in. wide. (Christie's) $17,336

## BUREAUX

A George III mahogany bureau, the fitted interior inlaid with narrow checkered lines and the front fitted with four long graduated drawers, 36in. wide. (Lawrence Fine Art) $3,094

A walnut and feather-banded bureau with rectangular top and hinged slope above a fitted interior with three graduated drawers below, on later bun feet, early 18th century, 39in. wide. (Christie's S. Ken) $5,541

A walnut bureau, the hinged flap enclosing a fitted interior with drawers and pigeon-holes above four long graduated drawers, on bracket feet, early 18th century, 36in. wide. (Christie's S. Ken) $5,541

A Dutch walnut and floral marquetry bombé bureau, the hinged sloping flap enclosing a fitted interior and well above three long drawers, on splayed bracket feet with sabots, late 18th century, 44½in. wide. (Christie's S. Ken) $14,851

Italian baroque walnut slant front desk, early 18th century, fall front opening to three drawers and a compartment, on turned legs, 33in. wide. (Skinner Inc.) $1,800

An early 19th century mahogany bureau, the fall front enclosing an interior of drawers and pigeonholes around a removable cupboard inlaid with leafy ovals, 40¼in. wide. (Bonhams) $1,815

A Dutch marquetry bombé cylinder bureau, the cylinder opening in conjunction with a pull-out slide revealing fitted interior, 40in. wide. (Lawrence Fine Art) $13,231

Chippendale mahogany carved slant lid desk, Massachusetts, 18th century, refinished, old brasses, 41¾in. wide. (Skinner Inc.) $4,750

A walnut bureau, the hinged sloping flap enclosing a fitted interior above four long graduated drawers on bracket feet, 36in. wide. (Christie's S. Ken) $1,807

## BUREAUX

Chippendale cherry slant top desk, Norwich-Colchester, Connecticut area, 1760–1800, replaced brasses, 41¼in. wide.
(Skinner Inc.) $2,800

A William and Mary stained burr-elm bureau attributed to Coxed and Woster, inlaid overall with pewter lines and crossbanded with kingwood, on bracket feet, 26in. wide.
(Christie's) $15,246

Chippendale birch slant lid desk, New England, circa 1800, the interior of small drawers and valanced compartments, 41½in. wide.
(Skinner Inc.) $1,600

Anglo/Indian calamander tambour cylinder desk, first quarter 19th century, tambour top enclosing a fitted interior above a leather lined writing surface, 41¼in. wide.
(Skinner Inc.) $6,000

A French Second Empire tulipwood, marquetry and gilt metal-mounted cylinder bureau of Louis XVI design, the cylinder door inlaid with a musical trophy, on square tapering legs with gilt sabots, 51½in. wide.
(Christie's S. Ken) $7,758

A George III mahogany bureau with sloping flap enclosing drawers and pigeon holes, four graduated long drawers below, 30in. wide.
(Bearne's) $2,444

A mid George III mahogany bureau, the hinged slope enclosing a fitted interior above four graduated drawers, 39in. wide.
(Christie's S. Ken) $2,610

Dutch Neoclassical walnut and marquetry cylinder bureau, second quarter 19th century, scalloped apron on square tapering supports, 34½in. wide.
(Butterfield & Butterfield) $3,025

A George III mahogany bureau, the fall front inlaid with chevron banding, with four long graduated drawers below, on ogee bracket feet, 38½in. wide.
(Bonhams) $2,865

## CABINETS

Napoleon III boulle side cabinet, third quarter 19th century, base with serpentine apron and block feet, with floral and mask ormolu mounts throughout, 60½in. wide.
(Skinner Inc.) $2,400

A black japanned, brass-mounted and gilt chinoiserie decorated double-domed cabinet-on-chest of Queen Anne design, on bun feet, 49½in. wide.
(Christie's S. Ken) $5,541

A Dutch satinwood Wastafel cabinet, the two doors decorated with lacquered panels with chinoiserie scenes, the top lifting to reveal folding shelves, late 19th/early 20th century, 36in. wide. (Lawrence Fine Art) $3,414

A Dutch rosewood and floral marquetry display cabinet of canted outline, the arched upper section with a molded cornice above a pair of glazed doors flanked by glazed panels, on bun feet, late 18th/early 19th century, 59½in. wide.
(Christie's S. Ken) $12,191

A Victorian walnut and marquetry side cabinet applied throughout with gilt brass mounts and inlaid with floral sprays, 76in. wide.
(Bearne's) $8,084

A mahogany dental cabinet by the American Cabinet Co Two Rivers Wisconsin, the upper part with three glazed-door compartments, 40¼in. wide.
(Christie's S. Ken) $1,351

A Regency mahogany side cabinet with pierced Grecian motif brass galleried top above two doors with brass grille panels, 52½in. wide.
(Christie's S. Ken) $2,129

An Art Nouveau music cabinet, in mahogany, the central door with copper plaque embossed with stylized flower and quotation *If music be the food of love play on*, 1.50m. high.
(Phillips) $1,595

Rare classical mahogany veneer artifact cabinet, Boston, circa 1820, upper case with ratchets to receive shelves, lower case has ten graduated pull-out drawers, 44in. wide.
(Skinner Inc.) $3,400

## CABINETS

A Regency design satinwood and gilt decorated side cabinet of broken D-shaped outline with a rosewood banded top above two frieze drawers with grill doors below, 56in. wide.
(Christie's S. Ken) $9,974

An Art Deco coal box attributed to S.S. Henry, of cuboidal form, the front door opening from the top to reveal a metal coal bucket, 80cm. high.
(Phillips) $836

A Chinese hardwood side cabinet with raised sides to the cleated top, on square supports, 84¾in. wide.
(Bearne's) $940

Dutch pine china cabinet, late 18th century, triangular pediment with Greek key frieze, above a pair of glazed cabinet doors, 48in. wide.
(Skinner Inc.) $1,500

A French breakfront contrabuhl side cabinet, the central cupboard door with a raised Classical figure and trophies, 5ft. 2in. wide.
(Woolley & Wallis) $10,724

A mid-19th century amboyna and partridgewood secrétaire display cabinet in the French manner, set with Sèvres-style panels, 24in. wide.
(Bearne's) $6,392

One of a pair of early Victorian pollard oak Elizabethan side cabinets in the manner of Richard Bridgens, each with a strapwork, scroll and dot trellis carved back centered by a rosette, each 64in. wide.
(Christie's S. Ken)
(Two) $4,876

Art Deco bar cabinet, England, circa 1930, manufactured by George Berlin and Sons Ltd, Sureline Furniture, interior with lighted compartment, approximate height 48in.
(Skinner Inc.) $150

One of a pair of Regency mahogany side cabinets, each with a rectangular banded top with brass border above two frieze drawers and brass grill doors, 40in. wide.
(Christie's S. Ken)
(Two) $6,650

## CABINETS

A George III mahogany side cabinet with eared rectangular breakfront top above one long central cedar-lined drawer, on turned feet, 62in. wide.
(Christie's) $58,080

A French walnut cabinet à deux corps, inset with black-veined marble tablets, in two sections, carved with Leda and the Swan and Diana and a stag, second half 16th century, 40in. wide.
(Christie's) $19,305

A Regency brass-inlaid rosewood side cabinet with later white marble top, the frieze with three tablets inlaid with scrolling foliage, on paw feet, 71in. wide.
(Christie's) $11,676

A George III green, black and gold japanned cabinet-on-stand mounted with copper hinges and escutcheons in the Japanese style, decorated with chinoiserie scenes, 38½in. wide.
(Christie's) $46,464

A pair of Louis XV black and gilt-japanned and lacquer encoignures, each with later bowed liver marble top above a bowed door incorporating a Chinese lacquer panel, 28in. wide.
(Christie's) $14,913

A black and gilt-japanned cabinet-on-stand, decorated overall with chinoiserie scenes of birds and figures in a landscape, the stand with chain pattern frieze on cabriole legs, early 18th century, 40½in. wide.
(Christie's) $8,492

A Flemish silver-mounted parcel-gilt, tortoiseshell, ebony, rosewood and marquetry cabinet-on-stand, the scroll broken cresting carved with the Virgin and Child and Saint John, on shaped giltwood feet, 76in. wide.
(Christie's) $121,550

A mid Victorian inlaid walnut credenza with ledged back above a central pair of doors with oval panels of scroll marquetry flanked by column uprights and glazed compartments, 72½in. wide.
(Christie's S. Ken) $10,021

A Portuguese colonial rosewood and bone-inlaid cabinet with rectangular top and fall-front inlaid with foliate scrolls, the sides with carrying-handles, early 18th century, 23½in. wide.
(Christie's) $8,580

## CABINETS

A North Italian cabinet with bone inlay and carrying handles, the ebonized stand with spiral supports, 20in. wide.
(Greenslades) $4,471

A 17th century Flemish ebonized, decorated and tortoiseshell cabinet-on-stand, the interior and reverse of the doors, backs and drawer fronts with paintings, 3ft. 2in. wide.
(Phillips) $20,875

Shibayama style inlaid lacquer shodana, Meiji period, with an upper section of hinged double-doors, decorated to the front with Genso teaching the flute to Yokihi, 37¾in. high.
(Butterfield & Butterfield) $4,675

A pair of ormolu-mounted citronnier side cabinets banded overall in amaranth, each with canted rectangular carrara marble top with pierced three-quarter gallery, 35in. wide.
(Christie's) $22,175

A red and gilt-lacquer cabinet-on-stand, the cabinet decorated overall with chinoiserie figures, buildings and birds in a landscape, on a giltwood stand, 48in. wide.
(Christie's) $10,890

A George III mahogany cabinet banded overall in tulipwood and inlaid with ebonized and boxwood stringing, the bowed top centered by an oval above two bowed doors, 51in. wide.
(Christie's) $17,424

A French Provincial mahogany side cabinet with two paneled doors enclosing a shelf flanked by two narrow paneled doors, 18th century, 50in. wide.
(Christie's) $9,653

Shibayama style inlaid gold lacquer and wood cabinet, Meiji period, carved in high relief with prunus and songbirds, 48in. wide.
(Butterfield & Butterfield) $7,150

A 17th century Milanese ebonized coromandel and ivory inlaid table cabinet, fitted with nine drawers about a central enclosed cupboard with incised and inlaid Classical military figure, fruit, grotesques, flowers and landscapes, 2ft. 1½in. wide.
(Phillips) $8,004

A Regency mahogany four division canterbury, the slatted divisions with curved top rails with two drawers below, 1ft. 5½in.
(Phillips) $3,828

A William IV rosewood canterbury with three C-scroll and leaf carved divisions, on turned legs, brass toes and castors, 21½in.
(Hy. Duke & Son) $1,400

A George IV rosewood canterbury, the rectangular top with four pierced curved rails and one frieze drawer, 19in. wide.
(Christie's) $3,703

A19th century burr walnut canterbury/whatnot, raised on turned columns over a canterbury section set on a drawer set base.
(Michael Newman) $969

A Victorian burr-walnut upright canterbury, the rectangular top with a pierced three-quarter brass gallery and long frieze drawer, 23½in. wide.
(Christie's S. Ken) $1,930

A mid-Victorian walnut canterbury whatnot inlaid overall with boxwood stringing and tulipwood banding, 22in. wide.
(Christie's S. Ken) $3,802

A George IV mahogany four division canterbury, on ring turned tapered legs terminating in brass cappings and castors, 1ft. 6in. wide.
(Phillips) $2,675

A William IV rosewood canterbury the laurel carved four division slatted rectangular top above a base drawer on turned legs, 22in. wide.
(Christie's S. Ken) $3,065

Victorian walnut canterbury, the three section top on turned spindle supports, two drawers to base with brass handles.
(G.A. Key) $735

One of six Hepplewhite period carved mahogany dining chairs, the slightly balloon shaped backs with arched top rails and pierced vase splats.
(Phillips) (Six) $2,725

A pair of 18th century Dutch walnut veneered elm and floral marquetry dining chairs in the Queen Anne style, the balloon shaped backs with mask inlaid top rails.
(Phillips) $2,531

One of a set of six Victorian mahogany dining chairs, the waisted hoop backs with leafy scroll slats on faceted baluster legs.
(Bonhams) (Six) $1,369

One of a set of six mid-Victorian mahogany dining chairs, each with shaped balloon back, on cabriole legs.
(Christie's S. Ken)
(Six) $2,129

A pair of early 19th century Dutch mahogany floral marquetry and brass strung music chairs, with bar top rails and lyre shaped splats.
(Phillips) $1,168

Queen Anne side chair, New Hampshire, circa 1800, original stained surface with later varnish, replaced splint seat, 43½in. high.
(Skinner Inc.) $2,700

One of six Gustav Stickley dining chairs, circa 1907, three horizontal slats, new seats in cream colored leather, 37½in. high.
(Skinner Inc.)
(Six) $3,100

A pair of late Victorian walnut and ebonized hall chairs in the manner of Charles Bevan, each with chamfered toprail.
(Christie's S. Ken)
(Two) $1,065

Chippendale carved mahogany side chair, Philadelphia, 1750–90, old refinish, 39½in. high.
(Skinner Inc.) $130,000

One of a set of nine French ormolu-mounted mahogany dining-chairs, each with pierced rectangular back with lyre-shaped splat, late 19th century. (Christie's)
(Nine) $15,169

One of a set of fourteen early Victorian oak dining chairs, including two open armchairs. (Christie's S. Ken)
(Fourteen) $9,309

One of a set of four Hepplewhite period carved mahogany wheelback chairs, the circular backs with vase-shaped radiating splats with central roundels.
(Phillips) (Four) $1,653

One of a pair of fine early 18th century Chinese carved hardwood dining chairs in the Queen Anne style, the balloon-shaped backs with solid vase splats decorated in relief with interlaced strapwork.
(Phillips)
(Two) $62,640

One of a set of four Italian Empire gray-painted and parcel-gilt side chairs, the toprail carved with anthemia on monopodia legs headed by anthemia, and lotus leaves, on paw feet, first quarter 19th century. (Christie's)
(Four) $19,503

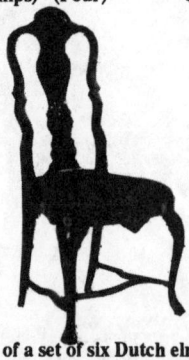

One of a set of six Dutch elm and walnut marquetry dining chairs, each inlaid with a bird perched amongst flowers, the uprights and shaped seat frames inlaid with trailing flowers.
(Bearne's)(Six) $14,100

One of a pair of early George III Irish mahogany dining chairs, the backs with pierced X-centered splats carved with C-scrolls and foliage to the clasped ends of the top rails.
(Phillips) (Two) $1,740

One of a pair of George III mahogany side chairs, each with waved rectangular back and serpentine seat covered in associated 18th century close-nailed gros and petit point needlework. $4,670

One of a set of six George III mahogany dining chairs in the Hepplewhite taste, with shield shaped backs with husks and scrolled end top rails, and two elbow chairs of a later date.
(Phillips)
(Eight) $3,306

## DINING CHAIRS

One of a set of four George IV hall chairs by Gillows of Lancaster, each with cartouche shaped back carved with C-scrolls and centered by a coat-of-arms with a bugle horn.
(Christie's) $5,742
(Four)

One of a set of eight George III rosewood dining chairs, including two armchairs, after a design by George Hepplewhite, the shield-shaped backs carved with husk chains.
(Bonhams) (Eight) $7,258

One of a set of ten mahogany dining-chairs, each with curved paneled horizontal toprail and pierced arcaded splat, on square tapering fluted legs.
(Christie's) (Ten) $9,900

One of a set of six George III mahogany dining-chairs, each with waved toprail and pierced vase-shaped splat, on square chamfered legs joined by stretchers.
(Christie's)
(Six) $6,465

One of a set of sixteen mahogany dining chairs of George II design, the concave arched back with pierced interlaced splat above green leather upholstered seats, on cabriole legs with claw-and-ball feet.
(Christie's S. Ken)
(Sixteen) $38,789

One of a pair of Italian Empire giltwood side chairs, each with paneled toprail carved with foliage and splat in the form of crossed arrows centered by a flowered roundel, on turned tapering legs. (Christie's)
(Two) $6,934

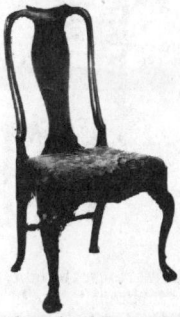

One of a pair of George I carved red walnut dining chairs, the balloon shaped backs with paper scroll crestings and solid vase splats.
(Phillips) (Two) $3,828

One of a pair of George III mahogany dining-chairs, each with arched back and pierced vase-shaped splat with a patera, on square chamfered legs.
(Christie's) $1,683

One of a set of six George III mahogany dining-chairs, each with arched toprail and pierced vase-shaped splat, and an open armchair but of later date.
(Christie's)
(Seven) $8,316

## DINING CHAIRS

Painted decorated child's bowback Windsor side chair, New England, 1790–1810, gold striping on light blue ground, 24¾in. high.
(Skinner Inc.) $1,800

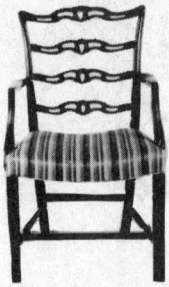

Two of a set of eight George III style mahogany dining chairs, 20th century, raised on molded square legs.
(Skinner Inc.)
(Eight) $1,700

One of a set of six painted and decorated Windsor chairs, Pennsylvania, circa 1835, original light green paint, 33⅝in. high.
(Skinner Inc.)
(Six) $1,900

German walnut Black Forest chair, late 19th century, the shaped upholstered back and circular seat within a naturalistic frame, 37in. high.
(Skinner Inc.) $800

A pair of chairs designed by E.W. Pugin, oak with upholstered seats, the curving back legs continuing to form vertical supports joined at the top by curved back legs.
(Christie's) $5,975

One of two Bruno Mathsson chairs, Sweden, circa 1940, laminated beech with upholstered webbing in brown, 33in. high.
(Skinner Inc.) $650

One of a set of seven William IV mahogany dining chairs, including two with arms, with solid curved cresting rails above turned horizontal splats.
(Lawrence Fine Art)
(Seven) $4,268

Two of a set of fourteen Anglo Colonial William IV hardwood dining chairs, each with a deep arched toprail and shaped center rail above a drop-in seat.
(Christie's S. Ken)
(Fourteen) $8,866

A beech Art Nouveau chair, the horizontal back splat inlaid with three stylized buds, the woven upholstered seat on four legs, with stretchers between.
(Phillips) $228

## DINING CHAIRS

William and Mary banister back side chair, New England, 18th century, dark varnish, replaced splint seat.
(Skinner Inc.) $950

Two of a set of eleven late Victorian oak dining chairs, each with a classical pierced foliate carved cresting above a padded back and seat.
(Christie's S. Ken)
(Eleven) $1,807

A 'Paris' chair, by André Dubreuil, constructed of welded sheet steel, the shield-shaped backrest supported on triangular pillar.
(Christie's) $2,774

One of a pair of Chippendale carved mahogany side chairs, Massachusetts, circa 1790, refinished.
(Skinner Inc.) $500

A pair of Morris & Co. ebonized side chairs, each with turned treble bar top rails and cross splat.
(Christie's) $2,241

Chippendale mahogany carved side chair, probably Delaware, late 18th century, refinished.
(Skinner Inc.) $2,600

Queen Anne carved walnut upholstered side chair, Rhode Island, circa 1750, refinished, worn old leather upholstery.
(Skinner Inc.) $8,500

Two of a set of six Regency simulated rosewood-on-beech dining chairs, the rope-carved rail and inlaid brass tablet backs above cane filled seats, on saber legs.
(Christie's S. Ken)
(Six) $5,098

One of a pair of Dutch walnut side chairs inlaid with birds, urns and foliate marquetry, on cabriole legs with pad feet, 19th century.
(Christie's S. Ken)
(Two) $1,552

One of a pair of mahogany library open armchairs of George III style, each with padded waved rectangular back, on cabriole legs carved with acanthus and claw-and-ball feet. (Christie's) Two $10,890

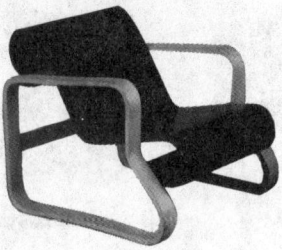

'Piamio', a laminated birch armchair designed by Alvar Aalto, the black painted back and seat formed from a single piece. (Christie's) $3,069

A George III later painted and carved elbow chair, attributable to the workshop of Thomas Chippendale, the oval upholstered panel back with pierced riband and laurel swag cresting. (Phillips) $43,807

A George III carved beechwood open armchair, in the Adam manner, the reeded husk entwined frame with a padded serpentine seat and oval padded back. (Phillips) $13,434

An Empire ormolu-mounted mahogany fauteuil and chaise, each with padded rectangular back and bowed seat covered in patterned close-nailed red silk, on saber legs headed by lotus leaves and paterae on paw feet. (Christie's) $6,501

One of a pair of Venetian giltwood open armchairs, each with padded cartouche-shaped back, the molded frame carved with S-scrolls and centered by rockwork, on cabriole legs, regilt. (Christie's) (Two) $5,634

A Regency mahogany bergère with rectangular padded back, on square tapering legs and brass caps, partially rerailed; and another en suite of later date. (Christie's) (Two) $4,752

A Charles X ormolu-mounted mahogany tub bergère, the seat-rail applied with anthemia and stars, on saber legs headed by paterae, later blocks, minor restorations. (Christie's) $1,950

A George II carved walnut open armchair of Gainsborough design, with a stuffover rectangular back and seat, on cabriole legs with pad feet. (Phillips) $11,682

A Regency mahogany tub bergère with curved arched reeded backrail, the padded back and bowed seat covered in close-nailed green velvet.
(Christie's) $4,138

A Carlo Bugatti two-seat sofa, the vellum-covered rectangular backrest painted with bamboo and arabic script and decorated with a beaten copper circular medallion, with tassel fringe.
(Christie's) $5,729

A Regency rosewood library open armchair, on X-frame support and brass caps, one cap stamped *COPES PATENT*, lacking reading stand.
(Christie's) $2,200

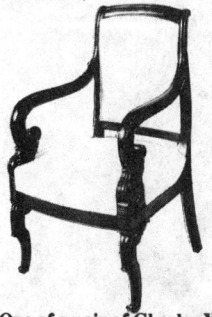

One of a pair of Charles X mahogany fauteuils, each with carved paneled toprail, the arms with scrolled anthemia-supports, on saber legs headed by lotus leaves.
(Christie's)
(Two) $6,068

One of a pair of Regency white painted and parcel gilt bergère chairs in the manner of Morel and Hughes, the curved top rails with fluted guilloche ornament with acanthus leaf and rosette terminals.
(Phillips)
(Two) $31,152

One of a set of four George III cream painted and parcel gilt armchairs, in the Louis XV manner, on cabriole legs with leaf carved feet.
(Bonhams)
(Four) $10,950

An Empire mahogany and parcel-gilt bergère, the sides decorated with anthemia, on square tapering legs headed by Roman masks, on paw feet, lacking mounts, possibly North European.
(Christie's) $15,169

A Queen Anne carved walnut wing armchair with stuffover back, outswept padded scroll arm supports and bowed seat, on cabriole legs.
(Phillips) $13,629

A Regency brass-mounted mahogany library open armchair with scrolled cane-filled back, on turned legs and ribbed brass caps.
(Christie's) $5,445

## EASY CHAIRS

A mid-George III mahogany and blue upholstered Gainsborough armchair with an arched upholstered back, outswept arms and square molded legs joined by stretchers.
(Christie's S. Ken) $3,814

A mahogany wing armchair of Queen Anne design, the back, scrolling arms and seat upholstered in figured pink damask, on cabriole legs.
(Christie's S. Ken) $1,606

George III mahogany library chair, third quarter 18th century, blind fret and floral carved arms, raised on blind fret-carved square legs.
(Skinner Inc.) $600

A giltwood easy chair with a padded outscrolled back and scroll arms with foliate carved terminals trailing to bellflowers, late 19th century.
(Christie's S. Ken) $2,106

Empire style mahogany bergere, 19th century, raised on stylized cabriole legs, ending in hoof feet and casters.
(Skinner Inc.) $2,000

Louis XV beechwood fauteuil, mid 18th century, carved serpentine seat rail, raised on molded cabriole legs, 36½in. high.
(Skinner Inc.) $1,700

Italian Renaissance Revival walnut throne chair, signed *L. Frullini, Firenze*, third quarter 19th century, with scrolling acanthus and dragons, 64in. high.
(Skinner Inc.) $5,000

A George IV mahogany bergère, the arms carved with anthemia, on ring turned tapering legs headed by paterae and brass caps.
(Christie's) $1,960

A George III mahogany open armchair in the French taste, with padded cartouche-shaped back, scrolled arms and serpentine seat.
(Christie's) $3,267

## EASY CHAIRS

An early Victorian mahogany open armchair, on X-frame supports, with Buckingham Palace inventory mark VR BP No 361 1866.
(Christie's) $4,356

Art Nouveau upholstered armchair, possibly Karpin Furniture co., early 20th century, carved fruitwood frame, 37½in. high.
(Skinner Inc.) $700

Federal mahogany lolling chair, New England, circa 1800, with molded arms and legs, old surface, 42in. high.
(Skinner Inc.) $5,100

A walnut wing armchair of Queen Anne design, scrolling arms and seat upholstered in figured brocade, on cabriole legs with pad feet.
(Christie's S. Ken) $3,325

A Maurice Dufrene giltwood bedroom chair, the arched back with wreath motif continuing into reeded decoration on arms.
(Christie's) $858

A Carlo Bugatti ebonized and rosewood corner chair, the arched toprail on three turned columns with beaten brass panels and elaborate fringe.
(Christie's) $2,660

A Neoclassical blue and gilt-painted open armchair with striped upholstery, the rectangular padded back with a toprail carved with bellflowers, circa 1800.
(Christie's S. Ken) $1,995

A 'Napoleon' chair, made by the firm of Aldam Heaton, the upholstered rounded angular back-rest with low scroll leg support.
(Christie's) $7,256

A George IV simulated rosewood bergère, the scrolled rectangular padded back, arms and squab seat covered in red cotton, the arms with anthemion terminals.
(Christie's) $3,049

## EASY CHAIRS

One of a pair of Empire mahogany fauteuils with rectangular padded backs, the downwardly curving arms with reeded and floral carved decoration.
(Phillips) (Two) $3,115

A gilt-silver and green-painted grotto rocking chair with back and seat in the form of a scallop shell, with scrolling dolphin arms, supported by seahorses riding on the backs of sea serpents.(Christie's) $4,501

One of a pair of Louis XV style giltwood fauteuils, branded *Jean Mocqué, à Paris*, each with cartouche-shaped over-upholstered back.
(Christie's East) $4,620

One of a matched pair of Louis XV giltwood bergères, each with outward-scrolling channeled arm-terminals and cabriole legs headed by shells, re-gilded, stamped *I. POTHIER*.
(Christie's) $21,505

One of a pair of Louis XVI giltwood fauteuils à la reine, the channeled frame with foliate finials, the arms with scrolled terminals on stop-fluted supports, on turned tapering stop-fluted legs.
(Christie's) $12,155

One of a pair of Louis XVI white-painted fauteuils à la reine, the channeled arms with scrolling terminals on turned tapering fluted legs headed by paterae, each stamped *G. IACOB*.
(Christie's) $9,350

One of a pair of Louis XV beechwood chaises basses en ottomane by Nicolas Heurtaut, the scrolling high backs and shaped seats upholstered in yellow silk velvet.
(Christie's) $29,920

One of a pair of Empire giltwood fauteuils, the toprails carved with halved flowerheads and dolphins above flowerhead and acanthus sprays.
(Christie's) $26,180

One of a pair of George III mahogany open armchairs, on channeled cabriole legs headed by anthemia on scrolled feet, both with repairs to front legs.
(Christie's) $5,544

## EASY CHAIRS

A Russian ormolu-mounted mahogany bergère, the reeded armrests with arched rectangular terminals supported by winged female masks, early 19th century. (Christie's) $63,580

A Venetian giltwood throne chair with padded cartouche-shaped back, the molded frame carved with acanthus, the backrail centered by a vase of pomegranates, 19th century. (Christie's) $4,334

One of a pair of Louis XVI giltwood fauteuils à la reine, the channeled frame carved with oak leaves and acorns, the back with pomegranate finials. (Christie's) $14,960

One of a pair of Louis XVI fauteuils, the molded frame carved with guilloche on turned tapering fluted legs headed by paterae. (Christie's) $14,086

A Louis XVI giltwood tabouret de pieds attributed to Jean-Baptiste-Claude Sené, possibly supplied for royal use at Versailles. (Christie's) $39,270

One of a set of ten Italian ebonized and parcel-gilt armchairs, on square legs with flat stretchers and paw feet, basically 19th century, 60in. high. (Christie's) $35,536

One of a pair of Empire white-painted and parcel-gilt fauteuils, the arms with tapering sphinx-headed supports, the tapering turned legs headed by long leaves, stamped *CRESSENT*. (Christie's) $28,050

One of a set of three Louis XV walnut fauteuils, each with cartouche-shaped back, padded arms and bowed seat covered in close-nailed floral cut-brown velvet. (Christie's) $13,090

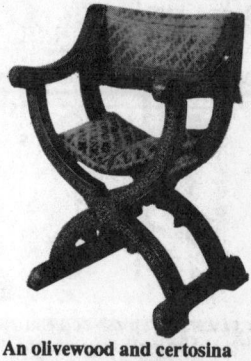

An olivewood and certosina X-frame open armchair, on X-frame supports and block feet, 17th/18th century, possibly Syrian or Hispano-Moresque. (Christie's) $3,034

## ELBOW CHAIRS

One of a set of seven George III carved mahogany dining chairs in the Hepplewhite taste, the slightly balloon shaped backs with trefoil top rails, on molded square tapered legs.
(Phillips) $7,308

One of a pair of walnut fauteuils, the channeled toprail carved with acanthus and rockwork, on cabriole legs headed by cabochon-encrusted rockwork on scrolling feet.
(Christie's) $12,342

One of a matched pair of yew and elm Windsor Gothic open armchairs, with shaped saddle-seat, the cabriole legs joined by bowed stretchers, on pad feet, 18th century.
(Christie's) $5,363

A mahogany open armchair with waved eared toprail centered by rockwork with pierced interlaced splat, on square chamfered fluted legs.
(Christie's) $891

One of a pair of ebonized and parcel-gilt open armchairs each with a double-caned paneled back, the arm supports and saber legs carved in the form of a leopard monopodia with wings.
(Christie's) $5,940

One of a set of ten Hepplewhite period carved mahogany dining chairs, the shaped balloon arched backs with anthemion crestings, and another pair of dining chairs of a later date.
(Phillips)
(Twelve) $34,800

One of a set of ten ash and elm dining-chairs including two open armchairs, on turned legs joined by turned stretchers and pad feet, first half 19th century, Lancashire/Cheshire.
(Christie's) $6,006

A North Italian simulated rosewood and parcel-gilt klismos armchair, on turned reeded tapering legs, first quarter 19th century. $11,594
(Christie's)

A Charles II oak child's chair with rectangular paneled back carved with a lozenge, the solid-seat on turned legs joined by square stretchers, lacking finials.
(Christie's) $8,580

## ELBOW CHAIRS

One of a pair of Regency brass-inlaid open armchairs, each with curved toprail and horizontal splat with ebonized balls, on saber legs.
(Christie's) (Two) $9,801

A Napoleon III rosewood prayer seat with hinged padded back and seat covered in patterned needlework, on X-shaped support.
(Christie's) $1,228

One of a set of eight George III mahogany dining chairs, the backs with horizontal curved bar top rails and horizontal ebony strung splats.
(Phillips) (Eight) $6,090

A Cromwellian oak open armchair, the paneled back with scrolled tablet cresting carved *THOMAS CORBETT 1657* flanked by two lions, on turned legs joined by stretchers.
(Christie's) $6,006

An English walnut open arm chair designed by Sir Edwin Lutyens, on turned legs incorporating the characteristic Lutyens 'Delhi Bell' motif, with stool en suite.
(Christie's) $13,871

A set of ten George III style mahogany 'ribbon back' dining chairs in the manner of Thomas Chippendale, including two armchairs.
(Christie's East)
(Ten) $39,600

One of a set of six Regency mahogany dining-chairs including an open armchair with curved paneled toprail and horizontal splat centered by a tablet flanked by anthemia, and two others of a later date.
(Christie's)
(Eight) $9,504

A Makers of Simple Furniture laminated birch armchair designed by Gerald Summers, cut and shaped to form a curved top rail with central splat and curved arms extending into plank legs. $10,230
(Christie's)

One of a set of fourteen elm ladder back chairs, including three open armchairs, with rush seats on turned legs joined by turned stretchers, late 18th/early 19th century.
(Christie's) $11,798

## ELBOW CHAIRS

One of a set of eight mahogany dining chairs, including two with arms, each with solid cresting rail, seven early 19th century.
(Lawrence Fine Art)
(Eight) $3,841

Painted turned child's high chair, Bergen County, New Jersey, late 18th century, worn old green paint, replaced rush seat.
(Skinner Inc.) $700

L. & J.G. Stickley rocker, circa 1910, no. 837, concave crest rail over four vertical slats, spring cushion seat, 39in. high.
(Skinner Inc.) $475

Twig armchair, 20th century, shaped arms and back comprised of Southern woods, 49in. high.
(Skinner Inc.) $475

A pair of Robert 'Mouseman' Thompson oak armchairs, each with horseshoe arms and back, carved with two cats' heads and shaped terminals, dated 1928.
(Christie's) $3,841

One of a set of six William IV mahogany dining chairs, each with bowed bar toprail and scroll carved horizontal splat, on baluster-turned tapering legs.
(Christie's S. Ken)
(Six) $4,259

A Sheraton painted open armchair, the open back with fluted column uprights, decorated panel top rail and lattice splat, on spiral turned legs.
(Phillips) $1,849

A George III beechwood simulated bamboo cockpen open armchair, the waved rectangular back and arms filled with interlocking ovals.
(Christie's) $3,485

Child's painted sack-back Windsor chair, New England, late 18th century, painted black, 25in. high.
(Skinner Inc.) $400

## ELBOW CHAIRS

Maple folding chair, third-quarter 19th century, beaded and wool worked needlepoint back and seat raised on turned legs.
(Skinner Inc.) $150

Painted ladderback armchair, England or America, 18th century, (significant paint loss and restoration), 48½in. high.
(Skinner Inc.) $175

A George III mahogany 'cockpen' armchair, with chinoiserie fretwork back, on square chamfered legs.
(Bonhams) $973

One of a pair of Biedermeier fruitwood armchairs, second quarter 19th century, with down-curved open arms, raised on saber legs, 37in. high.
(Skinner Inc.)
(Two) $2,300

A pair of red-painted and parcel-gilt open armchairs of Regency style decorated overall with foliage, on turned tapering legs.
(Christie's) $3,703

One of a set of five Regency mahogany dining chairs including one open armchair, on ring-turned tapering legs.
(Christie's S. Ken) $1,839

L. & J.G. Stickley fixed back armchair, Fayetteville, New York, circa 1910, no. 438, four horizontal back slats, 24½in. high.
(Skinner Inc.) $700

Child's painted and decorated settee, America, circa 1840, light green ground with green and yellow pinstriping and pink roses, 24¾in. wide.
(Skinner Inc.) $1,300

A William IV mahogany bergère with deep bowed caned paneled back and downswept arms terminating in scrolls.
(Christie's S. Ken) $1,646

## CHESTS OF DRAWERS

A George III mahogany serpentine chest with a molded top containing two short and three long drawers between blind fret angles, 3ft. 11in. wide. (Phillips) $4,867

Gustav Stickley six-drawer chest, circa 1907, no. 902, reverse V splashboard, two half-drawers over four graduated drawers, signed with red decal, 52½in. high. (Skinner Inc.) $4,250

A George III mahogany chest, the top with a molded edge, containing a brushing slide and four graduated drawers, on bracket feet, 3ft. (Phillips) $2,531

Federal mahogany inlaid bureau, Middle Atlantic States, 1795–1810, old surface, replaced brasses, 44½in. wide. (Skinner Inc.) $4,250

A Queen Anne walnut chest of two short and three long drawers, with quartered top inlaid with feather bands, on bracket feet, 39½in. wide. (Lawrence Fine Art) $3,948

Federal mahogany inlaid butler's desk, probably Middle Atlantic States, circa 1800, refinished, brasses replaced, 42in. wide. (Skinner Inc.) $1,700

A mahogany serpentine chest of four long drawers, surmounted by a slide, the top with a molded edge and on bracket feet, 19th century, 41½in. wide. (Lawrence Fine Art) $4,268

A mahogany semainier inlaid with urns, birds and foliate marquetry in the Dutch taste, fitted with seven long graduated drawers, on plinth base stamped *Maple & Co.*, 27in. wide. (Christie's S. Ken) $6,206

A George I walnut bachelor's chest with a hinged rectangular top with re-entrant corners, the interior quarter veneered, 3ft. wide. (Phillips) $8,177

## CHESTS OF DRAWERS

**Federal maple with bird's-eye maple and mahogany veneer chest of drawers, New Hampshire, circa 1800, brasses probably original, 42¼in. wide. (Skinner Inc.) $1,000**

**A Robert 'Mouseman' Thompson oak chest of drawers, the rectangular, molded and chamfered top above two short and three long drawers, 91.5cm. wide. (Christie's) $2,251**

**Birch chest of drawers, New England, circa 1800, refinished, original brass pulls, 36in. wide. (Skinner Inc.) $2,000**

**Federal mahogany veneered inlaid bureau, New England, circa 1810, drawer front cross-banded in curly maple, 39½in. wide. (Skinner Inc.) $1,300**

**A Dutch walnut and marquetry small bombé chest of three long drawers with waved edge to the top, shell apron and ball and claw feet, 34in. wide. (Lawrence Fine Art) $7,469**

**Painted pine blanket chest, New England, circa 1750, old red paint, replaced brasses, 38¾in. wide. (Skinner Inc.) $1,500**

**Federal mahogany veneered bowfront bureau, Pennsylvania, early 19th century, replaced brasses, signed on back *W.H. Spangler, Ephrata. Pa.*, 42in. wide. (Skinner Inc.) $1,600**

**An Aesthetic Movement burr-maple chest of drawers, the rectangular top above two short and four long drawers with ebonized stringing, 96cm. wide. (Christie's) $2,251**

**Federal mahogany veneer and cherry inlaid bowfront bureau, Connecticut River Valley, circa 1800, 41in. wide. (Skinner Inc.) $3,500**

## CHESTS OF DRAWERS

A Federal inlaid and flame birch veneered mahogany chest of drawers, Portsmouth, New Hampshire, 1790–1810, the rectangular top with bowed front edged with crossbanding and stringing, on French feet, 40in. wide.
(Christie's) $27,500

A Queen Anne walnut high chest of drawers, Pennsylvania, 1740–1760, the upper section with coved cornice above three short and three long thumb-molded drawers, 41½in. wide.
(Christie's) $16,500

A fine Chippendale carved mahogany block front chest of drawers, Massachusetts, 1760–1780, with four graduated long drawers over conforming base molding above a shell-carved pendant, on ogee bracket feet, 37⅜in. wide.
(Christie's) $22,000

A black and gold-japanned chest decorated overall with chinoiserie figures, birds and landscapes, on bracket feet, basically early 18th century, 38in. wide.
(Christie's) $3,861

The important Gilbert family matching Queen Anne walnut high chest of drawers and dressing table, Salem, Massachusetts, 1750–1770, on cabriole legs with pad feet, 38in. wide. (Christie's) $165,000

A fine Chippendale mahogany reverse serpentine chest of drawers, Massachusetts, 1760–1780, with four graduated long drawers with cockbead surrounds over a conforming base molding, on ogee bracket feet, 37in. wide. $20,900
(Christie's)

A fine George III mahogany serpentine chest, containing four long cockbeaded drawers, having a shaped apron, on slender splayed feet, 4ft. 6in. wide. (Phillips) $14,200

A fine Shaker maple cupboard with chest of drawers, Mount Lebanon, New York, mid-19th century, the molded top above a paneled cupboard door opening to a single shelf, 94in. high. (Christie's) $22,000

A Chippendale carved mahogany reverse-serpentine chest of drawers, Massachusetts, 1775–1790, with molded edge reverse-serpentine front above a conforming case, 41in. wide.
(Christie's) $8,250

## CHESTS OF DRAWERS

A George III mahogany serpentine chest, with a slide above two short and four graduated mahogany-lined long drawers on angled bracket feet, 40in. wide.
(Christie's) $10,725

A mahogany chest of American Queen Anne Boston style with molded waved rectangular top, the block front with four graduated long drawers, on cabriole legs and claw-and-ball feet, 32½in. wide.
(Christie's) $5,363

A good late 17th century walnut and burr walnut chest, of mellow golden color, on bracket feet, the drawers retaining some contemporary patterned lining paper, 38¼in. wide.
(Tennants) $7,700

A George III mahogany serpentine chest, the eared top inlaid with chevron banding above four graduated long drawers, on splayed bracket feet, 42½in. wide.
(Christie's) $17,424

A kingwood and tulipwood semainier inlaid with fruitwood lines, the molded D-shaped mottled gray marble top above six short drawers, 12¼in. wide.
(Christie's) $10,285

A mid-Georgian mahogany bachelor's chest with molded folding top above two short and three long drawers, on bracket feet, 33¾in. wide.
(Christie's) $26,136

A mid-Georgian mahogany bachelor's chest, the rectangular molded folding top with re-entrant corners above four graduated drawers, the sides with carrying-handles, 32¾in. wide.
(Christie's) $14,520

A mid-Georgian mahogany upright chest, the rectangular top above two short and four graduated long drawers on bracket feet, 16in. wide.
(Christie's) $22,264

A George III mahogany chest with molded eared serpentine top above a slide and four graduated mahogany-lined drawers, 41in. wide.
(Christie's) $18,419

## CHESTS ON CHESTS

A mid-George III mahogany chest-on-chest with a molded dentil cornice above three short and six graduated long drawers, on bracket feet, 46in. wide.
(Christie's S. Ken) $8,866

A George III mahogany chest on chest with two short and three long drawers, the lower part with a slide above three long drawers, on bracket feet pierced with scrolls, 43in. wide.
(Lawrence Fine Art) $6,068

Maple high chest on frame, Goffstown, Bedford or Henniker, New Hampshire, probably by Major John or Lieutenant Samuel Dunlap, late 18th century, 77½in. high.
(Skinner Inc.) $18,000

Maple tall chest, probably New York state, circa 1800, refinished, replaced brasses, 41¼in. wide.
(Skinner Inc.) $1,900

Spanish walnut vargueno, mid 17th century, with gilt metal mounts and elaborately fitted compartment fitted with various drawers, 41½in. wide.
(Skinner Inc.) $8,000

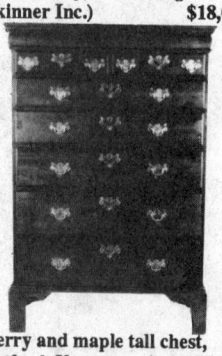

Cherry and maple tall chest, Thetford, Vermont, circa 1800, refinished, replaced brasses, 38¼in. wide.
(Skinner Inc.) $4,000

A George III mahogany chest on chest, the Greek key and blind fret cornice above three short and one long drawer with a double drawer fall front below, on bracket feet, 50in. wide.
(Bonhams) $3,629

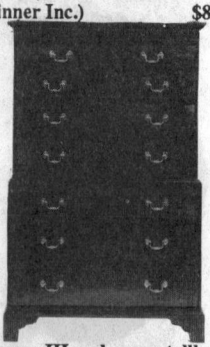

A George III mahogany tallboy, the molded rectangular cornice with Greek key decoration above a blind fretwork molding and two short and three graduated long drawers, on bracket feet, 44in. wide.
(Christie's) $3,564

A George III mahogany chest on chest, the dentil molded cornice above two short and three long graduated drawers, the lower section with three long graduated drawers, on bracket feet, 44in. wide.
(Bonhams) $1,916

## CHESTS ON CHESTS

Chippendale style cherry chest on chest, America, circa 1900, 88½in. high.
(Skinner Inc.) $5,000

A George III mahogany chest on chest, the molded cornice above two short and three long graduated drawers, on splayed feet, 45¾in. wide.
(Bonhams) $1,751

A George III mahogany secretaire tallboy with two short and three graduated long drawers flanked by fluted canted corners, 43½in. wide.
(Bearne's) $3,269

An early 18th century walnut chest on chest, the upper part with a molded cornice above three short and three long graduated drawers between reeded angles, on bracket feet, 3ft. 4in. wide. $15,660
(Phillips)

A mid-18th century mahogany chest-on-chest of small proportions, with two short and two long drawers to the upper section, three graduated long drawers below, 27½in. wide.
(Bearne's) $1,166

A George III mahogany tallboy with dentil cornice, brushing slide and on bracket feet, 41¼in. wide.
(Bearne's) $1,880

A late George III mahogany tallboy with molded and reeded cornice, satinwood-veneered frieze with shell medallions, on shaped bracket feet, 46½in. wide. (Bearne's) $1,354

A George III mahogany chest on chest, the lower section with a brushing slide above three long drawers, 42in. wide.
(Bonhams) $2,334

A mid-18th century mahogany tallboy, with original brass handles and escutcheons, on bracket feet with wood castors, 41½in. wide.
(Bearne's) $2,145

A tortoiseshell and bone-inlaid chest, the rectangular top and sides inlaid with a lozenge-pattern, above five cedar-lined drawers, the central drawer with arched recess, 26¾in. wide. (Christie's) $4,719

A William and Mary walnut and oyster-veneered cabinet-on-stand, banded overall with fruitwood and molded rectangular cornice, above two doors enclosing eleven drawers around a central cupboard, 43in. wide. (Christie's) $34,320

A Spanish walnut vargueno with rectangular top and fall-front applied with red velvet-backed lozenges enclosing a fitted interior, on scrolled block feet, 41¾in. wide. (Christie's) $17,160

A German ebony and ivory-inlaid cabinet-on-stand decorated overall with foliate scrolls, the molded rectangular top above two doors each inlaid with an oval, mid-17th century, possibly Dresden, 35in. wide. (Christie's) $9,752

A Goanese rosewood, teak and bone-inlaid cabinet-on-stand inlaid overall with stars on concentric circles, the cabinet with eight short drawers and two deep short drawers, late 17th century, 36in. wide. (Christie's) $52,008

A Louis XIII ebony cabinet-on-stand in the manner of Jean Mace of Blois, the two doors with roundels carved with scenes depicting the Rape of Europa and the Bull and Venus bathing attended by Diana and her Nymphs, 43in. wide. (Christie's) $10,725

A Venetian cedarwood and penwork cabinet-on-stand with later rectangular hinged top enclosing compartments, above two arcaded doors each with a standing man with a dog, mid-17th century, 20in. wide. (Christie's) $4,290

A Dutch ebony and bone-inlaid cabinet-on-stand with molded rectangular top above two doors with geometrical inlay enclosing a fitted interior with ten paneled drawers around a pillared door, second half 17th century, 36in. wide. (Christie's) $10,402

An Iberian ebonized, painted and gilt cabinet-on-stand of 16th century style, decorated overall with foliate scrolls and groteschi, 19th century, 26¾in. wide. (Christie's) $5,148

## CHIFFONIERS

19th century rosewood chiffonier with satinwood inlay, double glazed doors, and raised gallery top, with mirror, 36in. wide.
(Jacobs & Hunt) $1,275

A Regency rosewood, ebonized and parcel-gilt chiffonier, the raised superstructure with brass three-quarter gallery on column supports, the lower section with galleried rectangular top above a cupboard door, 36in. wide.
(Christie's) $5,940

An Empire carved mahogany chiffonier, the shelved superstructure with foliate scroll crestings and lion mask scroll uprights with flowerheads and foliage, 4ft. 2in. wide.
(Phillips) $6,960

A Louis XV lacquered-brass mounted, rosewood and tulipwood chiffonier with molded rounded rectangular brown and gray mottled marble top above six drawers, 23½in. wide.
(Christie's) $8,235

A pair of Regency mahogany dwarf chiffoniers, the open shelved superstructure with graduated shelves and pierced Vitruvian scrolled cresting and sides, 3ft. wide.
(Phillips) $9,000

One of a pair of George III satinwood open bookcases, one painted with roses, the other with pansies, on square tapering legs and brass caps, restoration to legs, 24in. wide.
(Christie's)
(Two) $61,952

A Shapland and Petter oak sideboard, the rectangular cornice overhanging a central reserve decorated with a copper relief panel of stylized flowers above shelf, 228cm. wide.
(Christie's) $9,207

A George III mahogany bonheur-du-jour, the rectangular top with a tambour-shutter enclosing mahogany-lined drawers and pigeon-holes, on bracket feet, 35¾in. wide.
(Christie's) $3,485

19th century Maltese cupboard with double panel doors and full length drawer, 4ft. 8in. wide.
(Jacobs & Hunt) $975

## COMMODES & POTCUPBOARDS

Chippendale cherry roundabout commode chair, refinished, 32¾in. high.
(Skinner Inc.) $2,000

A pair of Holland and Sons oak bedside cabinets, the chamfered rectangular top above cupboard doors, on chamfered and turned legs with gothic arch aprons, 93.6cm. high.
(Christie's) $1,637

A George III mahogany serpentine-fronted bedside commode, the part-galleried hinged top and paneled sides above a hinged flap enclosing a well, on square legs, 22½in. wide.
(Christie's) $2,574

A George III mahogany converted commode on square legs, 19½in. wide.
(Christie's S. Ken) $703

A matched pair of mahogany bedside cabinets inlaid with ebonized and fruitwood lines, each with square top on square tapering legs joined by an X-framed stretcher, 14in. square.
(Christie's) $3,168

A French walnut bedside cabinet, on square legs and splayed feet joined by a platform under-tier, 16in. wide.
(Christie's S. Ken) $426

A Regency mahogany bowfront three-step commode, each step with leather lining, on ring-turned legs, 17½in. wide.
(Christie's S. Ken) $2,106

Pair of George III mahogany bedside tables, late 18th century, with ebonized stringing, serpentine apron, tapering legs, 20in. high.
(Skinner Inc.) $4,000

A George III mahogany night commode, the rectangular three-quarter galleried top above a pair of doors, on square legs, 21½in. wide.
(Christie's S. Ken) $1,205

## COMMODE CHESTS

A Venetian giltwood commode, the molded serpentine top above one long drawer carved with S-scrolls, the pierced waved frieze carved with rockwork, 49in. wide.
(Christie's) $5,418

Classical Revival mahogany veneer commode, Eastern America, mid 19th century, brasses replaced, 25½in. wide.
(Skinner Inc.) $900

A Continental small walnut commode of three long drawers with molded decorations, on short supports with shells and ball and claw feet, late 18th/19th century, 34½in. wide.
(Lawrence Fine Art) $2,347

A North European Neo-classical giltmetal-mounted mahogany commode inlaid overall with fruitwood and ebonized lines with canted rectangular top above three graduated long drawers, the lower two centered by tablets, late 18th century, possibly Polish, 37in. wide.
(Christie's) $24,921

A pair of North Italian Empire ormolu-mounted bedside commodes, each with associated gray marble top with single frieze drawer above a cupboard door, probably Lombardy, 19in. wide.
(Christie's) $9,968

A Louis XVI ormolu-mounted tulipwood and amaranth commode with rounded rectangular breakfront red and white veined light brown marble top, above three drawers each inlaid with flower-filled entrelac pattern, stamped *N. PETIT*, 52½in. wide.
(Christie's) $26,004

Swedish rococo elmwood and ormolu mounted commode, mid 18th century, the serpentine molded top above bombé case with three drawers, 41½in. wide.
(Skinner Inc.) $8,000

A Louis XVI style ormolu-mounted mahogany marquetry and parquetry commode, circa 1900, after J.H. Riesner, 62in. wide.
(Christie's East) $11,000

A Louis XV walnut serpentine-fronted commode with three long drawers, fluted rounded corners, shaped apron and on short cabriole legs with scroll feet, 48½in. wide.
(Bearne's) $5,640

## COMMODE CHESTS

An ormolu-mounted kingwood, tulipwood, parquetry and marquetry commode in the manner of BVRB, the eared molded serpentine brèche d'alep marble top above two long drawers, late 19th/early 20th century, 61in. wide. (Christie's) $12,791

One of a Harlequin pair of Venetian cream lacquer bombé commodes painted overall with floral sprays and scrolls in pastel shades with simulated marble shaded serpentine tops, 60½in. wide. (Christie's) (Two) $30,338

A Louis XV ormolu-mounted amaranth commode inlaid overall à quatre faces, with eared molded arc-en-arbalette brown fossil marble top above two short and one long drawer, 51½in. wide. (Christie's) $15,169

A Louis XV kingwood bombé commode banded in tulipwood with later serpentine gray and orange fossil marble top, above two long drawers with waved apron mounted with C-scrolls and acanthus, stamped *L BOUDIN JME*, 38½in. wide. (Christie's) $10,835

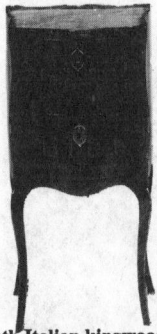

A South Italian kingwood comodino banded overall with tulipwood, the serpentine gray marble top with three-quarter gallery above two paneled drawers between keeled angles, third quarter 18th century, probably Sicilian, 17in. wide. (Christie's) $21,670

A Transitional giltmetal-mounted mahogany, amboyna and fruitwood commode by J. Caumont with molded breakfront mottled gray marble top above three long drawers, stamped *J. CAUMONT*, 35¼in. wide. (Christie's) $11,919

A South German walnut and fruitwood commode, inlaid overall with satinwood lines and scrolls with eared serpentine top above three graduated long drawers with waved apron, mid-18th century, 48½in. wide. (Christie's) $29,255

A Louis XV rosewood and kingwood crossbanded parquetry bombé commode en tombeau surmounted by a molded gray marble top, containing two short and two long drawers, 4ft. 4in. wide. (Phillips) $17,523

A Regency lacquered brass-mounted kingwood bombé commode with associated serpentine liver marble top above two short drawers divided by a concealed drawer above two long drawers, stamped *A CRIAERD JME*, 50in. wide. (Christie's) $18,420

An ormolu-mounted amaranth, parquetry and marquetry commode after J.H. Riesener, with partridgewood panels and inlaid overall with boxwood and ebonized lines, late 19th century, 64½in. wide.
(Christie's) $14,107

A Louis XV style ormolu-mounted tulipwood and kingwood parquetry commode à vantaux, circa 1900, after Antoine Gaudreaux, with a serpentine molded rouge royal marble top, 67¼in. wide.
(Christie's East) $20,900

A fine 18th century Italian carved walnut and tulipwood crossbanded commode of serpentine undulating outline and tapering form, the top with a molded edge and rounded corners, on molded cabriole legs, 4ft. 11in. wide.
(Phillips) $190,806

A Louis XV ormolu-mounted tulipwood and kingwood commode with associated molded serpentine mottled gray marble top above two short and two long drawers, on angled bracket feet, 38½in. wide.
(Christie's) $13,002

A Louis XV style ormolu-mounted kingwood and Vernis Martin meuble d'appui, late 19th century, with a serpentine-molded liver and gray marble top, 43in. wide.
(Christie's East) $4,950

A harewood, mahogany-banded, marquetry and gilt metal-mounted demi-lune commode in the style of Mayhew and Ince, on foliate molded brass feet, 43in. wide.
(Christie's S. Ken) $77,578

An 18th century South German walnut, crossbanded and inlaid commode of undulating outline, the top veneered with two crossbanded squares, having a molded edge, on bun feet, 3ft. 1in. (Phillips) $8,177

A fine Louis XV style ormolu-mounted mahogany and marquetry commode, third quarter 19th century, twice stamped *G. Durand*, with a serpentine breche d'Alep marble top, 34¾in. wide.
(Christie's East) $7,700

An 18th century French Provincial carved fruitwood, walnut and oak bowfront commode of small size, surmounted by a Sicilian jasper molded top, containing three long drawers, 2ft. 10in. wide.
(Phillips) $4,672

## CORNER CUPBOARDS

A red-stained ash corner cupboard, designed by Richard Norman Shaw, with gilt gesso decoration by J. Aldam Heaton, 194cm. high.
(Christie's) $5,548

Walnut inlaid wall cabinet, Chester County area, Pennsylvania, 1720–60, tulip and berry line inlay on drawer front, 24 3/4 in. high.
(Skinner Inc.) $6,000

Empire style ormolu mounted mahogany vitrine, late 19th century, triangular pediment over a glazed door, 32in. wide.
(Skinner Inc.) $2,500

An attractive George III mahogany bow front hanging corner cupboard, with shallow molded cornice over shaped shelves enclosed by a pair of bowed paneled doors, 2ft.2in. wide. (Spencer's) $1,595

A George III mahogany upright corner cabinet, with a molded cornice, the upper part with an arched cupboard enclosed by a pair of fielded panel doors, 9ft. 11in. high.
(Phillips) $2,920

An 18th century Continental tulipwood and purple heart marquetry upright corner cabinet, the upper part with a cavetto cornice fitted with adjustable shelves, having a shaped apron on splayed ogee bracket feet, 3ft. 9in. wide.
(Phillips) $5,841

A George III mahogany corner cupboard in two sections inlaid overall with checkered banding with molded dentil cornice and broken pediment carved with roses, 47in. wide.
(Christie's) $9,900

A Dutch polychrome-painted and parcel-gilt bow-fronted corner cupboard, painted with a kneeling woman offering bread to a group of soldiers, second half 18th century, 45 1/2 in. high.
(Christie's) $1,931

A fine Edwardian mahogany and satinwood inlaid double corner cupboard, the molded overhanging cornice with sunburst frieze, 89cm. wide.
(Phillips) $3,686

## CORNER CUPBOARDS

Painted slant back cupboard, New England, early 19th century, later glass pulls, green paint, 81½in. high.
(Skinner Inc.) $2,900

A George II carved mahogany hanging corner cupboard with swan neck pediment, rosette terminal and dentil cornice, 4ft. 4in. high.
(Phillips) $2,262

A George III mahogany corner cabinet, with flowerhead terminals and dentiled frieze above two paneled doors enclosing a green-painted interior, 37in. wide.
(Christie's) $3,647

George III oak corner cupboard, second half 18th century, with a reeded frieze above two sets of paneled doors flanked by reeded angles, 4ft. 3in. wide.
(Butterfield & Butterfield) $2,750

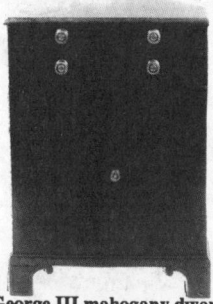

A George III mahogany dwarf corner cabinet, the top with a molded edge with two drawers and a cupboard below, 1ft. 11in. wide.
(Phillips) $3,115

A late 18th/early 19th century Dutch carved mahogany, marquetry and checker strung serpentine upright corner cupboard with canted angles, on ogee bracket feet, 3ft. 7in. wide.
(Phillips) $6,230

Federal cherry glazed inlaid corner cupboard, probably Pennsylvania, early 19th century, refinished, 47in. wide.
(Skinner Inc.) $3,250

A Queen Anne walnut hanging corner cupboard, the broken arched pediment above an arched fielded panel cupboard door, 33in. wide.
(Bonhams) $4,393

An attractive George III mahogany bow front hanging corner cupboard, with swept molded cornice over a frieze inlaid with a stylized swan, 2ft. 8in. wide.
(Spencer's) $1,264

## CUPBOARDS

One of a pair of Louis XV ormolu-mounted amaranth, kingwood and marquetry encoignures by Laurent Rochette, each with molded gray and orange fossil marble top, 35in. wide. (Two)
(Christie's) $12,935

An early Victorian satinwood linen cupboard with molded rectangular inverted breakfront top above two paneled doors, flanked on either side by six mahogany and cedar-lined drawers, 95in. wide.
(Christie's) $6,970

A George III mahogany bow-fronted clothes press, the upper section with arched paneled cresting above two paneled doors, the base with two short and two long mahogany-lined drawers, 50in. wide.
(Christie's) $6,098

A George III mahogany serpentine side cabinet, crossbanded overall in satinwood and inlaid with trails of grapes and vine leaves and with ebonized lines in an interlocking oval pattern, 40½in. wide. $36,784
(Christie's)

A Dutch walnut and marquetry serpentine-fronted corner cabinet, profusely inlaid with vases and baskets of flowers, cherubs and birds perched amongst foliage, 52in. wide.
(Bearne's) $11,656

A George III mahogany side cabinet inlaid overall with a rosewood band, the serpentine top with foliate-inlaid corners and gadrooned edge above a pair of doors, 39in. wide.
(Christie's) $11,616

An Anglo-Indian vizagapatam padouk-wood and engraved ivory clothes-press decorated overall with scrolling foliage and flowerheads, the dentiled cornice with broken pediment, late 18th century, 56in. wide.
(Christie's) $134,354

A Louis XVI ormolu-mounted mahogany side cabinet with canted rectangular white marble top above one long paneled drawer filled with entrelac pattern above two paneled doors mounted with paterae, stamped *G. DESTER*, 49in. wide.
(Christie's) $99,682

An early-Victorian cast-iron-mounted oak gothic clothes-press designed by A.W.N. Pugin, the cabinet-work by Gillows, the metal-work by Hardman and Iliffe, 47½in. wide.
(Christie's) $12,584

## CUPBOARDS

A Welsh oak tridarn of good patination, the top tier on turned supports tied by stretchers, on square section feet, 33in. wide, 17th century.
(Bonhams) $10,654

A Tuscan walnut and brass mounted credenza, enclosed by a pair of panel doors applied all over with cartouche molded panels and brass boss and studded ornament, on bracket feet, 6ft. wide. $7,788
(Phillips)

One of a pair of Regency plum-pudding mahogany cupboards, with gothic arcaded molding, the interior with arched molding and single shelf, on reeded bun feet, 17½in. wide.
(Christie's) (Two) $14,520

A Louis-Philippe maple and marquetry commode, by Georges-Alphonse Jacob Desmalter, with a frieze drawer above a pair of cupboard doors inlaid with Classical scenes, 50½in. wide.
(Bonhams) $4,393

A walnut cabinet with moulded rectangular top inset with a serpentine marble slab, above a paneled door inset with a pietra dura panel inlaid with a flower-vase within an arched niche, the cabinet 17th century, 28in. wide.
(Christie's) $10,835

A James I oak and parquetry press cupboard in two sections, the molded rectangular cornice above a paneled central section flanked by two conforming doors, on carved baluster supports, 37½in. wide.
(Christie's) $7,722

A George III mahogany cellaret, the top with one rectangular well and D-shaped section with spindle gallery, the central divide with carrying handle, 25in. wide. (Christie's) $3,861

A 17th century Yorkshire oak press cupboard on turned bulbous supports, center cupboard with canted sides and marquetry decoration to the panels, 50½in. wide.
(Andrew Hartley) $6,613

A late 18th century North Italian marquetry and crossbanded bedside cabinet, in the manner of Maggiolini, enclosed by a panel door depicting Mercury, 1ft. 9in. wide. (Phillips) $10,850

## DAVENPORTS

A Regency rosewood davenport, the sliding top with tooled leather inset to the sloping flap and a hinged pen and ink side drawer, 19in. wide.
(Bearne's) $3,384

A Regency rosewood davenport with hinged sliding rectangular top with pierced three-quarter gallery and red leather-lined flap enclosing two mahogany-lined drawers, 15½in. wide.
(Christie's) $7,801

A Regency rosewood davenport with a hinged pencil drawer and slide to the side above four drawers with dummy drawers to the reverse, 20in. wide.
(Christie's S. Ken) $4,301

A late Victorian walnut and marquetry davenport, the paneled door to the side enclosing four drawers, on scroll feet, the marquetry panels probably German, late 18th century, 26¼in. wide.
(Christie's S. Ken) $1,525

A mid-Victorian walnut piano top davenport, the rising superstructure with doors and pigeon-holes above a hinged fall enclosing an interior, 23¾in. wide.
(Christie's S. Ken) $4,290

A George IV rosewood davenport, the sliding box top with a spindled baluster three-quarter gallery, on plinth base, 18½in. wide.
(Christie's S. Ken) $3,077

A laburnum davenport with leather-lined slope and fitted interior above a pen drawer and four drawers, 19th century, 21in. wide.
(Christie's S. Ken) $1,070

A William IV carved mahogany davenport of small size, the ratcheted top with inset tooled leather surface and gadrooned edge, 1ft. 8in. wide.
(Phillips) $3,828

A late Victorian ebonized davenport banded in burr walnut, 22in. wide.
(Dreweatt Neate) $1,521

## DAVENPORTS

An early Victorian rosewood davenport, the inset leather-lined sloping flap enclosing a maple lined interior, 19¼in. wide.
(Christie's S. Ken) $1,205

A Victorian walnut davenport, the piano front lifting to reveal a pull-out writing slide with pen and ink recesses, drawers and slope, 23in. wide.
(Lawrence Fine Art) $4,944

Dutch colonial rosewood Davenport desk, first half 19th century, slanted writing surface enclosing a compartment with drawers, 22in. wide.
(Skinner Inc.) $1,000

A William IV rosewood davenport with spindle filled three-quarter gallery, tooled leather inset to the sloping flap, 23½in. wide.
(Bearne's) $1,471

A William IV rosewood davenport, the rectangular sliding box top with a leather-lined hinged sloping flap below a spindled three-quarter gallery, 20½in. wide.
(Christie's S. Ken) $6,776

Victorian walnut davenport, the rising lid serpentine formed having a green leather inset, the back superstructure with three quarter pierced gallery, 23in. wide.
(G.A. Key) $1,793

19th century walnut veneered davenport desk with walnut three-quarter gallery above slope front with fitted interior on 'piano' brackets.
(Michael Newman) £1,000

Victorian walnut and inlaid davenport, fitted stationery box top, four drawers and four opposing dummy drawers, 21in. wide.
(G.A. Key) $3,686

A Victorian walnut davenport with ledge back, rectangular top and hinged leather-lined writing slope inlaid with Classical and foliate motifs, 21in. wide.
(Christie's S. Ken) $968

## DISPLAY CABINETS

A Dutch burr-walnut display-cabinet with arched molded cornice centered by acanthus scrolls and two glazed doors above a bombé base, mid 18th century, 78in. wide.
(Christie's) $19,503

A George III satinwood and marquetry breakfront side cabinet of coffer form in the style of Mayhew and Ince with rectangular stepped top inlaid with a fan oval centered by a bacchic mask, 55in. wide.
(Christie's) $81,312

An Edwardian painted satinwood display cabinet with all-over ribbon-tied trailing floral and bell-flower ornament, on square tapering legs with spade feet, 54½in. wide.
(Christie's S. Ken) $10,021

A Victorian ormolu-mounted amboyna display cabinet with eared rectangular white marble top with molded rosewood rim above a glass-fronted door and sides, 26½in. wide.
(Christie's) $2,455

A fine pair of Regency mahogany dwarf cabinets in the Gillow's manner, banded with satinwood and outlined throughout with boxwood and ebony stringing, 31½in. wide.
(Bearne's) $63,333

An Edwardian satinwood and painted display cabinet inlaid overall with boxwood and ebonized lines, the lower section with one door with an oval painted with a vase of flowers, on splayed bracket feet, 45in. wide.(Christie's) $7,775

An ormolu-mounted kingwood vitrine-cabinet, the stepped top with three-quarter spindle gallery above one long arched glazed door, late 19th century, 50in. wide.
(Christie's) $8,464

A Regency amaranth, satinwood and ebony display cabinet-on-stand, with a glass-fronted door enclosing a shelf, flanked by two paneled doors, 50in. wide.
(Christie's) $9,009

A Dutch oak and marquetry vitrine, the arched molded cornice centered by a later shell, above a pair of rectilinear astragal glazed doors, 75½in. wide, second quarter 18th century.(Bonhams) $13,172

A Edwardian inlaid mahogany display cabinet, the center cupboard with arched door and drawer under, 4ft. wide. (Greenslades) $1,278

A fine quality ebonized and inlaid satinwood and fruitwood display cabinet, raised on square tapering legs, 32½in. x 63in. high. (Anderson & Garland) $3,720

A Louis XVI ormolu-mounted tulipwood and mahogany parquetry vitrine, with a rectangular eared ocher marble top above a frieze, 41½in. wide. (Christie's East) $22,000

A Louis XIV ormolu-mounted boulle and ebony bibliothèque, the molded cornice with egg-and-dart ornament, the frieze with foliage, above a pair of double glazed paneled doors, early 19th century, 61in. wide. (Christie's) $14,025

A Regency Irish brass-inlaid satinwood and ebony side cabinet by J. Dooly & Sons with breakfront D-shaped top with reeded edge above a glazed door enclosing two shelves, 36½in. wide. (Christie's) $14,520

A Chippendale painted poplar corner cupboard, mid-Atlantic States, 1760–1780, the upper part with a molded cornice with canted corners above a pair of arched glazed cupboard doors, 82in. high. (Christie's) $2,640

A Regency brass-mounted rosewood display-cabinet, with pierced arcaded three-quarter gallery above two glazed doors with arcaded glazing bars, 41in. wide. (Christie's) $12,584

A Dutch chestnut bookcase, with broken pediment above a dentil frieze and two glazed doors enclosing shelves, the lower section with two paneled doors, late 18th century, 84½in. high. (Christie's) $8,151

Oak Art Nouveau design display cabinet with two leaded glazed doors with inlaid decoration on shaped supports, 47½in. wide. (Bigwood) $1,365

## DRESSERS

An elaborate Art Nouveau dresser, possibly designed by Gustave Serurrier Bovy, in light oak, the superstructure having a central glass-fronted cupboard flanked by recesses, 206cm. high.
(Phillips) $2,587

A fine George II oak sideboard, the molded rectangular top crossbanded in mahogany, above three similarly banded drawers, 79in. wide.
(Bonhams) $6,198

A Robert 'Mouseman' Thompson oak dresser, the overhanging rectangular top with carved frieze and inscription *J.M.C 1929*, on bracket feet, 169cm. wide.
(Christie's) $1,921

A fine George II oak dresser, the lower section with three frieze drawers above a pair of fielded panel cupboard doors flanking an arched door, 72½in. wide.
(Bonhams) $9,298

A Dutch Art Nouveau dresser by Hoogenstraaten & Voom of Utrecht, the superstructure having two central glass paneled doors flanked by two further angle doors, 180cm. high.
(Phillips) $1,393

A mid-Georgian oak dresser, the cavetto molded cornice above a pierced scroll frieze and three shelf plate rack, on cabriole legs and pad feet, 80½in. wide.
(Bonhams) $3,680

An oak dresser with associated rack, fitted with three geometrically carved drawers on turned legs joined by stretchers, late 17th century, restored, 73in. wide.
(Christie's S. Ken) $4,812

A George III oak Lancashire dresser base crossbanded in mahogany, with a hinged rectangular top over six dummy drawers and three real drawers, 67in. wide.
(Hy Duke & Son) $1,488

Country Federal glazed tiger maple cupboard, Western Pennsylvania or Ohio, 19th century, 45¼in. wide.
(Skinner Inc.) $3,500

## DRESSERS

Pine server, Canada, 18th century, interior with three shelves, refinished, imperfections.
(Skinner Inc.) $950

A mid-Georgian oak dresser, of good color, the molded rectangular top above three frieze drawers and a shaped apron, 75½in. wide.
(Bonhams) $11,235

Louis XV provincial walnut buffet, mid 18th century, the rectangular molded top over two drawers, over a pair of paneled cabinet doors, 54in. wide.
(Skinner Inc.) $2,000

An early 19th century oak dresser with molded cornice, three open shelves, on simple turned supports joined by an undertier, 71in. wide.
(Bearne's) $5,312

An 18th century oak Welsh dresser, the delft rack with shallow swept and stepped molded cornice, over a deep scalloped frieze, 6ft. 8in. wide.
(Spencer's) $8,395

An early 19th century oak dresser with four open shelves, three frieze drawers, triple-arched underframe and on chamfered square supports, 56in. wide.
(Bearne's) $3,102

An Art Nouveau oak dresser, the mirrored superstructure having a crest with two supports, 1.68m. high.
(Phillips) $1,459

A George III pine dresser, the molded cornice above a two shelf plate rack, the lower section with three frieze drawers above a pair of fielded arched panel cupboard doors, 54in. wide.
(Bonhams) $3,099

An Arts and Crafts oak dresser, attributed to Ambrose Heal, the plain sides extending to form the supports, 137cm. wide.
(Lawrence Fine Art) $1,054

## KNEEHOLE DESKS

A Regency mahogany pedestal desk with rectangular leather-lined top and three drawers to each side, on plinth base, 72in. wide.
(Christie's) $8,492

An English walnut corner twin-pedestal writing table designed by Sir Edwin Lutyens, the triangular top with faded red leather writing surface, 96cm. wide.
(Christie's) $29,876

A George III carved rosewood partners pedestal desk, the top with inset tooled leather surface and foliate carved molded edge, on plinth bases, 5ft. wide.
(Phillips) $6,090

A Louis XIV marquetry and ebony bureau mazarin, on later supports, the rectangular top inlaid with a basket of flowers on a dais flanked by birds and butterflies, 4ft. wide.
(Phillips) $33,099

An early Georgian walnut kneehole desk with molded rectangular top above one drawer and six short drawers around a recessed fielded paneled cupboard door 30¾in. wide.
(Christie's) $12,738

A fine Louis XV style kingwood parquetry and ormolu bombé bureau rognon, on outswept legs terminating in cast scrolling sabots, 50in. wide, late 19th century.
(Bonhams) $13,370

A George III mahogany kneehole desk with molded rounded rectangular top above one long drawer fitted with a slide and compartments and six short drawers, on bracket feet, 40in. wide.
(Christie's) $4,356

A Queen Anne walnut knee-hole desk inlaid overall with featherbanding with molded rectangular quarter-veneered top, with one long and six short drawers, 34in. wide.
(Christie's) $9,653

An Italian tulipwood, parcel-gilt, ebonized and ivory-inlaid bureau Mazarin in the style of Luigi Prinotto, banded overall with kingwood, inlaid overall with geometric strapwork and foliage, circa 1730, 52in. wide.
(Christie's) $56,100

## KNEEHOLE DESKS

A Betty Joel kidney-shaped twin-pedestal desk, the top inset with green leather, pierced for a desk light, above two curved frieze drawers with carved scallop handles, 244cm. wide.
(Christie's) $5,122

A North European ormolu-mounted walnut pedestal desk with rounded rectangular balze-lined top, the frieze with one long drawer mounted with griffins flanking a roundel, second quarter 19th century, North European, possibly German or Russian.
(Christie's) $93,500

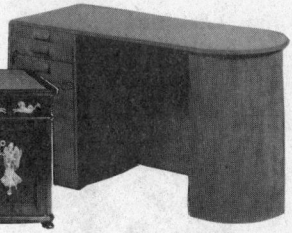

A Makers of Simple Furniture laminated beechwood kneehole desk designed by Gerald Summers, the overhanging rectangular top with D-end, 72.5cm. high.
(Christie's) $921

A George III mahogany pedestal partners' desk, the canted rectangular green leather-lined top with fluted frieze with one long solid-mahogany drawer with compartments, 61in. wide.
(Christie's) $20,168

A Louis XIV premier partie boulle bureau Mazarin, the rectangular top inlaid with dancing figures amid strapwork and foliage after Bérain, on kingwood cabriole legs and foliate sabots, 48in. wide.
(Christie's) $26,180

A Louis XIV contre partie boulle bureau Mazarin, inlaid in pewter, brass, ebony and tortoiseshell, in the manner of André-Charles Boulle, the rectangular overhanging top inset with a panel of tooled leather, 2ft. 7in. high.
(Phillips) $36,540

A Louis XIV giltmetal-mounted rosewood, tortoiseshell and brass-inlaid boulle bureau Mazarin inlaid overall with winged beasts, birds, fruiting vines and scrolling foliage, 48in. wide.
(Christie's) $28,050

A Restauraton mahogany bureau à cylindre with rounded rectangular black fossil marble top with three frieze drawers above the solid cylinder enclosing a bird's-eye maple interior, 58¾in. wide.
(Christie's) $9,101

A Chinese Export black, aubergine and gilt-lacquer kneehole desk decorated overall with chinoiserie landscape scenes, on shaped bracket feet, 43¼in. wide.
(Christie's) $8,276

## LINEN PRESSES

An oak linen press by Edward Barnsley, of plain form and construction, the chest having two long drawers with two short above, 168cm. high.
(Phillips) $2,388

George III mahogany linen press, circa 1800, rectangular cornice over a pair of paneled doors, on bracket feet, 79½in. high.
(Skinner Inc.) $1,100

An early 19th century mahogany linen press with molded cavetto cornice, two crossbanded paneled doors, four graduated long drawers below and on splayed bracket feet, 55in. wide.
(Bearne's) $1,798

A George III mahogany linen press, the oval panel doors with rosewood banding, the lower section with two short and two long drawers, on splayed legs, 48¾in. wide.
(Bonhams) $2,101

A George III mahogany and rosewood banded linen press, the dentil molded cornice above a pair of paneled doors and two short and two graduated long drawers, 49in. wide.
(Christie's S. Ken) $3,657

A Regency mahogany linen press, inlaid overall in boxwood stringing, the lower section with two short and two long drawers, on splayed feet, 49½in. wide.
(Bonhams) $1,910

A mid-George III oak press cupboard with molded cornice above a pair of arched paneled doors, 47in. wide.
(Christie's S. Ken) $1,839

A George III oak clothes press with two doors, each with two fielded panels, two short and two long drawers below, 63½in. wide. (Bearne's) $2,350

A George IV mahogany linen press, the arched scroll carved cornice above a pair of figured arched panel cupboard doors, on spirally lobed feet, 47in. wide.
(Bonhams) $1,815

## LOWBOYS

An early Georgian walnut and oak side table, with two drawers flanking a kneehole drawer, on cabriole legs and pad feet, 32in. wide.
(Christie's) $10,725

An early 18th century oak lowboy, the rectangular top with deep crossbanding, re-entrant corners, with short drawer flanked by two deep short drawers, 2ft. 8in. wide.
(Spencer's) $2,008

A George II 'red walnut' and mahogany lowboy, containing three drawers in the arched apron, on cabriole legs with pad feet, 2ft. 6in. wide.
(Phillips) $7,350

A Georgian oak lowboy, with molded rectangular top above two deep drawers flanking a kneehole drawer, on cabriole legs and pad feet, 30in. wide.
(Christie's) $2,789

A George II mahogany lowboy, the rectangular top with thumb molded edge, a long drawer to the frieze over a shaped scroll apron set with two further small drawers, 2ft. 6in. wide.
(Spencer's) $3,960

A mid Georgian oak lowboy, the molded rectangular top above three drawers around the shaped apron, 33in. wide.
(Bonhams) $1,710

A George I walnut lowboy, the molded rectangular top above three drawers around the shaped apron, on cabriole legs and pad feet, 29½in. wide.
(Bonhams) $2,660

A George II mahogany side table with molded rounded rectangular top above three drawers and waved apron, on cabriole legs headed by acanthus, 29in. wide.
(Christie's) $10,296

A late George I oak lowboy, the crossbanded top above one shallow and two deeper drawers, on square section cabriole legs, 25½in. wide.
(Bonhams) $930

## SCREENS

A Dutch six-leaf painted leather screen decorated with a musician seated before a pagoda, 18th century, each leaf: 22in. x 96½in.
(Christie's) $6,793

A painted leather six-leaf screen, painted by a follower of Pierre Mignard with the Muses of Music, Geometry, Painting, Astronomy, Horology and Poetry, late 17th century, each leaf 21¼in. x 77½in.
(Christie's) $17,765

An Italian pale-green painted and parcel-gilt three-leaf screen, the arched paneled side leaves carved on one side with putto heads headed by a coronet and on the other painted with kneeling angels, assembled in the 19th century, 82in. x 37in.
(Christie's) $4,767

A well painted six-leaf screen, depicting a panoramic view of shrines, castles, temples and village houses around Lake Biwa, in sumi, gofun and color on a gold paper background, early 18th century, each leaf approx. 107 x 46cm.
(Christie's) $21,670

'The Salutation of the Dawn', a painted and gilded screen, by Jessie Bayes, designed in the manner of a medieval manuscript, 54cm. x 68cm.
(Phillips) $2,334

A Louis XVI giltwood fire-screen (écran de cheminée) by Jean-Baptiste-Claude Sené with adjustable screen with a Beauvais tapestry panel, and another en suite of later date with a Louis XVI Beauvais tapestry panel en suite, 30¾in. wide.
(Christie's) $25,245

An Empire ormolu-mounted burr-maple fire-screen (écran de cheminée) with later gros-point floral needlework panel and pierced scrolling cresting, possibly German, 26½in. wide.
(Christie's) $4,675

## SCREENS

A Chinese polychrome-painted four-leaf screen painted with a woman holding swords and posing for an artist at a table, 19th century, each leaf: 25in. wide; 74in. high.
(Christie's) $7,524

A Louis XV style giltwood firescreen, late 19th century, with cartouche-shaped tapestry panel with silver thread ground depicting a peacock, 41¾in. high.
(Christie's East) $1,540

A Chinese black, silver and gilt-lacquer eight-leaf screen decorated on both sides with butterflies amidst bamboo plants, 19th century, each leaf: 83in. x 21¾in.
(Christie's) $10,190

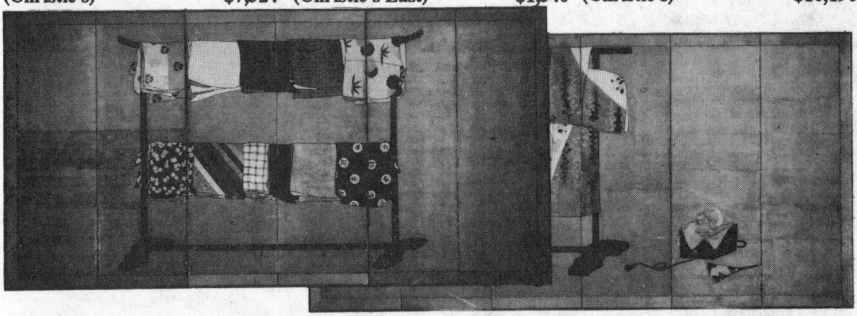

A superb pair of six-leaf screens, painted in sumi, color and gofun on gold painted silk, with Ta ga sode 'Whose sleeves?' motif, one with folded robes on a rack and the other with three robes hung on a rack, unsigned, each leaf 174.3 x approx. 60cm.
(Christie's) $99,682

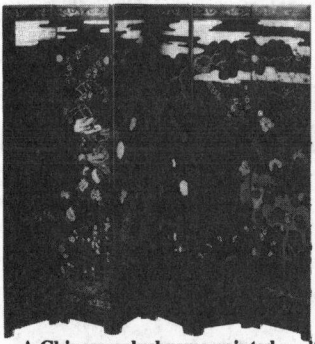

A Chinese polychrome painted six-leaf coromandel screen painted with figures and buildings by the sea and boats in a mountain landscape on a hardwood ground, 19th century, each leaf: 14¼in. x 68½in.
(Christie's) $4,246

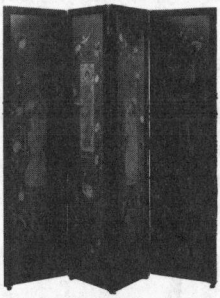

'Song, Drama, Poetry and Music', an English four-leaf embroidered screen, each panel in mahogany frame, embroidered in greens, reds, blues, pinks and yellows against a green ground, 192.9cm. high.
(Christie's) $2,864

A Dutch painted leather six-leaf screen painted in imitation of coromandel lacquer with a palace courtyard with courtiers and other figures, distressed, 18th century, each leaf: 21¼in. x 90in.
(Christie's) $6,793

## SECRETAIRE BOOKCASES

A Regency mahogany secretaire bookcase inlaid overall with ebonized and satinwood lines with domed cornice above two geometrically-glazed doors enclosing three shelves, on splayed bracket feet, 93in. wide. (Christie's) $8,712

A George III brass-inlaid mahogany breakfront bureau-bookcase, with four glazed doors filled with gothic arcading bars and lined with pleated green silk, with Bramah lock. (Christie's) $16,335

A padouk and ebonized secretaire-bookcase, the lower section with fitted secretaire-drawer above three long drawers, on bracket feet, 18th century, 33in. wide. (Christie's) $11,979

Federal cherry and flame birch veneer desk and bookcase, New England, circa 1815, refinished, replaced brasses, 40in. wide. (Skinner Inc.) $3,750

A George IV mahogany secrétaire bookcase, the dentil molded cornice above a pair of astragal glazed doors, the lower half in two sections, on bracket feet, 43in. wide. (Bonhams) $2,008

Federal mahogany glazed desk and bookcase, New England, circa 1810, refinished, brasses old replacements, 40½in. wide. (Skinner Inc.) $2,200

A George III mahogany secrétaire bookcase, the molded dentil cornice with broken pediment centred by a patera, the lower section with fitted secrétaire drawer, on ogee bracket feet, 49½in. wide. (Christie's) $5,346

A George III satinwood secrétaire bookcase banded overall with rosewood and inlaid with boxwood, 37in. wide. (Christie's) $21,780

A Biedermeier cherrywood and ebonized bureau bookcase, the molded rectangular cornice with two obelisk-shaped finials, above two trellis-filled doors, on square tapering legs, first half, 19th century, 47½in. wide. (Christie's) $20,587

## SECRETAIRES

A North German Empire mahogany Schreibschrank, the stepped upper section with a panel cupboard door flanked by rounded corners and turned columns, 43½in. wide, circa 1835. (Bonhams) $5,424

A George III mahogany secrétaire chest with molded rectangular top above a paneled secrétaire drawer enclosing a fitted interior above three graduated long drawers, on bracket feet, 34in. wide. (Christie's) $3,564

A Spanish walnut vargueno in two sections, the iron-bound top section with rectangular top and fall-front enclosing a fitted gilt and arcaded interior of twelve drawers around a cupboard. (Christie's) $23,595

An Italian walnut and marquetry secrétaire à abattant, the frieze drawer above a fall front inlaid with an oval depicting rural figures and goats, 32in. wide, 19th century. (Bonhams) $16,720

A William and Mary walnut secrétaire-on-chest with molded cornice, one long drawer and a fall-front with fitted interior, 42in. wide. (Christie's) $13,943

A Queen Anne burr walnut secrétaire-on-chest with molded rectangular top above one long drawer and fall-front enclosing a fitted interior, 42in. wide. (Christie's) $10,725

A Louis XV amaranth and tulipwood secrétaire à abattant inlaid with boxwood stringing with molded shaped brown fossil marble top above one long drawer and a fall-front enclosing a fitted interior, 37½in. wide. (Christie's) $8,235

A rare late 18th/early 19th century neo-Classical Continental mahogany papier-mâché and ormolu mounted secrétaire à abattant of narrow proportions, 2ft. wide. (Phillips) $26,100

A Louis XVI ormolu-mounted amaranth, kingwood, tulipwood and parquetry secrétaire à abattant by J.G. Schlichtig with canted rectangular bardiglio marble top, inlaid overall with cube pattern, 31in. wide. (Christie's) $14,736

## SETTEES & COUCHES

Classical Revival carved mahogany veneered upholstered sofa, light green silk watered moreen upholstery, 86½in. long.
(Skinner Inc.) $800

Painted and carved country sofa, probably Pennsylvania, 19th century, original olive green paint, 73½in. wide.
(Skinner Inc.) $1,700

Painted and decorated settee, Pennsylvania, early 19th century, all-over light green paint with stencil decoration, 72in. wide.
(Skinner Inc.) $750

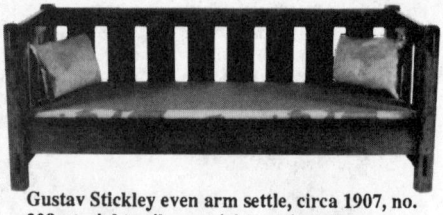

Gustav Stickley even arm settle, circa 1907, no. 208, straight rail over eight vertical slats on back, three on each end, with Southwestern designs, 76in. long.
(Skinner Inc.) $8,500

A Biedermeier satinbirch sofa with pedimented back and side finials, the arms with applied half columns with scroll capitals, mid 19th century.
(Christie's S. Ken) $2,807

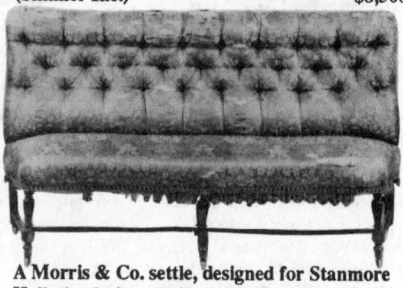

A Morris & Co. settle, designed for Stanmore Hall, the design attributed to George Jack, the rectangular button back and padded seat upholstered with 'flower garden' fabric, 76in. wide.
(Christie's S. Ken) $3,080

Italian Neoclassical fruitwood settee, late 18th century, pierced interlaced gothic back, bowed seat rail, 64in. long.
(Skinner Inc.) $1,700

A William IV rosewood sofa, the scrolled rectangular padded back, arms and seat with two bolsters upholstered in close-nailed red silk damask, on turned tapering legs.
(Christie's) $3,920

## SETTEES & COUCHES

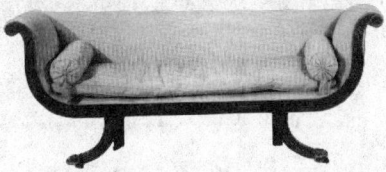

A Regency mahogany and green moire upholstered sofa with a padded back and dual scroll ends above a padded seat, on reeded splayed legs, 86in. wide.
(Christie's S. Ken) $4,876

Federal mahogany sofa, New England, early 19th century, old refinish, 74¼in. long.
(Skinner Inc.) $950

Rococo Revival walnut upholstered settee, third-quarter 19th century, grape vine and floral carved serpentine molded crest rail, raised on cabriole legs, 66in. wide.
(Skinner Inc.) $1,100

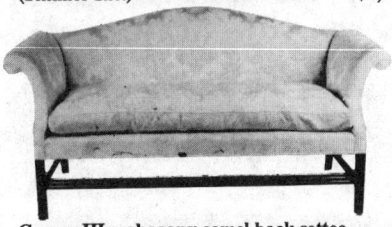

George III mahogany camel back settee, arched upholstered back with scrolled arms over rectangular seat raised on blind fret carved H-form stretcher, 63in. wide.
(Skinner Inc.) $1,700

A George III giltwood sofa, the shaped fluted paddedback, seat and arms covered in pale blue cotton, on fluted square tapering legs, 86in. wide
(Christie's) $3,485

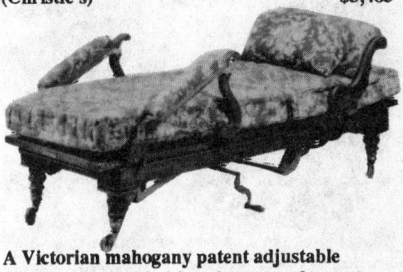

A Victorian mahogany patent adjustable daybed, the double-hinged rectangular seat adjusting by means of a winding handle, 80in. wide.
(Christie's S. Ken) $1,155

A mid Victorian carved walnut button-back sofa with bowed back and serpentine fronted seat between open padded scroll arms on cabriole legs, 65in. wide.
(Christie's S. Ken) $1,065

Federal mahogany sofa, probably New England, circa 1810, refinished, 80in. long.
(Skinner Inc.) $700

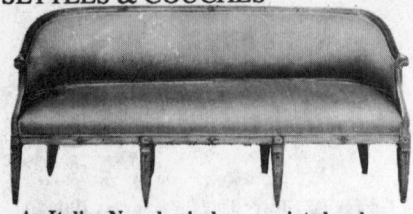

An Italian Neo-classical gray-painted and parcel-gilt canapé, the arms with scrolled terminals and downswept supports, the square tapering fluted legs headed by roundels, circa 1800. (Christie's) $5,236

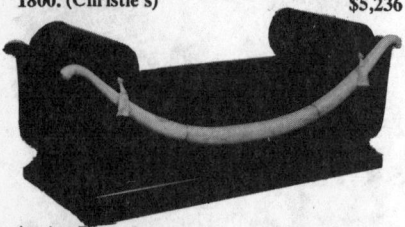

An Art Deco ebony, macassar and vellum covered day bed, the rectangular gondola-shaped form with vellum covered molding on plinth base, with band of bone inlay, 81cm. wide. (Christie's) $10,230

A William and Mary walnut sofa, covered in nailed later turkey work, on faceted baluster legs joined by conforming stretchers, possibly Flemish, 68in. wide. (Christie's) $11,798

An Italian giltwood canapé, the molded frame carved with flowerheads, rockwork and foliate scrolls, mid-18th century, the seat-frame partly reinforced, 77in. wide. (Christie's) $12,155

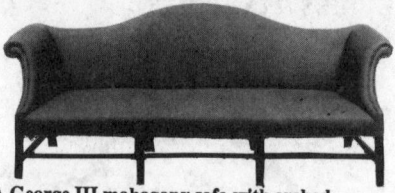

A George III mahogany sofa with arched padded back, on square chamfered legs joined by square stretchers, later blocks, restorations to back legs, 94in. wide. (Christie's) $3,080

A walnut sofa, covered in close-nailed 17th century and later Flemish tapestry, on turned legs joined by turned stretchers, on bun feet, 63in. wide. (Christie's) $6,435

A French walnut sofa, the channeled backrail and seat-rail centered by flowerheads, on cabriole legs, restorations and some replacements, basically mid-18th century and adapted, 42½in. wide. (Christie's) $5,201

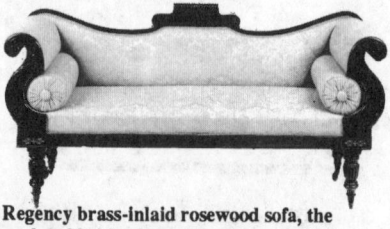

A Regency brass-inlaid rosewood sofa, the waved padded back centered by a scrolled tablet inlaid with paterae, the seat-rail carved with anthemia on turned reeded legs, the back legs plain, 75in. wide. (Christie's) $6,336

## SETTEES & COUCHES

L. & J.G. Stickley prairie settle, Fayetteville, New York, circa 1912, no. 220, wide flat arms and crest rail supported by corbels over inset panels, 84½in. wide.
(Skinner Inc.) $19,000

Federal carved mahogany sofa, possibly New England, circa 1800, refinished, 76in. long.
(Skinner Inc.) $1,200

Lifetime Furniture day bed, Hastings, Michigan, circa 1910, shaped crest rail over nine vertical slats at each end joined by seat and lower rail forming three arches, 77¾in. long.
(Skinner Inc.) $1,800

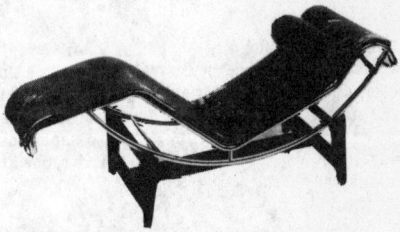

A tubular chromium-plated chaise longue designed by Le Corbusier and Charlotte Perriand, the adjustable seat upholstered in brown and white pony skin, on black painted steel base.
(Christie's) $1,637

Painted and stencil decorated Windsor day bed, New England, circa 1820's, fold-out hinged sleeping area supported by four wooden pinned legs, allover original yellow paint with gold and black fruit and leaf decoration, fold-out, 49½ x 80⅝in.,
(Skinner Inc.) $1,600

A.J. & J. Kohn bentwood two-seater settee, designed by Gustave Siegel, with woven rush seat, the back pierced with an array of arrow motifs, 122cm. wide.
(Phillips) $1,094

Classical mahogany and maple veneer sofa, probably Boston, circa 1815, refinished, 80in. wide.
(Skinner Inc.) $1,800

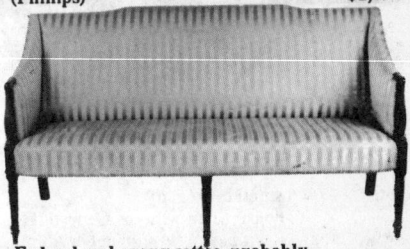

Federal mahogany settee, probably Massachusetts, circa 1810, (blue silk upholstery with water stain) 66½in. wide.
(Skinner Inc.) $5,750

## SIDEBOARDS

A George III mahogany serpentine sideboard, the central bowed drawer flanked by a deep drawer and a cupboard door, on square tapered legs, 73½in. wide.
(Bonhams) $3,890

A late Georgian mahogany serpentine sideboard fitted with a central drawer flanked by two deep drawers, all with kingwood crossbandings, 53in. wide.
(Lawrence Fine Art) $5,228

A Regency mahogany and ebony-strung bowfront sideboard fitted with a central frieze drawer and arched apron drawer flanked by a deep cellaret drawer with lead-lined interior, 62in. wide.
(Christie's S. Ken) $5,320

A Victorian carved mahogany sideboard, the crested back above a rectangular re-entrant top with three frieze drawers and three panel doors below, 65in. wide.
(Christie's S. Ken) $2,130

American Rococo Revival walnut and burl walnut credenza and overmantel mirror, third-quarter 19th century, raised on a plinth base, 59½in. wide.
(Skinner Inc.) $2,300

Lifetime Furniture sideboard, Grand Rapids, Michigan, circa 1910, mirrored backboard, three central drawers flanked by cabinet doors over long lower drawer, 60½in. wide.
(Skinner Inc.) $500

A late Georgian small mahogany sweep front sideboard fitted with a drawer above a tambour cupboard, on six turned supports, 48in. wide.
(Lawrence Fine Art) $4,268

A George III mahogany sideboard inlaid overall with boxwood and ebonized stringing on square tapering legs and block feet, 51in. wide.
(Christie's) $7,623

Rare Gustav Stickley sideboard, circa 1902, the top shelf galleried on three sides, unsigned, 48in. wide.
(Skinner Inc.) $3,500

## SIDEBOARDS

A George III mahogany breakfront sideboard, the rectangular bowed top above central drawer and a recessed drawer flanked by a double drawer and two short drawers, 60in. wide.
(Christie's) $10,890

A George III mahogany and chevron strung sideboard, on square tapering legs with collared feet, now fitted with castors, 4ft. 7in. wide.
(Phillips) $3,309

Federal mahogany veneer sideboard, New York, circa 1800, three inlaid drawers above a central cupboard flanked by bottle drawers and end cupboards, 67½in. wide.
(Skinner Inc.) $8,000

An Anglo-Indian rosewood sideboard, the rectangular center section with pierced backboard centered by an anthemion, flanked by a pair of cellarets of octagonal shape with ribbed lids, circa 1830, 94in. wide.
(Christie's) $2,239

A George III mahogany sideboard with bowfronted rectangular top, inlaid with boxwood and ebonized lines and satinwood fan-shaped paterae, on square tapering legs and spade feet, 42¾in. wide.
(Christie's) $5,148

Gustav Stickley sideboard, circa 1907–12, no. 816, plate rack on rectangular top, long drawer over two central drawers, 48in. wide.
(Skinner Inc.) $1,600

A Regency mahogany breakfront sideboard, on ring turned tapered legs, the whole outlined with ebony cockbeadings, 67in. wide.
(Bonhams) $4,380

A George III mahogany, kingwood crossbanded and inlaid bowfront sideboard of small size, on square tapered legs on ogee arched stringing terminating in spade feet, 4ft. 2in. wide.
(Phillips) $7,788

Federal mahogany veneered inlaid sideboard, Massachusetts, circa 1790, right cupboard door simulated, right end with hinged cupboard door, 67in. wide.
(Skinner Inc.) $7,500

## STANDS

A mahogany kettle stand, with hexagonal solid galleried top, on ring-turned vase-shaped shaft, 20½in. high.
(Christie's) $1,960

George III mahogany library steps, late 18th century, rectangular molded hinged top opening to eight steps, 49½in. high.
(Skinner Inc.) $2,150

A George III mahogany dumb-waiter with three circular graduated tiers, each with waved gallery on tripod base with splayed legs, 48in. high.
(Christie's) $4,138

A Regency mahogany dumb-waiter with three circular tiers, the lower two with drop-leaves on a ring-turned shaft, 21in. diameter.
(Christie's) $3,049

A Carlo Bugatti vellum-covered and pewter inlaid center-piece, the ebonized cross-shaped rotating superstructure inlaid in pewter with oriental motifs, with four end drawers, each with turned handle, 73cm. high.
(Christie's) $7,366

Grain painted candlestand, New England, early 19th century, faux rosewood, 25¼in. high.
(Skinner Inc.) $2,100

One of a pair of Regency mahogany cutlery and plate stands, each with a central carrying handle and white-painted metal-lined interior, each 28in. wide.
(Christie's S. Ken)
(Two) $5,763

A George III walnut wool winder with twin adjustable spools and shaped tray top stand on splayed baluster legs, 23in. wide.
(Christie's S. Ken) $919

A Gallé marquetry tray on stand, inlaid in various fruitwoods with five sailing boats, on carved trestle ends, 78cm. high.
(Christie's) $1,637

## STANDS

Mahogany veneered octagonal tilt top candlestand, Rhode Island, early 19th century, cross banded veneer and cockbeading in outline, 28¾in. high.
(Skinner Inc.) $1,900

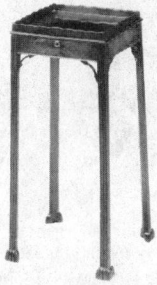

A mahogany urn-stand of George III style, the square top with waved solid gallery, the paneled frieze with candle-stand, 19th/20th century, 11½in. square.
(Christie's) $3,267

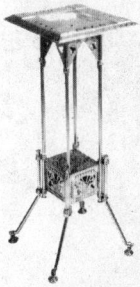

An Aesthetic Movement brass pedestal, the square top with shallow well, supported on triangular brackets and four tubular columns, 82cm. high.
(Christie's) $1,280

A William IV rosewood pedestal teapoy, the telescopic circular molded top enclosing recesses and twin boxed caddies, 21½in. diameter.
(Christie's S. Ken) $1,313

A set of George IV metamorphic mahogany library steps, with four rectangular red leather-lined treads on turned and baluster supports, 36in. wide.
(Christie's) $8,276

A gothic painted wood pedestal, probably designed by the office of William Burges, the square overhanging molded entablature supported on a column with cushion capital, 79cm. high.
(Christie's) $4,268

An early Victorian walnut folio stand with twin-flap with plain bars, on plain end supports and bun feet, 32in. wide x 44in. high, closed.
(Christie's S. Ken)
$5,541

A pair of Regency parcel-gilt and simulated rosewood torchères, on baluster shaft with triple scroll monopodia and concave-sided paneled triangular base, on bun feet, 88in. high.
(Christie's) $11,979

Arts & Crafts umbrella stand, probably Europe, early 20th century, shaped flat sides with spade trailing to circle cut-out, 22in. wide.
(Skinner Inc.) $300

## STOOLS

L. & J.G. Stickley footstool, Syracuse and Fayetteville, New York, circa 1918, no. 397, signed with decal, 20in. wide.
(Skinner Inc.) $475

One of a pair of Regency mahogany foot stools after a design by George Smith, the scrolling sides carved with anthemia on ribbed bun feet, minor restorations, 15¾in. wide.
(Christie's)
(Two) $3,564

An Aesthetic Movement ebonized rectangular chest-stool, decorated front and back with carved gilt emblematic roundels, 89.7cm. wide.
(Christie's) $4,695

A Chippendale period carved mahogany stool with a stuffover needlework seat, on pierced angular chamfered legs with Gothic ogee and pierced fretwork.
(Phillips) $6,425

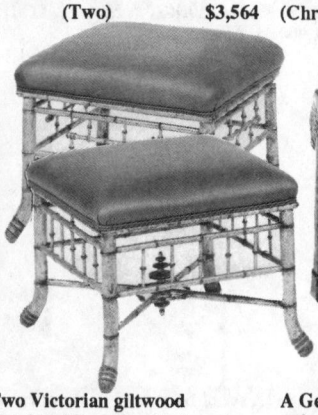

Two Victorian giltwood simulated bamboo stools each with square padded seat covered in green cotton, on turned saber legs joined by X-shaped stretchers, 19in. wide.
(Christie's) $5,940

A George III Gothic cream-painted stool, the waved arcaded seat-rail carved with pigs and pierced with trefoils, on square tapering legs headed by satyr masks, 16in. wide.
(Christie's) $2,673

A mahogany stool, the rectangular padded seat covered in close-nailed floral patterned needlework on eared cabriole legs headed by lion-masks, on paw feet, 26½in. wide.
(Christie's) $6,336

An Italian walnut stool of Renaissance design, the uprights in the form of lion heads joined by foliate carved spiral-turned stretchers, 35½in. wide.
(Christie's S. Ken) $3,990

A Regency white-painted and parcel-gilt stool, on X-framed legs carved with flowerheads and cleft feet joined by a baluster stretcher, 19¾in. wide.
(Christie's) $3,960

## STOOLS

A walnut stool with rectangular seat, the waved frieze carved with acanthus on cabriole legs headed by lion-masks and paw feet, 28in. wide.
(Christie's) $3,366

A Regency mahogany footstool after a design by George Smith, of lotus-carved S-scroll form with reeded rails and on bun feet. (Bearne's) $592

A George III carved mahogany window seat frame, the scroll ends with serpentine front fluted seat rail with oval paterae, on fluted tapered legs.
(Phillips) $5,256

One of a pair of Swedish Gustavian cream-painted and parcel-gilt Neo-classical stools, the seat-rail carved with guilloche pattern, on turned tapering fluted legs headed by paterae, last quarter 18th century, 18in. wide.
(Christie's)
(Two) $3,251

A pair of Queen Anne carved walnut oval stools, on cabriole legs with foliate and flowerhead carved knees terminating in claw and ball feet.
(Phillips) $21,750

A Louis XVI giltwood tabouret, with fluted frieze, the turned tapering stop-fluted legs headed by paterae on toupie feet, 23½in. wide.
(Christie's) $3,467

An oak stool by A.W.N. Pugin, the upholstered square seat on rounded carved 'X'-shaped trestle ends with stylized paw feet.
(Christie's) $1,707

A William IV mahogany music stool on an acanthus carved stem and three leaf capped scroll feet, 20in. high.
(Lawrence Fine Art) $747

A George IV gilt stool, on fluted 'X'-shaped supports with acanthus capitals, tied by a fluted stretcher, 36½in. wide.
(Bonhams) $1,242

## STOOLS

A mahogany stool with rounded rectangular padded seat on cabriole legs carved with acanthus, 19th century, 23in. wide.
(Christie's) $5,519

A Regency mahogany stool, on X-scrolling supports applied with paterae and joined by stretchers, 19in. wide.
(Christie's S. Ken) $693

A Charles I oak joint stool with molded rectangular top on slightly splayed turned spreading legs joined by square stretchers and block feet, 18½in. wide.
(Christie's) $2,789

A George III cream-painted and parcel-gilt stool, the waved channeled seat-rail centered by flowerheads, on cabriole legs headed by flowerheads, 19½in. wide.
(Christie's) $2,335

Victorian music stool, four turned legs and central column, brass claw and glass ball feet.
(G.A. Key) $300

One of a pair of walnut stools each with padded rectangular seat on cabriole legs headed by acanthus on claw-and-ball feet, later blocks, 24in. wide.
(Christie's)
(Two) $9,009

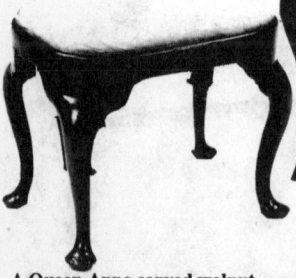

A Queen Anne carved walnut stool, having an arched seat rail, on cabriole legs with C-scroll carved spandrels to the knees.
(Phillips) $4,500

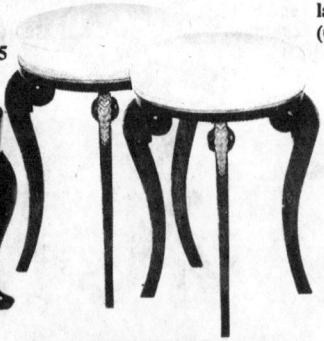

A pair of Regency simulated rosewood circular music stools on splayed legs with overlapping gilt metal ornament and roundels.
(Phillips) $1,914

A Dutch walnut and marquetry window seat, 29½in. wide.
(Dreweatt Neate) $936

## STOOLS

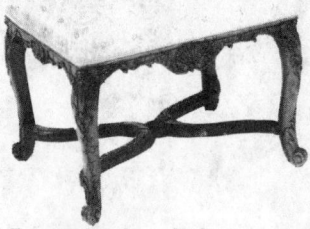

A Regency beechwood tabouret, the waved seat-rail centered with scallop-shells and carved with acanthus, on cabriole legs headed by scrolls and husks, 21in. wide.
(Christie's) $8,976

A classical carved and gilt mahogany piano stool, Baltimore, 1820–1830, on three acanthus-carved and gilt paw feet, 32 7/8in. high.
(Christie's) $2,420

An oak stool, the rectangular top covered in nailed red wool, on spirally-twisted legs joined by conforming stretchers, 28in. wide.
(Christie's) $1,180

A George IV round adjustable music stool with a mahogany frame.
(Dreweatt Neate) $624

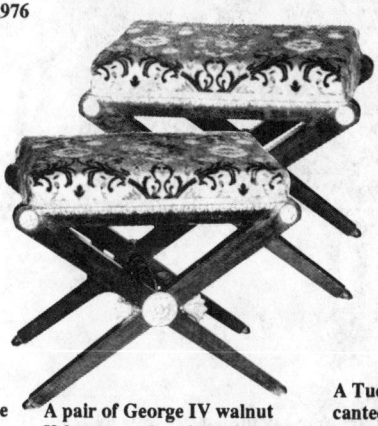

A pair of George IV walnut X frame stools, with brass escutcheons, 23in. x 16 1/2in.
(Dreweatt Neate) $3,705

A Tudor oak stool with later canted rectangular plank seat and waved arcaded apron, on faceted legs joined by arcaded stretchers, legs shortened, mid-16th century, 17 1/2in. wide.
(Christie's) $9,653

A Napoleon III giltwood stool attributed to A.M.E. Fournier, with waved rope-twist apron and conforming legs and stretchers, 21in. diameter.
(Christie's) $6,501

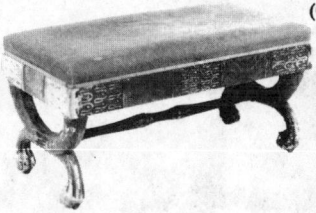

One of a pair of Regency simulated rosewood, simulated bronze and parcel-gilt stools, the seat-rail carved with lotus-leaves, on X-frame end-supports, 35 1/2in. wide.
(Christie's)
(Two) $52,272

A William IV mahogany rectangular stool in the manner of Bullock, 15in. wide.
(Dreweatt Neate) $585

SUITES

**A Victorian parcel-gilt and polychrome-painted gothic suite comprising: a sofa and a pair of open armchairs each with square back, pointed finials and arcaded toprail, on turned legs carved with lotus leaves and ball feet, 74in. wide.**
**(Christie's) $6,138**

**A rare Irish pearwood Art Nouveau three-piece suite by James Hayes, comprising; a two-seat sofa and two side chairs, each upholstered with brown leather, the frames carved with naturalistic forms, the shaped legs with carved feet reminiscent of cloven hooves.**
**(Christie's) $11,253**

**An English Art Deco leather upholstered three-piece suite, the sofa with cloud-shaped arms and back upholstered in gray leather with walnut stringing to arms, 162.5cm. length of sofa.**
**(Christie's) (Three) $7,366**

## SUITES

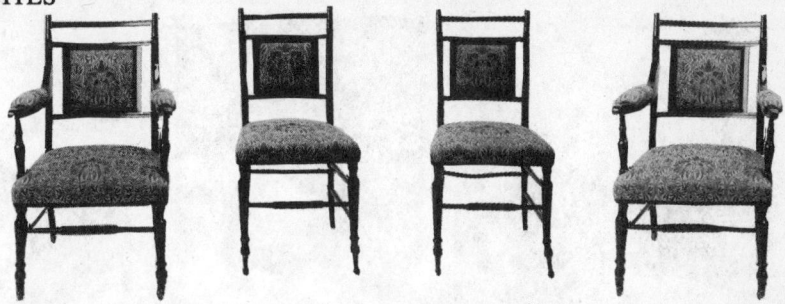

**An Aesthetic movement suite, consisting of four side chairs, two armchairs and a settee, all ebonized, incised with gilt lines and circular floral motifs, with turned front legs.**
**(Phillips)** **$1,592**

**A suite of rootwood furniture formed of links, comprising: a pair of chairs with planked seats and a pedestal table with planked top, late 19th century.**
**(Christie's)** **$7,623**

**An Art Deco three-piece suite, consisting of a three-seater settee with two matching armchairs, the solid wooden rounded geometric frame veneered with walnut, upholstered, with matching cushions, 175cm. long.**
**(Phillips)** **$3,781**

## SUITES

**An Art Deco burr-walnut and satinwood bedroom suite, comprising: a 'Lit Double', a pair of bedside cabinets, a dressing mirror and a wardrobe with overhanging rectangular top.**
**(Christie's) $3,218**

**An Art Deco dining suite, probably Hille, veneered in light walnut, consisting of: a table, a sideboard of geometric form, a small buffet and eight chairs en suite.**
**(Phillips) $8,169**

**Three pieces of Limbert furniture, Grand Rapids, Michigan, circa 1910, open arm rocker, and matching armchair, both with straight crest rail, open-arm settle, with straight crest rail.**
**(Skinner Inc.) (Three) $1,200**

## SUITES

**An Italian three-piece 1950s suite, comprising a chaise-longue and two armchairs, each of curvilinear form, upholstered in dark blue and ivory, on short tapering cylindrical legs, with swivel feet.**
**(Christie's)** **$2,145**

**An Art Deco maple dining room suite, comprising: a dining table, a similar side table, a set of six dining chairs with arched rounded back, a three tiered trolley and a glazed display cabinet.**
**(Christie's S. Ken)** **(Ten)** **$3,465**

**Assembled suite of Edwardian satinwood seat furniture, circa 1900, comprising a settee and two tub chairs, each back and seat caned, raised on square tapered legs, 37in. high.**
**(Skinner Inc.)** **$3,800**

## CARD & TEA TABLES

Classical mahogany and rosewood veneer card table, probably Boston, circa 1815, refinished, 36in. wide.
(Skinner Inc.) $850

Federal mahogany and mahogany veneer inlaid card table, New York, circa 1800, refinished, 35 3/4in. wide.
(Skinner Inc.) $2,600

A Regency kingwood scissor-action tea-table with hinged D-shaped top crossbanded in satinwood on four downward-scrolling legs with brass caps, 36in. wide.
(Christie's) $5,445

A George III mahogany tea table, on foliate headed cabriole legs with pad feet, two spandrels replaced, restorations, 36in. wide.
(Christie's S. Ken)
$1,936

A George II red walnut tea table with circular fold-over top, two quadrant frieze drawers and on shell-carved cabriole legs, 30in. wide.
(Bearne's) $3,269

Federal mahogany and birch veneer card table, Massachusetts or New Hampshire, circa 1800, 35 3/4in. wide.
(Skinner Inc.) $7,000

Late Classical carved mahogany card table, probably New York State, circa 1830, old surface, 36 3/4in. wide.
(Skinner Inc.) $1,100

An Edwardian satinwood-tulipwood-banded and painted D-shaped card table of Sheraton design, the folding baize-lined top painted with a musical trophy and ribbon-tied garlands of summer flowers, on square tapering legs, 36in. wide.
(Christie's S. Ken) $6,206

Classical mahogany carved card table, New England, early 19th century, 35in. wide.
(Skinner Inc.) $425

## CARD & TEA TABLES

One of a pair of Regency rosewood card-tables, each with D-shaped red baize-lined top above a well, on tapering octagonal shaft and concave-sided rectangular platform base, 36in. wide.
(Christie's) Two $4,792

An attractive Edwardian rosewood envelope card table, the square swivel top with four triangular leaves, each inlaid with a neo-Classical urn and foliage, 1ft. 10in. wide.
(Spencer's) $1,584

Classical carved mahogany veneer card table, Middle Atlantic States, circa 1830, some refinish, 36in. wide.
(Skinner Inc.) $1,000

One of a pair of George III painted and satinwood card-tables crossbanded with rosewood and decorated overall with swags of flowers, scrolling foliage and husks, on square tapering legs, 36in. wide.
(Christie's)
(Two) $20,790

An Arts and Crafts inlaid oak card table, attributed to William Birch, the square top with four hinged triangular panels above arched aprons and plank legs, 74.6cm. high.
(Christie's) $1,330

A late Victorian giltwood card table of Adam design with rectangular baize and leather-lined top above a fluted and foliate carved frieze, 38in. wide.
(Christie's S. Ken)
$4,259

An early George III mahogany card table, the baize-lined interior above frieze drawers on club legs, restored, 30in. wide.
(Christie's S. Ken) $1,444

A mahogany and rosewood strung D-shaped card table with a swiveling baize-lined top, on four later fluted column supports and quadripartite platform, first quarter 19th century.
(Christie's S. Ken) $1,884

A George III mahogany card-table with hinged eared serpentine top, the beaded edge carved with paterae, 36in. wide.
(Christie's) $6,534

## CARD & TEA TABLES

A Regency rosewood card-table, the rounded rectangular baize-lined swivel-top inlaid with a band of scrolling foliage on four scrolled downswept legs, 36in. wide.
(Christie's) $5,227

A late Regency rosewood tea table, on four acanthus carved hipped outswept legs, 36in. wide.
(Bonhams) $1,278

A Regency rosewood and brass inlaid card table, on a baluster and lobed column, concave plinth and outswept legs, 36in. wide.
(Bonhams) $2,483

A Regency mahogany crossbanded and inlaid card table, the D-shaped baize lined top banded in amboyna and rosewood, 3ft. wide.
(Phillips) $3,115

A mid-Georgian mahogany card-table with canted rectangular top enclosing a green baize-lined interior with candle-rests, on cabriole legs headed by acanthus, 29in. wide.
(Christie's) $7,524

A George III satinwood card table, the purpleheart banded top above a similarly banded frieze, on square tapered legs, 35½in. wide.
(Bonhams) $4,015

Classical mahogany card table, New York or New Jersey, circa 1830, refinished, 36in. wide.
(Skinner Inc.) $1,900

An early Victorian mahogany card table with rectangular swiveling fold-over top enclosing a baize lined interior, 36¼in. wide.
(Christie's S. Ken) $2,130

Federal mahogany veneered card table, New England, early 19th century, refinished, 36½in. wide.
(Skinner Inc.) $750

## CARD & TEA TABLES

A Regency brass inlaid rosewood card table with fold-over swivel top inlaid with a continuous band of trailing flowers and leaves, 36in. wide.
(Lawrence Fine Art) $4,055

A Regency rosewood and brass inlaid D-shaped card table with lyre-shaped support on quadripartite platform with four splayed legs, 36in. wide.
(Christie's S. Ken) $6,582

A George IV mahogany card table, on four turned column supports with lotus caps, and a beaded concave plinth, on scroll feet, 36in. wide.
(Bonhams) $1,337

A George III concertina-action card table with canted rectangular hinged lid with counter wells and plain frieze with egg-and-dart molding, on cabriole legs, 33½in. wide.
(Christie's) $12,276

George II mahogany card table, circa 1750, raised on acanthus carved cabriole legs ending in ball and claw feet, 33¾in. wide.
(Skinner Inc.) $1,500

Federal mahogany inlaid demilune card table, probably Rhode Island, circa 1800, refinished, 33¾in. wide.
(Skinner Inc.) $1,000

Federal mahogany inlaid card table, Rhode Island, circa 1800, old refinish, 35¾in. wide.
(Skinner Inc.) $4,200

A Regency rosewood card table, on a broadening square column, concave plinth and hipped outswept legs, 36in. wide.
(Bonhams) $1,528

Federal mahogany card table with mahogany and birch veneers, Portsmouth, New Hampshire, circa 1800, 36in. wide.
(Skinner Inc.) $9,500

## CENTER TABLES

A Victorian walnut center table, the oval quarter veneered top above fluted and baluster column end supports, 54in. wide.
(Bonhams) $1,369

Renaissance Revival walnut center table, third quarter 19th century, the inset marble top above a carved pedestal with four fluted supports, 30½in. high.
(Skinner Inc.) $1,000

A mid-Victorian inlaid walnut and giltmetal mounted center table, the eared serpentine top with floral and foliate scroll inlay, on cabriole legs, 34in. wide.
(Christie's S. Ken) $1,773

A George IV ash and elm center table with circular segmented tilt-top inlaid with a star in ebony and burr walnut, 36in. diameter.
(Christie's) $5,940

A late Regency rosewood center table on twin ring-turned end-standards, each on splayed legs headed by roundels, 36in. wide.
(Christie's S. Ken) $1,636

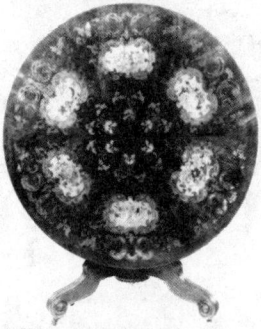

A Victorian rosewood and marquetry center table, the circular top segmentally veneered, each segment centered by a cartouche incorporating birds and foliage, 48½in. wide.
(Bonhams) $4,198

A George IV rosewood center table with a beaded kidney-shaped top, on dual splayed lappeted legs with paw feet, 38in. wide.
(Christie's S. Ken) $3,325

An Empire mahogany center table surmounted by a circular dished gray marble top with a veneered frieze, raised on five cylindrical columns with ormolu capitals, 4ft. 5in. diameter.
(Phillips) $12,460

A William IV rosewood and parcel-gilt center table with rectangular black slate top inset with bluejohn and marble squares, on paneled end-supports headed by paterae, 32in. wide.
(Christie's) $28,314

## CENTER TABLES

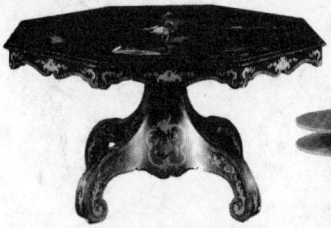

**An early Victorian mahogany, ebony and marquetry center table attributed to E.H. Baldock, the octagonal tilt-top with simulated rosewood leather-lined rim, 56in. wide.**
**(Christie's) $17,305**

**An Art Deco veneered center table, having an oval top and similar under shelf, 77cm. high.**
**(Phillips) $458**

**A Regency grained pine center table with associated gray marble top on four S-scroll supports applied with roundels, 59in. wide.**
**(Christie's S. Ken) $2,599**

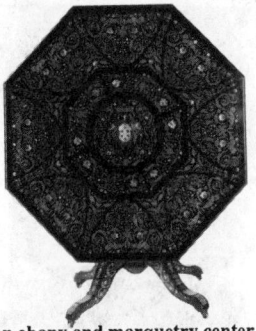

**An ebony and marquetry center table, the octagonal tilt-top profusely inlaid with ribbon-tied stylized Medici foliate panels heightened with mother-of-pearl, 19th century, 49½in. wide.**
**(Christie's) $15,048**

**Marquetry and laminated wood center table, 20th century, inlaid with various woods, raised on cabriole legs, 29¾in. diameter.**
**(Skinner Inc.) $750**

**A George IV satinwood-veneered center table, the twelve-sided tip-up top with rosewood and mahogany crossbanding, 35¾in. wide.**
**(Bearne's) $1,598**

**A mid Victorian walnut center table on turned cabochon carved shaft and three foliate carved splayed legs, 30in. diameter.**
**(Christie's S. Ken) $1,452**

**A mid-Georgian mahogany center table with rounded rectangular top and waved frieze centered by scallop shells, on cabriole legs headed by acanthus, 31½in. wide.**
**(Christie's) $6,930**

**An Italian gray-veined Carrara marble center table, the circular top inlaid with various marbles with central radiating motifs and borders with butterflies, birds and flowers, 35½in. wide.**
**(Christie's S. Ken) $7,758**

## CONSOLE TABLES

A Louis XVI style giltwood console table with a white marble top over a fluted frieze, on eight fluted tapering legs, 97in. wide.
(Hy Duke & Son) $3,720

One of a pair of William Kent design giltwood pier tables, each with a rectangular mottled white marble top above a Vitruvian scroll frieze with eagle support, 45½in. wide.
(Christie's S. Ken)
(Two) $9,974

Louis XV style carved walnut console table, late 19th century, raised on four S-scroll supports and acanthus carved feet, joined by a rocaille-carved stretcher, 39in. high.
(Butterfield & Butterfield)
$4,125

A Regency simulated rosewood and parcel-gilt console table with molded D-shaped white-veined marble top, on turned tapering legs, inscribed *Mrs Golding & Glass*, 43½in. wide.
(Christie's) $5,944

A Louis XV giltwood console table with later serpentine mottled green marble top and pierced frieze carved with flowerheads, 32in. wide.
(Christie's) $7,854

A Swedish Empire giltwood console table with rectangular gray marble top above a lappeted frieze, on scrolled dolphin supports and stepped base, early 19th century, 30¾in. wide.
(Christie's) $5,851

Régence style carved giltwood console table, 19th century, with an acanthus carved frieze, raised on foliate carved scroll supports, 33½in. high.
(Butterfield & Butterfield)
$4,675

One of a pair of satinwood, marquetry and giltwood demi-lune pier tables, each with a top centered by classical urns, on tapering fluted legs with turned foliate carved feet, each 39in. wide.
(Christie's S. Ken)
$19,949

A Louis XV giltwood console table with gray serpentine marble top above a frieze pierced and carved with rockwork, C-scrolls and flowerheads, 45in. wide.
(Christie's) $10,285

## CONSOLE TABLES

A Charles X rosewood and marquetry console table inlaid overall with paterae and anthemia, with D-shaped mottled white marble top, on bun feet, 58in. wide.
(Christie's) $3,684

An Art Deco console table in walnut veneer, the rectangular top held by two splayed solid supports, 150cm. long.
(Phillips) $684

One of pair of Louis XVI mahogany and ormolu mounted console dessertes, by Conrad Mauter, with concave canted sides surmounted by contemporary fossilized marble tops, 4ft. 3in. wide.
(Phillips)
(Two) $112,926

A Louis XV giltwood console table with molded eared serpentine brèche violette top, the waved apron carved with interlocking chain pattern and centered by a pair of ribbon-tied bagpipes, 34in. wide.
(Christie's) $39,006

A pair of William IV carved giltwood consoles surmounted by rectangular white marble tops, the ogee molded friezes with pierced foliate scroll aprons.
(Phillips) $2,725

A Southern Italian giltwood console table with molded eared serpentine white marble top, the pierced frieze carved with flowerheads, acanthus and rockwork, mid-18th century, possibly Neapolitan, 46in. wide.
(Christie's) $6,935

A William IV rosewood console table with rectangular white marble top above foliate carved scroll uprights and mirrored back, 29in. wide.
(Christie's S. Ken) $1,162

One of a pair of Louis XVI white-painted consoles, the pierced fluted friezes carved with foliage on fluted scrolling supports edged with ropetwist, 21¼in. wide.
(Christie's)
(Two) $8,976

A brass-mounted mahogany console-dessert with D-shaped molded canted gray marble top above one panelled drawer and a paneled door enclosing a shelf, 42½in. wide.
(Christie's) $4,334

## DINING TABLES

A mahogany breakfast table with oval tilt-top crossbanded in satinwood and banded with kingwood, on turned shaft and quadripartite base, 67½in. wide. (Christie's) $6,970

A Regency mahogany breakfast table with rounded rectangular tip-up top on four hipped splayed legs, 59in. wide. (Christie's S. Ken) $2,420

A Victorian walnut and amboyna parcel gilt oval top table, the quarter veneered top crossbanded and inlaid with stringing, 42 x 60in. (Lawrence Fine Art) $6,402

A Regency mahogany breakfast table with a rounded rectangular tip-up top above a spiral turned shaft, on four splayed reeded legs, 49in. wide. (Christie's S. Ken) $3,990

A George IV brass-inlaid rosewood center table, inlaid overall with alternating paterae and sycamore leaves with circular tip-up top, 47¼in. diameter. (Christie's S. Ken) $6,206

A George III rosewood breakfast table banded overall with fruitwood and ebonized stringing with rounded rectangular tilt-top, 70in. wide. (Christie's) $13,034

A Regency mahogany breakfast table with rounded rectangular rosewood banded top on baluster-turned shaft and four splayed legs, 33in. wide. (Christie's S. Ken) $1,742

A Louis XVI mahogany dining-table with two D-shaped end-sections and turned tapering legs with brass caps, 58in. wide. (Christie's) $7,585

One of a pair of early Victorian burr-elm breakfast tables, each with an oval top, on a turned and leaf-and-berry carved shaft with oval platform, 58in. wide. (Christie's S. Ken) (Two) $6,206

A Victorian carved walnut 'Capstan' extending dining table, the circular top opening to accomodate two sets of eight leaves of a different radius. (Phillips) $26,284

L. & J.G. Stickley dining table, no. 720, circa 1912, overhanging top supported by five legs, signed *"The Work of L. & J.G. Stickley"*, 54in. diameter. (Skinner Inc.) $2,400

An early Victorian rosewood breakfast table, the circular top with a tongue and dart border on a bulbous pillar and tripod carved support, 56in. diameter. (Lawrence Fine Art) $3,094

## DINING TABLES

Louis XVI style walnut dining table, circular top raised on fluted legs, 72in. diameter.
(Skinner Inc.) $400

Charles and Ray Eames segmented base table, design date 1972, manufactured by Herman Miller, rosewood veneer top, 78in. long.
(Skinner Inc.) $600

A Regency mahogany breakfast table with a circular reeded tip-up top and baluster turned shaft, on four splayed reeded legs, 60in. diameter.
(Christie's S. Ken) $6,650

A Victorian burr walnut center table, the spreading stem and four splayed legs carved overall with stylized foliage, 61in. wide.
(Bearne's) $3,196

A Regency mahogany breakfast table, the crossbanded rounded rectangular tilt top on quadripartite support, with hipped reeded scroll legs with brass paw feet, 55in. wide.
(Christie's) $5,445

A Regency parcel-gilt rosewood and burr-elm center table, on a canted concave-sided spreading triangular support with ropetwist and scroll angles, 53in. diameter.
(Christie's) $20,691

A William IV mahogany breakfast table, the circular tip-up top with arcaded frieze hung with finials, 48in. diameter.
(Christie's S. Ken) $3,465

Limbert dining table, circa 1910, circular top over arched skirt connecting to four square legs, 51in. diameter.
(Skinner Inc.) $1,100

A mid Victorian burr-walnut breakfast table with oval quarter veneered tilt-top on quadripartite hipped splayed legs and scroll feet, 54 x 41in.
(Christie's S. Ken) $1,258

A George III mahogany breakfast table, with rounded rectangular tilt-top on a baluster shaft and downswept reeded legs, 56in. wide.
(Christie's) $4,792

A Capstan mahogany extending dining table, the circular revolving top opening to incorporate two sets of leaves, on a reeded quadripartite base terminating with claw-and-ball feet, 67in. diameter.
(Christie's S. Ken) $26,598

A Regency rosewood and brass-inlaid breakfast table with a rounded rectangular tip-up top above a faceted column and quadripartite platform with gilt foliate ornament, 41in. wide.
(Christie's S. Ken) $6,206

## DRESSING TABLES

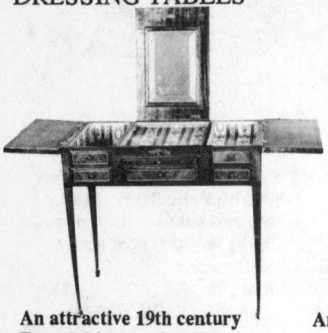

An attractive 19th century French kingwood enclosed dressing table for a lady, raised upon square tapering supports terminating in brass spade feet, 2ft. 7in. wide.
(Spencer's) $1,700

An Edwardian inlaid mahogany dressing table with shield-shaped adjustable plate flanked by two drawers to either side, on square tapering legs with trailing husks and spade feet, 40in. wide.
(Christie's S. Ken) $1,219

A black and gilt-japanned dressing-table decorated overall with figures, geese and houses in a chinoiserie landscape, on turned tapering legs with brass caps, 42in. wide.
(Christie's) $5,148

An unusual George II mahogany dressing table, the caddy top above two short and one long drawer, with two deeper drawers below, flanking the arched recess, 28in. wide.
(Bonhams) $1,719

A Dutch mahogany and marquetry bombé dressing chest, the rectangular plate on shaped supports, above four long graduated drawers, on paw feet, 35in. wide.
(Bonhams) $7,361

A George III fustic dressing-table crossbanded in kingwood, the stepped rectangular top with hinged central section enclosing a formerly fitted interior, 40in. wide.
(Christie's) $8,712

A George III mahogany dressing-table with molded rectangular top above three frieze drawers above a pair of recessed doors, the sides with carrying-handles, 36in. wide.
(Christie's) $6,195

'Morel', a macassar ebony and ivory dressing table, designed by Jacques-Emile Ruhlmann, 1921–22, the circular mirror in electroplated frame pivoting on horse-shoe pedestal, 51.5cm. wide. (Christie's) $9,790

A George III carved mahogany and ebony strung bowfront sideboard or dressing table of small size, in the manner of Gillows, 3ft. 6in. wide.
(Phillips) $5,220

## DRESSING TABLES

George I walnut dressing table, second-quarter 18th century, molded rectangular top above a single frieze drawer, 32¼in. wide.
(Skinner Inc.) $500

One of a pair of Regency mahogany dressing-tables, each with twin-flap rectangular top enclosing a mirror and lidded compartments on tapering turned reeded legs, 32in. wide.
(Christie's)
(Two) $3,397

A Robert 'Mouseman' Thompson oak dressing table, with rectangular cheval mirror on rectangular, molded and chamfered top, on two pedestals each with three short drawers and eight octagonal feet, 106.7cm.
(Christie's) $3,887

An early Victorian satinbirch dressing table with two swing-frame mirrors fitted with ten drawers on rounded rectangular plinth base, 63in. wide.
(Christie's S. Ken) $1,452

Stickley Brothers chest of drawers, circa 1912, rectangular swivel mirror, two short drawers over three long drawers, 44in. wide.
(Skinner Inc.) $400

A Louis XV ormolu mounted kingwood, tulipwood crossbanded and marquetry poudreuse or coiffeuse with cartouche shaped panels of floral sprays veneered à quatre faces, 3ft. 2in. wide.
(Phillips) $20,443

Queen Anne walnut dressing table, early 18th century, on cabriole legs ending in pad feet, 28½in. wide.
(Skinner Inc.) $950

A late Regency oak dressing table, in the manner of George Bullock, on bulbous turned legs tied by a concave platform stretcher, 34¼in. wide.
(Bonhams) $1,337

Queen Anne dressing table, New England, 18th century, refinished, replaced brasses, 33in. wide.
(Skinner Inc.) $12,000

## DROP LEAF TABLES

A mid-Victorian mahogany Sutherland table, on turned supports and dual scroll feet joined by a stretcher, 36in. wide.
(Christie's S. Ken) $426

Federal cherry inlaid breakfast table, New England, circa 1810, refinished, 18¼in. wide.
(Skinner Inc.) $500

A George III mahogany supper table with serpentine shape top above one drawer and with wire-mesh enclosing the sides, 33in. x 39in. extended.
(Lawrence Fine Art) $16,181

A Victorian walnut Sutherland table with well-figured quarter-veneered shaped oval top, 41in. wide.
(Bearne's) $1,471

A Dutch mahogany and floral marquetry triangular drop-flap table on foliate carved cabriole legs with claw and ball feet, 33in. wide.
(Christie's S. Ken) $2,131

Classical mahogany veneer breakfast table, probably Boston, circa 1815, the drop leaves over four curving beaded legs, 42in. wide.
(Skinner Inc.) $750

A George II Cuban mahogany oval drop leaf dining table, fitted an end frieze drawer with a brass ring handle, the plain turned legs on hoof feet, 4ft. 10in. wide.
(Woolley & Wallis) $4,024

A George II mahogany drop leaf dining table, raised upon turned and tapering supports terminating in pad and block feet, 4ft. 4in. long extended.
(Spencer's) $907

A George II mahogany drop-leaf dining table with oval molded top, on club legs, 59in. wide.
(Christie's S. Ken) $4,433

## DROP LEAF TABLES

An early Victorian mahogany Sutherland table, on twin-column end-supports and downswept legs joined by a turned stretcher, with brass caps, 41¾in. wide.
(Christie's) $3,184

A Chippendale mahogany drop-leaf table, Salem, Massachusetts, 1760–1780, the molded oval twin-flap top above an arching, shaped skirt on cabriole legs and ball-and-claw feet, 53in. wide.
(Christie's) $8,800

A mid-Victorian walnut Sutherland table, on turned supports and dual scroll feet joined by a stretcher, 36in. wide.
(Christie's S. Ken) $542

A Napoleon III amboyna, parcel ebonized and marquetry table à volets, the rectangular top with elliptical leaves, 43in. wide.
(Bonhams) $2,101

A Victorian burr-walnut Sutherland table, on turned tapering column end-standards and foliate carved splayed legs, 35½in. wide.
(Christie's S. Ken) $1,007

Federal cherry breakfast table, New England, circa 1810, refinished, replaced brass pull, 32½in. wide.
(Skinner Inc.) $800

A George III mahogany hunt-table with oval twin-flap top on square molded legs and four gatelegs joined by molded stretchers, 95in. long.
(Christie's) $12,584

A Federal figured maple drop-leaf table, New England, 1800–1820, the rectangular top with two drop leaves above a plain apron, on square tapering legs, 55½in. wide.
(Christie's) $4,400

Edwardian rosewood Sutherland table with marquetry and bone inlay, on turned ring legs with baluster bottom stretcher, 24in. wide.
(G.A. Key) $650

## GATELEG TABLES

A George III mahogany spider gateleg table with rectangular twin-flap top, on turned legs joined by conforming stretchers and block feet, 31in. wide.
(Christie's) $2,396

Oak gate-legged dining table, 18th century, twin plank top and leaves, two drawers, turned supports, 57in. opened.
(G.A. Key) $4,074

An early Victorian mahogany Sutherland table, the rounded rectangular twin-flap top inlaid with ebonized lines on twin-column end-supports, 41¾in. wide, open.
(Christie's) $2,396

A George III mahogany spider gateleg table with eared serpentine twin-flap top, on turned legs joined by turned stretchers on claw-and-ball feet, 35¾in. wide.
(Christie's) $26,004

A Chinese Export huali miniature gateleg table inlaid overall in mother-of-pearl with foliage and domestic utensils, the circular twin-flap top inlaid with birds in trees, bats' wings and butterflies, late 18th/early 19th century, 26in. diameter.
(Christie's) $6,067

A George II mahogany gate-leg dining-table on turned tapering legs joined by turned and square stretchers, on pad feet, restorations to underside and top, 48in. wide.
(Christie's) $9,653

An oak gateleg dining-table, the oval twin-flap top with single later frieze drawer on baluster and square legs joined by square stretchers, early 18th century, 49in. wide.
(Christie's) $4,934

An oak gateleg table with elliptical leaves and two end drawers, on baluster and bobbin turned supports, 51¼in. wide, basically late 17th century.
(Bonhams) $2,280

An early 18th century walnut gateleg table with an oval top, shaped frieze and on baluster-turned legs, 43in. wide.
(Bearne's) $1,354

## GATELEG TABLES

An oak gate-leg table with oval twin-flap top with one drawer to the end, on spirally-twisted legs joined by square stretchers on bun feet, 63½in. wide.
(Christie's) $6,006

An oak gate-leg table, the rectangular top with two hinged leaves on baluster turned legs joined by stretchers, 17th century, 69in. long.
(Christie's S. Ken) $1,891

Georgian oak gate-legged dining table, three plank top, turned legs, united by stretchers, 53in.
(G.A. Key) $2,214

A George III mahogany spider gate-leg table, on turned legs joined by conforming stretchers, 33in. wide.
(Christie's S. Ken) $2,574

An oak gate-leg table with oval hinged top on bobbin-turned supports joined by stretchers, 58in. wide.
(Christie's S. Ken) $3,080

A Charles II walnut gateleg table, previously with a drawer, on baluster-turned legs joined by square stretchers, on turned feet, 32¼in. wide.
(Christie's) $12,584

A Queen Anne oak oval gate-leg table with single frieze drawer on baluster turned legs, with molded stretchers, on scrolling feet, 58in. wide.
(Christie's) $3,861

An oak gate-leg table, the demi-lune fold-over top on baluster column supports joined by stretchers, 37½in. wide.
(Christie's S. Ken) $2,738

Antique American William & Mary gate-leg table in maple and curly maple, drawer of pine and poplar secondary woods, top open 49in. x 61in.
(Eldred's) $2,860

## LARGE TABLES

Regency mahogany four pedestal dining table, with reeded edges above four turned columnar supports, raised on four reeded downswept legs ending in brass paw feet, 136½in. long.
(Skinner Inc.) $7,500

A late Regency mahogany extending dining table, in the manner of Gillows, supported on five lobed tapering legs, including five extra leaves, 161in. wide.
(Bonhams) $5,730

Walnut and cherry tavern table, probably New York State, 18th century, old surface, 53½in. wide.
(Skinner Inc.) $2,300

Regency style double pedestal mahogany dining table, 20th century, reeded edge, raised on a carved baluster support on tripartite base, 85in. long (extended).
(Skinner Inc.) $1,700

An oak dining table, designed by M.H. Baillie-Scott, of rectangular shape on two trestle supports, each composed of twin turned baluster columns on square plinths and shaped transverse base, circa 1897, 183cm. long.
(Christie's) $6,829

A brass-mounted William IV mahogany wine table, the semi-circular top with a hinged semi-circular removable section and two hinged flaps, on turned tapering reeded legs, 73in. wide.
(Christie's) $8,712

A Regency mahogany drinking table, the semi-circular top with associated D-shaped inner section and two side flaps, on turned tapering reeded legs, 86in. wide.
(Christie's) $8,276

Italian baroque walnut refectory table, with a central long drawer flanked by drawers, raised on scrolling supports joined by a stretcher, 80½in. long.
(Skinner Inc.) $2,,000

## LARGE TABLES

A William IV mahogany extending dining-table with two D-shaped ends and five extra leaves, on turned tapering reeded legs and brass caps, 147in. wide.
(Christie's) $9,801

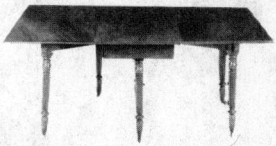

A Regency mahogany drop-leaf dining table, with a rectangular twin-flap top, on reeded tapering legs with gate-leg action, 70in. wide, extended.
(Christie's S. Ken) $3,768

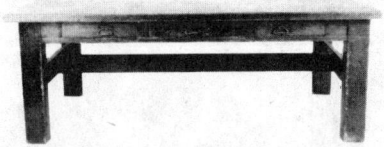

Large six drawer library table, circa 1915, rectangular top over six drawers, large post legs with side stretchers, 86in. long.
(Skinner Inc.) $1,000

A Regency mahogany extending dining-table with two D-shaped end-sections, one with hinged section and gateleg action, with two extra leaves, on turned tapering reeded legs with brass caps, 95½in. wide.
(Christie's) $6,970

A George IV mahogany extending dining-table with two D-shaped end-sections, on turned ribbed legs and giltmetal caps, 103in. wide.
(Christie's) $11,979

An oak refectory table, designed by Margaret Butterfield, for the Choir School, All Saints, Margaret Street, London, 1850–1859, 90cm. wide, 152cm. long.
(Christie's) $3,201

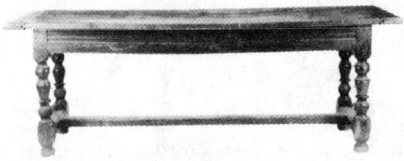

Continental baroque walnut refectory table, rectangular top above molded frieze, raised on turned legs joined by a stretcher, 89in. long.
(Skinner Inc.) $3,100

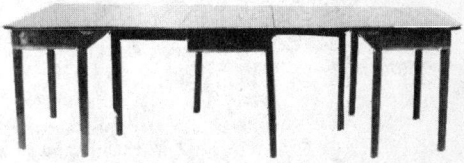

George III mahogany three-part dining table, late 18th century, D-shaped end flanking a rectangular center section, inlaid with stringing, 98¾in. wide.
(Skinner Inc.) $2,500

## OCCASIONAL TABLES

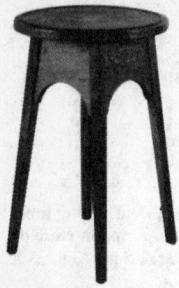

'Quaint Furniture' cafe table with copper top, Grand Rapids, Michigan, circa 1915, no. 2615, signed with metal tag, 18¼in. diameter.
(Skinner Inc.) $650

An Anglo-Italian ebonized two-tier etagère, the rectangular tiers with finely turned ivory balustrade gallery, 30in. wide, 19th century.
(Bonhams) $5,293

A Regency mahogany dumb-waiter with two circular tiers on brass column supports and spirally-reeded baluster stem, 21¼in. diameter.
(Christie's) $2,178

A late George III drum top table, by W. Priest, the circular top with a leather inset above four real and four mock drawers.
(Bonhams) $3,468

A set of 19th century mahogany and rosewood quartetto tables, the rounded rectangular tops on dual turned splayed end supports, 2ft. wide.
(Phillips) $2,920

Early Gustav Stickley table, circa 1902–03, no. 439, round top with four cut-in leg posts, 30in. diameter.
(Skinner Inc.) $1,100

A George III mahogany twin tier dumb waiter with revolving dished tops and reeded edges, on tripod splayed legs, 2ft. diameter top.
(Phillips) $1,363

An ormolu-mounted rosewood, marquetry and parquetry center table with two graduated shaped rectangular tiers inlaid with flowerheads on a cube-pattern ground, early 20th century, 34½in. wide.
(Christie's) $2,633

A mahogany tripod table, the circular top with raised waved rim on a fluted base carved with acanthus, on cabriole legs headed by cabochons, 17in. diameter.
(Christie's) $4,158

## OCCASIONAL TABLES

A Victorian walnut pedestal table, the circular tilt-top inlaid with various segmented veneered woods on a spiral turned shaft with splayed legs, 16in. wide.
(Christie's S. Ken) $1,205

A Gothic Revival invalid's table, the top on adjustable slide with two reading slopes on a hexagonal four-footed pedestal base, 90cm. long.
(Phillips) $1,653

A Regency penwork tripod table, the circular top decorated with a checkerboard within foliate borders interspersed with chinoiserie panels of birds and figure, on arched downswept legs, 23½in. diameter.
(Christie's) $1,198

A Regency ormolu-mounted mahogany and parcel-gilt occasional table with later rectangular black leather-lined top on column end-supports with lotus leaf terminals, 23¼in. wide.
(Christie's) $3,168

A William IV mahogany three tier dumb waiter with serpentine acanthus and gadrooned rectangular galleried top, on brass castors, 50½in. wide.
(Christie's S. Ken) $1,839

An Egyptian carved wood and shell-inlaid occasional table, the rectangular top intricately carved with scrolling foliage and a geometric design, 27½in. wide.
(Bearne's) $752

A satinwood drum table banded in walnut with circular red leather-lined top, the frieze with four drawers and four false drawers, 23in. diameter.
(Christie's) $2,376

A mahogany silver table, the rounded rectangular top with a raised molded rim above two frieze drawers, 33¾in. wide.
(Bonhams) $1,910

A George III mahogany dumb-waiter, the three graduated circular dished tiers on ring-turned spiral carved supports, 42½in. high.
(Christie's S. Ken) $2,502

## OCCASIONAL TABLES

Chippendale mahogany carved tilt-top tea table, Boston, 1760–80, old surface, 35in. diameter.
(Skinner Inc.) $4,100

William IV rosewood reading/duet table, with two adjustable flaps and single drawer, carved column on tripartite base, 31in. wide. (G.A. Key) $1,250

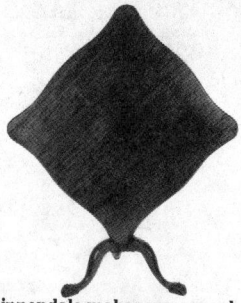

Chippendale mahogany carved tilt top tea table, probably Middle Atlantic States, late 18th century, refinished, 30¼in. high.
(Skinner Inc.) $1,500

A Regency ormolu-mounted mahogany occasional table, the square top banded in maple, the baluster shaft on concave-sided triangular base with scrolling feet, 17¾in. wide.
(Christie's) $2,970

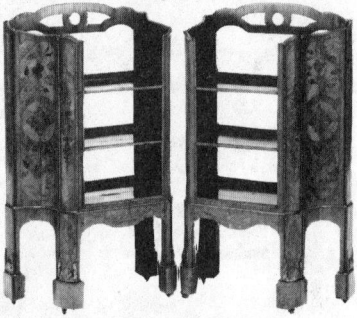

A pair of Louis XV ormolu-mounted kingwood and end-cut floral marquetry bibliothèques basses inlaid overall with ebonized and fruitwood lines and inlaid with leaves and flowerheads, English 19th century.
(Christie's) $153,340

A Transitional ormolu-mounted tulipwood, harewood, amaranth and marquetry guéridon or table de chevet, the circular top with pierced entrelac gallery inlaid with flowerpots and an ink tray within a laurel wreath, 13in. diameter.
(Christie's) $28,171

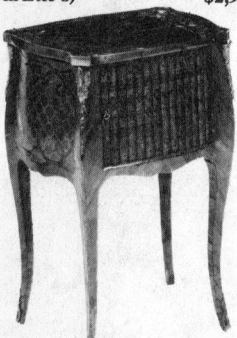

A Louis XV ormolu-mounted tulipwood, kingwood and end-cut marquetry guéridon with a tambour shutter with later leather book-spines, on cabriole legs with foliate sabots, 19½in. wide.
(Christie's) $14,960

Gustav Stickley table, circa 1912–16, no. 626, round top on four legs, joined by arched cross stretchers with finial, 40in. diameter.
(Skinner Inc.) $1,200

One of a pair of Spanish walnut-kingwood and marquetry corner tables, late 18th century/early 19th century, possibly Majorca, 32in. wide.
(Christie's) $13,002

## OCCASIONAL TABLES

Chippendale mahogany carved tilt top table, Philadelphia, circa 1765, old refinish, bird cage fixed in place, 32in. diameter.
(Skinner Inc.) $11,000

A Regency mahogany bagatelle table, with hinged rectangular top opening to reveal a green baize-lined playing surface with nine numbered wells and two corner compartments, 96in. wide.
(Christie's) $6,794

An ormolu-mounted tulipwood, kingwood and marquetry table à écrire, the reading-slope flanked by two hinged silk-lined wells, on cabriole legs with foliate sabots, 26in. wide.
(Christie's) $46,750

A mahogany occasional table, the oval top with waved gallery on tripod base with downswept legs headed by acanthus, 27½in. wide.
(Christie's) $5,307

Pair of Edwardian satinwood virtine tables, circa 1900, horseshoe shaped glass-inset top, raised on square tapered legs, 27¼in. high.
(Skinner Inc.) $2,200

An ormolu-mounted mahogany jardinière with hexagonal top and paneled frieze applied with alternating cornucopia and lyre-and-quiver motifs, 27in. wide.
(Christie's) $2,384

A set of Regency carved rosewood and crossbanded quartetto tables, attributed to Gillows of Lancaster, the rectangular top veneered in amboyna, burr walnut and satinwood, 1ft. 11¼in. x 1ft. 3¾in.
(Phillips) $4,867

An ormolu-mounted amaranth, harewood and stained beech tricoteuse inlaid overall with ebonized and boxwood stringing, inlaid with lozenges, the rectangular top with D-shaped ends and hinged front, 30in. wide.
(Christie's) $11,919

A George III mahogany architect's table, the rectangular molded top with easel support and mechanical book rest, 3ft. wide.
(Russell Baldwin & Bright) $9,114

## PEMBROKE TABLES

A Regency mahogany Pembroke table, on a ring turned vase shaped column support, circular plinth and hipped reeded outswept legs, 36in. wide.
(Bonhams) $1,528

A George IV mahogany Pembroke table, the frieze with two drawers and two simulated drawers, on turned pedestal carved with acanthus, 38in. wide.
(Christie's) $9,009

A George III satinwood Pembroke table, crossbanded with mahogany and edged with amaranth, the rectangular twin-flap top above a single frieze drawer, 42½in. wide.
(Christie's) $4,138

A George III mahogany Pembroke table, outlined in boxwood stringing, on square tapering legs headed by oval fan paterae, 29in. wide.
(Bonhams) $3,103

A George III satinwood Pembroke table, the rounded rectangular twin-flap top crossbanded with kingwood, on square tapering legs with kingwood block feet, 41½in. wide. (Christie's) $6,970

A George III style satinwood Pembroke table, the kingwood crossbanded oval top outlined in barber pole stringing, 35¾in. wide.
(Bonhams) $2,008

A George III mahogany Pembroke table banded overall in kingwood with oval twin-flap top and single frieze drawer, 37in. wide.
(Christie's) $3,703

A mahogany oval Pembroke table, the top with rosewood and satinwood bands edged with stringing, fitted with one drawer and on four square tapering supports, 18th century.
(Lawrence Fine Art) $2,135

A George III satinwood Pembroke table with molded serpentine twin-flap top inlaid with three amboyna oval panels, on square tapering mahogany legs with satinwood panels and pendant husks, 36¾in. wide.
(Christie's) $13,552

## PEMBROKE TABLES

A George III mahogany and marquetry Pembroke table, with oval twin-flap top centered by an oval inlaid with a stylized flowerhead with a satinwood border inlaid with entwined ribbon and flowerheads, 42in. wide. (Christie's) $11,484

Early 19th century mahogany Pembroke table with end drawer, standing on four turned ringed legs with brass castors, 36in. wide. (G.A. Key) $732

A Federal figured maple Pembroke table, eastern Connecticut or Rhode Island, 1795–1825, on square tapering legs joined by an X-shaped stretcher, 29$^{3}/_{8}$in. high. (Christie's) $6,050

A Regency ebony Pembroke table inlaid with brass lines, the rectangular twin-flap top edged with milled brass border, on spirally-turned tapering legs, 38in. wide. (Christie's) $52,272

A George III satinwood and marquetry Pembroke table, the oval top with rosewood crossbanding and the center with a large oval shell motif, 28in. wide. (Lawrence Fine Art) $16,855

A George III satinwood marquetry, white-painted and parcel-gilt Pembroke table, the top possibly by Thomas Chippendale with serpentine molded twin-flap top with central ammonite flower and conch shell-medallion, 37$^{1}/_{4}$in. wide. (Christie's) $21,296

A George III mahogany Pembroke table with oval twin-flap top, on square tapering legs and brass caps, one caster lacking, 38in. wide. (Christie's) $2,178

A George III mahogany Pembroke table, the oval flap top banded in harewood with stringing, 30in. wide. (Woolley & Wallis) $1,915

A Regency mahogany Pembroke table with rounded rectangular twin-flap top, on turned tapering legs and brass caps, 40in. wide. (Christie's) $2,376

## SIDE TABLES

A mahogany side table, designed by Gordon Russell, with inlaid ebony and sycamore decoration, the rectangular top with undulating sides, 92cm. wide.
(Christie's) $7,256

George III satinwood side table, circa 1800, inlaid with bellflowers, raised on square tapered legs, 49in. wide.
(Skinner Inc.) $4,000

A William Burges ebony sidetable inlaid with ivory, the rectangular top with shaped edges above rectangular shelf and arched end supports.
(Christie's) $30,690

A George II mahogany side table, the thumbnail molded rectangular top with indented corners, on turned tapering legs, 33¼in. wide.
(Bonhams) $2,101

A Louis Philippe mahogany side table with rectangular Carrara marble top above frieze drawer, 38in. wide.
(Christie's S. Ken) $1,742

A Regency oak side table with rectangular top above a drawer with divided interior, on turned legs joined by a square H-shaped stretcher, 30in. wide.
(Christie's) $3,762

One of a pair of foliate painted satinwood pier tables with serpentine eared tops cross-banded in rosewood, (modern) 39¼in. wide.
(Christie's S. Ken)
(Two) $1,355

One of a pair of giltwood side tables, each surmounted by an eared top of Verde Antico marble above a beaded and meander frieze centered by a tablet hung with husk swags, on cabriole legs, late 19th century, each 47in. wide.
(Christie's S. Ken)
(Two) $8,201

A Baltic grained beech mahogany and parcel-gilt pier table with rectangular top above a gilt foliate frieze on scroll supports, mid 19th century, 37in. wide.
(Christie's S. Ken) $1,355

## SIDE TABLES

One of a pair of mahogany side tables banded overall with satinwood, each with D-shaped top on square tapering channeled legs and block feet, the top 18th century, 62in. wide.
(Christie's) Two $22,473

A satinwood side table with rectangular breakfront top and concave center section inlaid with a thuya oval and checkered lines, on square tapering legs, 44in. wide.
(Christie's) $10,296

An Edwardian parcel-gilt painted satinwood pier table, with a serpentine D-shaped crossbanded top decorated with a foliate swag and a demi-lune panel, 57½in. wide.
(Christie's East) $7,700

A Dutch small 'D' shape mahogany side table, with two tambour cupboards above conjoined circles, and on three fluted and tapering supports, 20½in. wide.
(Lawrence Fine Art) $1,707

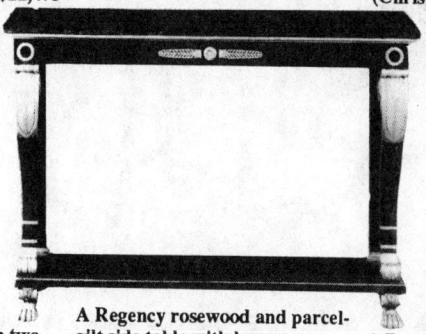

A Regency rosewood and parcel-gilt side table with large rectangular top, the plain frieze with late ormolu wreath and anthemia mounts, on S-scroll front supports, 54in. wide.
(Christie's) $4,792

A Regency mahogany demi-lune pier table with veined white marble top, and mirrored back flanked by giltwood semi-columns, 23½in. wide.
(Bearne's) $1,166

An Adam period satinwood and marquetry pier table, with similarities to the work of Ince and Mayhew, the elliptical top crossbanded in rosewood and tulipwood with central radiating fan lunette, 3ft. 9in. wide.
(Phillips) $15,576

An 18th century Irish mahogany side table with associated molded rectangular carrara marble top, the waved frieze carved with acanthus and centered by an eagle, on cabriole legs, 35½in. wide.
(Christie's) $6,534

A mahogany side table with mottled rectangular breccia marble top above a molding carved with flowerheads, the frieze applied with scrolling acanthus and strapwork, 48in. wide.
(Christie's) $6,336

## SOFA TABLES

A Regency brass-inlaid rosewood sofa table with rectangular twin-flap top, the frieze with two mahogany-lined drawers flanked by lotus, on splayed end-supports, 54½in. wide, open.
(Christie's) $13,068

A Regency mahogany sofa table inlaid overall with boxwood and ebonized lines, the rounded rectangular twin-flap top crossbanded in fruitwood and rosewood, 61½in. wide.
(Christie's) $10,890

A mahogany and gilt metal-mounted sofa table, on scroll supports with anthemion mounts, on dual splayed legs joined by a shaped stretcher, first quarter 19th century, 59in. wide.
(Christie's S. Ken) $7,758

A Regency brass-mounted rosewood sofa table, with two paneled drawers mounted with beading and two false drawers on plain end-supports, 61¾in. wide.
(Christie's) $12,738

A Regency mahogany small sofa table inlaid overall with ebony stringing with rounded rectangular twin-flap top, 30½in. wide.
(Christie's) $8,067

A George III mahogany sofa table, the crossbanded top inlaid with boxwood stringing, above two frieze drawers, 59½in. wide.
(Bonhams) $9,168

A Regency rosewood sofa table, outlined in boxwood and ebony stringing, on curved 'X'-shaped end supports, tied by a pole stretcher, 60½in. wide.
(Bonhams) $2,555

A Regency rosewood sofa table, the frieze with two cedar-lined drawers and two false drawers, on vase-shaped end-supports joined by an arched stretcher, 58¾in. wide.
(Christie's) $11,676

A late Regency mahogany sofa table with two drawers opposite two dummy drawers, on solid trestle end supports joined by turned stretcher, 41½ x 61in. extended.
(Lawrence Fine Art) $4,268

## SOFA TABLES

A Regency mahogany sofa table, fitted with two drawers opposite two dummy drawers on a U shape support with four fluted saber legs, 50¾in. wide. (Lawrence Fine Art) $5,548

An unusual Regency rosewood sofa table with unusual sprung hinged top, containing two recessed panel drawers and dummy drawers to the reverse, 5ft. x 2ft. 4in. (Phillips) $6,619

A Regency rosewood sofa table banded overall with satinwood and inlaid with boxwood and ebonized stringing, on square end-supports and downswept legs with brass caps, 57½in. wide, open. (Christie's) $8,276

A Regency rosewood sofa table, the two central shaped flat supports on a rectangular platform with four hipped splayed legs, 55½in. wide. (Bearne's) $3,269

A Regency mahogany, rosewood crossbanded and inlaid sofa table, the hinged top with rounded corners containing two drawers in the frieze, 5ft. 2in. x 2ft. 3in. (Phillips) $3,894

A George III mahogany, boxwood strung and rosewood crossbanded sofa table, on standard end uprights united by a turned stretcher and dual splayed end supports, terminating in brass paw cappings and castors, 3ft. 2in. wide. (Phillips) $4,698

A late Regency mahogany sofa table, on twin baluster turned columns and stepped arched downswept legs terminating in brass cappings and castors, 4ft. 10in. wide. (Phillips) $5,220

A Regency mahogany crossbanded and brass strung sofa table, the hinged, rosewood crossbanded top with cut corners containing two drawers in the frieze, 4ft. 11in. x 2ft. 4in. (Phillips) $3,504

A Regency rosewood sofa table inlaid with brass lines and cut-brass foliate motifs, 28¼in. high by 58in. wide. (Bearne's) $2,656

## WORK BOX & GAMES TABLES

A late George III mahogany work table, on tapered legs with a cross stretcher, 17¾in. wide. (Dreweatt Neate) $3,315

A Regency mahogany games table, the rounded rectangular twin-flap top crossbanded in kingwood, with sliding central section, the reverse with chessboard, 59in. wide. (Christie's) $4,792

An attractive William IV mahogany teapoy, the slightly tapering square top with acanthus carved edge, on fluted scroll feet, 14in. square. (Spencer's) $908

An attractive Regency parquetry decorated rosewood teapoy/work table, on four outward splayed square tapering supports terminating in brass acanthus sheathed caps and castors, 1ft. 4in. wide. $3,402 (Spencer's)

A mid Victorian rosewood work table, the rectangular shaped top having frieze drawer opening to reveal a maple wood fitted interior, 58cm. wide. (Phillips) $1,006

An Anglo Indian rosewood sewing table of unusual design, the revolving top with rectangular box inlaid with ivory, 23in. wide. (Lawrence Fine Art) $1,169

A Regency rosewood work-table with hinged green leather-lined reading-slope above two mahogany-lined drawers, formerly with work-basket, 46in. wide. (Christie's) $2,972

A classical carved mahogany work table, Philadelphia, 1815–1825, on four saber legs with carved scrolled knees and cast foliate brass casters, 20in. wide. (Christie's) $3,850

A Regency rosewood and parcel-gilt games table with rectangular sliding top, the reverse with a checkerboard enclosing a backgammon board, the D-shaped end-sections with pierced brass gallery, 31½in. wide. (Christie's) $10,890

## WORK BOX & GAMES TABLES

Early Victorian rosewood worktable, circa 1844, octagonal molded top enclosing a fitted interior, ending in claw and ball feet, 30½in. high.
(Skinner Inc.) $950

Italian rococo walnut games table, shaped rectangular top, raised on cabriole legs ending in shaped pad feet, 43in. wide.
(Skinner Inc.) $3,200

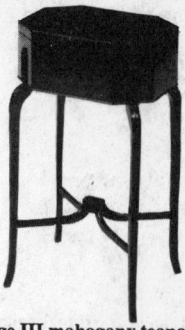

A George III mahogany teapoy with octagonal hinged lid enclosing three lidded boxes, the reeded spreading legs headed by lotus leaves, 16¾in. wide.
(Christie's) $4,752

A George III inlaid rosewood work table, the elongated octagonal top and frieze outlined with sharks'-tooth banding, originally with work bag.
(Bearne's) $3,384

A Regency mahogany games-table, the rounded rectangular top with sliding checkerboard and well with backgammon board, 35½in. wide.
(Christie's) $5,148

An early 19th century mahogany work table in the Empire style, the rectangular top enclosing a fitted interior, 20½in. wide.
(Bearne's) $1,348

A Biedermeier mahogany teapoy with hinged octagonal lid inlaid with boxwood and ebonized lines enclosing a fitted interior with lidded compartments above a cream-painted silk-lined well, 20½in. wide.
(Christie's) $2,970

One of a pair of Regency rosewood work-tables inlaid with boxwood lines, each with a rectangular canted twin-flap top, 31in. wide, open.
(Christie's)
(Two) $14,520

A Victorian walnut teapoy, with circular hinged cover, quarter veneered in burr walnut, opening to reveal a foliate carved rosette to the inner cover, 1ft. 4in. diameter.
(Spencer's) $302

## WORK BOX & GAMES TABLES

Classical carved mahogany veneered work table, Boston, 1820–30, the central fitted veneered drawer above similar frame drawer for the wooden work bag, 30½in. high. (Skinner Inc.) $1,800

A Regency kingwood games table with rectangular leather-lined twin-flap top opening to reveal a checkerboard, with single frieze drawer above a blue pleated silk work-box, 31½in. wide. (Christie's) $3,564

Classical carved mahogany veneered work table, probably New York, 1820s, two working and two simulated drawers, 15½in. wide. (Skinner Inc.) $425

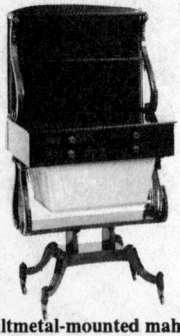

A giltmetal-mounted mahogany work table the superstructure with two shelves on S-scrolled supports, the lower section with rectangular top banded in rosewood above two drawers, first quarter 19th century, 45in. high. (Christie's) $6,930

Classical cherry and rosewood veneer gilt-stenciled worktable, Middle Atlantic States, circa 1815, 20¾in. wide. (Skinner Inc.) $1,500

A Regency brass-mounted rosewood games table with removable square leather-lined sliding top, the reverse with checkerboard, enclosing a well with later backgammon board, 28in. wide. (Christie's) $5,940

Classical mahogany and mahogany veneer work table, Rhode Island, circa 1830, on a veneered swiveling pedestal, 20¾in. wide. (Skinner Inc.) $450

A mid-Victorian yewwood-veneered octagonal work table with hinged top, on acanthus-carved tripod base, 28¼in. high. (Bearne's) $1,144

Classical Revival mahogany veneered carved work table, probably New York or New Jersey, circa 1830m, with brass inlay, 24in. wide. (Skinner Inc.) $700

## WORK BOX & GAMES TABLES

Painted and grained work table, possibly Pennsylvania, second quarter 19th century, with smoke grained top, 25½in. wide. (Skinner Inc.) $2,200

A Regency rosewood and marquetry work-table inlaid with bands of scrolling foliage with rounded rectangular twin-flap top fitted with central removable panel enclosing silk-lined interior, 30in. wide. (Christie's) $2,614

Federal mahogany veneered work table, New York, 1810–30, top drawer fitted, replaced brasses, 22½in. wide. (Skinner Inc.) $4,000

A Regency satinwood work table with purpleheart lines to the rectangular top, two long drawers above a false drawer and on lyre supports, 22½in. wide. (Bearne's) $5,925

A Dutch mahogany and marquetry games table inlaid throughout with birds, butterflies, floral sprays and scrolling foliage, 34½in. wide. (Bearne's) $4,512

A Regency rosewood games table, the top with pierced brass gallery to each shaped flap, the sliding reversible central section inlaid with a chessboard, 39in. wide. (Bearne's) $7,763

An early 19th century mahogany work table, the rounded rectangular top with two drop flaps, raised upon ring turned tapering supports, 2ft. 3in. wide extended. (Spencer's) $1,278

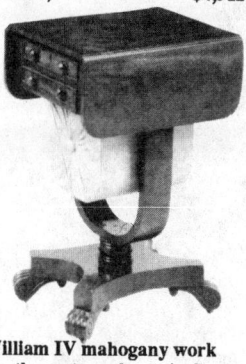

A William IV mahogany work table, the rectangular twin-flap top above two frieze drawers, the lower enclosing sliding well, 31 x 20¾in. (Christie's S. Ken) $1,646

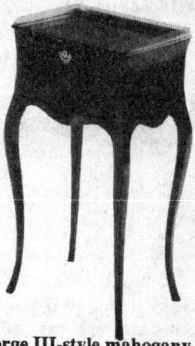

A George III-style mahogany bombé work table in the French manner, with three-quarter pierced brass gallery, 15¾in. wide. (Bearne's) $1,015

## WRITING TABLES & DESKS

A late Victorian mahogany kneehole writing table inlaid with marquetry, rosewood and zebra wood bands, on square tapering legs and spade feet, 41in. wide.
(Christie's S. Ken) $4,211

A French Second Empire tulipwood, marquetry and gilt metal-mounted cylinder bureau of Louis XVI design, the cylinder door inlaid with a musical trophy, on square tapering legs with gilt sabots, 51½in. wide.
(Christie's S. Ken) $7,758

An Arts & Crafts inlaid oak desk, the rectangular top with bow front, covered in red leather above three short drawers, 149cm. wide.
(Christie's) $3,003

Gustav Stickley desk, circa 1912, letter file with two small drawers on rectangular top over two half drawers, 22¾in. wide.
(Skinner Inc.) $700

Gustav Stickley slant lid desk, Eastwood, New York, circa 1907, gallery top, slant lid front over single drawer with brass v-pulls, 30in. wide.
(Skinner Inc.) $1,000

A George III satinwood and mahogany writing-table inlaid overall with ebonized and boxwood lines crossbanded with tulipwood, the D-shaped top and drawer inlaid in penwork, 41in. wide.
(Christie's) $9,801

A Regency mahogany and boxwood strung library table, containing six drawers in the frieze, on standard and dual splayed end supports terminating in brass cappings and castors, 4ft. x 2ft. 6in.
(Phillips) $4,672

Federal mahogany and mahogany veneer lady's desk, New England, circa 1810, the veneered doors open to an interior of small drawers, 39⅛in. wide.
(Skinner Inc.) $1,000

An early Victorian mahogany and brass-bound military pedestal desk with a rectangular leather-lined top above three frieze drawers about the kneehole, 51in. wide.
(Christie's S. Ken) $6,206

## WRITING TABLES & DESKS

A good Regency rosewood and rosewood grained library table, on lyre-shaped end supports, and gilt metal paw feet, 58¼in. wide.
(Bonhams) $13,505

An Edwardian mahogany kidney-shaped kneehole desk inlaid with boxwood lines and satinwood banded borders, on square tapering legs, labelled *Hamptons, Pall Mall, London*, 55in. wide. (Christie's S. Ken) $5,985

A William IV mahogany double-sided writing table with blue tooled leather inset and bead and reel edge to the top, 54½in. wide.
(Bearne's) $3,473

A George III mahogany bonheur du jour, inlaid overall with boxwood stringing, the low galleried superstructure with three satinwood veneered drawers, 28½in. wide.
(Bonhams) $3,056

A George III mahogany bonheur-du-jour banded in satinwood and inlaid overall with boxwood stringing, the rectangular hinged top with three-quarter gallery enclosing a baize-lined well, on brass paw feet, 36in. wide. $14,850
(Christie's)

An Edwardian mahogany lady's bonheur du jour, the shelf flanked by carved flap front stationery compartments, 3ft. wide.
(Woolley & Wallis) $1,819

A satinwood Carlton House desk inlaid with ebonized lines, the D-shaped superstructure with pierced brass gallery with six cedar-lined drawers around a leather-lined reading slope, 41½in. wide.
(Christie's S. Ken) $6,650

A thuya-veneered and partridgewood roll-top bureau de dame with rising firescreen back, 16in. wide, French, mid-19th century.
(Bearne's) $846

A William IV rosewood library table with rounded rectangular leather-lined top above frieze drawers, 42in. wide.
(Christie's S. Ken) $1,452

## WRITING TABLES & DESKS

A Victorian inlaid and parcel gilt center writing table with leather inset top above a shallow frieze drawer, 53½ x 25in.
(Lawrence Fine Art) $8,323

Gustav Stickley desk, circa 1902–03, rectangular top over two banks of four short drawers, 54in. wide.
(Skinner Inc.) $2,200

A French ormolu-mounted rosewood, mahogany and burr walnut writing table inlaid overall with boxwood and harewood, on toupie feet, mid-19th century, 55in. wide.
(Christie's) $9,207

A George III mahogany library table, the rectangular top with replacement pale green tooled hide, 3ft. 6in. wide.
(Woolley & Wallis) $4,788

Federal mahogany veneer lady's desk, New England, circa 1810, old refinish, pulls replaced, 38¼in. wide.
(Skinner Inc.) $850

A George III mahogany roll-top desk with tambour shutter enclosing a fitted interior with baize-lined reading-slope, on square tapering legs, 37in. wide.
(Christie's) $5,227

A good George III mahogany writing table, on molded square section legs headed by open 'C'-scroll brackets, 39in. wide.
(Bonhams) $8,213

Edwardian satinwood and painted cylinder desk. circa 1900, the roll top painted with central medallion, raised on square tapering legs, 36½in. wide.
(Skinner Inc.) $4,250

An ormolu-mounted kingwood and marquetry table à écrire with crossbanded kidney-shaped top inlaid with end-cut marquetry foliage, 24¼in. wide.
(Christie's) $2,445

## WRITING TABLES & DESKS

A late Victorian brass-mounted rosewood bureau plat, of Louis XV style, the shaped rectangular red leather-lined top above a waved frieze with three drawers, on cabriole legs, 54in. wide.
(Christie's) $5,729

A Louis XVI style ormolu-mounted plum pudding mahogany bureau plat in the manner of J.H. Riesener, with a shaped rectangular ormolu-molded top, 78½. wide.
(Christie's East) $20,900

A mid-Victorian ormolu-mounted amaranth, bird's eye maple, and marquetry writing-table inlaid overall with mahogany banding and floral bouquets, on cabriole legs with foliate sabots, 57in. wide.
(Christie's) $7,366

Heywood Wakefield painted wicker desk, late 19th century, shelved superstructure above a rectangular writing surface, 37in. wide.
(Skinner Inc.) $800

A Victorian ormolu-mounted tulipwood bonheur du jour, mid-19th century, with a stepped rectangular three-quarter pierced galleried superstructure, 36¾in. wide.
(Christie's East) $4,620

Louis XVI style tulipwood and kingwood marquetry desk, 19th century, recessed marble top, raised on saber legs, 32in. wide.
(Skinner Inc.) $3,750

A Napoleon III ormolu-mounted ebonized table milieu, third quarter 19th century, on spirally tapering ormolu legs with foliate cap feet, 36¼in. wide.
(Christie's East)
$28,600

An American walnut roll-top desk, with a D-shaped tambour top enclosing a fitted interior with three frieze drawers below.
(Christie's S. Ken)
$2,310

A Louis XVI ormolu-mounted mahogany and fruitwood marquetry table en encrier in the manner of J.H. Riesener, with shaped rectangular ormolu-molded top, 42¾in. wide.
(Christie's East) $15,400

## TRUNKS & COFFERS

Painted six-board chest, New England, early 19th century, lidded till, red paint, shaped bootjack ends, 47½in. wide.
(Skinner Inc.) $425

Sculptured hardwood trunk, attributed to Wendell Castle, mid 20th century, domed top on rectangular base, 45in. wide.
(Skinner Inc.) $6,000

Painted dower chest, Pennsylvania, late 18th century, all-over blue-green paint, some original brasses, 50½in. wide.
(Skinner Inc.) $1,200

Child's painted and decorated blanket box, Pennsylvania, first quarter 19th century, decorated with red, yellow, black and green, 15in. wide.
(Skinner Inc.) $11,000

A Momoyama period rectangular coffer and flat overlapping cover richly decorated in aogai and gold and brown lacquer with a hishigata (lozenge or diamond shape) design, filled alternately with shippo-hanabishi, kikko and other geometric patterns, late 16th century, 107.8 x 65.6 x 73.7cm. high.
(Christie's) $60,676

Grain painted six-board chest, New England or New York State, early 19th century, red and yellow graining to simulate mahogany, 36in. wide.
(Skinner Inc.) $375

An 18th century South German walnut and marquetry dome top coffer of tapering form, banded and inlaid with interlaced strapwork, 3ft. 11in. wide.
(Phillips) $2,141

A Chinese black and gilt lacquer chest-on-stand decorated overall with chinoiserie scenes, the domed lid decorated with figures holding nets, the sides with carrying-handles, late 18th century, 34in. wide.
(Christie's) $3,920

A 17th century later decorated chest of Armada type, painted with flowers, the hinged top with pierced interlaced engraved plate concealing a locking mechanism, 2ft. 4½in.
(Phillips) $779

## TRUNKS & COFFERS

**An 18th century Italian walnut cassone, the front with an armorial shield, grotesque mask and supported by mermen between atlantes and caryatid pilaster stiles, 2ft. 4in. wide.**
**(Phillips) $876**

**Grain painted and decorated six-board chest, Albany County, New York, 1810–35, the sides and front grained to simulate mahogany, 42in. wide.**
**(Skinner Inc.) $1,900**

**A giltmetal-mounted walnut coffer, banded overall with ebony, the repoussé mounts with birds among flowerheads and foliage, Flemish or North German, late 17th century, 24in. wide.**
**(Christie's) $6,970**

**An 18th century Italian carved walnut cassone, with later hinged top and paneled front with keyhole cartouche between mermaids flanked by caryatids, 2ft. wide.**
**(Phillips) $1,070**

**Grain painted blanket chest, New England, second quarter 19th century, all-over ocher and burnt umber simulated mahogany graining, 38in. wide.**
**(Skinner Inc.) $1,400**

**A James I oak coffer, the rectangular top above a rosette and null carved front, on trestle supports, 35in. wide.**
**(Bonhams) $5,036**

**A Continental walnut coffer, the domed top carved in relief with an armorial flanked by mounted warriors, 46in. wide.**
**(Bearne's) $1,278**

**Louis XVI provincial walnut dough box, late 18th century, serpentine molded lifting lid opening to a lined interior, 38in. high.**
**(Skinner Inc.) $1,400**

**A 17th century oak coffer, the top divided into three panels, the similarly paneled front with a frieze carved with a repeating foliate design, 39¼in. wide.**
**(Bearne's) $1,128**

## TRUNKS & COFFERS

An oak blanket chest designed by Gordon Russell, the lid with three wrought-iron strap hinges terminating in 'fleur-de-lys', with carved borders top and bottom, dated 20.6.27, 166.5cm. wide.
(Christie's) $8,110

An 18th century Swedish painted pine marriage chest, 43in. wide.
(Dreweatt Neate) $624

Painted and decorated six-board chest, New England, 19th century, all-over green paint with colored panels decorated with Rufus Porter-type trees, 43in. wide.
(Skinner Inc.) $1,900

A Chinese coffer-on-stand, the rectangular domed top with a central cartouche with Chinese landscapes of pavilions within a border of inlaid mother-of-pearl, with English carrying handles, the coffer 18th century, 39¼in. wide.
(Christie's) $7,920

A George III mahogany and brass-mounted campaign medicine chest, on later stand with square tapering legs, 20in. wide.
(Christie's S. Ken) $1,906

A Spanish leather, brass bound and studded coffer chest, the front with fall-flap enclosing two drawers, late 17th century, 42in. wide.
(Christie's S. Ken) $1,280

A George III mahogany chest enclosed by a hinged coffered rectangular lid above brass side carrying handles, 51in. wide.
(Christie's S. Ken) $1,482

An oak cellaret of cassone form carved with putti, birds, lions and fruit, 34½in. wide.
(Christie's S. Ken) $2,567

A Charles II brass-studded leather coffer decorated overall with stylized flowers and scrolling foliage with rectangular domed lid, the front with entwined dolphin and birds, 46in. wide.
(Christie's) $858

## TRUNKS & COFFERS

An Italian, Roman, walnut cassone, the molded rectangular stepped lid carved with acanthus enclosing a plain interior with drainage hole, the front and sides of waisted shape carved with flowerheads, late 16th century, 68½in. wide.
(Christie's) $8,668

A 19th century mahogany rectangular cellaret on paw feet.
(Dreweatt Neate) $2,243

A Venetian cedarwood coffer, the front incised and inlaid with lions and birds flanking a tree, on later bracket feet, first half 17th century, 69½in. wide.
(Christie's) $3,647

A Chinese black-lacquer and chinoiserie chest, on a pine stand profusely carved with dragons and emblems of happiness, 42in. wide.
(Christie's S. Ken) $6,006

A Cromwellian oak chest with molded rectangular hinged top enclosing a well above a panel carved with a coat-of-arms, on stile feet, with later staining, 52in. wide.
(Christie's) $6,006

17th/18th century oak coffer, having a three paneled front with rosette carvings and bottom drawers, 3ft. 9in. wide.
(G.A. Key) $567

Late 18th early 19th century oak dower chest with brass carrying handles to the front and sides, 4ft. 3in. wide.
(G.A. Key) $624

Painted pine blanket box, possibly New York, early 19th century, the lift top opens to a well with open till, 47in. wide.
(Skinner Inc.) $3,100

A late 16th/early 17th century Continental dome top painted leather and wrought iron bound coffer, of Islamic influence, Italian or Flemish.
(Phillips) $5,675

## WARDROBES & ARMOIRES

A French Provincial walnut and elm armoire, with a pair of triple shaded panel cupboard doors, on short cabriole legs, 52¾in. wide, mid 18th century.
(Bonhams) $2,850

A Franco-Flemish walnut armoire with molded rectangular cornice above a paneled frieze carved with vases and foliage above three pairs of paneled doors, incorporating some earlier panels, 180in. wide.
(Christie's) $13,943

An oak wardrobe designed by Peter Waals, of rectangular form, the two cupboard doors each with four panels and wooden latch, 182.5cm. high.
(Christie's) $4,268

A fine Dutch mahogany armoire, the pair of paneled cupboard doors applied with ribbon and tassel tied pendant husk swags and urns, 68in. wide, late 18th century.
(Bonhams) $6,840

A Dutch mahogany and marquetry armoire with molded dentil cornice above two fielded paneled doors each inlaid with vases of flowers, birds and butterflies, 70in. wide.
(Christie's) $14,086

A Flemish oak, walnut, ebony and ebonized armoire with fielded paneled frieze flanked and divided by volutes above a pair of small fielded paneled doors and a larger conforming pair of doors, late 17th century, 60½in. wide.
(Christie's) $9,653

A Robert Thompson Mouseman oak cupboard, of rectangular two door construction with adze-finish, carved with a mouse, 108.5cm. wide.
(Lawrence Fine Art) $2,530

A stained oak Arts & Crafts wardrobe, the paneled door having a beaten copper panel with a design of birds and trees towards its top.
(Phillips) $756

A late Georgian mahogany breakfront wardrobe with central arched pediment above a pair of doors, 90in. wide.
(Spencer's) $1,024

## WARDROBES & ARMOIRES

A handsome George III mahogany wardrobe, the pair of rectangular panel cupboard doors crossbanded in rosewood and outlined in boxwood stringing, 55¾in. wide. (Bonhams) $2,865

A George II mahogany wardrobe in the style of Giles Grendey, with later broken pediment cornice with dentil molding centered by a giltwood armorial device, 52¾in. wide. (Christie's) $5,663

A Regency mahogany wardrobe probably by Gillows, with molded cornice above two molded paneled doors enclosing hanging space, 51in. wide. (Christie's S. Ken) $2,502

A Dutch mahogany armoire with two paneled doors carved with ribbon-tied paterae and baskets of flowers flanked by fluted column-angles, late 18th century, 105½in. high. (Christie's) $17,336

A Franco-Flemish oak wardrobe with molded rectangular cornice above a pair of hinged paneled double doors each carved with Romayne busts headed by foliate scrolls, 72in. wide. (Christie's) $7,508

Late Victorian inlaid mahogany wardrobe in the Adam taste, circa 1880, the upper panels inlaid with ribbon-tied wreaths suspending pendant husks, 45in. wide. (Butterfield & Butterfield) $1,430

Gustav Stickley two-door wardrobe, circa 1907, two paneled doors with copper pulls opening to reveal two compartments, 34⅛in. wide. (Skinner Inc.) $5,000

A George III oak wardrobe inlaid overall with mahogany, the lower section with seven false drawers and two long drawers, on shaped bracket feet, 71¼in. wide. (Christie's) $2,360

An 18th century French oak armoire with two doors each with three shaped fielded panels and on bun feet, 58in. wide. (Bearne's) $1,716

## WASHSTANDS

An unusual early 19th century mahogany wash basin and stand. (Lawrence Butler) $950

A William IV mahogany washstand, the rectangular top with a rising central section and flap ends, 41½in. wide extended. (Hy Duke & Son) $651

George III mahogany wash stand with lifting top revealing a central void to house wash basin, 17in. square. (G.A. Key) $720

A French Empire mahogany basin stand with circular dished top, small drawer and on a 'lyre' support, 16in. wide. (Bearne's) $508

A George III mahogany pedestal toilet stand, the folding rectangular top enclosing bowl apertures above a simulate drawer front, 23in. wide. (Christie's S. Ken) $1,180

A George III mahogany bow fronted corner washstand with cut-out from basin and a single drawer on splay legs. (Abbotts) $285

A George III mahogany lady's toilet stand, the serpentine hinged top enclosing a fitted interior and adjustable plate, 26¾in. wide. (Christie's S. Ken) $1,171

A George IV mahogany wash stand with a pair of hinged flaps enclosing a pull up swing frame toilet mirror, cut out basin and beaker stands, 33in. x 34in. high. (Anderson & Garland) $1,027

A late George III satinwood and amaranth banded corner washstand with a hinged galleried back enclosing a fitted interior, on splayed legs, 26½in. wide. (Christie's S. Ken) $2,660

## WHATNOTS

A George III mahogany whatnot with five tiers, on square end-supports each with splayed finial and brass caps, 48in. high.
(Christie's) $6,970

A Victorian figured walnut three tier whatnot, on turned tapered legs terminating in castors, 23in. wide. (Spencer's) $785

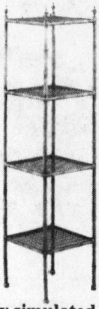

A Regency simulated bamboo whatnot with four square cane-filled tiers headed by vase-shaped finials, 50½in. high.
(Christie's) $4,138

A Victorian rosewood four tier corner whatnot, 23in. x 48in. high.
(Dreweatt Neate) $975

A pair of early Victorian mahogany whatnots, one with a lower part with a cupboard and the other with open top with divisions for magazines, 51in. high. (Lawrence Fine Art)
$3,146

A George IV rosewood four-tier whatnot, the tiers supported on baluster turned columns, with a drawer to the base, on turned legs, 18¼in. wide.
(Bonhams) $1,643

A William IV mahogany whatnot of four tiers with a pierced gilt-metal gallery around the top tier, 66in. high.
(Lawrence Fine Art)
$6,292

A mid Victorian walnut canterbury whatnot, the serpentine top with a three-quarter fret-carved gallery, 24in. wide.
(Christie's S. Ken) $1,839

A Napoleon III ormolu-mounted kingwood, amaranth and marquetry étagère with three kidney-shaped tiers each inlaid with a cartouche, 32in. high.
(Christie's) $1,129

## WINE COOLERS

A George IV mahogany wine cellaret of sarcophagus shape, the hinged cover with central raised panel, on plinth base, 29½in. wide.
(Lawrence Fine Art) $1,600

A William IV feathered mahogany sarcophagus wine cooler, with fruit cast brass carrying handles to the sides, on paw feet, 42in. wide.
(Bonhams) $3,056

One of a pair of William IV wine coolers, each with molded rectangular top around a lead-lined well, with gadrooned sides and feet, 35in. wide.
(Christie's) Two $16,854

A George III mahogany cellaret, of octagonal form, bound in brass, the hinged top enclosing a lead-lined interior, 25in. wide.
(Bonhams) $4,745

Limbert cellarete, circa 1908, no. 751, rectangular top projecting over single drawer with square copper pulls, 24¾in. wide.
(Skinner Inc.) $1,000

A George III mahogany wine cooler, the hinged rectangular lid enclosing an interior with compartments, the sides with brass carrying handles, on square tapering legs, 21in. wide.
(Christie's) $3,960

A Regency mahogany and ebony-strung wine cooler with square canted hinged top, enclosing a lead-lined interior, on turned tapering fluted legs, 16½in. wide.
(Christie's S. Ken) $3,990

A George III mahogany cellaret-on-stand, banded with rosewood, the hinged square top enclosing a later mahogany tray and compartments, 15¾in. wide.
(Christie's) $3,366

A George III solid amboyna cellaret, with brass carrying handles to the sides, the hinged top enclosing an interior fitted with divisions, 20½in. wide.
(Bonhams) $3,438

## WINE COOLERS

A Regency mahogany wine cooler with a brass-bound rounded rectangular body enclosing a tin liner, 35in. wide.
(Hy Duke & Son) $2,790

A Regency mahogany wine cooler of rectangular shape with lead-lined interior and lead tray, on rosewood paw feet, 32½in. wide.
(Christie's) $4,792

A Regency mahogany sarcophagus wine cooler, the lid with a gadrooned rim above a paneled front and sides, 29½in. wide.
(Bonhams) $1,433

A George III mahogany cellaret, with hinged serpentine-fronted square top enclosing a foil-lined interior with compartments, on square tapering legs, 16in. wide.
(Christie's) $4,246

A George III mahogany wine cellaret, on a stand with four canted supports with brass castors, 25in. wide.
(Lawrence Fine Art) $4,719

A late George III mahogany cellaret of octagonal form, the ebony strung lid opening to reveal a converted interior, 20in. wide.
(Hy Duke & Son) $2,790

A George III carved mahogany and brass bound oval wine cooler, on foliate carved square tapered legs, brass cappings and castors, 2ft. wide.
(Phillips) $2,784

A Chinese Export black-lacquer and gilt decorated octagonal cellaret on a later stand with an overall trellis design centered by oval floral medallions, first quarter 19th century, 25in. wide.
(Christie's S. Ken) $3,103

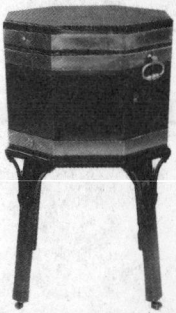

A George III mahogany brass bound octagonal wine cooler, the hinged top with molded edge opening to reveal a lead lined divided interior.
(Phillips) $5,568

A Doulton terracotta urn, the squat body decorated with trailing grape vine motif, on circular socle, 40in. high.
(Christie's) $773

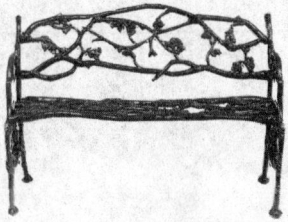

A green-painted cast-iron bench, the pierced back, sides and seat cast with leafy branches, 50½in. wide.
(Christie's) $1,933

One of a pair of lead figures of eagles with wings outstretched, standing on square bases with cut corners, 24in. high.
(Christie's)(Two) $1,628

A white-painted cast-iron chair, the pierced floral back above a drop-in pierced seat and scrolled cabriole legs.
(Christie's) $1,323

One of a pair of Verona marble seats, the curved backs with lion mask terminals with paw feet, centred by an anthemion motif, 30in. high, and a table of rectangular oval form.
(Christie's)
(Three) $14,245

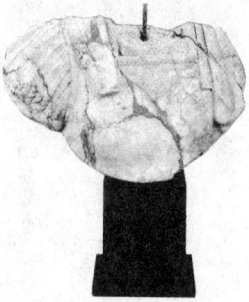

A variegated white marble bust, lacking head, the torso dressed as a Roman Emperor, 15½in. high.
(Christie's) $2,239

A terracotta jardinière, on twist turn support with three addorsed figures of swans, on circular rocky naturalistic base, 35½in. high.
(Christie's) $2,849

A magnificent Italian marble group of Galatea riding a dolphin, by Leopoldo Ansiglioni, the alluring naked nymph reclining against her dolphin, her arms reaching back and entwined about his tail, circa 1880, 54½in. high overall.
(Christie's) $174,240

One of a pair of white-painted cast-iron urns of Campana form, the beaded rims above foliate arabesques, mask-and-loop handles, 29½in. high.
(Christie's)(Two) $1,425

A cast-iron double-sided garden bench, the end pieces decorated with eagle-mask hand terminals, on paw feet, 57in. wide.
(Christie's) $3,867

A cast-iron plant stand, the scrolled framework supporting six circular and pierced stands, 39½in.
(Christie's) $712

A large pair of English white lionesses, after the Antique, reclining, their tails curled about their haunches, on rectangular bases, 19th century, 42½ x 25 x 14⅜in.
(Christie's) $90,024

A terracotta plinth, the square top formed as a capital with acanthus leaf scrolls, the circular knopped shaft applied with trailing grapevines, 41in. high.
(Christie's) $1,016

A pair of lead fountain masks, depicting Winter and Spring, of Baroque influence, spouts issuing from their mouths, raised on cloud motifs, 21in. high.
(Christie's) $4,070

A large bronze group, depicting Hebe, the cup-bearer for the Gods, proffering ambrosia from the cup to Jupiter's eagle, on oval naturalistic base signed *C. BUHOT*, 65¾in. high.
(Christie's) $32,560

An 18th century white marble part urn, the bowl with fluted mask-and-loop handles, carved with anthemion and stiff leaf decoration, the base 22in. high.
(Christie's) $3,867

A green-painted cast-iron garden bench, the pierced scrolled back on S-scrolled end supports, 28½in. wide.
(Christie's) $509

Marble bird bath, 20th century, circular basin, decorated throughout with scrolling acanthus and anthemion, 27in. diameter.
(Skinner Inc.) $1,600

A white marble bust of the Apollo Belvedere, after the Antique, the head turned to sinister and with draped shoulders, on socle, 30¼in. high. (Christie's) $5,291

A Coadestone urn of oval form, with lion-mask ring handles, rosette frieze and stiff leaf decoration, 36in. diameter. (Christie's) $15,263

Lead figural fountain head, first half 19th century, in the form of a standing naked infant strangling a cockerel, 33in. high. (Butterfield & Butterfield) $1,870

Charming lead garden figure of a little girl and her rabbit, circa 1930, standing on a rockwork base, 31½in. high. (Butterfield & Butterfield) $825

A Regency wrought-iron arch, centered by a scrolled spike, above a fan overdoor, 120 x 78½in. (Christie's) $1,526

Monumental cast-stone figure of Diana holding a bow and drapery across her thighs, leaning with her right arm around her deer, 7ft. 1in. high. (Butterfield & Butterfield) $3,300

Continental carved carrara marble sundial in the Neoclassical taste, probably Italian, second half 19th century, on a concave sided plinth, 41in. high. (Butterfield & Butterfield) $2,200

Large cast-stone planter on stand, 19th century, on an associated rusticated square pedestal, 35½in. high. (Butterfield & Butterfield) $1,980

A white marble figure of a bathing Venus, clutching draperies to her midriff, on circular shaped base, signed *R.J. Wyatt, Fecit, Roma*, 60½in. high. (Christie's) $11,193

A glazed stoneware sun-dial plinth, on addorsed swan support, and square sloping base, incorporating a bronze sun-dial inscribed *Thomas Grice, 1705*, 34½in. high.
(Christie's) $1,628

A white-painted cast-iron gothic armchair, the pierced back and down-curved arm-rests on iron slat seat.
(Christie's) $712

One of a pair of Italian Verona marble tazze, the circular dishes with molded rims and gadrooned bodies, with square bases, 29in. diameter.
(Christie's)
(Two) $10,175

A fine Italian white marble figure of a Greek slave girl, by Scipione Tadolini, the maiden shown lightly clad, her hair elaborately dressed in a chignon and head-dress, second half 19th century, 65½in. high the sculpture.
(Christie's) $163,680

Pair of large cast-stone fruit baskets on stands, raised on a lobed hemispherical stand above a fluted spreading socle, 45in. high. (Butterfield & Butterfield)
$5,225

A 19th century white marble figure of Rebecca at the Well, seated on a rocky outcrop in pensive mood, with water jar at her feet, signed indistinctly, on naturalistic base, 55in. high.
(Christie's) $16,280

A filled terracotta plinth of cylindrical form, the shaft decorated with a frieze of classical figures, 41in. high.
(Christie's) $366

One of a pair of Indian white marble urns of spherical form with fluted bodies, 19in. diameter.
(Christie's) (Two) $1,323

One of a set of six white-painted cast-iron chairs, the waisted backs above pierced seats and cabriole legs.
(Christie's) (Six) $1,425

## BEAKERS

A finely cut Biedermeier tumbler with an oval panel intaglio carved with a figure of Psyche amidst flowers, 13.5cm.
(Phillips) $711

A German green-tinted small flared beaker with allover honeycomb-molding beneath a ribbed rim, 15th century, 9.5cm. diameter.
(Christie's) $1,805

A small German glass tumbler, probably Nuremberg, engraved with the sun over a hillside town, 8.8cm., 18th century.
(Bearne's) $1,396

An interesting German beaker with three arcaded panels engraved with a sportsman carrying a gun and restraining his dog, 13.2cm.
(Phillips) $860

A pair of lithyalin green tinted remembrance beakers from the workshop of Friedrich Egermann, of faceted, waisted form, 11cm.
(Phillips) $2,431

A Bohemian clear glass flared beaker engraved with a scene of the Last Supper, the reverse inscribed *Das heil Abendmal*, 12cm.
(Phillips) $673

An engraved cylindrical tumbler decorated with a continuous scene of a standing figure of Britannia, with facet-cut footrim, circa 1800, 11.5cm. high.
(Christie's) $807

Bohemian white and cranberry overlay spa glass, mid 19th century, with six vertical panels each with a named engraved and gilt architectural view, 5in. high.
(Butterfield & Butterfield) $357

A Bohemian tumbler engraved on one side with a peasant holding a fishing rod, a dog at his side, 11.5cm.
(Phillips) $673

## BOTTLES

'Reeds/Bitters' bottle, lady's leg, bubbly glass, amber, sloping collar with bevel-smooth base, 12½in. high, America, 1820–80. (Skinner Inc.) $175

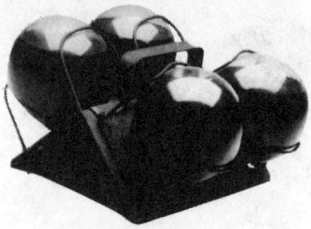

Fire grenade rack with four grenades, with brass label 'Pyro-Ball/International/Staten Island/ New York City'. (Skinner Inc.) $125

'Dr. Caldwells/Herb Bitters' bottle, triangular, amber, sloping collar with ring-smooth base, 12½in. high, America, 1870–80. (Skinner Inc.) $125

Fire grenade, patented Aug. 8, 1871, square with round panels, original contents, cobalt blue, 5⅞in. high. (Skinner Inc.) $175

Warners 'Log Cabin-Extract-Rochester NY' labeled medicine bottle, with box in mint condition, 8⅛in. high. (Skinner Inc.) $130

'Barnums/Hard Fire/Ext-Diamond' fire grenade, patented June 25, 1869, square with indented round panels, aqua, 6in. high. (Skinner Inc.) $275

Ruby glass bottle vase, 19th century, the metal of a deep rich purplish-red tone, 10½in. high. (Butterfield & Butterfield) $2,200

Regency mahogany traveling cellaret, the fitted interior with six bottles and stoppers, 11¼in. wide. (G.A. Key) $1,203

'AM Bininger & Co.' labelled cannon shaped whiskey bottle, label *Great Gun Gin* with woman holding flag and man with goblet and rifle, 12½in. high, America, 1861–1864. (Skinner Inc.) $950

## BOTTLES

Santa Claus figural bottle, Husted on lower side, colorless round flat collar-smooth base, 12½in. high, 1880–1900.
(Skinner Inc.) $30

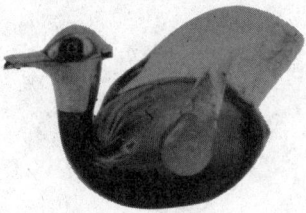

A novelty duck amber glass bodied sauce bottle with silver head spout, the hinged cover set with glass eyes, 6¼in., Akers & Co. Birmingham 1919.
(Woolley & Wallis) $813

'Mohawk Whiskey Pure Rye' Indian figural whiskey bottle, original red sealing wax around half of lip, 12⅝in. high, America, 1870–80.
(Skinner Inc.) $650

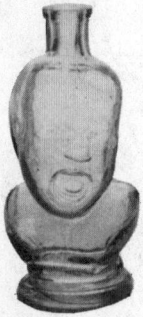

Crying baby figural bottle, colorless, (one small chip on underside of base), 6in. high, 1875–90.
(Skinner Inc.) $100

An attractive small wine bottle of shouldered onion shape with a pronounced string ring, 15cm.
(Phillips) $279

'S.O. Dunbar/Taunton/Mass' medicine bottle, with frayed and stained label reading *Fluid Magnesia, prepared by S.O. Dunbar, Taunton, Mass*, 5⅝in. high, America, 1840–60.
(Skinner Inc.) $230

A sealed wine bottle for Jesus College Common Room, in dark green glass of mallet shape, 20.5cm.
(Phillips) $632

Fancy cologne bottle, square with upward diamond-like points on edge, excellent deep amethyst color, 6¾in. high New England, 1860–80.
(Skinner Inc.) $550

Pineapple figural bitters bottle, bright medium green, double collared lip-iron pontil, 8½in. high, America, 1855–65.
(Skinner Inc.) $1,100

## BOTTLES

**Fancy barber's bottle, nine panels on bulbous body with diamond design, cranberry, with colorless petaled applied lip, 6 1/2 in. high.**
**(Skinner Inc.) $70**

**Tea kettle ink bottle, barrel shaped, medium sapphire blue, no closure, 2 1/4 in. high.**
**(Skinner Inc.) $550**

**Melon sided barber bottle, opalized yellow green, rolled lip-smooth base, 7 1/4 in. high.**
**(Skinner Inc.) $70**

**A well-engraved Bohemian bottle of shouldered cylindrical shape, engraved with a continuous stag-hunting scene, 14.5cm.**
**(Phillips) $1,295**

**An 'onion' serving-bottle of olive-green tint with kick-in base, the applied scroll handle with pincered thumbpiece, circa 1725, 16.5cm. high.**
**(Christie's) $1,592**

**A sealed wine bottle of cylindrical shape in dark olive glass, with a circular seal inscribed *Colonel Wood's Madiera 1797*, 27.5cm.**
**(Phillips) $316**

**A very rare octagonal sealed wine bottle, of flattened octagonal shape in mid-green glass with a tapering neck, 1740, 21cm.**
**(Phillips) $2,604**

**Early snuff bottle, rectangular with chamfered corners, mouth slightly offset, deep green, very bubbly glass, 4 5/8 in. high, probably New England, 1800–40.**
**(Skinner Inc.) $250**

**'Log Cabin/Sarsaparilla/ Rochester NY' sarsaparilla bottle, golden amber, round blob lip-smooth base, 9in. high, America, 1885–1895.**
**(Skinner Inc.) $50**

'Warners/Safe/Remedies Co.' labeled medicine bottle, full label with contents and neck label, 6 fl. oz., golden amber, 7 3/8 in. high.
(Skinner Inc.) $80

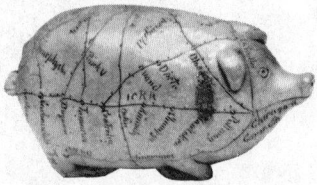

Anna-type pottery railroad guide pig, large railroad map around body, mint condition, 4in. high, probably Anna Pottery, Anna, Illinois, 1890.
(Skinner Inc.) $3,700

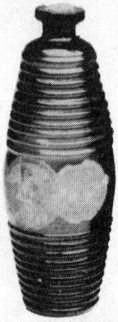

'Greeley's Bourbon/Bitters' labeled bitters bottle, barrel shape, 95% label, light smokey olive green, 9 1/8 in. high, America, 1860–80.
(Skinner Inc.) $550

Enameled cordial bottle, with multi-colored scene of bird and florals, pewter screw threads complete, no cap, 6 1/2 in. high, Bohemia, mid 18th century.
(Skinner Inc.) $325

Skull figural poison bottle, deep cobalt, 4 1/4 in. high, America, 1880–90.
(Skinner Inc.) $950

A dated enameled rectangular bottle and stopper, the sides with diaper-pattern and with applied milled bands to the angles, perhaps Scotland, 1767, 18.5cm. high.
(Christie's) $1,168

'Hathaways/Celebrated/ Stomach/Bitters' labeled bitters bottle, square, amber, 80% black and white label, 10in. high, America, 1870–80.
(Skinner Inc.) $150

Pinch bottle, half pint, 24-ribs swirled to the left, smoky sapphire blue, flaring lip-pontil scar, 9 1/2 in. high, probably Germany, mid 18th century.
(Skinner Inc.) $450

Bininger barrel whiskey bottle, dark amber, double collared lip-pontil scar, 8in. high, America 1861–64.
(Skinner Inc.) $155

## BOTTLES

Paneled cologne bottle, 12-sided, rare rolled over lip, deep emerald green, smooth base, 4¾in. high, New England, 1860–80.
(Skinner Inc.) $400

'Suffolk Bitters' – 'Philbrook and Tucker' figural pig bitters bottles, medium golden amber, flattened collared lip, 10in. high, America, 1870–80.
(Skinner Inc.) $450

'Rohrers-Expectoral/Wild/Cherry/Tonic' medicine bottle, amber, sloping collar with bevel-iron pontil, 10¾in. high, America, 1860–70.
(Skinner Inc.) $100

Early snuff bottle, rectangular with beveled edges, oliver green, applied lip-smooth base, 6¾in. high, New England, early 19th century.
(Skinner Inc.) $175

Midwestern globular bottle, 24-ribs swirled to the left, deep golden amber, rolled lip-pontil scar, 7¾in. high, 1820–50.
(Skinner Inc.) $325

Early utilitarian bottle, cylinder with slightly wider base, applied string ring below lip, olive green, pontil scar, 5⅞in. high, 1780–1830.
(Skinner Inc.) $550

A Nuremburg engraved bottle, the compressed globular body with Cupid holding a heart and bow, on a circular foot, circa 1700, 25cm. high.
(Christie's) $4,034

'EG Booz's/Old Cabin/Whiskey' bottle, cabin shaped, deep golden amber, quart, Whitney Glassworks, Glassboro, New Jersey, 1860's.
(Skinner Inc.) $1,100

Moses figural Poland Springs mineral water bottle, unusual flared lip, green, 10⅞in. high.
(Skinner Inc.) $175

## BOWLS

An Art Deco frosted green glass bowl set in a chromed metal stand on a bakelite base, 32.5cm.
(Bearne's) $222

A Gallé enamel painted, acid-etched and gilded two-handled jardinière, the smoky-green tinted glass with polychrome enamel painted decoration of grasshoppers, a butterfly and a cicada amongst foliage and mushrooms, 31.2cm. diameter.
(Christie's) $39,820

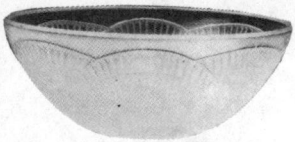

A Lalique opalescent bowl, cataloged 'Vase Coquilles', 24cm.
(Bearne's) $586

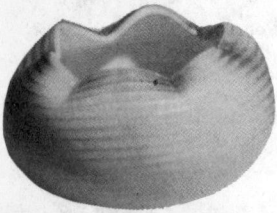

A rainbow 'mother-of-pearl' small bowl of compressed form with crimped inverted rim, the base marked *PATENT*, perhaps Stevens & Williams, circa 1885, 11.5cm. diameter.
(Christie's) $444

A cut shallow oval bowl with sunray center, the sides with a wide band of diamonds beneath a Vandyke-pattern rim (slight bruising), circa 1815, 30cm. wide.
(Christie's) $887

A 'mother-of-pearl' circular bowl of compressed globular form with crimped inverted rim, perhaps Stevens & Williams, circa 1885, 16.5cm. diameter.
(Christie's) $480

Pattern molded bowl, broken swirl, 16-ribs swirling to the right, lead glass, sapphire blue, pontil scar, 4 7/8 in. wide, possibly early Pittsburg piece.
(Skinner Inc.) $300

Louis XVI style gilt-bronze-mounted cut glass center bowl, on a square plinth with four leaf-cast outswept feet, 8 3/8 in. high.
(Butterfield & Butterfield) $550

A Loetz white metal overlay bowl, clear glass splashes with golden iridescence, decorated with curvilinear flowers and foliage, 5 1/4 in. high.
(Christie's S. Ken) $407

'Perruches', a Lalique opalescent bowl, the blue-stained glass molded with a band of budgerigars perched amid foliage, 24cm. diameter.
(Christie's) $5,148

A 'Le Verre Français' cameo glass jardinière, of yellow tone streaked with turquoise-green overlaid with red glass shading to reddish-brown, 17.50cm. high.
(Phillips) $1,751

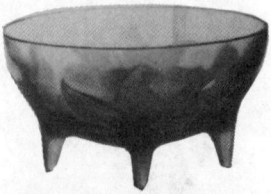

'Lys', a Lalique opalescent bowl, the clear and satin-finished glass molded with four lilies, the stems forming the feet of the bowl, 23.9cm. diameter.
(Christie's) $1,792

## BOWLS

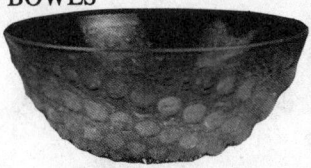

A Lalique opalescent glass bowl, of circular form, the exterior molded with graduated bubbles spiraling towards the base, 20.5cm. diameter.
(Lawrence Fine Art) $675

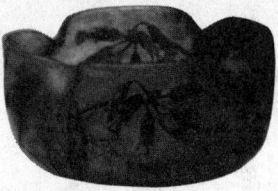

A Daum acid-etched and enameled bowl, the mottled opaque yellow and pink glass decorated with enamel painted polychrome cowslips, 15cm. diameter.
(Christie's) $2,389

'Perruches'. A Lalique opalescent glass bowl molded with love birds amid flowering prunus branch heightened with blue staining, 23.5cm. diameter.
(Phillips) $1,330

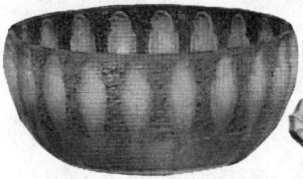

'Perruches', a Lalique opalescent glass bowl, the exterior molded in relief with a band of budgerigars perched on foliage, $9^{1}/_{4}$in. diameter.
(Christie's S. Ken) $3,132

One of a pair of George III oval cut glass baskets and stands, $10^{5}/_{8}$in. wide.
(Dreweatt Neate)
(Two) $1,599

Webb gem cameo multi-layered bowl, unusual olive green layered in red, mauve and white, $5^{1}/_{2}$in. diameter.
(Skinner Inc.) $2,500

A Venetian enameled deep bowl, gilt with a wide band of scale ornament embellished with enameled dots in white, iron-red, green and blue, circa 1500, 24cm. diameter.
(Christie's) $5,095

A brandy-warmer or sauce-pan, the circular slightly waisted bowl with allover honeycomb molding beneath an everted rim with pouring lip, mid-18th century, 13.5cm. wide.
(Christie's) $849

A 'Façon de Venise' tazza, the shallow circular bowl with traces of granular gilding to the rim, Antwerp or perhaps South Netherlands, 16th century, 19.5cm. diameter.
(Christie's) $12,012

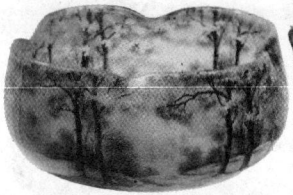

A Daum acid-etched and enamel painted bowl, the mottled clear, green and yellow glass decorated with polychrome enameled wooded landscape, 19.8cm. diameter.
(Christie's) $4,290

A Venini 'Vetro Pezzato Arlecchino' bowl, designed by Fulvio Bianconi, the patchwork design made up of irregular rectangles in green, blue, red and clear cased glass, 16.5cm. diameter.
(Christie's) $6,864

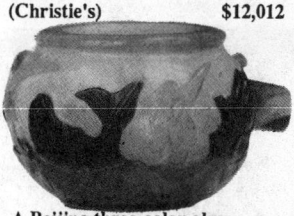

A Beijing three-color glass overlay bird-feed cup, the globular body carved through layers of blue, red and green to a milky white ground with a fish swimming in a lotus pond, 18th century, 5cm. wide.
(Christie's) $2,988

## BOWLS

A Gabriel Argy-Rousseau pâte-de-verre pedestal glass bowl, the exterior molded with a green and blue vine leaf pattern, 13cm. diameter.
(Bearne's) $5,459

Blown sugar bowl, flaring lip with applied threading extending to mid body, 7⅝in. high, attributed to Saratoga Mt. Glassworks, Saratoga, New York, mid 19th century.
(Skinner Inc.) $2,900

An Irish oval turnover bowl cut with a band of facets, the turnover rim with alternate prismatic cutting, (chips to footrim), circa 1800, 31cm. wide.
(Christie's) $1,571

A fine glass combination bowl and comport cut with panels containing flower heads within diamond borders, 32.5cm.
(Bearne's) $273

'Ondine', a Lalique opalescent glass bowl, the under side molded with six sea sprites, with wheel-carved signature *R. Lalique France*, 21cm. diameter.
(Christie's) $1,566

Clear pressed glass compote, in thumbprint pattern, height 9in., diameter 10in.
(Eldred's) $121

An Almaric Walter pâte-de-verre hexagonal footed bowl in shades of blue, 4in. diameter.
(Christie's S. Ken) $300

Fine English footed pressed glass punch bowl, in diamond point pattern, height 9½in., diameter 10–12in.
(Eldred's) $99

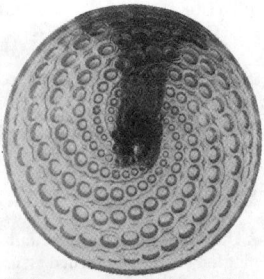

A Lalique opalescent bowl with beads graduating inside and forming a swirling pattern, 20cm. long.
(Phillips) $534

## BOWLS

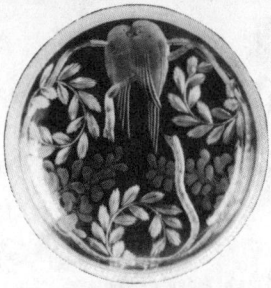

Libbey lovebirds cut glass bowl, shallow form in the Wisteria pattern with crosshatch border, 8in. diameter.
(Skinner Inc.) $400

Freeblown bowl, with witch ball cover, widely flaring lip, applied solid foot, greenish aqua, 8in. high.
(Skinner Inc.) $300

A cased glass bowl designed by A Mazzega, of flaring form with everted rim, white glass cased in green.
(Christie's S. Ken) $240

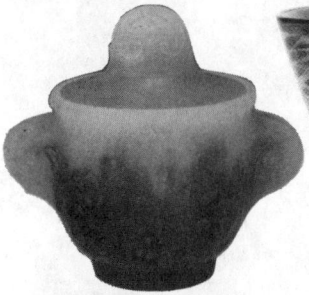

An Almaric Walter pâte-de-verre cache-pot, modeled by H. Bergé, the mottled white and blue pot molded with green and red leaves and berries, 13cm. high.
(Christie's) $4,308

A Graal bowl by Lindean Mill, the flared form on short circular foot, the blue tinted glass with purple stylized birds amid foliage, 14cm. high.
(Christie's) $598

Freeblown sugar bowl, Clevenger Brothers, crimped on bottom, deep pinkish amethyst, pontil scar, 3⅝in. high, New Jersey, 1930's.
(Skinner Inc.) $150

A good slice, hob nail, diamond and fan cut glass punch bowl and stand, the tulip shaped bowl with undulating scalloped rim, 13in. diameter.
(Spencer's) $334

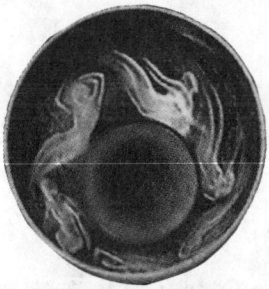

'Ondines', a Lalique opalescent glass bowl, the exterior molded in relief with a band of undulating sea nymphs, 8in. diameter.
(Christie's S. Ken) $770

Cranberry glass stemmed bowl on circular foot, 7in. diameter.
(G.A. Key) $175

## CANDLESTICKS

A pair of Venini black and white glass candlesticks each modeled as kneeling blackamoors holding baskets, 6¾in. high.
(Christie's S. Ken) $964

A set of four late 19th century Murano gilt heightened and white enameled glass three light candelabra, each with a central branch flanked by two scrolling arms, 21in. high.
(Christie's S. Ken)
(Four) $4,477

One of a pair of Venini candlesticks designed by Fulvio Bianconi, each modeled as a white jacket on a tripartite coatstand, 8¼in. high.
(Christie's S. Ken)
(Two) $2,784

An opaque taperstick, the cylindrical nozzle with everted rim and the domed foot painted with loose bouquets and scattered flowers, South Staffordshire, circa 1760, 18.5cm. high. $1,062
(Christie's)

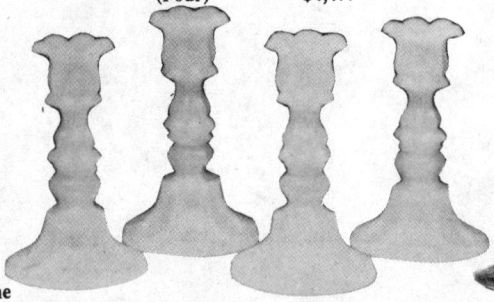

Four pressed glass Clambroth candlesticks, Sandwich Glass Company, Massachusetts, 1840–60, all with petal bobeches, 7in. high.
(Skinner Inc.) $350

A pedestal-stemmed candlestick, supported on a beaded knop above an octagonally molded pedestal section, circa 1750, 20.5cm. high.
(Christie's) $1,478

Pair of pressed glass candlesticks, Sandwich Glass Company, Massachusetts, 1850–65, 9in. high.
(Skinner Inc.) $950

A 'Cristallo Ceramie' double branch candelabra attributed to Apsley Pellat, the square stem set with a medallion containing a sulphide of an historical gentleman, 40cm.
(Phillips) $996

Pair of cranberry to clear candlesticks, classic baluster form with faceted paneling, 9½in. high.
(Skinner Inc.) $100

## CANDY CONTAINERS

**Rabbit family candy container, with all original gold paint, no closure.**
**(Skinner Inc.) $400**

**Piano candy container, with tin closure, mint condition.**
**(Skinner Inc.) $150**

**Rocking horse with clown candy container, bluish tinted glass, no closure, few base chips.**
**(Skinner Inc.) $90**

**Kewpie candy container, standing by barrel with 100% paint, perfect closure with coin slot.**
**(Skinner Inc.) $145**

**Village log cabin candy container, complete with glass liner.**
**(Skinner Inc.) $500**

**Rabbit pushing chick in shell cart candy container, excellent example, all original complete paint.**
**(Skinner Inc.) $425**

**Telephone candy container, with cork top and cardboard shield *when empty have me refilled at H B Waters & Co., Boston, Mass,* 5 1/8 in. high.**
**(Skinner Inc.) $350**

**Liberty Motors airplane candy container, excellent condition with 100% paint, complete.**
**(Skinner Inc.) $3,500**

**Crowing chicken candy containers, with all original paint, colorful contents and closure.**
**(Skinner Inc.) $220**

**Duck with large bill candy container, with most of its original paint.**
**(Skinner Inc.) $125**

**Opera glass candy container, opaque white glass, tin screw on closures, perfect condition.**
**(Skinner Inc.) $150**

**Uncle Sam's hat candy containers, with original paint, one small base chip.**
**(Skinner Inc.) $30**

## DECANTERS

A very attractive Bohemian cased decanter and stopper, the ruby body cased in white and green opaline glass, 28cm.
(Phillips) $4,183

A 19th century boulle and rosewood decanter box, holding four cut-glass decanters, decorated with gilt floral sprays, six similar glasses and five others, 13in. wide.
(Bonhams) $1,242

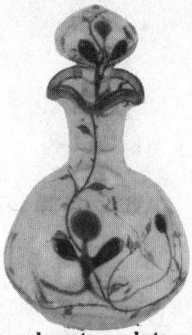

A liqueur decanter and stopper by Moser of Karlsbad, decorated with floral motifs and trailing stems in mauve, ruby and green glass appliqués, 17.5cm. high.
(Phillips) $1,070

A Hukin & Heath electroplated tantalus designed by Dr. Christopher Dresser, the open rectangular square-section frame with sliding and locking front stretcher, registration lozenge for 1879, 28cm. high.
(Christie's) $10,670

A Gallé enameled decanter and stopper, the green tinted glass polychrome enameled with the suit of hearts picture cards flanked by an ace and ten, 34.8cm. high.
(Christie's) $5,287

A mahogany and marquetry decanter box, the interior divided into four compartments each with cut-glass decanter, 8in. wide.
(Christie's) $792

A pair of green glass mallet decanters, with panel cut decoration and spire stoppers, 13in. high.
(Spencer's) $788

A German silver-mounted cut fluted tapering oval clear glass decanter, with an elaborate leaf-capped handle, 13in.
(Christie's S. Ken) $948

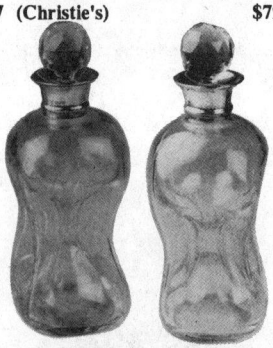

A pair of silver mounted decanters, circa 1910, each of pinched quatrefoil section with facet cut spherical stopper, 27.5cm. overall, Sheffield, 1910.
(Lawrence Fine Art) $232

## DECANTERS

An Irish decanter and 'Waffle' stopper, possibly Belfast, of ovoid shape with a rib-molded lower section and two double-milled collars, 27cm.
(Phillips) $1,793

A pair of amethyst gilt-decorated decanters and stoppers for Hollands and Brandy, of club shape, named in gilt within linked navette, early 19th century, 30.5cm. high.
(Christie's) $2,218

A Hukin & Heath electroplated metal-mounted decanter, designed by Dr. Christopher Dresser, with wooden handle, registration lozenge for 1881, 22cm. high.
(Christie's) $1,637

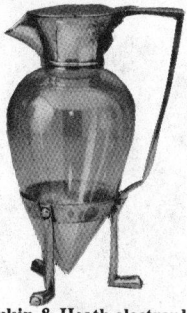

A Hukin & Heath electroplated metal and glass 'crow's foot' decanter, designed by Dr. Christopher Dresser, stamped *H&H*, and with registration lozenge for 1878, 24cm. high.
(Christie's) $25,575

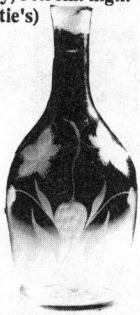

An engraved ale decanter of mallet shape, the shoulder with a pendant hop-spray flanked by two ears of barley, circa 1775, 26.5cm. high.
(Christie's) $679

A Guild of Handicraft decanter, designed by C.R. Ashbee, the green Powell glass mounted with a hammered silver neck set with five chrysoprase, with London hallmarks for 1903, 23cm. high.
(Christie's) $3,841

A nest of three Continental glass decanters in a circular holder pierced and stamped with rococo flowers and foliage, overall height 9¾in.
(Christie's S. Ken) $1,378

A pair of unusual Venetian or Bohemian millefiore decanters and stoppers of globe and shaft form, 31.5cm.
(Phillips) $1,992

A traveling decanter set, the case of plain rectangular form veneered in pollard oak, bound in cut-brass, 12¼in. wide, mid-19th century.
(Bearne's) $1,466

## DISHES

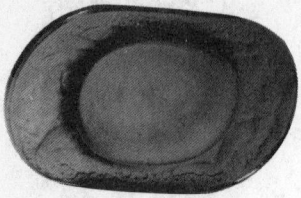

'Medicis' or 'Quatre Figurines', a Lalique emerald green ashtray, with molded decoration of four sirens and a running border of flowerheads, 15cm. long.
(Christie's) $2,787

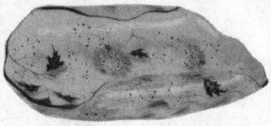

A Gallé gilded and enameled dish, the clear glass decorated with gilt and polychrome enameled umbel flowers, 30cm. long.
(Christie's) $1,716

'Archers', a Lalique frosted glass ashtray, the rim molded with vignettes of naked Greek archers, heightened with gray staining, 4½in. diameter.
(Christie's S. Ken) $516

'Gorgette', a Lalique opalescent bonbonnière, the circular slightly domed cover molded with three dragonflies, 21cm. diameter.
(Christie's) $3,916

A 'Façon de Venise' tazza, the shallow tray with a concentric pink lattimo thread enclosed within two white threads, probably Liège, late 16th century, 14.5cm. high.
(Christie's) $2,335

'Martigues', a Lalique opalescent glass dish the underside molded in relief with a band of spiny fish, 14¼in. diameter.
(Christie's S. Ken) $4,283

'Poissons', a Lalique opalescent glass dish, the underside molded in relief with a spiraling pattern of fish, 11¾in. diameter.
(Christie's S. Ken) $516

A Venetian latticinio tazza in vetro a retorti, decorated with vertical bands of lattimo thread and gauze, on a conical foot, 17th century, 16.5cm. diameter.
(Christie's) $23,353

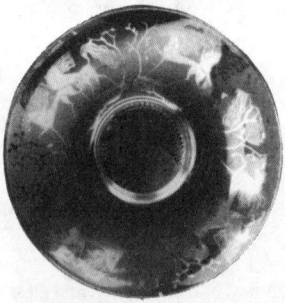

An Austrian Art Deco circular green glass dish, with silver deposit decoration of prancing horses, 12½in. diameter.
(Christie's S. Ken) $92

## DRINKING SETS

European Art glass cordial service for eight, in the Lobmeyr manner, polychrome enamel floral swag and scroll decoration centering garden portait reserves, 8in. high.
(Skinner Inc.) $825

A Victorian ormolu liqueur casket with beveled glass panels, fitted with sixteen small engraved drinking glasses, and at each corner a small decanter, 16½in. wide x 13¼in. high.
(Christie's S. Ken) $1,907

A Victorian liqueur set of a rectangular two handled tray and six glass liqueur tots with pierced holders of rococo design, by Harry Atkin, Sheffield, 1897, 9oz.
(Lawrence Fine Art) $1,448

Seven piece amberina group, three punch cups, tumbler, two squared celery vases, swirl patterned cruet.
(Skinner Inc.) $605

Cranberry enameled lemonade set, attributed to Mount Washington Glass Company, pitcher with six glasses, 10¾in. high.
(Skinner Inc.) $605

A Stuart enameled glass harlequin cocktail set, the shaker of tapering cylindrical form with chromed metal mount and cover, 8¾in. high.
(Christie's S. Ken) $187

'Adam and Eve', an Orrefors cocktail set designed by Edward Hald in 1935, comprising cylindrical decanter with black applied foot and stopper, 8¼in. high.
(Christie's S. Ken) $774

A Delveaux enameled glass part lemonade set, possibly by Leerdam, decorated in blue, black and white, height of jug 7¼in.
(Christie's S. Ken) $405

An Art Deco glass decanter set, comprising: a decanter of tapering, faceted form with six cylindrical, faceted glasses en suite.
(Phillips) $716

## FIGURES

A Venini Commedia dell'Arte figure, designed by Fulvio Bianconi, of a clown, performing a handstand, on a circular black base.
(Christie's S. Ken) $3,641

'Suzanne au Bain', a Lalique amber glass figure, molded as a nude girl standing, her arms outstretched supporting a drape, 23cm. high.
(Christie's) $42,900

A Vistosi metal and glass stylized bird, the free-blown purple glass form internally decorated with three bands of purple and green irregular rectangles, 27.5cm. high.
(Christie's) $1,716

A Venni lattcino stylized glass figure of a bird perched on a bell-shaped platform, 10¾in. high.
(Christie's S. Ken) $921

A pair of glass horse heads, designed by Archimede Seguso, the dark blue glass covered with white fragments, Murano, Made in Italy, 16.5cm. high.
(Christie's) $1,566

An Art Deco frosted glass model of a naked female, in Venus de Milo stance, supported on square black glass base, signed *'Joz 30'*.
(Phillips) $1,026

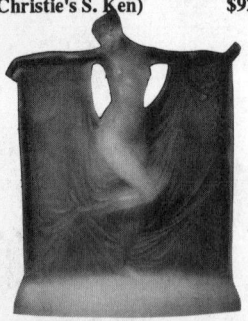

'Suzanne', a Lalique opalescent glass figurine modeled as a naked girl, her arms outstretched to reveal a cascade of loose fitting drapery, 23cm. high.
(Phillips) $27,230

A Nuutajarvi stylized figure of a bird designed by Toikka, of hollow cased white glass, 8in. high.
(Christie's S. Ken) $240

An Art Deco polished glass luminere by Gueron Cazeaux, modeled as a naked woman wearing batwing cape, on stepped wood base, 15in. high.
(Christie's S. Ken) $1,290

## FLASKS

A Central European dated tailor's spirit-flask, enameled in colors with accoutrements of the tailor's trade, the reverse with an inscription and the date *1771*, 14cm. high.
(Christie's) $1,663

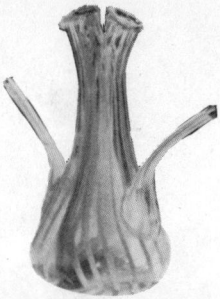

A Spanish latticinio cruet-flask with opposing slender curved spouts, Barcelona or Catalonia, late 17th/18th century, 17cm. high.
(Christie's) $832

Franklin-Dyott portrait flask, deep amber, sheared lip-pontil scar, pint, Kensington Glassworks, Philadelphia, 1826–30.
(Skinner Inc.) $1,900

A German engraved flask and screw-cap cover, the flattened oviform body with a dragon-fly alighting on the hump of a camel, perhaps Nuremburg, circa 1700, 28.5cm. high.
(Christie's) $7,431

Concentric ring eagle historical flask, light green, sheared lip-pontil scar, approximate pint, probably New England Glassworks, Cambridge, Massachusetts, 1820s–30's.
(Skinner Inc.) $4,000

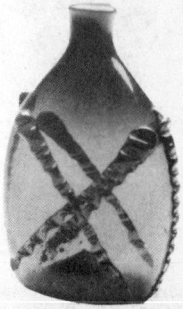

Whimsey flask, chestnut-form with X-pinched rigaree pattern on each side, olive green, sheared lip-pontil scar, 7¼in. high, New England, early 19th century.
(Skinner Inc.) $1,500

Pitkin-type flask, 36 ribs swirled to the left, olive amber, sheared lip-pontil scar, 5in. high, New England, 1790–1830.
(Skinner Inc.) $190

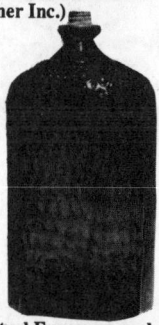

A Central European amber-tinted spirit-flask of rectangular section with allover honeycomb molding, second half of the 18th century, 15cm. high.
(Christie's) $2,772

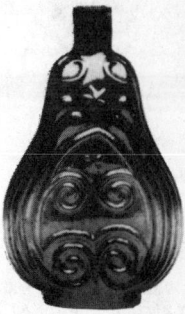

Scroll flask, bright tobacco amber, sheared lip-pontil scar, quart, America, 1840–60.
(Skinner Inc.) $150

## GOBLETS

A Vedar enameled glass goblet, of clear glass, the bowl decorated in colors with a frieze of semi-naked maidens, 19.3cm. high, signed *Vedar III*.
(Lawrence Fine Art) $159

A 19th century Bohemian ruby flash goblet, etched with herd of deer in a woodland clearing, 37.5cm. overall.
(Allen & Harris) $969

Bohemian white and cranberry overlay glass goblet, mid 19th century, enameled with floral bouquets or cut with blocks of diamonds, 6¾in. high.
(Butterfield & Butterfield) $605

A large Bohemian standing goblet in ruby glass gilt with foliage, the deep cup-shaped bowl with castellated rim, 37cm.
(Phillips) $2,431

A pair of glass goblets, each bowl engraved with national emblems, hops and barley, dated 1829, 13.4cm.
(Bearne's) $627

A large Dutch-engraved light baluster shipping goblet, the funnel bowl with a ship in full sail with sailors in the rigging, circa 1750, 25cm. high.
(Christie's) $7,762

A baluster goblet, the funnel bowl with a tear to the solid lower part on an inverted baluster stem enclosing a circle of beads, circa 1715, 15.5cm. high.
(Christie's) $1,016

A lithyalin goblet of marbled blue/gray color, the ovoid hexagonal bowl with raised cut bosses, perhaps Johann Zich, Waldviertel, circa 1832, 15.5cm. high.
(Christie's) $2,033

A Bohemian amber flashed goblet, the bowl engraved with hounds in a forest glade, 24cm.
(Bearne's) $597

## GOBLETS

An engraved facet-stemmed goblet perhaps executed by a German hand, the stem with swelling waist knop cut with diamond facets, mid-18th century, 21.5cm. high.
(Christie's) $1,201

A German green-tinted puzzle goblet (Scherzgefas), the waisted funnel bowl with a central column supporting a detachable figure of a stag, 17th century, 35.5cm. high.
(Christie's) $11,677

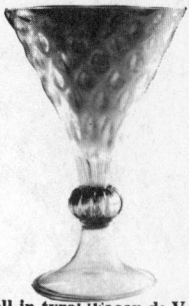

A Hall-in-tyrol 'Façon de Venise' large goblet, the flared funnel bowl lightly molded with an allover 'beech-nut' pattern, perhaps workshop of Sebastian Höchstelter, 16th century, 26cm. high.
(Christie's) $31,845

An interesting and well engraved Bohemian topographical goblet and cover, with a large rectangular panel engraved with a view of 'Das e.Hof u Nationaltheater zu Munchen', 25.5cm.
(Phillips) $2,232

Two Orrefors goblets designed by Gunnar Cyrén, each with deep bowl on thick cylindrical colored stem and circular foot, 8¼in. high.
(Christie's S. Ken) $1,474

A large and finely engraved Bohemian ruby overlay goblet and cover, engraved with a sportsman and his hound on one side and two stags on the reverse, 47cm.
(Phillips) $5,580

A Beilby white enameled goblet with deep bucket bowl, enameled in white with a border of fruiting vine and leaves, 18.5cm.
(Phillips) $5,976

An interesting 'Façon de Venise' vetro a retorti goblet with entwined corkscrew spirals, above five knops and a tall conical foot, 16.5cm. high.
(Phillips) $3,720

A tall Bohemian goblet with deep rounded bucket bowl, engraved with three putti in scroll bordered panels, 28cm.
(Phillips) $1,594

## JARS

Pair of yellow Peking glass ginger jars and covers, circa 1900, the ovoid sides of each carved in deep relief, 6 3/8 in. high. (Butterfield & Butterfield) $1,980

Bear figural pomade jar, removable head, deep amethyst, 3 3/4 in. high, New England, 1870–90. (Skinner Inc.) $130

An early 19th century glass jar, cover and stand, each piece cut with a diamond design within a serrated rim, 23.4cm. high. (Bearne's) $448

Jeweled Crown Milano biscuit jar, with pale yellow and orange mottled floral background, 5in. high. (Skinner Inc.) $425

A collection of eleven 19th century deep bottle-green and brown specie jars, with numbered, gilt oval labels, 14 1/2 in. high. (Christie's S. Ken) (Eleven) $2,317

Mount Washington Crown Milano biscuit jar, with shaded gold-amber color handpainted with leafy brown and green stalks, 7 1/2 in. high. (Skinner Inc.) $550

A pair of pedestal sweetmeat jars and covers set on square stepped bases, the body and cover cut with scrolls and vertical flutes, 32.5cm. (Bearne's) $546

A 19th century glass specie-jar, with painted and gilded royal coat of arms and gilded lid, 35in. high. (Christie's S. Ken) $685

A pair of cut jars and covers with mushroom finials, with spiral fluted decoration on square star cut bases, 11 1/2 in. high. (Christie's S. Ken) $805

## JUGS & PITCHERS

A Hukin & Heath silver, glass and ivory decanter, the design attributed to Dr. Christopher Dresser, faceted cut glass, with London hallmarks for 1882, 22.5cm. high.
(Christie's) $3,478

A Daum carved, acid-etched, and applied jug, with long pulled spout, the clear, blue and green glass overlaid with mottled brown, green and yellow leaves and berries, 17cm. high.
(Christie's) $16,056

A blue overlay oviform jug, decorated with panels painted in colors and gilt with flowers, 12in. high.
(Christie's S. Ken) $4,026

Liberty Bell centennial pitcher, applied ribbed handle, three piece mold, colorless, 9in. high.
(Skinner Inc.) $500

A 'Façon de Venise' diamond-engraved ewer of slightly straw-tinted metal, decorated with panels of flower-sprays, scroll and dot ornament, Spain or Italy, early 17th century, 17cm. high.
(Christie's) $3,397

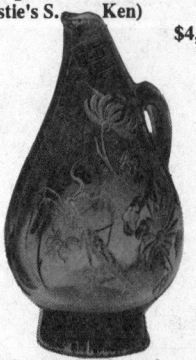

A Gallé enameled jug, of swollen form pinched at sides, with pulled lip and applied handle, the amber tinted glass with polychrome enameled wild flowers and praying mantis, 18.2cm. high.
(Christie's) $7,049

Mount Washington Royal Flemish pitcher, with extensive marine decoration including realistic fish, seashells and oceanic plant-life, 8½in. high.
(Skinner Inc.) $2,000

Daum cameo glass scenic pitcher, cameo etched overall in a riverside landscape with full length trees, 10½in. high.
(Skinner Inc.) $1,600

An American Aesthetic Movement white metal hot water jug, the oviform body extravagantly applied with pine-needles, 7in. high.
(Christie's S. Ken) $1,028

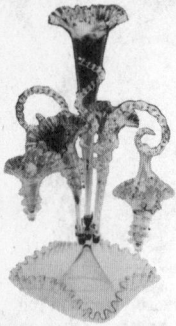

A cranberry tinted and clear glass épergne, with central trumpet shaped vase with frilled rim, 22in. high.
(Spencer's) $760

'Deux Figurines', a Lalique molded and engraved glass clock, of arched form, the clear and satin-finished glass molded in intaglio with two scantily clad maidens, 38.7cm. high.
(Christie's) $31,328

An attractive Cranberry glass centerpiece, the semi-ovoid bowl with minaret rim, all-over decorated in gilt with wild flowers and grasses within plain gilt borders, 16in. high.
(Spencer's) $622

'Blind Heart in Hell', a glass charger by Steven Newell, the acid-textured clear glass with amber and blue overlay, 1990, 53.5cm. diameter.
(Christie's) $4,268

A Tiffany Studios bronze and marbled glass photograph frame, the green and red patinated metal of openwork vine and trellis design, 24cm. high., (Phillips) $778

A Venetian diamond engraved plate in clear glass, with folded rim, the border with flowers, 23.5cm.
(Phillips) $1,029

A mid-Georgian beechwood cruet stand with five spirally-molded bottles of various sizes each with ivory top, on spreading circular base, 12in. high.
(Christie's) $2,376

Pair of Louis XVI style gilt-bronze-mounted cut glass urns, with upstanding foliate handles issuing from female masks at the shoulder, 16¾in. high.
(Butterfield & Butterfield) $1,980

Frosted cut glass ice bucket with metal swing handle, inscribed *Lalique, France* to base.
(G.A. Key) $291

## MISCELLANEOUS

A clear glass épergne, the central trumpet vase with frilled rim applied with a wrythen prunted band, 21in. high.
(Spencer's) $840

A very unusual glass teapot and cover, of globular shape with a trailed loop handle, wide spout and stylized bird finial, 15.5cm.
(Phillips) $1,793

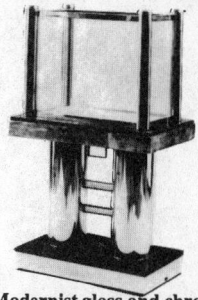

A Modernist glass and chrome metal fish tank, with polished copper column supports at each corner, on polished steel rectangular base inset with amber-tinted glass, 130.5cm. high.
(Christie's) $8,593

A Lalique frosted glass ice bucket, the exterior molded in relief with naked Bacchanalian figures amongst foliage, 9in. high.
(Christie's S. Ken) $774

'Amor and Alcestis', a Morris & Co. stained glass panel designed by Edward Burne-Jones, from Chaucer's Legend of Goode Wimmen, 48cm. high, 54.5cm. wide.
(Christie's) $23,474

A Venini photograph frame, of rectangular design, the glass rope twist frame internally decorated with bubbles and flakes of gold foil, 7in. high.
(Christie's S. Ken) $405

A finely painted Bohemian standing cup with castellated rim, the ruby cup-shaped bowl with eight oval white panels painted with figures, 28.5cm. high.
(Phillips) $2,244

'Coutard, Masque de Femme No. 2', a Lalique square frosted glass plaque molded in relief with the face of a young woman, 12½in. square.
(Christie's S. Ken) $2,027

A rare syllabub glass with funnel bowl applied with 'double B' handles, on an annular knop and terraced foot, 10.5cm.
(Phillips) $518

## PAPER WEIGHTS

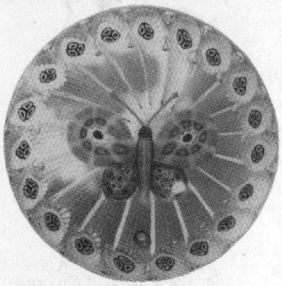

A Paul Ysart butterfly weight, the hovering insect with orange body and antennae, the wings in white and orange, 7cm.
(Phillips) $972

A 19th century slate paper weight of shaped outline, the center with an oval micro mosaic inlay of the Temple of Vesta, 7in. wide, overall.
(Christie's S. Ken) $903

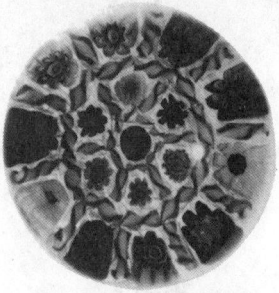

A Clichy green and white 'barber's pole' checker weight, the central pink rose surrounded by two circles of spaced canes, mid-19th century, 6.5cm. diameter.
(Christie's) $4,805

A Baccarat primrose paperweight, the five-petaled flower in pink with white edging, star cut base, 6.5cm.
(Phillips) $595

A Clichy double-overlay faceted concentric millefiori mushroom weight, the tuft with four circles of colored canes including one of alternate mauve-edged white roses, mid-19th century, 7.3cm. diameter.
(Christie's) $13,306

A Clichy 'sodden snow' patterned millefiori weight, the opaque-white ground embedded with a central green florette, 8cm.
(Phillips) $785

A flower weight attributed to Paul Ysart, the central four petaled flower with five fleshy green leaves, 7.5cm.
(Phillips) $449

A small Clichy style swirl paperweight, the alternate bright blue and white staves radiating from a large pink, white and green central cane, 2in. diameter.
(Spencer's) $380

A rare St. Louis pear and cherry in a basket paperweight, the unusually large pear shaded in pale yellow, 8cm.
(Phillips) $3,785

## PAPER WEIGHTS

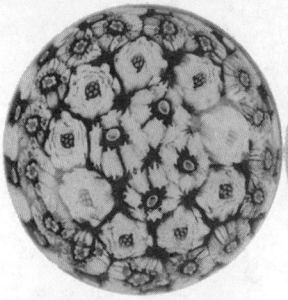

**A millefiori glass paperweight, the four central white and green cut canes surrounded by two concentric circles, 6cm. diameter.**
**(Spencer's) $760**

**A small clear glass paper weight with pansy decoration.**
**(Spencer's) $698**

**A Clichy blue ground paperweight, with central pink and white cane within a border of green canes, 5.5cm.**
**(Phillips) $558**

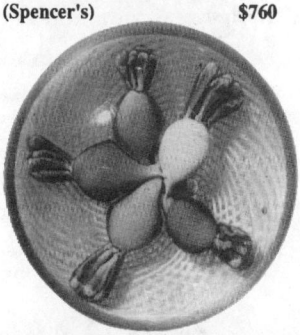

**An unusual St. Louis vegetable weight with five vegetables in an opaque white trellis basket, 6.5cm.**
**(Phillips) $797**

**'Grenouille', a Lalique amethyst-tinted glass paperweight modeled as a seated frog, 2 3/4in. high.**
**(Christie's S. Ken) $8,567**

**A Baccarat white double clematis paperweight, the flower set within a garland of alternate blue and white canes, 6cm. diameter.**
**(Spencer's) $1,011**

**A Clichy flower weight, the daisy-like flower with white petals tipped in pink and with pink dots about the pale-green center, mid-19th century, 7.5cm. diameter.**
**(Christie's) $7,762**

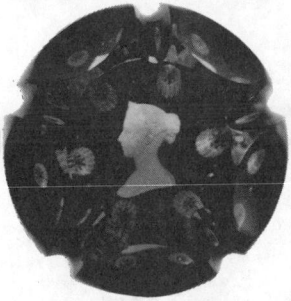

**A Clichy faceted amethyst-ground garlanded sulphide weight, the profile of Queen Victoria to the left, mid-19th century, 7.2cm. diameter.**
**(Christie's) $2,587**

**A Clichy purple and white swirl weight, the alternating colored staves radiating from a yellow-centered pink and white pastry-mold cane, mid-19th century, 8cm. diameter.**
**(Christie's) $1,146**

## SCENT BOTTLES

Webb cameo tri-color perfume, layered in pink and white, cameo cut and carved with delicate morning glory blossoms, 4¼in. high.
(Skinner Inc.) $1,700

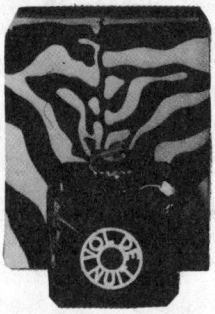


'Vol de Nuit' for Guerlain, a shaped square bottle molded as a sunburst design, one side enclosing the pierced gilt title, sealed 3¾in. high.
(Bonhams) $175

An English cameo glass scent bottle of shield shape, the deep ruby ground overlaid in white and carved with a spray of nasturtium like flowers, 9.5cm.
(Phillips) $860

A small Lalique glass scent bottle and stopper of Capricorne design.
(Spencer's) $8,200

'Liu'. An opaque black perfume bottle and stopper, for Guerlain, of chamfered cuboidal form with a square section stopper, 8cm. high.
(Phillips) $260

A faceted bell-shaped scent bottle with hexagonal stopper, 7½in. high.
(Christie's S. Ken) $107

A square blue scent-flask for the Indian market, decorated in red, green and gilt with radiating arrangements of stylized fruit, the glass perhaps Venice and 16th/17th century, 14cm. high.
(Christie's) $517

'Ketty', a clear and frosted bottle of rounded triangular form, flanked by seated nude female figures, 5⅜in.
(Bonhams) $679

Gallé cameo glass perfume bottle, baluster form of frosted opalescent yellow layered with red-orange, 6in. high.
(Skinner Inc.) $750

## SCENT BOTTLES

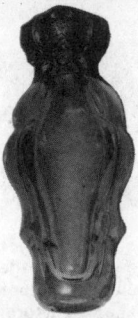

A gold-mounted glass scent-bottle, of shaped flattened form, the hinged cover and mount elaborately chased and engraved, 19th century, 3¾in. high.
(Christie's) $1,287

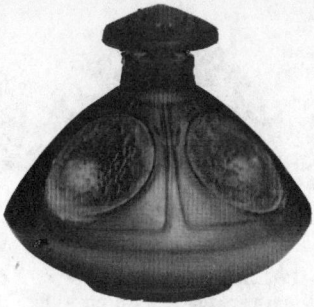

'Quatre Soleils', a Lalique amber-tinted scent bottle and stopper, the angular bulbous body molded with four chrysanthemum flowerheads each with gold foil backing, 7.2cm. high.
(Christie's) $27,885

'Ambre d'Orsay', a Lalique black glass scent bottle and stopper, the square section tapering body molded with four classical maidens at the corners, 13.3cm. high. $1,287
(Christie's)

English cameo double perfume, of unusual gemel form brilliant blue teardrop layered in white, each vial cameo cut and carved in floral motif, 4¾in. long.
(Skinner Inc.) $925

'Volubilis', an Art Deco perfume bottle and stopper, of tapering design molded in relief with flowers and foliage, 4½in. high.
(Christie's S. Ken) $829

'Le Nouveau Gardenia', a Lalique clear glass perfume bottle and stopper for Coty, intaglio molded to each facet with a fairy clutching at a long stemmed flower, 13.60cm. high.
(Phillips) $4,474

A Cristallerie de Pantin cameo brûle-parfum, the yellow opalescent body overlaid in pink with pendant trails of fuschia, 6in. high.
(Christie's S. Ken) $1,000

'Fougères', a Lalique clear glass scent bottle and stopper, molded in relief with an oval green stained panel centered with the head and shoulders of a woman in floral gown, 9.20cm. high. (Phillips) $9,394

'Sans Adieu', a Lalique Art Deco green glass perfume bottle for Worth, the stopper formed as six graduated circular discs, 10.90cm. high.
(Phillips) $1,070

## SHADES

A Tiffany bronze and leaded glass lamp shade, the irregular rectangular mottled green panes in vertical bands, stamped marks, 20in. diameter.
(Christie's S. Ken) $1,646

Leaded glass lamp shade, of green graduated segments with four sets of blue squares at lower edge, 10½in. diameter.
(Skinner Inc.) $15,400

Cased Art glass lamp shade, of deep emerald green textured and cased to opal white, decorated with gilt enhanced stylized foliate elements, 14in. diameter.
(Skinner Inc.) $412

Gone-with-the-Wind glass lamp shade, with etched and gilt enameled alternating dragon and wreath with quiver decoration, 9½in. high.
(Skinner Inc.) $450

Leaded glass hanging shade, attributed to Duffner & Kimberly, with green wreath and swag design incorporating red-amber flame designs, 24in. diameter.
(Skinner Inc.) $600

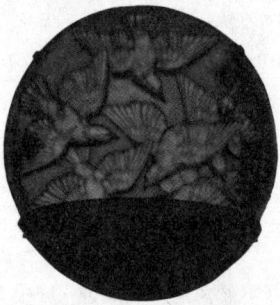

'Hirondelles', a Lalique wall-light, with molded decoration of five swallows in flight, above a hemispherical satin-finished shade, 47.5cm. diameter.
(Christie's) $16,326

'Boule de Gul', a Lalique hanging light, composed of two hemispherical and eight rectangular glass panels, linked by metal rings to form a globe, 45cm. high.
(Christie's) $21,450

A Sabino hanging light, the metal frame mounted in three tiers with satin-finished panels, each with molded decoration, 60cm. high.
(Christie's) $3,218

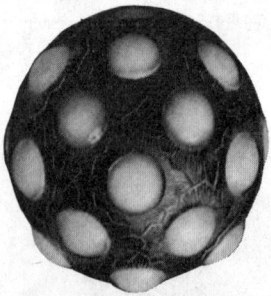

'Soleil', a Lalique opalescent glass shade, of semi-spherical form molded in relief with interlocking sunburst motifs, 12in. diameter.
(Christie's S. Ken) $1,842

## TANKARDS

A baluster coin-tankard with a gadrooned lower part and applied scroll handle, supported on a hollow knop enclosing a George III sixpence dated 1787, 16cm. high.
(Christie's) $1,016

A baluster coin-tankard and a cover, with gadrooned lower part, the base set with a George III silver threepence dated *1762*, circa 1765, 19cm. high.
(Christie's) $892

An engraved baluster tankard with scroll strap handle, applied with a trailed thread above gadrooning and on a circular foot, circa 1765, 18cm. high.
(Christie's) $591

A baluster coin tankard with a George II sixpence of 1757 trapped in the short stem to a spreading foot, 14cm.
(Phillips) $655

German pewter-mounted green glass flagon, late 19th century, the body decorated in enamel with a heraldic armorial on a ground of raised enamel lunettes, 15in. high.
(Butterfield & Butterfield) $440

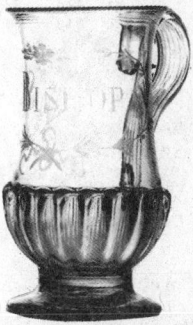

A baluster tankard with a ribbed strap handle, ribbed rim and molded with basal flutes, 14cm.
(Phillips) $636

## TANTALUS

A fine late Victorian tantalus, with three square decanters and four glasses, with games drawer below, 14in. high.
(Bearne's) $1,174

An Art Deco electroplated and cut-glass two-division tantalus with central locking carrying handle, 11½in. high.
(Bearne's) $1,444

A late Victorian metal mounted oak box pattern tantalus, with three cut glass decanters, 35cm.
(Phillips) $660

## VASES

A Daum, acid-etched and enamel painted vase, with mottled blue and white ground encased in clear glass, decorated with polychrome enameled wooded river landscape, 11.5cm. high.
(Christie's) $2,574

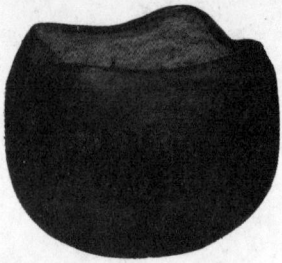

A Daum carved, acid-etched and enamel painted vase, the mottled amber and yellow glass decorated with brown enamel painted sailing boats, 11.5cm. high.
(Christie's) $6,435

A Daum carved and acid-etched landscape vase, the mottled pale amber and orange glass overlaid with a coastal landscape and sailing boats, 24.1cm. high.
(Christie's) $3,003

A Daum carved and acid-etched double-overlay vase, the mottled yellow ground cased in clear glass, and overlaid in brown and light amber hazelnut branches, 17.5cm. high.
(Christie's) $3,218

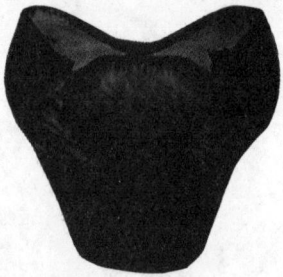

A Cristallerie de Pantin carved and acid-etched cameo vase, the iridescent clear glass overlaid with red flowering fuchsias, with acid-etched signature, 11cm. high.
(Christie's) $1,502

A Daum acid-etched and enameled cameo vase, the mottled yellow glass overlaid with polychrome enamel painted orchids, 34.1cm. high.
(Christie's) $8,580

A Daum carved and acid-etched double overlay vase, the mottled amber and pink glass overlaid in mottled green and red with wheel-carved poppies, 23.5cm. high.
(Christie's) $30,030

A Loetz vase, dimpled globular body, cylindrical neck with flared rim, the green glass decorated with silver-blue iridescent oil splashes, 20.3cm. high.
(Christie's) $995

A Daum carved and acid-etched double-overlay vase, the mottled orange, red and clear glass overlaid in green and brown with a wooded river landscape, 31cm. high.
(Christie's) $4,719

## VASES

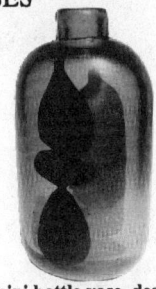

A Venini bottle vase, designed by Fulvio Bianconi, the amber-tinted glass inlaid with deep amber and white abstract forms, 23cm. high.
(Christie's) $12,870

A Daum acid-etched and enameled vase, the mottled clear, blue and green glass decorated with polychrome enameled wooded river landscape, 12.1cm. high.
(Christie's) $3,861

'Paysage Vosgien', a Gallé carved and acid-etched double-overlay landscape vase, the pale amber glass overlaid in purple and blue with a farm in a wooded mountainous landscape, 43.5cm. high.
(Christie's) $77,220

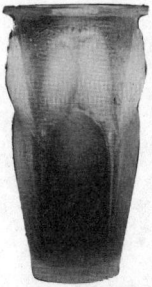

'Ceylan', a Lalique opalescent glass, vase, molded with four pairs of budgerigars perched amid foliage, blue staining, 24.2cm. high.
(Christie's) $4,778

A Gallé intrecalaire, intaglio carved 'verrerie parlante' vase, the clear glass decorated internally with mottled green, yellow and amber oxide striations, overlaid in red, with intaglio decoration of a seahorse among various seaweeds, 11cm. high.
(Christie's) $55,748

'Vase à Pekin', a Gallé carved and acid-etched fire-polished vase, the jade-colored glass overlaid with purple lotus flower, 21cm. high.
(Christie's) $11,798

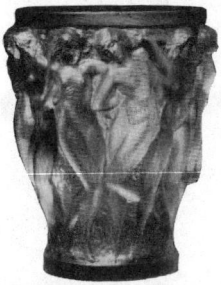

'Bacchantes', a Lalique blue-stained vase, the flared cylindrical body molded in relief with nude female dancing figures, 24.5cm. high.
(Christie's) $18,915

A Gallé carved and acid-etched double-overlay vase, the yellow glass overlaid with blue and purple flowering clematis, 12.5cm. high.
(Christie's) $6,435

A Georges Dumoulin vase, the clear heavy glass internally decorated with air bubbles and green and blue marbling, engraved G. Dumoulin, circa 1930, 22.5cm. high.
(Christie's) $3,186

## VASES

A Daum carved, acid-etched and enamel painted vase, the mottled clear, blue and green glass decorated with polychrome enameled wooded river landscape, 44.2cm. high.
(Christie's) $9,009

A large Schneider glass vase of baluster shape, internally mottled in mauve shading to purple towards the base, 47cm. high.
(Phillips) $876

A Gallé cameo glass vase, the body showing through as yellow glass, overlaid with brown etched away to leave a design of irises, 18.5cm. high.
(Phillips) $1,393

'Oursin', a Lalique turquoise stained vase, the clear and satin-finished glass molded with protruding bubbles, with acid-stamped signature *R. Lalique France*, 19cm. high.
(Christie's) $2,389

Roycroft silver washed vase with Steuben glass insert, East Aurora, New York, no. 248 in the 1926 catalog, 6in. high.
(Skinner Inc.) $250

'Domremy', a Lalique black-stained vase, the satin-finished glass molded with flowering thistles, with molded signature *R. Lalique*, 21.5cm. high.
(Christie's) $1,991

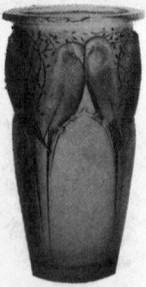

'Ceylan'. A Lalique opalescent glass vase of flared cylindrical form, molded with pairs of lovebirds perched amid prunus blossom, 24cm. high
(Phillips) $3,383

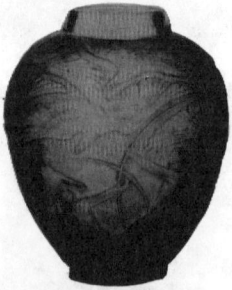

'Archers', a Lalique grey-stained vase, of ovoid form with chamfered neck, the satin-finished glass molded with archers and eagles, 26.5cm. high.
(Christie's) $6,371

A Daum carved and acid-etched vase, the mottled clear and yellow glass overlaid in dark and light amber with flowering sweet peas; 38.7cm. high.
(Christie's) $5,376

## VASES

A Daum carved, acid-etched and enamel painted vase, the acid-textured ground of mottled white glass, decorated in cameo with polychrome enameled wooded and mountainous landscape, 49.5cm. high.
(Christie's) $13,943

'Fontainebleau', a Lalique grey-stained vase, the clear and satin-finished glass molded with fruiting vine branches, with acid-stamped signature *R. Lalique*, 17.7cm. high.
(Christie's) $1,991

A Daum carved, acid-textured and enameled vase, the mottled opaque and yellow glass decorated in amber, green and blue with blackberry branches, 34cm. high.
(Christie's) $6,371

A Loetz vase, with two applied angular handles, the body of purple glass decorated with iridescent green and blue oil splashes, 21cm. high.
(Christie's) $1,716

A Daum carved, acid-etched and enamel painted vase, the mottled clear and white glass decorated with a polychrome enameled wooded river landscape and hills, 33.5cm. high.
(Christie's) $8,580

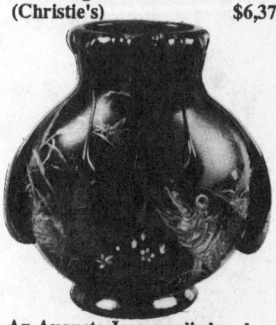

An Auguste Jean applied and enameled glass vase, the iridescent purple glass decorated in polychrome enamel and gilding with a pike rising towards a grasshopper perched on a waterplant, 23cm. high.
(Christie's) $3,783

A Vedar enamel painted glass bottle-vase, on wide flaring foot, the clear glass decorated with polychrome enamel painted berry laden branches and various insects, 37cm. high.
(Christie's) $1,593

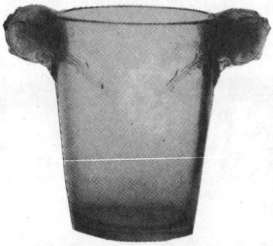

'Chamarande'. A Lalique opalescent twin-handled vase of bucket shape, the handles molded to form two circular clumps of flowering briers, 19.7cm. high.
(Phillips) $1,691

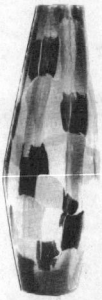

A Venini 'Vetro Pezzato Arlecchino' vase, the patchwork design made up of red, green, blue and clear cased glass, 28cm. high.
(Christie's) $13,943

## VASES

A Venini 'Occhi' vase designed by Tobia Scarpa, the cased red and black glass compressed to form irregular 'windows', 6in. high.
(Christie's S. Ken)
$11,137

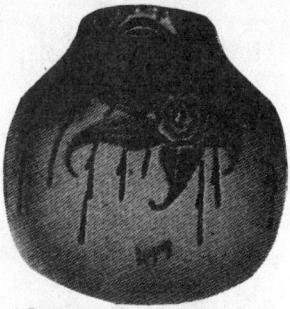

A Legras acid-etched and enameled glass vase, decorated in red and black with stylized flowers and foliage, 5in. high.
(Christie's S. Ken) $553

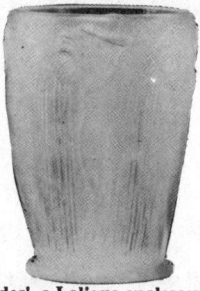

'Danäides', a Lalique opalescent footed vase, molded in relief with a frieze of naked women pouring water from pitchers, stained blue, 7¼in. high.
(Christie's S. Ken)
$5,140

'Martin-Pêcheurs', a Lalique clear and frosted glass vase, intaglio molded with birds amongst foliage, stained green, 9½in. high.
(Christie's S. Ken)
$8,567

Dale Chihuly Macchia series studio glass vase, of opaque to translucent sky-blue, decorated in molten state with horizontal striping, 17in. wide.
(Skinner Inc.) $6,050

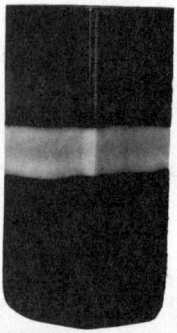

A Venini square section vase, dark emerald green glass with powder blue stripe around the center, 9¾in. high.
(Christie's S. Ken)
$2,356

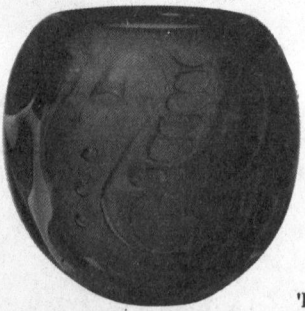

An early Orrefors 'Ariel' glass vase designed by Edvin Ohrström, of aquamarine tone and internally decorated with air bubbles of abstract forms, 15cm. high.
(Phillips) $7,780

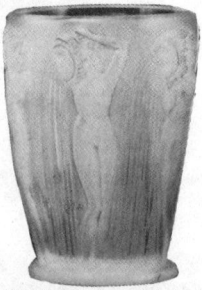

'Danäides', a Lalique opalescent footed vase, the exterior molded in relief with a frieze of women pouring urns from their shoulders, stained blue, 7¼in. high.
(Christie's S. Ken)
$5,997

'Tourbillons', a Lalique yellow glass vase, of bucket form, the thick walled body molded in deep relief with abstract scrolling, 8in. high.
(Christie's S. Ken)
$17,134

## WINE GLASSES

A color-twist wine-glass with a stem with a solid twisted cobalt-blue core entwined by two opaque threads, on a conical foot, circa 1765, 16.5cm. high. (Christie's) $1,592

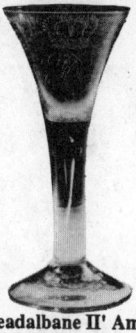

The 'Breadalbane II' Amen glass, of drawn-trumpet shape, the bowl engraved in diamond-point with a crown above the Royal cipher of King James VIII, 1745–50, 17cm. high. (Christie's) $50,592

A color-twist wine-glass, the bell bowl, the stem with an opaque corkscrew core edged with translucent cobalt-blue thread, circa 1765, 16.5cm. high. (Christie's) $4,038

A color-twist wine-glass with a bell bowl, the double-knopped stem with an opaque gauze core entwined with translucent turquoise, brown and opaque-white threads, circa 1765, 16cm. high. (Christie's) $2,760

A 'Façon de Venise' winged wine-glass, the stem with an elaborate coiled section enclosing white threads , Venice or Low Countries, 17th century, 12.5cm. high. (Christie's) $6,369

A polychrome enameled armorial opaque-twist wine-glass attributed to William Beilby, the funnel bowl enameled in yellow heightened in iron-red, black, white and gilt, circa 1765, 15.5cm. high. (Christie's) $18,045

A tartan-twist wine-glass, the stem with an opaque corkscrew core edged in brick-red and translucent green entwined by two opaque threads, circa 1765, 16cm. high. (Christie's) $6,369

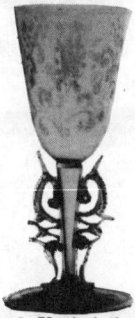

A 'Façon de Venise' diamond-engraved winged-glass, the funnel bowl decorated with flower-sprays supported on a hollow tapering stem,, Low Countries, 17th century, 17.5cm. high.(Christie's) $2,123

A 'Façon de Venise' flute, the slender funnel bowl supported on a merese, the stem with a wrythen-molded section, The Netherlands, 17th century, 26.5cm. high. (Christie's) $14,861

## WINE GLASSES

**A light baluster wine glass with pan-topped bowl engraved with a border of vines, the stem with a teared central knop, 15cm. (Phillips) $518**

**A bell-bowled wine-glass on multi-spiral air-twist stem with applied knop, 6in. high. (Christie's S. Ken) $278**

**A Lynn wine glass, the horizontally ribbed bowl on an opaque twist stem of a pair of spiral tapes, 13.8cm. (Phillips) $797**

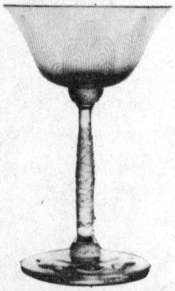

**'Fountains', a Baccarat crystal drinking glass, designed by Georges Chevalier, the bell-shaped bowl with engraved decoration on long, swollen stem and circular foot, 15.4cm. high. (Christie's) $557**

**A fine stipple and diamond point engraved Newcastle Armorial wine glass engraved in Holland, the rounded funnel bowl with the arms of William V of Orange, 19cm. (Phillips) $5,197**

**A façon de Venise wine glass, the funnel bowl 'nipt diamond waies', set in two rings above a hollow-blown quatrelobed knop, 13.3cm., end 17th century. (Phillips) $2,244**

**A rare cider glass, the tall funnel bowl cut and engraved with two fruiting apple branches united by a simple ribbon, 18.3cm. (Phillips) $3,187**

**A wine glass with slightly lipped ogee bowl engraved with six-petaled roses linked by leaf meander, 15.6cm. (Phillips) $438**

**A very unusual facet-cut wine glass, the heavy bowl deeply cut with diamond facets, on an opaque twist stem, 11.8cm. (Phillips) $478**

## WINE GLASSES

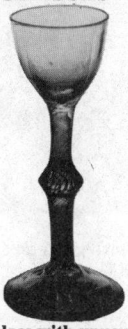

**A wine glass with unusual ribbed shallow ogee bowl, the multiple opaque twist stem with a central swelling knop, 15cm.**
**(Phillips) $299**

**A wine glass with large bell bowl, the multiple air twist stem with shoulder and central knops, 18cm.**
**(Phillips) $517**

**An unusual composite stemmed wine glass, the bell bowl with solid base containing spiral tears, 16.8cm.**
**(Phillips) $637**

**A rare wine glass possibly of Jacobite significance, the pan-topped bowl engraved with a border of a stylized passion flower, rose, honeysuckle and sunflower, 18cm.**
**(Phillips) $996**

**An interesting and amusing Schwarzlot decorated glass, the small cup-shaped bowl decorated with an amusing scene of an irate woman belaboring a man with a stick, 9.3cm., probably Silesian.**
**(Phillips) $411**

**A Beilby wine glass, the small ogee bowl enameled with grapes and vine tendrils, the opaque twist stem with a multi-ply corkscrew, 15.3cm.**
**(Phillips) $2,390**

**A Jacobite wine glass with round funnel bowl engraved with a six-petaled rose and a single bud, 16cm.**
**(Phillips) $1,693**

**A wine glass, the ogee bowl engraved with trailing vines, the air twist stem with a pair of mercurial corkscrews, 15.4cm.**
**(Phillips) $478**

**A baluster wine glass with bell bowl, the stem with a teared swelling knop between shoulder a basal knops, 16.5cm.**
**(Phillips) $637**

A fine French octagonal vari-colored gold and piqué tortoiseshell snuff-box, the cover piqué with a windmill on a hill, by Adrien-Jean-Maximilien Vachette, Paris, 1789–90, 2⅝in. long.
(Christie's) $39,600

A rare gold zodiac figure, standing barefoot on a tripod base, wearing an armor-like studded suit with a long tunic and shoulder pads, 12th/13th century, 13cm.
(Christie's) $20,273

A Swiss rectangular gold snuff-box, the hinged cover chased and engraved with Naval Trophies, the engine-turned walls and base with laurel and bead border, maker's mark *C C S*, 19th century, 3⅜in. long.
(Christie's) $6,171

A Swiss rectangular gold snuff-box set with a Roman micro-mosaic, showing Rinaldo and Armida, in a wooded landscape setting, by S. Chaligny, Geneva, circa 1820, 3¾in. long.
(Christie's) $41,173

A gold-mounted enamel and gemset rock-crystal parasol-handle, engraved with sunflowers around the stem and set with red stones, late 19th century, 2⅜in. long.
(Christie's) $1,950

An important Frederick Augustus III oval gold and hardstone snuff-box, set on all sides with a Zellenmosaik of rural landscapes, by Johann Christian Neuber, Dresden, circa 1770, 3⅜in. long.
(Christie's) $82,280

A 'Scottish' barrel-shaped gold-mounted agate vinaigrette, formed of hardstone staves and engraved gold hoops, 19th century, 2½in. high.
(Christie's) $5,634

A very rare pair of inscribed beaten gold lotus cups, each with straight tapering sides thinly beaten and chased with two tiers of lotus petals, Tang Dynasty, 9.8cm. diameter.
(Christie's) $42,680

A George II gold scent-bottle case set with two panels of moss agate, circa 1755, with velvet lining, 1½in. high.
(Christie's) $2,017

A rare gold foliate box and cover, the cover chased with two lions amidst flower-sprays within a band of raised dots and flower-heads, Liao Dynasty, 6cm. wide.
(Christie's) $34,144

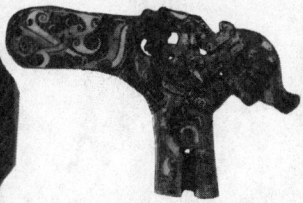

An archaic gold and silver-inlaid bronze axe-head, cast at the angle with openwork dragons biting the blade and gripping the shaft socket, Warring States, 13cm. wide.
(Christie's) $14,938

A fine engraved gold singing bird box by Georges Reymond, Geneva, the movement providing song and motions to head, beak and wings of feathered bird, circa 1805–1815, 71mm. long.
(Christie's New York) $35,200

A Roman rectangular micro-mosaic plaque, depicting a view of St. Peter's Square, in gilt-metal frame with suspension ring, 19th century, $3^5/_8$in. wide.
(Christie's) $3,960

A Louis XVI gold-mounted glass scent-flask, the front applied with an oval vari-color gold medallion chased and engraved with flowers and foliage, Paris, 1777–78, 4in. long.
(Christie's) $2,600

A Swiss oval enameled gold snuff-box, the cover painted with a couple in a garden with a fountain and statue in the background, Geneva, circa 1800, maker's mark MC, $2^5/_8$in. long.
(Christie's) $5,544

A Louis XV shaped gold and agate snuff-box, the convex cover hinged at one end and set with two panels of agate in borders chased and engraved with foliage, by Nicholas Bouillerot, Paris, 1728–29, $2^3/_8$in. long.
(Christie's) $6,501

A Swiss rectangular vari-colored gold snuff-box, the cover chased and engraved with a female winged demi-figure between eagles, Geneva, circa 1815, maker's mark *M M*, possibly for M. Marchinville, $3^1/_8$in. long.
(Christie's) $5,544

A fine George II cartouche-shaped gold snuff-box, the interior of the lid set with an enamel portrait of Mary, Countess of Bute by Christian Friedrich Zincke, circa 1750, $2^3/_4$in. wide.
(Christie's) $71,280

A Royal Doulton 'Seriesware' plate painted with a typical golfing scene inscribed *He hath a good judgment who relieth not wholly on his own*, 10¾in. diameter.
(Christie's) $354

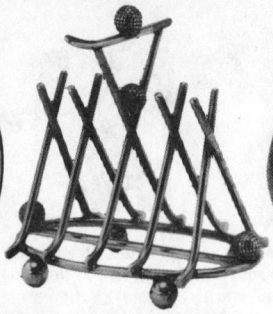

An electroplated four-division toast rack, the divisions modeled as crossed golf clubs, 5½in. wide.
(Christie's) $473

A silvered metal pocket watch with circular white enamel dial in a golf ball shaped case, 1½in. diameter.
(Christie's) $295

Golf Illustrated Magazine: vol. XXVI to LXVIII inclusive and LIII and LIV, bound red cloth.
(Phillips) $46,540

A Winter Evening by W. Dendy Sadler (1854–1923), engraving by James Dobie, signed by the artist and engraver, printed on Japanese vellum, 13 x 9in.
(Christie's) $591

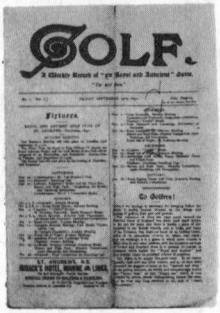


A copy of 'Golf' No. 1, Vol. 1, dated Friday, 19th September, 1890.
(Christie's) $551

A Royal Doulton baluster jug for Colonel Bogey Whisky, 7½in. high.
(Christie's) $3,938

A brass gutty golf ball mold for 'The Trophy' dimple pattern golf ball, the mold stamped John White & Co.
(Christie's) $3,938

A pottery tobacco jar, the green ground transfer printed with an oval panel of a golfer, 5½in. high.
(Christie's) $827

# GOLFING ITEMS

A painted lead figure of a golfer and his caddy, 3in. high.
(Christie's) $433

Pottery tee plaque, hole No. 15, Houlets Haunt.
(Christie's) $433

A silver golf trophy for the Irish Open Amateur Championship 1935, 15in. high, on ebonized plinth.
(Christie's) $1,871

Hutchinson, H.G., Aspects of Golf, a rare paperback booklet, London 1900, illustrated paper cover, fly-leaf signed *Garden G. Smith*.
(Phillips) $13,425

A framed lithograph of Tom Morris, as a middle-aged man, circa 1870, 17½ x 12¼in.
(Christie's) $1,772

Hilton, H. and Smith, G.G, The Royal and Ancient Game of Golf, London 1912, limited de luxe edition 46/100, bound ivory vellum.
(Phillips) $7,160

A Pen-nee Golf pin-ball game, 17½in. high.
(Christie's) $1,083

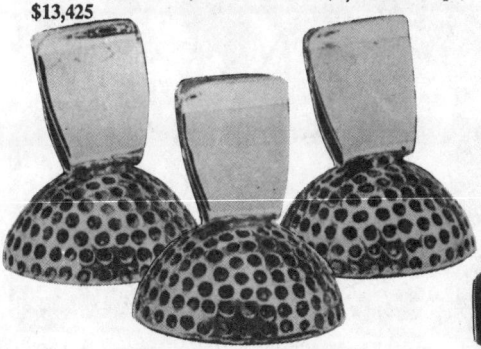

Three of a set of six silvered metal menu holders, the bases modeled as golf balls, each 1½in. diameter.
(Christie's) (Six) $788

A bronze of Harry Vardon having driven, on greenstone shaped base, by Hal Ludlow for Elkington.
(Phillips) $3,938

A scared-head wooden putter by J. Jameson, the head stamped *J. Jameson*, re-gripped, circa 1890.
(Christie's) $3,347

John Wallace (George Pipeshank): Saturday Morning, Reiss Golf Club, Wick, Caithness, watercolor, signed lower right and dated 1895, 36.5 x 54.5cm.
(Phillips) $48,330

A rare scared-head long-nosed short spoon by Sandison of Aberdeen, the head stamped *L.G. Sandison, Aberdeen*, circa 1860.
(Christie's) $17,721

A golden beechwood headed play club by Munro, the head also stamped with owner's initials *W.M.K.*, and 41in. shaft.
(Phillips) $7,518

Golfiana or A day at Gullane, an extremely rare pamphlet of golfing poems, privately printed, presumably in Edinburgh, in 1869, 15 pages.
(Phillips) $32,220

A good feather ball by J. Gourlay, the ink written weight 28.
(Phillips) $14,320

A play club in dark gold stained beech by J. Wilson, with 44½in. shaft.
(Phillips) $12,530

The Heath Robinson Golf Course by Wiliam Heath Robinson (1872–1944), signed, watercolor, 16½ x 23in., painted for Peek Freans Biscuits.
(Christie's) $33,473

A scared-head long-nosed driver by Robert Forgan, the shaft stamped *R. Forgan and Son, St. Andrews*, rubberized grip, circa 1870.
(Christie's) $3,938

A scared-head wooden niblick by Peter Paxton, the head stamped *P. Paxton*, re-gripped, circa 1875.
(Christie's) $3,938

Garden Grant Smith RSW, Crossing Jordan, watercolor, signed lower right *Garden Grant Smith RSW*, Pau 1892, 34 x 47cm.
(Phillips) $35,800

A scared-head long-nosed driver by George Fernie, the head stamped *G. Fernie*, circa 1865.
(Christie's) $2,953

A fine and unused feather-filled golf ball by Allan Robertson, stamped *Allan* and inscribed *29*, circa 1840.
(Christie's) $27,500

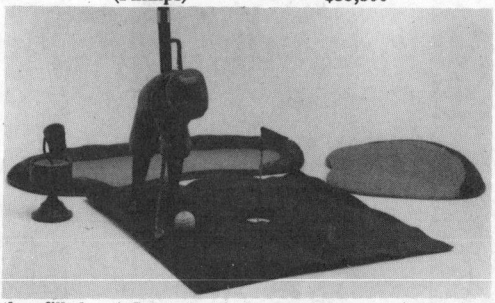

A Schoenhut indoor golf game: 'set No. G/10, in original box with instructions, comprising: a 'Tommy Green' figure, a water hazard, and a putting green, etc.
(Christie's) $827

A good feather ball by J. Gourlay, indistinctly written, ink weight 30.
(Phillips) $10,740

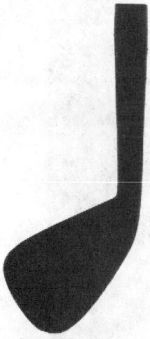

A blacksmith-made track iron with 5½in. hosel and hand-hammered and well-dished face, the grip lacking, circa 1790.
(Christie's) $51,194

The Golf Match by Arthur P. Dixon (fl. 1884–1916), signed, oil on board, 7¾ x 11¾in.
(Christie's) $15,752

A scared-head long-nosed long spoon by Hugh Philp, the head stamped *H. Philp*, circa 1840.
(Christie's) $11,814

**Angel, Paramount, 1937, one-sheet, linen backed, 41 x 27in.**
**(Christie's East) $2,860**

**The New Frontier, Republic, 1935, one-sheet, linen backed, 41 x 27in.**
**(Christie's East) $5,720**

**Dimples, 20th Fox, 1936, one-sheet, linen backed, 41 x 27in.**
**(Christie's East) $2,640**

**Her Wedding Night, Paramount, 1930, one-sheet, linen backed, 41 x 27in.**
**(Christie's East) $3,300**

**Flying Pat, Paramount, 1920, one-sheet, linen backed, 41 x 27in.**
**(Christie's East) $1,870**

**The Mysterious Dr. Fu Manchu, Paramount, 1929, one-sheet, linen backed, 41 x 27in.**
**(Christie's East) $2,530**

**Red Headed Woman, MGM, 1932, one-sheet, linen backed, 41 x 27in.**
**(Christie's East) $10,780**

**Shall We Dance, RKO, 1937, one-sheet, linen backed, 41 x 27in.**
**(Christie's East) $6,050**

**The Young Rajah, Paramount, 1922, one-sheet, linen backed, 41 x 27in.**
**(Christie's East) $3,410**

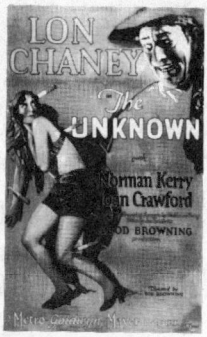


The Unknown, MGM, 1927, one-sheet, linen backed, 41 x 27in.
(Christie's East) $12,100

The Grim Game, Paramount-Artcraft, 1919, one-sheet, linen backed, 41 x 27in.
(Christie's East) $12,650

Go Into Your Dance, First National, 1935, one-sheet, linen backed, 41 x 27in.
(Christie's East) $3,520

Doubling for Romeo, Goldwyn, 1922, one-sheet, linen backed, 41 x 27in.
(Christie's East) $1,870

The Round Up, Paramount, 1920, one-sheet, linen backed, 41 x 27in.
(Christie's East) $4,400

Tarzan and his Mate, MGM, 1934, one-sheet, linen backed, 41 x 27in.
(Christie's East) $5,720

Son of the Golden West, FBO, 1928, one-sheet, linen backed, 41 x 27in.
(Christie's East) $1,870

The Suitor, Vitagraph, 1920, one-sheet, linen backed, 41 x 27in.
(Christie's East) $1,045

Prodigal Daughters, Paramount, one-sheet, linen backed, 41 x 27in.
(Christie's East) $1,430

**The Son of the Sheik, United Artists, 1926, half-sheet, unfolded, 22 x 28in.**
**(Christie's East) $2,750**

**Citizen Kane, RKO, 1941, half-sheet, unfolded, 22 x 28in.**
**(Christie's East) $3,850**

**The Jazz Singer, Warner Brothers, 1927, 24-sheet, linen backed, 9 x 20 feet.**
**(Christie's East) $18,700**

**Platinum Blonde, Columbia, 1930, three-sheet, linen backed, 81 x 41in.**
**(Christie's East) $4,620**

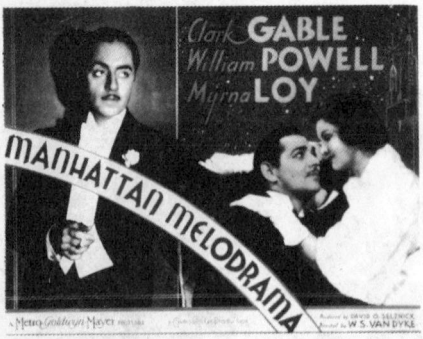


**Manhattan Melodrama, MGM, 1934, half-sheet, unfolded, 22 x 28in.**
**(Christie's East) $3,190**

**The American Venus, Paramount, 1926, six-sheet, linen backed, 81 x 81in.**
**(Christie's East) $3,740**

**The Pilgrim, First National, 1923, six-sheet, linen backed, 81 x 81in.**
**(Christie's East) $12,650**

**Way Out West, MGM, 1937, half-sheet, unfolded, 22 x 28in.**
**(Christie's East) $3,190**

**The Cabinet of Dr. Caligari, Goldwyn, 1921, one-sheet, linen backed, 41 x 27in.**
**(Christie's East) $37,400**

**American Entertainment Co., ca. 1900, one-sheet, linen backed, 28 x 41in.**
**(Christie's East) $3,740**

**The Wizard of Oz, MGM, 1939, half-sheet, unfolded, 22 x 28in.**
**(Christie's East) $11,000**

**She Done Him Wrong, Paramount, 1933, six-sheet, linen backed, 81 x 81in.**
**(Christie's East) $5,720**

A late 19th century Moscow School icon of the Pokrov, overlaid with a repoussé silver oklad, 15in. x 12in.
(Christie's S. Ken) $1,050

A 19th century Russian icon of the Mother of God of the Sign, 12¼in. x 10½in.
(Christie's S. Ken) $630

An 18th century Russian icon of the Virgin of Joy to Those who Grieve, overlaid with a silver gilt oklad, 11½in. x 9½in.
(Christie's S. Ken) $840

A late 19th century Russian icon of Nine Chosen Saints, including Markarii, Avksentii, Evstratii, Evgenii, and Orest with the apostle Peter, 10¼in. x 9in.
(Christie's S. Ken) $735

A 19th century Russian icon of the Transfiguration, the Saviour brightly robed, with standing and kneeling saints before Him, 14in. x 12in.
(Christie's S. Ken) $798

A late 19th century Russian icon of The Mother of God Kazanskaya, in a silver repoussé and engraved oklad, 7in. x 5¾in.
(Christie's S. Ken) $1,366

A 19th century Russian icon of the Vladimirskaya Mother of God, overlaid with a silver oklad, 10½in. x 8¾in.
(Christie's S. Ken) $945

A 17th/18th century Cypriot icon of the Mother of God of the Sign, 30in x 25in.
(Christie's S. Ken) $2,941

A 19th century Russian icon of the Baptism of Christ, with the Forerunner and angels, the Lord Sabaoth above, 8¾in. x 6¾in.
(Christie's S. Ken) $882

An 18th century Russian icon of the Kazanskaya Mother of God, 14in. x 11½in.
(Christie's S. Ken) $1,576

A 19th century Russian icon of St. George and the Dragon, within a chased brass basma, 12¼in. x 10½in.
(Christie's S. Ken) $1,050

A 19th century Greek icon of St. Nicholas, the Miracle Worker, 14in. x 10½in.
(Christie's S. Ken) $420

A late 19th century Russian icon of The Old Testament Trinity, realistically painted, with Abraham and Sarah in attendance, 14in. x 12¼in.
(Christie's S. Ken) $1,933

An 18th century Italo-Cretan icon of the Hodigitria Mother of God, 19in. x 15in., in a carved wood and gesso frame.
(Christie's S. Ken) $7,983

A 19th century Russian icon of the Mother of God of the Sign, traditionally painted on gilt ground, Christ with an applied halo, 7¼in. x 6¼in.
(Christie's S. Ken) $1,680

A 19th century Russian icon of St. John the Forerunner, with the Christ Child, 17½in. x 14½in.
(Christie's S. Ken) $1,050

A late 19th century Finift icon of the Appearance of the Mother of God to St. Serafim of Sarov, in a silver engraved frame, St. Petersburg 1886, 7½in. x 6in.
(Christie's S. Ken) $1,156

A 19th century Russian icon of Six Chosen Saints, including Catherine, Barbara, Mitrophan and Harlampy, 12¼in. x 10½in.
(Christie's S. Ken) $882

A four-case fundame inro decorated in hiramakie and heidatsu with chrysanthemum flower-heads, signed *Tsunekawa* (or Josen) *saku*, with red tsubo seal, 19th century, 7.8cm. high.
(Christie's) $2,167

A four-case fundame inro decorated in hiramakie, kirikane, togidashi, aogai, metal foil and silver inlay, signed *Koma Kansai*, 19th century, 9cm. high.
(Christie's) $15,488

A four-case inro richly decorated in hiramakie, aogai and kirikane on a hirame ground with a cicada on a gourdvine, signed *Kajikawa*, 18th century, 8.9cm. high.
(Christie's) $7,744

A large four-case inro decorated in hiramakie, okibirame, kimpun and togidashi with a dragon arising from the sea in clouds of vapour, signed *Koma Kyoryu saku*, late 18th century, 12cm. high, with a walrus ivory ryusa style manju netsuke attached.
(Christie's) $8,131

A large kinji ground two-case oval inro, in the shape of Daikoku's treasure bag, decorated in Shibayama style with Ebisu with an abacus seated before an account book and Daikoku counting coins watched by a mouse, unsigned, 19th century.
(Christie's) $16,456

A four-case kinji inro decorated in gold and silver hiramakie, takamakie, kirikane, nashiji and inlaid in Shibayama style, one side with a tea-house girl watching a samurai falling from a bench, signed *Teimin*, late 19th century, 10cm. long.
(Christie's) $11,616

A four-case inro decorated in hiramakie, togidashi and makibokashi with Nitta no Yoshisada casting a sword into the sea as an offering to the gods, signed *Inagawa*, with red tsubo seal, 19th century, 8.2cm. high.
(Christie's) $4,259

An unusual four-case inro inlaid in ivory and shell with masks, fans and musical instruments connected with Gagaku and the Noh theatre, unsigned 19th century, 7.8cm. high.
(Christie's) $3,484

A three-case roironuri inro decorated in raden, red and gold hiramakie with a flower arrangement in a wicker basket, signed *Shutoho*, 19th century, 7.3cm.
(Christie's) $3,034

A three-case hirame inro decorated in silver, gold and gray hiramakie with three red-capped cranes on the reverse cypress saplings, signed *Koma Yasutada saku*, 19th century, 7.3cm. high.
(Christie's) $8,131

A tsuishu four-case inro carved with a flower arrangement in a Chinese-style basket, signed *Yosei tsukuru*, 19th century, with a tsuishu ojime carved with peonies, 8.2cm. (Christie's) $3,251

A four-case hirame inro decorated in hiramakie and okibirame with yamabushi-no-oi, the robe container of a warrior monk, standing in an ivy-clad landscape beneath a maple, unsigned, 19th century, 8.2cm.
(Christie's) $6,068

A five-case inro decorated in takamakie, hirame and okibirame with a long-tailed pheasant perched on a rock among peonies, signed Toshosai Hozan, 19th century, 9.2cm.
(Christie's) $4,767

A fine four-case inro decorated in hiramakie on a hirame ground with a flock of cranes among pine trees beside a waterfall, others alighting on the reverse, signed *Toyo saku*, with red lacquer seal, 19th century, 8.3cm.
(Christie's) $14,086

A four-case kinji inro decorated in gold and silver hiramakie and kirikane with a blossoming plum tree, with young shoots springing from a gnarled trunk, signed *Gyokujunsai*, 19th century, 9cm. high.
(Christie's) $4,259

An unusual single-case cherry-wood inro containing four cases and a cover, formed as an oi or backplate of a yamabushi, signed *Haritsuo*, probably 18th century, with a silver filigree ojime, 9.9cm. high.
(Christie's) $4,259

A three-case stained boxwood inro shaped as a cicada, its eyes inlaid in black horn, unsigned, 19th century, 10.2cm. long, with an attached tooth netsuke carved as a half-eaten gourd with a mouse on top.
(Christie's) $5,201

A four-case gold hirame ground inro decorated in gold hiramakie, takamakie, kirikane and foil, decorated with tree peony, signed, 19th century, 8.2cm. long.
(Christie's) $5,420

A late 17th century French $2^{7}/_{8}$ inch brass equinoctial ring dial, signed on the meridian ring *Pierre Sevin, AParis*, the bridge with sliding pinhole sight engraved with calendar scales.
(Christie's S. Ken) $3,282

A fine and rare 19th century lacquered brass goniometer, signed on the vertical circle *Aug. Oertling, Berlin No. 2840*, with silvered scale and magnifier, $10^{1}/_{2}$in. high.
(Christie's S. Ken) $10,039

A good 19th century lacquered brass compound monocular and binocular 'Van Huerck' microscope, the tripod support signed, *W. Watson & Sons.*
(Phillips) $6,290

A Stanley transit theodolite, the telescope with rack and pinion focusing, mounted in trunnion, with silver inset verticals and horizontal circles of degrees, 13in. high.
(Henry Spencer) $797

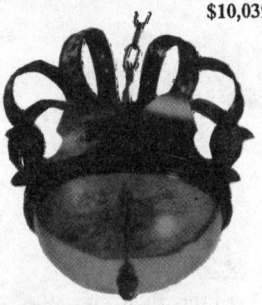

An 18th century Danish suspended deckhead compass, with dry card signed *RASMUS KOCH I KIOBENHAVN 1772*, $8^{1}/_{2}$in. diameter.
(Christie's S. Ken) $2,124

An early 19th century $3^{3}/_{4}$ inch celestial globe, with makers label inscribed *SMITHS CELESTIAL GLOBE*, the constellations named and lightly colored, $6^{3}/_{4}$in. high.
(Christie's S. Ken) $2,703

A rare Hygrophant early hygrometer for measuring relative air humidity with turning drum measurement, circa 1929.
(Auction Team Köln) $96

An early 19th century 'Jones Most Improved' monocular microscope, on a turned pillar with folding tripod stand signed *Dollond London*, 1ft. $5^{3}/_{4}$in. high.
(Phillips) $2,035

An 18th century 3 inch brass reflecting telescope, signed on the back plate *B. MARTIN*, with screw-rod focusing, mirrors and eye-piece.
(Christie's S. Ken) $1,255

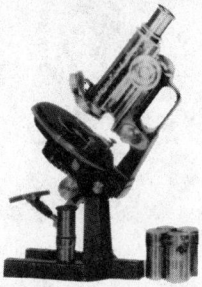

A microscope by Zeiss, with lacquered brass body on black 'jug-handle' stand, coarse and fine focusing, 12in. high.
(Christie's S. Ken) $593

A late 17th century silvered brass compass, the octagonal plate signed *Ieremius Kögler Dantzig Fecit 1680* with well engraved compass rose, iron needle with brass cap, 2⁷/₈in. wide.
(Christie's S. Ken) $1,544

A brass theodolite by OTTO FENNELL SOHNE CASSELL No. 19813 with telescope, graduated bubble levels, the enclosed scale with micrometer adjustment.
(Christie's S. Ken) $425

An early 19th century 16in. terrestrial globe, inscribed *J. & W. Cary, Strand, March 1st 1816 with corrections and additions to 1839*, 3ft. 8½in. high.
(Phillips) $11,100

A brass cannon-dial signed *F BARKER & Sons* with calendar dial, engraved quadrant on three pad feet, 9¾in. diameter in plush lined carrying case.
(Christie's S. Ken) $1,255

A late 19th century oxidized and lacquered brass transit theodolite, signed on the silvered compass dial *Stanley, Gt. Turnstile, Holborn, LONDON*, 13½in. wide.
(Christie's S. Ken) $1,448

A 19th century brass transit theodolite, the telescope with rack and pinion focusing, signed *Troughton & Simms, London*, in a fitted mahogany box.
(Phillips) $1,480

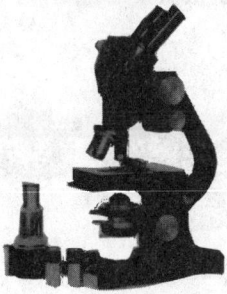

A black enameled "Bactil Binocular" microscope by W. Watson & Sons Ltd., in fitted mahogany case, 17in. high, with accessories.
(Christie's S. Ken) $381

Swiss precision watchmaker's milling machine on mahogany plinth with drawer, brass with almost complete set of equipment, circa 1880.
(Auction Team Köln) $531

A brass reflecting telescope by Nairne & Blunt, with terrestrial eyepiece, on folding tripod stand, late 18th century, 25½in. length of body tube.
(Christie's New York)
$1,540

A rare 18th century 2¾ inch terrestrial globe, with label inscribed *A Terrestrial GLOBE G: Adams No. 60 Fleet Street LONDON*, the colored paper gores showing Anfon's Voyage.
(Christie's S. Ken)
$6,945

A fine and rare mid 19th century heliostat, signed on the drum *J.T. Silbermann invteur, Soleil Fecit à Paris, No. 7*, on tripod stand with lock and three adjustable feet, 15in. high.
(Christie's S. Ken)
$11,583

The Portable Astronomical Pantoscope, original US patent 1865. Shows 'position of the heavenly bodies in relation to the horizon, the equator and the ecliptic!'
(Auction Team Köln)
$4,332

A fine brass universal equinoctial ring dial, the pivoted horizon ring engraved with 24-hour Roman chapters graduated at five-minute intervals, probably English, late 17th century, 15cm. diameter.
(Christie's New York)
$3,520

A fine early 19th century lacquered and silvered brass equinoctial dial, signed on the hour-ring *Watkins & Hill Charing Cross* with inner hour scale, spring loaded gnomon, 3¾in. long.
(Christie's S. Ken)
$2,124

A fine engraved gilt metal horse pedometer and watch by Ralph Gout, London, the verge watch movement with pierced balance cock chased with trophy of arms, circa 1800, 55.5mm. diameter of pedometer.
(Christie's New York)
$9,350

A late 18th century lacquered brass oak and paper planetarium, the finely printed paper planetary dial inscribed *A TABLE of the principal AFFECTIONS of the PLANETS, Jany St. 1794*, 14in. wide.
(Christie's S. Ken)
$7,722

A late 19th century brass transit, by Cary, the telescope with 'V' and bead sights, the axis with vertical circle divided in four quadrants, 19½in. high.
(Christie's S. Ken)
$2,703

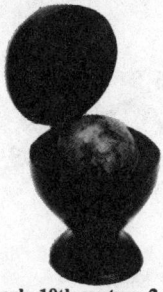

An early 19th century 2 inch terrestrial globe, inscribed *Model of the Earth by J. Manning*, 13¾in. high.
(Christie's S. Ken) $1,834

An early 19th century brass 2½in. reflecting telescope, with turned support and folding tripod stand in a fitted mahogany box.
(Phillips) $962

American celestial globe, J. Wilson & Sons, 1826, Albany St. New York, on a mahogany tripod base, 36½in. high.
(Skinner Inc.) $1,200

A fine semi-miniature marine chronometer, the silvered dial signed *Arnold London*, with Government mark within seconds dial at VI, blued spade hands, flat glass, the top-plate similarly signed, early 19th century, dial diameter 63mm.
(Christie's) $5,225

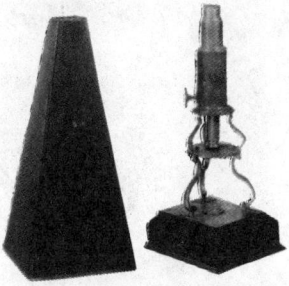

An early 19th century brass 'Culpeper-Type' compound monocular microscope with rack and pinion focusing and circular stage between three 'S'-scroll supports, 1ft. 2½in. high.
(Phillips) $1,018

An 18th century brass gunner's-caliper signed on one arm Geo. Adams, with scales for Inches, Guns, Brafs Guns, and Proof, 12in long opened, and with circular and semi-circular protractors.
(Christie's S. Ken) $1,004

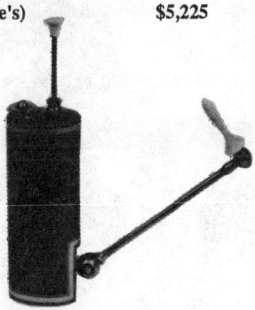

A Maw pattern enema pump with ivory plunger handle and articulated nozzle, the reservoir of oval form decorated with gilt banding, in leather case, 10½in. long.
(Christie's S. Ken) $463

An early 19th century German fruitwood diptych dial, unsigned, with colored paper vertical dial and horizontal plate, 2⅝in. long.
(Christie's S. Ken) $251

A rare late 18th century lacquered brass miniature refracting telescope, signed *Dollond, London*, the 1¼ inch lens covered with a screw-on dust cap.
(Christie's S. Ken) $3,089

**A Salter Improved No 5 typewriter, by Geo. Salter & Co., West Bromwich, with gilt lining and decoration.**
**(Christie's S. Ken) $5,082**

**Orrery 'Trippensee Planetarium, Detroit, Michigan', early 20th century, painted wood, various metals and printed paper, 25½in. wide.**
**(Skinner Inc.) $750**

**An Odell typewriter with linear index mechanism, on ornamentally cast iron base, with retail plate of Perry & Co. Ltd.**
**(Phillips) $930**

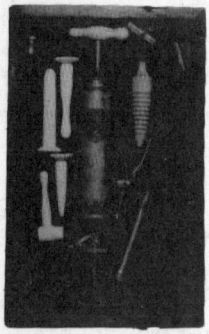

**A late 19th century brass enema syringe by S. Maw Son & Thompson, complete with accessories in mahogany case 12in. wide.**
**(Christie's S. Ken) $385**

**A Lambert typewriter, No. 2924, in maker's bentwood carrying case, with transfer to front.**
**(Phillips) $815**

**An oak cased Ericsson Telephones Ltd Magneto telephone.**
**(Spencer's) $441**

**A brass equinoctial dial, with silvered compass and two levels under glass, signed *Cox, London*, 11.2cm. diameter.**
**(Allen & Harris) $1,375**

**Antique ship's binnacle and compass by James Morton Ltd, Sunderland, in brass and oak with bearing sight and prism, height overall 56in.**
**(Eldred's) $550**

**A miniature terrestrial globe inscribed within a circle *CARY'S/Pocket/GLOBE;/ agreeable/to the latest/ DISCOVERIES/LONDON*, 3½in. diameter.**
**(Bearne's) $1,730**

A set of counter-top scales signed on the porcelain slab *J. White & Sons Auchtermuchty Est 1715*, with brass central carrying handle and weights pan, 19½in. wide.
(Christie's S. Ken) $318

A Lambert typewriter, by Lambert Typewriter Co., New York, with blue and gilt lines and oak case with transfer.
(Christie's S. Ken) $847

A Merritt typewriter with linear index, in original carrying case, with roll inker and ink tube in original packing case.
(Phillips) $875

A fine 19th century lacquered brass 'double telescope' surveying level, signed on the silvered dial *Pistor and Martins BERLIN*, 10¼in. high.
(Christie's S. Ken) $6,425

A George III pocket chronometer by John Arnold, circa 1785, with 1¾in. diameter enameled dial, now in later mahogany case as a boudoir clock, 7in. high.
(Bearne's) $8,460

Automatique Dubuit platen machine, desk top model for printing small items like business cards, circa 1920.
(Auction Team Köln) $157

A rare Fitch typewriter with downstroke action and plate of the Fitch Typewriter Company Ltd., London.
(Christie's S. Ken) $6,089

An early 19th century 12 inch celestial globe, the label inscribed *CARY'S NEW CELESTIAL GLOBE*, 35in. high.
(Christie's S. Ken) $5,019

Rare American Momsen lung, the first well-known submarine escape device.
(Eldred's) $88

A Norris A51 annealed iron smoother with twin-thread adjustment, the cutter 5¾in. long.
(Christie's S. Ken) $318

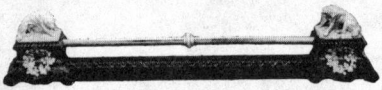

An ormolu, bronze and steel adjustable fender with seated dogs and molded rectangular plinths mounted with fruiting wreaths, on scroll feet, mid-19th century, 53in. wide.
(Christie's) $3,292

An iron figure of a Sphinx, French, late 19th century, the mythological creature at rest, the base inscribed in raised letters *VAL D'OSNE*, 20½ x 40½in.
(Christie's East) $3,300

Cast iron architectural ornament, America, late 19th/ early 20th century, in the form of an eagle with outstretched wings, 21in. high.
(Skinner Inc.) $700

Pair of Victorian black-painted cast-iron urns, each fluted flaring form on a circular fluted socle, 34½in. high.
(Butterfield & Butterfield) $2,200

Hand forged steel rocker, 20th century, bent steel, with tufted upholstered suede back and seat, 45in. high.
(Skinner Inc.) $250

An early Victorian red-painted and gilt coal scuttle, the sides with lion-mask handles and decorated with eagles, lions and horses, 14in. wide.
(Christie's) $1,287

A pair of French cast iron torchères, each modeled as putto holding a torch with glass shade above his head, one inscribed *Pelees*, late 19th century, 56in. high.
(Christie's) $5,643

Continental black-painted cast-iron urn in the Neoclassical taste, second half 19th century, the handles modeled as satyr masks with rams' horns, 24in. high.
(Butterfield & Butterfield) $1,210

An iron koro and cover on tripod feet, the squat body with three elaborately pierced silver cloisonné lappet panels depicting a dragon, ho-o bird and karashishi among flowers, 19th century, 12.8cm. high.
(Christie's) $6,068

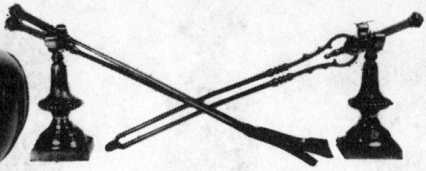

A set of early Victorian ormolu and steel fire-irons, each with pineapple finial, and a pair of Regency ormolu and steel andirons.
(Christie's) $3,564

The Skier. Attributed to Manuel Felguerez Barra. Signed *"Felguerez"* on the figure, painted steel, 10in. high.
(Skinner Inc.) $300

A gothic wrought-iron Paschal candlestick designed by John Loughborough Pearson, the deep circular drip-pan with cylindrical nozzle of foliate decoration, 175cm. high.
(Christie's) $6,402

Pair of Continental black-painted cast-iron urns, second half 19th century, the side handles formed as lion masks each supporting a winged seated putto, 24½in. high.
(Butterfield & Butterfield) $2,750

Painted and decorated baby carriage, America, late 19th century, ground painted white and heightened with blue and yellow, 56in. long.
(Skinner Inc.) $550

North African brass-mounted iron storage chest, 18th century, with arched top and embossed designs, 58in. wide.
(Skinner Inc.) $1,500

Coalbrookdale cast iron umbrella stand to hold twelve umbrellas, with pierced sides and carrying handles, approx. 24in. wide.
(G.A. Key) $468

A silvered cast iron group of a mare and her foal, on a naturalistic base, 12in. high.
(Christie's S. Ken) $665

A Victorian tole peinte wine cooler, repainted with flower borders and stylized flowerheads, with removeable liner, 62cm. long.
(Allen & Harris) $591

One of a pair of cast-iron urns and stands, each with a circular waisted body, on spreading foot and square base, on a square plinth, the urns: 22in. high.
(Christie's) (Two) $517

A fine inlaid iron plaque worked in high relief and enameled with monkeys playing tug of war, signed, Meiji period, 18.5cm. x 27.75cm.
(Hy. Duke & Son) $5,250

A late Victorian polychrome and painted tole bird-cage of architectural form, with trefoil-mounted raised turret cresting, the upper canted rectangular level with cusped arches, 70½in. wide.
(Christie's) $4,950

An Art Nouveau cast-iron fire surround, the circular top molded with a naked kneeling maiden in a cartouche, 1.70m. high. (Phillips) $2,237

An early 19th century white-painted wrought-iron garden seat, the oval sectioned back above a slatted seat, 61½in. wide.
(Christie's) $1,300

Flemish enamel stove with oven with attractive colored Art Nouveau decoration, oven with heat regulator, attachable to wall or chimney, circa 1910.
(Auction Team Köln) $512

A J & E Stevens painted cast iron 'Creedmoor Bank', designed by James Bowen, marksman firing at target, 6½in. high.
(Christie's S. Ken) $437

An iron tetsubin of cylindrical form, the sides with a dragon in low relief rising amongst clouds two small handles, 19th century, 14cm. high.
(Christie's) $786

A wrought-iron plant stand of demi-lune outline, with six graduated shelves, 74in. wide.
(Christie's) $700

A 'Jolly Nigger' mechanical money bank, in the form of a negro wearing a top hat, 21.5cm. high.
(Phillips) $150

A white-painted cast-iron seat, with shaped arm supports and triple slat wooden seat, on shaped legs, 57in. wide.
(Christie's) $925

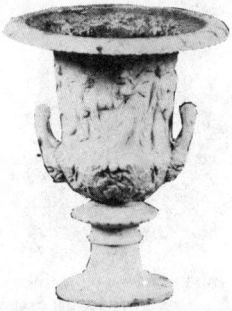

One of a pair of white-painted cast-iron krater urns, after the Borghese vase, each with an egg-and-dart rim above a Bacchic frieze, 18¼in. high.
(Christie's) (Two) $885

A white-painted cast-iron jardinière, cast with stylized foliate brackets, on scrolled trefoil supports with black-painted octagonal foot, 19th century, 40½in. high.
(Christie's) $2,400

One of a pair of cast-iron urns and covers, the fluted body with a gadrooned rim and lower section, on stepped circular foot, 30in. high.
(Christie's) (Two) $1,570

A green-painted cast-iron fountain, with two circular tiers, the first supported by two cherubs, 19th century, 57in. high overall.
(Christie's) $2,600

Two of a set of four mauve-painted cast-iron urns and covers, after the antique, each with anthemion decorated lid, 31½in. high.
(Christie's)
(Four) $9,240

A black and white painted cast-iron fountain, by Walter Macfarlane & Co. Glasgow, the circular pediment headed with acanthus and scrolls, 66in. high.
(Christie's) $3,325

An ivory carving of a seated man, a tortoise emerging from a cut down wooden barrel filled with water in front of him, 3¾in. long, signed Meiji period.
(Bonhams) $392

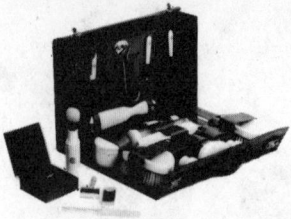

A gentleman's tan pigskin dressing case, with ivory fittings monogrammed C.E.F., 26 x 38cm.
(Onslow's) $393

'Posing', an ivory figure carved from a model by Ferdinand Preiss, of a naked maiden, on a green onyx plinth, signed in the onyx *F. Preiss*, 10cm. high.
(Christie's) $1,432

An ivory carving of two dignitaries, one standing pouring from a vessel, the other seated, 4in. high, Meiji period.
(Bonhams) $1,026

'Naked maiden', an ivory figure, carved from a model by Ferdinand Preiss, on a green onyx circular dish, 20cm. high.
(Christie's) $3,432

An ivory okimono of Bashiko the Chinese doctor healing a dragon, the physician bending forward to examine the mouth of his patient, signed *Mansanari*, late 19th century, 10.8cm. high.
(Christie's) $3,484

An ivory okimono of a sennin conjuring a dragon from a bowl, the sennin dressed in a loose-fitting and partially-covering garments, signed *Nobusane*, late 19th century, 14.4cm. high.
(Christie's) $1,452

A German ivory lidded tankard, the sides finely carved in relief with an animated hunting scene, with riders, hounds and bears, 19th century, 9in. high.
(Christie's) $8,593

A late 19th century Japanese carved ivory figure of a middle aged game hunter, standing wearing a short sleeved tunic tied at the waist, 8in. high.
(Spencer's) $716

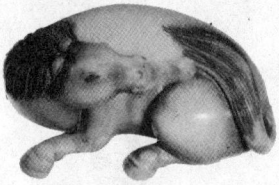

An ivory okimono of a recumbent horse, its head turned to the rear, its mane and tail engraved and stained, unsigned, style of Rantei, 19th century, 4.8cm. long.
(Christie's) $1,517

An ivory group of The Three Sake Tasters and a sake bowl, their faces most expressively carved, the tasters wearing robes and tasseled girdles, the figures signed *Mitsuaki*, 19th century, 21.5cm. high.
(Christie's) $32,912

A wood and ivory carving of an oni on a turtle in two sections to constitute a box, the ivory oni crouching and scowling in a wicked fashion, signed *Sekkosai Masayoshi*, late 19th century, 15.3cm. long.
(Christie's) $2,129

An ivory peach-shaped carving with a scholar and three young attendants beside a pavilion next to trees on a rocky river bank, 18th/19th century, 15cm. wide.
(Christie's) $1,707

Pair of Dieppe ivory figures of young women, mid 19th century, a wood-gatherer and a figure holding a bird in nest, 14½in. high.
(Skinner Inc.) $9,500

A late 19th century ivory Japanese model of the takarabune, the seven gods on the canopied two tiered deck, each with their respective attributes, 11in. tall.
(Spencer's) $1,790

An ivory basket and cover, of lobed circular shape, with a domed lid and twin high loop handles, 9½in. high.
(Lawrence Fine Art) $422

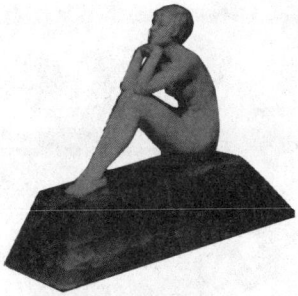

'Thoughts', an ivory figure carved from a model by Ferdinand Preiss, of a young woman seated with knees drawn up supporting bent elbows, signed on the base, 4½in. high.
(Christie's S. Ken) $2,130

'Lighter than Air', a bronze and ivory figure, cast and carved from a model by Ferdinand Preiss, of a female figure poised holding a glass sphere above her head, 33.5cm. high.
(Christie's) $7,832

Large ivory okimono of a fisherman, 20th century, standing in peasant garb with his body slightly turning to the right as he pulls up on his bamboo fishing rod, 6½in. high.
(Butterfield & Butterfield) $1,045

One of two carved and painted ivory plaques, Meiji period, with stained and incised details, each within carved hardwood frames, 8in. x 6⅝in.
(Butterfield & Butterfield) (Two) $3,025

Large uncarved 19th century sperm whale's tooth, on a turned wood base, height 6½in.
(Eldred's) $715

'Butterfly dancers', a bronze and ivory group cast and carved from a model by Prof. Otto Poertzel, of two ballerinas dancing in formation, 41.5cm. high.
(Christie's) $18,233

Fine pair of American 19th century scrimshaw vases, made from whale's teeth with notch-carved edges inset with two turned wood bands.
(Eldred's) $1,980

A painted ivory figure carved from a model by Ferdinand Preiss, of a young woman wearing green halter-neck bathing costume, signed on ivory base, 7½in. high.
(Christie's S. Ken) $1,936

A Japanese one piece ivory figure, of a courtesan, wearing scroll and foliate carved robes, 15in. high.
(Spencer's) $1,253

A Vizigapatan ivory workbox in the form of a house, engraved with penwork, the hinged lid enclosing a fitted interior, late 18th century, 6¾in. wide.
(Christie's) $11,616

A Goanese group of the Christ Child as The Good Shepherd, the young boy seated holding a lamb on his lap, 8in. high, late 17th/early 18th century.
(Bearne's) $2,350

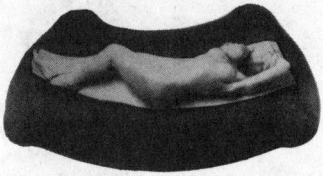

T.H. Paget, ivory reclining female nude, the young woman depicted lying full length, 20¾in. long, signed.
(Bearne's) $3,948

A German ivory figure of Venus with Cupid, the goddess lightly clad, her long hair falling down her back, carrying the winged Cupid on her shoulder, 19th century, 9in. high.
(Christie's) $3,683

An ivory figure of a mother reclining, her head resting on her hand and a child suckling at her breast, Meiji period, 17.5cm.
(Hy. Duke & Son) $960

Large ivory okimono of a potter, Meiji period, the elderly man shown standing beside a persimmon and small stool supporting stacked plates, 8in. high.
(Butterfield & Butterfield) $1,540

A Japanese carved ivory group of a woodcutter, the smiling man cutting a half-sawn tree trunk, Meiji period, signed, 7½in. high.
(Bearne's) $884

An ivory okimono of a young woman teaching a boy to walk on bamboo stilts, signed, Meiji period, 17cm. high.
(Hy. Duke & Son) $1,485

Large ivory okimono, Meiji period, featuring two dozen oni of various sizes clamoring about the gigantic temple bell of Miidera, 7¾in. high.
(Butterfield & Butterfield) $3,850

An impressive pair of ivory temple ornaments with double pagoda roofs above carved hexagonal bodies, 25in. high.
(G.E. Sworder) $4,650

An unusual Anglo-Indian carved ivory miniature chiffonier, the upper section with mirror back and scroll supports, 19th century, 7in. high.
(Bearne's) $919

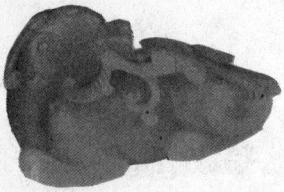

A celadon jade carving of a bixie, the recumbent animal turning its horned head back while grasping a lingzhi spray in its mouth, 18th/19th century, 9.5cm. long.
(Christie's) $2,134

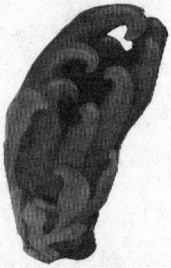

A gray jade carving of a finger citron, the curling fingers issuing from a gnarled leafy stem, 18th century, 10.5cm. high.
(Christie's) $2,134

A gray and russet jade bull, carved recumbent with its legs tucked into its body, with naturalistically detailed openwork horns curling back to its neck, Ming Dynasty, 13.5cm. long.
(Christie's) $11,737

A speckled gray jade bowl the spreading foot and flaring rim each delicately incised with a thin horizontal groove, the semi-translucent gray stone heavily dappled with black flecks, an incised Qianlong six-character mark, 14.3cm. diameter.
(Christie's) $1,921

Small jadeite censer and cover of compressed globular form raised on three paw feet, 4 3/4 in. high.
(Butterfield & Butterfield) $1,430

A pale celadon jade flattened baluster vase, the spherical body incised and gilt to one face with fishermen in a mountainous river landscape, the jade 18th century, the decoration possibly later, 19.2cm. high.
(Christie's) $3,201

An oval grayish-brown jade plaque, Ming dynasty or earlier, the slightly convex top carved with two stylized taotie with snake-like bodies on a finely-incised ground, 2 7/8 in. wide.
(Christie's) $5,627

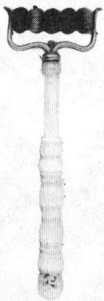

A celadon jade back massager with a pale celadon jade handle ornately carved with stylized buds and petals and an openwork lingzhi cluster at one end, mid Qing Dynasty, 26.5cm. long.
(Christie's) $8,536

A pair of linked jade bangles, Ming dynasty, each carved as two confronted archaistic crouching dragons, the stone of even light brownish tone, 2in. diameter.
(Christie's) $5,184

A celadon and russet jade boulder carved from a broad stone to one face with two deer on a river bank below pine trees, 18th century, 19cm. long.
(Christie's) $7,469

A celadon jade boulder group, well carved with the eight horses of Mu Wang and an attendant below pine trees at the base of a precipitous cliff, 18th century, 18.5cm. wide.
(Christie's) $5,975

A pale celadon jade censer and cover, carved around the body with interlaeed archaistic kui dragons divided by horizontal bands of flanges, Qianlong, 19cm. wide.
(Christie's) $2,561

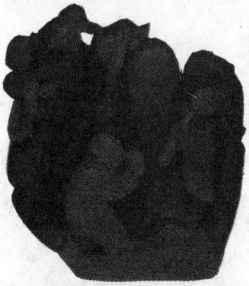

A celadon jade carving of Shoulao and a boy, standing among rockwork and a fruiting peach tree, Shoulao with a staff and ruyi sceptre, the boy holding up a small peach, mid Qing Dynasty, 10cm. high.
(Christie's) $4,268

A pale celadon jade figure of a camel naturalistically carved and detailed with a thick mane, bushy tail and thick hair on the top of the humps and legs, Qing Dynasty, 19cm. wide.
(Christie's) $5,762

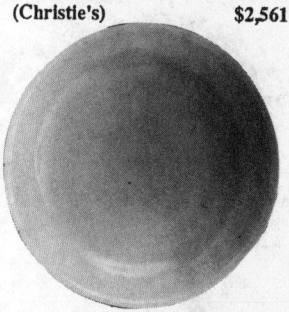

A large celadon jade dish, the shallow sides rising to a flaring rim from a crisp foot ring, the stone of very even milky tone, 18th century, 27.2cm. diameter.
(Christie's) $6,829

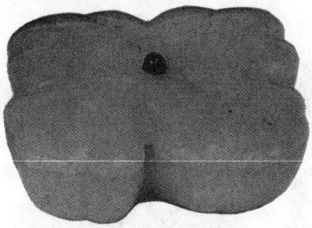

A moghul jade cosmetic box and cover comprising four petal-shaped compartments, the shallow cover of a similar design inset with ruby-colored stone bead, 18th century, 8cm. wide.
(Christie's) $3,201

A very fine jadeite figure of Guanyin, carved from a highly translucent stone with attractive bright apple-green suffusions as the Goddess of Mercy wearing loose-fitting robes tied at the waist, 6in. high.
(Christie's) $148,093

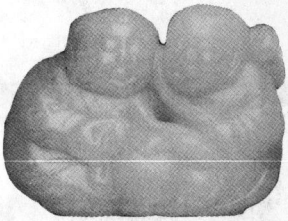

A white jade group, 18th century, carved from a stone of pale celadon tone with the Hehe Erxian, both wearing loose-fitting robes, 2¾in. long.
(Christie's) $2,968

An Austro-Hungarian 'peacock' brooch, its body set with mother-of-pearl, its wings set with small half pearls, 7cm. long.
(Phillips) $250

An unusual H.G. Murphy gold 'tortoise' brooch, the creature having a green-stained chalcedony shell and garnet eyes, 3.5cm. long.
(Phillips) $398

An attractive plique-a-jour enameled 'peacock' pendant, the creature's body set with mother-of-pearl, its wings and neck blue enameled, 7cm., probably Austro-Hungarian.
(Phillips) $716

A topaz and diamond brooch, the oval shaped topaz collet set at the center within a double row border of cushion-shaped similarly set diamonds.
(Lawrence Fine Art) $2,223

A half-pearl and ruby brooch, designed as a graduated half-pearl crescent supporting a gold owl with ruby eyes.
(Lawrence Fine Art) $1,143

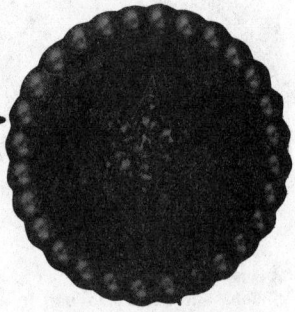

An enamel, diamond and half-pearl brooch, circa 1880, the circular plaque of blue guilloché enamel set at the center with a star motif pavé-set.
(Lawrence Fine Art) $381

A gold and pietra dura oval brooch, the central oval hardstone mosaic depicting a dove within a gold frame.
(Bearne's) $510

A late 19th century gold and diamond flower brooch with six petals pavé-set with old-mine brilliant-cut stones.
(Bearne's) $17,710

An antique gold locket, last quarter of the 19th century, of large oval shape engraved with scrolled motifs.
(Lawrence Fine Art) $447

An Omar Ramsden pendant, the silver openwork backed with red enamel, the foliate border studded with small red garnets.
(Christie's) $1,494

A large interlaced 'C' brooch set with a double row of diamonds (approximately 14 cts.)
(Woolley & Wallis) $10,836

A kunzite and diamond ring, the large step-cut kunzite within a border of circular-cut claw-set diamonds.
(Lawrence Fine Art) $4,023

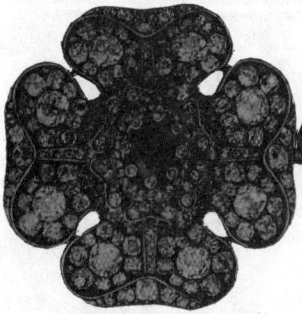

A mid-19th century gold, ruby and diamond flower brooch, with four petals, pavé-set with old-mine brilliants, centering in a larger oval ruby.
(Bearne's) $13,090

An amethyst and diamond brooch/pendant, last quarter of the 19th century, the oval shaped amethyst within a foliate border pavé and collet-set with rose-cut stones.
(Lawrence Fine Art) $1,588

A gold, enamel and tortoiseshell brooch, circa 1880, the oval tortoiseshell of a young woman and elderly gentleman within a blue guilloché enamel and scrolled border.
(Lawrence Fine Art) $1,355

By and after Francesco Bianchi, an oval shell carved cameo depicting Pope Leo XIII, contained in a silver gilt filigree pendant mount.
(Spencer's) $576

An attractive French pendant locket of triangular shape, formed as a moth in silver-colored metal with golden linear detail, 5cm.
(Phillips) $557

A large oval shell cameo brooch, carved depicting two classical female figures with the Greek goddess 'Minerva' in a gold frame.
(Bearne's) $924

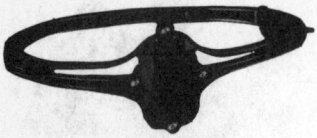

**An amethyst and half-pearl hinged bangle, claw-set at the front with a scissor-cut amethyst collet-set on each side with a half-pearl.**
**(Lawrence Fine Art)**
**$1,271**

**An emerald and diamond ring, the step-cut emerald collet-set within a border of cushion-shaped diamonds.**
**(Lawrence Fine Art)**
**$7,411**

**An antique gold hinged bangle, the front decorated with corded wire and ivy leaves.**
**(Lawrence Fine Art)**
**$1,059**

**An oval shell cameo portrait brooch depicting a young girl with a lion, her hair adorned with grapes and vine leaves.**
**(Bearne's)**
**$1,360**

**A Georg Jensen circular enameled silver brooch, depicting a cherub in flight amid stars and holding a flaming torch, 4.70cm. diameter.**
**(Phillips)**
**$973**

**An 18ct gold Victorian Scottish agate brooch, claw-set at the center with a mixed-cut citrine.**
**(Lawrence Fine Art)**
**$1,506**

**A 19th century gold and pietra dura oval pendant, the hardstone panel depicting a floral spray within a gold frame.**
**(Bearne's)**
**$459**

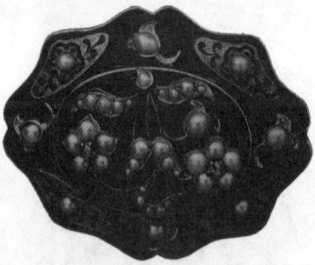

**A mid-19th century black enameled gold oval mourning brooch with central 'forget-me-not' design in half-pearls and rose-diamonds.**
**(Bearne's)**
**$515**

**A Victorian gold and rock crystal reverse intaglio, painted as a kingfisher flying above the water's edge.**
**(Lawrence Fine Art)**
**$3,378**

A garnet set stiff hinged bangle, with central cluster flanked by two lines of pavé set faceted stones.
(Spencer's) $448

A 15ct gold, diamond and half-pearl brooch, designed as a dove of peace, with a rose-cut diamond eye and decorated with half-pearls.
(Lawrence Fine Art) $521

An Egyptianesque brooch by Georg Adam Scheid, formed as a winged scarab with Swiss lapis body and blue and green enameled wings, 5.5cm. wide.
(Phillips) $796

A Victorian gold and shell cameo brooch, last quarter of the 19th century, the oval plaque carved as two female profiles, an owl and a dove, within a gold beaded border.
(Lawrence Fine Art) $2,413

A mid-19th century enameled gold and seed-pearl hinged bangle and matching drop earrings.
(Bearne's) $2,406

An early 19th century gold, seed-pearl and hair plait memorial brooch with central hair miniature, dated 1831.
(Bearne's) $385

An enamel, diamond and half pearl brooch/pendant, circa 1875, of marquise shape, painted with three cherubs seated on a cloud.
(Lawrence Fine Art) $4,826

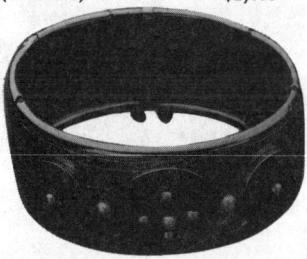

A 19th century French gold, agate, seed-pearl and diamond-mounted hinged bangle, inset with seed-pearls and rose diamonds.
(Bearne's) $588

An unusual Art Nouveau plique-a-jour and diamanté pendant, the ivory and mother-of-pearl bust mounted in a gilt white-metal setting, 12.9cm. long.
(Christie's) $5,729

A nashiji toilet box decorated in takamakie with chrysanthemum beside a rock-lined stream, a woman's traveling cloak in the foreground, the chrysanthemums inlaid with silver dewdrops, unsigned, circa 1600.
(Christie's) $60,676

A nashiji suzuribako, decorated in gold and silver hiramakie and kirikane with a youth playing a flute while seated on the back of an ox, signed *Iwami*, 18th century, 23.6 x 21.4cm.
(Christie's) $3,872

A three-tiered kashibako decorated with blossoming cherry trees by the banks of the Yoshino River in hiramakie, hirame and okibirame, unsigned, 19th century, 12 x 9.8 x 8.2cm.
(Christie's) $14,086

A gold lacquer kobako and domed cover richly decorated in hiramakie, fundame and nashiji, the all-over design of suzumemon, blossoming boughs and bamboo leaves and stalks, circa 1700, 8cm. high.
(Christie's) $1,950

A pair of carved red lacquer armchairs carved in mirror image, the high back with three panels, the center depicting the Queen of the West, 18th/19th century, 111cm. high.
(Christie's) $25,608

A nest of seven Chinese Export red, black and gilt lacquer corner tables of graduated size decorated overall with blossom, late 19th/20th century, 73½in. high, stacked.
(Christie's) $1,960

A large lacquer dish decorated in gold hiramakie, hirame and nashiji inlaid in Shibayama style depicting a cockerel and a hen under plum and chrysanthemum blossoms on a gold ground, late 19th century, 36.2cm. diameter.
(Christie's) $2,817

A gold lacquer skull attended by three ivory oni, the three demons with stained detail and decorated with accoutrements in Shibayama style, unsigned, 19th century, overall height 20cm.
(Christie's) $14,520

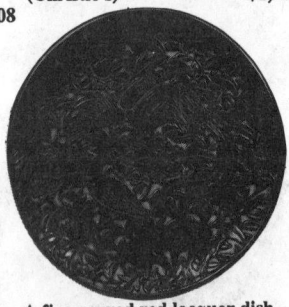

A fine carved red lacquer dish, the front carved through to a buff ground to depict a brace of pheasant perched and fluttering among a dense field of blossoming peony, Ming Dynasty, 29.5cm. diameter.
(Christie's) $17,072

A pewter-rimmed bunko, the cover and sides decorated in hiramakie and gold and silver foil with aki-no-nanakusa on a hirame ground, unsigned, 17th century, 38.7 x 32.1 x 12cm.
(Christie's) $19,360

A lacquer koro formed as a cockerel and hen on an alarm drum on a four-legged stand, decorated in hiramakie, togidashi and gyobu, late 19th century, 24.1cm. high.
(Christie's) $9,101

A silver-rimmed circular wood kogo, the exterior simulating bamboo and the interior with the full moon seen among clouds in silver and gold togidashi, Meiji period, 11cm. diameter.
(Christie's) $2,904

A gold gyobu ground lacquer kodansu, each side decorated with mountainous water landscape, the front of the door with a hut and a water-wheel beneath a willow tree, 19th century, 9cm. high.
(Christie's) $4,259

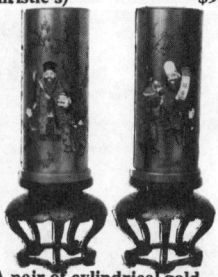

A pair of cylindrical gold lacquered wood vases decorated in gold and silver takamakie, hiramakie and kirigane and inlaid with wood and ivory with Fikurokuju and Daikoku standing under blossoming boughs, late 19th century, 52cm. high.
(Christie's) $16,253

A Korean black lacquered cabinet with metal fittings and inlaid with mother-of-pearl, the compartments comprising a lower single drawer below two smaller drawers, 19th century, 31cm. high.
(Christie's) $5,033

A red lacquer four-tier box and cover, carved around the sides with chrysanthemum, lotus and peony meanders, the top depicting a sage and lion beneath a pine tree, 17th/18th century, 16cm. high.
(Christie's) $1,814

A carved marbled lacquer stand, of cinquefoil shape raised on five cabriole legs braced by a continuous cinquefoil stretcher, 17th/18th century, 23cm. wide.
(Christie's) $7,469

A large export lacquer medallion, the oval plaque decorated in gold hiramakie on a roironuri ground with a bust portrait of Pieter Breughel the Elder, 18th century, 22.5cm. high.
(Christie's) $3,467

A Gallé carved and acid-etched double-overlay lamp, the milky-white glass overlaid with orange and yellow nasturtium, supported by a bronze naturalistic base, 38.5cm. high.
(Christie's) $18,233

Glass and brass table lamp, with reverse painted border design in yellow with sylized green and red floral motif, 16in. diameter.
(Skinner Inc.) $650

A Gallé carved and acid-etched lamp, with bronze mount, cast from a model by Pondany, the glass shade of mushroom-cap form with undulating rim, 53.5cm. high.
(Christie's) $9,009

An early 20th century bronzed metal three light candelabrum, in the form of a street lamp, modeled with a figure of a swaggering young man, his hands in his cummerbund, 36in. high overall.
(Christie's S. Ken) $733

An early 19th century Siena marble oil lamp, the lobed elongated urn shaped reservoir with winged dragon handle, 5½in. high.
(Christie's S. Ken) $2,544

A Gallé carved and acid-etched, double-overlay table lamp, the yellow glass overlaid in royal blue and purple with harebells, the base and shade with carved signatures *Gallé*, 61cm. high.
(Christie's) $75,658

A Daum carved and acid-etched double-overlay lamp, the shade of stepped conical form, with yellow ground overlaid in red and burgundy with a wooded river landscape, 32cm. high.
(Christie's) $12,870

An early Victorian brass two light oil lamp, the reservoirs with vine chased holders, supported by a figure of Hercules, 33in. high.
(Christie's S. Ken) $1,933

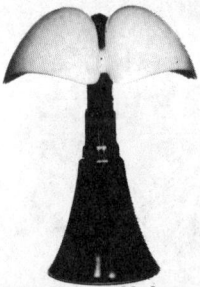

'Pipistrello', a table lamp designed by Gae Aulenti, for Martinelli Luce, the telescopic stainless steel pedestal on a black enameled conical foot, 91cm. maximum height.
(Christie's) $1,692

A Gallé carved and acid-etched double-overlay lamp, with mushroom-cap shade, the yellow glass overlaid with purple and blue marguerites, 39.2cm. high.
(Christie's) $55,770

An unusual 19th century Austrian twin light oil lamp, centered by a carved wood and polychrome figure head of Diana the Huntress with bow and sheaf of arrows, 38in. wide.
(Christie's S. Ken) $1,323

A Gallé carved and acid-etched double-overlay table lamp, with mushroom-cap-shade, the yellow and red-tinted glass overlaid with red stylized flowers and fruit, 55.5cm. high.
(Christie's) $68,640

Rose mandarin porcelain and brass kerosene lamp, 19th century, porcelain cylinder with brass base and fixture, 12in. high.
(Skinner Inc.) $600

A William IV bronze colza-oil lamp, in the manner of Thomas Messenger, in the form of a rhyton horn with lotus leaf top and fruiting finial, 9½in. wide.
(Christie's) $2,178

Austrian bronze lamp with Gallé Cameo glass shade, base after Friedrich Gornick, late 19th century, with stag and doe beneath trees, signed, 23½in. high.
(Skinner Inc.) $6,000

Leaded glass table lamp, umbrella-form shade of segmented white glass panels with swag and blossom elements, 18in. diameter.
(Skinner Inc.) $350

An early 19th century Dutch repoussé brass octagonal hall lantern, the domed cupola with suspension loop, 17in. high.
(Christie's S. Ken) $407

An important A S.A.L.I.R. 'vaso Veronese', designed by Vittorio Zecchin, the traditional Venetian shape pierced with elaborate and intricate acid-cut fretwork of a hunting scene, 51cm. high.
(Christie's) $47,190

A Royal Doulton group entitled 'The Flower Seller's Children', H.N.1206, withdrawn 1949, mounted as a table lamp.
(Bearne's) $674

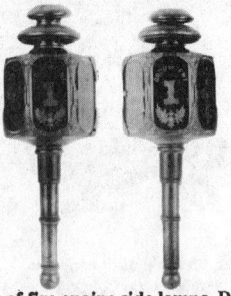

Pair of fire engine side lamps, De Voursney Bros. 9 Broome Street, New York, late 19th century, each with two blue, one red and clear etched glass panels, 19½in. high.
(Skinner Inc.) $2,100

A Birmingham Guild of Handicrafts hammered brass table lamp, the pagoda shade with shaped finial, mounted on a pedestal base formed by four shaped and hammered rods, circa 1893, 51cm. high.
(Christie's) $8,362

A Loetz iridescent glass table lamp, with bronze base formed as two Art Nouveau maidens standing amid flowers, 51cm. high.
(Phillips) $1,751

Copper oil lamp, executed by Mary Steere Batchelder, 39 Hancock St., Boston, circa 1907, 13in. high.
(Skinner Inc.) $1,700

A figural bronze and glass table lamp, cast from a model by Pohl, with three young women wearing diaphanous robes, dancing around the central column, total height 52cm.
(Phillips) $1,751

An Art Nouveau iridescent glass and metal table lamp, with domed Pallme Konig shade of pink tone, 37.50cm. high.
(Phillips) $2,237

A pair of Moorcroft 'Iris' pattern lamp bases, with white piped slip decoration, covered in polychrome glazes on a buff and cobalt blue crackelé ground, 37.2cm. height of base.
(Christie's) $1,195

Scheier Pottery lamp base, circa mid 20th century, large ovoid form, sgraffito decorated with man, woman and child, 16in. high.
(Skinner Inc.) $1,100

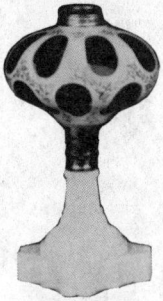

Cut overlay glass lamp with pressed glass base, New England, circa 1870, white glass heightened with gilt, 40in. high.
(Skinner Inc.) $425

Art Deco lamp, circa 1925, fan-shape mica covered metal shade with patinated metal standard and base, 13$^{3}/_{8}$in. high.
(Skinner Inc.) $350

A Daum carved and acid-etched landscape table lamp, with tricorn-shaped shade pinched at each corner, the base of mottled yellow glass tinged with red, 45.5cm. high.
(Christie's) $13,943

Gustav Stickley porch lantern, circa 1907, wrought iron frame in flat black painted finish, with textured amber glass panels, 15in. high.
(Skinner Inc.) $700

A pair of Louis XVI style ormolu-mounted malachite veneered vases mounted as lamps, 19$^{1}/_{2}$in. high.
(Christie's East) $8,800

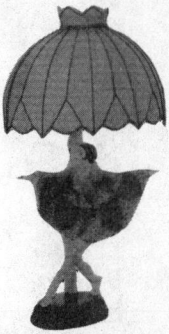

'The Butterfly Girl', a Goldscheider ceramic figural lamp, designed by Lorenzl, modeled as a girl wearing a combined tunic and cape, 52.50cm. high.
(Phillips) $6,710

Hammered copper and mica table lamp, probably upstate New York, with strapwork dividing four panels, 20in. high.
(Skinner Inc.) $2,100

Hammered copper and mica table lamp, early 20th century, with three mica panels on urn shape standard.
(Skinner Inc.) $400

R. Guy Cowan Pottery table lamp, Cleveland, Ohio, circa 1925, metal shade of square flaring form, simulating mica, 19$^{1}/_{2}$in. high.
(Skinner Inc.) $1,000

A marble bust of a girl by A. Piazza, Italian, 19th century, truncated at the shoulders, 18in. high.
(Christie's East) $1,100

Italian carved carrara marble group of two putti, circa 1900, both naked but for scanty draperies, 29in. high.
(Butterfield & Butterfield) $3,025

A marble bust of Spring by Salvatore Albano, Italian, 19th century, the maiden truncated at the waist, 26¾in. high.
(Christie's East) $5,280

'Psyche of Capua', a white marble torso, after the Antique, Le Pecoraro, Italian, late 19th century, 18½in. high.
(Christie's East) $1,100

A pair of Italian alabaster and brass urns, the gadrooned body with two handles and centered by a bacchic mask on a pinched socle and stepped square base, late 18th century, 18¾in. high.
(Christie's) $5,634

An Italian alabaster figure of a young fisherboy, crouching on a rocky outcrop, signed *R. Romanelli 1876*, 24¾in. high.
(Bonhams) $1,872

'Il Spinario', an alabaster figure after the Antique, the seated boy leaning over to draw a thorn from his foot, 17⅝in. high.
(Christie's East) $880

Carved white marble group, Cupid and Psyche, after Canova, late 19th century, on a rockwork mound, 15in. high.
(Butterfield & Butterfield) $825

An alabaster group of Apollo and Daphne after Gianlorenzo Bernini, Apollo chasing a nymph as she metamorphoses into a laurel tree, 26¼in. high.
(Christie's East) $1,320

A white marble bust of a Bacchante in the Renaissance style, truncated as a herm, 21in. high.
(Christie's East) $2,200

A Japanese large white marble figure of Buddha, seated on the back of a Kylin, on a rocky oblong plinth, 38in. high.
(Spencer's) $3,401

A French marble bust of Marie-Antoinette, after Jean-Antoine Houdon, her hair elaborately dressed and crowned with roses, 19th century, 29in. high.
(Christie's) $3,762

A white marble allegorical figure of Autumn by Pasquale Romanelli, Italian, 19th century, 22¾in. high.
(Christie's East) $3,080

Pair of monumental gray marble footed urns in the Neoclassical taste with foliate swags and swan neck handles, 45in. high.
(Butterfield & Butterfield) $4,400

'Augustus of Prima Porta', a variegated marble group, after the Antique, 33½in. high.
(Christie's East) $8,250

An Italian carved alabaster figure group of the birth of Venus by Fliaccini, circa 1880, inscribed *Prof. H. Fliaccini, Florence*, 23½in. high.
(Christie's East) $11,000

An Italian white marble group of the Wrestlers, after the Antique, the two naked athletes locked in combat, 19th century, 18¼in. high.
(Christie's) $4,138

An allegorical white marble bust of Spring, Continental, 19th century, the young maiden with various flowers at her bosom, 21in. high.
(Christie's East) $2,090

An English white marble bust of a young boy, his head turned to the right, his short hair with curls, first half 19th century, 15in. high.
(Christie's) $3,267

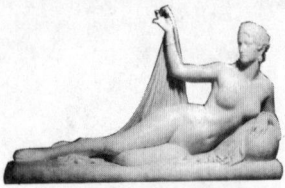

A fine Italian white marble figure of Juno, from the workshop of Lorenzo Bartolini, the naked goddess reclining against an embroidered cushion, first half 19th century, 32in. long.
(Christie's) $13,068

An English white marble bust of a young girl, by Donald Campbell Haggart, her hair partially held in a bow, inscribed and dated on the back *D.G. HAGGART. SCR. 1902*, early 20th century, 19¼in. high the bust.
(Christie's) $2,251

An Italian white marble bust of Rebecca, by P. Morelli, the alluring girl wearing an oriental headdress with pendants, her long hair plaited, one plait falling over her left shoulder, late 19th century, 30in. high with socle.
(Christie's) $11,867

A pair of rouge marble and ormolu vases, as table lamps, the ovoid bodies with twin handles and foliate swag ornament, 16¾in. high, overall.
(Christie's S. Ken) $2,438

An Italian white marble group of Ganymede and Jupiter's eagle, after the Antique and Cellini, the young god shown naked, his curling hair held by a head band, 19th century, 26¼in. high.
(Christie's) $2,940

A 19th century white marble bust of a young boy, shown looking slightly to sinister, on turned socle base, 15¾in. high.
(Christie's S. Ken) $1,773

A large white marble bust depicting The Lord of the Isles, the bearded figure with long flowing hair and draped shoulders, signed on back *J. Hutchison Sc, Edinr*, 32in. high.
(Christie's) $2,239

A Swiss marble group of Ruth the Gleaner, by Heinrich Maximilian Imhof, shown walking forward modestly attired gathering grain, mid 19th century, 39⅜in. high.
(Christie's) $8,184

A French white marble bust of Marie-Antoinette, in the style of Simon-Louis Boizot, looking to dexter, her hair elaborately dressed with pearls and a large bow, 19th century, 34$^{1}/_{8}$in. high.
(Christie's) $6,138

A large white marble group of two children on a swing, by Alessandro Lazzarini, the boy wearing a hat and with his trousers rolled up, his young sister holding on to him, late 19th century, 40$^{1}/_{8}$in. high the sculpture.
(Christie's) $94,116

An English white marble bust of a Vestal Virgin, looking slightly downwards, her veil drawn forwards over her shoulders, first half 19th century, 15$^{1}/_{2}$in. high.
(Christie's) $6,098

An Italian white marble figure of a dancer, after Antonio Canova, the maiden with her head tilted to her right and her right hand to her chin, first half of 19th century, 31$^{1}/_{2}$in. high.
(Christie's) $5,115

A pair of marble and gilt bronze urns, the mottled white and green marble forming the baluster body, with gilt bronze feet decorated with stylized foliage, 19th century, 6$^{1}/_{4}$in. high.
(Christie's) $2,396

A fine English white marble bust of a maiden, by Holme Cardwell, with delicate classical features, her hair swept into a graceful chignon, signed and dated *HOLME CARDWELL SCULPt ROMA 1868*, mid-19th century, 23$^{1}/_{2}$in. high.
(Christie's) $4,501

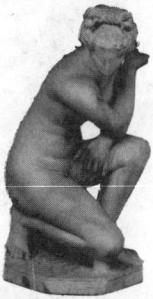

A mid-19th century Italian white marble figure of the crouching Venus, after the Antique, signed *G. Andreoni, Pisa*, a vase at her feet, 34in. high.
(Christie's) $8,140

A 19th century Italian marble panel, carved in low relief with the Virgin and Child, 26$^{1}/_{2}$ x 16$^{3}/_{4}$in.
(Christie's S. Ken) $1,552

An early 19th century sculpted white marble bust of Pericles, his helmet with raised figures of Hercules, Centaurs and animals, 27in. high.
(Christie's S. Ken) $7,758

A Kalliope table model with central spring lift on central spindle, with fifteen 23.5cm. discs, good loud tone.
(Auction Team Köln)
$1,889

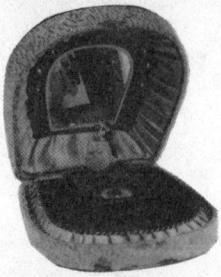

Luxus Necessaire-Etui with music box and dancing couple, melody 'Tales from the Vienna Woods' couple retract on closure, circa 1920.
(Auction Team Köln) $204

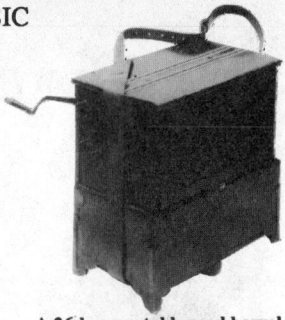

A 26-key portable reed barrel organ with eight-air barrel in varnished case with fretwork front panel and leather carrying strap, 19in. wide.
(Christie's S. Ken)
$2,629

A 15⅝in. table Polyphon disc musical box with single comb movement, in walnut case with inlaid panel and monochrome print to lid, with fifty discs.
(Phillips) $3,492

A 19.58in. upright Polyphon with coin mechanism and drawer in typical walnut case with pediment, 51½in. high, with thirty-nine discs.
(Christie's S. Ken)
$9,203

Stella disc music box, Switzerland, circa 1900, playing 17 ¼-inch discs on a single comb, handle wound, mahogany case with oak leaf carving, 28½in. wide.
(Skinner Inc.) $2,600

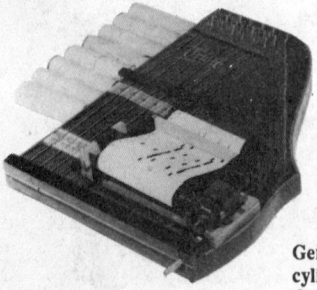

A Triola mechanical zither with 25-note roll mechanism and twenty-four hand-played strings, on ebonized base.
(Christie's S. Ken)
$4,092

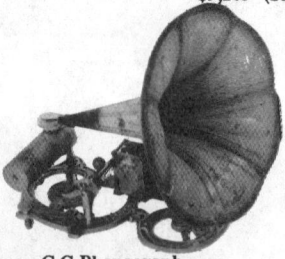

German C G Phonograph cylinder player with finely decorated cast socle and horn in the form of a convolvulus head with French 4 minute adapter and 2 each 2 min and 4 min cylinders, only one other example known, 1903.
(Auction Team Köln) $1,732

Very rare Polyphon, the first model without spring winding, still with hand cranked direct drive. With nine 16.5cm. discs, circa 1890.
(Auction Team Köln)
$1,064

Glass fronted gramophone, with dealer's label, *Chas. Knishott, Cardiff*, with tin for needles, in working order, horn with fine floral decoration, circa 1905.
(Auction Team Köln) $709

A cabinet roller organ, twenty-note organette in gilt stenciled oak case, with seventeen cobs.
(Phillips) $1,746

An 11¼in. Regina disc musical box, with twin combs, in carved walnut case of Gothic style, with seventeen discs.
(Phillips) $3,104

A good H.M.V. Model 460 table grand gramophone with Lumiere pleated diaphragm, gilt fittings in quarter-veneered oak case.
(Phillips) $2,134

A Gramophone & Typewriter Ltd 'Melba' gramophone pedestal, ebonized with gilt incised Art Nouveau floriate decoration, 39in. high, circa 1905.
(Christie's S. Ken) $2,864

A large cabinet phonograph incorporating a Model A Edison Triumph mechanism 45035 with two-speed pulley and Diamond B reproducer, 49in. high.
(Christie's S. Ken) $3,887

A rare E.M.G. tropical portable gramophone with E.M.G. two-spring soundbox, gooseneck tone-arm and internal horn, circa 1928, and eight albums of records.
(Christie's S. Ken) $1,125

An E.M.G. Mark IX hand-made gramophone with electric motor, E.M.G. two-spring soundbox on swan-neck tone arm, in oak case with 23in. papier mâché horn.
(Phillips) $3,104

A Cabinetto 25-note organette in gilt stenciled walnut case with instructions and National Musical Cabinetto importers' label, 17½in. wide.
(Christie's S. Ken) $1,330

Eternola Portablofon gramophone with octagonal wooden base and red horn.
(Auction Team Köln) $1,889

An Edison GEM phonograph with original horn serial no. 3146330.
(Michael Newman) $361

Columbia Graphophone, in working order, horn connection possibly renewed, circa 1905.
(Auction Team Köln) $552

A 15⅝in. upright Polyphon with double comb, dual coin mechanism, in walnut case with glazed door, 35in. high, with one disc.
(Phillips) $6,014

A twenty-three key portable barrel piano, playing eight airs, in mahogany case with pierced fretwork grille, 36½in. high.
(Phillips) $1,455

Wurlitzer model A 500 'Victory' jukebox, circa 1948, in a black walnut case with stenciled mirrored panels depicting trophies, Pierrot and Harlequin, 5ft. 5½in. high.
(Butterfield & Butterfield) $4,950

An Edison disc phonograph, official laboratory model with Diamond reproducer, lateral cut adapter and William and Mary style case, 50½in. high.
(Christie's S. Ken) $876

A 19th century walnut cased musical box and table base, the musical box with comb and cylinder movement with white metal lyre cast soft/loud pedal, 41in. wide overall.
(Spencer's) $6,585

An HMV Model 193 re-entrant tone chamber gramophone with 5A soundbox, the oak case of Jacobean design, 44½in. high, 1930.
(Christie's S. Ken) $8,327

An upright 25¼ inch Symphonion disc musical box with side-by-side combs, coin mechanisms and drawer, 95½ in. high.
(Christie's S. Ken) $16,720

A hand-turned Tinfoil phonograph with brass mandrel on steel threaded arbor with hand wheels at each end, with brass bearings on turned supports with screw release, 15in. wide.
(Christie's S. Ken) $6,545

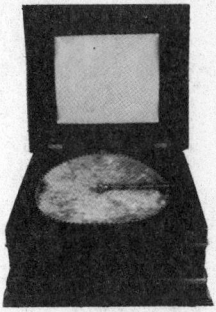

Regina disc music box, circa 1880, table model, 10 x 21 x 18in., mahogany serpentine case, banjo attachment, duplex comb, having thirty 15½in. discs.
(Du Mouchelles) $2,200

A Regina Corona 27 inch self-changing disc musical box, with double-spring motor, coin mechanism, double combs on horizontal bedplate and magazine below containing twelve discs, 66in. high
(Christie's S. Ken) $24,640

A 'Grand Format' musical box by Nicole Frères, playing four overtures, with lever-wind, engraved silver tune sheet in rosewood veneered case, 27½in. wide. Accompanying this musical box is a letter (written in French) from Nicole Freres to their London agents, dated April 1860.(Christie's ) $54,780

Unnamed and hitherto unknown music automat, with 5 tunes, 15cm. metal cylinders with complete 57 tooth tone comb, 2 part spring winding and two mechanical dolls, in wooden case with wall attachment, circa 1890.
(Auction Team Köln) $29,926

Old 'Symphonium Simplex' musical box, complete with discs.
(Lawrence Butler) $800

A rare mahogany cased Edison Gem phonograph, now with combination gearing and K reproducer, the mahogany case with *Edison Gem Phonograph* banner transfer.
(Christie's S. Ken) $1,936

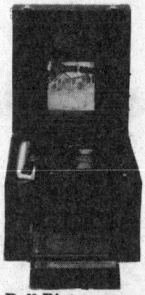

An Edison Bell Picturegram portable gramophone with Edison Bell 'Era' soundbox and drawer containing panoramic picture apparatus, circa 1925.
(Christie's S. Ken) $2,112

**One of a pair of early Victorian gilt gesso mirrors, each with rounded rectangular plate, the eared mirrored frame applied with flowers and foliage, 85 x 52in.**
**(Christie's) Two $12,632**

**An early 18th century carved and later decorated overmantel in the manner of William Kent, the rectangular central aperture with ribbon and rosette molded border, 5ft. 6in. wide.**
**(Phillips) $14,790**

**A giltwood mirror with later rectangular plate, the rusticated frame headed by an asymmetrical acanthus scroll cresting, the pierced sides carved with flowerheads, 55 x 26in.**
**(Christie's) $6,098**

**A giltwood mirror of George II style with later rectangular beveled plate, the frame with ribbon and flower-molded border, with a mask of Diana flanked by acanthus, 66 x 37½in.**
**(Christie's) $6,098**

**A William and Mary walnut and floral marquetry cushion frame mirror, the surround with ebonized reserved panels inlaid with vases of flowers and foliate sprays, 3ft. 8½in. x 3ft. 1½in.**
**(Phillips) $9,570**

**A George I gilt and gesso wall mirror with later beveled plate within a foliate and strapwork border, the broken scroll cresting egg-and-dart molded with flowerhead terminals, 3ft. 8in. x 1ft. 11in. (Phillips) $8,700**

**A George III giltwood mirror with shaped rectangular plate, the pierced frame carved with C-scrolls, rockwork, acanthus and flowerheads, 38in. x 22in.**
**(Christie's) $12,276**

**A Regency giltwood mirror with circular convex plate and ebonized slip, the molded frame applied with balls and stars, 30in. diameter.**
**(Christie's) $3,960**

**A Regency giltwood mirror with convex circular plate, ebonized slip and molded frame applied with balls, the plate possibly resilvered, 42in. x 22in.**
**(Christie's) $3,366**

A giltwood mirror with eared rectangular plate, the frame carved with C-scrolls, rockwork and flowerheads with asymmetrical acanthus cresting, 66 x 34in. $8,276
(Christie's)

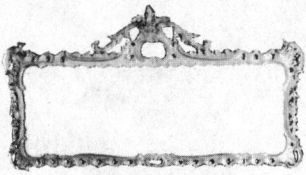

A George III giltwood overmantel mirror, the frame carved with rockwork, C-scrolls and acanthus and pierced with quatrefoils, 29in. x 57in.
(Christie's) $12,870

A George III giltwood mirror, the rope-twist frame encircled by rope-tied vine-shoots with grapes, 52in. x 30in.
(Christie's) $13,860

A giltwood mirror with rectangular plate, the eared frame carved with egg-and-dart, with broken pediment cresting centered by an armorial device, 59in. x 38in. $3,960
(Christie's)

A carved and giltwood square wall mirror designed by Eric Gill, with carved inscriptions *'My love is like a red red rose that's newly sprung in June, My love is like a melody that's sweetly played in tune'*, 55.7cm. square.
(Christie's) $9,603

One of a pair of Dieppe ivory mirrors, each with beveled oval plate and eared rectangular frame applied with seahorses, putti and masks on a bed of seaweed, late 19th century, 33in. x 20in.
(Christie's) (Two) $6,501

A George II walnut and parcel-gilt mirror with beveled rectangular plate, the cresting with egg-and-dart moulding and broken pediment centered by a lion-mask, 50in. x 27in.
(Christie's) $8,316

A Continental baroque style stained pine mirror, 19th century, intricately carved with trailing foliage and putti, 75in. high.
(Christie's East) $9,900

A George III giltwood mirror, the pierced sides carved with C-scrolls and rockwork, the apron similarly carved, 49in. x 27in.
(Christie's) $7,524

A red and gilt-japanned toilet-mirror decorated overall with chinoiserie figures in landscapes, with later arched beveled plate, basically early 18th century, 37¾in. high.
(Christie's) $3,267

A Regency style gilt convex girandole, the plate within an ebonized slip and molded frame, surmounted by a displaying eagle, 44 x 33½in., late 19th century.
(Bonhams) $1,433

George II giltwood mirror, circa 1740, swan's neck pediment and shell-carved frieze, 56in. high.
(Skinner Inc.) $4,000

Giltwood looking glass, America, second quarter 19th century, 52in. high.
(Skinner Inc.) $1,500

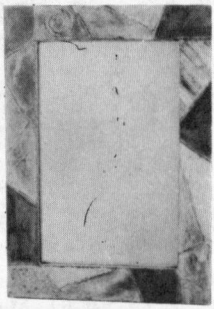

Wall mirror, designed and executed by Paul Evans, third quarter 20th century, anodized and painted metal frame, 34½in. high.
(Skinner Inc.) $350

A George II walnut and parcel gilt mirror, the rectangular beveled plate surmounted by an egg-and-dart carved cornice above onset corners, 43 x 27in.
(Bonhams) $1,719

A George III gilt mirror, the later shield shaped plate within a beaded frame surmounted by a Classical urn and a feather plume, 40 x 17½in.
(Bonhams) $860

A Chippendale style mahogany and parcel gilt triple plate overmantel, surmounted by a shaped crest with gilt ho-ho bird finial, 55 x 50½in.
(Bonhams) $1,186

Chippendale mahogany looking glass, labeled Peter Grinnell & Son, Providence, Rhode Island, early 19th century, 39in. high.
(Skinner Inc.) $550

Chippendale parcel-gilt mahogany looking glass, England, late 18th century, 42½in. high.
(Skinner Inc.) $2,300

A late 18th century/early 19th century giltwood and gesso mirror frame, boldly carved with flowerheads, foliage and scrolls, 32 x 28in.
(Christie's S. Ken) $903

A giltwood mirror with cartouche-shaped plate, the eared frame carved with acanthus, the apron centered with a scallop-shell, 19th century, 29 x 21in.
(Christie's) $614

Federal giltwood and eglomisé looking glass, America, early 19th century, 58¾in. high.
(Skinner Inc.) $1,200

A good Regency gilt and parcel ebonized girandole, the octagonal plate within an ebonized slip and sphere applied frame, 32 x 16½in.
(Bonhams) $3,650

Chippendale mahogany looking glass, England, late 18th century, shaped crest centering a gilt foliate device, 29in. high.
(Skinner Inc.) $750

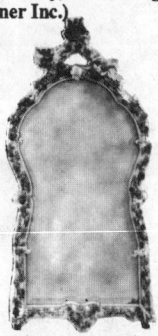

An extremely large and impressive Continental mirror, with beveled edge and with a porcelain surround encrusted with colored flowers and scrolls, 203cm. tall.
(Phillips) $8,366

A George III mahogany dressing mirror, with shield-shaped glass plate on 'S'-supports, 23½in. high.
(Bearne's) $1,222

Giltwood girandole mirror, England, early 19th century, 40in. high.
(Skinner Inc.) $2,900

A painted wood model of the topsail schooner 'Anne Marie' in 52in. glazed wood case.
(Anderson & Garland) $698

A Bing painted tinplate clockwork twin-funnel 'American-outline' ocean liner 'Columbia', with single screw, deck fittings and detail, circa 1906, 26in. long.
(Christie's S. Ken) $7,524

A large tinplate model of a toy torpedo battle ship, 'The Olympia', the hull made in four parts, 156cm. long, 26cm. wide, fitted with spirit fired boiler and commercially produced German engine finished in black, 20cm.
(Phillips) $9,260

Two builders 1/4in.: 1ft. scale models of the torpedo boat destroyers H.M.S. 'Cheerful' and H.M.S. 'Viper' built by R. & W. Hawthorn, Leslie & Co. Ltd. Engineers and Shipbuilders, Newcastle-Upon-Tyne, mounted side by side in the original mahogany table mounted bronze framed glazed case, 86 1/4in. long.
(Christie's) $25,454

An early 20th century model of the brig 'Marie Sophie' by L.D. Taylor, the two masted ship painted in blue and white, with standing rigging, planked deck and hatches with lift off covers, 41in. long overall.
(Spencer's) $1,366

A carved and stained wood model of a 16th century three masted galleon, circa 1920, with metal sails, fully rigged and with various deck details, 46in. long overall.
(Spencer's) $335

A 20th century model of a fully rigged 4 masted barque with planked wooden hull.
(R.K. Lucas) $580

An early 19th century Prisoner of War bone model ship, 13in. overall.
(Dreweatt Neate) $2,243

A Carette painted tinplate steam ocean-going steamship, the horizontal boiler with usual fittings, single oscillating cylinder to propellor shaft and flywheel, circa 1905, on a wooden base, 21in. long.
(Christie's S. Ken) $7,524

A detailed 1/4in.: 1ft. scale builder's model of the Train Ferry Steamer 'Drottning Victoria', Trelleborg, built by Swan Hunter & Wigham Richardson Ltd., 30 x 91in.
(Christie's) $15,664

Chinese Export bone model of an English frigate, 19th century, with mother-of-pearl inlaid rosewood base, glass case, 23in. long.
(Skinner Inc.) $9,350

Wooden ship model of the New Bedford whaler 'Alice Mandell', well detailed, height 24in.
(Eldred's) $1,870

A spirit fired 4-4-0 locomotive and 8 wheeled bogie tender, finished in black with red and gold detailing, circa 1909, slight chipping.
(Phillips) $6,341

A Märklin hand-painted bogie Midland Railway family saloon, with opening roof, detailed interior, opening doors and seated figures, circa 1907.
(Christie's S. Ken) $2,517

A clockwork 4-4-0 Paris-Lyon Mediterranee painted tinplate 'windcutter' locomotive and 6 wheeled tender CV 1022, finished in dark green with gold and red banding and lining, circa 1905.
(Phillips) $7,833

A 3-rail electric 20v 4-8-2 ME locomotive and 8 wheeler tender finished in pale green, dark green and red.
(Phillips) $6,714

Hornby control system: lever frame and 'Windsor' signal cabin, in original boxes, with adjustable No. 2 20in. control rail, two control points and nine rod guide brackets, circa 1925.
(Christie's S. Ken) $766

A Hornby Series 'Palethorpes' sausage van, in original box, circa 1939.
(Christie's S. Ken) $832

A 3-rail electric 4-4-2 NBR locomotive and tender No. CE 6513021, finished in brown with red, yellow and black lining, excellent condition, tender sticky.
(Phillips) $2,984

A 3-rail electric, 20v, 4-6-2 HS pantograph locomotive, finished in brown with orange lining and black roof, slight retouching.
(Phillips) $6,341

A spirit fired NBR 4-4-2 locomotive and 6 wheeled tender No. 4021, finished in brown with red, yellow and black lining.
(Phillips) $2,798

A large well engineered horizontal twin cylinder steam plant driven by a separate boiler, the twin cylinders mounted in tandem, lacks boiler, overall 64cm. long.
(Phillips) $933

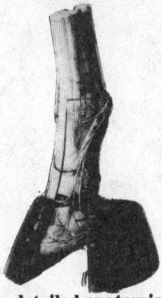

A finely detailed anatomical model of a horse's fetlock, showing the arteries, veins, small bones, muscles and tendons, the top inscribed *Anatomic Clastique du Dr. Auzoux, 1914.*
(Lawrence Fine Art) $1,100

A red aluminium 1/10 scale model Lancia F1 D50 by Michele Conti with leather upholstery, one of four made in 1955 specially for Gianni Lancia.
(Finarte) $16,008

A Märklin spirit-fired 'Three in One' convertible steam engine, single-cylinder over-type, in original box without lid, 1920's, 8in. long.
(Christie's S. Ken) $700

Ducrette and Roger of Paris, a well detailed brass, vertical hot-air engine with glass enclosed piston driving flywheel, 39cm. high.
(Phillips) $709

A well engineered model of a single-cylinder side-rod horizontal mill engine built by G.B. Houghton, Rochester, 7¼ x 11in.
(Christie's S. Ken) $1,748

A well engineered approx. 3in. scale model of a six-wheeled undertype steam engine wagon 'Lensford Dragon' built by A. Pickering, 30 x 69in.
(Christie's S. Ken) $10,285

An exhibition standard ⅛in. scale model of an Oxfordshire wagon, circa 1830, built from plans drawn from the original wagon by John Thompson, 8½ x 32½in.
(Christie's S. Ken) $494

A well engineered and presented model stationary steam set built by D.J. Moir, 1976, overall, 24 x 30¼in.
(Christie's S. Ken) $1,851

**A 1953 Alfa Romeo 1900 C Sprint Mk II, chassis no. 01320 one of less than 300 models built, with right hand drive.**
**(Finarte) $87,150**

**1959 BMW 600, engine no: 142 873, two cylinders, 582 c.c., left hand drive, introduced in August 1957 as a four seat alternative to the Isetta.**
**(Christie's) $2,079**

**1924 Rolls-Royce Twenty, engine no. G867 with boat-tail fabric covered bodywork 2/4 seater by Maloney, Sydney, and V.M. Engineering, Adelaide, black fabric, green paintwork, with green leather upholstery, and 6 cylinder push rod overhead valve engine, 3127 cc.**
**(Christie's) $63,501**

**1922 Hispano-Suiza H6B 1922 Rothschild Coupe Limousine, coachwork by J. Rothschild et Fils, Rheims and Auscher, France, engine no. 300521, engine; six-cylinder, 100mm. bore, 140mm. stroke, 6.5-litres; shaft-driven overhead camshaft with non-detachable head and nitrided steel liners.**
**(Christie's New York) $330,000**

**1937 2½ Litre S.S. Jaguar 100, with original factory standard 2 seater bodywork with original mudguards, and weather equipment, in silver gray paintwork, with red leather upholstery, and 6 cylinder push rod operated overhead valve engine.**
**(Christie's) $186,276**

**1938 4½ Litre Bentley Tourer, engine no. T8BT, with open four seater, four door "All weather" Sports Tourer bodywork by Vanden Plas (England) Ltd, with hood, hood bag, tonneau cover and wind up windows, and 6 cylinder push rod overhead valve engine.**
**(Christie's) $203,210**

**1960 Jaguar XK 150 fixed-head coupe, engine no. VA11719, color: white with red interior, specification: engine; six-cylinder, twin-overhead camshaft 83mm. bore, 106mm. stroke, 3,442 c.c.**
**(Christie's) $37,620**

**1966 A.C. Cobra 427 MK.III 2-seater sports, coachwork by A.C. Cars and Shelby American Cobra, engine; Ford V8 cylinder 6,997 c.c, bore and stroke 107.4mm. x 96mm. (427 cu. in) 425 b.h.p. at 5,600 r.p.m.**
**(Christie's New York) $396,000**

1925 Morris Cowley Occasional four door tourer, engine no: 101191, four cylinders, right hand drive, finished in beige with tidy green interior, and complete apart from the battery.
(Christie's) $19,750

1955 Fiat 1100 four door saloon, engine no: 212 739, four cylinders, left hand drive, finished in gray with red trim and upholstery.
(Christie's) $1,559

1929 Bentley 4½-litre Mulliner Tourer, engine no. FB3304, coachwork: Arthur Mulliner four-seater Touring Body, color: dark green, black fabric, green leather upholstery and carpets, engine; four-cylinder in line 4398 c.c., bore and stroke 100mm. x 140mm., C.R. 5.3:1, 110 b.h.p. at 3,500 r.p.m.
(Christie's) $338,580

1961 Ferrari 250GT short wheelbase Berlinetta, coachwork Pininfarina design, built by Scaglietti, engine no. 2417, color: red with black interior (left-hand drive), engine; V.12, 60°, 73mm. (2.87in.) bore, 58.8mm. (2.31in.) stroke, 2,953 c.c., 180.2 cu. in., single overhead cam per bank, two Marelli distributors.
(Christie's New York) $2,200,000

1913 Philos four-seater tourer, engine no. 14081, color: green bodywork, black wings with black leather upholstery, engine; ballot, four-cylinder in-line monobloc, 1,131 c.c., 8 h.p., bore and stroke 60mm. x 100mm. Bosch magneto, Zenith carburettor.
(Christie's) $11,286

1938 Roll-Royce Phantom III, engine no. E48Z with Sedanca-de-Ville bodywork by H.J. Mulliner and Co. London, open drive, with division and swivel mounted occasional seats, with white paintwork, fawn cloth upholstery, and 60 degree V12 cylinder engine.
(Christie's) $127,001

1946 Packard Custom Super Clipper 7 passenger limousine, engine no: 2150-2757, 8 cylinders, 5838 c.c., left hand drive, the front seats leather and with a glass divide between the driver's compartment and the rear.
(Christie's) $7,456

1930 Aston Martin 1½ Litre International, coachwork by Bertelli, engine no. 567, color: blue coachwork and brown leather interior, engine: 4 cylinder 1495cc 69.3mm. x 99mm. 56 bhp at 4250 RPM.
(Christie's) $92,515

1964 ASA 1000 GT Coupe, chassis no. 01080, coachwork: Bertone Two Door Coupe, engine; four-cylinder in-line, 1,032 c.c., bore and stroke 69mm x 69mm., compression ratio 9.1:1, 97 b.h.p. at 6,800 r.p.m., single overhead camshaft.
(Christie's) $27,274

1975 Renault Alpine A110 2 door coupe, chassis no. 7479, engine no. 0209359, color: white and yellow with black interior, specification: rear engine, four-cylinder, 73mm. bore, 77mm. stroke, 1,289 c.c., 9.5:1 compression, 85 b.h.p. (DIN) at 6,000 r.p.m.
(Christie's) $16,929

A 1933 Fiat 508 Balilla, chassis no. 19888, three gear, excellent condition.
(Finarte) $16,452

A 1933 BMW 303 Spider 2-door saloon, chassis no. 45973.
(Finarte) $44,463

1927 Type 40 Bugatti 4 cylinder with replica Grand Sport 2/3 seater bodywork with pointed tail in blue paintwork, with black leather upholstery and 4 cylinder, 72mm bore engine.
(Christie's) $101,606

A very rare Isotta Fraschini Type FENC 10/14HP (1909) engine replaced in the 1910s by an American Cripps Booth 4-cylinder 1300 cc valve in head model.
(Finarte) $84,483

1930 Cadillac V-16 Madam X Imperial Landaulette, coachwork by Fleetwood. Body no. 3, Cadillac Style no. 4108 C, engine; 45 degree V-16; 3in. 76.2mm. bore; 4in. 101.6mm, stroke; 452.6cu. in. 7,412 c.c.
(Christie's New York) $522,500

1929 Mercedes-Benz SSK (Specification), engine no. 66543, engine; six-cylinder; overhead camshaft; 100mm. bore, 150mm. stroke, 7,065 c.c.; 170 b.h.p., or 220 b.h.p. with supercharger engaged at 3,300 r.p.m.
(Christie's New York) $990,000

1963 Mercedes-Benz 190SL two door coupe, engine no. 12192820003825, color: white with red upholstery, specification; engine; four-cylinder, single overhead camshaft 85mm. bore, 83.6mm. stroke, 1,897 c.c., 120 b.h.p. gross at 5,700 r.p.m.
(Christie's) $34,798

A 1950 Buick 50L Super Sedan, chassis no. 15892395, with V8 124 H.P engine, excellent condition.
(Finarte) $14,229

A 1965 Ford Mustang Convertible 289, chassis no. 8TO1C146048 with 8 cylinder, 289 brake hp engine, automatic gearbox and contemporary radio-stereo 8.
(Finarte) $20,454

1970 Jaguar E-Type Series II Roadster, engine no. 7R 9221-9, color: regency red with black interior, specification: engine; 92.07mm. bore, 106mm. stroke, 4,235 c.c., twin overhead camshafts 265 b.h.p. gross at 5,400 r.p.m.
(Christie's) $63,954

1961 Ferrari 250 GT SWB Berlinetta, engine no. 3281, with Pininfarina designed 2 door, 2 seater steel and aluminium paneled G.T. Coupe bodywork built by Scaglietti in metallic green paintwork, with green leather upholstery, and 60 degree V12 cylinder engine.
(Christie's) $1,185,395

A 1970 Maserati Ghibli, chassis no 115.1634, with 8 cylinder overhead cam engine.
(Finarte) $78,258

A 1977 Mercedes Benz 450 SEL 6.9, chassis no. 116.03612002473 one of only 7,380 models produced between 1975 and 1980.
(Finarte) $17,785

1934 Talbot 105 Vanden Plas Tourer, engine no. AV188, coachwork by Vanden Plas, engine; six-cylinder in-line, 2,969 c.c., bore and stroke 75mm. x 112mm., pushrod-operated vertical OHV.
(Christie's) $141,075

1964 A.C. Cobra 289 two-seater sports, coachwork by A.C. Cars, Thames Ditton, engine; Ford V8 cylinder 4,727 c.c.
(Christie's New York) $225,500

A 1955 Jaguar Mk VII, chassis no. 738092, with 3.4 litre 6 cylinder, twin overhead cam, twin carburettor engine, excellent condition.
(Finarte) $36,462

1965 Morris Mini Cooper '1275' S ex works rally car, engine no. XSP 3068-2, color: tartan red with white roof, specification: engine; four-cylinder pushrod, transmission; BMC 4 speed and reverse gearbox. full works competition specification.
(Christie's) $122,265

1932 Rolls Royce Phantom II rolling chassis, engine no: TR45, six cylinders, 7.7 litre, right hand drive and a standard long chassis when first delivered in 1932 to the Parisien coachbuilder Maurice Proux who built a Sedanca body for it.
(Christie's) $33,264

1927 Austin Seven Chummy two door open tourer, engine no: M31108, four cylinders 8 h.p., one of the best loved cars of the 1920s and 1930s.
(Christie's) $15,592

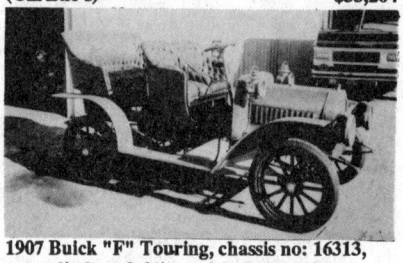

1907 Buick "F" Touring, chassis no: 16313, two cylinders, 2.6 litre, right hand drive, driven by a single chain with two forward gears and one reverse.
(Christie's) $17,671

1931 Rolls-Royce Phantom 1 Marlborough Town Car, coachwork by Brewster, engine no. 22499, engine; six-cylinders in blocks of three, 107.95mm. (4.25in.) bore, 139.7mm. (5.5in.) stroke, 7,668 c.c. pushrod-operated overhead valves.
(Christie's New York) $319,000

1913 Sunbeam 12/16 hp., engine no. 6488, the original factory-built four seater Torpedo Tourer bodywork by Sunbeam, with folding fabric hood, and side curtains, dark green paintwork with green leather upholstery, and 4 cylinder side valve fixed head engine.
(Christie's) $67,736

**1951 Jaguar XK120 roadster, engine no: KF75068, six cylinder, 3,442 c.c., left hand drive.**
**(Christie's) $17,671**

**1926 Bentley 3 Litre "Speed Model", engine no. LT1589, with fabric covered Weymann lightweight saloon bodywork by J. Gurney Nutting and Co. Ltd, London in red and black with red leather upholstery, and 4 cylinder engine.**
**(Christie's) $123,999**

**1969 Eagle (Santa-Ana) Indy single-seat race car, chassis no. 702, Manufacturer: All American Racers Inc, Santa Ana, California, color: dark blue with sponsor graphics as driven by Dan Gurney.**
**(Christie's New York) $143,000**

**1926 Type 30 Bugatti 8 cylinder, engine no. 277, with original 4 seater 4 door tourer bodywork by Lavocat et Marsaud, Paris, in black paintwork, with red vinyl upholstery, and straight 8 cylinder, 60mm bore x 88mm stroke engine.**
**(Christie's) $211,678**

**A 1974 Lamborghini Espada Mk III, chassis no. 9248, 12 cylinder engine, with original leather upholstery.**
**(Finarte) $69,363**

**1953 Alfa Romeo 1900C Sprint, engine no: AR130800630, four cylinder in line, 2000cc, left hand drive. At present this Alfa Romeo is stripped to the bare metal, however it is believed to be complete and was mechanically sound before being laid up.**
**(Christie's) $35,343**

**1928 Austin Seven Chummy two door open tourer, engine no: M58553, four cylinders, 747 c.c., right hand drive, the black interior is tidy, however the maroon paintwork needs some attention.**
**(Christie's) $8,732**

**1910 Doriot Flandrin Parant – DFP, engine no: 1042, 4 cylinders, believed to be a 10/12 HP model of 1.6 litre.**
**(Christie's) $26,103**

A Heuer divided stopwatch, 50mm. diam. in black rubber protective casing.
(Finarte) $400

A complete 'fruit and smoking' service in yellow cut glass, personally commissioned in not more than 12 sets by Enzo Ferrari as Christmas gifts for his closest collaborators in the 1960s.
(Finarte) $2,490

Metal ashtray mounted with an Alfa Romeo 158, made by Alfa to celebrate their victory in the World Championship in 1950.
(Finarte) $1,335

A Mingozzi designed lithograph 'V^a Corsa in salita Vittoria Cansiglio, 1 July 1928, 36 x 45cm.
(Finarte) $249

An Englebert advertising poster showing Tazio Nuvolari's Alfa Romeo B type P3, winner of the 1935 German Grand Prix, French text, 44 x 62cm.
(Finarte) $1,068

Monaco, 1er et 2 juin 1952, lithograph in colors by B. Minne, 48 x 31in.
(Christie's New York) $8,250

An original radiator grill for the Alfa Romeo 1750, complete with enamel badge.
(Finarte) $1,602

1971 Ferrari 365 GTB/4 Daytona hand-carved wood engine, a unique work of art with every piece accurately reproduced in nine different types of wood.
(Christie's New York) $26,950

Gold Lemania wristwatch, the round face with Ferrari inscription 1950s.
(Finarte) $4,092

Carlo Brianza, an extremely fine and detailed 1:10 scale model of a 1976 Ferrari 512BB constructed in brass and aluminium, presented on a wooden plinth and enclosed in a case, 21in. long.
(Christie's New York) $11,000

Large illuminated 'Ferrari Service' sign in double sided flexiglas complete with electrics, 1970s, 77 x 178 x 17cm.
(Finarte) $5,514

1936/7 Auto Union C Type Model, length 24in., the 1936 and 1937 V-16 6.1-litre, 520 b.h.p., C Type Auto Union was one of the world's most powerful and spectacular Grand Prix cars.
(Christie's New York) $55,000

A poster designed by Paolo Cassa for the XXIV Mille Miglia Brescia, 11–12 May 1957, 70 x 100cm.
(Finarte) $5,514

A watercolor by Giovanni Alloisi, showing a red Cisitalia in competition, drawn for the XXI Italian Grand Prix at the Monza Autodrome on 3 September 1950, 52 x 70cm.
(Finarte) $2,133

A Maserati poster with a Maserati valve in the foreground, designed by Adriani, 1941, 68 x 103cm.
(Finarte) $2,313

Abarth & C sign with scorpion and script in relief in wood on yellow, blue and red painted metal base, 1950s, 47 x 56 x 3.5cm.
(Finarte) $1,155

Moto MV Agusta Agenzia enamel shield, red base, 48 x 48cm., slightly worn.
(Finarte) $400

An IWC stopwatch with black face and white numerals, inscribed on reverse 'R J Beattie Seaman, Prix de Berne, August 23rd 1936.'
(Finarte) $2,490

A chromium-plated and enameled Frazer Nash Car Club badge, the reverse stamped 74.
(Onslow's) $669

A sales brochure for Carrosserie Van Den Plas, color plates by Rene Lelong, French text, hard bound, circa 1914.
(Onslow's) $738

A CIJ tinplate clockwork Alfa Romeo P2, finished in silver with brown seats, nickel-plated water, oil and petrol filler caps, leather bonnet straps, 54cm. long.
(Onslow's) $5,720

Coolie Motor Oil printed tin 1 quart can.
(Onslow's) $211

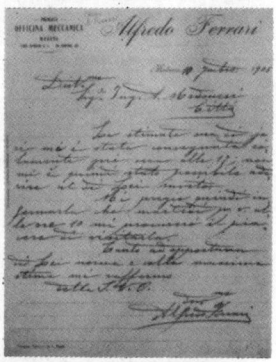


Letter from Alfredo Ferrari (father of Enzo) to engineer Modonesi of Modena, saying that he will visit him in the next few days as requested, dated 10 September 1905 with Ferrari's signature.
(Finarte) $623

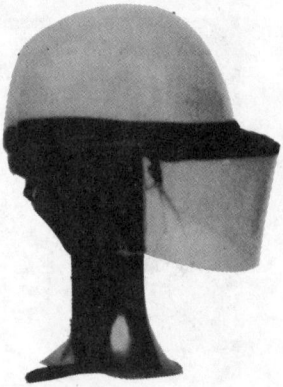

Herbert Johnson 1930's crash helmet and visor, large size.
(Onslow's) $616

A chromium-plated and enameled Automobile Club of America badge with 1929 date label surmounted with eagle.
(Onslow's) $704

Rapiditas Rivista Universale D'Automobilismo, Vol 1 no 1, 1906, plates some color, French, English and German text.
(Onslow's) $2,952

An AA Committee Club badge, surmounted by a pennant decorated with a circle enclosing an AA design, 6¼in. high.
(Christie's) $846

A brass Smith's speedometer calibrated 5–80, 9cm. diameter.
(Onslow's) $493

A sales brochure for the Alfa Romeo 8C Mod including Gran Sport Spyder 2-seater, Open 4-seater and Racing Type (Monza), English text, 1931.
(Onslow's) $1,292

A pair of brass vintage sportscar ventilators for scuttle mounting, each 20cm high.
(Onslow's) $229

Michael Watson, 1933 Monaco Grand Prix, Varzi in the Bugatti Type 51 leading Nuvolari in the 8C Monza Alfa Romeo, watercolor, signed, 25½ x 20½in.
(Christie's New York) $1,100

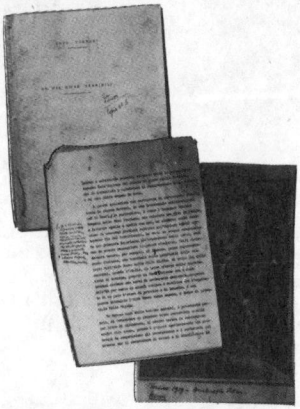

Original typescript of Enzo Ferrari's book 'La mei gioie terribile' consisting of 167 sheets, with margin notes in violet ink, mostly by Enzo Ferrari.
(Finarte) $18,231

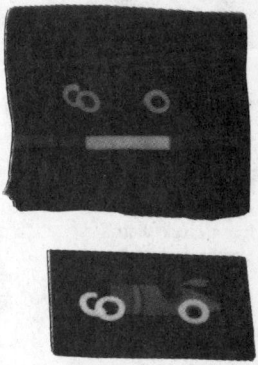

A wool and felt purse with matching scarf depicting Bugatti racing car, 1920's.
(Onslow's) $88

A YAC divided stopwatch, 1/10 seconds, in wooden case, inscribed on reverse 'Giulio Cabianca, 26.7.1959, Trieste-Opicina, 1° Assoluto'.
(Finarte) $1,335

A tempera picture by Antonio de'Giusti showing Nigel Mansell in a Ferrari F1/90 and Gerard Berger in a Maclaren Mp4/5B during the 1990 Mexico Grand Prix, 83 x 58cm.
(Finarte) $3,735

Nurburgring programme 'Grosser Preis von Deutschland 26th July 1936'.
(Onslow's) $430

A fine violin by Jean Baptiste Vuillaume in Paris, circa 1840, bearing his original undated label.
(Phillips)
$60,600

A fine composite violin, the back, ribs and scroll by Giuseppe Guarneri, filius Andrea, labeled *Joseph Guarnerius.*
(Christie's)
$55,440

A fine Italian violoncello by Carlo Tononi labelled *Carlo Tononi Bolognese/Fece in Venetia l'A 1730.*
(Christie's)
$240,240

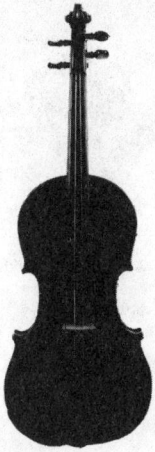

A fine violin by the Voller Brothers, labeled *Francesco Stradivarius*, the two-piece back cut on the slab.
(Christie's)
$24,167

A fine Italian violin by Guiseppe Rocca labeled *Joseph Antonius Rocca/fecit Taurini/anno Domini 18*, the one-piece back of handsome medium curl.
(Christie's)
$111,540

A fine Italian violin by Giovanni Pressenda labelled *Joannes Franciscus Pressenda q. Raphael/fecit Taurini anno Domini 1837.*
(Christie's)
$102,245

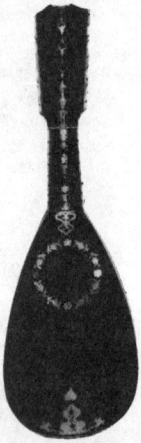

A handsome mandolin circa 1760 attributed to a member of the Vinaccia family, the shaped boxwood pegs for twelve strings.
(Phillips)
$2,626

A good Italian violin attributed to Gaetano Antoniazzi labeled *Antoniazzi Gaetano Cremonese/fece a Milano l'anno 1897.*
(Christie's)
$8,316

An Italian violin by Giovanni Battista Guadagnini labeled *Joannes Baptista filius Laurentji Gua/dagnini fecit Placentiae 174?.* (Christie's) $164,472

A fine Italian violin by Goffredo Cappa, bearing a manuscript label, the one-piece back of small curl. (Christie's) $40,656

A rare early guitar bearing the maker's manuscript label Fait par moy Antonie Aubry A Mirecourt 1739. (Phillips) $4,242

An important violin by Antonio Stradivari labeled *Antonio Stradivari Cremonensis/Faciebat Anno 1720.* (Christie's) $1,776,940

A fine Italian violin by Camillo Camilli labeled *Camillo Camilli/Fecit in Mantova/Anno 1742.* (Christie's) $74,360

A fine French violoncello, school of Bernadel, unlabeled, the two-piece back of handsome wood cut on the slab. (Christie's) $36,839

A fine mandolin by Gennaro & Alle Vinaccia bearing the maker's signed label in Naples dated 1893, with case. (Phillips) $848

An Italian violin labeled and branded *C. Candi Genova*, two-piece back of medum curl, the ribs and scroll similar. (Christie's) $10,164

A rare violin by Hendrik Jacobs bearing the label *Hendrik Jacobs me fecit in Amsterdam 1714.*
(Phillips)
$13,315

A grenadilla oboe d'amore by Louis, thumbplate system with regular octaves, length 25 3/8 in.
(Christie's)
$7,064

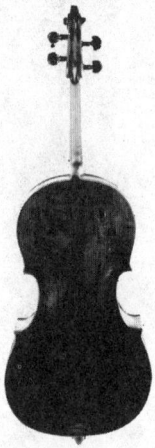

An interesting composite Cremonese violoncello, circa 1670, bearing a fictitious label.
(Christie's)
$30,338

A six-keyed glass flute by Claude Laurent, silver keys and end-cap, sounding length 21 5/16 in.
(Christie's)
$11,919

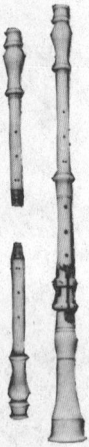

A two-keyed ivory oboe by J. Panormo, silver-gilt octagonal padded keys, the C key with fishtail touchpiece.
(Christie's)
$5,544

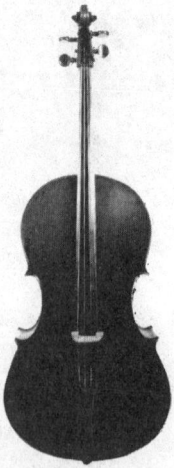

A violoncello by Eugenio Degani bearing the maker's label *Dieci Medaglie di Merito. Fecet Venezia Anno 1894.*
(Phillips)
$23,045

A rare one-keyed ivory flageolet, circa 1830, by F. Tabard, gold square-padded key, length 10 7/16 in.
(Christie's)
$3,142

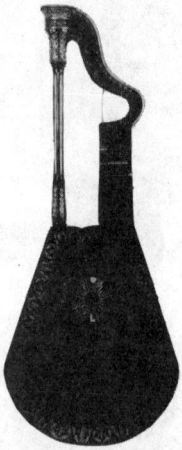

A fine dital harp by Edward Light at Foley Place London, circa 1790, overall length 32 5/8 in.
(Phillips)
$2,121

A boxwood alto recorder by Johann Heinrich Eichentopf, unmounted, length 19½in.
(Christie's) $2,045

An Irish harp by John Egan 30 Dawson Street Dublin and bearing on the brass name plate a Coat of Arms.
(Phillips) $2,535

A dancing master's kit, faintly labeled in manuscript, the cigar-shaped back decorated with painted scene.
(Christie's) $5,851

A viola d'amore, unlabeled, the two-piece flat back of small curl, the ribs similar, the pegbox of a later date.
(Christie's) $1,571

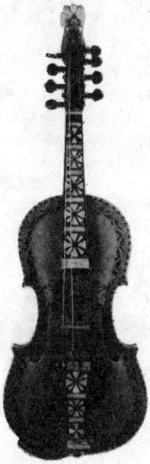

A Hardangerfele violin circa 19th century Swedish, bearing a repair label.
(Phillips) $1,252

A good six-keyed ivory flute by Thomas Cahusac, with three corps de rechange, silver mounts.
(Christie's) $3,718

A rare and important violin of the early Brescian School, circa 1610, by Gasparo da Salo or Giovanni Paolo Maggini.
(Phillips) $42,895

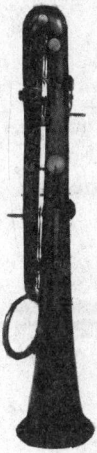

A brass ophicleide, by Henry Smith Wolverhampton, circa 1818–1884, 12 keys, overall length 43in.
(Phillips) $819

An ivory netsuke of two hares, their eyes inlaid in brown horn, signed in an oval reserve *Rakuzan*, circa 1800, 4.3cm.
(Christie's) $5,201

An ivory netsuke depicting Kanyu sitting leaning against a low table stroking his beard while reading a military treatise, signed *Kinryusai*, late 19th century, 4.2cm. wide.
(Christie's) $1,084

An ivory netsuke of a wild boar asleep on a bed of leaves, its engraved and stained hair largely worn smooth, unsigned, Kyoto school, 18th century, 5cm. long.
(Christie's) $8,235

A stained wood netsuke carved as a snail and an aubergine on a pumpkin, signed *Shigemasa to*, early 19th century, 4.5cm. wide.
(Christie's) $2,384

An ivory netsuke of a macaque monkey sitting holding a persimmon between its feet and a shishimai headdress on its head, signed *Masatami*, late 19th century, 4cm. high.
(Christie's) $2,600

A wood netsuke depicting a human skull entwined by a snake, its body passing through the left orbit, its head with black inlaid eyes, unsigned, 19th century, 3.5cm. high.
(Christie's) $2,600

A finely carved ivory netsuke of a group of three rats clustered together, signed in a rectangular reserve *Masaka*, late 19th century, 3.5cm. wide.
(Christie's) $5,634

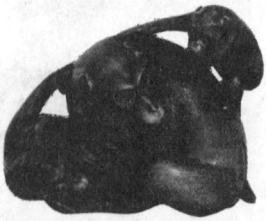

A well-detailed ivory netsuke of a monkey with two young ones, signed in an oval reserve *Naomitsu*, 19th century, 4.5cm. wide.
(Christie's) $1,950

An ivory netsuke of a man kneeling to polish the character Shin, signed *Ogura* (*Tomoyuki*), late 19th century, 5cm. long.
(Christie's) $1,192

A boxwood netsuke group depicting Yama Uba the mountain woman and sennin with her son Kintaro and a bear-cub, signed *Toto Shugetsu*, 19th century, 5.7cm.
(Christie's) $2,167

An ivory netsuke of a terrapin or freshwater tortoise with a young one on its back, signed *Garaku*, circa 1800, 5cm. long.
(Christie's) $2,059

An ivory netsuke of a tiger sitting looking behind it, its tail curled along its back, unsigned, Kyoto school, style of Tomotada, 18th century, 4.5cm.
(Christie's) $2,384

An ivory netsuke depicting Kanyu standing stroking his beard, his retainer Chow Tsang beside him, signed *Shounsai* (*Shounsai Joryu of Edo*), late 18th century, 5cm. high.
(Christie's) $2,059

A well-detailed stained boxwood netsuke of the toad and decayed well-bucket model, signed *Masakatsu* (of Ise-Yamada, son of Masanao I), 19th century, 4cm. high.
(Christie's) $1,625

An unusual stained boxwood netsuke depicting Santa Claus holding a small Christmas tree, surrounded by three boys, signed *Gyokuzan*, circa 1900, 6.2cm. high.
(Christie's) $1,950

An ivory okimono-style netsuke Raijin the God of Thunder setting out as a traveler with his drum on his back and a young oni carrying a persimmon at his side, signed *Tomomasa to*, late 19th century, 5cm. high.
(Christie's) $14,204

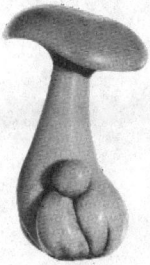

A well-modeled ivory netsuke depicting a mushroom, a young unopened mushroom growing at its base, unsigned, late 19th century, 6.5cm. high.
(Christie's) $4,767

A wood netsuke depicting two sumo wrestlers, one attempting the Kawazu throw, signed *Gessho*, 19th century, 6cm. high.
(Christie's) $2,817

A pressed and pierced metal magic lantern with fluted chimney and lens, 11½in. high.
(Christie's S. Ken) $285

A green-metal body bookform The Rotoscope Folding Stereoscope Apparatus with sprung photograph holder, eyepiece section with lenses, and six Rotary Photo photographic stereocards.
(Christie's S. Ken) $213

A burr walnut Brewster-pattern stereoscope with hinged lid, rear ground glass screen, and viewing hood.
(Christie's S. Ken) $1,745

British projection lantern for max 19 x 19cm. slides, having wood and brass Petzval type optics with gear drive and red filter equipped for 21cm. diam. condensor, original gas burner.
(Auction Team Köln) $434

A 19th century box stereoscope, the case decorated with flowers on a black ground.
(Michael Newman) $664

A mohagany-body bi-unial magic lantern with a pair of two-draw brass bound lenses each with rack and pinion focusing, all in a fitted combined container.
(Christie's S. Ken) $3,643

A metal-body upright magic lantern type 720 by Ernst Planck, Germany, with gilt-metal decoration lens, chimney and illuminant.
(Christie's S. Ken) $405

A mahogany body table Achromatic Stereoscope by Smith, Beck and Beck, with a pair of focusing eyepieces and original mirror.
(Christie's S. Ken) $925

A cardboard-body New Patent Jewel Kaleidoscope by London Stereoscopic Co., with brown morocco-leather finish, and ball-socket mounting section.
(Christie's S. Ken) $1,548

A metal bodied Flickergraph optical toy with viewing lens, handle and one reel, printed paper labels *For use with the Animated Pictorial.*
(Christie's S. Ken) $619

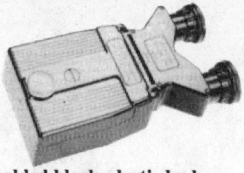

A molded black-plastic body OTHEO Stereo Viewer x5 with red illuminant button and a pair of focusing eyepieces by Ernst Leitz Canada Ltd., in maker's fitted box.
(Christie's S. Ken) $1,065

A mahogany-body Kinora viewer with inlaid-wood decoration and a picture reel no. 273 showing a white polar bear.
(Christie's S. Ken) $1,113

A wood body electrically-operated wall-mounted stereo viewer proclaiming *40 different pictures. You see ten for 3d and 3-D Beauty Parade* featuring stereoscopic pairs of posed nude and semi-nude women.
(Christie's S. Ken) $2,429

A red and black painted Mutoscope viewer with hand crank, coin slot, viewing hood, internal reel no. 7529 featuring Charlie Chaplin.
(Christie's S. Ken) $2,631

A 20 x 14cm. Polyrama Panoptique viewer with diced-green paper covered body, brass fittings, and black leather bellows with thirteen day and night views.
(Christie's S. Ken) $1,230

A mahogany-body pedestal Scott's Patent Stereoscope with rack and pinion focusing eyepiece section, with plaque *Negretti & Zambra.*
(Christie's S. Ken) $1,107

A mahogany sliding box camera obscura front section with lens and turned wood lens cap, body stamped By His Majestys Special Appointment. Jones, (Artist.) London.
(Christie's S. Ken) $811

A mahogany and brass-fitted biunial magic lantern with a wood-mounted snow effect mechanical slide with printed label *E.H. Wilkie*, in a fitted wooden box.
(Christie's S. Ken) $1,812

**Lebanon: 1939 25 livres.**
**(Phillips) $906**

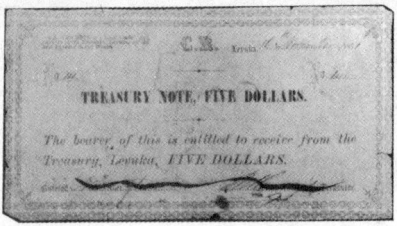


**Fiji: 1871 $5 Treasury note.**
**(Phillips) $888**

**Bank of England Note, E.M. Harvey: £10 29 June 1920 issued at Manchester.**
**(Phillips) $506**

**France: 1720 La Banque Royale 1,000 livres, 3mm nick top edge otherwise good.**
**(Phillips) $414**

**New Zealand: 1886 (?) National Bank of New Zealand £20 issued at Auckland, difficult to be precise with handwritten date but note very well preserved and extremely rare.**
**(Phillips) $2,775**

**New Caledonia: 1921 500 francs, most attractive design with allegorical figures left and right, note overstamped "Annule" and with small tear top of center crease.**
**(Phillips) $1,517**

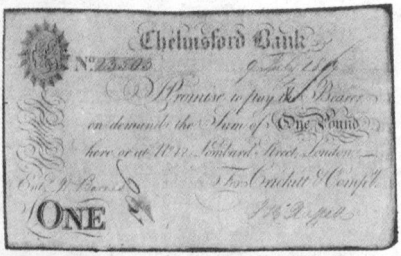


**Chelmsford Bank: £1, 1819 Crickitt & Co. fully printed on back as 'Bank of Crickitt, Russell & Co., Chelmsford'.**
**(Phillips) $217**

**Mauritius: 1815 (c.) Colonial Bank of Mauritius Bourbon and Dependencies 5 crowns unissued.**
**(Phillips) $590**

**Canada: 1900 Dominion $4.**
**(Phillips) $552**

**Germany: 1924 20 billion marks.**
**(Phillips) $295**

**British West Africa: 1954 Currency Board £5, pinholes.**
**(Phillips) $374**

**China: 1917 Yokohama Specie Bank $10 issued at Hankow.**
**(Phillips) $1,443**

**Bank of England Note, George Forbes: £5 24 May 1871, Forbes was the first Chief Cashier to have his printed signature on Bank of England notes, extremely rare.**
**(Phillips) $8,880**

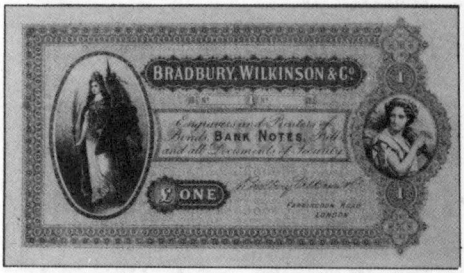


**Great Britain: Bradbury Wilkinson & Co. advertising note 1880 (c.), uniface, brown and black on face with large vignette at left of allegorical woman.**
**(Phillips) $185**

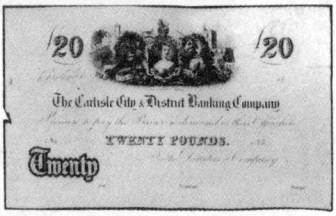


**Carlisle City & District Banking Company: £20 proof by Lizars, small piece missing left side.**
**(Phillips) $202**

**Provincial Bank: £10 September 1852 issued at Galway, split along middle and overstamped 'Cancelled'.**
**(Phillips) $453**

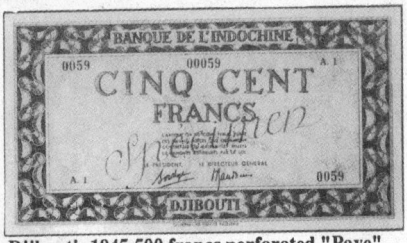


Djibouti: 1945 500 francs perforated "Paye" and with "Specimen" handwritten across face.
(Phillips) $674

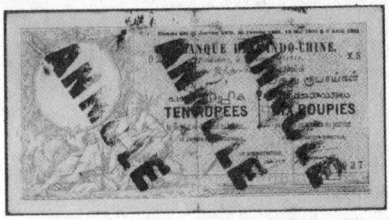


French India: 1919 10 roupies overstamped "Annule" three times.
(Phillips) $438

Great Britain, Bank of England Note, K.O. Peppiatt: £100 15 March 1937.
(Phillips) $573

Italy: 1867 100 lire handsigned by Garibaldi at right.
(Phillips) $337

Cape Verde: 1941 50 escudos.
(Phillips) $303

French Indo-China: 1925 Banque de L'Indochine 100 piastres issue perforated "Specimen".
(Phillips) $1,146

Northern Bank Ltd: £100 1919.
(Phillips) $349

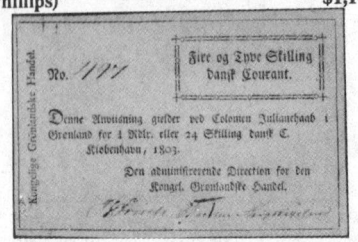


Greenland: 1803 24 skilling, early and rare.
(Phillips) $1,938

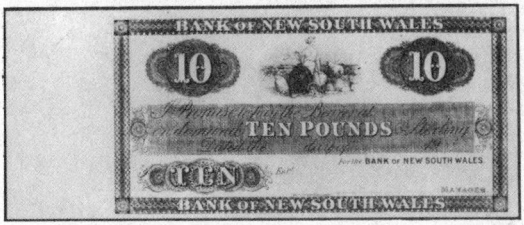


New Zealand: 1923–34 Bank of New South Wales £10 specimen.
(Phillips) $337

Mauritius: 1942 1 rupee emergency issue.
(Phillips) $977

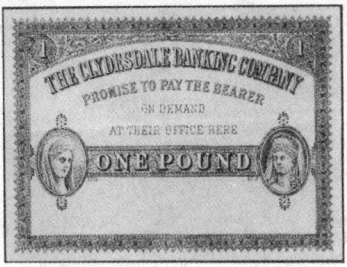


Clydesdale Banking Company: £1 proof/ artwork in green and purple.
(Phillips) $337

Bank of England Note, J.G. Nairne: £5 21 February 1910 issued at Plymouth.
(Phillips) $7,751

Great Britain: Bradbury Wilkinson advertising note in red and black for "Biglietti di Banca" with large allegorical vignette at left.
(Phillips) $160

Bank of Scotland: £1 February 1893 signed by J.F. Stormonth Darling.
(Phillips) $426

Great Britain, J. Bradbury: 10/- August 1914.
(Phillips) $809

Ulster Bank: £100 Specimen in black on white 1920.
(Phillips) $371

New Zealand: 1925 Nank of New South Wales £20 perforated 'Specimen'.
(Phillips) $444

Great Britain: Robert Owen 1 Hour 'Labor Exchange' note, handsigned and dated 17 September 1832, plus card token for 1/6 hour.
(Phillips) $433

Ceylon: 1881 Oriental Bank Corporation 5 rupees issued at Colombo, attractive Bradbury Wilkinson engraving.
(Phillips) $670

U.S.A.: 1917 $10,000 Gold Certificate, payable to the 'Federal Reserve Board', uniface and perforated across portrait 'Payable only to The Treasurer of the US'.
(Phillips) $681

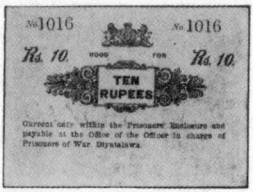


Ceylon: 1900 10 rupees issued at Diyatalawa Camp.
(Phillips) $506

Russia: 1919 Banque de L'Indochine 500 rubles Specimen prepared for Allied Forces brown with central vignette of Marianne.
(Phillips) $1,480

Netherlands: 1888 Munt-Biljet for 10 gulden, few pinholes left side.
(Phillips) $2,945

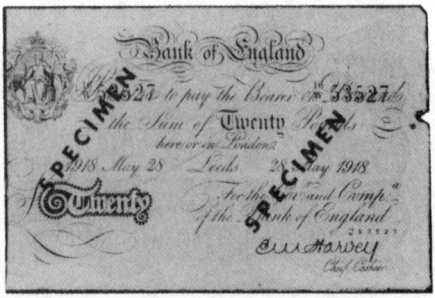


Bank of England Note, E.M. Harvey: £20 28 May 1918 issued at Leeds.
(Phillips) $809

Great Britain, J. Bradbury: £1 August 1914, heavy center crease.
(Phillips) $472

Djibouti: 1945 1,000 francs overstamped "Annule" and with four small punch-holes.
(Phillips) $1,180

Isles de France et de Bourbon: 1780 (c.) 6 livres tournois, officially rebacked and re-numbered.
(Phillips) $1,011

El Salvador: 1925, El Banco Salvadoreno 100 colones Waterlow color trial in brown, orange and green, two punch-holes.
(Phillips) $167

Australia: 1882 (c.) Federal Bank of Australia £1 (2), £5, £10, £20 and £50 "Specimen" notes of Bradbury Wilkinson & Co., one of the £1 notes is payable at Sydney with the others all at Melbourne.
(Phillips) $3,370

Great Britain: £1 trial in green, brown and blue on watermarked paper (210 x 155mm) with large white margin which has "Passed" penciled in twice.
(Phillips) $1,356

Germany: 1907 Deutsch-Asiatische Bank $10 issued at Tientsin.
(Phillips) $1,382

Sudan: 1884 20 piastres, Siege of Khartoum, hectographic signature.
(Phillips) $253

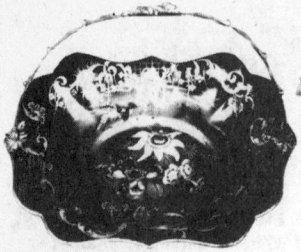

A fine 19th century papier mâché cake basket, the central panel painted with a passion flower, roses and a mythical bird, 11½in. wide.
(Michael Newman) $606

A Victorian inlaid and painted small papier mâché writing slope with glass inkwells.
(Greenslades) $410

A Regency papier mâché rectangular tray with monochrome flowers and leaves on a crimson ground within an oak leaf and anthemia border, 32¼ x 24½in.
(Christie's) $3,049

An attractive lacquered papier mâché face screen of ornate mirror shape, painted with a scene of Magdalen College Oxford, 11¼in. wide, circa 1850.
(Bonhams) $420

Black lacquered papier mâché rectangular box, the lid painted with a picture of a woman as 'Autumn', Brunswick, Stobwasser, early 19th century, 6cm. long.
(Kunsthaus Lempertz) $2,003

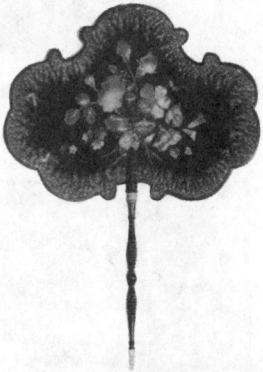

One of a pair of lacquered papier-mâché hand held face screens, of ornate mirror shape, each inlaid with a central mother of pearl floral bouquet, 11in. wide.
(Bonhams) $256

An early Victorian papier-mâché tray, decorated in gilt and mother-of-pearl with a cockatoo in an exotic garden, 2ft. 6¾in. wide.
(Phillips) $1,266

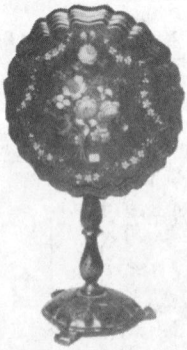

Victorian papier mâché snap top table, painted with flowers and inlaid with mother of pearl detail, 24in. wide.
(G.A. Key) $441

A 19th century papier-mâché tray, decorated overall with gilt heightened leaves and flowers, circa 1840, 2ft. 7¾in. wide.
(Phillips) $1,947

A good 19th century shaped rectangular black papier mâché tray, the center painted with lilies, the border dripping foliated scrolls, 31½in. wide. (Anderson & Garland) $2,529

A Victorian mother-of-pearl inlaid black lacquer papier mâché tilt-top table, mid 19th century, attributed to Bettridge and Jennins, 43¼in. high. (Christie's) $3,000

Victorian black papier mâché tray with gilt detail to edges and painted floral center, having mother of pearl inlays, 23 x 19in. (G.A. Key) $435

One of a pair of lacquered papier-mâché hand held screens, of ornate mirror shape, painted with landscape scenes after Constable, 10¾in. wide. (Bonhams) (Two) $821

Pair of Chinese lacquered papier mâché vases, 18th/19th century, with incised polychrome landscape and floral reserves on black ground, 13in. high. (Skinner Inc.) $1,540

A Victorian mother-of-pearl inlaid black lacquer tilt-top table, mid 19th century, with a scalloped circular top above a baluster turned support on S-scrolling legs, 43in. high. (Christie's) $2,600

A lacquered papier-mâché blotter, the front painted with a bouquet of garden flowers, heightened with tinted inlaid mother of pearl leaves and petals, 12in. x 9in., circa 1835. (Bonhams) $164

A Victorian papier mâché work table decorated with painted flowers and gilt scrolls, 18½ x 31in. high. (Anderson & Garland) $2,079

A Regency papier-mâché tray decorated with chinoiseries, the two central figures of elders seated at a table taking tea, 2ft. 6¼in. wide. (Phillips) $1,168

A Tudric planished pewter bowl raised upon four fluted cabriole supports terminating in trefoil feet, with cut card type terminals, 13in. wide over feet terminals.
(Spencer's) $256

Pair of Chinese Export polychrome pewter figural pricket candlesticks, early 19th century, each a kneeling gentleman, 12½in. high.
(Skinner Inc.) $7,150

A W.M.F. electroplated pewter letter tray, the oval tray cast in relief with an Art Nouveau maiden reclining beside a lily pond, 10in. wide.
(Christie's S. Ken) $1,178

Pewter flagon, Roswell Gleason, Dorchester, Massachusetts, mid 19th century, 10in. high.
(Skinner Inc.) $450

A Continental Art Nouveau pewter plaque, with the bust head of pre-Raphaelite maiden, flanked by curved uprights, 21cm. wide.
(Spencer's) $119

A late 18th century japanned metal coffee pot, the stepped domed cover with urn finial, the urn shaped body with gilt decoration.
(Phillips) $3,828

A mid-18th century French pewter lavabo cistern with flat back, serpentine front and twin cherub cast handles, 10¼in. high.
(David Lay) $300

A pair of W.M.F. twin handled pewter vases, decorated in relief with tendril-like entrelacs, on splayed quatrefoil base, 35cm. high.
(Phillips) $1,010

Pewter coffee pot, Josiah Danforth, Middletown, Connecticut, early 19th century, 11in. high.
(Skinner Inc.) $1,100

An 18th century pewter pedestal punch bowl with pricked inscription *The London Punch House, 1760*, 10in. diameter. (Greaves, Son & Pilcher) $819

An 18th century pewter inkstand with removable ink and pounce pots, center taperstick and wax drawer, engraved *For y use of y Great Vestry Room, Samuel Cooper.* (Greaves, Son & Pilcher) $1,463

A mid-18th century French pewter soup pail with tapering ribbed body, the handle swinging from mask cast loops, 8½in. diameter. (David Lay) $300

Pewter claret jug decorated with embossed Art Nouveau designs, circa 1870. (Spencer's) $390

A pair of pewter W.M.F. candelabra with nymphs entwined around tendrils which form the sconces, on spreading bases, 25cm. high. (Phillips) $1,724

A German pewter Guild flagon of conical form, with scroll thumbpiece, the cover with an heraldic lion supporting a shield with owner's initials, 25½in. high, Wismar, circa 1670. (Christie's S. Ken) $5,320

A Charles I pewter flagon with straight sided body incised with lines, and engraved *Kingstone* 1633, 13in. high. (Lawrence Fine Art) $2,280

'For Old Times ' Sake'. A pair of Liberty & Co. 'Tudric' twin-handled vases of cylindrical shape, 20cm. high, impressed *'Tudric and 010'* to base. (Phillips) $570

One of three pewter fluid lamps, 19th century, two with acorn front, one with strap handle, marked *Curtis, New York*, the largest lamp 9¾in. high. (Christie's) (Three) $385

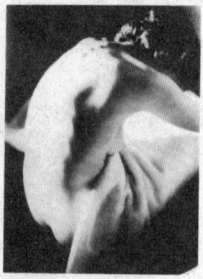

Max Dupain, 'The Little Nude', 1938, printed 1980s, gelatin silver print, 19¾ x 15¼in., signed and dated in pencil on image, titled in pencil on mount.
(Christie's) $660

Lewis Carroll, 'Sir Henry Taylor, 12 Earls Terrace', probably October 1863, albumen print, 8⅝ x 6⅞in., arched top.
(Christie's) $1,980

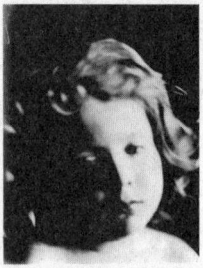

Julia Margaret Cameron, Untitled, child portrait, circa 1864–65, albumen print, 11½ x 9¼in., mounted on card, ink manuscript credit and caption *From Life not Enlarged*, on mount.
(Christie's) $24,200

Lewis Carroll, 'George MacDonald with his daughter Lilia in the garden of 12 Earls Terrace', 14 October 1863, albumen print, 9⅜ x 7½in.
(Christie's) $5,720

Cecil Beaton, HRH Princess Marina, 1949, gelatin silver print, 14 x 12in., mounted on card, photographer's signature in colored pencil with date and signature *Marina* in ink on mount.
(Christie's) $1,012

Bill Brandt, Jack B. Yeats in his Dublin studio, 1946, gelatin silver print, image size 9 x 7⅝in., photographer's signature in ink on margin, matted, framed.
(Christie's) $2,530

Norman Parkinson, Golfing – Simpson's Suits, Le Touquet, 1939, printed later, gelatin silver print, 15½ x 11in., matted, signed and dated '39 in ink on mount.
(Christie's) $2,420

Anon, Harbour scene, [1850s–60s], large ambrotype, 9¾ x 9¾in., gilt frame.
(Christie's) $186

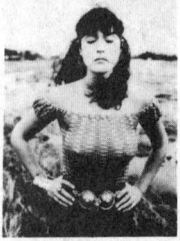

Willem Diepraam, 'Peggy Amsterdam 1975', gelatin silver print, image size 18 x 12¼in., signed, titled and dated in ink on reverse.
(Christie's) $880

**Rudolph Dührkoop, Portrait of Hermann Bahr, circa 1912, carbon print, 8 1/2 x 6 3/8 in., photographer's blindstamp signature and date on image, ink credit stamp on verso.**
**(Christie's) $660**

**Ida Kar, Barbara Hepworth, 1954, gelatin silver print, 11 1/4 x 10in., signed in crayon on image matted.**
**(Christie's) $1,100**

**Henri Cartier-Bresson (b. 1908), Joseph Albers, circa 1950s, gelatin silver print, 11 5/8 x 7 3/4 in., photographer's ink credit stamp and numbers *11121 43* in pencil on verso.**
**(Christie's) $880**

**Eugène Atget (1857–1927), 'Ancien Ecole de Médecin Rue de l'Hôtel Colbert, 1898, albumen print, 8 3/4 x 7in., titled and numbered 3531 in pencil by photographer on verso.**
**(Christie's) $1,430**

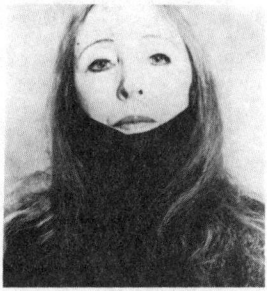

**Irving Penn, Portrait of Anais Nin, 1971, platinum – palladium print, image size 19 x 19in., number 7 of 20 matted, framed.**
**(Christie's) $2,310**

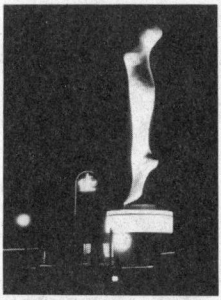

**Max Yavno (1911–85), 'The Leg', 1949, printed later, gelatin silver print, 19 1/4 x 15 1/4 in., matted, signed *Yavno* in pencil on mount.**
**(Christie's) $1,100**

**Attributed to Lewis Carroll, self portrait, circa 1863, albumen print, 4 x 3 1/8 in., arched top, mounted on card titled in ink Charles Lutwidge Dodgson (Lewis Carroll).**
**(Christie's) $9,900**

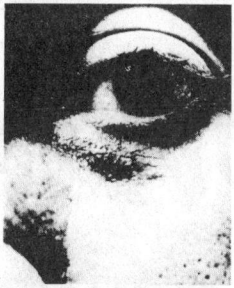

**Bill Brandt, Antonio Tapies, 1964, printed 1970s, gelatin silver print, 28 x 23 1/2 in., mounted on board, photographer's ink credit stamp on verso.**
**(Christie's) $2,640**

**Anon possibly Baron Von Stillfried, Japanese costume studies, 1870s, concertina album containing eleven hand-tinted albumen prints, approx. 7 3/4 x 9 3/4 in.**
**(Christie's) $1,540**

George Davison (1856–1930), 'The Onion Field (An Old Farmstead),' 1890, photogravure, image size 6 x 8in., signed in pencil in margin, framed.
(Christie's) $1,144

Lewis Carroll, 'Greville Matheson MacDonald at Elm Lodge Hampstead', July 1863, albumen print, oval 8¾ x 6⅞in.
(Christie's) $4,400

Manuel Alvarez Brazo (b. 1902), Female nude, circa 1970s, platinum/palladium print, image size 7¼ x 9¾in., signed in pencil in the margin, matted.
(Christie's) $2,860

Edouard Boubat (b. 1923), 'France 1949', gelatin silver print, 15 x 11¼in., mounted on card, signed in ink on mount, photographer's credit, title and date on verso.
(Christie's) $880

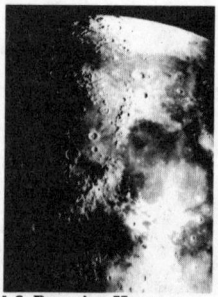

Paul & Prospère Henry 'Photographie Lunaire – Corne Nord – 29 Mars 1890', albumen print, 8¾ x 6⅝in., mounted on card, titled, with detail *Age de la Lune 215 heures. Agrandissement direct 15 fois.*
(Christie's) $9,240

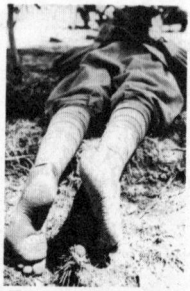

Alfed Eisenstaedt (b. 1898), 'Ethiopia – a soldier who fought in puttees and bare feet against Mussolini's armies in 1935', gelatin silver print, image size 9½ x 6½in.
(Christie's) $550

Dr. Ernest G. Boon, Child portraits, circa 1900–1910, six platinum prints, 5 x 4¼ to 11 x 9¼in.
(Christie's) $990

Lewis Carroll, 'Irene [MacDonald], Flo Rankin, Mary [MacDonald] at Elm Lodge', July 1863.
(Christie's) $16,500

Roger Fenton,, 'Jupiter', circa 1857, salt print, 12 x 9⅝in., titled and numbered *1120–1/0½* in pencil on reverse.
(Christie's) $836

Danny Lyon (b. 1942), 'Mary, Santa Marta', 1960s, printed later, gelatin silver print, $8^1/_2$ x $12^1/_2$in., pencil title, signature and number *11/78/2* on verso, matted, framed.
(Christie's) $1,100

Lewis Carroll, 'Irene', July 1863, oval albumen print, $8^3/_4$ x 7in.
(Christie's) $19,800

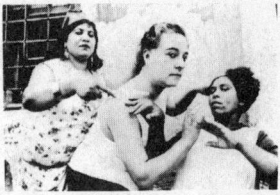

Henri Cartier-Bresson, 'Alicante, Spain, 1933', printed later, gelatin silver print, image size $9^1/_2$ x $14^1/_4$in., signed in ink and with photographer's blindstamp in margin, matted.
(Christie's) $4,180

Henri Cartier-Bresson, Coco Chanel, circa 1950s, gelatin silver print, image size 10 x $6^5/_8$in., photographer's ink credit stamp, title and other pencil annotations on verso.
(Christie's) $1,100

Eugène Atget, 'Rouen – Rue Malpalu(?)', 1907, albumen print, $8^1/_2$ x 7in., titled and numbered 335 in pencil by photographer on verso.
(Christie's) $990

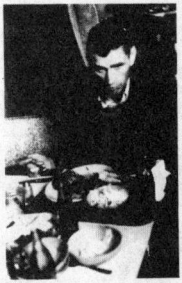

Robert Frank, 'San Francisco 1956', printed 1970s, gelatin silver print, $13^1/_4$ x 9in., signed and titled in ink in margin, matted, framed.
(Christie's) $1,210

Lewis Carroll, Xie Kitchin, 1873, albumen print, $4^1/_4$ x $3^1/_2$in., numbered 2033 in the negative and in ink on verso.
(Christie's) $1,430

After Julia Margaret Cameron, 'The Kiss of Peace', 1869, printed 1890, photogravure, image size $8^1/_2$ x $6^3/_4$in., arched top, printed title in margin.
(Christie's) $764

Dr. Ernest G. Boon, FRPS (d. 1959), 'The Dead Bird,' circa 1905, platinum print, 11 x $9^1/_2$in.
(Christie's) $836

Alfred Ellis, two photographs: 'Mr. Oscar Wilde' and Oscar Wilde and friend, circa 1880s, albumen cabinet cards.
(Butterfield & Butterfield)
$550

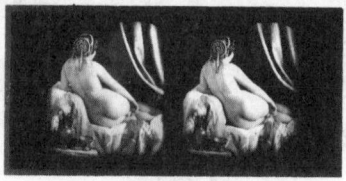

Anon, Reclining nude (inspired by Ingres), 1850s, stereoscopic daguerreotype, hand-tinted, gilt highlights, paper-taped.
(Christie's) $14,960

Julia Margaret Cameron, 'Paul & Virginia', 1867–70, albumen print, 10½ x 8½in., mounted on card.
(Christie's) $4,862

Weegee, 'New Year's Eve at Sammy's-on-the-Bowery', 1943, printed later, gelatin silver print, 8¼ x 12⅝in., *The Weegee Collection* blindstamp in the margin.
(Butterfield & Butterfield)
$770

Bert Stern, 'The Last Sitting', a portfolio of 10 Ektacolor prints, 1962, printed 1978, each measuring 19 x 18½in., each signed and numbered.
(Butterfield & Butterfield)
$3,300

Henri Cartier-Bresson, 'Rue Mouffetard', 1954, printed later, 14 x 9⅜in., signed in ink and the photographer's blindstamp in the margin.
(Butterfield & Butterfield)
$3,850

Ansel Adams, 'Moonrise, Hernandez, New Mexico', circa 1942, printed circa 1976, gelatin silver print, 15¼ x 19⅜in., signed in pencil on the mount.
(Butterfield & Butterfield)
$8,250

Frantisek Drtikol, Fat boy posing, 1925, gelatin silver print, 8⅞ x 6¾in., photographer's blindstamp with date on recto.
(Christie's) $1,122

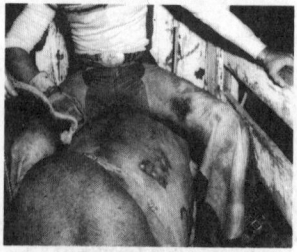

Susan Felter, 'Roy (red chaps) riding bull', 1978, Cibachrome, 13 x 16⅞in., signed and dated in the margin, signed and dated in pencil on the reverse.
(Butterfield & Butterfield)
$522

David Octavius Hill & Robert Adamson, John Henning, mid 1840s, calotype, 8 x 6in., matted and framed.
(Christie's) $1,402

William Klein, 'Three heiresses, Greece', 1963, printed later, gelatin silver print, 9 x 13½in., signed, titled and dated in pencil on verso.
(Butterfield & Butterfield) $550

Brassaï, 'Salvador Dali', 1932, printed later, gelatin silver print, 11¾ x 8½in., signed and numbered *11/30* in red ink in the margin.
(Butterfield & Butterfield) $1,100

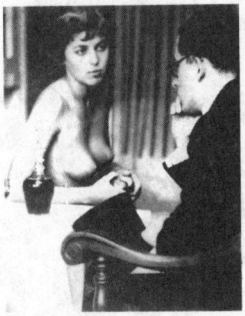

Josef Britenbach, 'Dr. Riegler and J. Geno', 1933, printed later, photogravure, 12 x 9½in., the photographer's estate blindstamp.
(Butterfield & Butterfield) $660

Diane Arbus, 'A family one evening at a nudist camp', 1965, printed later by Neil Selkirk, gelatin silver print, 15 x 15in., dry mounted covering the signature in ink.
(Butterfield & Butterfield) $1,045

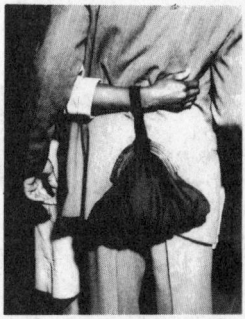

Weegee, Hands and Purse, circa 1940s, gelatin silver print, 13½ x 10¾in., the photographer's name stamp (three times) on verso.
(Butterfield & Butterfield) $715

Edward S. Curtis, 'Aphrodite, (Spirit of the Sea)', circa 1920, blue-toned gelatin silver print, 10½ x 13½in., signed with the *Curtis LA* copyright insignia.
(Butterfield & Butterfield) $1,430

Yousef Karsh, 'Albert Einstein', 1948, printed later, gelatin silver print, 17 x 15⅞in., signed in ink on the mount.
(Butterfield & Butterfield) $990

Imogen Cunningham, 'Magnolia blossom', 1925, printed 1930s, gelatin silver print, 7½ x 9⅜in., signed in pencil on the mount.
(Butterfield & Butterfield) $15,400

A Louis XV style parcel-gilt 'Vernis Martin' grand piano, by Erard, decorated by Lucien Simonnet, with a shaped top with gadrooned edge, on cabriole legs with foliate scrolling feet and casters, 80in. long.
(Christie's) $41,800

Late 18th century English mahogany table piano, signed *JOSHUA DANE, BEDFORD ROW, LONDON*, on square tapered legs.
(Duran) $1,875

Late 19th century inlaid burr walnut upright piano by Waldemar, Berlin, 145cm. wide.
(Duran) $1,355

An overstrung grand pianoforte, 7¼ octaves by John Broadwood & Sons, in a satinwood case inlaid with boxwood lines and amaranth bands.
(Phillips) $3,555

A baby grand piano, designed by Jacques Adnet, for Gaveau of Paris, of rosewood, on three tapering rectangular section legs, with matching upholstered stool.
(Christie's) $17,160

A fine Louis XVI style ormolu-mounted satinwood and parquetry grand piano, dated 1901, by Erard, with an ormolu-molded shaped rectangular hinged top, 84½in. long.
(Christie's East) $18,700

An upright piano, by Fred Baier, the body of lacquered mustard yellow, orange and hot pink, incorporating a traditional 'Welmar' piano, 1990, 172.5cm. wide. (Christie's) $18,139

A boudoir grand pianoforte by Gaveau Paris, the satinwood case with banded borders on turned tapering fluted legs.
(Christie's S. Ken) $6,013

A grand pianoforte by John Broadwood & Sons, in a mahogany case with a rosewood interior, the turned legs and lyre-shaped pedal board enriched with ebony, circa 1817.
(Christie's) $12,569

An Art Deco Strohmenger baby grand piano and stool, in bleached burr walnut, the semi-circular body having three arches under solid supports meeting at the pedals.
(Phillips) $13,421

A Bechstein boudoir grand piano, the walnut case on three pairs of tapering square legs with brass castors, 6ft. 9in.
(Bearne's) $3,015

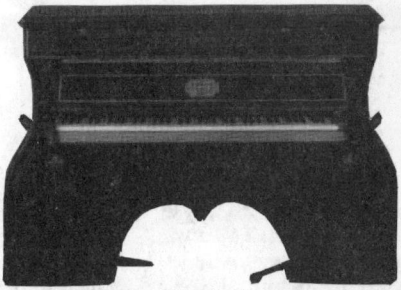

Late 19th century flame mahogany and marquetry upright piano by S. Mercier, Paris.
(Hôtel de Ventes Horta) $3,400

An Italian early seventeenth century carved, gilded and marbled frame, the centers and corners with panels of scrolling acanthus leaves, 53¼ x 42½in. (Christie's S. Ken) $13,552

A South German eighteenth century carved frame, with pierced c-scrolls, surmounted with a heraldic eagle, overall size 11 x 8½in. (Christie's S. Ken) $1,258

A Dutch seventeenth century tortoiseshell frame, 13½ x 17¼in. (Christie's S. Ken) $9,293

A Spanish seventeenth century carved, gilded and painted frame, with scrolling acanthus outer edge, 45⅛ x 39in. (Christie's S. Ken) $3,160

An Anglo-Dutch carved frame, circa 1660, centered with a coat of arms and surmounted with scrolling acanthus leaves, overall size 26½ x 22¼in. (Christie's S. Ken) $6,741

A South German seventeenth century carved, gilded and ebonized frame, with various ripple and wave moldings, 25⅜ x 23¼in. (Christie's S. Ken) $1,510

An Italian late sixteenth century carved, gilded and painted cassetta frame, with raised outer edge, 41¼ x 33in. (Christie's S. Ken) $15,799

Italian baroque giltwood picture frame, circa 1700, carved with acanthus scrolls and putti, the inner frame carved with laurel leaf clusters, 78½in. high. (Skinner Inc.) $6,000

A Flemish nineteenth century carved ebonized frame, with various color marble inlays under glass, 27¼ x 24¾in. (Christie's S. Ken) $1,881

A Spanish seventeenth century carved, gilded and painted frame, the corners and centers with acanthus leaves, 65¼ x 53in.
(Christie's S. Ken)
$14,520

A Spanish seventeenth century carved, gilded and painted frame, with stepped outline and pierced scrolling acanthus leaves, overall size 39¼ x 33in.
(Christie's S. Ken)
$10,533

An Italian seventeenth century carved and painted frame, with bar-and-treble-bead outer edge, 42 x 37½in.
(Christie's S. Ken)
$3,581

An oval French Empire frame, with acanthus leaf raised outer edge, and stiff leaf sight edge, 12 x 11⅜in.
(Christie's S. Ken)
$581

An Italian seventeenth century carved tabernacle frame, the broken pediment supported on a pair of doric columns, 22½ x 15¾in.
(Christie's S. Ken)
$2,107

A Provincial Louis XIV carved and gilded laurel leaf corner frame, the central panels with engraved and gadrooned sight edge, 15¾ x 13¾in.
(Christie's S. Ken)
$1,549

An English eighteenth century carved and gilded swept frame, the c-scroll corners flanked by pierced s-scrolls, 37 x 32¼in.
(Christie's S. Ken)
$1,580

A Spanish seventeenth century carved and gilded frame, with acanthus and c-scroll corners and centers in high relief, 36 x 31in.
(Christie's S. Ken)
$16,456

A Venetian eighteenth century carved and painted frame, the corners with granito foliage and flowers, 35½ x 42½in.
(Christie's S. Ken)
$6,320

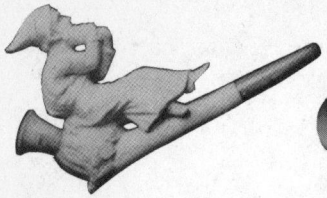

Cheroot holder of a gnome stroking his beard, amber stem, fitted case, 5in. long.
(Skinner Inc.) $150

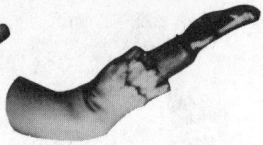

Woman's leg cheroot holder, silver ferule, amber stem, no case, 4½in. long.
(Skinner Inc.) $150

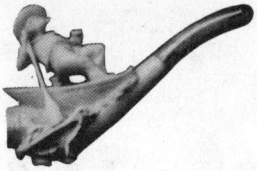

Gondolier cheroot holder, amber stem, missing adaptor, fitted case, 4½in. long.
(Skinner Inc.) $125

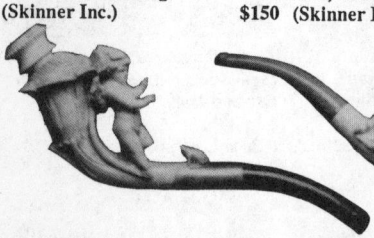

Cupid with frog cheroot holder, silver ferule, amber stem, fitted case, 6in. long.
(Skinner Inc.) $150

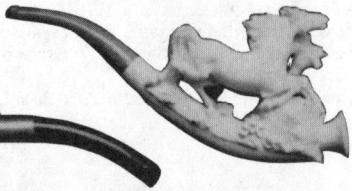

Cheroot holder of a pair of running horses, amber stems, fitted cases, 7in. long.
(Skinner Inc.) $225

A massive meerschaum pipe bowl, carved with figures and hounds hunting bears, 7½in. long.
(Christie's S. Ken) $381

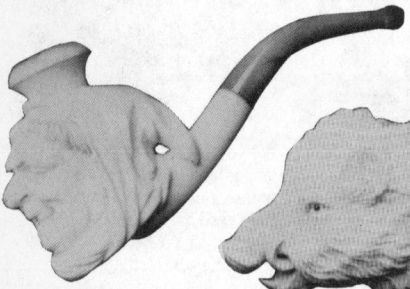

Monk's head cheroot holder, amber stem, fitted case, 6¾in. long.
(Skinner Inc.) $950

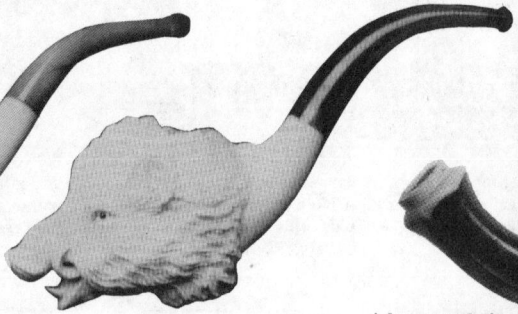

Boar's head pipe, amber stem, fitted case, 9in. long.
(Skinner Inc.) $1,100

A hexagonal pipe-head painted with figures in regional Eastern costumes above molded gilt ribs and green foliage, circa 1840, 9cm. long.
(Christie's) $338

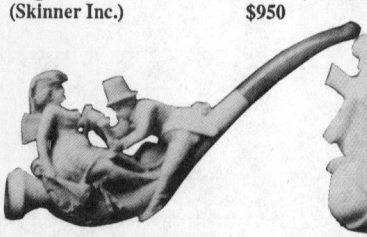

Cheroot holder of champagne drinkers, amber stem, fitted case, 5½in. long.
(Skinner Inc.) $325

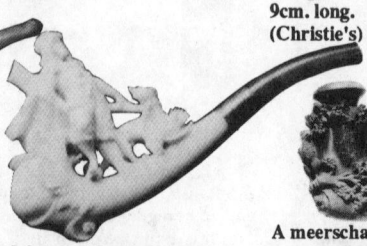

Arab hunter cheroot holder, silver ferule, amber stem, fitted case, 6in. long.
(Skinner Inc.) $500

A meerschaum pipe, the bowl carved with the figures of a fox and a bird, fitted with an amber stem, 3¾in. high.
(Christie's S. Ken) $261

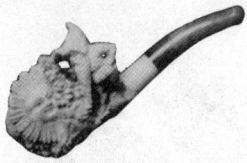

Gnome cheroot holder, with sun and trees, amber stem, fitted case, 4¼in. long.
(Skinner Inc.) $150

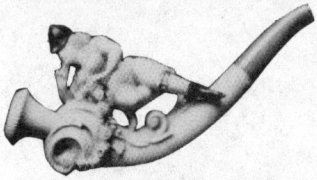

Female jockey cheroot holder, ebonized accents, amber stem, fitted case.
(Skinner Inc.) $225

A meerschaum pipe, the bowl modeled as an open flowerhead and carved with a running deer, 2¾in. high.
(Christie's S. Ken) $321

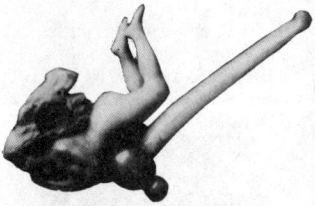

Cheroot holder of a fairy, amber stem, adaptor missing, fitted case, 5in. long.
(Skinner Inc.) $375

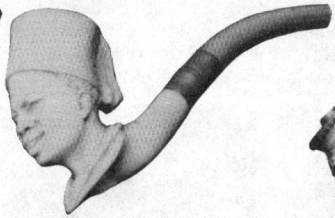

Pipe of a North African man, wearing a fez, amber ferule and stem, fitted case, 6½in. long.
(Skinner Inc.) $250

Pipe of soldiers drinking, silver fittings, no stem or case, 4½in. long.
(Skinner Inc.) $550

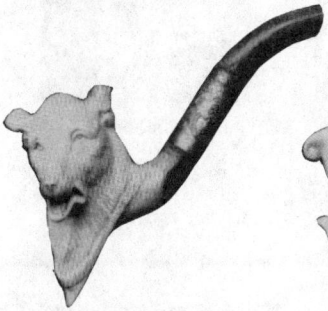

Wolf's head pipe, metal ferule, amber stem, fitted case, 7in. long.
(Skinner Inc.) $200

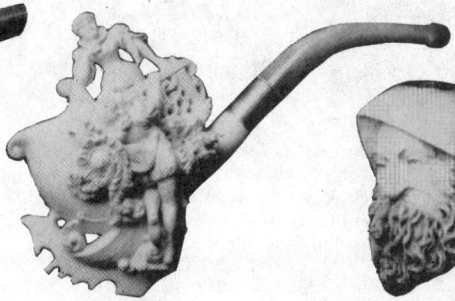

Romeo and Juliet pipe, inscribed silver ferule, amber stem, fitted case, 9½in. long.
(Skinner Inc.) $1,100

Pipe of a bearded and hooded man, silver ferule hallmarked Birmingham, amber stem, no case, 7½in. long.
(Skinner Inc.) $400

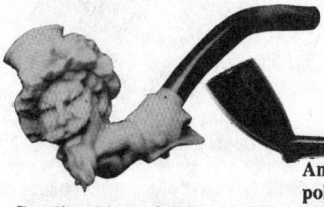

Cavalier cheroot holder, held by the neck, amber stone, fitted case, 5½in. long.
(Skinner Inc.) $375

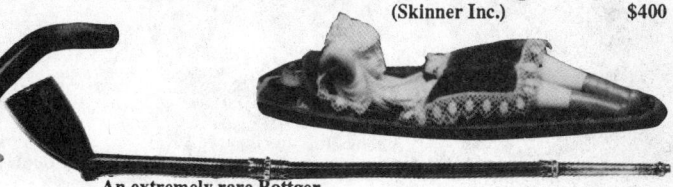

An extremely rare Bottger polished red stoneware pipe with small funnel shaped bowl, on a long slender cylindrical stem, total length 27.5cm.
(Phillips) $19,920

Set of three "Naughty" cheroot holders of a young woman, torso and pair of legs, amber stem, fitted case, 1½–3½in. long.
(Skinner Inc.) $650

Samuel Cooper (1609–1672), a young gentleman, in black doublet, slashed sleeves to reveal white, large lawn collar trimmed with lace, his long curly hair falling over his shoulders, oval, $3^{1}/_{8}$ in. high.
(Christie's) $35,838

Richard Cosway, R.A. (1742–1821), a lady, possibly Lady Elizabeth Lindsay, in décolleté white and gold dress with frilled border, cloudy background, oval, 2in. high.
(Christie's) $25,883

Richard Gibson (1615–1690), Sir Henry Blount, facing right, in black doublet and white lawn collar, fair curly hair, on vellum, oval, $2^{1}/_{4}$ in. high.
(Christie's) $35,838

Simon Jacques Rochard (1788–1872), a lady, in low-cut white dress with jeweled rim and belt, wearing a red cloak, the curly hair falling over her left shoulder, rectangular, 3in. high.
(Christie's) $2,588

Samuel Shelley (1750–1808), Lady Jane Caledon and her child, seated before a red curtain, she wears a black dress, white fichu and blue bandeau, the child wears a white tunic, rectangular, 5in. high.
(Christie's) $2,389

Sir William John Newton (1785–1869), Lord Verulam, in brown coat, white waistcoat, a gold, red and white striped robe over his shoulders, rectangular, 5in. high.
(Christie's) $1,195

George Engleheart (1750–1829), a lady, in white dress, blouse and figured veil falling over her shoulders, wearing a pearl necklace, signed with initial, oval, $3^{3}/_{4}$ in. high.
(Christie's) $3,982

John Hoskins (fl. circa 1645), Lady Mary Glamham, in low-cut black dress trimmed with white lace and brooch at corsage, wearing pearl necklace and earrings, signed with initials and dated 1648, oval, $2^{7}/_{8}$ in. high.
(Christie's) $35,838

Peter Oliver (circa 1594–1647), the Countess of Pembroke, in orange and black striped dress with jeweled border, white fichu and high ruff, wearing earrings and a jewel in her hair, oval, $2^{1}/_{8}$ in. high.
(Christie's) $37,829

Christian Friedrich Zincke (circa 1683–1767), a lady, in décolleté blue dress with a bouquet of pink and white flowers at her corsage, enamel, gilt-metal mount, oval, 2in. high. (Christie's) $2,957

Charles Boit (1662–1727), James Fitz-James, Duke of Berwick, in armor and white stock, ermine lined red cloak, enamel, signed on the reverse, oval, 1¼in. high. (Christie's) $3,802

Christian Friedrich Zincke (circa 1683–1767), a gentleman, in gold-laced blue coat, red waistcoat, frilled white shirt and stock, enamel, oval, 1⅝in. high. (Christie's) $1,901

John Comerford (circa 1770–1832), Philip, 3rd Lord Hardwicke, in jeweled white coat, red cloak and sash, wearing the Collar Chain, Gorge and Mantle of the Most Noble Order of the Garter, rectangular, 4in. high. (Christie's) $1,593

Miniature of three children and a cat, American School, 19th century, watercolor on ivory 4¾ x 3¾in. (Skinner Inc.) $16,000

English School, circa 1820, Lady Verulam, standing three-quarter length before an iron trellis, in green dress with white underslip and cashmere stole, rectangular, 4⅞in. high. (Christie's) $995

Susan Penelope Rosse (circa 1652–1700), after Samuel Cooper (1609–1672), Frances Stuart, Duchess of Richmond, wearing a pearl necklace and drop earrings, against a cloud background, oval, 3½in. high. (Christie's) $12,672

Jean-Baptiste-Jacques Augustin (1759–1832), a lady, seated before an architectural background, in décolleté white dress and red scarf, holding a laurel wreath, signed and dated 1800, circular, 3⅝in. diameter. (Christie's) $7,566

Richard Gibson (1615–1690), Elizabeth Capell, Countess of Carnarvon, in low-cut blue dress with scalloped edge over white underslip, diamond and pearl clasps at shoulder and corsage, oval, 3¼in. high. (Christie's) $29,568

English School, circa 1810, an officer, in naval uniform and gold epaulette, white shirt and black stock, gilt-metal frame, oval, 2½in. high.
(Christie's) $498

Gervase Spencer (fl. circa 1745), a lady, in gold embroidered blue dress and white ruff collar, wearing a gold-rimmed blue cap, dated London 1748, oval, 1⅞in. high.
(Christie's) $4,380

Horace Hone, A.R.A. (1754–1825), captain Lambert Brabazon, in naval uniform with gold epaulettes, gray waistcoat, white shirt and black stock, signed with initials and dated (18)06, oval, 1⅞in. high.
(Christie's) $1,294

Louis Marie Autissier (1772–1830), a gentleman, in black coat with high collar, white waistcoat, frilled shirt and cravat, signed and dated 1809, oval, 2⅞in. high.
(Christie's) $896

Louis-Marie Sicardi (1746–1825), a lady, in décolleté light blue dress gathered with gold brooch at her corsage, her hair dressed with blue ribbons, signed and dated 1797, circular, 2⅞in. diameter.
(Christie's) $7,566

Thomas Hargreaves (1774–1847), a gentleman, in blue coat, white waistcoat and cravat, curly blond hair, gold frame, oval, 2¾in. high.
(Christie's) $796

English School, circa 1790, a gentleman, in brown coat with large gold buttons, white waistcoat and cravat, powdered hair, gold frame, oval, 2½in. high.
(Christie's) $1,196

William Grimaldi (1751–1830), Prince William of Gloucester, in gold figured blue coat with red collar and cuffs, the background with red curtain and pillar, oval, 4⅛in. high.
(Christie's) $9,955

Thomas Forster (fl. circa 1700), Sir Thomas Pope Blount, in flowing robes and cravat, full-bottomed wig, plumbago, signed and dated 1700, oval, 4¼in. high.
(Christie's) $2,534

English School, circa 1790, an officer, in scarlet uniform possibly of the Monmouth Yeomanry Cavalry, with blue facings, silver lace and pouch-belt, oval, 2⅝in. high.
(Christie's) $1,155

John Smart (1742–1811), Colonel Charles Reynolds, in black coat, black-lined white waistcoat, frilled shirt and cravat, signed with initials and dated 1810, oval, 3½in. high.
(Christie's) $13,937

Attributed to Philip Jean (1755–1802), an officer, in scarlet uniform with black facings, large silver buttons and epaulette, white waistcoat and cravat, powdered hair en queue, oval, 2¾in. high.
(Christie's) $2,190

Frederick Buck (1771-circa 1840), a purser, in naval uniform with gold buttons and anchor on the facings, wearing long sideburns, oval, 3in. high.
(Christie's) $796

Louis-Lié Périn-Salbreux (1753–1817), a lady, in décolleté white dress and hood, a striped red scarf round her shoulders, holding a flower basket, circular, 3in. diameter.
(Christie's) $9,556

Circle of Thomas Richmond (1771–1837), a young lady, in frilled white dress, tied with light blue ribbon, her long hair gathered with a blue hairband, oval, 3in. high.
(Christie's) $1,196

Attributed to Cornelius Durham (fl. circa 1850), a little boy, in light blue coat and waistcoat, an open white shirt with large frilled collar, silver frame, oval, 2⅞in. high.
(Christie's) $299

Peter Cross (1630–1716), Captain Roper, in armor, wearing a full-bottomed wig which falls over his shoulders, a white cambric scarf tied round his neck, oval, 3¼in. high.
(Christie's) $11,946

William Grimaldi (1751–1830), a lady, seated half length on a red chair, in décolleté white dress and matching bandeau, the chin resting on her hand, oval, 4in. high.
(Christie's) $6,371

Louis Icart, Méditation, drypoint with aquatint part printed in colors, finished by hand, 1930, on wove paper, signed in pencil with the artist's blindstamp, 15½ x 19½in. (Christie's S. Ken) $9,578

After Hieronymous Bosche (circa 1450–1516), Die Blau Schuyte, engraving, circa 1559, first state (of two), a very fine, clear impression of this very rare print, printed with tone and wiping marks, 226 x 295mm. (Christie's) $49,192

Ethelbert White (1891–1972), The Barge Breakers; Regents Canal; Sawing logs; The Weeping Ash; Plowmans' Cottage; The River Bank; and The Hamlet, wood engravings, 5½ x 7in. (Christie's S. Ken) $809

Jemmy's Return, publisher Robert Sayer, mezzotint with extensive hand coloring, published in London, 1786; on wove with margins, 13¾in. x 9⅞in. (Phillips) $443

Andy Warhol, Marilyn, silkscreen, printed in colors, 1967, signed in pencil and stamp numbered *75/250* on reverse, published by Factory Addition, New York, 36in. x 35⁷⁄₈in. (Phillips) $46,202

Albrecht Dürer, The Entombment, from the engraved Passion, engraving, 1512, a Meder a-b impression, 4⅝in. x 2⅞in. (Phillips) $3,018

After Wafflard, Le Chien de L'Hospice, stipple engraving printed in colors, engraved by Dibart, published by Barise, Bernard and Vilquin, Paris, 19¼in. x 13½in. (Phillips) $221

After George Stubbs, A.R.A., The Horse and Lioness, by B. Green, mezzotint, third (final) state, indistinct watermark, published by R. Sayer, London 1791, with margins, 17½ x 22½in. (Christie's S. Ken) $1,703

Framed colored lithograph, depicting the 'Fairy Sisters', Cassie and Victoria Foster, advertised by Barnum & Bailey as the 'Smallest Persons in the World', 53in. x 39in. (Eldred's) $1,540

After John Boultbee, The Durham Ox, by J. Whessel, mixed method engraving printed in colors, published by J. Day, 1802, laid on stretcher, lesser defects, 21 x 25in.
(Christie's S. Ken) $2,022

Mortimer Menpes, portrait of James Abbott McNeill Whistler, seated, with arms folded, etching, signed in pencil, on wove, with margins, slightly time-stained, 7 3/4in. x 5 3/4in.
(Phillips) $805

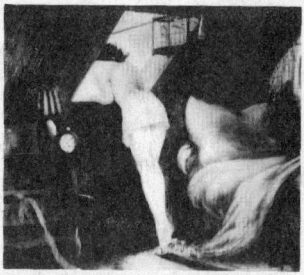

'Attic Room', by Louis Icart, etching and drypoint, printed in colors, signed lower right, Copyright 1940, 37.5 x 44cm.
(Christie's) $9,009

'Symphony in Blue', by Louis Icart, etching and drypoint, printed in colors, signed lower right, © Copyright 1936, 59.2 x 49.7cm.
(Christie's) $6,435

Felix Vallotton, La Paresse, woodcut, 1896, on wove paper, a fine impression, signed and numbered *109* in blue crayon, from the edition of about 180, with margins, 177 x 222mm.
(Christie's) $11,919

After John James Audubon, 'Lesser Tern', plate CCCXIX, Havell edition, 1836, engraving, etching, aquatint and hand coloring, 38 x 25 3/8in.
(Skinner Inc.) $1,500

Thomas Goldsworth Dutton, Her Majesty's iron cased screw steam frigate 'Black Prince', tinted lithograph, printed by Day & Son, published by W. Foster, London, 1862, 16 x 24in.
(Christie's S. Ken) $851

Henri de Toulouse-Lautrec, Le Divan Japonais, lithograph printed in colors, 1892–3, on buff wove paper, a fine impression, the colors good and strong, 800 x 622mm.
(Christie's) $56,760

Louis Icart, Fumée, etching with drypoint part printed in colors, finished by hand, 1926, signed in pencil, with the artist's blindstamp, 15 x 20in.
(Christie's S. Ken) $5,534

"The Life of a Fireman, The Metropolitan System", 1866, image size 17¼ x 26¼in.
(Skinner Inc.) $1,300

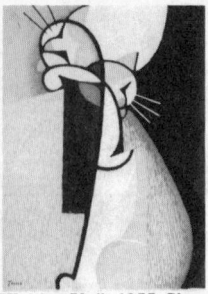

"Cat Waking Up", 1955. Signed "Tomoo" in the plate l.l. and "T. Inagaki" in pencil l.r., color woodblock on paper, image size 23 x 16¾in.
(Skinner Inc.) $650

Thomas Mann Baynes, View of the North Bank of the Thames from Westminster Bridge to London Bridge, hand-colored lithograph after Lt. Col. Trench, printed on silk, published 1825, 8⅝in. x 220in.
(Phillips) $1,272

Henri de Toulouse-Lautrec, Au Concert, lithograph printed in colors, 1896, on cream wove paper, Wittrock and Adriani's third (final) state with the lettering, a very good impression, 320 x 255mm.
(Christie's) $39,006

After Pieter Brueghel the Elder, a Man of War with the inscription *Die Scip 1564*, by F. Huys, engraving, 1565, first state (of two), a very fine, strong impression, printed with tone, 240 x 187mm.
(Christie's) $5,298

After John James Audubon, 'American Flamingo', plate CCCCXXXI, Havell edition, 1838, 38 x 25⅝in.
(Skinner Inc.) $14,000

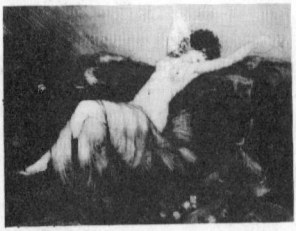

'Smoke', by Louis Icart, etching and drypoint, printed in colors, signed lower right, © Copyright 1926 by Les Graveurs Modernes, 38.1 x 51.5cm.
(Christie's) $6,435

Playing cards, 'Jeu des Nouveaux Cris de Paris', a deck of 32 hand-colored engraved cards, in original pictorial box, circa 1880.
(Christie's S. Ken) $899

'Leda and the Swan', by Louis Icart, etching and drypoint, printed in colors, signed lower right with artist's blindstamp, *Copyright 1934 by L. Icart Cty. N.Y.*, 52cm. x 80cm.
(Christie's) $18,601

'Before the Raid' by Louis Icart, etching and drypoint, printed in colors, signed lower right, 46.5 x 56.5cm.
(Christie's) $5,115

After James Ward, Jem Ward's picture of the Great Fight between Tom Sayers and J.C. Heenan, tinted lithograph, 1860, published by F.R. Scofield, Brixton, 27¼in. x 40in.
(Phillips) $262

'Papillon II', by Louis Icart, etching and drypoint, printed in colors, signed lower right Copyright 1936, 18.5 x 24cm.
(Christie's) $9,438

Dr. Robert John Thornton, publisher, Tulips, from the Temple of Flora, after P. Reinagle, by R. Earlom, mezzotint, printed in colors, finished by hand, first state (of two), published London, 1798, 18¾ x 14in.
(Christie's S. Ken) $4,044

Albrecht Dürer, the Martyrdom of Saint Catherine, woodcut, circa 1498, a very fine Meder a-b impression, the break in the contour of the mountain perhaps just beginning, without the breaks in the lower borderline by which Meder provides his b categorisation, 388 x 254mm.
(Christie's) $75,680

'Michelle', by Erté, a serigraph, printed in colors, on wove paper, signed in pencil, numbered 198/300, printed and published by The Chicago Serigraph Workshop, Chicago, Illinois, November 1980, with margins, mounted and framed, 63.2 x 46cm.
(Christie's) $1,228

"Camping Out, 'Some of the Right Sort'", 1856, (Conningham, 777). Lithograph with hand coloring on paper, image size 19 x 27¼in.
(Skinner Inc.) $950

After John James Audubon, 'Raven', plate CI, Havell edition, engraving, etching, aquatint and hand coloring, 38⅛ x 25½in.
(Skinner Inc.) $850

'Martini', by Louis Icart, etching and drypoint, printed in colors, signed lower right with artist's blindstamp, numbered 52 *Copyright 1932 by L. Icart Sty. N.Y.*, 34cm. x 44cm.
(Christie's) $9,790

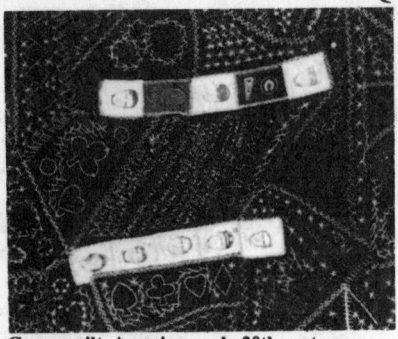

**Crazy quilt, America, early 20th century, comprised of various silk and velvet patches including printed tobacco silks depicting baseball players, 68 x 74in. (Skinner Inc.) $700**

**A Tree of Life variation quilt, composed of black and yellow sprigged cottons arranged as a series of trees, 74in. x 64in., American, late 19th century. (Christie's S. Ken) $650**

**A pieced and appliqued cotton quilted coverlet, American, mid 19th century, worked in red and green cotton with forty-two squares of various designs including floral motifs, 67 x 80in. (Christie's) $5,000**

**A pieced and appliqued cotton quilted coverlet, Mary Swartz, Shiloh, Ohio, 1853, the central floral medallion with appliqued tulips, posies and roses in yellow, red and green cotton, 80 x 78in. (Christie's) $5,000**

**A pieced and appliqued cotton quilted coverlet, Hawaii, 20th century, with four elaborate fern-like spokes radiating from the openwork center medallion, 80 x 90in. (Christie's) $1,100**

**A pieced and appliqued cotton quilted coverlet, North Carolina, circa 1850, worked in the Whigs defeated and rose pattern with red cotton and with green and yellow calico, 84 x 88½in. (Christie's) $1,650**

A pieced cotton quilted coverlet, Pennsylvania, 1860, with a central pieced blue calico square comprised of nine pieced fugitive yellow stars from which radiate vertical and horizontal blue calico bands with pieced yellow stars, 78 x 87in.
(Christie's) $1,600

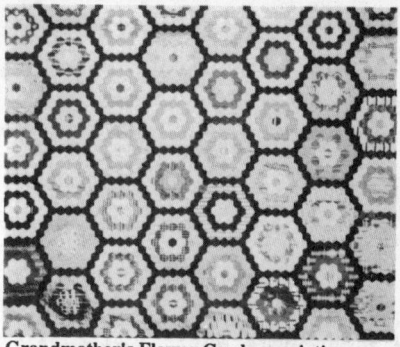

A Grandmother's Flower Garden variation patchwork coverlet composed of various figured silks arranged in a series of hexagons, 76 x 88in., circa 1850.(Christie's S. Ken) $522

A patchwork cover top, composed of long hexagon patches of various figured silks, including tartan, 82in. square, with original templates intact, circa 1850s.
(Christie's S. Ken) $374

Pieced, appliqued and embroidered silk and velvet crazy quilt, initialed *L.A.S. 1885*, silk backing, 6ft. x 6ft. 1in.
(Skinner Inc.) $700

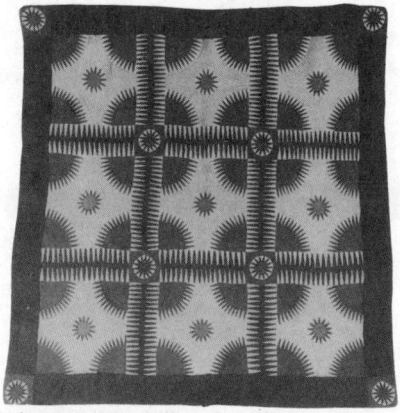

A pieced cotton quilted coverlet, American, late 19th century, worked in nine blocks of New York Beauty pattern embellished with star flower medallions, 88 x 88in.
(Christie's) $1,430

A framed patchwork quilt, composed of various floral printed patches arranged around a central panel, with the name *Eliza Westray, 1812* worked in blue silk, 86 x 92in.
(Christie's S. Ken) $903

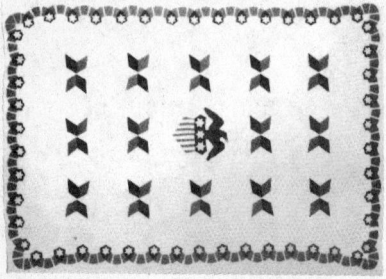

Pieced and appliquéd quilt, America, late 19th/ early 20th century, red, white, navy blue and brown patches arranged in patriotic design, heightened with diamond, 89 x 66in.
(Skinner Inc.) $850

Crazy quilt, America, late 19th century, various velvet and silk patches, arranged in fan pattern and heightened with embroidery, 80 x 62in.
(Skinner Inc.) $700

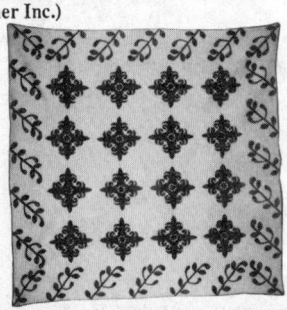

Appliquéd quilt, America, 19th century, pattern of shaped medallions enclosed by a vine border worked in red and green printed cotton patches and heightened with compotes of flowers, 88 x 89in.
(Skinner Inc.) $750

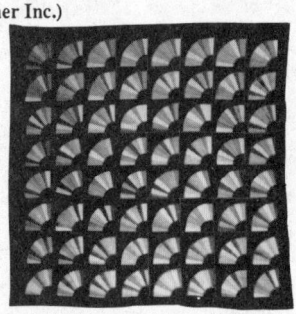

Patchwork Amish coverlet, probably Pennsylvania or Ohio, early 20th century, fan pattern worked in cotton sateen in solid shades of purple, blue, green, pink, yellow, brown and black, 81 x 77in.
(Skinner Inc.) $650

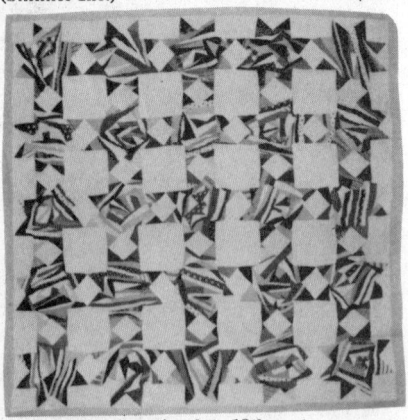

Pieced quilt, America, late 19th century, a "crazy star" pattern worked in various calico patches, heightened with diamond and parallel line quilting, 81 x 86in.
(Skinner Inc.) $500

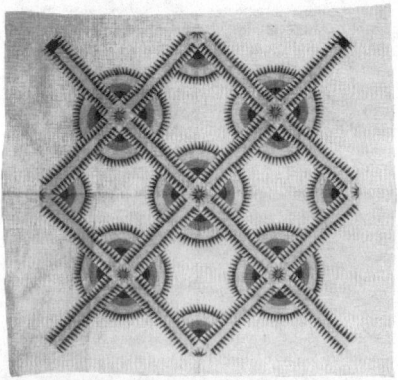

A pieced and appliqued cotton quilted coverlet, American, circa 1870, worked in a New York Beauty pattern variation with five full circles quartered by intersecting sawtooth-edged bands, 84 x 74in.
(Christie's) $550

Album quilt, America, mid 19th century, floral, pictorial and geometric squares marked with various solid and printed cotton patches, 84 x 84in.
(Skinner Inc.) $2,800

Crazy quilt, America, late 19th century, various color satin and velvet patches embellished with floral, figural and geometric embroidery, 78 x 70in.
(Skinner Inc.) $400

Embroidered wool coverlet, America, first half 19th century, the madder homespun ground embroidered with wool yarns in shades of blue, green, pink and yellow.
(Skinner Inc.) $1,200

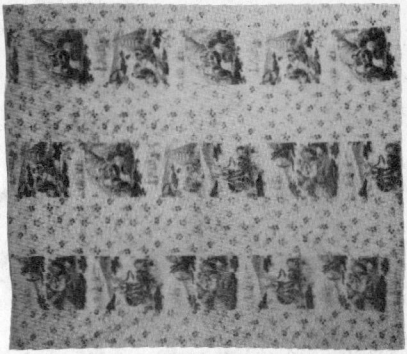

Strip quilt, early 19th century, comprised of bands of copper plate printed "British Naval Heroes", 86 x 91in.
(Skinner Inc.) $475

Pieced, appliquéd and embroidered silk and velvet crazy quilt, America, late 19th century, 70 x 70in.
(Skinner Inc.) $950

Appliquéd quilt, possibly Pennsylvania, with cross stitch inscription *Pieced by Grand Mother Statira Pease, Aged 82 Years May 8th 1856*, heightened with conforming floral and diamond quilting, 70 x 72in.
(Skinner Inc.) $700

An Ekco Model 313 AC mains receiver in horizontal brown bakelite case, 16¾in. wide, circa 1930, and a Celestion speaker in mahogany case.
(Christie's S. Ken) $368

A Gecophone 'Victor 3' three-valve receiver in crinkle finish metal case with hinged lid, and an Orphean horn speaker.
(Christie's S. Ken) $348

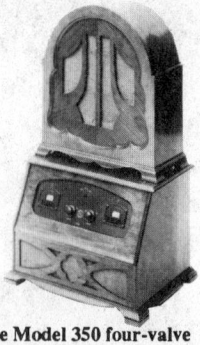

A Pye Model 350 four-valve receiver in horizontal walnut case with sloping control panel above fret, 17in. wide, and a Celestion Model 79 speaker in arched case.
(Christie's S. Ken) $450

An Ekco R.S.2 3-valve mains receiver in Art Deco style brown bakelite case with triple speaker grille, 16¼in. high.
(Christie's S. Ken) $225

A Gecophone Type BC 2001 3-valve receiver in walnut case with door enclosing control panel and battery compartment below.
(Christie's S. Ken) $920

A Pilot Model U-650 six-valve receiver in upright walnut veneered case with circular tuning dial with 'Magic Eye', 19½in. high.
(Christie's S. Ken) $532

An Ekco Type AD65 AC/DC mains receiver in circular brown bakelite case with semi-circular dial, 15½in. diameter.
(Christie's S. Ken) $389

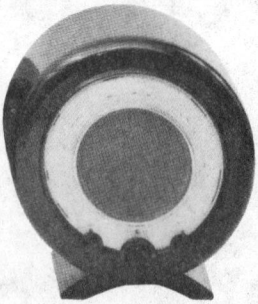

An Ekco Type A22 AC mains receiver in circular black bakelite case with circular dial, 13¼in. diameter.
(Christie's S. Ken) $982

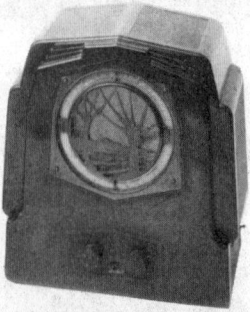

An Ekco Type BS3 AC mains receiver in black Art Deco case with oxidized metal grille formed as stylized trees, 17¾in. high.
(Christie's S. Ken) $716

Ko-Yoshiya, Japanese tinplate Planet Robot finished in metallic blue and red with battery operated remote-control, 22cm. high.
(Phillips) $153

An unusual silver Horikawa Attacking Martian robot, in original box.
(Christie's S. Ken) $689

A Yonezawa for Cragstan battery-operated tinplate 'Mr Robot', same body pressing as 'Talking Robot', 1960's.
(Christie's S. Ken) $568

A Nomura painted tinplate 'Battery Operated Mechanised Robot' ("Robbie the Robot"), with black body, red arms and feet, circa 1956, 13in. high.
(Christie's S. Ken) $2,729

A Yonezawa friction drive tinplate 'Talking Robot' with battery operated speech mechanism, retailed by Cragstan, in original box, circa 1960's
(Christie's S. Ken) $823

Ko-Yoshiya, Japanese tinplate clockwork Planet Robot finished in black and red, with sparking face in color picture box, 22cm. high.
(Phillips) $374

A Horikawa battery operated tinplate 'Fighting Robot', with transparent plastic chest cover, 1960's.
(Christie's S. Ken) $400

A Yonezawa 'Space Explorer' No. 802, finished in brown, transforming from a TV set into a battery operated walking robot, in original box, early 1960's.
(Christie's S. Ken) $975

Alps-Shoji, battery operated Robot Television Spaceman, 38cm. including aeriel, in working order.
(Phillips) $289

An album cover, The Travelling Wilburys, signed on the front by George Harrison and Tom Petty in black and blue felt pen.
(Christie's S. Ken) $295

David Bowie, original photomontage artwork for Fashion 12 inch and 7 inch single covers, 1980, signed and inscribed by artist Edward Bell.
(Christie's S. Ken) $1,580

An album cover, Never Mind The Bollocks Here's The Sex Pistols, Virgin Records, 1977, signed *Rotten, Jones, Sid V., Paul Cook – at Virgin and Boogie!*
(Christie's S. Ken) $843

An illustrated souvenir concert programme, New Victoria Theatre, 24th August, 1976, signed on the cover *Luck, Fats Domino.*
(Christie's S. Ken) $590

An Epiphone Bard acoustic guitar, in natural finish, and corresponding case stenciled with white lettering *Cream*, played by Eric Clapton circa 1966–1968.
(Christie's S. Ken)
$10,533

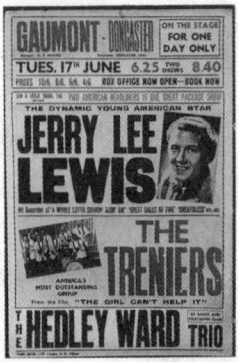


A rare concert bill for Jerry Lee Lewis's canceled tour, advertising a concert at the Gaumont Theatre, Doncaster, 1958, 15 x 10in.
(Christie's S. Ken) $800

Live Aid, a color machine-print photograph of Paul McCartney and Pete Townshend carrying Bob Geldof on their shoulders during the Live Aid concert, signed by all three subjects.
(Christie's S. Ken) $1,053

A rare page of handwritten lyrics, Cars Hiss By My Window – a song on The Doors' last album, L.A. Woman, 1971, on yellow lined paper, inscribed at head of page *J.M./Doors.*
(Christie's S. Ken)
$5,477

A presentation 'Gold' disc, Morrison Hotel, *Presented to The Doors To Commemorate The SaleOf More Than One Million Dollars Worth.*
(Christie's S. Ken)
$2,528

**The Blues Brothers, an album cover, Briefcase Full of Blues, 1978, signed and inscribed *Dan Akroyd and Stay Cool, John Belushi.***
**(Christie's S. Ken) $1,159**

**An album cover, Born To Run, signed on the front by Bruce Springsteen, Clarence Clemons, Max Weinberg, Danny Federici, Garry Tallent, Roy Bittan and Nils Lofgren.**
**(Christie's S. Ken) $590**

**An album cover, Andy Warhol, signed by subject in black felt pen, 12 x 12in.**
**(Christie's S. Ken) $1,159**

**A copy of the Glasgow Evening Citizen newspaper, Saturday, 5th October, 1963, autographed by all four Beatles in blue biro, 23½ x 16in.**
**(Christie's S. Ken) $800**

**Stevie Wonder, a presentation 'Gold' disc, *Presented to Stevie Wonder to recognise the sale, in the United Kingdom, of more than £250,000 worth of the album 'Songs in the Key of Life' 1976.***
**(Christie's S. Ken)**
**$2,528**

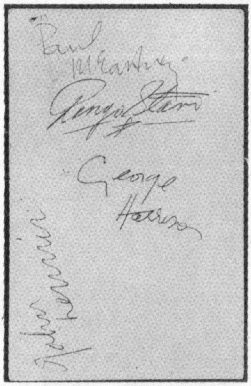


**The Beatles, a Parlophone Records publicity postcard, circa 1962, signed on the reverse by each member of the group, 3½ x 5½in.**
**(Christie's S. Ken) $506**

**Jim Morrison, a piece of paper signed and inscribed *Cheers Morrison*, in common mount with a half-length machine-print photograph.**
**(Christie's S. Ken)**
**$2,949**

**A black-and-white print of the four Beatles performing on stage during rehearsals for The Royal Variety Performance, 4th November 1963, 3½ x 3½in., sold with negative and copyright.**
**(Christie's S. Ken) $1,264**

**A presentation 'Gold' disc, *Presented to The Jackson Five to commemorate the sale of more than 500,000 copies of the Motown Records album, "Dancing Machine".***
**(Christie's S. Ken) $948**

**A group photograph, circa 1964, signed by John Lennon, Paul McCartney, Ringo Starr and George Harrison, 6½ x 8½in., framed.**
**(Christie's S. Ken) $1,475**

**A souvenir table lamp, the yellow metal base and paper shade printed with the Beatles portraits and their facsimile signatures, 12in. high.**
**(Christie's S. Ken) $506**

**An early promotional postcard for Come On and I Wanna Be Your Man 1963, signed on the front by each member of The Rolling Stones, 4¼ x 5½in.**
**(Christie's S. Ken) $548**

**Jimi Hendrix, a silk screen print poster in gouache and gilt, 50 x 38in.**
**(Christie's S. Ken) $548**

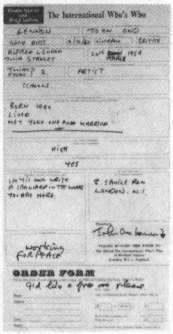


**An entry form for The International Who's Who 1969–1970, completed in Lennon's hand, giving various personal details, signed John Ono Lennon, with ink receipt stamp dated 21 May 1969, 16 x 9in.**
**(Christie's S. Ken) $4,424**

**Keith Richards, signed 8" x 10", full length playing guitar, slight smudging.**
**(T. Vennett-Smith) $61**

**A publicity photograph by Robert Whitaker, 1966, signed by all four members of the group in two different colored inks, 7½ x 6in.**
**(Christie's S. Ken) $843**

**Michael Jackson's grey and blue denim hat decorated with an elaborate pattern of colored sequins and mirror-work, inscribed *Mike* in pencil inside the brim.**
**(Christie's S. Ken) $800**

**Chubby Checker, signed and inscribed vintage 8" x 10", full length in classic 'twist' pose, slight corner creasing.**
**(T. Vennett-Smith) $57**

David Bowie, original photomontage for Scary Monsters album cover, signed by artist Edward Bell, dated 1980, 10½ x 13in., framed.
(Christie's S. Ken) $4,213

John Somerville, Imagine, limited edition, polished bronze of John Lennon, 1983, numbered 4 from an edition limited to 20.
(Christie's S. Ken) $3,581

Peter Sander TV cartoon series, 1964 –The Performing Beatles, gouache on celluloid, 8⅝ x 13½in., This image was used on the cover of a Beatles Tour programme, 1965.
(Christie's S. Ken) $1,159

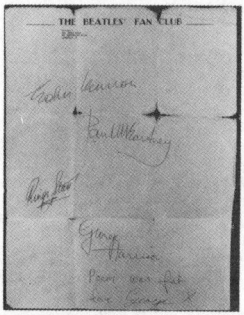


A sheet of The Beatles' Fan Club headed paper signed by all four members of the group in blue biro and additionally signed and inscribed by George Harrison *Poem was fab love George x.*
(Christie's S. Ken) $632

The Sex Pistols, a promotional poster for Never Mind The Bollocks, signed by all members of the band including Sid Vicious, Jonny Rotten, Paul Cook, Steve Jones and Malcolm McLaren, 35 x 24½in.
(Christie's S. Ken) $1,791

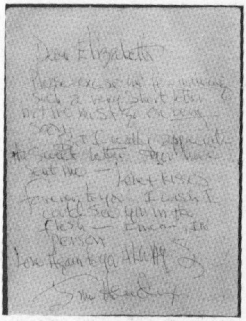

An autograph letter signed to a fan by Jimi Hendrix [n.d. but 1967], written prior to a performance, *I wish I could see you in the flesh – I mean in person.*
(Christie's S. Ken) $2,738

An album, A Hard Day's Night, Parlophone, 1964, signed on the back cover by all four members of The Beatles in black biro.
(Christie's S. Ken) $948

An autographed tambourine, the clear perspex skin signed and inscribed *Thanks for your help! Cheers Phil Collins 89* and annotated with self portrait caricature of a drummer.
(Christie's S. Ken) $674

The Beatles, an official fan club card, 1963, the Dezo Hoffmann photograph signed by each member of the group in black biro, 4¼ x 5½in.
(Christie's S. Ken) $800

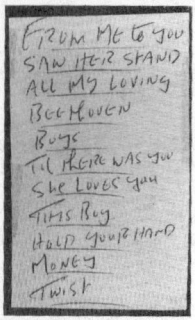


A rare handwritten playlist by John Lennon for a Beatles concert 1964, with ten abbreviated song titles, 3¾ x 2½in.
(Christie's S. Ken) $3,792

A pair of slate-gray suede shoes fastening at the side with a brass clip with maker's name *Thom McAn*, worn by Buddy Holly during the late 1950s.
(Christie's) $774

A small lock of hair mounted beside a machine-print photograph of Lennon on a page from an autograph album signed and inscribed *Love from "Bald" John Lennon.*
(Christie's S. Ken) $737

A black leather biker's jacket decorated on the back with chrome studs and a hand-painted design, used in George Michael's Freedom video.
(Christie's) $2,948

A set of four Bobb'n Head Beatles character dolls, each composition with spring mounted enlarged head, by Car Mascots Inc., 1964, 8in. high.
(Christie's S. Ken) $379

John Somerville, Mick Jagger, Limited edition, bronze, numbered 2 from an edition limited to 20, signed by the sculptor, 25in. high.
(Christie's S. Ken) $2,317

The Beatles, an album, A Hard Day's Night, Parlophone, 1964, signed on the back cover by all four members of the group.
(Christie's) $1,013

A Fender Stratocaster guitar, in metallic aquamarine, the body signed by Mark Knopfler in gold felt pen; with corresponding Fender case.
(Christie's S. Ken) $1,264

A baking tray, signed on the base by John and Yoko in blue and black felt pen and dated 1969, 4¾in. diameter.
(Christie's) $553

A studio photograph by Robert Freeman of The Beatles holding umbrellas, 1963, signed by each member of the group, 12 x 15in. (Christie's S. Ken) $2,107

A wide-brimmed black felt hat allegedly owned by John Lennon and worn by him in the photograph on the cover of A Spaniard In The Works, 1965. (Christie's S. Ken) $1,791

An ivory crepe shirt and a rust colored cotton cap, worn by David Bowie in the 1969 film Love You Till Tuesday. (Christie's S. Ken) $1,159

Sam Cooke, Dion and others, a rare early concert poster from The Vets Memorial Auditorium, Columbus, Fri October 4th, 8:15pm, 1963, featuring Sam Cooke, Dion, Bobby Blue Bland, TNT with Al Braggs, 35½ x 22in. (Christie's) $1,382

A set of four glasses, each transfer printed with an individual facial portrait of a Beatle and their names, 4in. high, circa 1964. (Christie's S. Ken) $316

The Beatles, an illustrated page from a concert programme at the Winter Gardens, Margate, circa 1963, signed by each member of the group, 9 x 5¾in. (Christie's) $1,013

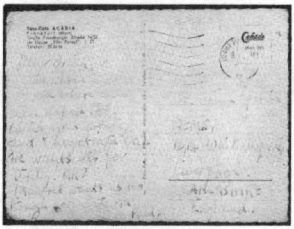

Paul McCartney, an early autograph postcard picturing Tanz-Café Acadia, Frankfurt, signed, to Brian Epstein regarding a possible booking. (Christie's) $921

A Gibson Les Paul Deluxe, in black, maple neck and rosewood fingerboard, the body signed *Les Paul* and *Les Paul Jr.* in silver felt pen. (Christie's S. Ken) $6,320

A piece of paper inscribed to a fan, annotated with a psychedelic doodle and signed *Love & Kisses to you FOREVER, Jimi Hendrix EXPERIENCE.* (Christie's) $884

East Anatolian Yastik, late 19th/ early 20th century, the column of four rust rectangles each inset with a hooked diamond, 2ft. 10in. x 1ft. 8in.
(Skinner Inc.) $200

Northwest Persian saltbag, early 20th century, the horizontal panels with brocade decoration, 1ft. 9in. x 1ft.
(Skinner Inc.) $300

Yomud Ensi rug, West Turkestan, late 19th/early 20th century, the chestnut brown field quartered into rectangles, 5ft. 11in. x 4ft.
(Skinner Inc.) $475

Kazak prayer rug, Southwest Caucasus, late 19th century, four gabled rectangular medallions in midnight and royal blue, 4ft. 3in. x 3ft.
(Skinner Inc.) $650

Fachralo Kazak rug, Southwest Caucasus, late 19th century, the red field with two blue and one green joined horizontal medallions, 4ft. x 3ft. 4in.
(Skinner Inc.) $3,250

Avar rug, Northeast Caucasus, late 19th century, the bold red "many-necked house" design decorates the medium blue field, 4ft. 10in. x 3ft.
(Skinner Inc.) $450

Shirvan rug, East Caucasus, last quarter 19th century, rows of red, ivory and royal blue flowerheads decorate the midnight blue field, 5ft. 8in. x 4ft. 2in.
(Skinner Inc.) $2,400

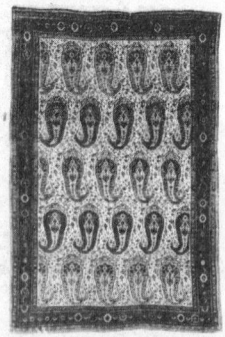

Senneh rug, Northwest Persia, late 19th century, staggered rows of large elaborately drawn boteh in shades of royal blue, red, rose, gold and blue-green, 7ft. x 4ft. 10in.
(Skinner Inc.) $3,000

Bahktiari rug, Southwest Persia, early 20th century, the square grid enclosing palmettes, weeping willow motifs, and blossoming branches, 7ft. 2in. x 4ft. 8in.
(Skinner Inc.) $2,500

Shirvan Kelim, East Caucasus, last quarter 19th century, broad red and navy blue bands inset with ivory and red stepped hexagons, 10ft. 8in. x 5ft. 6in.
(Skinner Inc.) $750

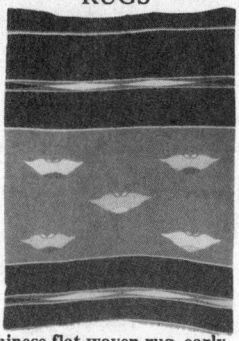

Chinese flat-woven rug, early 20th century, the center soft coral panel with five lime and ivory elliptical floral motifs, 5ft. 8in. x 4ft. 5in.
(Skinner Inc.) $300

Kurdish corridor rug, Northwest Persia, late 19th century, the midnight blue field features an overall diamond lattice, 9ft. 10in. x 5ft.
(Skinner Inc.) $800

Northwest Persian rug, late 19th/early 20th century, the bright red field with large ivory indented medallion, 6ft. 3in. x 4ft. 11in.
(Skinner Inc.) $600

Yomud Salatshak, West Turkestan, early 20th century, columns of midnight blue, red, apricot and ivory geometric figures, 4ft. 6in. x 3ft. 10in.
(Skinner Inc.) $800

Kurd pictorial rug, Northwest Persia, late 19th century, the ivory field features a horse and rider, lion and family group, 5ft. 8in. x 3ft. 4in.
(Skinner Inc.) $425

Malayer Sarouk rug, West Persia, early 20th century, the rose and sky blue scalloped circular medallion rests on the navy blue field, 6ft. 6in. x 4ft. 8in.
(Skinner Inc.) $1,800

Karapinar rug, Central Anatolia, late 19th/early 20th century, the large ivory and green hexagonal medallion nearly covers the light red-brown field, 5ft. 4in. x 3ft. 10in.
(Skinner Inc.) $1,300

Lori Pambak Kazak rug, Southwest Caucasus, late 19th/early 20th century, three characteristic navy and medium blue octagonal medallions decorate the red field, 9ft. x 5ft.
(Skinner Inc.) $750

Southeast Anatolian Kelim, late 19th century, the ivory field with two columns of large stepped medallions in shades of moss green, soft red, brown, denim blue, magenta and mustard, 4ft. 6in. x 3ft. 7in.
(Skinner Inc.) $800

Konya area prayer rug, Central Anatolia, mid 19th century, (small areas of restoration), 5ft. 2in. x 3ft. 8in.
(Skinner Inc.) $14,000

Malayer-Sarouk prayer rug, West Persia, second half 19th century, the midnight blue abrashed field supports the triple column prayer arch, 6ft. 3in. x 4ft. 3in.
(Skinner Inc.) $6,000

Kazak rug, Southwest Caucasus, late 19th century, the central ivory octagonal medallion flanked by two navy blue stepped medallions, 8ft. x 6ft. 5in.
(Skinner Inc.) $2,750

Baluch bagface, Northeast Persia, last quarter 19th century, the red octagonal medallion surrounded by animal and geometric motifs, 2ft. 8in. x 2ft. 8in.
(Skinner Inc.) $550

Konagend rug, Northwest Caucasus, early 20th century, the sky blue and rose central medallion flanked by four abrashed red octagons, 5ft. 6in. x 3ft. 9in.
(Skinner Inc.) $1,800

Shirvan rug, East Caucasus, late 19th century, the abrashed mustard-gold field with octagonal lattice of palmettes, 5ft. 6in. x 3ft. 10in.
(Skinner Inc.) $1,600

Shirvan rug, East Caucasus, late 19th century, the dark brown field with six columns of confronting animals, 5ft. x 4ft. 3in.
(Skinner Inc.) $3,000

Shirvan rug, East Caucasus, late 19th century, the ivory field with overall Chi-Chi design in shades of dark red, blue, rose and beige, 5ft. 6in. x 3ft. 8in.
(Skinner Inc.) $1,100

Malayer rug, West Persia, late 19th century, in shades of blue, rose, gold and light teal, 6ft. 8in. x 4ft. 6in.
(Skinner Inc.) $1,600

Kuba rug, Northeast Caucasus, late 19th century, the gold field with rows of flowering shrubs, 3ft. 10in. x 2ft. 11in.
(Skinner Inc.) $850

Quchan Kurdish rug, Northeast Persia, late 19th century, the so-called hauzi design of two navy blue rectangular medallions with six gabled and square projections, 7ft. 9in. x 5ft. 5in.
(Skinner Inc.) $4,000

Karabagh prayer rug, South Caucasus, late 19th century, the diamond lattice of red, sky blue, gold and green flowering plants covers the midnight blue field, 4ft. 5in. x 2ft. 8in.
(Skinner Inc.) $1,500

One of a pair of Soumak bags, Northwest Persia, South Caucasus, second half 19th century, the ivory star-filled hooked octagon rests on a teal blue field, both 1ft. 8in. by 1ft. 6in.
(Skinner Inc.)
(Two) $2,750

Kazak rug, Southwest Caucasus, late 19th century, the red field contains the Lori Pambak design of a large elongated octagonal ivory medallion, 10ft. 2in. x 5ft. 10in.
(Skinner Inc.) $7,000

Shirvan rug, East Caucasus, late 19th/early 20th century, the abrashed brick red field lavishly decorated with human figures and animals, 5ft. 6in. x 3ft. 9in.
(Skinner Inc.) $4,250

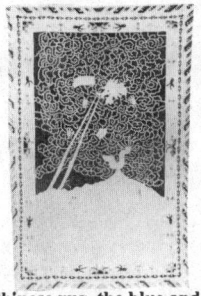

A Chinese rug, the blue and beige field with cloudbands, dragon and geometric motifs within a beige border, 7ft. 9in. x 5ft. 3in.
(Christie's S. Ken) $1,064

Karagashli rug, East Caucasus, late 19th century, two stepped diamond medallions flanked by two bright red flowerheads decorate the navy blue field, 6ft. 6in. x 3ft. 10in.
(Skinner Inc.) $2,700

A mid 17th century unfinished linen sampler with six bands of reticella work, depicting strawberries and acorns, 90 x 13cm., English.
(Phillips) $1,748

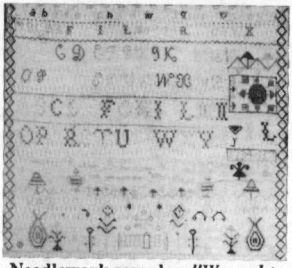

Needlework sampler, *"Wrought by Roxanne Lyard of Cabot, Vt. aged 20, born December the 23rd, 1801–21"*, rows of alphabets over inscription and panel, 12¾ x 14½in.
(Skinner Inc.) $600

A needlework sampler worked in colored silks with the alphabet by Mary Barne, February 26 1785, 16¾ x 11½in.
(Christie's) $741

Needlework sampler, worked by *"Sarah Elizabeth Wright, Aged 18 Years"*, Massachusetts, dated *"1821"*, 15¾ x 17in.
(Skinner Inc.) $1,100

Needlework sampler, *Betsy Patten born September 1802, aged 11 A.D. 1812 Mary Cummings instructress*, Westford, Massachusetts, 17 x 17in.
(Skinner Inc.) $450

Needlework sampler, *"Sally Harringtons Work 1808"*, New England, worked in silk threads, 25 x 19½in.
(Skinner Inc.) $2,100

Needlework sampler, *Chloe E. Trask's work wrought in the year 18...*, probably Massachusetts, worked in silk threads, 15¾ x 16½in.
(Skinner Inc.) $650

An early 19th century sampler of silk cross-stitch on tammy cloth, portraying a house with a green roof in a garden with a fence, worked by Jane Peskett aged 10 years, 1824, English, 40 x 32cm.
(Phillips) $840

Needlework sampler, probably England, dated 1804, worked in shades of red, green, blue and cream silk threads, 12¾in. wide.
(Skinner Inc.) $300

Needlework sampler, *Rachel McClure, New York, 1760*, worked with silk threads in shades of blue, green, yellow and brown, 16 x 14in.
(Skinner Inc.) $4,250

Needlework sampler, *Mary L. Montagu, A.D. 1828 AE 11 yrs.*, worked in silk threads in shades of black, green, blue and tan, 18¾ x 13¾in.
(Skinner Inc.) $150

Needlework sampler, worked by *"Ruthy Long Poor born Oct. 28 1801, Aged 13"*, Newburyport, Massachusetts, 1814, 11¼ x 8¾in.
(Skinner Inc.) $800

An early 19th century sampler, *Mary Ann Healey's work July 28 1809*, the undyed tammy cloth ground designed with a central prayer worked in black cross-stitch, English, 41.5cm. x 30.5cm.
(Phillips) $1,517

A mid 19th century needlework sampler, wool on canvas, depicting a colorful bead eyed bird in a stylized tree, by *'Emma Collinson Aged 9 years 1844'*, 47 x 43cm.
(Phillips) $662

A late 18th century needlework sampler by Isabella Cunningham, the linen ground worked in blue, green, yellow, ivory and crimson silk threads, 38cm. x 30cm.
(Phillips) $846

Needlework sampler, *Sally Goss*, probably Pennsylvania, rows of alphabets above inscription and verse over a panel of flowering trees, 11½ x 15¾in.
(Skinner Inc.) $1,600

Late 18th century English sampler, depicting a house, figure of a Major Domo, trees, flowers, and more, 11in. x 13in.
(Eldred's) $468

An early 19th century sampler dated 1803, by *Ann Wilson Aged 11*, the tammy cloth ground worked in colored silk threads with pious verse and family names, Scottish, 44.5cm. x 32cm.
(Phillips) $971

Clemens Müller hand cranked plinth machine with chain stitch, circa 1875.
(Auction Team Köln) $336

German Casige child's sewing machine, 1918.
(Auction Team Köln) $428

Jones swivel shuttle machine in original wooden case, circa 1885.
(Auction Team Köln) $296

A Whight & Mann Prima Donna sewing machine, with good gilt decorations and instructions.
(Phillips) $1,745

Clemens Müller chain stitch sewing machine without gripper on attractive 3 footed stand by E Pruchner, formerly E Boissier, Berlin, circa 1875.
(Auction Team Köln) $2,027

Union Special industrial sewing machine by the Union Special Machine Co Chicago USA, circa 1910.
(Auction Team Köln) $141

The Gresham bow shuttle machine circa 1875, without shuttle.
(Auction Team Köln) $663

Weir chain stitch machine described as 'The Globe', 1885, in original metal case, without shuttle.
(Auction Team Köln) $390

German Casige child's sewing machine made in 'British Zone', circa 1950.
(Auction Team Köln) $124

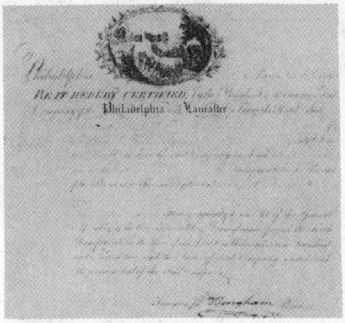

**Philadelphia and Lancaster Turnpike Road 1795, One share, the earliest known U.S. certificate with a vignette, black print on vellum, hand signed by W. Bingham. (Phillips) $404**

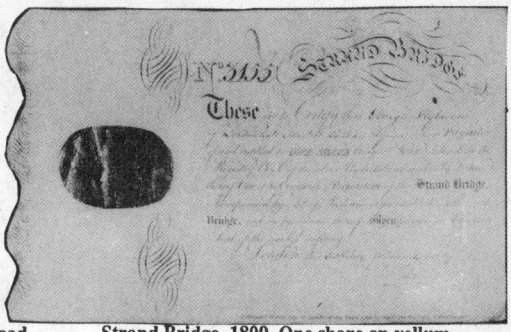

**Strand Bridge, 1809. One share on vellum. Large gold embossed seal depicting the bridge. (Phillips) $623**

**South Africa: The Great Kruger Gold Mining Co. Ltd. 1889. £1 shares, several attractive vignettes. (Phillips) $337**

**Spain: Compania General De Coches De Lujo. Madrid 1909, bearer share cert. for 1 x 500 Pesetas, large vignette of coach and horses. (Phillips) $169**

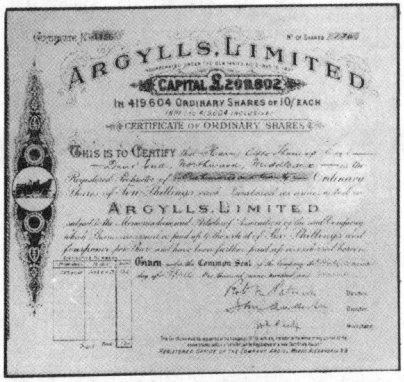

**Argylls, Ltd. 1909. Ord. 10/- shares, very early car manufacture, vignette of car of that period, embossed seal depicting the car. (Phillips) $126**

**Whitehead Aircraft (1917) Ltd. 1919. Deferred 1/- Ordinary shares. Vignettes of biplanes and busy airfield, also large biplane in R.A.F. markings on underprint. Yellow/black on white. (Phillips) $404**

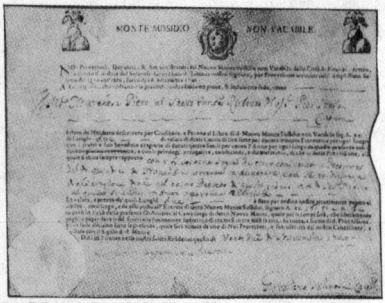


**Italy: Monte Sussidio Non Vacabile della Citta di Firenze 22nd November 1700, an interest bearing deposit receipt di Luoghi "Due", paying 4% per annum.**
**(Phillips) $539**

**Japan: Osaka City Harbour Construction Loan 6%, 1933. 1,000 Yen bearer bond with coupons, attractive vignettes of Osaka Bay and Castle.**
**(Phillips) $843**

**The Michigan Central Railroad 1881 $5,000 bond issued to W.H. VANDERBILT and signed by C. VANDERBILT as Vice President.**
**(Phillips) $736**

**The Pere Marquette Transportation Co. 1897. One $1,000 Bond. 200 bonds issued for the payment in construction of the car ferry steamboat called "The Pere Marquette".**
**(Phillips) $214**

**Republic of China 6% 2 Year Gold Treasury Notes 1919. $1,000 bond with original coupons and 14 script certificates attached.**
**(Phillips) $472**

**Italy: Monte Della Citta di Firenze 6th July 1752, an interest bearing deposit receipt di Luoghi "Quattro", paying 3% per annum.**
**(Phillips) $640**

**The Mobile & Alabama Grand Trunk Railroad Co. 1874, large attractive $1,000 bond with five vignettes.**
**(Phillips) $843**

**Union Gold Mining Company 1834, bearer certificate for 5 x $100 shares. Incorporated as a Chartered Company in January 1834, by an Act of the Legislature of Virginia, United States of North America. Corporate Seal of the Company at Philadelphia.**
**(Phillips) $539**

**Deal and Walmer Coalfield, Ltd. 1912. £1 Ordinary shares. Vignettes of Deal Castle and Walmer Castle.**
**(Phillips) $101**

**Tattersall's (of Chicago) Ltd. 1891. £5 shares. Capital £52,500. Cert. No. 5 for 5 Founders shares and Cert. No. 84 for 20 Ordinary shares.**
**(Phillips) $135**

**Italy: Monte Redimi Bile Secondo della Citta di Firenze 14 July 1734, an interest bearing deposit receipt di Luoghi "Ventidue", paying $3^1/_2$% per annum.**
**(Phillips) $472**

A fine lacquer and Shibayama kodansu, the exterior decorated on three sides with wheeling cranes and on the top with a bird of prey, Meiji period, 12.75cm. high.
(Hy. Duke & Son) $14,000

A spherical tripod koro and cover, decorated in Shibayama style on a gold lacquer ground, the body with birds on a blossoming branch and two oni at kubi-hiki represented in shippo, signed *Gyokukendo*, late 19th century, 19cm. high.
(Christie's) $13,552

A silver filigree mounted Shibayama inlaid ivory tray, the center with a peacock standing majestically on a rocky outcrop and a peahen below, signed *Naoyuki*, Meiji period (1868–1912), 30.1cm. long.
(Christie's) $6,068

Red lacquer corner cabinet with gilt lacquer and mother-of-pearl overlay panels, Meiji period, the upper section with a curved curio shelf above two sliding doors overlaid in Shibayama style, 32in. wide.
(Butterfield & Butterfield) $7,150

A Shibayama tusk vase decorated with geese, butterflies, bees, dragonflies, flowering grasses and chrysanthemums, Meiji period, 14.5cm. wide.
(Hy. Duke & Son) $700

A fine lozenge-shaped gold lacquer vase, the sides decorated in gold hiramakie, takamakie, okibirame, kirikane, kimpun, hirame and Shibayama style with Shoki searching for oni in the stream, unsigned, 19th century, 18.5cm. high, with European fitted box.
(Christie's) $19,360

A pair of silver vases decorated in Shibayama style on a gold lacquer ground, the panels depicting birds perched on flowering boughs and panniers, signed *Teiko*, Meiji period (1868–1912), 17cm. high.
(Christie's) $8,235

A late 19th century Japanese Shibayama ivory tusk section vase, applied with carved and stained ivory reliefs of a young lady wearing fine robes, 1ft. 3in. high.
(Spencer's) $3,401

A Shibayama box and cover, carved in low relief with branches inhabited with doves, the lid with a finial of a hen and chicks, 3¼in. high.
(Lawrence Fine Art) $759

Malcolm Campbell postcard, inscribed *with my best wishes.*
(Onslow's) $352

A full length photograph of Winston Churchill seated on a horse 11 x 9½in. mounted on card signed *W.S. Churchill, 1948.*
(Christie's S. Ken) $2,567

Richard Seaman signed postcard.
(Onslow's) $651

Tsar Nicolas II, a head and shoulders portrait photograph, signed and inscribed *Nicolas, Balmoral, Sept. 1896*, mounted on card, 11½ x 7in.
(Christie's S. Ken) $3,637

Oscar Wilde, a head and shoulders portrait photograph, signed and inscribed *Bobbie, from his friend OW*, mounted on card, 9½ x 7¼in.
(Christie's S. Ken) $3,209

A cabinet card studio portrait of the young Winston Churchill in tropical uniform probably taken in Egypt prior to the Omdurman campaign, 1898, signed *Winston*, 8 x 5in.
(Christie's S. Ken) $5,134

A three quarter length portrait photograph by Hugh Cecil of H.R.H. Prince Edward in Admiral's full dress uniform, signed and inscribed *Edward, 1939*, 12½ x 10½in.
(Christie's S. Ken) $599

Winston Churchill, a head and shoulders portrait photograph 5½ x 4½in. mounted on card signed *W.S. Churchill.*
(Christie's S. Ken) $1,284

A portrait photograph of H.M. Queen Victoria, by A. Bassano, signed and inscribed *Victoris R.I. 1899*, mounted on card, 12½ x 10½in.
(Christie's S. Ken) $1,498

Al Jolson, signed 7" x 5", head and shoulders, corner crease.
(T. Vennett-Smith) $181

Apollo 11, signed and inscribed color 8" x 10" by Neil Armstrong, Michael Collins and Buzz Aldrin, three quarter length in space mount.
(T. Vennett-Smith) $411

Enrico Caruso, signed postcard, Buenos Aires 1915.
(T. Vennett-Smith) $191

Anna Pavlova, signed postcard, full length dancing, slightly trimmed to edges, some foxing to image.
(T. Vennett-Smith) $115

Trapp Family, a rare signed and inscribed 8" x 10" of the Trapp Family Singers, shown seated around a table.
(T. Vennett-Smith) $497

Andrew Lloyd Webber, signed 8" x 10", head and shoulders, minor stain to image.
(T. Vennett-Smith) $143

Sir Winston S. Churchill, signed postcard, full signature, head and shoulders, as Minister of the Navy, photo by Elliott and Fry.
(T. Vennett-Smith) $955

Adolf Hitler, signed, in pencil, portrait profile, smiling, oval image, rare, apparently signed for Heinrich Heim, Martin Bormann's Adjutant.
(T. Vennett-Smith) $649

King George V, signed 6" x 8.25", full length in ceremonial dress, 1898, weaker signature.
(T. Vennett-Smith) $181

Galina Ulanova, signed 8" x 10", full length dancing.
(T. Vennett-Smith) $105

Tony Zale and Rocky Graziano, signed 8" x 10", in boxing pose.
(T. Vennett-Smith) $59

Gustave Carpentier (1860–1956; French Composer), good signed and inscribed 6" x 4.25", head and shoulders, 1924.
(T. Vennett-Smith) $267

Ronald Reagan, signed 8" x 10", head and shoulders.
(T. Vennett-Smith) $171

Charles Lindbergh, signed 5" x 7.5" heavystock magazine photo, full length standing in front of the Spirit of St. Louis at Curtiss Field a few days prior to his historic airflight, 1927.
(T. Vennett-Smith) $1,241

Claudia Muzio, signed and inscribed 7" x 9.25", head and shoulders, Buenos Aires 1933.
(T. Vennett-Smith) $220

Anna Pavlova, boldly signed postcard, full length dancing with, but not signed by, Novikoff, in 'Amarilla'.
(T. Vennett-Smith) $248

Dwight D. Eisenhower, signed 8" x 10", to lower white border, with typed inscription, 'For Margaret Montgomery Zogbaum'.
(T. Vennett-Smith) $191

Neil Armstrong, signed and inscribed color 8" x 10", half length wearing spacesuit.
(T. Vennett-Smith) $229

Edith Piaf, signed and inscribed postcard, in French, rare, slight corner creasing.
(T. Vennett-Smith) $250

Jascha Heifetz, signed and inscribed 12" x 7.5", head and shoulders playing violin, "To A.E. Warren, In rememberance of my first concert in Calcutta Jascha Heifetz", 1927.
(T. Vennett-Smith) $325

Fats Waller, signed postcard, in green ink, full length seated, playing piano.
(T. Vennett-Smith) $191

Nellie Melba, good signed sepia postcard, full length in costume as Margarette.
(T. Vennett-Smith) $267

Captain Robert F. Scott, signed 5.25" x 7.5", half length in uniform, photo by J. Thomson of London.
(T. Vennett-Smith) $764

Grace Kelly, signed color 6" x 4", as Princess, full length seated surrounded by family.
(T. Vennett-Smith) $92

Mike Tyson, signed color 8" x 10", three quarter length in boxing pose.
(T. Vennett-Smith) $143

Colonel Gadaffi, signed color 5.25" x 7.25", head and shoulders, scarce, corner crease.
(T. Vennett-Smith) $95

Marc Chagall, signed magazine photo, in blue crayon, to lower white border.
(T. Vennett-Smith) $267

**Sir Winston S. Churchill, signed piece, in full, laid down to blue card beneath original 10" x 8" photo of Churchill and the Queen outside 10 Downing Street.**
**(T. Vennett-Smith) $382**

**Lord Alfred Tennyson, signed Carte-de-Visite photo, half length profile, rare in this form.**
**(T. Vennett-Smith) $344**

**Apollo 11, a good color signed 8" x 10" by Neil Armstrong, Buzz Aldrin and Michael Collins, showing Aldrin walking on the moon.**
**(T. Vennett-Smith) $583**

**Christine Keeler, signed and inscribed 8" x 10", a reproduction of the famous photograph by Lewis Morley showing Keeler, full length naked, sat on chair, signed and dated 1989.**
**(T. Vennett-Smith) $105**

**Queen Elizabeth II and Prince Philip, signed Christmas card, 1957, signed beneath color photo of The Queen and Prince Philip with Prince Charles, Princess Anne and two corgis.**
**(T. Vennett-Smith) $382**

**Richard Strauss, signed postcard, head and shoulders, in darker portion, corner clipped and slight tear to left of image.**
**(T. Vennett-Smith) $306**

**Josephine Baker, signed 4.25" x 5.75", full length.**
**(T. Vennett-Smith) $159**

**Gene Tunney, signed 7.5" x 9.5", head and shoulders, photo by Apeda of New York.**
**(T. Vennett-Smith) $153**

**Babe Ruth, irregularly trimmed 5.75" x 6.75" signed newspaper photo, full length seated by a long row of baseball bats.**
**(T. Vennett-Smith) $783**

A silhouette of a gentleman, painted on plaster, by John Miers, in ebonized wood frame. (Phillips) $260

American School, 19th century, silhouette family portrait, 12 x 19in. wide, in gilt wood frame. (Skinner Inc.) $750

American school, 19th century silhouette portrait of a Masonic gentleman, with Masonic devices and the initials *J.W.*, $4^{1}/_{4}$ x $6^{5}/_{8}$in. (Skinner Inc.) $750

American School, 19th century, Four silhouettes, Three Children and a Lady, unsigned, each cut-out and enhanced with watercolor, $2^{3}/_{4}$ x $3^{7}/_{8}$in. (Skinner Inc) $550

Miers and Field, circa 1820, Captain W.C. Lemprière, in uniform of the Royal Artillery, silhouette on plaster, oval, $3^{1}/_{4}$in. high. (Christie's) $498

H.A. Frith, two children standing full-length in a landscape, the eldest handing the other a rose, dated 1846, rectangular, 8in. high. (Christie's S. Ken) $1,931

John Meirs, a gentleman, in profile to the right, in coat and frilled cravat, signed, gold frame, oval, $1^{5}/_{8}$in. high. (Christie's S. Ken) $429

## ARGYLES

A Sheffield plate cylindrical argyle with acanthus and beaded edging, detachable cover and wood scroll handle.
(Bearne's) $698

A George IV Sheffield plate argyle, in the manner of Robert Gainsford, the baluster body chased with foliage, 6¼in. high.
(Woolley & Wallis) $735

An Edwardian gadrooned cylindrical argyle, in the late 18th century taste, with a wicker-covered scroll handle, Charles Stuart Harris and Son, London 1907, 4¾in., 14.25oz.
(Christie's S. Ken) $808

## BASINS

A George III Irish cauldron sugar basin on lions' mask and paw feet, later-decorated with punch-beaded spiral fluting, 5¾in., 9oz.
(Christie's S. Ken) $737

A French silver-gilt oval basin, the everted rim applied with oval vignettes, a nymph riding hippocamps, sea monster, palmettes and scrolls, by Marc-Augustine Lebrun, Paris 1821–1838, 14½in. long, 942grs.
(Christie's) $8,910

A George III Irish punch-beaded and spiral-fluted cauldron sugar basin on shell and hoof feet, Matthew West, Dublin 1787, 5in., 5.25oz.
(Christie's S. Ken) $1,095

## BASKETS

A fine George II two-handled bread basket, by Paul de Lamerie, the sloping sides of simple pierced trellis-work with interlaced flat-chased grooved strands, 8.5cm. high, 33cm. long, 1731, 40.5 ozs.
(Phillips) $201,200

An Art Deco style roll basket, 13in. long, rounded rectangular, ribbed interior and angled side handles, Birmingham, 1937, 19 ozs.
(Bonhams) $642

A George V two-handled oval fruit basket, the handles in the form of mermaids seated on shells, 15in. long overall, William Comyns, London 1914, 1336 gms, 42.9 oz.
(Bearne's) $1,771

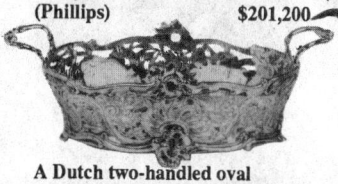

A Dutch two-handled oval basket, the slightly shaped sides pierced and engraved with vines, foliage and scrolls, by Rudolph Sondag, Rotterdam, 1766, 11in. overall width, 597grs.
(Christie's) $15,922

A late Victorian quatrefoil pierced cake basket on applied shell and scrolling foliate feet, James Dixon & Son, Sheffield 1900, 12¼in., 20.25 oz.
(Christie's S. Ken) $1,348

A George III silver-gilt oval basket, on spreading foot pierced and chased with palmettes and anthemion ornament, by Thomas Arden, 1805, 13¼in. long, 54oz.
(Christie's) $12,870

## BASKETS

A George III swing-handled oval cake basket, with foliate festoons and openwork swing handle on spreading base, 12in. long, William Plummer, London 1774, 592 gms, 19.0 oz.
(Bearne's) $1,579

A George I two-handled circular bread basket, on pierced and ropework foot, the basketwork sides with similar ropework border, by David Willaume, 1723, Britannia Standard, 11¼in. diameter, 32oz.
(Christie's) $12,342

A George III bread basket, with everted wire work sides, the swing handle of cable design, 1762 (maker's mark poorly struck), 32cm., 22 oz.
(Lawrence Fine Art) $2,435

A Victorian sweetmeat basket, with beaded borders and beaded swing handle, the sides engraved with ferns and ivy, on oval pedestal base, London, 1856.
(Bonhams) $622

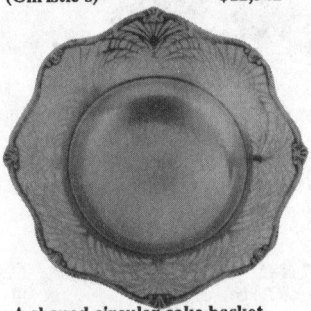

A shaped circular cake basket pierced with stylized shells and with an applied shell and foliate tim, on a rising circular foot, Adey Brothers, Birmingham, 10in., 14oz.
(Christie's S. Ken) $736

Charles T. and George Fox, early Victorian naturalistic sugar basket, blue glass liner, London 1840, 8.5 oz.
(Woolley & Wallis) $1,006

A George III circular bread basket, chased with a broad band of flutes and engraved with a band of anthemion ornament, by Joseph Felix Podio, 1806, 10½in. diameter, 32oz.
(Christie's) $4,117

A George III sugar basket, with bright cut engraved floral decoration, swing handle and pedestal foot, 1786, 15.5cm., 8.5oz.
(Lawrence Fine Art) $772

A fine early Victorian cake basket, embossed with rococo foliage sprays, having a swing handle, on a shaped floral embossed foot, 10½in. diameter, George John Richards, London 1848, 21 oz.
(Woolley & Wallis) $1,587

## BASKETS

An oval cake basket, 14¾in. long, with reeded borders, above bright-cut engraved foliate sides, London, 1795, by Robert and David Hennell, 27 oz.
(Bonhams) $3,680

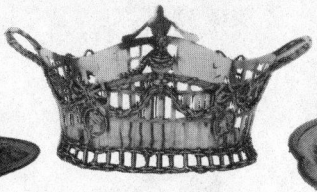

A Dutch small two-handled oval basket, the pierced sides applied with portrait busts, husk festoons and ribbon ornament, by Johannes Janse(n), Rotterdam, 1777, 7½in. overall width, 266grs.
(Christie's) $4,671

A Victorian gadrooned shaped oval swing-handled cake basket on a beaded rising oval foot, John Newton Mappin, Sheffield 1882, 12in., 21.25 oz.
(Christie's S. Ken) $944

A George III circular fruit basket, with looped wirework sides, reeded borders and similar swing handle, by John Wakelin and Robert Garrard, 1797, 11¾in. diameter, 41oz.
(Christie's) $11,918

A George III beaded, pierced and bright-cut oval swing-handled pedestal sugar basin fitted with a blue glass liner, London 1784, incuse mark, 6¾in. overall, 8oz. free.
(Christie's S. Ken) $987

A George III sweatmeat basket, pierced in a design of scrolls between swags and paterae, by Thomas Daniell, 1783, 17cm., 4.5oz.
(Lawrence Fine Art) $869

A George III sugar basket, with swing handle, the body with floral bright cut engraved decoration, by Solomon Hougham, 1793, 17cm., 7.5 oz.
(Lawrence Fine Art) $1,059

A French oval fruit basket, the bowl formed from woven wirework, the rim and crossed scroll handles formed as grape laden vine tendrils, circa 1880, 20½in. long, 5,593grs.
(Christie's) $10,835

A George III sweetmeat basket, by Henry Chawner, the sides with linear and foliate bright-cut decoration, on shaped pedestal base, London, 1792.
(Bonhams) $739

## BEAKERS

A small beaker, the sides engraved with opposed leaves and initials and date 1756, 18th century, Scandinavian, 5.5cm. (Lawrence Fine Art) $734

A C.R. Ashbee hammered silver beaker, the base with an openwork frieze of stylized trees set with seven cabochon garnets, London hallmarks for 1900, 11.5cm. high, 205 grams. gross. (Christie's) $3,841

An Edwardian parcel-gilt tapering beaker and cover on ball feet, chased with rococo flowers and scrolling foliage, Child & Child, London 1903, 5¼in., 8.75oz. (Christie's S. Ken) $590

A French late 18th/early 19th century bell-shaped beaker engraved with foliage and shells, Louis-Jacques Berger, Paris 1798/1809, 5in., 5.75 oz. (Christie's S. Ken) $629

A pair of George III plain beakers, each on molded rim foot, engraved with a crest and monogram, 1773, maker's mark *M.S.* or *S.W.*, 2⅞in. high, 5oz. (Christie's) $3,684

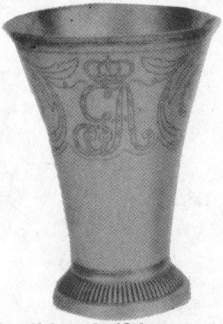

A Swedish early 19th century gilt-lined tapering beaker on a fluted rising circular foot, engraved with wriggle-work, stylized foliage and trellis-work, 8½in., 14.25oz. (Christie's S. Ken) $1,540

A Victorian parcel-gilt prize beaker in the late 17th/early 18th century Continental style, engraved with portraits of famous people with Liverpool connections, by George Fox, 1890, 13.5cm. high, 11 ozs. (Phillips) $2,616

An Art Nouveau beaker, the body stamped with flowers, foliage and scrollwork decoration, Mappin and Webb, Sheffield 1901, 6in., 13.5oz. (Christie's S. Ken) $619

A German silver gilt tapering cylindrical beaker, the body with a broad band of tear drop ornament on a punched ground, by Christoph Zorer, Augsburg, 1570–1575, 4¾in. high, 208grs. (Christie's) $14,861

## BOWLS

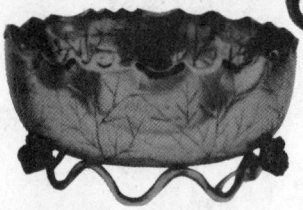

A Hukin & Heath electroplate rose bowl with crimped rim, the sides stamped with stylized branches and engraved with initials, 10in. diameter.
(Christie's S. Ken) $128

An Edwardian gilt-lined two-handled rose bowl on four stylized bracket feet, the bowl embossed with a Celtic band, London 1908, 10in. diameter, 64oz.
(Christie's S. Ken) $2,517

An Edwardian bowl, the center and shaped border pierced with scrolls and trellis work, by J. Dixon & Sons, Sheffield, 1908, 33cm., 52oz.
(Lawrence Fine Art) $3,185

A plain hexagonal sugar bowl, on six curved feet and with foliate pierced rim, by Omar Ramsden, 1935, 4½in. wide, 7oz.
(Christie's) $1,168

A late Victorian foliate-chased boat-shaped pedestal fruit bowl on a shell and foliate-chased domed circular base, Goldsmiths & Silversmiths Co. Ltd., London 1900, 12¾in., 34.75oz.
(Christie's S. Ken) $2,420

A late Victorian part spiral-fluted rose bowl on a rising circular foot and with a molded rim, William Hutton & Sons Ltd., London 1895, 8¾in., 20oz. free.
(Christie's S. Ken) $871

A French late 18th of early 19th century two-handled oval bowl and cover, the sides pierced, stamped and chased with classical figures, Etienne Janety, Paris, 6½in. overall.
(Christie's S. Ken) $1,164

A Continental molded oval fruit bowl on openwork rococo floral, foliate and trellis-work feet, bearing import marks for London 1899, 13¼in., 55oz.
(Christie's S. Ken) $5,959

A Georg Jensen footed bowl, the lightly hammered gadrooned bowl decorated beneath with trailing vines, on a stepped foot, 25.5cm. diameter, 1050 grams.
(Christie's) $3,432

## BOWLS

A 19th century Russian and shaded enamel circular bowl decorated with bats, clouds and circular panels, 4¼in. diameter, maker's mark *A. Postnikov*, Moscow 1874, 254 gms.
(Bearne's) $1,502

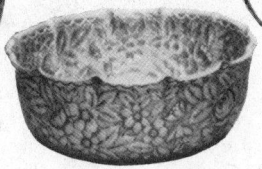

Frederick Smith repoussé sterling fruit bowl, Denver, circa 1889, round with scalloped rim, 15 troy ozs.
(Skinner Inc.) $400

A Victorian two-handled oval bowl, with leaf-capped handles and on spreading base, 16½in. over handles, Atkin Brothers, Sheffield 1896, 2216 gms, 71.2 oz.
(Bearne's) $3,561

A German late 19th/early 20th century circular fruit bowl, fitted with a clear glass liner, Eugen Marcus, 8in. diameter.
(Christie's S. Ken) $674

A silver rose bowl by Bernard Cuzner, the rounded bowl with rolled rim decorated with a repoussé rose briar frieze with five applied stylized rose heads, Birmingham hallmarks for 1911, 18.5cm. high.
(Christie's) $25,608

A Victorian circular punch bowl with shaped rim in monteith style with masked scroll edging, 13in. diameter, London 1900, 1685 gms, 54.1 oz.
(Bearne's) $3,080

A large silver-mounted Chinese kraak porcelain bowl, decorated in blue and white with panels of trees, flowers and birds between columns, the silver rim engraved with acanthus leaves, early 17th century, 14¼in. diameter.
(Christie's) $13,371

A James Dixon & Sons sugar bowl and cover, designed by Dr. Christopher Dresser, the spherical body flanked by two curved handles, model number 2273 and registration lozenge for 1880, 9.5cm. high.
(Christie's) $587

Hand hammered sterling silver bowl, R. Wallace & Sons Mfg. Co., Wallingford, Connecticut, with applied rim and four plaques of Austrian style geometric motifs, 4⅝in. diameter.
(Skinner Inc.) $100

## BOWLS

A rare James II monteith, the body plain apart from simple lobing in panels, by George Garthorne, 1685, 31cm., 42 oz. (Lawrence Fine Art) $80,465

A French 19th century foliate-pierced shaped oval fruit bowl applied with a rococo scrolling foliate rim, 16in., 27 oz. (Christie's S. Ken) $854

A late 19th century French silver-mounted engraved and frosted glass oval fruit bowl, on a decorated silver base on four bun feet, 8½in. long. (Bearne's) $866

Kirk repoussé silver monteith, Baltimore, 1846–61, chased floral decoration, removable goblet holder with 1852 inscription, 10¾in. diameter, approximately 46 troy oz. (Skinner Inc.) $2,700

A circular shallow bowl, on tapering shaped hexagonal foot, with openwork knop above, by Omar Ramsden, 1928, 5⅝in. high, 12oz. (Christie's) $3,703

A large rose bowl, engraved with a coat of arms and presentation inscription to *A.J. Webbe, 1893*, the interior gilt, by C.S. Harris, 1892, 35cm., approximately 60 oz. (Lawrence Fine Art) $3,176

A Limited Edition tapering circular punch bowl, the body applied with four shaped oblong cartouches cast and chased with vignettes of animals, retailed by Tessiers, 10¼in., 47.75oz. (Christie's S. Ken) $1,180

A Victorian novelty rose bowl modeled as a waterlily, supported by leaves at either side, the junction applied with a frog, by Hukin & Heath, 1885, 25.6cm. diameter, weighable 40.5 ozs. (Phillips) $3,018

A Liberty & Co. Cymric silver and copper bowl, the shallow conical silver bowl with everted rim set with band of cabochon nephrites, with Birmingham hallmarks for 1901, 20.7cm. diameter, 680 grams. gross. (Christie's) $2,134

## BOXES

An attractive Edwardian silver box and cover by Nathan and Hayes, of plain rectangular form, Chester 1901, 37 grams. 6cm. wide.
(Spencer's) $138

A German silver-gilt double spice box, the interior with central divider, the hinged cover engraved with latticework and scrolls on a matted ground, by Johann Pepfenhauser, Augsburg, 1735–6, 2in. long, 80grs.
(Christie's) $3,684

A Norwegian mid 18th century oval tobacco box, the lid engraved with birds, trees and a garden urn, 4 4/5in.
(Christie's S. Ken) $887

A Wiener Werkstätte white-metal box, with hinged cover, decorated with a repoussé frieze of a stag and bird amid stylized trees, 8.8cm. long.
(Christie's) $4,895

A C.R. Ashbee hammered silver spice box and cover, set with seven cabochon garnets, stamped *C R A* with London hallmarks for 1899, 9.5cm. high, 145 grams. gross.
(Christie's) $2,881

A late Victorian toilet box in the Carolean taste, engraved with chinoiseries, Ho-ho birds, stylized flowers, foliage and fruit, George Lambert, London 1886, Britannia Standard, 5in., 17oz.
(Christie's S. Ken) $1,791

A late Victorian oblong cedar-lined cigarette box, the hinged cover cast and chased with an inn scene in the style of Tenniers, Birmingham 1895, 5 1/2in.
(Christie's S. Ken) $1,369

A late 17th/early 18th century oval tobacco box engraved with armorials, unmarked, circa 1700, 9.8cm. long, 5 ozs.
(Phillips) $805

A Scandinavian 19th century oval sugar box or tea caddy on floral and foliate feet, Zethelius, 6 1/2in., 19oz.
(Christie's S. Ken) $1,276

## CANDELABRA

One of a pair of Old Sheffield plate three-light candelabra, with tapering stem, reeded scroll branches, square drip pans, and detachable nozzles, circa 1810, 19¾in. high. (Two) (Christie's) $1,584

A pair of plated three-light candelabra, the rounded rectangular bases, drip pans and detachable nozzles with gadroon edging, 21¼in. high, Mappin & Webb. (Bearne's) $693

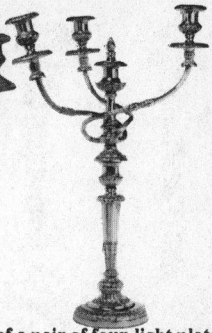

One of a pair of four-light plated candelabra, with three reeded scroll branches and central light each with similar socket, by Matthew Boulton & Co., circa 1815, 25¼in. high. (Christie's) (Two) $6,930

A Victorian six light candelabrum centerpiece, the fluted stem with foliage terminals, with three bi-furcated scroll branches and vase-shaped fluted sockets and detachable nozzles, by Barnard and Co., 1842, 30½in. high, 343oz. (Christie's) $16,456

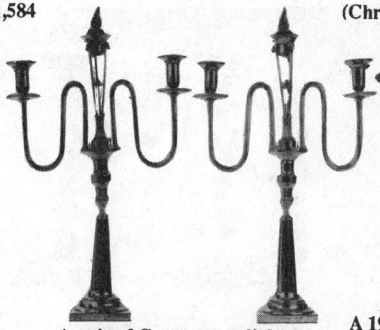

A pair of German two light candelabra, with two reeded branches and central openwork tripod with applied rams' masks and flame finial, by Johann Gottlieb Kohlheim, Berlin, circa 1800, 20¾in. high, weight of branches 1437grs. (Christie's) $3,908

A 19th/20th century five-light candelabrum, with beaded edging, reeded branches and sconces decorated with ribbon tied festoons, William Hutton and Sons Ltd., London 1899, 19¾in. overall height of candelabrum, 41.3 oz weight of branches. (Bearne's) $2,310

A Danish three-light candelabrum, with baluster stem and vase-shaped socket, by Christian Werum, Copenhagen, probably 1762, 18½in. high, 1439grs. (Christie's) $3,908

One of a pair of modern small three branch three light candelabra, from a single stick in the George I style, on stepped hexagonal base, London 1965, maker's mark *RC*., 2309 grammes total. (Spencer's)(Two) $1,787

A pair of Sheffield plate three-light candelabra, the circular bases, tapering stems, drip pans and detachable nozzles with gadroon edging, 20in. high, Matthew Boulton, Sheffield. (Bearne's) $1,482

## CANDLESTICKS

A pair of Sheffield plate table candlesticks, the stems designed as bound palms on tapering square bases with beaded edging, 12¾in. high.
(Bearne's) $732

A pair of late Victorian tapersticks in the George III style, with detachable square sconces, London 1890, by Henry Wilkinson and Co., loaded, 12cm. high.
(Spencer's) $893

A pair of German early 19th century baluster candlesticks on foliate and berry-decorated rising square bases, 9½in., 17 oz.
(Christie's S. Ken) $1,798

A pair of table candlesticks of Regency design, the baluster stems and shaped circular bases embossed with cartouches between flower swags, by Leopold Ltd., 1908, 25cm., loaded. (Lawrence Fine Art) $1,694

A set of four George II cast candlesticks with fluted baluster columns and shell decorated knops, 23cm. high, by William Gould, 1746, 101.25 ozs.
(Phillips) $13,078

A good pair of George II table candlesticks, the baluster stems and shaped rectangular bases embossed with shells within gadroon borders, by Ebenezer Coker, 1759, 27.5cm., original scratch weight 47.5 oz.
(Lawrence Fine Art) $5,082

A pair of electroplated Corinthian column table candlesticks, the square bases decorated with rams masks, 11¾in. high.
(Bearne's) $347

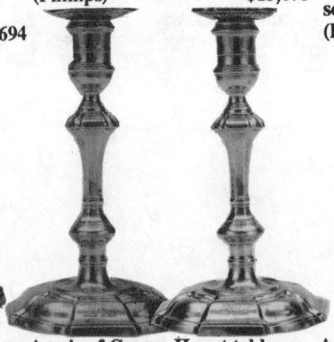

A pair of George II cast table candlesticks, with shaped circular bases and knopped stems, 7in. high, John Gould, London 1736, 26.6 oz.
(Bearne's) $6,545

A pair of table candlesticks, the tapering stems headed by double sided Bacchanalian masks, possibly central European, circa 1800, 30cm., loaded.
(Lawrence Fine Art) $4,659

## CANDLESTICKS

An early pair of George III cast candlesticks, in the rocaille style, 28cm. high, by Arthur Annesley, 1760, 52 ozs. (Phillips) $7,646

A pair of George VI candlesticks, the plain oval sockets raised upon swept oval columns, Birmingham 1945, by A & J Zimmerman Ltd., 6in. high. (Spencer's) $671

A pair of George II cast candlesticks, 8¾in. high, the shaped circular bases cast with shells, London 1757, by John Hyatt and Charles Seymour. (Bonhams) $3,293

A pair of George III Corinthian candlesticks, on plain sloping square bases and with gadroon borders, engraved with a crest, 31cm. high, by John Carter, 1770. (Phillips) $5,030

A good set of four George III Irish candlesticks with 'cotton reel' nozzles and holders, John Walker, Dublin circa 1775, 11.5 oz. (Woolley & Wallis) $11,223

A pair of George III table candlesticks, the circular bases with fluted borders and engraved with a coat of arms, by John Parsons & Co., Sheffield, 1790, 28cm., wood based. (Lawrence Fine Art) $4,447

A George III pair of Corinthian candlesticks, with cast acanthus capitals and incurved square nozzles, 29cm. high, by John Parsons & Co., Sheffield, 1789. (Phillips) $4,426

A pair of Victorian Corinthian column dressing table candlesticks, 6in. high, Mappin Brothers, Sheffield 1898, loaded. (Bearne's) $1,059

An attractive pair of George III small candlesticks, the baluster urn shaped sockets with flange rims, Sheffield 1780, probably by Fenton Creswick and Co., 19cm. high. (Spencer's) $1,393

## CASTERS

Peter, Anne and William Bateman, pepper muffineer, 5 3/4 in. high, with reeded borders on domed circular base, London, 1804, 3 oz. (Bonhams) $426

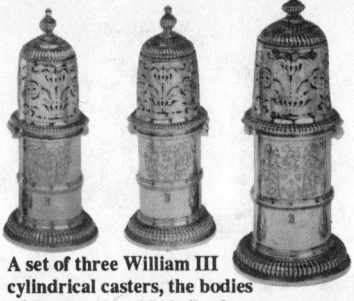

A set of three William III cylindrical casters, the bodies with central molded rib, the covers with bayonet fittings, by Joseph Ward, 1698, 6 1/4 in. and 7 3/4 in. high, 23oz. (Christie's) $17,485

A George I cast sugar dredger, of baluster octagonal form, engraved with a crest, 15cm. high, by Charles Adam, 1718, 4.75 ozs. (Phillips) $1,610

A pair of George III reeded vase-shaped casters, the waisted and engraved tops with vase-shaped finials, London 1804, 5 3/4 in. (Christie's S. Ken) $689

A matched pair of late Victorian gadrooned and spiral-fluted sugar casters on foliate-chased gadrooned circular bases, Edward Hutton, London 1892 and William Hutton & Sons Ltd., London 1896, 8in. and 7 3/4 in., 15.75oz. (Christie's S. Ken) $1,081

A pair of George II sugar casters, 6in. high, Warwick form on domed circular bases, London, 1748, by Samuel Wood, 12 oz. (Bonhams) $1,395

An early 18th century style baluster sugar caster with molded body band and bayonet fittings, 8in., 9.25oz. (Christie's S. Ken) $432

A set of four George III style baluster casters, having pierced corners, on cast collet feet, Goldsmiths & Silversmiths Co., London 1935, 16 oz. (Woolley & Wallis) $1,161

A George II large inverted pear-shaped sugar caster, the pierced domed cover with baluster finial, by Samuel Wood, 1756, 10in. high, 22oz. (Christie's) $4,034

## CENTERPIECES

A George III epergne and mirror plateau, the epergne on four fluted and foliage columns with lions' paw feet, by Matthew Boulton and Plate Company, Birmingham, 1810, the epergne 10½in. high. weight of epergne 95oz.
(Christie's) $20,570

A Victorian four-branch epergne, the four scroll branches each terminating in a detachable circular dish and with similar larger central dish, by Walter and John Barnard, 1894, 8in. high, 75oz.
(Christie's) $6,171

An Art Nouveau Edward VII dessert stand centerpiece of hammered design, 13in. high, Hamilton and Inches, Edinburgh 1904, 2228 gms, 71.6 oz.
(Bearne's) $2,406

A large French parcel-gilt centerpiece, the central hardstone plinth supporting a detachable loosely draped female figure, the ground signed *H. Wadere*, circa 1897, 34½in. high, gross 25,860grs.
(Christie's) $29,700

A Victorian parcel gilt dessert stand, the vine tendril stem flanked by bacchanti, the openwork frame above with applied pendant grapes and vine leaves, by J.S. Hunt, 1858, 12½in. high, 62oz.
(Christie's) $5,760

A Victorian vase-shaped centerpiece and cover, the stem formed as three female figures, the bowl cast and chased with a horserace and numerous figures on horseback, by John S. Hunt, 1861, 20in. high, 266oz.
(Christie's) $13,790

An early George V centerpiece, the central trumpet vase flanked by three smaller trumpet vases, the whole with cast reel and bobbin borders, Sheffield 1913, 906 grammes.
(Spencer's) $970

An attractive late Victorian horn cornucopia table centerpiece, the horn with plated swept rim and stepped beaded frieze, on a foliate cast quadruped base, approximately 30in. high.
(Spencer's) $895

An early Victorian five-light candelabrum centerpiece and mirror plateau, the base engraved with a coat-of-arms, crest and presentation inscription dated 1843, by Richard Sawyer, Dublin, 1843, height overall 25in., 254oz.
(Christie's) $10,890

## CHAMBERSTICKS

A rare George IV silver-gilt chamber candlestick, with flower petal socket, cylindrical nozzle and tendril handle, by Philip Rundell, 1821, 4¼in. diameter, 6oz.
(Christie's) $3,684

A George II plain circular chamber candlestick with rising scroll handle and waisted socket, John Cafe, London 1756, 6½in., 9.25oz.
(Christie's S. Ken) $1,314

A George III chamberstick, 3in. high, with gadrooned border, flying scroll handle and engraved crest, London, 1816, by Samuel Whitford II, 9 oz.
(Bonhams) $814

A matched pair of George III chambersticks complete with scissor-type snuffers and conical extinguishers, one by Robert & Samuel Hennell, 1810, the other by Hennell & Terry, 1813.
(Phillips) $5,634

C.R. Ashbee, a Guild of Handicrafts bedroom candlestick, raised hammered border chased with branches of stylized leaves and berries, London 1900, 7oz.
(Woolley & Wallis) $1,552

A pair of early Victorian Sheffield plate bedroom candlesticks, with leaf scrolls to the borders.
(Woolley & Wallis) $735

A George III chamber candlestick, with flying scroll handle and extinguisher, marked on base and extinguisher by Ebenezer Coker, 1766, 10cm., 10.5oz.
(Lawrence Fine Art) $888

A George III chamberstick, 4¼in. high, with gadrooned border, vase-form socket with detachable nozzle and scroll handle, Sheffield, 1803, by John Watson, 8 oz.
(Bonhams) $736

A George III miniature chamber candlestick, the circular base, nozzle and conical extinguisher engraved with crest, 3in. diameter, Peter, Anne and William Bateman, London, 1802, 96 gms, 3.0 oz.
(Bearne's) $520

## CHOCOLATE POTS

A French 19th century baluster chocolate pot, with a polished rosewood octagonal side handle, applied with shell decoration, 9in., 21.50oz. gross.
(Christie's S. Ken) $1,089

A pair of Edward VII chocolate pots of flared cylindrical form with ebony side handles, 7¼in. high, maker's mark *D.F.*, London 1904, 586 gms, 18.8 oz.
(Bearne's) $866

A Belgian pear-shaped chocolate pot, the body chased with swirling fluting, foliage and festoons of husks, Mons, 1773, maker's mark *G* a coronet above, 13¼in. high, gross 1,206grs.
(Christie's) $39,600

## CIGARETTE CASES

A late Victorian cigarette case lined in red leather, the hinged cover enameled en grisaille with a facsimile of the cover of Punch magazine, Birmingham, 3in.
(Christie's S. Ken) $337

A German cigarette case, one side engraved with an armorial, the lid enameled with three naked women relaxing by a lake, London 1902, 3²/₅in.
(Christie's S. Ken) $2,006

A German Art Nouveau silver and enameled cigarette case, depicting in naturalistic colors a Mucha-style girl, 8.50cm. long, maker's marks for Heinrich Levinger.
(Phillips) $1,459

A Victorian novelty cigarette case, the name and address and franked postage stamp in enamel to the front, 4in., London 1883.
(Woolley & Wallis) $503

A white metal rectangular hinged cigarette case, decorated in niello to a design by Gerard Sandoz, 5in. long.
(Christie's S. Ken) $2,033

A Russian rectangular gilt-lined cigarette case, the lid stamped with a bird of prey in a mountainous wooded landscape, modern, 4¹/₁₀in.
(Christie's S. Ken) $556

## CLARET JUGS

A George III reeded vase-shaped pedestal claret or hot water jug with wicker-covered scroll handle, John Denziloe, London 1788, 12in., 20.75 oz. gross.
(Christie's S. Ken) $1,795

A Victorian silver-gilt-mounted fern-engraved oval claret jug cut with monograms and a crest, in a fitted case, E.H. Stockwell, London 1871, 7in.
(Christie's S. Ken) $1,980

Victorian silver-gilt claret jug, Stephen Smith, London, 1856, with frieze of animals and masks, 13½in. high, approximately 39 troy oz.
(Skinner Inc.) $2,600

A Victorian silver-mounted bottle-shaped clear glass claret jug with star-cut base, Findley & Taylor, London 1889, 13½in.
(Christie's S. Ken) $1,475

A pair of Victorian silver-gilt mounted glass claret jugs, the neck mounts chased with flowers and foliage on a matted ground, by W. and G. Sissons, Sheffield, 1869, 9½in. high.
(Christie's) $7,479

A Victorian large vase-shaped claret jug, the cork stopper with melon finial surmounted by two doves, by Hunt and Roskell, 1881, 15½in. high, gross 57oz.
(Christie's) $4,731

A Victorian silver-mounted vase-shaped claret jug, the glass engraved with palmettes and beading, with bracket handle, by William Gough, Birmingham, 1869, 11¼in. high.
(Christie's) $2,079

A Victorian plain vase-shaped claret jug, with entwined double serpent handle, hinged domed cover and bunch of grapes finial, by John S. Hunt, 1860, 12in. high, 30oz.
(Christie's) $3,684

An Edwardian claret jug, with floral repoussé decoration and scroll handle, by J&T, Sheffield, 1901, 28cm.
(Lawrence Fine Art) $1,525

## CLARET JUGS

A late Victorian silver-mounted spiral-fluted cut-glass oval claret jug with scroll handle, M.J.J., Birmingham 1896, 9½in.
(Christie's S. Ken) $528

A James Dixon & Sons electroplated claret jug designed by Dr. Christopher Dresser, with angled handle, the conical body with tapering cylindrical neck and triangular spout, 21.7cm. high.
(Christie's) $21,340

A Continental Art Nouveau silver-mounted plain tapering clear glass claret jug with star-cut base, bearing import marks for London 1903, 9in.
(Christie's S. Ken) $1,159

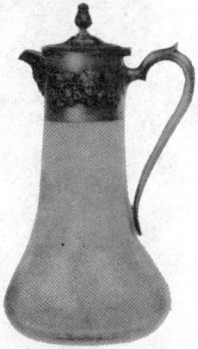

A Victorian style silver-mounted flaring glass claret jug with star-cut base, the body decorated with vines.
(Christie's S. Ken) $1,306

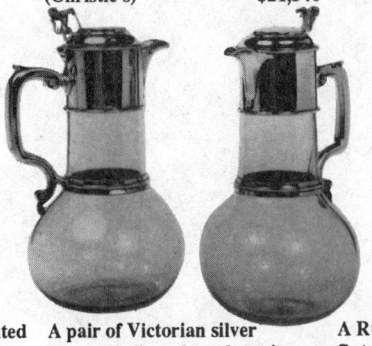

A pair of Victorian silver mounted clear glass claret jugs, each with bracket handle, molded spout and hinged domed cover, by C.F. Hancock, 1882, 10½in. high.
(Christie's) $10,296

A Russian silver-mounted spiral-fluted tapering oval clear glass claret jug cut and engraved with arabesques, 13½in.
(Christie's S. Ken) $1,685

A Victorian silver-mounted engraved glass claret jug, 9¾in. high, John Figg, London 1875 (glass foot chipped).
(Bearne's) $1,287

A late Victorian shaft and globe claret jug, with elaborate fruiting vine mounts, beaded loop handle and hinged cover, 13in. high over handle.
(Spencer's) $756

An Elkington electroplate mounted engraved glass claret jug, the cylindrical glass body engraved with fruiting vines on a spreading base, 11in. high, Elkington marks for Newhall Street, 1891.
(Bearne's) $809

## COASTERS

A pair of George IV circular coasters, the everted rims with acanthus, shell and rose bud edging, 6¼in. diameter, maker's mark *W.S.*, London 1823.
(Bearne's) $2,406

A set of four Victorian plated tall circular wine coasters, the sides pierced with trellis-work and putti harvesting vines, 5¾in.
(Christie's S. Ken) $2,851

A pair of William IV Sheffield plate decanter stands, the paneled sides with grapevine pierced borders, turned wood bases.
(Woolley & Wallis) $851

A set of four George III wine coasters, 5¼in. diameter, with ivory insets, pierced sides and beaded borders, Sheffield, 1775.
(Bonhams) $4,068

A set of four George III gadrooned circular open-work wine coasters applied with die-stamped and chased trailing vine sides, John Roberts & Co., Sheffield 1809, 5½in.
(Christie's S. Ken) $8,847

A set of four William IV silver-gilt wine coasters, each on wood base, the sides pierced and engraved with scrolls, foliage and lattice-work, by Paul Storr, 1833 and 1834.
(Christie's) $22,627

A pair of George III circular wine coasters, pierced with slats and with gadrooned borders and wood bases, by Thomas Jackson, 1772.
(Christie's) $4,767

A pair of William IV silver-gilt wine coasters, the sides pierced with vine leaves and grapes, with reed-and-tie and vine tendril borders, by John Settle and Henry Williamson, Sheffield 1830. (Christie's) $7,405

An almost matched pair of part-fluted molded circular wine coasters, John Bridge, London 1823 and Messrs. Barnard, London 1834, 6½in.
(Christie's S. Ken) $2,135

## COFFEE POTS

An Edwardian Irish plain cylindrical coffee biggin in the early 19th century taste, with a foliate-decorated spout, J.S., Dublin 1902, 7¾in., 22.75oz. gross.
(Christie's S. Ken) $736

A George II plain tapering cylindrical coffee pot, with wood side handle, curved spout, hinged domed cover and bell-shaped finial, by Paul Crespin, 1732, 7¼in. high, gross 19oz.
(Christie's) $7,920

A George III coffee pot, 8½in. high, with everted gadroon border and leaf-chased spout and angled wooden handle, London, 1819, 25oz.
(Bonhams) $1,190

A George I plain tapering octagonal coffee pot, with curved octagonal spout, molded borders and domed cover, by Edward Vincent, 1723, 9½in. high, gross 25oz.
(Christie's) $31,845

A George II tapering coffee pot, the upper and lower parts of the body chased with flowers, foliage and scrolls, by John Swift, 1752, 10½in. high, gross 33oz.
(Christie's) $3,564

A George II tapering cylindrical coffee pot, engraved with a coat-of-arms and flat-chased with bands of scrolls, shells, strapwork and latticework, by John White, 1737, 8½in. high, gross 24oz.
(Christie's) $5,417

A George II plain tapering coffee pot on a spreading circular foot, with a foliate-chased and capped rising curved spout, Thomas Farren, London 1738, 8½in., 22.50oz. gross.
(Christie's S. Ken) $3,080

An important George II tapering cylindrical coffee pot, with curved spout terminating in an eagle's head and with hinged slightly domed cover and bud finial, by Paul de Lamerie, 1742, 87½in. high, gross 23oz.
(Christie's) $86,680

A Regency part-fluted tapering coffee biggin on a spreading circular foof with a part-fluted squat curved spout, Rebecca Emes and Edward Barnard, London 1813, 8in., 22.75oz. gross.
(Christie's S. Ken) $774

## COFFEE POTS

George III baluster coffee pot, London, 1770–71, maker script "JS", pineapple finial above a leaf-wrapped spout, 10½in. high, approximately 32 troy oz. (Skinner Inc.) $3,750

A Portuguese early 19th century molded oblong coffee pot on ball feet, maker's initials *T.I.C.*, Lisbon 1814–1816, 9½in., 38 oz. gross. (Christie's S. Ken) $1,348

A French 19th century pear-shaped coffee pot on scrolling foliate feet and with a foliate-chased rising curved spout, 9in. high, 18.75 oz. (Christie's S. Ken) $719

A George III Provincial coffee pot with domed cover, acorn finial and gadroon borders, ivory handle and scalloped spout, by Langlands & Robertson, Newcastle, 1784, 33.5cm. high, 29 ozs. (Phillips) $5,030

A George IV coffee pot, 8in. high, with angled handle and everted cape with beaded border, London, 1824, by William Elliott, 16 oz. (Bonhams) $1,201

A George III coffee pot, on circular foot, scroll handle and domed cover with pineapple finial, by James Stamp (probably), 1775, 26cm., 25.5 oz. (Lawrence Fine Art) $5,082

An Edwardian plain tapering coffee pot in the 18th century taste, Goldsmiths & Silversmiths Co. Ltd., London 1909, 10¼in., 18.25oz. gross. (Christie's S. Ken) $686

A George II coffee pot, 6in. high, on molded foot with faceted spout and wooden scroll handle, London, 1731, by Samuel Lea, 12 oz. (Bonhams) $2,324

An attractive George II coffee pot, 9in. high, on spreading circular foot with leaf-capped curved spout, London, 1748, by Thomas Whipham, 21 oz. (Bonhams) $3,099

## COFFEE POTS

An early 19th century Continental plain bellied coffee pot with scroll handle and leaf and bud finial, N.B., 6in.
(Christie's S. Ken) $786

A George II baluster coffee pot, later-chased with arabesques and engraved with a contemporary armorial surrounded by rococo flowers and foliage, Benjamin Gignac, London 1750, 10¼in., 30oz. gross.
(Christie's ) $1,716

A German plain pear-shaped coffee-jug, with a molded drop to the short curved spout, by Martin Friedrich Muller, Berlin, 1735–45, 11½in. high, gross 1056grs.
(Christie's) $13,371

A George II coffee pot, with molded scroll spout and wood handle, the bun shaped cover with turned finial, by John Pero, 1738, 23cm., 24 oz.
(Lawrence Fine Art) $5,929

A Swedish 19th century fluted baluster coffee pot with a rising curved spout, and engraved with rococo scrolling foliage, 8½in., 17oz.
(Christie's ) $965

A coffee pot with straight tapering spout, wood scroll handle and domed cover with bun finial, maker's mark *N.G.*, circa 1730, 23cm., 24 oz.
(Lawrence Fine Art) $5,082

Paul Storr, coffee jug on stand, of Neo Classical design, with gadroon molding and engraved with a coat of arms, 13¼in., London 1803, 53.5 oz.
(Woolley & Wallis) $10,062

A George III coffee pot, the hinged cover, spout and spreading base with banded edging, 10¾in. high, Daniel Smith and Robert Sharp, London 1780, 813 gms, 26.1 oz.
(Bearne's) $5,967

A George III beaded pear-shaped coffee pot on a rising foot, with a bead and foliate-chased rising curved spout, possibly Thomas Heming, London 1779, 12in., 30 oz. gross.
(Christie's S. Ken) $3,820

## CREAM JUGS

A George III cow creamer, the curled tail forming the handle and with hinged back-flap chased with foliage and with applied fly, by John Schuppe, 1768, 5¾in. long, 4oz.
(Christie's) $18,419

A George IV cream jug, 3½in. high, with gadrooned border and leaf-chased reeded strap handle on four ball feet, London, 1823, by William Burwash, 6 oz.
(Bonhams) $232

An early Victorian gilt-lined compressed pear-shaped cream jug on crouching figure feet and with a mask spout, London 1843, overall length 6¼in., 16.75oz.
(Christie's S. Ken) $1,015

A George III cream jug of helmet shape with gadroon border, scroll handle and pedestal foot, by Charles Clark, 1765, 9cm.
(Lawrence Fine Art) $463

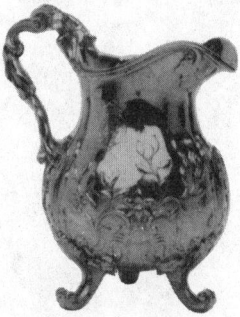

A George IV silver-gilt pear-shaped cream jug, chased with flowers, foliage and scrolls, engraved with a Royal crest and Garter Motto, by Paul Storr, 1820, 10oz.
(Christie's) $5,940

A George III cream jug, with reeded borders and reeded angled handle, London, 1796, by Samuel Hennell.
(Bonhams) $368

A George II cream jug, 3¾in. high, inverted pear-shape, punch bead border and double scroll handle, London, 1770, 2 oz.
(Bonhams) $271

An Irish George III cream jug, with cut away borders and wide lips banded to belly, Dublin, circa 1770, 6 oz.
(Bonhams) $659

Peter and William Bateman cream jug, with reeded borders, above prick engraved and bright-cut sides, London, 1805, 6 oz.
(Bonhams) $310

## CRUETS

A George III silver-gilt Warwick cruet, on four shell and scroll feet and with central detachable handle, by John Delmester, 1761, 9in. high, 37oz.
(Christie's) $9,108

A George III cruet with four contemporary bottles, two casters and a mustard pot of cut glass with silver mounts, maker's mark *C.C.*, 1804, 20cm.
(Lawrence Fine Art) $2,329

A Victorian novelty quatrefoil four-cup egg cruet, the detachable egg cups modeled as riding boots, the center with crossed riding crops, 6¼in. overall.
(Christie's S. Ken) $1,079

Joseph & Albert Savory, a William IV egg cruet, the circular wire work frame with a central foliage scroll ring handle, London 1836, 22 oz.
(Woolley & Wallis) $1,200

An early Victorian cruet, the mustard pot and caster with contemporary silver mounts, Birmingham 1845, Messrs. Lias, London.
(Woolley & Wallis) $658

A fine early Victorian oil and vinegar cruet, by Robert Hennell, London 1840, 18.5 oz. weighable silver.
(Woolley & Wallis) $3,386

A Hukin and Heath four-piece electroplated cruet, designed by Dr. Christopher Dresser, with patent registration marks for 1879, 13cm. high.
(Christie's) $1,287

An old Sheffield plate eight bottle cruet stand, of slightly shaped rounded rectangular form, Sheffield 1822, by Smith, Tate, Hoult and Tate.
(Spencer's) $695

A Georgian style six bottle cruet stand, of bombé oval form with central spade handle, raised upon four acanthus leaf shell and rosette cast feet.
(Spencer's) $318

A silver-gilt mounted two-handled coconut bowl, the straps pierced with latticework, the bowl carved with stylized foliage, the mounts unmarked, Central European, probably 16th century, 4¼in. high.
(Christie's) $6,501

A Victorian electro-plated two-handled football trophy of highly ornamental form, the lid surmounted by a female figure depicting Victory, the underside inscribed, *Kerr and Philips, Silversmiths, Glasgow*, 26½in. high.
(Christie's) $1,016

A Regency four-cup shaped square egg cruet on leaf and floral-capped lion's paw feet, Rebecca Emes & Edward Barnard, London 1812, 7¾in., 26.50oz.
(Christie's S. Ken) $1,171

A George II silver-gilt two-handled cup and associated cover, on domed circular foot, the body with applied rib and with leaf-capped scroll handles, by John Laver, 1771, the cover by Peter Archambo and Peter Meure, 1751, 15in. high, 98oz.
(Christie's) $5,348

A late Victorian cup and cover, 15½in. high, with two leaf-capped scroll handles, the domed pull-off cover with egg-shaped finial, Birmingham, 1894, 33 ozs.
(Bonhams) $778

A small two-handled cup by Charles Fox, 4½in. high, with two foliate mounted scrolling side handles, the sides chased with scrolls and foliage, London, 1834, 7 ozs.
(Bonhams) $369

A Commonwealth wine cup, the tapering bowl chased with flutes, the foot and bowl with matted shaped-oval panels, 1650, maker's mark *E.T.* crescent below, 3½in. high, 2oz.
(Christie's) $16,252

A William and Mary parcel-gilt tumbler cup, the sides stamped with a broad band of matting and with molded rim, probably 1694, maker's mark indistinct, 2¼in. high.
(Christie's) $2,167

A George III coconut cup, 6½in. high, the bulbous circular bowl carved with figures, palm trees and hearts, silver rim hallmarked for 1809.
(Bonhams) $146

An Edwardian two handled trophy cup, on a domed foot repoussé with flower heads and scrolls, London 1901, by Stephen Smith, 620 grammes.
(Spencer's) $516

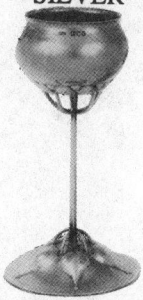

A Guild of Handicraft silver chalice, supported on wire work brackets and pentagonal stem, the flanged foot with repoussé decoration, with London hallmarks for 1902, 21.5cm. high, 275 grams.
(Christie's) $811

Gorham Martelé sterling presentation loving cup, Rhode Island, circa 1902, 11in. high, approximately 92 troy oz.
(Skinner Inc.) $6,500

A Victorian large silver-gilt inverted bell-shaped cup and cover, by James Garrard, 1890, with wood plinth applied with two silver-gilt plaques, one engraved *"THE GOODWOOD CUP, 1892"*, 18½in. high, 163oz.
(Christie's) $17,820

A German silver-mounted coconut cup and cover, the nut with three applied straps and with tapering cylindrical neck and detachable domed cover, by Samuel Kesborer, Ulm, circa 1595, 10¼in. high.
(Christie's) $60,676

A large Victorian two-handled trophy cup, 10½in. high, the sides engraved with diaper-worked panels and chased with 'C'-scrolls, ferns and other foliage, London, 1849, by Samuel Hayne and Dudley Carter, 31 ozs.
(Bonhams) $1,089

A German silver-gilt cup, formed as the standing figure of a lady, her skirt chased and engraved with stylized foliage and scrolls, by Abraham Tittecke (Dittecke), Nuremburg, circa 1600, 5½in. high, 153grs.
(Christie's) $53,460

Chinese Export silver egg set and stand, Khecheong, Canton, mid 19th century, six cups and spoons, 8in. high, approximately 28 troy oz.
(Skinner Inc.) $2,600

A Victorian two-handled parcel-gilt cup and cover, the handles formed as standing figures of fame, the cover with standing knight in armor finial, by Stephen Smith, 1871, 27½in. high, 170oz.
(Christie's) $6,284

## DISHES

A Victorian shaped oval sweet meat dish heavily chased with flowers and scrolling foliage, 10½in. long, London 1898, 9.9oz.
(Bearne's) $478

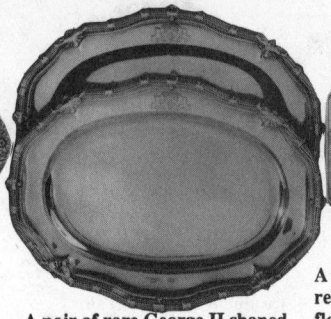

A pair of rare George II shaped-oval meat dishes, each with shell, foliage and reeded border, later engraved with a coat-of-arms, by Nicholas Sprimont, 1743, 13½in. long, 50oz.
(Christie's) $18,513

A Spanish octagonal dish, repoussé and chased with birds, flowers and foliage, Cordoba, early 18th century, maker's mark not identified, Fiel Contraste Francisco Alonso del Castillo, 15½in. wide, 450grs.
(Christie's) $3,609

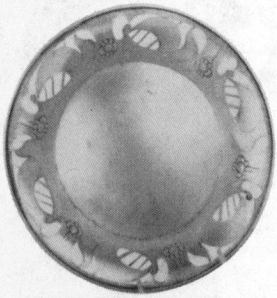

A Guild of Handicraft silver dish, designed by C.R. Ashbee, the border decorated with a pierced frieze of stylized galleons, London hallmarks for 1906, 20.5cm. diameter, 250 grams.
(Christie's) $1,024

A William IV circular butter dish, formed as a pail with swing handle, engraved with cypher, crest and Garter Motto, by Robert Garrard, 1834, 4¾in. diameter, 11oz.
(Christie's) $3,960

A late Victorian shaped-circular dish, the broad waved border chased with acorns and oak leaves, by Gilbert Marks, 1898, Britannia standard, 16¾in. diameter, 56oz.
(Christie's) $9,051

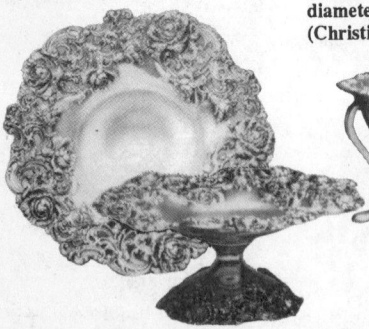

Pair of Black, Starr & Frost sterling compotes, circa 1880, rim and foot pierced with bold flowers, 11in. diameter, approximately 56 troy oz.
(Skinner Inc.) $2,300

Reed & Barton sterling chafing dish, early 20th century, on cabriole legs with paw feet, 10½in. high, approximately 81½ troy oz.
(Skinner Inc.) $1,400

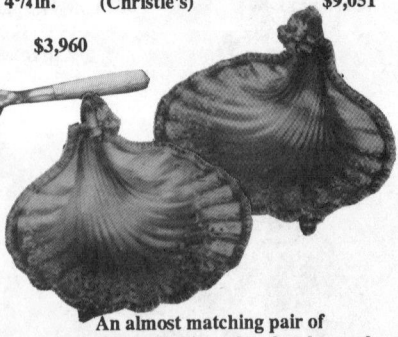

An almost matching pair of silver-gilt pierced and gadrooned shell-shaped bonbon dishes on cast and applied dolphin feet, Goldsmiths & Silversmiths Co. Ltd., London 1914 and 1917, 6in. and 5¾in., 21.25oz.
(Christie's S. Ken) $2,253

## DISHES

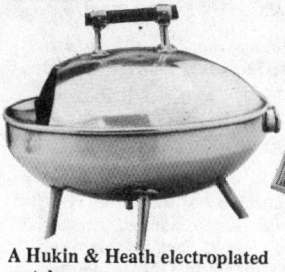

A Hukin & Heath electroplated metal spoon-warmer, supported on four spike feet, oval body, angular bar handle, the bar of ebonized wood, 14.5cm. high. (Christie's) $1,740

A Victorian octagonal butter dish, cover and stand, with vertical handles to the sides and flower finial to the slightly raised cover, by E.J. and W. Barnard, 1837, 20oz. (Christie's) $3,168

An attractive Arts and Crafts Movement butter dish and cover of compressed circular shape, the hammered surfaces chased with stylized chrysanthemum motifs, 6cm. high, 12.5cm. diameter, by H. Haseler, Birmingham, 1911, 14 ozs. (Phillips) $1,811

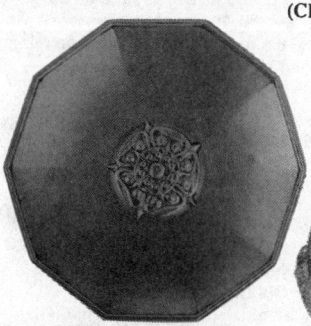

A small ten-sided dish with a molded border, decorated in the center with an applied boss, modeled as a Tudor rose, 15cm. diameter, 1932, 6.5 ozs. (Phillips) $563

A silver-gilt swan bon-bon dish, 5in. long, the cut-glass oval body with silver-gilt neck and head. (Bonhams) $293

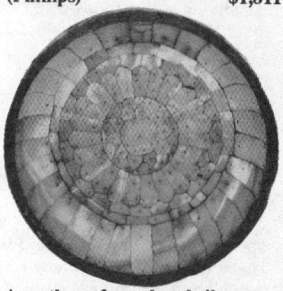

A mother-of-pearl and silver-mounted circular shallow dish, the center of flowerhead pattern engraved with the date 1568, possibly German, 10in. diameter. (Christie's S. Ken) $4,876

A pair of George II butter shells, engraved with an armed griffin crest, on webbed feet, S. Herbert & Co., London 1757, 7.5 oz. (Woolley & Wallis) $1,664

Austrian silver figural compote, late 19th century, chased shell form bowl supported by Bacchus and child, 14 1/8in. high, approximately 44 troy oz. (Skinner Inc.) $2,400

A pair of Victorian shaped-circular entrée dishes and covers, with gadrooned borders, by William Moulson, 1857, 10 1/2in. diameter, 86oz. (Christie's) $4,767

## FLATWARE

A Scottish Provincial toddy ladle, the plain bowl with monogram engraved to base, Aberdeen, circa 1810, maker's mark *WJ*.
(Bonhams) $291

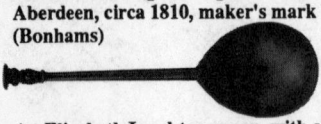

An Elizabeth I seal-top spoon, with a gilt elongated baluster fluted terminal, pricked with initials *EW*, pear-shaped bowl, 16.5cm. long, by W. Cawdell, London, 1589.
(Phillips) $1,610

A Guild of Handicraft silver butter knife, designed by C.R. Ashbee, with wirework 'cage' handle set with a pale green stone, with London hallmarks for 1900, 50 grams. gross.
(Christie's) $854

A Liberty & co. silver and enamel ceremonial spoon, designed by Archibald Knox, the shaped handle with elaborate entrelac design and blue-green and red enamel, Birmingham hallmark for 1900, 20.5cm. long, 95 grams. gross.
(Christie's) $6,402

An early George II hash spoon by Mary Lofthouse, the base of the bowl engraved with initials I.W.I., London 1732, 186 grams, 42cm. long.
(Spencer's) $2,362

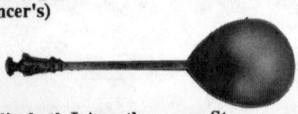

An Elizabeth I Apostle spoon, St. Bartholomew, the cast gilt figure terminal finely modeled with an esprit nimbus, 17.5cm. long, maker's mark an orb and cross, London, 1582.
(Phillips) $3,018

A spoon with rat-tail bowl and dog nose terminal, with engraved initials *PC*, Exeter, 1701 (maker PE), 19.5cm.
(Lawrence Fine Art) $1,271

A George III Stilton scoop, 9¾in. long, with baluster stem and tapering cylindrical handle, London, 1792, by George Smith.
(Bonhams) $252

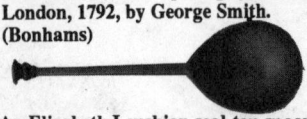

An Elizabeth I cushion seal-top spoon, the surface of the gilt seal prick-dotted with initials *RI*, pear-shaped bowl, 15.5cm. long, maker's mark *W* in a radiant circle, London, 1561.
(Phillips) $1,811

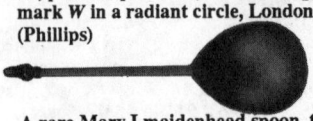

A rare Mary I maidenhead spoon, the cast female terminal gilt, the bowl fig-shaped, 15.5cm. long, maker's mark, crescent enclosing a mullet, London, 1557.
(Phillips) $3,622

A pair of George III Irish basting spoons, 12¼in. long, Old English pattern with crests engraved to terminals, Dublin, 1795, maker's mark *L&B*, 6 oz.
(Bonhams) $504

A spoon with rat-tail bowl and embossed scroll work, the terminal with shell and scroll decoration and initials RC, circa 1700, 19.5cm.
(Lawrence Fine Art) $805

An Edward VI Apostle spoon, St. James the Greater, the cast gilt figure terminal finely modeled, with a pierced nimbus and holding in his right hand a pilgrim's staff, 18cm. long, by Nicholas Bartlemew (sic), London, 1548.
(Phillips) $9,658

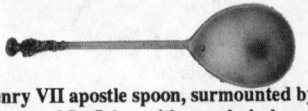

A Henry VII apostle spoon, surmounted by the gilt figure of St. John, with rayed nimbus, 1508, maker's mark illegible.
(Christie's) $8,640

## FLATWARE

A George IV meat skewer, 11¼in. long, beveled blade and pierced loop terminal, London, 1825, 3 oz.
(Bonhams) $232

A Henry VIII hexagonal seal-top spoon, plain, of reasonable good gauge, with gilt hexagonal terminal, fig-shaped bowl, 15cm. long, maker's mark a basket, London, 1532.
(Phillips) $3,823

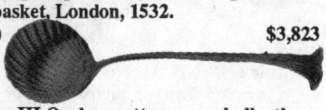

A George III Onslow pattern soup ladle, the cast terminal inscribed on the reverse with initials, maker Thomas Evans, London 1772, 4.5 oz.
(Woolley & Wallis) $735

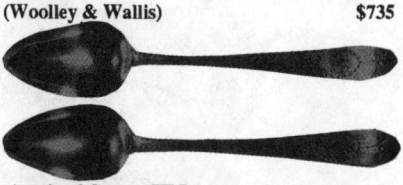

A pair of George III Irish serving spoons, 9¾in. long, Old English pattern bright-cut engraved with zig-zag border, Dublin, 1802, by John Power, 4 oz.
(Bonhams) $310

A pair of William IV cast naturalistic sugar nips, oak bough decorated, William Theobalds, London 1834.
(Woolley & Wallis) $252

A Guild of Handicraft silver butter knife, designed by C.R. Ashbee, with twisted wirework 'cage' handle set with a faceted amethyst, with London hallmarks for 1905, 35 grams. gross.
(Christie's) $462

A 19th century Russian enameled silver ladle, 8½in. long overall, maker's mark 84 standard mark, St. Petersburg, 95gms.
(Bearne's) $919

An early Victorian Stilton scoop by Martin Hall and Co., the silver cased handle stamped with strapwork and beading, Sheffield 1854.
(Spencer's) $554

A Charles II rare Provincial ascribed trefid spoon, plain, egg-shaped bowl, 19cm. long, punched twice with the maker's mark *EM* for Edward Mangie, Hull, circa 1666.
(Phillips) $644

A Guild of Handicraft silver jam spoon, designed by C.R. Ashbee, set with abalone, with London hallmarks for 1906, 45 grams. gross.
(Christie's) $384

A very rare Henry VII Apostle spoon, St. James the Greater carrying a pilgrim's staff, length 18cm., punched in the bowl with an early variation of the crowned leopard's head, and on the stem with a obscure maker's mark representing a Gothic L (?) and the date letter for London, 1490.
(Phillips) $40,240

A rare William and Mary Provincial ascribed lace back trefid spoon, embossed on the back of the egg-shaped, ribbed rat-tail bowl, 17cm. long, by Thomas Hebden, Hull, circa 1690.
(Phillips) $2,012

A mid Victorian silver traveling apple corer, the hollow handle of slightly tapering cylindrical form with screw on corer, Birmingham 1854, by John Tongue, 31 grammes.
(Spencer's) $398

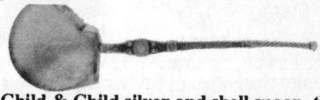

A Child & Child silver and shell spoon, the bowl formed by a thin scallop shell having subtle nacreous sheen, 26cm. long, 1903.
(Phillips) $622

## FRAMES

An Edward VII shaped square photograph frame, chased and pierced with figs amongst scrolls and foliate festoons, 10in. high, London 1902.
(Bearne's) $770

A Victorian heart-shaped dressing table mirror, within a frame of scrolling foliage, masks, drapes and trelliswork, 11in. high, William Comyns, London 1897.(Bearne's) $866

An Art Nouveau silver shaped oval photograph frame with easel support, John and William Deakin, Birmingham 1904, 12in. high.(Christie's S. Ken) $465

An Art Nouveau silver photograph frame, the shaped square frame with floral repoussé decoration, one corner with drape motif, Birmingham hallmarks for 1904, 15.8cm. high.
(Christie's) $1,991

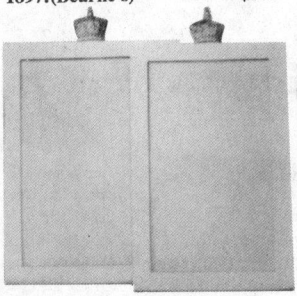

A plain oblong photograph frame with easel support and crown surmount, Mappin and Webb, London 1911, 13¼in., and a matching smaller photograph frame, 13in.
(Christie's S. Ken) $973

A William Hutton and Sons silver and enamel picture frame, with repoussé entrelac decoration, the top corners decorated with blue-green enamel, London hallmarks for 1903, 19.3cm. high.
(Christie's) $2,987

A Victorian heart-shaped photograph frame, decorated with cherubs faces amongst scrolling flowers and foliage, 7½in. high, William Comyns, London 1897.
(Bearne's) $578

A decorative Edwardian photograph frame, in the Art Nouveau style with ivy on a wood back, 1901, 24.8cm. high x 21.5cm. wide.
(Phillips) $6,036

A Liberty and Co. silver photograph frame, the top and base decorated with band of mistletoe, stamped maker's mark *L & Co.* and Birmingham hallmarks for 1892, 21.3cm. high.(Christie's) $1,593

## GOBLETS

Paul Storr silver-gilt goblet, $4^{3}/_{4}$in. high, with an applied frieze of Classical females linked by floral swags, London, 1814, 5.5 oz.
(Bonhams) $3,487

A pair of goblets, the thistle shape bodies with a girdle molding above fluting, $7^{1}/_{2}$in., Peter and William Bateman, London 1806, and William Bateman, London 1818, 23.5oz.
(Woolley & Wallis) $1,692

A C.R. Ashbee hammered silver goblet, the foot with a radiating repoussé pattern of stylized buds, London hallmarks for 1899, 12cm. high, 300 grams.
(Christie's) $1,067

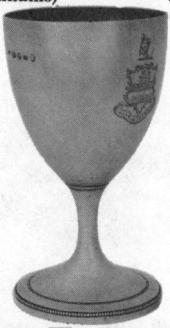

A George III goblet, engraved with a coat of arms, the circular foot with beaded border, by William Allen II, 1787, 15.5cm., 7.5oz.
(Lawrence Fine Art) $734

A mid Victorian wine ewer and matching pair of goblets, the high curved lip and applied with a bacchanalian mask, London 1874, mark *F.E.*, 1464 grammes total. (Spencer's) $3,580

A William III goblet, with cylindrical stem and tapering conical bowl, engraved with stylized strapwork, scrolls and foliage, by Robert Peake, 1701, $6^{1}/_{4}$in, 11oz. $4,246
(Christie's)

A Spanish silver-gilt chalice, on large circular foot chased with four coats-of-arms between winged cherubs masks and scrolls, Zamora, 17th century, $9^{1}/_{2}$in. high, 722grs.
(Christie's) $5,520

A pair of George III goblets and covers, the lower part of the bowl with applied acanthus leaves, the tapering covers with similarly chased acanthus leaves and with acorn finials, by D. Smith and R. Sharp, 1773, $9^{1}/_{4}$in. high, 32oz. (Christie's) $7,920

A Victorian gilt-lined and beaded goblet on a foliate, floral and thistle-chased rising circular foot, D. & C. Hands, London 1867, $7^{1}/_{2}$in., 10.75 oz.
(Christie's S. Ken) $629

## INKSTANDS

A late Victorian ink stand, with beaded border and foliate engraved rim, the floriform stamped central panel supporting a diamond and slice cut globular glass ink well, 15.5cm. diameter.
(Spencer's) $313

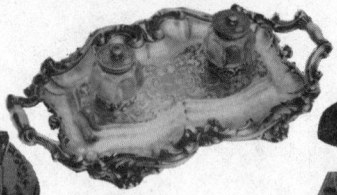

Richard Sibley, a fine early Victorian inkstand, the center chased with leafy scrolls and engraved with the contemporary coat of arms of Butler, 13in. wide, London 1840, 26oz.
(Woolley & Wallis) $5,771

An unusual horn and plated inkwell and bell, designed as two dolphins, on a wooden plinth, 43cm.
(Lawrence Fine Art) $1,004

A large two-handled oblong treasury inkstand, with three internal inkwells labelled *RED*, *WRITING* and *COPYING*, engraved with the Prince of Wales crest, by Elkington and Co. Ltd., Birmingham, 1903, 12in. long, 117oz.
(Christie's) $8,228

An unusual Continental inkstand on a rising oval base, the inkwell itself finely-modeled and chased as the head of a wild boar resting on scrolling oak leaves, Berthold Muller, London 1910, 7in., 41 oz.
(Christie's S. Ken) $3,483

A Batavian silver writing tray comprising a pen box with hinged lid and finial handle and shaped trefoil tray, on three molded animalistic feet, by Jurriaan van Kalker, circa 1725–1730, 24cm. wide, 38 oz.
(Christie's) $19,360

A William IV shaped-oval inkstand, the shaped sides and bottle holders pierced with foliate scrolls and gadrooned rims, by Edward Farrell, 1836, 12¾in. long, 59oz.
(Christie's) $6,068

An Old Sheffield plate globe inkstand on a reeded rising circular foot, applied with paterae and drapery swags, 8½in. overall.
(Christie's S. Ken) $710

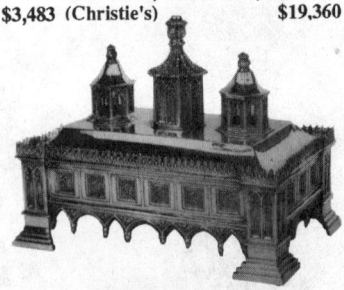

A Victorian oblong inkstand, surmounted by two pierced octagonal inkwells, each with hinged cover, and a similar hexagonal central wafer box, by Joseph Angell, 1855, 14¼in. long, 92oz.
(Christie's) $5,760

## JUGS

George III silver covered wine jug, Peter and Ann Bateman, London 1795, bright cut decoration, approximately 31 troy oz.
(Skinner Inc.) $2,000

A 19th century French silver colored metal hot water jug, the hinged gadrooned cover with applied pomegranate finial, Paris mark, 17cm. high.
(Spencer's) $774

A George III hot water jug, 11¼in. high, with fluted spout and wicker-bound scroll handle, London, 1768, by Augustin Le Sage, 26 oz.
(Bonhams) $2,131

A George III wine jug, the body of elongated baluster form, engraved with a coat of arms and on pedestal foot, by Boulton & Fothergill, Birmingham, 1775, 34cm., 20 oz.
(Lawrence Fine Art) $2,118

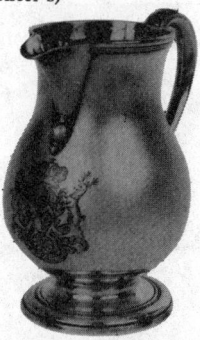

A George II plain pear-shaped beer jug, with baluster drop to the curved lip and harp-shaped handle, by William Darker, 1729, 7½in. high, 24oz.
(Christie's) $9,751

A good George III wine jug, the domed cover with pineapple finial, scroll handle and square pedestal base with ball feet, maker's mark *Morson & Stephenson*, 1772, 33cm., 36 oz.
(Lawrence Fine Art) $7,199

A Victorian molded oval hot water jug in the 18th century taste, on a rising foot, Richard Sibley, London 1871, 6¾in., 13 oz.
(Christie's S. Ken) $1,079

A Victorian wine jug, the elongated baluster body engraved with panels of strapwork, shaped cover with turned finial and scroll handle, by Robert Hennell, 1863, 25cm., 16 oz.
(Lawrence Fine Art) $805

A late 19th century electroplated lidded jug in the style of an adapted 18th century tankard, 8¼in. high.
(Bearne's) $500

A Victorian wine jug, the body engraved with panels of fruit and an inscription dated 1867 surrounded by scrollwork, by Henry Holland, 1867, 35cm., 26oz. $1,930
(Lawrence Fine Art)

An Elizabeth I silver-mounted tigerware jug, chased with foliage and bead ornament, the cylindrical neck mount engraved with strapwork and foliage, by John Jones, Exeter, circa 1575, 8in. high. $8,910
(Christie's)

An Edwardian plain vase-shaped hot water jug on a rising circular foot, with a reeded shoulder mount, Goldsmiths & Silversmiths Co. Ltd., London 1905, 11¾in. $465
(Christie's S. Ken)

A good Victorian wine jug of baroque design, the silver mounts repoussé with shells and flowers, female caryatid handle, 1898 (maker's mark obscured), 35cm. $2,124
(Lawrence Fine Art)

A Regency jug, richly embossed with fruit and foliage, scrolls to the crested cartouche, 7½in., Alice & George Burroughs, London 1818, 27oz.
(Woolley & Wallis) $1,791

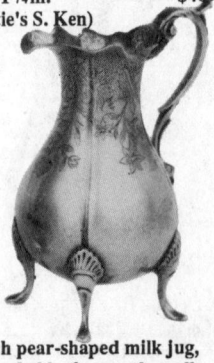

A Dutch pear-shaped milk jug, with beaded leaf-capped scroll handle and shaped rim, by Wijnand Warneke, Amsterdam, 1792, 5½in. high, 266grs.
(Christie's) $3,034

A late Victorian beaded cylindrical jug applied with a foliate-cast scroll handle and with a shell-fluted cast spout, Chester 1897, 4½in., 10.75oz.
(Christie's S. Ken) $803

A highly unusual milk jug, by Charles Fox, 4⅞in. high, the body chased with hare coursing scenes, London, 1830, 12.5oz.
(Bonhams) $3,477

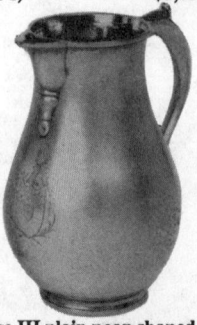

A George III plain pear-shaped beer jug, with leaf-capped scroll handle and molded rim and spout, 1780, maker's mark erased, 7in. high, 21oz.
(Christie's) $4,356

## MISCELLANEOUS SILVER

A Victorian figure of a donkey and cart, the silver gilt two wheeled cart with spindle sides, 1891, 16 oz.
(Lawrence Fine Art) $4,023

A George III fish slice, 11½in. long, oval pierced blade engraved with a monogram, London, 1800, by John Emes.
(Bonhams) $271

A set of six Art Nouveau silver buttons, cast with a portrait of a girl, Chester 1902.
(Spencer's) $224

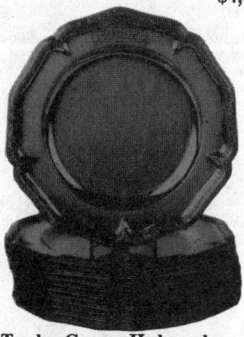

Twelve George II shaped-circular dinner plates, with reed-and-tie borders, by George Hindmarsh, 1740, 9½in. diameter, 238oz.
(Christie's) $20,570

A Continental model of a two masted nef, the hull chased with panels of Mercury and Europa, the prow formed as a dolphin, Chester import marks for 1909, 26¾in. high, 96oz.
(Christie's) $5,760

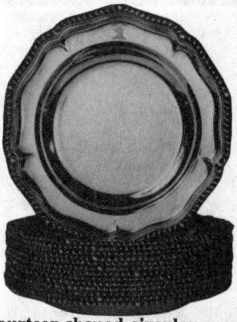

Fourteen shaped-circular soup plates, each with gadrooned border, thirteen by William Brown, twelve 1835, one 1834; and one by John S. Hunt, 1860, 10in. diameter, 310oz.
(Christie's) $12,342

A French large wine barrel and stand, the stand with X-shaped frame and stretcher, the barrel with two dolphins mask spouts, the stand stamped *C. Bayard*, late 19th century, 27½in. high overall.
(Christie's) $10,285

An Italian parcel gilt circular wine taster, the center chased with a recumbent sleeping dog within a border of stylized foliage, Turin, probably mid 17th century, 5¼in. diameter, 117grs.
(Christie's) $22,627

A spherical bezoar stone holder and stand, the holder pierced overall with foliage and with gilt liner and stone, the stand by Adey Bellamy Savory, 1826, the holder probably Middle Eastern, 18th century, 5in. high.
(Christie's) $10,696

## MISCELLANEOUS SILVER

A late Victorian trump marker, the silver fascia stamped with scrolls and foliage the color decorated ivorine marker with silver slides. Birmingham mark, 3in. wide.
(Spencer's) $348

An unusual late Victorian candle snuffer modeled as a pair of bellows, by James Bell & Louis Wilmott, 1900 and inscribed with retailer's name *H. Wells, Shrewsbury.*
(Phillips) $602

An 18th century English wine taster, part lobed decorated border, the reverse engraved with a coronet within a grape border.
(Woolley & Wallis) $1,084

A Hukin & Heath electroplated metal and cut-glass condiment holder, designed by Dr. Christopher Dresser, complete with two original spoons, registration lozenge for 1878, 9cm. high.
(Christie's) $4,501

A Victorian card case decorated in high relief with a panoramic view of a cathedral or minster, by Nathaniel Mills, Birmingham, 1846.
(Phillips) $1,509

A spirit barrel, the cut glass body with silver mounts, including bung, spigot and on a stand of trestle design, Birmingham, 1927, 24cm.
(Lawrence Fine Art) $1,588

A James Dixon & Sons electroplated condiment holder, designed by Dr. Christopher Dresser, the wide circular base on three ball feet, 20.8cm. high.
(Christie's) $1,566

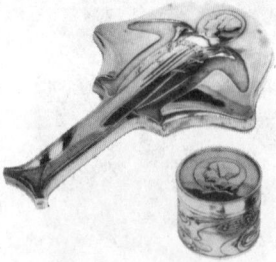

A Goldsmiths' and Silversmiths' Co. silver handmirror, designed by Kate Harris, and a Goldsmiths' and Silversmiths' Co. silver box and cover, London hallmarks for 1990.
(Christie's) $1,991

A table bell, of domed form decorated with scrolls and with two winged cherub masks, the finial cast as a young girl playing a tambourine, stamped *925F*, 4in. high.
(Spencer's) $354

## MISCELLANEOUS SILVER

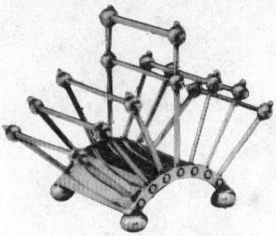

A Hukin & Heath electroplated articulated metal letter-rack, designed by Dr. Christopher Dresser, with three movable supports on either side, stamped *H&H 2555*, 12.5cm. high.
(Christie's) $1,023

An inlaid silver ox and ceremonial cart, the ox standing foursquare with head raised, chased with foliate scrolls in relief, the hooves and harness gilt, late Qing Dynasty, 47cm. long.
(Christie's) $8,536

French silver gilt powder jar, Paris, circa 1900, compressed cylindrical body with chased spiral fluting and leaf motif, signed *A. Bucher*, approximately 10 troy oz.
(Skinner Inc.) $1,000

A Guild of Handicraft silver biscuit barrel, designed by C.R. Ashbee, with green Powell glass liner, the lid with red enamel and wirework finial, with London hallmarks for 1900, 20.5cm. high, 475 grams. gross.
(Christie's) $7,682

A large white metal petrol-burning table lighter with clock mounted to the front, the matt gilt dial with stepped bezel, 10 x 8cm.
(Christie's S. Ken) $295

A silver koro, the pierced spherical body worked in colored shippo and gilt with a continuous decoration of insects amongst a dense mass of mixed flowers and plants, late 19th century, 15.4cm. high.
(Christie's) $5,420

A WMF figure of a blacksmith, $10^1/_2$in. high, the well modeled figure pictured by his anvil with a hammer in hand, on ebonized rectangular plinth.
(Bonhams) $389

Charles Stuart Harris, set of twelve Edwardian silver gilt dessert plates, the matt borders embossed with foliate scrolls and birds, $9^1/_4$in. diameter, London 1902–09, 217 oz.
(Woolley & Wallis) $8,708

A Georg Jensen cocktail shaker, with two handles each shaped as fruiting vines, cylindrical lid with pine finial, stamped maker's mark, 24.5cm. high, 500 grams.
(Christie's) $3,982

## MISCELLANEOUS SILVER

A casket in 17th century style, the octagonal body and domed cover with repoussé decoration of panels of fruit, Continental, 18cm., 20oz.
(Lawrence Fine Art) $1,699

A novelty cocktail shaker modeled as a bell, Asprey & Co. Ltd., Birmingham 1946, 10¼in., 25oz. gross.
(Christie's S. Ken) $913

A Continental model of a pig, the detachable head with an appealing quizzical expression, Berthold Muller, bearing import marks for Chester 1899, 5¼in., 7.75oz.
(Christie's S. Ken) $1,126

A George III honey pot formed as a bee skep, on circular stand with reed-and-tie borders, by Paul Storr, 1797, 4½in. high, 14oz.
(Christie's) $35,640

An Art Nouveau three-handled coupe, the twisted whiplash handles curving up from the base and joining the body with foliate terminals, Charles Edwards, London 1904, 8¼in. high, 12oz.
(Christie's S. Ken) $387

A George II triangular kettle stand, on three lion's paw feet and with molded foliate scroll border, by William Peaston, 1752, 10½in. wide, 22oz.
(Christie's) $3,397

An electroplated spoon warmer in the form of a nautilus shell with bright-cut decoration on rocky base with shell handle, 5¾in. high.
(Bearne's) $147

A plain cylindrical measure, with molded borders and tapering cylindrical handle with ring top, circa 1800, diameter of bowl 4¼in., 16oz.
(Christie's) $4,671

A French circular chamber pot, with scroll handle applied with fruit and foliage and with everted molded rim, by Veyrat, Paris, circa 1880, 9¼in. diameter, 1,126grs.
(Christie's) $2,970

## MISCELLANEOUS SILVER

An amusing German minaudiere, embossed on the front with two cats and a kitten in a wicker basket, 9.50 x 6.50cm., bearing marks for Louis Kuppenheim of Pforzheim, and '900'.
(Phillips) $1,167

A George II wax-jack, on three claw-and-ball feet and with cylindrical stem, maker's mark *C.N.*, circa 1755, 5½in. high.
(Christie's) $2,760

An Austro Hungarian silver gilt oval casket, chased overall with eagles, foliage and rococo ornament, the hinged cover containing two oval portrait miniatures, the box apparently 1855, 6in. wide.
(Christie's) $3,609

Twelve Old Sheffield plate shaped-circular dinner plates, with molded gadrooned borders, engraved with a coat-of-arms and later initials M & S, circa 1780, 9½in. diameter.
(Christie's) $2,970

A cup holder, the openwork frame of a trellis of roses having a leaf decorated handle, inscribed *Omar Ramsden me fecit*, London 1927, 6.5oz.
(Woolley & Wallis) $597

An Edwardian oblong card case die-stamped with an Art Nouveau profile bust portrait of a maiden with flowing hair and elaborate headdress, Chrisford & Norris, Birmingham 1905, 3¾in..
(Christie's S. Ken) $632

A Victorian shaped rectangular card case, bright-cut with floral and foliate decoration, George Unite, Birmingham 1891.
(Christie's S. Ken) $319

A Victorian novelty conical cigar lighter modeled as a candle snuffer, applied with a scroll handle and engraved with an initial and coronet, L.D., London 1883, 6¼in.
(Christie's S. Ken) $813

An Art Nouveau circular plaque stamped in high relief with a classical maiden seated in a garden, stamped with Sheffield hallmarks, 11½in. diameter, 11oz.
(Christie's S. Ken) $658

## MUGS

A George II plain baluster pint mug, with a molded rim and double scroll handle, Robert Albin Cox, London 1752, 4¾in., 7.75oz.
(Christie's S. Ken) $1,306

A mug, the tapering cylindrical body plain, apart from an engraved reeded band and molded rim foot, by Timothy Ley, William III or Queen Anne, possibly 1701, 9cm., 6 oz.
(Lawrence Fine Art) $1,376

A Victorian Aesthetic Movement mug, the body finely engraved with Japanese style swallows, foliage, half-circular and geometric patterns, 10cm. high, Edward Charles Brown, 1879, 6 ozs. (Phillips) $604

An Indian Colonial 19th century gilt-lined campana-shaped christening mug, the fluted body chased and applied with flowers and foliage and with a molded rim, Hamilton & Co., Calcutta circa 1860, 4½in., 9oz.
(Christie's S. Ken) $453

A Queen Anne mug of tapering form, with a reeded band and plain thumbpiece to scroll handle, 10cm. high, by Humphrey Payne, 1710, 6.7 ozs.
(Phillips) $1,308

A George II baluster mug later-chased with rococo flowers and scrolling foliage and on a rising circular base, Humphrey Payne, London 1744, 4½in., 11.75oz.
(Christie's S. Ken) $965

A George III plain baluster mug with leaf-capped scroll handle and spreading foot, probably by John Deacon, 1774, 12.3cm. high, 10.5 ozs.
(Phillips) $905

A fine early Victorian campana shape half pint mug, chased and embossed with a cow and sheep in pastoral landscape, 5¼in., John Evans II, London 1839, 6.5 oz.
(Woolley & Wallis) $851

A late 17th century tapering mug with a molded rim and applied fluted scroll handle, the body engraved with two reeded bands, possibly Norwich, 3¾in.
(Christie's S. Ken) $858

## MUGS

A Victorian mug, 5 3/8 in. high, the fluted campana-shaped body chased with floral clusters, London, 1840, by Rawlins and Sumner, 10 ozs.
(Bonhams) $622

A Charles II globular mug, the body flat chased with Chinoiserie figures and foliage, by George Garlthorne, 1683, 4 1/4 in. high, 8oz.
(Christie's) $9,900

A Victorian silver-gilt campana-shaped christening mug on a domed circular base applied with classical musicians, George Adams, London 1858, 5in.
(Christie's S. Ken) $792

A George III plain baluster mug, with a scroll handle and spreading circular foot, engraved with a monogram, 13cm. high, maker's mark *WF* in Gothic script, 1765, 12.25 ozs.
(Phillips) $905

A George II mug of circular baluster form with engraved inscription on spreading base, 4 1/2 in. high, maker's mark *R.B.*, London 1738, 360 gms, 11.7 oz.
(Bearne's) $1,117

A large George III plain mug of tapering shape with flared lip, applied girdle and leaf-capped scroll handle, by Peter & Anne Bateman, 1791, 16cm. high, 20.5 ozs.
(Phillips) $2,213

A late George II mug by Isaac Cookson, on a skirt foot, the scrolling and rescrolling handle with heart shaped terminal, Newcastle 1750, 577 grams, 16cm. high over handle.
(Spencer's) $1,255

An early Victorian christening mug of paneled waisted cylindrical form, engraved with a presentation inscription, and panels of diapering and foliage, London 1853, maker's mark *RD*, 127 grams.
(Spencer's) $277

A George III plain baluster mug with leaf-capped scroll handle and spreading foot, by Francis Crump, 1762, 10.25cm. high, 6.75 ozs.
(Phillips) $704

## MUSTARDS

A fine George IV mustard pot, the melon paneled body and hinged cover chased and embossed with foliage, William Elliott, London 1823, 5 oz.
(Woolley & Wallis) $677

A George III mustard pot, 3¾in. high, with shell and 'C'-scroll border leaf-capped strap handle on three scroll supports, London, 1819, by Sarah and John William Blake, 7 oz.
(Bonhams) $387

A George IV mustard pot, 3½in. high, circular, with gadrooned border and double scroll handle on raised circular foot, London, 1822, by Joseph Biggs, 5 oz.
(Bonhams) $232

A French vase-shaped mustard pot, the bowl chased with a band of foliage and with double serpent scroll handle, Lille, circa 1755, maker's mark *I.B.H.*, 5¼in., 274grs.
(Christie's) $5,634

A pair of Ramsden and Carr silver mustard-pots, supported on four pad feet, cylindrical blue glass liners, stamped maker's mark RN & CR and London hallmarks for 1903, 7cm. high.
(Christie's) $597

John Denziloe, pierced drum shape mustard pot, with gothic fret sides, blue glass liner, London 1773.
(Woolley & Wallis) $929

An unusual Victorian mustard pot, 3½in. high, the flat hinged cover engraved with a crest and with an applied frog thumbpiece, London, 1850, by Charles and George Fox, 7 ozs.
(Bonhams) $1,323

A large Regency mustard pot, the hinged cover with a cast flower finial, cast satyr mask scroll handle, John Wakefield, London 1819, 9.5 oz.
(Woolley & Wallis) $1,122

A C.R. Ashbee hammered silver mustard pot, set with three amber cabochons, original clear glass liner, stamped *C R A* with London hallmarks for 1900, 6.5cm. high, 100 grams. gross.
(Christie's) $1,707

## MUSTARDS

A Victorian mustard pot, 2¾in. high, with molded borders, double scroll handle, the flat cover with pierced thumbpiece and engraved monogram, *London, 1853, by Martin Hall and Company*, 5 ozs.
(Bonhams) $447

A good George IV gilt-lined molded circular mustard pot, the body cast and chased with game birds in a mountainous landscape, Charles Price, London 1823, overall length 4¾in., 10oz.
(Christie's S. Ken) $1,791

A George III mustard, circular with gadrooned border, oval thumbpiece and angled handle, the flat-winged cover engraved with a crest, *London, 1815*.
(Bonhams) $584

A Victorian mustard pot, 3½in. high, on rim foot with scroll handle, the raised hinged cover with baluster finial revealing detachable blue glass liner, London, 1844, by Hayne and Carter, 5 ozs.
(Bonhams) $467

A Regency oval mustard pot, with a clear glass liner, artichoke finial and domed hinged cover engraved with a crest and motto, Philip Rundell, London 1820, 3¼in.
(Christie's S. Ken) $1,277

A George III mustard pot, with bands of bright cut decoration, domed cover, by Crispin Fuller, 1792 (with a salt spoon of 1808), 9cm.
(Lawrence Fine Art) $1,197

A George III mustard pot, 3¾in. high, with beaded borders and scroll handle, the hinged domed cover with urn finial, detachable blue glass liner, London, 1786, by Thomas Shepherd.
(Bonhams) $1,751

A Victorian circular mustard pot with hinged cover, plain, engraved crests, 5.72oz., with blue glass liner.
(Phillips) $188

A George III mustard pot, 3¼in. high, the domed hinged cover with shell thumbpiece and urn finial, London, 1810, by Emes and Barnard, 5 oz.
(Bonhams) $387

## PITCHERS & EWERS

Kirk repoussé silver covered pitcher, Baltimore, 1846–61, recumbent deer finial, chased floral and village landscape decoration, 9in. high, aproximately 33 troy oz.
(Skinner Inc.) $1,800

Silver ewer, Crosby, Morse & Foss, Boston, circa 1850, 14in. high, approximately 32 troy oz.
(Skinner Inc.) $750

An Italian fluted baluster ewer on a shaped circular domed foot, applied with a cast double scroll handle, Venice or Padua, 7¼in., 13.25oz.
(Christie's S. Ken) $1,877

A Spanish plain cylindrical ewer, the spout cast with a bearded mask, scrolls and foliage, 17th century, marked only *REISS*, 7¾in. high, 825grs.
(Christie's) $19,800

An impressive Victorian ewer, 14½in. high, with loop handle and domed hinged cover, London, 1871, by Stephen Smith, 27oz.
(Bonhams) $1,181

A Victorian parcel-gilt ewer, the vase-shaped body repoussé and chased with putti, hops and acanthus foliage, by Elkington & Co., Birmingham, 1864, in fitted wood case, 12in. high, 51oz.
(Christie's) $7,643

A Danish oval ewer, with fluted knop and harp-shaped handle, the fluted body of shaped outline, by Silvert Thorsteinsson, Copenhagen, 1786, 9½in. high, 612grs.
(Christie's) $3,086

A Victorian plated lidded baluster ewer, with cast boar's head terminal, and domed hinged cover with cast rampant horse finial, 1885, 14¼in.
(Christie's S. Ken) $2,070

A George III wine ewer, 12½in. high, with beaded borders and leaf mounted wooden scroll handle, London, 1773, by Daniel Smith and Robert Sharp, 30 oz.
(Bonhams) $3,874

## PORRINGERS

A Guild of Handicraft twin-handled hammered silver porringer, the wirework handles set with a triangular panel with repoussé decoration of stylized leaves and each set with an amber cabochon, with London hallmarks for 1900, 210 grams. gross.
(Christie's) $2,774

A porringer, 5½in. diameter, spiral fluted to lower body, beaded double-scroll handles and stylized foliate chasing to base, London, 1908, 5.5oz.
(Bonhams) $311

A Guild of Handicraft twin-handled silver porringer and cover with spoon, the cover with turquoise and wirework finial set with mother of pearl, with London hallmarks for 1903, 340 grams. gross.
(Christie's) $6,402

A Carolean style compressed pear-shaped porringer and cover chased with a lion and a unicorn surrounded by elaborate rococo flowers and foliage, George Fox, London 1905, Britannia Standard, 5in. overall, 12oz.
(Christie's S. Ken) $383

A Charles II two-handled porringer, with beaded scroll handles and chased with a band of foliage and with a vacant oval cartouche, 1660, 3½in. wide, 7oz.
(Christie's) $4,034

A Victorian porringer and cover in Charles II style, with chased and repoussé decoration of a lion, unicorn and flowerheads, maker's mark *WC/JL*, 1897, 16cm., 22.5oz.
(Lawrence Fine Art) $1,351

A George III porringer, 3in. high, with ropetwist band and two double-scroll handles, London, 1769, by Thomas Cooke II and Richard Gurney, 4 oz.
(Bonhams) $1,511

A William and Mary part spiral-fluted porringer applied with scroll handles and with a rope-twist body band, maker's initials *W.G.*, London 1691, 7½in. overall, 9.50oz.
(Christie's S. Ken) $2,323

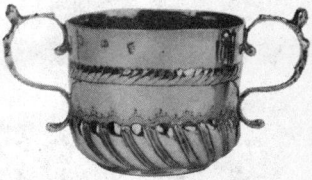

A Commonwealth two-handled porringer, the lower part of the body chased with spiral flutes and with a band of ropework above, 1659, maker's mark *R.N.*, 3in. high, 6oz.
(Christie's) $2,167

## SALTS & PEPPERS

One of a pair of Elkington & Co. Victorian salts, with blue glass liners, Birmingham 1852, 8 oz. (Woolley & Wallis) (Two) $387

A matched pair of 18th century double lipped salts, on shaped oval bases, gilt interiors, one London, 1756, the other with rubbed marks, possibly by David Hennell. (Bonhams) $700

A Guild of Handicraft lidded hammered silver salt dish, set with a cabochon amethyst, with green Powell glass liner, with London hallmarks for 1904, 5.5cm. high, 50 grams. gross. (Christie's) $598

A pair of Victorian circular salts cast and pierced with scrolls, festoons and acanthus with blue glass liners, 3¼in. diameter, John and Henry Lias, London 1840. (Bearne's) $643

A C.R. Ashbee hammered silver salt stand, the vertical supports with openwork design of stylized trees set with heart-shaped amber cabochons, London hallmarks for 1900, 5cm. high, 50 grams. gross. (Christie's) $896

A pair of Victorian parcel-gilt shell-shaped salts, the shells chased with flutes and with rococo borders, by Robert Garrard, 1861, 4¼in. long, 17oz. (Christie's) $5,520

A George III good set of four cauldron salts, the bellied circular bodies finely chased with sprays of flowers and leaves, by Thomas Holland II, 1808, 34 ozs. (Phillips) $5,090

A pair of Victorian octagonal salts, each applied with a coat-of-arms and Royal monogram, the detachable tapering cover with beaded finial, by James Garrard, 1897, 5in. high, 12oz. (Christie's) $5,940

David Hennell, set of four early George III oval salts, on shell applique legs, with hoof feet, London 1762, 12 oz. (Woolley & Wallis) $813

## SAUCE BOATS

A pair of George V oval sauce boats, each on three shell capped feet, 8in. long, Goldsmiths and Silversmiths Company Ltd., London 1932, 750 gms, 24.1 oz.
(Bearne's) $1,001

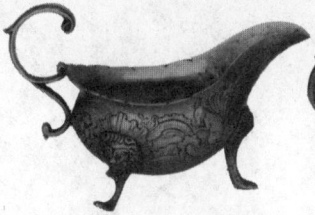

A George III Irish sauceboat with repoussé decoration of a dog, bird and squirrel among scrollwork, Dublin, circa 1765 (maker's mark poorly struck), 7.5oz.
(Lawrence Fine Art) $927

Two Victorian sauce boats of George III design, the boat shape bodies with floral repoussé decoration, maker's mark *J.A.*, 1854/1859, 16.5cm., 14.5 oz.
(Lawrence Fine Art) $1,101

Two plain oval sauceboats, with shaped rims and upcurved scroll handle engraved with acanthus foliage, 18th century, marks not identified, 1137grs.
(Christie's) $6,994

A pair of fine George I plain two-handled double-lipped sauceboats, each on spreading oval foot and with molded rim, by George Wickes, 1725, 7½in. long, 26oz.
(Christie's) $43,340

A pair of George II fluted shaped-oval sauceboats, each with leaf-capped scroll handle and reeded rim, by John Jacobs, 1739, 7¼in. long, 29oz.
(Christie's) $10,890

A pair of George III large shaped-oval sauceboats, each body applied with a similar band and with leaf-capped scroll handle and gadrooned rim, by Thomas Robins, 1811, 9½in. long, 48oz.
(Christie's) $11,313

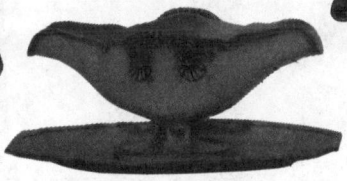

A French late 19th century two-handled double lipped oval sauce boat with shaped reeded border and fitted oval stand, 10in. wide.
(Christie's S. Ken) $629

A pair of fine George II plain double-lipped sauceboats, each with molded shaped rim and faceted double scroll handles, by Peter Archambo, 1729, 8½in. long, 37oz.
(Christie's) $46,706

## TANKARDS

A good Charles II-style tankard, 'C' scroll thumbpiece, scroll handle and molded foot rim, Robert Frederick Fox, London 1915, 27 oz.
(Woolley & Wallis) $1,161

A Continental large cylindrical three-handled tankard and cover, the body and cover inset with various thalers of Saxony, Austria, etc., London import marks for 1892, 15in. high, 104oz. (Christie's) $5,554

A good Queen Anne-style tankard, the flat cover with inscription and twist thumbpiece, Carrington & Co., London 1920, 27.5 oz.
(Woolley & Wallis) $1,084

A George II lidded baluster quart tankard on a rising circular foot, with a molded body band, probably Richard Bayley, London 1750, 7¾in., 25 oz.
(Christie's S. Ken) $3,259

A Scandinavian plain parcel-gilt cylindrical tankard, with scroll handle, ball thumbpiece and hinged, slightly domed cover, possibly by Henrik Moller of Stockholm, circa 1660, 5¾in., 796grs.
(Christie's) $6,171

A Queen Anne tankard, possibly Irish, the body finely engraved with armorials, the cover stepped domed and with a cast scroll thumbpiece, 19cm. high overall, apparently unmarked, circa 1705, 24 ozs.
(Phillips) $1,811

A George III plain baluster tankard with applied girdle, domed cover, chair-back thumbpiece, the handle terminating in a heart motif, by Jacob Marsh of John Moore I, 1764, 21.5cm. high, 27.5 ozs.
(Phillips) $4,426

An unusual George III tankard, 9in. high, with a broad band of vines, leaves and 'C'-scrolls chased against a stippled ground, London, 1818, by William Bateman I, 44 oz.
(Bonhams) $2,712

An early George I Britannia standard tankard by John Wisdome, of slightly tapering cylindrical form with applied girdle, London 1718, 663 grammes, 17cm. high.
(Spencer's) $4,244

## TEA & COFFEE SETS

A five piece tea service, of lobed oval baluster form raised upon four stylized paw feet, Sheffield 1935, and a matching two handled tray, London 1936, 3599 grams total gross.
(Spencer's) $2,611

A four-piece part spiral-fluted molded oblong tea service, the teapot and hot water jug with ebonized wood bracket handles, Viners, Sheffield 1925, 61 oz. gross.
(Christie's S. Ken) $1,685

A Chinese three-piece teaset, the sides chased with bamboo fronds against a stippled ground, the teapot with flat hinged cover.
(Bonhams) $797

Frank Smith sterling six piece tea and coffee service, circa 1930, Woodlily pattern, approximately 54 troy oz.
(Skinner Inc.) $3,000

A Hukin & Heath electroplated metal three-piece tea-set, designed by Dr. Christopher Dresser, comprising: a tea-pot, milk jug and two-handled bowl, each piece on four short curly feet, registration lozenge for 1878, 8.5cm. height of teapot.
(Christie's) $9,207

A James Dixon & Son three-piece electroplated metal tea-set, designed by Dr. Christopher Dresser, the globular bodies supported on three curving feet, with angular spout, curving handles, registration lozenge for 1880, 10.5cm. height of teapot.
(Christie's) $15,345

An Arts and Crafts style spot-hammered four-piece tea service on curved feet, possibly Charles Edwards, London 1919, height of hot water jug 8in., 51.75 oz. gross.
(Christie's S. Ken) $2,023

A Puiforcat four-piece white metal and ivory tea and coffee service, comprising: a coffee-pot with lid, a teapot with lid, a sugar basin with lid and a cream jug, 15.5cm. height of coffee-pot. (Christie's) $12,942

## TEA CADDIES

A George II oval tea caddy fitted with a lock and with a flat hinged cover with foliate and acorn finial, William Vincent, London 1776, 4½in., 11oz. (Christie's S. Ken) $3,004

A pair of George II vase-shaped tea caddies and circular bowl and cover, chased overall with flowers, foliage and scrolls, by Samuel Taylor, 1751, 27oz. (Christie's) $5,944

An electroplated mid-18th century style tea caddy with heavily chased chinoiserie decoration, the hinged cover with figure finial, 5¼in. high. (Bearne's) $423

A good George IV Irish tea caddy, the body of bombé shape with repoussé and chased decoration of flowers and scrolls, by W. Nolan, Dublin, 1828, 17cm., 16oz. (Lawrence Fine Art) $2,027

Two George II and George III oblong tea caddies, engraved with a foliage and trelliswork design, the covers with similar scroll borders, one by Edward Wakelin, circa 1755, the other by J. Langford and J. Sebille, 1764, 28oz. (Christie's) $6,930

A George III oblong tea caddy, the sides and cover finely engraved with ribbon ornament, festoons of husks and foliage, 1772, maker's mark *I.L.*, 4½in. high, 6oz. (Christie's) $3,185

A Victorian tea caddy in Indian taste, the engraved borders including a band of figures, animals and fish, by Richard Sibley, 1867, 9.5cm., 8.5oz. (Lawrence Fine Art) $734

A pair of George III oblong tea caddies, the sides chased with panels of scrolls enclosing Chinese figures and pagodas, by Robert Garrard, 1819, in a fitted silver-mounted and ivory case inlaid with flowers and foliage, 35oz. (Christie's) $16,830

A Queen Anne octagonal baluster tea caddy and cover, the detachable cover with shaped finial, the base engraved with initials, by Ebenezer Roe, 1711, 4¾in. high, 6oz. (Christie's) $3,366

A Victorian plain tapering tea kettle with rising curved spout, scroll handle and flattened rising hinged cover, Hunt and Roskell, London 1869, 12¾in., 46oz. (Christie's S. Ken) $1,316

A Victorian tea kettle on stand, 15¾in., in early 18th century style, Sheffield, 1862, Martin Hall and Company, 82oz. (Bonhams) $2,685

A German 19th century spiral-fluted compressed pear-shaped swing-handled tea kettle with fluted rising curved spout, Friedlander, 16in., 56.25oz. gross. (Christie's S. Ken) $1,220

A George II inverted pear-shaped tea kettle, by William Grundy, 1746, 14¼in. high, gross 61oz. (Christie's) $8,668

A Regency style part-fluted molded oblong tea kettle applied with a gadroon, shell, foliate and floral rim, by William Hutton & Sons Ltd., Sheffield 1911, 12¼in., 42.25oz. gross. (Christie's S. Ken) $1,007

A George II inverted pear-shaped tea kettle, stand and lamp, by John Jacobs, 1754, 15¼in. high, gross 76oz. (Christie's) $5,417

A Queen Anne plain pear-shaped tea kettle, stand and lamp, the kettle by John Jackson, 1708, the stand and lamp, circa 1710, maker's mark only, probably that of William Fawdery, 11in. high overall, gross 51oz. (Christie's) $11,880

An Edwardian part-fluted compressed globular tea kettle with rising curved spout, everted rim, ebonized wood handle and domed hinged cover, Heath & Middleton, London 1902, 10½in., 34.75oz. gross. (Christie's S. Ken) $736

A Dutch 19th century reeded tapering boat-shaped tea kettle with rising curved spout, ebonized wood swing handle and domed detachable cover, 15¾in. overall, 48oz. gross. (Christie's S. Ken) $1,423

## TEAPOTS

A George III circular teapot, with a band of anthemion ornament at the shoulder and curved spout, by Paul Storr, 1814, gross 26oz.
(Christie's) $4,937

A George IV compressed circular teapot, the body heavily chased with sea-scrolls, foliage and rocaille on a scale-work ground, Michael Starkey, London 1827, 4¼in., 18.50oz. gross.
(Christie's S. Ken) $1,210

A Victorian Irish tea pot, the body with reeded girdle, scroll handle, by R.S., Dublin, 1870, 23.5oz.
(Lawrence Fine Art) $1,004

A Victorian Scottish bullet teapot chased with arabesques and with two vacant scrolling foliate cartouches, Marshall & Summers, Edinburgh 1844, 6¼in., 21.75oz.
(Christie's S. Ken) $1,056

A George III beaded drum teapot with tapering angular spout, possibly Samuel Wood or Samuel White, London 1777, 4¾in., 14.75oz. gross.
(Christie's S. Ken) $1,355

A George III foliate and floral bright-cut molded oval teapot with rising curved spout, Andrew Fogelberg, London 1802, 6½in., 17oz. gross.
(Christie's S. Ken) $1,320

George III teapot and associated stand, Peter and Ann Bateman, London, 1792–93, approximately 15 troy oz.
(Skinner Inc.) $1,000

A George III teapot, 5½in. high, with 'bat-wing' fluted sides, angled spout and wooden scroll handle, London, 1792, by Henry Chawner, 14 oz.
(Bonhams) $1,937

A George III oblong teapot and stand with incurved, canted corners, the sides half-fluted below a wide engraved band of flowers and berries, by John Robbins, 1802, 21.25 ozs.
(Phillips) $3,219

An Irish George III teapot, 6½in. high, on domed circular base chased with a floral band, the mask mounted spout formed as an eagle's head and neck, Dublin 1818, by James Le Bass, 31 oz.
(Bonhams) $1,278

A George III teapot, 6in. high, with gadrooned border and long shaped handle on four ball feet, London, 1812, by Thomas Wallis and Jonathan Hayne, 19 oz.
(Bonhams) $969

A George III tea pot, with beaded borders, straight tapering spout and wood handle, the flat cover with pineapple finial, maker's mark *SW*, 1778, 15.5oz.
(Lawrence Fine Art) $1,583

## TEAPOTS

A George IV teapot, 6¼in. high, with leaf-capped reeded scroll handle and spout, London, 1821, by Emes and Barnard, 22oz. (Bonhams) $697

A Victorian teapot, the sides chased with scrolls and foliage, on shaped circular skirt foot, London, 1839, by Charles Gordon, 19½ ozs. (Bonhams) $1,128

A late George III teapot and stand by Robertson and Darling, the teapot of slightly tapering oval form, Newcastle 1795, 548 grams total gross. (Spencer's) $1,845

A George III beaded oval teapot, the body applied with two oval vignettes decorated with putti, Andrew Fogelberg & Stephen Gilbert, London 1784, 5½in., 17 oz. gross. (Christie's S. Ken) $1,348

A George I bullet-shaped teapot, with partly octagonal curved spout, the shoulder and almost flush cover engraved with masks, foliage and strapwork, by William Darker, 1731, 4in. high, gross 13oz. (Christie's) $7,584

A late George III teapot, of rounded rectangular cushioned form, the everted rim with cast gadrooned border, London 1811, by T. Robins, 498 grammes gross. (Spencer's) $560

A George III Irish tea pot, with a band of rose, shamrock and thistle decoration, the shoulders with gadroon and foliate border, by James Scott, Dublin, 1818, 29.5oz. (Lawrence Fine Art) $1,120

A George III Irish teapot, with prick engraved and bright-cut borders, and wooden loop handle, Dublin, circa 1780. (Bonhams) $930

A George IV bullet shaped teapot by Garrards, the flat hinged cover and shoulders later engraved and chased with scrolls, London 1824, 681 grams gross. (Spencer's) $1,075

A George III tea pot, with bright cut engraved bands and contemporary initials, straight tapering spout and domed cover, by Peter & Ann Bateman, 1794, 14.5 oz. (Lawrence Fine Art) $1,271

A George III tea pot and stand, with bright cut engraved bands and beaded borders, the stand with conforming borders, by John Mitchison, Newcastle, 1784/1786, 19 oz. (Lawrence Fine Art) $3,070

A George III tea pot and stand, with bright cut engraved decoration, the tea pot with domed cover and straight tapering spout, by Henry Chawner, 1788, 19.5oz. all in. (Lawrence Fine Art) $1,930

## TEAPOTS

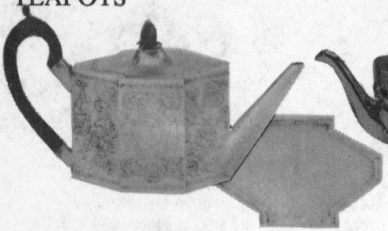

A George III shaped oblong teapot with tapering angular spout, polished wood scroll handle and domed hinged cover, Duncan Urquahart and Napthali Hart, London 1791, 6¼in., 17.75oz., gross.
(Christie's S. Ken) $1,980

A George III oval teapot, 6¼in. high, Charles Fox, London 1804, and a matching oval teapot stand, 6½in. long, Peter, Anne and William Bateman, London 1803, 563 gms, 18.1 oz.
(Bearne's) $1,117

Edward Cornelius Farrell, ogee teapot, in Britannia standard, chased in high relief with gun dogs, fowling pieces and game birds, London 1817, 24 oz. all in.
(Woolley & Wallis) $1,664

A George I plain pear-shaped octagonal teapot, with curved octagonal spout and domed cover with baluster finial, by Joseph Ward, 1717, 6in. high, gross 16oz.
(Christie's) $28,171

A teapot by William Ball, Baltimore, 1790–1800, with a conical cover, and a carved wood handle, 11½in. high, gross weight 28oz.
(Christie's) $9,350

A George I plain octagonal teapot, on narrow rim foot and with curved spout, hinged domed cover and baluster finial, by Joseph Clare, 1715, 6in. high, gross 14oz.
(Christie's) $19,800

A George III oval teapot on matching stand, the pot of straight sided oval section, 6¾in. long, Andrew Fogelberg, London 1799, 578 gms, 18.5 oz.
(Bearne's) $2,118

A German oval teapot and pear-shaped cream jug, each on molded foot with stylized leaf border, by J.C.W.P. Hessler, Hanau, circa 1825, 1,266grs.
(Christie's) $3,250

A teapot on stand after Paul Revere by George C. Gebelein, Boston, circa 1930, with a straight spout, a hinged domed oval cover, and a carved wood handle, 11¼in. wide, gross weight 28oz.
(Christie's) $2,090

## TOAST RACKS

A rare James Dixon & Sons electroplated toast rack, designed by Dr. Christopher Dresser, divisions with lunette shaped designs, central loop handle, 8.5cm. high.
(Christie's) $7,832

A George III seven bar toastrack, the arched wirework divisions supported on oval base, London, 1799, possibly by John Fountain.
(Bonhams) $387

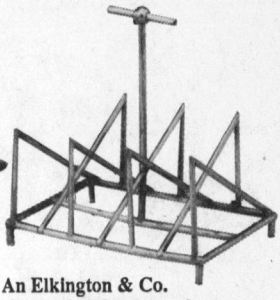

An Elkington & Co. electroplated toast rack, designed by Dr. Christopher Dresser, with a tall central 'T' base and three low triangular shaped supports on either side of it, 13.5cm. high.
(Christie's) $13,299

An unusual George III wirework shaped oblong toast rack of cage form, on baluster feet, Henry Chawner, London 1792, 4½in.
(Christie's S. Ken) $800

A six-division toast-rack, on four bun feet and with central bracket handle and a similar smaller four-division toast-rack, by Omar Ramsden, 1928 and 1932, 4in. and 3in. long, 13oz.
(Christie's) $2,123

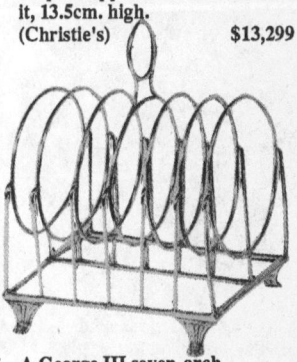

A George III seven-arch toastrack, the circular wirework divisions with arched side supports, London, 1801.
(Bonhams) $426

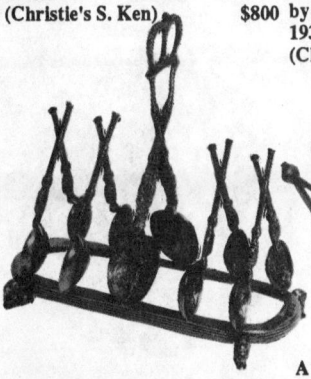

An unusual silver-gilt toastrack, the five divisions formed from crossed apostle spoons, and surmounted by a coronet handle, London, 1910.
(Bonhams) $251

A Hukin & Heath plated toastrack, designed by Christopher Dresser, the arched base on four bun feet supporting six pronged divisions, 12.50cm. high.
(Phillips) $428

A Guild of Handicraft toast rack, designed by C.R. Ashbee, the end panels with repoussé decoration of stylized trees, London hallmarks for 1906, 13cm. high, 220 grams.
(Christie's) $2,774

## TRAYS & SALVERS

A George IV two handled tray, with gadroon, shell and foliate border and leafy scroll handles, by William Bateman I, 1826, 66cm., approximately 114oz. (Lawrence Fine Art) $4,826

A Danish shaped-circular salver, with foliage border and the center engraved with a paterae, Copenhagen, circa 1740, maker's mark illegible, assaymaster Peter Nicolai von Haven, 11½in. diameter, 831grs. (Christie's) $3,291

A George V shaped rectangular two-handled tea tray, 27¼in. over handles, London 1918, 3866 gms, 124.3 oz. (Bearne's) $2,310

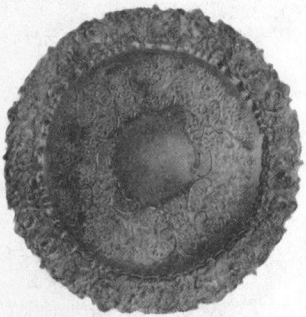

A William IV large shaped-circular salver, on four eagle, shell and foliage feet, chased with birds, flowers and foliage, by J.E. Terrey, 1831, 24¼in. diameter, 172oz. (Christie's) $7,817

A good Victorian tray, the center engraved with a coat of arms within elaborate borders of entwined roses, butterflies and peacocks, by the Fenton Brothers, Sheffield 1891, 67cm., 199oz. (Lawrence Fine Art) $8,687

A Victorian circular salver, with beaded edging on three tapering feet, 14in. diameter, Frederick Elkington, Birmingham 1879, 1035 gms, 33.2 oz. (Bearne's) $1,348

A Portuguese shaped-circular salver, engraved with a band of flowers and shell ornament and with chased shell and scroll border, Lisbon, circa 1780, 11½in. diameter, 605grs. (Christie's) $2,574

An Edwardian shaped oblong trinket tray die-stamped with rococo shells, flowers and scrolling foliage, William Hutton and Sons Limited, Birmingham 1905, 11½in., 9.75oz. (Christie's S. Ken) $659

An attractive salver, 16in., shaped circular with scroll border, on four shell-chased scroll supports, Sheffield, 1929, 58 ozs. (Bonhams) $1,245

## TUREENS

Regency Sheffield silver plated tureen, circa 1820, domed cover with gadrooned rim, with paw feet and foliate handles, 10in. high.
(Skinner Inc.) $1,300

A pair of George III sauce tureens and covers, of boat shape with beaded borders, the covers with leafy urn finials, by Thomas Evans, 1777, 42 oz.
(Lawrence Fine Art) $6,564

A Hukin & Heath electroplated metal tureen, designed by Dr. Christopher Dresser, with bone finial and cylindrical bar handle, on three spike feet, with registration lozenge for 1880, 25.5cm. high.
(Christie's) $12,276

A George IV two-handled shaped-oval bombé soup tureen and cover, with vine tendril and leaf handles and gadrooned, shell and foliage border, by William Ker Reid, 1826, 13in. wide, 162oz.
(Christie's) $14,399

A French plain oval two-handled soup tureen, cover and stand, the stand on four lion's paw feet and with a foliage and beaded frieze, by Jean-Nicolas Boulanger, Paris, 1798–1809, 14in., 6,950grs.
(Christie's) $16,252

A fine tureen and cover, designed by Georg Jensen, the bombé bowl with curved leaf and bud handles on four scroll feet with stem and flower head decoration, 31.5cm. long, 1980 grams.
(Christie's) $23,496

An Old Sheffield plate two-handled oval soup tureen and cover, with foliage handles and gadrooned border, the domed cover with similar detachable foliage ring handle, circa 1820, 16½in. wide.
(Christie's) $2,178

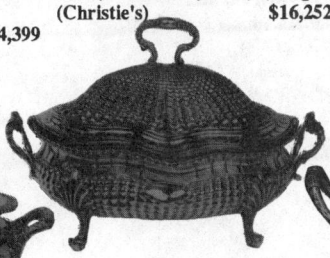

A George II quilted two-handled shaped-oval soup tureen and cover, with leaf-capped gadrooned scroll handles, the domed cover with similar handle, by Peter Archambo and Peter Meure, 1756, 15½in. long, 100oz.
(Christie's) $15,840

A George III two-handled circular partly-fluted soup tureen and cover, the bombé body with reeded and foliage handles, by John Edwards III, 1807, with plated liner, 11in. diameter, 109oz.
(Christie's) $15,840

## URNS

A Victorian two-handled vase-shaped tea urn with foliate decoration and on scrolling foliate feet, 20½in. high.
(Christie's S. Ken) $1,201

An Old Sheffield plate tea urn and cover, of melon fluted globular form engraved with a crest, 16in. high over finial.
(Spencer's) $995

Tiffany sterling coffee urn on stand, 1938–47, tapering fluted body cast with basketweave and Renaissance motifs, 15in. high, approximately 90½ oz.
(Skinner Inc.) $7,500

A George III two-handled circular tea urn, the lower part of the body chased with vertical fluting, with reeded and foliage handles and fluted spigot, by John Edwards III, 1810, 15in. high, 133oz.
(Christie's) $6,994

A George III two-handled circular tea urn, the plain body on fluted and foliage supports terminating in shells and sprays of fruit and acanthus foliage, by Benjamin Smith, 1819, the spirit lamp by Paul Storr, 1812, 15½in. high, gross 181oz.
(Christie's) $7,431

A George III part-fluted vase-shaped tea urn on a foliate-decorated and reeded shaped square base with ball feet, by John Emes, London 1801, 18¼in. overall, 92.50oz. gross.
(Christie's S. Ken) $4,257

A George III Irish tea urn, with cast rococo handles and gadroon borders, the spool shape cover with pineapple finial, by John Loughlin, Dublin, circa 1770, 48cm., 89 oz.
(Lawrence Fine Art) $2,541

A German two-handled fluted pear-shaped coffee urn, with scroll handles and domed cover, by Johann Georg Kloss, Augsburg, 1747/1749, 11¾in. high, 799grs.
(Christie's) $3,715

A George III two-handled vase-shaped coffee urn, chased with a band of waterleaves and bright-cut below the reeded rim with rosettes and wheatears, by Peter and Ann Bateman, 1799, 13¾in. high, gross 43oz.
(Christie's) $3,185

## VASES

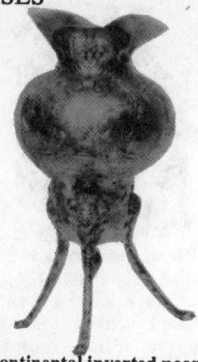

A Continental inverted pear-shaped vase on mask and paw feet, the body cast and chased with exotic birds, flowers and scrolling foliage, bearing import marks, 9¼in., 21oz.
(Christie's S. Ken) $1,064

A two-handled replica of the Warwick vase, the body chased and applied with masks, lions' pelts, foliage and trailing vines, by Barnard Brothers, 1908, height of vase 10½in., 118oz.
(Christie's) $8,234

A George III beaded, pierced and bright-cut swing-handled pedestal sugar vase with blue glass liner, Hester Bateman, London 1779, 6¼in. overall.
(Christie's S. Ken) $900

Black, Starr and Frost sterling vase, New York, early 20th century, with an overall chased flowering clematis vine, 14¾in. high, approximately 44 troy oz.
(Skinner Inc.) $2,800

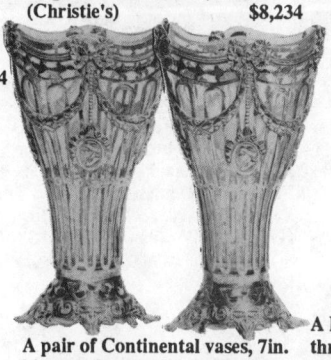

A pair of Continental vases, 7in. high, on floral and scroll pierced oval bases with leaf-chased bracket feet, circa 1880, Bertholdt Müller.
(Bonhams) $823

A Liberty and Co. 'Cymric' three-handled waisted vase, the handles enameled with entwined strap-work in shades of blue, green and purple, Birmingham 1901, 6¾in. high.
(Christie's S. Ken) $2,710

A pair of late 19th century electrotype vases of amphota shape, the body decorated in high relief with a procession of allegorical figures above a band of vine leaves and grapes, 28in. high.
(Christie's S. Ken) $1,773

An Edwardian silver-gilt gadrooned elongated campana-shaped vase, the body decorated with 18th century style figures, birds, flowers and scrolling foliage, D. & J. Wellby, London 1905, 7in., 12.75oz.
(Christie's S. Ken) $1,089

A matched pair of Neapolitan vases and covers, one repoussé with a bust portrait of Francis IV, the other repoussé with a victory scene depicting William of Orange, bears import marks for Birmingham 1902, 1714 grammes total.
(Spencer's) $4,613

## VESTA CASES

An Edwardian rectangular vesta case, the front enameled with a two-horse carriage in a rural landscape, Birmingham 1901. (Christie's S. Ken) $321

An Edwardian rectangular vesta case, one side enameled with a wasp, Birmingham 1905. (Christie's S. Ken) $513

A Victorian novelty vesta case modeled as a milkman's hand can of oval cylindrical form, by William Leuchars, 1875, 5.6cm. high. (Phillips) $704

A late Victorian rectangular vesta case chased on the cover in relief with a horse-racing scene, Chester, 1895, apparently no maker's mark. (Phillips) $523

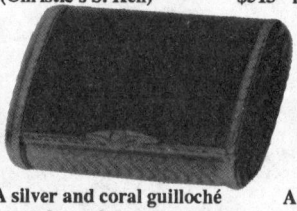

A silver and coral guilloché enamel match box, workmaster's stamp of Michael Perchin and Fabergé in Russian script, Petersburg 1905, 3½in. x 2¼in. (Woolley & Wallis) $1,838

A Continental gilt-lined vesta case, enameled with a standing lady dressed in black stockings and a camisole holding a cat in the gathered folds, 2in. (Christie's S. Ken) $676

## VINAIGRETTES

An early Victorian silver castle top vinaigrette, of rounded rectangular form depicting St. Pauls Cathedral, Birmingham 1842, probably by John Tongue. (Spencer's) $716

A Victorian combination horn-shaped scent bottle and vinaigrette applied with lattice-work decoration, T.J., London 1873, 4⅕in. (Christie's S. Ken) $513

York Minster, an early Victorian rectangular vinaigrette, the gilt interior with a pierced grille of a basket of flowers, 1¾in., John Tongue, Birmingham 1843. (Woolley & Wallis) $1,122

A George III oblong vinaigrette engraved with a portrait of Nelson in uniform within an oval surround inscribed with *England expects everyman will do his duty*, by Matthew Linwood, Birmingham, 1805, 3.5cm. long. (Phillips) $3,018

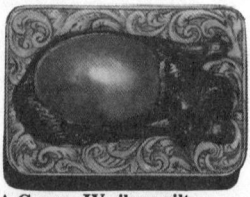

A George IV silver-gilt rectangular vinaigrette, the lid applied with a cast model of a Papillion dog, its back applied with a blister pearl, James Beebe, Birmingham 1824, 1½in. (Christie's S. Ken) $4,217

A Victorian rectangular silver-gilt vinaigrette, the lid chased in high relief with a view of York Minster within a cast border, Nathaniel Mills, Birmingham 1841. (Christie's S. Ken) $2,741

## VINAIGRETTES

A Victorian 'castle-top' vinaigrette chased in low relief with Abbotsford, by Nathaniel Mills, Birmingham, 1840.
(Phillips) $765

A Continental oval silver-gilt vinaigrette, the lid inset with a black pietra dura panel inlaid with two vari-colored hardstone butterflies, circa 1800, $1^{4}/_{5}$in.
(Christie's S. Ken) $1,054

A Victorian vinaigrette engraved with a view of Yorkminster, by Nathaniel Mills, Birmingham, 1843.
(Phillips) $704

A Continental gilt-lined casket-shaped vinaigrette, the base, sides and lid enameled with blue foliage, possibly French, circa 1800, $1^{1}/_{2}$in.
(Christie's S. Ken) $1,097

A Victorian silver-gilt vinaigrette, the cover chased in low relief with a view of Yorkminster, by Joseph Willmore, Birmingham, 1844.
(Phillips) $1,046

A Victorian shaped rectangular silver-gilt vinaigrette, the lid chased in high relief with a view of St. Pauls, Nathaniel Mills, Birmingham 1852, $1^{4}/_{5}$in.
(Christie's S. Ken) $4,850

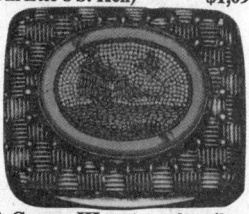

A George III rectangular silver-gilt vinaigrette, chased with a basket-weave effect, the lid inset with an oval micro-mosaic of a chariot, possibly Birmingham 1809, $1^{1}/_{2}$in.
(Christie's S. Ken) $380

A George IV oval silver-gilt vinaigrette, the lid cast with two wading birds within a heavy shell, scrollwork and floral border, Birmingham 1829, 2in.
(Christie's S. Ken) $1,582

An attractive 19th century Swiss gold and enamel vinaigrette, the engine-turned surfaces enameled in a translucent flesh-pink, maker's mark *MB & C* in lozenge, circa 1840.
(Phillips) $1,911

A Victorian rectangular gilt-lined vinaigrette, the lid chased in high relief with a view of Westminster Abbey, J.T., Birmingham, date letter indistinct, $1^{9}/_{10}$in. wide.
(Christie's S. Ken) $1,027

A William IV oval silver-gilt vinaigrette, the lid applied with a carved cameo plaque depicting Venus and Cupid within a cast border, Nathaniel Mills, Birmingham 1836, $1^{7}/_{10}$in.
(Christie's S. Ken) $1,898

A George IV rectangular silver-gilt vinaigrette, the lid chased with flowers and foliage, the grill pierced and engraved with scroll work, Nathaniel Mills, Birmingham 1826, $1^{7}/_{10}$in.
(Christie's S. Ken) $843

## WARMERS

A George III brandy warming saucepan with gadroon edging and turned wood handle, 9in. long, London 1807, 8.5oz.
(Bearne's) $515

A George II plain baluster brandy saucepan, with molded rim and lip and turned wood side handle, engraved with initials, by Robert Bailey, 1729, gross 6oz.
(Christie's) $1,089

A Queen Anne plain tapering circular brandy saucepan on a rim foot, maker's mark probably S. L., London 1713, Britannia Standard, 10¼in. overall, 9oz. gross.
(Christie's S. Ken) $1,685

## WINE COOLERS

A pair of George III two-handled partly-fluted wine coolers, the reeded angular handles springing from bearded male masks, by William Frisbee, 1807, 9¾in. high, 185oz.
(Christie's) $38,214

A pair of fine George III two-handled vase-shaped wine coolers, chased with bands of fluting and with lion's mask, shell and foliage bracket handles, by Paul Storr, 1810, 10in. high, 279oz.
(Christie's) $76,428

A pair of Old Sheffield plate two-handled wine coolers, the partly-fluted vase-shaped bodies applied above with a band of vines, circa 1820, 10in. high.
(Christie's) $2,970

## WINE FUNNELS

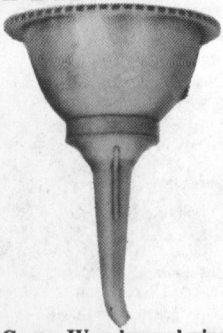

A George IV gadrooned wine funnel with curved spigot and shaped clip, William Bateman, London 1825, 4¾in.
(Christie's S. Ken) $885

A George III wine funnel, 4½in. high, plain circular with reeded rim and shaped rectangular hook, London, 1781, by Luke Hebden, 2½ ozs.
(Bonhams) $486

A George III beaded wine funnel with curved spigot and rounded clip, maker's initials possibly *I.L.*, London 1776, 4¾in.
(Christie's S. Ken) $380

Good white jade snuff bottle, late 19th century, carved as a ripe melon enclosed by leafy fruiting melon vines and a rat.
(Butterfield & Butterfield) $660

A glass overlay bottle, carved through a layer of red glass to the snowstorm ground, hefengdi, with a frog on a lotus spray to one face, 19th century.
(Christie's) $2,027

A green glass snuff bottle of flattened ovoid form carved in relief with gourds issuing from a leafy branch, stopper, 19th century.
(Christie's) $1,921

Mongolian silver-mounted jade snuff bottle, of pale green tone mottling to white with dark brown striations.
(Butterfield & Butterfield) $495

A large agate snuff bottle, well carved and incised through a dark skin with three Buddhistic lions playing on rockwork with ribbons, 19th century.
(Christie's) $1,921

A glass overlay ovoid snuff bottle, the pink bubble suffused ground overlaid in red with a carp on each side, 19th century.
(Bonhams) $336

An agate snuff bottle, the ocher inclusions carved to the front to form five monkeys in different postures staring at a bee, circa 1800.
(Christie's) $3,841

A metal and enameled snuff bottle of Meiping form, the body incised with scrolling foliage, 19th century.
(Bonhams) $224

A glass overlay snuff bottle each face carved through layers of black and red to a white ground with a horse tethered to a pine tree, 19th century.
(Christie's) $4,268

A late eighteenth century cartouche shaped gilt-metal mounted mother-of-pearl snuff box, carved with an extensive rural peasant scene, 3.2in.
(Christie's S. Ken) $601

A good Victorian snuff box, shaped rectangular, with all-over engraving of floral scrolls, by John Linnit, 1838, 9cm.
(Lawrence Fine Art) $907

Silver and enamel faux malachite and lapis snuff box, circa 1900, marked *800*, approximately 3 troy oz.
(Skinner Inc.) $300

A Staffordshire enamel circular box, the cover modeled in relief, the base decorated with floral sprigs and gilt scrollwork, 4.5cm.
(Phillips) $1,594

A Meissen gold-mounted waisted rectangular Purpurmalerei snuff-box painted in the style of Watteau with gallants and companions in idyllic landscapes, circa 1750, 7.5cm. wide.
(Christie's) $8,109

A Mennecy silver-mounted snuff-box and cover naturalistically modeled as an apple and colored in shades of yellow and purple with some dark blemishes, circa 1755, 6.5cm. diameter.
(Christie's) $1,387

A fine gilt lined snuff box, engraved *The passengers on The Falcon beg Capt. John Adams to accept this small token in admiration of his Seamanship on the passage to Port Sydney. 21st day of May 1829.*
(Woolley & Wallis)
$38,700

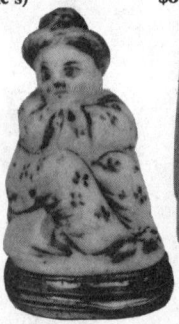

A Mennecy snuff-box as a seated man crouched on a mound base with his arms and legs crossed, circa 1750, 5.5cm. high.
(Christie's) $1,091

John Bettridge, George IV rectangular snuff box, with reeded sides, cast chased foliage thumbpiece, 2¾in., Birmingham 1823.
(Woolley & Wallis) $464

A Regency oval vari-colored gold and hardstone snuff-box, the cover set with a panel of mottled brown agate, by Alexander James Strachan, London, 1817, 3½in. long. (Christie's) $7,920

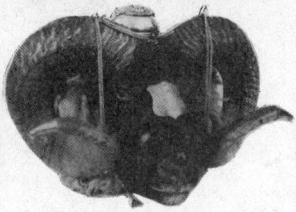

A silver mounted presentation ram's head snuff mill, the container applied with the regimental badge, complete with accoutrements, hallmarked Glasgow, 1890, 45cm. wide. (Phillips) $1,347

An 18th century copper-gilt snuff box of cartouche shape, chased with leaves, flowers and 'C' scrolls, the cover set with a panel of bloodstone, 6cm. wide, circa 1750. (Phillips) $382

A gold-mounted tortoiseshell smeeching-mull, the oval hinged cover with fluted thumbpiece, probably Scottish, mid 18th century, 2⅜in. high. (Christie's) $1,842

An attractive Staffordshire enamel casket-shaped box with hinged cover, painted in colors with vignettes of figures in landscapes, 7cm. (Phillips) $359

A fine late 17th/early 18th century oval gilt-lined snuff box, the lid engraved with many emblems purporting to relate to the Stuart monarchy and the Jacobite cause, possibly Lawrence Coles, circa 1697, 3⅛in. (Christie's S. Ken) $8,857

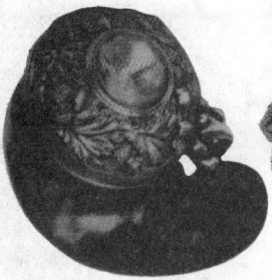

A Scottish 19th century silver-mounted horn snuff mull applied with a shield-shaped cartouche engraved with a crest and initials, unmarked, probably circa 1850, 3½in. (Christie's S. Ken) $648

A Victorian parcel-gilt rectangular snuff box, crested on a central escutcheon amongst scrolling acanthus, pheasants and a dog, 3½in. long, Charles Rawlins and William Summers, London 1839, 242 gms, 7.7 oz. (Bearne's) $1,059

A good 18th century copper-gilt snuff box of cartouche shape chased with a courting couple, by James Ferguson, 7cm. wide, circa 1745. (Phillips) $704

Flemish Verdure tapestry, 17th century, a pair of swans swim with a fountain behind in a wooded setting, 14ft. 7in. long.
(Skinner Inc.) $16,000

A European hunting tapestry, dated 1910, the scene of hunters with dogs attacking a stag with trees in the background, 10ft. 9in. x 9ft.
(Christie's East) $12,100

A tapestry, woven in many colors depicting a battle scene, 104 x 140in., Flemish, late 16th/ early 17th century.
(Christie's S. Ken) $8,030

'Moonlight', a woollen tapestry, designed by Howard Hodgkin, woven at the West Dean Tapestry Studio by Dilys Stinson, dated 1983, 149 x 121cm.
(Christie's) $8,536

An armorial tapestry woven in silks and wools with a coat-of-arms within scrollwork, late 16th century, probably Peruvian, reduced, cut and shut, some reweaving, 101½in. x 39½in.
(Christie's) $13,002

A Flemish tapestry woven in wools and silks depicting the infant Moses being offered by a maid to Pharaoh's daughter, surrounded by attendants and two huntsmen with dogs, second half 17th century, 131in. x 121in.
(Christie's) $21,670

A European tapestry, the scene comprising a queenly figure seated receiving gifts from several ladies in waiting with male onlookers, 7ft. 10in. x 6ft. 10in.
(Christie's East) $14,300

A Felletin verdure tapestry woven in silks and wools with travelers in a landscape with herons in a pond, the foreground with stylized flowerheads, late 17th century , 10ft. 2in. x 13ft. 6in.
(Christie's) $20,587

A tapestry fragment woven in silks and wools of an eagle with prey by a pool, probably Flemish, 18th century, 25½in. x 20¼in.
(Christie's) $1,287

A Flemish tapestry woven in silks and wools, after Teniers with peasants merrymaking beneath trees and a couple dancing, with a chateau and village beyond, mid-18th century, 9ft. 4in. x 13ft. 6in.
(Christie's) $47,674

A panel of early 17th century linen depicting a castle, male and female figures including a water carrier and horsemen, 2.30m x 24cm., Italian.
(Phillips) $478

Flemish Verdure tapestry fragment, 17th century, wooded scene with waterfowl, 8ft. 4in. wide.
(Skinner Inc.) $3,400

A Mortlake tapestry, woven in silks and wools with three frolicking boys and a goat in a garden, late 17th century, reduced, some areas of repair, 71in. x 73in.
(Christie's) $16,253

A tapestry panel, woven in many colors depicting Dido on the funeral pyre with a sword in her hand and Aeneas' armor at her feet, 80 x 56in., Flemish, 17th century.
(Christie's S. Ken) $5,220

A Flemish tapestry, woven in wools and silks, depicting a garden with statues and a landscape beyond with a castle on a hill, late 17th century, 99in. x 84in.
(Christie's) $6,864

A Flemish armorial tapestry woven in wools, centered by a coat-of-arms with two goats flanking an apple tree surmounted by a plumed helmet, late 16th century, 86½in. x 101in.
(Christie's) $18,420

A pair of Napoleon III tapestries, second half 19th century, signed *W. Geets*, depicting a man and a woman emblematic of Industry and the Arts, 165in. high.
(Christie's East) $11,000

An 18th century Soho tapestry depicting 'Ovid's Muse', from a series of Ovid's Metamorphoses, 5ft. 11in. x 6ft. 6in.
(Phillips) $21,320

A golden curly plushed covered teddy bear with cut muzzle snout, glass eyes, rexine type pads, with original Chad Valley swing ticket and label on foot pad, 21in. high.
(Christie's S. Ken) $487

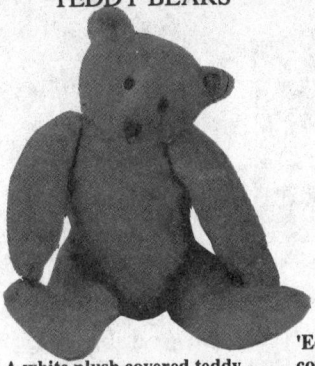

A white plush covered teddy bear with elongated limbs, pronounced snout, glass eyes, hump and Steiff button in ear, circa 1930's, 18in. high.
(Christie's S. Ken) $1,752

'Edward Bear', a blonde plush covered teddy bear with boot button eyes, cut muzzle , elongated limbs, with Steiff button in ear, circa 1905, 10in. high.
(Christie's S. Ken) $1,539

A straw gold plush covered teddy bear with elongated limbs, pronounced snout, glass eyes, and Steiff button in ear, probably circa 1909, 24in. high.
(Christie's S. Ken) $3,984

An unusual red plush covered teddy bear with pronounced snout, 16½in. high (eyes missing, plush worn, pads replaced) with an illustrated manuscripted story book of the bear's adventures written by the family's French governess in 1938. (Christie's S. Ken) $2,052

A golden plush covered teddy bear with cut muzzle, dark orange glass eyes, English, circa 1930's, 9½in. high (squeaker inoperative).
(Christie's S. Ken) $323

A golden plush covered teddy bear with elongated limbs, cut muzzle, glass eyes, wide apart ears, hump and growler, 21in. high.
(Christie's S. Ken) $1,439

A Steiff gold mohair plush teddy bear with wide apart rounded ears, black boot button eyes, 16in., 1911.
(Phillips) $1,610

A dark golden plush covered teddy bear with elongated limbs, low set wide apart ears, and red, white and blue ribbon rosette on chest, 12in. high.
(Christie's S. Ken) $681

A golden plush covered center seam teddy bear with boot button eyes, by Steiff, circa 1905, 20in. high (lacks stuffing in arms from loss of front paw pads).
(Christie's S. Ken) $1,408

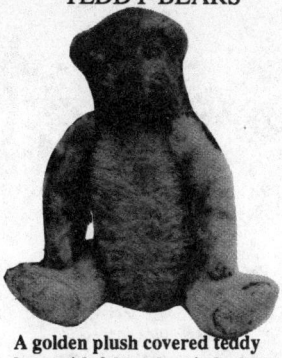

A golden plush covered teddy bear with felt pads, stitched nose, enlarged torso and forward placed ears, 15in. high.
(Christie's S. Ken) $283

A fawn plush covered Yes/No teddy bear with cut muzzle, glass eyes, down-turned paws and felt pads, sits 11in. high.
(Christie's S. Ken) $984

A blonde plush covered teddy bear with boot button eyes, dressed as a sailor in blue trousers, white jersey and blue beret, by Steiff, 8½in. high.
(Christie's S. Ken) $568

'Page Hop': a golden plush Yes/No bear dressed in red jacket, black felt trousers with bellboy cap, original Schuco swing ticket and price tag, circa 1928, 14½in. high.
(Christie's S. Ken) $4,478

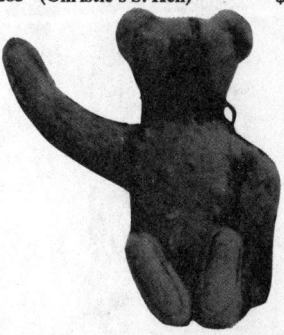

A dark golden plush covered teddy bear wearing a leather muzzle with lead, with Steiff button and white tag in ear, circa 1910, 12½in. high.
(Christie's S. Ken) $1,012

A deep golden plush covered teddy bear with boot button eyes, elongated limbs, wide apart ears, felt pads and hump, 22in. high.
(Christie's S. Ken) $818

A fine Steiff black mohair plush teddy bear with wide apart rounded ears, black boot button eyes, hump back and elongated felt pads, 19in, button in ear marked *Steiff*, 1912.
(Phillips) $16,096

A blonde plush covered teddy bear with cut muzzle, felt pads, squeaker and slight hump, probably by Merrythought, 16in. high.
(Christie's S. Ken) $410

A needlework panel, of natural linen, worked with a repeating pattern of grapes and vine leaves in black silk and gilt threads, 9in. x 13½in., English, late 16th century.
(Christie's S. Ken) $3,185

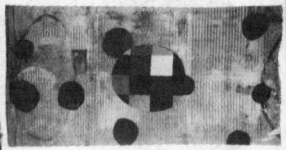

'Core', a cotton wall hanging by Ruston Aust, screen printed pink ground with hand-written script and painted yellow stripes, signed bottom center *Ruston Aust*, 1989, 254 x 121cm.
(Christie's) $1,494

Needlework picture, worked by a Mehitable Goddard, Sutton and Worcester, Massachusetts, circa 1770, inscribed with the initial *MM* and *The 24 chapter of Genesis*, 14½ x 10½in.
(Skinner Inc.) $7,000

An early 18th century banner wall hanging of linen boldly embroidered with couched metal thread and colored silks, 1.35m. x 65cm., Italian, later red silk lining.
(Phillips) $1,415

An early 19th century ivory silk handkerchief printed with Hackney Coach and Cabriolet Fares, Regulations and Acts of Parliament, 88 x 92cm., circa 1833.
(Phillips) $221

A late 18th century oval silkwork picture, the ivory silk ground, designed with a romantic youth playing a flute, 17cm. long, English.
(Phillips) $202

A late 18th century needlework embroidery of a hare and three leverets, executed in fine long and short stitch, possibly by Mary Linwood (1755–1845), English, 51cm. x 70cm.
(Phillips) $5,055

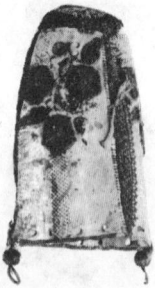

A late 16th/early 17th century kid sweet bag embroidered with stylized Tudor roses, red, gold and black thread, approximately 6in. top to bottom.
(Woolley & Wallis) $1,000

A late 18th century embroidered picture with charming harvest scene depicting laborers gathering sheaves of corn, English, 24.5 x 31.5cm., circa 1770.
(Phillips) $1,380

A needlework purse, worked in the shape of a frog, the front and back embroidered in green and brown shades of silk, 1½in. long, early 17th century.
(Christie's S. Ken) $2,972

A late 17th century petit point embroidered picture worked in wool and silk, portraying the coming of God's Angel to Abraham, 33cm. x 41cm., English, circa 1660.
(Phillips) $1,196

A Queen Victoria souvenir beadwork purse, the gilt clasp marked *Victoria June 28th, 1838* with floral beadwork.
(Woolley & Wallis) $144

A late 18th century chair back cover with colorful crewel work embroidery of a tree with bird and stylized peonies, roses and other flowers, 97cm. x 59cm.
(Phillips) $930

A needlework casket, worked in colored silks against an ivory silk ground, depicting the story of Joseph, 5½in. x 14in. x 10in., with key and wooden case, English, 1660.
(Christie's S. Ken) $159,225

A William Morris & Company embroidered wool portière designed by Henry Dearle, circa 1910, the central rectangular reserve embroidered with a flowering tree and song birds, 244 x 180.5cm.
(Christie's) $71,610

A mid-17th century needlework picture, the ivory satin silk ground worked in silk threads, showing Charles II and Catherine of Braganza, 29.5cm. x 26cm., circa 1660.
(Phillips) $1,112

Pair of Aubusson window surrounds, second half 19th century, floral bouquet with a pair of birds, 11ft. 10in. high.
(Skinner Inc.) $5,100

A mid-17th century embroidered cushion worked in silk and metal threads on ivory satin silk ground, having a small tassel at each corner, English, 26.5cm. x 31cm., circa 1660.
(Phillips) $1,112

A Distler lithographed tinplate clockwork London General double decker bus, with moving conductor, circa 1929.
(Christie's S. Ken)
$2,052

Painted and decorated baby carriage, America, 19th/20th century, painted light green and heightened with red and black pinstriping.
(Skinner Inc.)
$400

The American National Company, painted steel model of a Packard finished in red with red and yellow lining, 73cm. long.
(Phillips)
$2,196

A George III three storey painted wooden baby house, of three bays, with pedimented dentil cornice, 37½in. wide.
(Christie's S. Ken)
$5,240

A Bell-toy, with plush covered monkey seated on a cloth covered platform with three fretwork metal wheels below, 8in.
(Phillips)
$651

An early 20th century English dolls' house, the wooden superstructure with nine windows to the façade, 30in. high, probably G. & J. Lines, circa 1900–1910.
(Phillips)
$919

Lehmann, Japanese coolie in conical hat pulling rickshaw, with spring-motor action operating woman's fan and spoked wheels, 1930's.
(Christie's S. Ken)
$2,462

A jointed all-bisque monkey with molded face and hands, dressed in original crochet suit and hat, 2½in. high.
(Christie's S. Ken)
$109

Dinky rare 923 Heinz big Bedford van, tomato ketchup bottle variant, in original box.
(Christie's S. Ken)
$1,949

A Bing clockwork painted and lithographed tinplate 'United Motor Bus Company Ltd' London double-decker bus, circa 1912, 11in. long.
(Christie's S. Ken) $7,642

Fernand Martin, 'La Madelon casseuse d'assiettes', clockwork painted tinplate maid, dressed in blue with white apron and cap, circa 1913.
(Christie's S. Ken) $1,026

Dinky 943 Esso Leyland Octopus tanker, in original box.
(Christie's S. Ken) $410

A 19th century English wooden dolls' house, the deep red brick painted exterior having four gables, 64in. high, circa 1880.
(Phillips) $3,447

'Little Mocking Bird' painted tinplate clockwork musical box, with eccentric-driven bellows and rotating songbird, circa 1900, 4½in. wide.
(Christie's S. Ken) $1,128

A painted wooden dolls' house, simulating brickwork with slate roof, the base with shaped apron, furnished, 41in. high.
(Christie's S. Ken) $1,266

A gollywog, with cloth face, hands and shoes, comical eyes and mohair hair, with Deans Rag Book Co. stamp on bottom of foot, 13½in. high.
(Christie's S. Ken) $328

A painted wooden toy carter's dray with carved and painted dapple gray horses, 36in. long, possibly English, circa 1900.
(Christie's S. Ken) $584

A German painted tinplate clockwork nursemaid, with rocking upper torso, umbrella, apron, cap and eccentric walking action, circa 1910, 6½in. high.
(Christie's S. Ken) $985

Carette, a clockwork four seater Torpedo, hand painted in cream with green lining, lacking lamps, windscreen and two tires, 32cm. long.
(Phillips) $7,833

A wooden toy military ambulance, with opening rear doors and stretchers, 19in. long, marked *The Priory Toys*.
(Christie's S. Ken) $221

Citroen, painted tinplate clockwork petrol tanker finished in red and silver, 44cm., with electric lighting.
(Phillips) $1,492

An English wooden doll's house, the cream painted and simulated brick papered facade with eight windows, 51in. high, 1910, probably G. and J. Lines Bros.
(Phillips) $1,328

A Punch and Judy toy theater booth, the interior with painted landscape back drop, and four composition head puppets, theatre 16in. high.
(Phillips) $845

A 12-inch diameter black metal drum zoetrope mounted on a turned mahogany stand with 7½ inch diameter friction-drive wheel with handle.
(Christie's S. Ken) $1,518

A lithographed Penny Toy of a nodding goose on dark green wheeled undercarriage, 9cm., some rust.
(Phillips) $86

A clockwork wood and papier-mâché head-over-heels figure of a policeman, dressed in navy-blue felt uniform, 9½in.
(Phillips) $201

Unique Art Manufacturing Co. clockwork 'Kiddy Cyclist', fair haired young boy on tricycle, the wheels with lithographed animals, 23cm.
(Phillips) $386

An American clockwork tinplate streamlined record car finished in red with driver, 46cm.
(Phillips) $1,608

Lehmann, No. 686 clockwork open tourer with hood 'Berolina' finished in blue with gold lining and yellow fabric hood, 10.5cm.
(Phillips) $1,759

C.I.J., clockwork P2 Alfa Romeo racing car, early version, finished in green with shock absorbers, drum brakes, and treaded tires, circa 1927, 52cm.
(Phillips) $3,357

A German lithographed Penny Toy of a pram and child within, on four spoked wheels, 6.5cm., some wear and rust.
(Phillips) $172

A Schuco Mercedes 190SL Elektro-Phänomenal 5503, with accessories and instructions, in original box, circa 1959.
(Christie's S. Ken) $492

Painted composition cat squeak toy, America, late 19th century, painted white with orange and black markings seated on a bellows base, 7¾in. high.
(Skinner Inc.) $1,200

A clockwork lithographed dog with two puppies finished in brown and white with red collars, 17cm.
(Phillips) $160

'Felix the Cat', the plush covered head with black boot button eyes and wide smiling mouth, with swivel joints, 11in.
(Phillips) $161

A wooden pull-along horse, the painted dapple body with carved features, metal stud eyes and leather cloth saddle, 18in. high.
(Phillips) $443

Nomura, friction The Great Swanee River Paddle Steamer, colorfully lithographed with deck details and passengers, 27cm.
(Phillips) $156

Lehmann clockwork sailor dressed in white summer uniform discolored, 18.5cm. high, circa 1912.
(Phillips) $379

Ingap, clockwork lithographed motorcycle and rider finished in bright colors, 13cm.
(Phillips) $476

ALPS, TPS, battery operated Mercury Explorer spaceship with magic color dome finished in very bright primary colors, 20cm., boxed.
(Phillips) $110

Linemar battery operated Busy Secretary, the blond girl wearing spotty blouse and fluted skirt, 19cm. high., boxed.
(Phillips) $275

A lithographed Penny Toy of an Indian Elephant on green wheeled undercarriage, 10cm.
(Phillips) $165

Kellermann, a lithographed freewheeling negro on a tricycle, dressed as a clown in stripy trousers, 10cm. long.
(Phillips) $439

Schuco, felt and velvet mouse drinking from a flagon, 11cm.
(Phillips) $201

A Japanese battery operated tinplate pig farming wagon 'Pinkee' the farmer, 25cm.
(Phillips) $110

KKK battery operated open top saloon car finished in red with cream interior and working head lights, 21.5cm., boxed.
(Phillips) $137

A Steiff Mickey Mouse, the velvet covered head with felt ears and wide smiling mouth, 7in.
(Phillips) $547

ALPS battery operated Mystery car finished in two tone red and cream, the interior with lithographed detail, 30cm.
(Phillips) $952

Nomura, a tinplate battery operated doll dressmaker seated at her sewing machine, 17cm. high.
(Phillips) $146

ALPS clockwork lithographed Little Shoemaker dressed in stripy T-shirt and checkered jacket, 15cm., boxed.
(Phillips) $137

F. Martin, clockwork L'Eminent Avocat, 22cm. high, boxed in excellent to mint condition, with Code Civil.
(Phillips) $2,379

Schuco clockwork felt covered fox dressed in red jacket, blue trousers and yellow tie, carrying a lithographed tinplate clockwork suitcase, 13cm.
(Phillips) $210

Ingap, clockwork lithographed Dipsy car with young clown rider finished in red, yellow and pale blue, 12.5cm.
(Phillips) $230

Schuco, felt and velvet rabbit, the orange creature with large ears, green trousers, dancing with its pink infant, 15.5cm.
(Phillips) $238

J.E.P., large painted tinplate Rolls Royce open tourer finished in cream with red mudguards, lithographed 'wooden' running boards, 51cm., repainted, No. 7395 fatigue to driving shaft.
(Phillips) $1,865

A 1/10th scale cast aluminium model of the Alfa Romeo Type 158 Racing Car, finished in red and silver, 40cm. long, with original box.
(Onslow's) $5,720

Automobile mechanique André Citroen, a large clockwork four door saloon, finished in two tone blue with black roof, 53.5cm., 1920's.
(Phillips) $3,171

A wooden box-type dolls' house, of four bays and two stories painted on upper storey to simulate brickwork, 28in. wide, third quarter of the 19th century, English.
(Christie's S. Ken) $1,168

A Bing painted tinplate clockwork Maypole with rotating suspended figures, a girl in a red dress and apron, and two boys in blue, and gray suits, circa 1910, 11in. high.
(Christie's S. Ken) $3,467

A boxed clockwork toy, of two composition headed dolls swinging and dancing before a mirror, 11in. wide, circa 1870.
(Christie's S. Ken) $1,300

A painted wooden dolls' house, simulating stone with brick quoining and window and door surrounds, 37in. wide, late 19th century.
(Christie's S. Ken) $876

A flock covered Carton Boston terrier, with chain pull growl, moving lower jaw and glass eyes, 21in. long, French.
(Christie's S. Ken) $662

A beechwood child's perambulator, with gilt metal fittings, painted dark green, upholstered in American cloth, 52in. long, circa 1880.
(Christie's S. Ken) $1,083

Citroen, clockwork painted tinplate delivery lorry finished in red with black lining with electric lighting, boxed with key, 43cm.
(Phillips) $895

Schuco, clockwork Radio Car 5000 finished in maroon and cream, complete with key and instructions, boxed.
(Phillips) $3,357

A Distler gray battery-operated tinplate Porsche Electromatic 7500, with instructions, in original box.
(Christie's S. Ken) $1,217

A golden short plush covered lion on wheels, with curly plush blonde mane, by Steiff, circa 1913 (missing ears, growl inoperative).
(Christie's S. Ken) $606

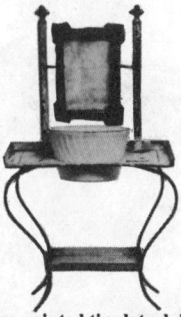

A cream painted tinplate dolls' house wash-stand, 8in. high, by Rock and Graner.
(Christie's S. Ken) $433

A painted wooden dapple gray rocking horse, on swing stand, 44in. long, by Lines Bros.
(Christie's S. Ken) $1,409

A papier mâché headed political toy modeled as Churchill, with frowning expression, remains of cigar, small bowler hat, and red bow tie, 10½in. high, circa 1920s.
(Christie's S. Ken) $175

Meccano: two nickel plated No. 5 Outfits, one in original wooden stained presentation box, mainly 1914–20.
(Christie's S. Ken) $303

A rare felt-covered Flip The Frog with Dean's Rag Book Co. Ltd., logo on one foot, *Made In England* on the other, 8in. high.
(Christie's S. Ken) $800

'Bahnhof' country station with entrance foyer, ticket collectors foyer, waiting rooms under a removable simulated tiled roof, 48cm. long.
(Phillips) $933

A clockwork painted tinplate horse with seated gentleman rider finished with blue tailed jacket, 15.5cm.
(Phillips) $403

A card model of a three bay stuccoed villa, laid out with a garden containing seven Grodnerthal dolls, 24in. wide, in glazed case, circa 1860.
(Christie's S. Ken) $758

Dinky, a rare half dozen trade pack of 106 'The Prisoner' mini-mokes, in original boxes and original cellophane wrapping.
(Christie's S. Ken) $1,231

Schuco 5300 Ingenico, the open top saloon car finished in bright red, the interior lithographed in green and checkered seats, 22cm.
(Phillips) $631

A Roly Poly blue and white rabbit with glass eyes and Steiff button in ear, 10½in. high with ears extended.
(Christie's S. Ken) $1,641

A felt rooster with wire framed feet, yellow, red and green feathers with Steiff button and original white tag, 1117, circa 1905–26.
(Christie's S. Ken) $1,026

A gray leather covered clockwork walking elephant, with bone tusks, glass eyes and serrated wheels on the feet, 10in. long, probably by Roullet et Decamps.
(Christie's S. Ken) $451

A German lithographed clown dressed in yellow checkered trousers, blue jacket with a spinner above his head, 11cm.
(Phillips) $62

Frog Hawker Hart Mark II Day Bomber, with accessories and instruction book, in original box, with Hamley's retail label, circa 1935.
(Christie's S. Ken) $1,846

Karl Bub printed tinplate clockwork Fire Brigade turntable ladder truck, with electric headlamps and four crew, circa 1931, 18in. long.
(Christie's S. Ken) $985

Ingap, clockwork lithographed twin funneled river boat, the main body finished in cream, on four silver spoked wheels, 15.5cm.
(Phillips) $337

A colored lithographic boxed sand toy, depicting Pierrot climbing up to a lady on a balcony with Harlequin preventing him with a stick, 8½in. high, published by Carre-Michels circa 1840.
(Christie's S. Ken) $1,436

A lithographed stand-up American policeman dressed in blue and white uniform, a lever behind enables the figure to raise and lower his arms, 21cm.
(Phillips) $168

Die Süd-Nord-Eisenbahn bei Erlangen, a colored lithograph sand toy, depicting a river scene with a train crossing a viaduct, 10½in. wide, Studio of Godefrey Engelmann, Alsace circa 1830.
(Christie's S. Ken) $3,180

A lithographed Penny Toy of a jigger dressed in red jacket, with yellow hat and trousers, on green box base, 9cm.
(Phillips) $231

A German papier-mâché sailor swallowing fish, the hand operated automaton with molded painted features, probably Sonneberg, late 19th century.
(Phillips) $1,341

A painted tinplate parlor maid chasing a mouse with a broom, dressed in pale blue dress with white collar, 19cm., probably by Martin.
(Phillips) $1,500

A tan leather Harrods gentleman's fitted dressing case, the interior finished in polished hide lined leather, 40 x 66cm.
(Onslow's) $286

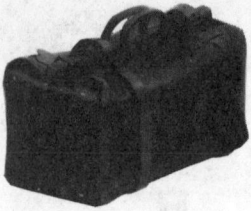

A fine large leather Gladstone bag, with key and straps, initialed M.W.H., little used with foul weather cover.
(Onslow's) $358

A Louis Vuitton brown grained leather suitcase, interior finished in canvas with two straps, labeled *Louis Vuitton Paris, Nice, Lille, London*, 55 x 34 x 18cm.
(Onslow's) $984

A Louis Vuitton Johnny Walker whiskey traveling drinks case, fitted for one bottle of whiskey, two bottles of mineral water, one packet of cheese biscuits, two glasses and ice container.
(Onslow's) $3,580

A Louis Vuitton gentleman's cabin trunk, bound in brass and leather with leather carrying handle, on castors, 91 x 53 x 56cm.
(Onslow's) $1,486

A Louis Vuitton special order tan pigskin gentleman's fitted dressing case, accessories include silver tooth brush, soap and talc containers, 54 x 32cm., circa 1930.
(Onslow's) $4,475

A Louis Vuitton shaped motor car trunk, covered in black material, interior with three matching fitted suitcases, 85 x 65 x 50cm.
(Onslow's) $6,265

A Louis Vuitton shoe secretaire, bound in leather and brass, fitted with twenty-nine shoe boxes with lids, one drawer and tray, 112 x 64 x 40cm.
(Onslow's) $7,697

A fine tan leather hat box by The Our Boys Clothing Company Oxford Street, with red velvet lining.
(Onslow's) $197

**A Louis Vuitton yellow fabric covered motor car suitcase, brass bound, with nickel-plated padlock shaped lock, 59 x 39 x 17cm.**
**(Onslow's) $633**

**A Louis Vuitton cabin trunk, vermin proof for use in the tropics, covered in zinc and brass bound, interior finished in white cotton, 85 x 49 x 47cm.**
**(Onslow's) $3,938**

**A Malles Goyard cabin trunk, covered in Malles Goyard patterned material, bound in leather and brass, 85 x 49 x 47cm.**
**(Onslow's) $716**

**A Louis Vuitton suitcase, No 761119, with key and leather LV luggage label, 62 x 40 x 17cm.**
**(Onslow's) $3,043**

**A Louis Vuitton shoe secretaire, fitted with thirty shoe boxes with lids, two large drawers top and bottom and tray, 112 x 64 x 40cm.**
**(Onslow's) $6,200**

**A Louis Vuitton gentleman's cabin trunk on castors, covered in LV material, fitted with three trays, one with compartments, 90 x 51 x 48cm.**
**(Onslow's) $1,969**

**A Garrison black fabric covered picnic service for six persons, complete with yellow and gold crockery, 56 x 40 x 30cm.**
**(Onslow's) $716**

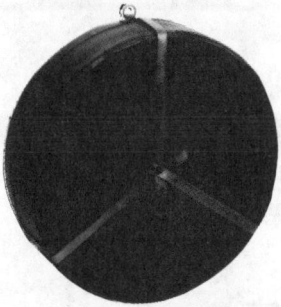

**A Louis Vuitton "Sac Chauffeur", the two circular halves covered in black material, the lower section watertight, 89cm diameter, circa 1905, designed to fit inside spare tyres.**
**(Onslow's) $5,370**

**A matching white hide suitcase and hat box by John Pound, with chromium-plated locks and foul weather covers, the suitcase 56 x 36cm.**
**(Onslow's) $501**

A molded copper gorse-and- sulky weathervane, American, circa 1875, the hatted rider with crop and reins in hand atop the sulky, 30½in. long.
(Christie's) $11,000

A gilded and molded copper peacock weathervane, attributed to A.L. Jewell and Company, Waltham, Massachusetts, active 1852-1867, the lifted head above a slender neck over a shaped body.
(Christie's) $16,000

A fine and rare molded and gilt copper. weathervane attributed to A.L. Jewell & Co., Waltham, Massachusetts, circa 1870, the galloping shell-bodied centaur, with drawn bow and arrow and shaped head and beard, 39in. long.
(Christie's) $33,000

A molded copper and cast zinc horse weathervane, A.L. Jewell and Co., Waltham, Massachusetts, 1850–1867, with cast head and applied ears above a molded body, 17in. long.
(Christie's) $4,950

Fine small index horse weather vane, J. Howard & Co., Bridgewater, Massachusetts, third quarter 19th century, 18in. high.
(Skinner Inc.) $4,000

A painted copper weather vane, depicting a running fox, 31in. long.
(Christie's) $244

A molded copper gilt bull weathervane. attributed to L.W. Cushing and Sons, Waltham, Massachusetts, circa 1875, with applied horns and cut ears, 29½in. long.
(Christie's) $6,050

Molded gilt copper and zinc weather vane, America, late 19th century, in the figure of the horse 'Colonel Patchen', 30in. long.
(Skinner Inc.) $1,100

An extremely rare and important molded copper and zinc horse-and-rider weathervane, J. Howard and Company, West Bridgewater, Massachusetts, circa 1860, 76½in. high, 36½in. wide.
(Christie's) $104,500

Copper weathervane, America, 20th century, in the form of a sailboat with directionals, 26½in. wide.
(Skinner Inc.) $400

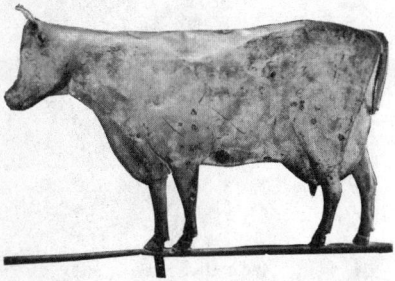

A large molded and gilt copper cow weathervane, American, late 19th century, with horns rising above copper ears and large molded eyes, 36in. long.
(Christie's) $3,850

Large copper cow weathervane, America, late 19th century, 28in. high.
(Skinner Inc.) $500

Rare carved sternboard from an admiral's gig, found on the Island of Malta, the brass framed pictorial panel with carved and polychromed decoration of Britannia flanked by a lion, 34in. wide.
(Eldred's) $1,870

Renaissance fruitwood figure of St. Dominick, 17th century, on one knee with one hand raised in prayer, 36in. high.
(Skinner Inc.) $1,700

A mid-Georgian brass-inlaid padoukwood tray in the style of John Channon with rectangular top, the gallery pierced with ovals, 18¾in. wide.
(Christie's) $8,712

A Regency mahogany birdcage with spindle-filled domed top, front and sides with ivory finials, the solid back with flap, 17¼in. high.
(Christie's) $3,900

A Bavarian stained oak seat in the form of a bear with outstretched arms, late 19th century, 51in. wide.
(Christie's S. Ken) $2,949

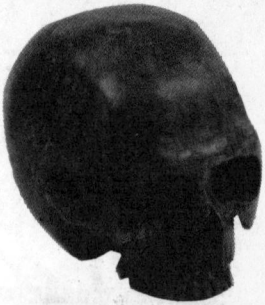

A carved wood skull, 7½in. high.
(Christie's S. Ken) $676

An Art Nouveau wood photograph frame, carved in relief with a young maiden dressed in flowing robes stretching up to a flower, 14in. high.
(Christie's S. Ken) $156

A pair of mahogany candlesticks with brass nozzles, fluted and ring-turned shafts and turned molded bases, 14in. high.
(Christie's) $693

A set of Dutch oak egg shelves, the arched back carved with *K I H ANNO 1723*, the front and sides decorated with chip carving with two arched pierced doors, first quarter 18th century, Friesian, 13in. wide.
(Christie's) $1,716

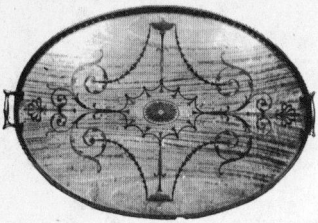

A 19th century satinwood and marquetry oval tray, 24in. wide.
(Dreweatt Neate) $819

An Akan female wood figure seated on a typical Ashanti stool, wearing a long skirt and sandals, the linear designs on her breasts and shoulders painted in white, 54cm. high. $141
(Phillips)

Carved and polychrome painted panel, Larraine Pasho, St. Albins, Vermont, circa 1940, 42¾ x 23¾in.
(Skinner Inc.) $375

A Swiss carved softwood model of a begging dog, on a molded naturalistic base stamped *BERGEN & CO INTERLAKEN*, late 19th/early 20th century, 31½in. high.
(Christie's) $14,107

A pair of polychrome-painted Venetian blackamoor torchères, each with a boy holding a torchère with a glass shade, 19th century, 69in. high.
(Christie's) $34,672

A painted wooden snuff or tobacco figure of a Scotsman, his right hand aloft holding a pinch of snuff, his left hand with a snuff mull, 37½in. high, 19th century.
(Bonhams) $3,293

An important large polychromed wood figure of Guanyin, Song dynasty, seated in rajalilasana, the right arm relaxed on the raised right knee, 61½in. high.
(Christie's) $310,993

One of a pair of giltwood wall brackets, with lotus-carved frieze above a tapering stiff-leaf-carved body and fruiting finial, 10½in. high.
(Christie's) $3,872

A Black Forest umbrella stand in the form of a standing bear with glass eyes and open mouth.
(Bearne's) $1,673

Carved and painted eagle and shield, attributed to John H. Bellamy, Kittery Point, Maine, late 19th century, 55in. wide. (Skinner Inc.) $5,000

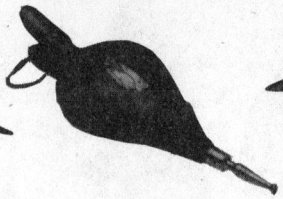

Painted and decorated bellows, America, 19th century, some paint loss, leather dry, 18¾in. high. (Skinner Inc.) $550

Challenge grade golden eye duck decoy, Mason Factory, Detroit, early 20th century, 15½in. long. (Skinner Inc.) $900

An important large polychromed wood figure of Guanyin, 12th/13th century, seated in rajalilasana on a rocky base issuing lingzhi, the right arm supported on the raised right leg, 60in. high. (Christie's) $345,817

A pair of large polychrome blackamoor torchères, Italian, 19th century, each formed as a young boy with feathered turban raised on a tripartite cushioned tabouret, 77½in. high. (Christie's East) $9,900

A pair of Continental giltwood and gesso wall brackets, the serpentine platform supported on a pierced tapering cartouche molded with foliate scrolls and flowers, 10¼in. across. (Phillips) $1,168

A good late 17th century Norwegian birchwood tankard, the lid carved GT.KL, two coats of arms surmounted by doves and 1693, 7¼in. high. (Woolley & Wallis) $87,500

A boxwood model of the takarabune with detachable models of the Seven Gods of Good Fortune and their various attributes on deck, unsigned, late 19th century, 48cm. long. (Christie's) $6,068

An 18th century French walnut carving, modeled as a basket hung with fruit, the lower part with a grotesque mask head and foliate scrolls, 8in. high, overall. (Christie's S. Ken) $1,064

Shaker maple dipper, 19th century, 6in. diameter.
(Skinner Inc.) $500

A late 18th century Russian mangle board, carved with roundels and geometric ornament, with horse handle, 28¼in. long.
(Christie's S. Ken) $562

Painted wooden hobby horse, New England, early 19th century, painted dapple gray with green saddle and heart-shaped supports, 51in. wide.
(Skinner Inc.) $1,200

A Norwegian lidded tankard of cylindrical form with slightly domed cover carved in relief with a lion, 9in. high, 18th century.
(Bearne's) $1,316

An early 16th century Flemish oak group of the Flagellation, guild mark of Antwerp, 7in. high, mounted on a later shaped oak base.
(Christie's S. Ken) $2,217

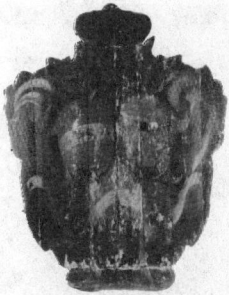

Italian polychrome wooden panel, 18th century, shaped and decorated as a heraldic crest, 72in. high.
(Skinner Inc.) $1,900

A Yoruba wood helmet mask for the Gelede festival, the smiling face with numerous exposed teeth and black and red rimmed pierced eyes, 41.5cm. high.
(Phillips) $493

A pair of Japanese bamboo vases, each of cylindrical form, carved in low relief with figures in a garden setting, 22in. high.
(Spencer's) $895

A Yoruba wood head-dress for the Egungun Society, egungun solde, the sharp-featured face with three horizontal scarifications on the cheeks and vertical ones on the brow, 28.5cm. high.
(Phillips) $114

A pair of mid 19th century fruitwood candle stands, the wide drip pans supported on barley twist columns with spreading circular bases, 36½in. high.
(Christie's S. Ken) $1,730

Two Venetian parcel gilt, polychrome and ebonized blackamoor torchères, each wearing a turban and a costume tied at the waist, 62¼in. high.
(Christie's S. Ken) $8,866

A pair of late 19th century stained beech candlesticks, the turned knopped columns with wide circular drip pans, 52¾in. high.
(Christie's S. Ken) $1,323

A monumental parcel-gilt, carved wooden panel, from H.M.S. Britannic, by Professor A.H. Gerrard, deeply carved and incised with a frieze of eight wild horses amid stylized foliage, 75cm. high x 270cm. wide.
(Christie's) $15,435

An early 19th century pin cushion designed as a crown of turned wood, inscribed *King George the fourth crowned July 19 1821.*
(Phillips) $202

Four red japanned wine coasters, with reeded sides and silver plated lion's mask and drop ring handles, circa 1800.
(Christie's) $4,752

A giltwood No Mask of a demon, his face with grimacing expression, inlaid glass eyes, 8¼in., Meiji period.
(Bonhams) $998

# INDEX


AA 504
Aalto, Alvar 292
Abarth & C. 503
AC Cobra 496, 500
Action Comics 23
Adam, Charles 584
Adams, Ansel 528
Adams, Geo. 455, 613
Adams, John 181
Adamson, Robert 529
Adey Brothers 574
Adnet, Jacques 530
Advertising 16-19
Aero Shell 18
Aeronautical Items 20, 21
Aitken, Mary 134
Akers & Co. 402
Akroyd, Dan 551
Albano, Salvatore 478
Albemarle Postage Stamp camera, The 86
Albin, Eleazar 66
Aldam Heaton 295
Aldrin, Buzz 568, 571
Alfa Romeo 496, 501, 502-505
Alfred and Darling & Co. 86
Alice Mandell 491
Allen II, William 603
Allen, Fred 133
Alloisi, Giovanni 503
Almaric Walter 408, 409
Alms dish 240, 241
American Camera Co. 87
American China 98-101
American Comics 22, 23
American Enertainment Co. 447
American School 572
American Venus, The 446
Amphora 101
Amusement Machines 24, 25
Andirons 240, 241
Andreoni, G. 481
Angel 444
Angell, Joseph 604
Anna Pottery 404
Annals of Sporting and Fancy Gazette, The 66
Anne Marie 490
Annesley, Arthur 583
Ansbach 148
Ansiglioni, Leopoldo 396
Ansonia Clock Co., The 21
Antiquities 26, 27
Antoniazzi, Gaetano 506
AR 125
Aramburu, Pedro Eugenio 50
Arbus, Diane 529
Archambo, Peter 596, 619, 629
Architectural Fittings 28, 29
Arden, Thomas 573
Argy-Rousseau, Gabriel 408
Argyles 573
Argyll and Sutherland Highlanders 35
Argylls Ltd. 563
Arita 102
Arms & Armor 30-48
Armstrong, Louis 59
Armstrong, Margaret 133
Armstrong, Neil 54, 568, 569, 571
Arnold & Richter 84
Arnold, John 457
Arts and Crafts 238, 274, 382, 390
ASA 498
Ashbee, C.R. 413, 576, 580, 586, 598, 600, 601, 602, 609, 614, 618, 627
Askew, Richard 130
Aspects of Golf 441
Asprey & Co. Ltd 610
Astaire, Fred 265
Aston Martin 497
Atget, Eugène 525, 527
Atkin Brothers 578
Atkin, Harry 415
Augustin, Jean-Baptiste-Jacques 537
Aulenti, Gae 474
Auliczek, Dominicus 178
Austin 500, 501
Autissier, Louis Marie 538
Auto Union 503
Autographed Documents 50-53
Automatons 60, 61
Automobile Club of America 504
Avengers, The 23

Babe Ruth 571
Baccarat 424, 425
Baetens 223
Bagian, Dr. James P. 56
Baier, Fred 531
Bailey, Banks & Biddle 210
Bailey, Robert 634
Baillie-Scott, M.H. 366
Baillon, J.B. 220
Baker, Josephine 51
Baker, Josephine 571
Baldock, E.H. 355
Baldwyn, C.H.C. 204
Ball, William 626
Bambi 247
Banham, D. 20
Bank of England 514-518
Bank of New South Wales 517, 518
Bank of Scotland 517
Banque de L'Indochine 516, 517
Baptiste, Jean 506
Barbedienne, F. 69
Bardot, Brigitte 263
Barker & Sons, F. 453
Barlow, Hannah 134
Barnard and Co. 581
Barnard Brothers 631
Barnard, E.J. & W. 599
Barnard, Edward 591, 596
Barnard, Messrs 590
Barnard, Walter and John 585
Barnasconi, M. 62
Barnsley, Edward 326
Barometers 62, 63
Barr, Flight & Barr 206
Bartlemew, Nicholas 600
Bartok, Bela 57
Bartolini, Lorenzo 480
Barton, Thomas 77
Barye, Antoine-Louis 71
Basins 573
Baskets 573-575
Bass, James Le 624
Bassano, A 567
Basser, Gamal Abdel 51
Batchelder, Mary Steere 476
Bateman, Hester 631
Bateman, Peter and Ann 605, 613, 624, 625, 630
Bateman, Peter and William 594, 602
Bateman, Peter, Anne and William 584, 586, 626
Bateman, William 620, 628, 634
Bates Tyres 17
Bath J.L. 218
Batman 22, 23
Battle of Life, The 67
Batty, Dora 180
Baubo 27
Baume & Mercier 235
Bayard, C. 607
Bayes, Jessie 328
Bayley, Richard 620
Baynes, Thomas Mann 542
Bayol, Gustave 94
Beakers 400
Beakers 576
Beatles, The 551-555
Beaton, Cecil 524
Beaumont Adams 41
Bedfordshire Yeomanry 39
Beds & Cradles 272-, 273
Beebe, James 632
Beilby, William 435
Bell Bros. 229
Bell, Edward 550
Bell, James 608
Bellamy, John H. 660
Belleek China 103
Belushi, John 551
Benches 396, 397
Beney, Robt. & Co 93
Bennett, Harve 261
Benson, J.W. 220, 233
Benson, W.A.S. 96
Bent, John 18
Bentley 496, 497, 501
Bergen & Co. 659
Berger, Louis-Jacques 576
Bergman, Ingrid 262, 265
Bergner, Carl 249
Berlin China 103, 104
Berlin, George & Sons Ltd. 283
Bernard et fils 225
Beromat 24
Bertion, L. 188
Bettridge and Jennins 521
Bettridge, John 636
Beyer, Johann Christian Wilhelm 148
Bianconi, Fulvio 410
Bianconi, Fulvio 416, 431
Biedermeier 83
Biggs, Joseph 614
Billingsley, William 129
Bilodeau, J.W. 19
Bingham, W. 563
Bininger, A.M. & Co 401
Binne, B. 502
Birch, William 351
Bird Bath 397
Birds of North America 65
Birks, Ron 118
Birmingham Guild of Handicrafts 476
Bittan, Roy 551

Bizarre 119
BL and St. Ives 161
Black, Starr & Frost 598, 631
Blaha, Col. John E. 56
Blake, Sarah & John William 614
Bleriot, Louis 57
Blues Brothers, The 551
Blum, Maxime 66
Blunt, Wilfred Jasper Walter 65
BMW 496, 498
Bobby Blue Bland 555
Bogart and Bacall 55
Boit, Charles 537
Bonheur, Isidore 69
Bookcases 274-275
Books 64-67
Boon, Dr. Ernest G. 526, 527
Boote, A.T. & R. 120
Booth, Edward Thomas 66
Booth, Jas. 219
Booz, E.G. 405
Boreman, Zachariah 129
Boscovitch, Roger Joseph 67
Bosio, Baron François-Joseph 71
Bottengruber, Ignaz 169
Böttger Hausmalerei 148
Bottles 401-405
Boubat, Edouard 526
Boucher, A. 72
Bouger, M. 73
Bouillerot, Nicholas 439
Boulanger, Jean-Nicolas 629
Boultbee, John 541
Boulton & Fothergill 605
Boulton, Matthew & Co. 581, 585
Bovy, Gustave Serurrier 322
Bow China 105
Bowers, A.G.F. 121
Bowie, David 550, 553, 555
Bowls 406-409, 577-579
Boxes 580
Boyer, Charles 262
Bracket Clocks 208, 209
Bradbury Wilkinson & Co. 515, 517
Bradbury, J. 517, 519
Braggs, Al. 555
Brandt, Bill 524, 525
Brassaï 529
Brazo, Manuel Alvarez 526
Breatplates 30, 31
Briade 258
Brianza, Carlo 503
Bridge, John 590
Bridgens, Richard 283
Briggle, Van 98
Britenbach, Josef 529
British China 106-110
Broadwood, John & Sons 530, 531
Brockbank & Atkins 227
Bronze 68-75
Brook & Son 35
Brooke, Rupert 51
Brooklands Aero Club 20
Brotherston & Son 229
Brown, Edward Charles 612
Brown, Harry 181
Brown, William 607
Bru 248, 250
Brummell, George B. 56
Brunswick Infantry Regt. 38
Bryans of Kegworth 24
Bryant, Fred. 223
Bucher, A. 609
Buchli, Col. James F. 56
Buck, Frederick 539
Buckets 76
Buffalo Bill 54
Bugatti 498, 501, 505
Bugatti, Carlo 293, 295, 340
Buhot, C. 397
Buhre, Pavel 211
Buick 499
Buick 500
Bullion 24
Bullock, George 266
Bunyan, Thos. 228
Bureau Bookcases 276, 277
Bureaux 278-281
Burges, William 374
Burleigh ware 106
Burroughs, Alice & George 606
Burton, Sir Richard, F. 50
Burwash, William 594
Bustelli 147
Butcher, W. & Sons Ltd 86
Butterfield, Margaret 367

Cabianca, Giulio 505
Cabinet of Dr. Caligari, The 447
Cabinets 282-285
Caddies & Boxes 77-83
Cadillac 498
Cafe, John 586
Cahusac, Thomas 509
Cain, Auguste Nicolas 69
Calamatta, J. 258
Calderwood & Son 33
Callas, Maria 55
Caltagirone 157
Calvert, Willm. 231
Cameras 84-89
Camerer Cuss & Co. 230
Cameron, Julia Margaret 524, 527, 528
Camilli, Camillo 507
Campania General De Coches De Lujo 563
Campbell, Malcolm 567
Candelabra 581
Candi, C. 507
Candlesticks 238, 240, 241, 256, 257, 410, 582, 583
Candy Containers 411
Cane Handles 90, 91
Canon Camera Co. 86
Canterburys 286
Canton 113
Capodimonte 156
Cappa, Goffredo 507
Car Mascots 92, 93
Card & Tea Tables 350-353
Cardew, Michael 110
Cardwell, Holme 481
Carlisle City & District Banking Co. 515
Carnegie, Andrew 51
Carousel Figures 94, 95
Carpeaux, J.B. 72
Carpentier, Georges 55
Carpentier, Gustave 569
Carr & Co. 19
Carriage Clocks 210,211
Carrier-Belleuse, Albert-Ernest 70
Carrington & Co. 620
Carroll, Lewis 524-527
Carrosserie Van Den Plas 504
Carter & Son 208
Carter, Dudley 597
Carter, John 583
Cartier 221, 226
Cartier-Bresson, Henri 525, 527, 528
Caruso, Enrico 568
Cary, J. & W. 453
Cased Sets 32, 33
Cassa, Paolo 503
Castel Durante 154, 155
Castelli 155
Casters 584
Caumont, J. 312
Cavelier, Pierre-Jules 71
Cawdell, W. 600
Cawfon, Jas. 216
Cazeaux, Gueron 416
CB 249
CC 595
Cecil, Hugh 567
CEF 462
Center Tables 354, 355
Centerpieces 585
Chad Valley 253 ,640
Chadburn, Alfred 493
Chagall, Marc 570
Chaligny, S. 438
Chambersticks 238, 586
Chambrelant 258
Chandeleliers 96, 97
Chanel 243, 260
Chaney, Lon Snr. 56
Channon, John 658
Chaplin, Charlie 59, 261, 265
Chaplin, Charlie 513
Charles II 52
Chase Brass and Copper Co. 239
Chatham & Gillingham Vol.
Chawner, Henry 575, 624, 625, 627
Checker, Chubby 552
Chelmsford Bank 514
Chelsea China 111, 112
Chelsea Keramic 99
Chenets 267
Cher 261
Chests of Drawers 302-305
Chests on Chests 306, 307
Chests on Stands 308
Chevalier, Georges 436
Chicago Serigraph Workshop, The 543
Chiffoniers 309
Child & Child 576, 601
Chimes, The 67
Chimot, Edouard 66
China 98-207
Chinese China 113-117
Chivers' Jellies 17
Chocolate Pots 587
Chrisford & Norris 611
Christian Dior 243
Christie, Agatha 56
Christmas Carol, A 67
Christophle & Cie 69
Chronometer 455, 457
Churchill, Winston S. 52, 53, 67, 567, 568, 571
Ciceri & Pini 63
Cigarette Cases 587
Circle Skill 24
Citizen Kane 446
Clapton, Eric 550
Clare, Joseph 626
Claret Jugs 588, 589
Clarice Cliff 118-119

Clark, Charles 594
Clemons, Clarence 551
Clevenger Brothers 409
Clichy 424, 425
Cliff, Clarice 118
Clift, Montgomery 58, 263
Clinton, Dewitt 101
Clock Sets 212-214
Clocks & Watches 208-235
Clodion, C.M. 69, 75
Cloisonne 236, 237
Clucking Hen 25
Clydesdale Banking Co. 517
CN 611
Coade 29
Coal scuttle 240, 241
Coalbrookdale 107
Coasters 590
Coats, Capt. Michael L. 56
Coca Cola 19
Cody, W.F. 54
Coffee Pots 591-593
Cohen, D. 62
Coker, Ebenezer 582, 586
Coles, Lawrence 637
Colinet, Cl. J.R. 75
Collins, Michael 568, 571
Collins, Phil 553
Colonial Bank of Mauritius 514
Columbia 446, 490
Columbia Graphophone 484
Columbus 24
Comerford, John 537
Commemorative China 120-122
Commode Chests 311-313
Commodes & Potcupboards 310
Compass 453
Complin, George 129
Comyns, William 573, 602
Condliff, James 219, 229
Console Tables 356, 357
Conti, Michele 495
Contreau, L. 211
Cooke, Sam 555
Cooke, Thomas 617
Cookson, Isaac 613
Coolie Motor Oil 504
Cooper 208
Cooper, Gary 54, 264
Cooper, Samuel 523, 536
Coper China 123
Coper, Hans 123
Copes 293
Copper & Brass 238-241
Corbett, Thomas 299
Corbusier, Le 337
Corkscrews 242
Corner Cupboards 314, 315
Costume 243-245
Cosway, Richard 536
Courthrope, Fred 238
Cowan Guy, R. Pottery 477
Cox, Robert 216, 612
CR 614
CRA 614
Crawford, Joan 262
Cream 550
Cream Jugs 594
Creamware China 124
Crespin, Paul 591
Cressent 297
Criaerd, Jme. A. 312
Cricket on the Hearth, The 67
Crickitt & Co. 514
Crosby, Gordon 92
Crosby, Morse & Foss 616
Cross, Peter 539
Crosse and Blackwell 17
Crown petrol 19
Cruets 595
Crump, Francis 613
CS 103
CSA Ltd. 110, 181
Cuff, I. 63
Cunningham, Imogen 529
Cupboards 316, 317
Cups 596, 597
Curtis, Edward S. 529
Cushing, L.W. & Sons 657
Cuzner, Bernard 578
Cyrén, Gunnar 419

d'Orleans, Marie 71
da Venezia, Domenico 196
Daggers 34, 35
Daisey Duck 247
Dane, Joshue 530
Daniell, Thomas 575
Darcy, G. 258
Darker, William 605, 625
Darwin, Charles 56
Daudet, Alphonse 66
Daum 407, 421, 430, 431-433, 474, 477
Davenport 108, 318, 319
Davis, W. & Sons 226
Davison, George 526
De Voursney Bros. 476
de Beaumont, E. 258
de la Mare, Walter 50
de la Rue, Thomas 271
de Morgan, William 167
Deacon, John 612
Deakin, John and William 602
Deal and Walmer Coalfield Ltd. 565
Dean, James 260
Deane & Son 32
Deane, Adams and Deane 33
Decanters 412, 413
Deck, Théodore 100
Dedham Pottery 98, 99
Defoe, Daniel 64
Degani, Eugenio 508
DeGrave Short and Fanner 239
Delft China 125-129
Delmester, John 595
Denigre 224
Denziloe, John 588
Denziloe, John 614
Deparcieux, Antoine 66
Déposé Tête Jumeau 248, 252, 253
Derby China 130, 131
Deruta 156
Descomps, Joë 73
Desmalter, Georges-Alphonse Jacob 317, 332
Dester, G. 316
Detective Comics 22, 23
Deutsch-Asiatische Bank 519
DF 587
Diamond Dyes 18
Diana 26
Dickens, Charles 67
Diepraam, Willem 524
Diers, Edward 183
Dietrich, Marlene 261, 265
Dillwyn A, & Co. 106
Dimples 444
Dining Chairs 287-291
Dining Tables 358-359
Dion 555
Dionysos 26
Dior, Christian 243
Dishes 414,598-599
Disneyana 246, 247
Display Cabinets 320, 321
Disraeli, Benjamin 56
Dixon, Arthur P. 443
Dixon, James & Son 42, 43, 573, 577, 578, 589, 608, 621, 627
Doccia 156, 157
Dodson, Richard 130
Dolland 452
Dolls 248-253
Domestic Equipment 254-255
Donald Duck 247
Dooly, J. & Sons 321
Doors, The 550
Doré, Gustave 74
Doriot Flandrin Parant 501
Doubling for Romeo 445
Doucai China 132
Doulton China 133-136
Doyle, Sir Arthur Conan 56
Dr Bone's X-Ray 25
Dr Harter's 19
Dr. Caldwells/Herb Bitters 401
Dresser, Christopher 162, 163, 238, 413, 421, 578, 589, 608, 621, 627, 629
Dressers 322, 323
Dressing Tables 360, 361
Dressler, Marie 59
Drew & Sons 210
Drinking Sets 415
Drop Leaf Tables 362, 363
Drottning Victoria 491
Drtikol, Frantisek 528
Dubreuil, André 231, 291
Ducommun, Henri 224
Ducrette and Roger 495
Duesbury, Wm. & Co. 130, 131
Duffner & Kimberley 428
Dufrene, Maurice 295
Dührkoop, Rudolph 525
Duke of Bronte 64
Dumbo 247
Dumoulin, Georges 431
Dunbarton, Jas. McInnes 208
Dunhill-Namiki 270, 271
Dunlap, Samuel 306
Dupain, Max 524
Durand, G. 227, 313
Durante, Castel 154, 155
Durantino, Francesco 154
Dürer, Albrecht 540, 543
Duret and Delafontaine 74
Durham, Cornelius 539
Dutchboy 24
Dutton, Thomas Goldsworth 541
Dutton, Willm. & Sons 217
Duvivier, Michel Joseph 145

Eagle 501
Eames, Charles and Ray 359
Earlom, R. 543
Eastman Kodak Co. 86
Easy Chairs 292-297, 298, 299
Eberlein, J.F. 173
Edison 484-485
Edward VIII 50, 52
Edwards, Charles 610, 621

Edwards, John 629, 630
Egan, John 509
Eichentopf, Johann 509
Eisenhower, Dwight, D. 53, 569
Eisenstaedt, Alfed 526
Ekberg, Anita 264
Ekco 548
El Banco Salvadoreno 519
Elastic Sportszalag 16
Elbow Chairs 300-301
Elevenses 24
Elizabeth, The Queen Mother 51
Elkin & Co. 106
Elkington & Co. 589, 604, 616, 618, 627
Elkington, Frederick 628
Elliott, William 592, 614
Ellis, Alfred 528
EM 601
Emes and Barnard 615, 625
Emes, John 630
Emes, Rebecca 591, 596
EMG 483
Enamel 256, 257
Engle, Joe 57
Engleheart, George 536
Epstein, Brian 555
Erard 530
Ernst Leitz Canada Ltd. 513
Ernst, Matthias 220
Erté 543
Essevi 139
ET 596
Eternola Portablofon 484
Eton Volunteer Rifle Corps 37
European China 137-139
European Watch & Clock Co. 222
Evans II, John 612
Evans, Paul 488
Evans, R.T. 215
Evans, Thomas 601, 629
Evans, W.F. & Sons 229
Evening gowns 243
Everill Propeller Corp 20
Ex-Lax 18
Extraordinary 25

Faenza 157
Fagioli, D. 63
Faguay, Pierre Le 72
Fairbanks, Douglas Snr. 264
Fairey Swordfish 21
Famille Rose China 140
Fans 258-259
Fantasia 246
Farini 154
Farrell, Edward 604
Farrell, Edward Cornelius 626
Farren, Thomas 591
Fats Domino 550
Fawdrey, William 623
FBO 445
FE 603
Federal Bank of Austrlia 519
Federal Reserve Board 518
Federici, Danny 551
Felter, Susan 528
Fenton Brothers 628
Fenton Creswick and Co. 583
Fenton, H. 136
Fenton, Roger 526
Ferara, Andrea 46
Ferguson, James 637
Fernie, George 443
Ferns of Great Britain and Ireland, The 65
Ferrari 497, 499, 502, 503
Ferrari, Alfredo 504
Ferrari, Enzo 502, 505
Ferry. H. 44
Fiat 497, 498
Figg, John 589
Figures 416
Film Memorabilia 260
Film Star Photographs 261-265
Findley & Taylor 588
Fiot, Maximilien-Louis Fiot 75
Fire irons 240, 267
Fire screen 241
Firegrates 266
Fireplace Furniture 267
Fireplaces 268, 269
First National 445, 447
Flaming Carrot Comics 23
Flasks 417
Flatware 600-601
Fleury l'Ainé 233
Fliaccini, Prof. H. 479
Flight & Barr 205, 207
Flora Superba 65
Flying Pat 444
Flynn, Errol 58,265
Focke-Wulf 21
Fogelberg, Andrew 624, 625, 626
Foley China 16, 141
Forbes, George 515
Ford 499
Ford, Harrison 260
Forgan, Robert 442
Forham & Co. 239
Forster, Thomas 538
Fountain Pens 270, 271
Fountain, John 627
Fournier, A.M.E. 345
Fox, Charles 574, 596, 626, 606
Fox, Charles and George 614
Fox, George 574, 576, 617
Fox, Robert Frederick 620
Frames 602
Frank, Robert 527
Franke and Heidecke 85
Frankenthal 147
Franklin-Dyott 417
Fraser Nash Car Club 504
Fraser, Lavra Gardin 20
Fremlins Ale 19
French China 142-145
Frères, Japy 213, 214, 226
Frères, Nicole 485
Freydanck, Carl Daniel 103
Frith, H.A. 572
Frodsham 222
Frodsham, Henry 63
Frog de Havilland 21
Fruit Grower's Guide, The 66
Frullini, L. 294
Fry's 18, 19
Fulper Pottery 98, 99
Fumo, Gaetano 156
Funkwerk Dresden 254
Furniture 272-395

G & JW Hawksley 43
Gable, Clark 263
Gadaffi, Colonel 570
Gainsford, Robert 573
Gallé 142, 340, 406, 412, 414, 421, 426, 431-433, 474, 475
Gally, P. 62
Garaku 511
Garden Statuary & Furniture 396-399
Garfield, John 59
Garibaldi 516
Garland, Jusy 58
Garlthorne, George 613
Garrard, James 597, 618
Garrard, Robert 575, 618,622 ,598
Garthorne, George 579
Gateleg Tables 364, 365
Gaucher, P. 188
Gaultier, François 249
Gaumont, L et Cie 86
Gauntlets 30, 31
Gaveau Paris 531
Gebelein, George C. 626
Gecophone 548
Geldof, Bob 550
Gennaro & Alle Vinaccia 507
George III 51
George V 52
George Washington: Patriot, Soldier, Statesman 65
Gere, Richard 260
German China 146-148
Gerrard, Prof. A.H. 662
Gessho 511
Ghost's Bargain, The 67
Gibbs, W. 228
Gibson, Richard 536, 537
Gienne, E. Berner 240
Gigantic Land-Tortoises, The 67
Gignac, Benjamin 593
Gilbert, Stephen 625
Gill, Eric 487
Gillois, Peter 81
Gillows 289
Gillray, James 124
Gilmour, Margaret 230
Gilroy, John 16
Girardot 74
Glass 400-437
Globes 452-457
Go Into Your Dance 445
Goblets 418, 419, 603
Goebel, William 106
Goebels 147
Gold 438-440
Goldscheider China 149
Goldsmith & Silversmiths Co 577, 584, 592, 598, 606, 608, 619
Goldwyn 445, 447
Golf Illustrated Magazine 440
Golf Match, The 443
Golfiana or A day at Gullane 442
Golfing Items 440-443
Goodyear 17
Gordon, Charles 625
Gordon, Thos. 219
Gough, William 588
Gould, John 582
Gould, William 582
Goupy, Marcel 144
Gourlay, J. 442, 443
Gout, Ralph 454
Graal 409
Grable, Betty 264
Graham, George 219
Gramophone & Typewriter Ltd. 483
Grandmother Duck 247

Grant, Gary 54
Grant, John 217
Gratchev, A. 72, 74
Graziàno, Rocky 569
Great and Small Game of Africa 67
Great Kruger Gold Mining Co. Ltd. 563
Greeley's 404
Green Lantern 23
Grego, A. 62
Gregoire, Jean Louis 72
Gregory, J.M. 494
Grenadier Regt. 37
Gretna Green, The Smithy 24
Gricci, Guiseppe 154, 156
Grice, Thomas 399
Griffen, Joseph 44
Grim Game, The 445
Grimaldi, William 538, 539
Grimes, Thos. 219
Grinnell, Peter & Son 488
Grip Tester 25
Grueb Faience Co. 100
Grueby Pottery 98
Grundy, William 623
Guadagnini, Giovanni Battista 507
Guameri, Giuseppe 506
Guerlain 426
Guild of Handicraft Ltd 238
Guinness 16
Günther, Albert C.L.G. 67
Gurney, Richard 617
Gyokujunsai 451
Gyokukendo 566

Hadley, James & Sons 205-207
Hagenauer 239
Haggart, David Campbell 480
Hale, W. 207
Halford, Robt. H. 212
Hall, J.H. 44
Hall, Martin & Co. 601, 615, 623
Hamada, Shoji 150
Hamilton & Co. 612
Hamilton and Inches 585
Hamilton Crighton & co 34
Han Dynasty 26
Hancock, C.F. 589
Hands, D. and C. 603
Handscomb, E. 209
Hardman and Iliffe 316
Hardy, Oliver 261, 264
Hare, George 85
Hargreaves, Thomas 538
Haritsua 451
Harris, C.S. 579
Harris, Charles Stuart 609
Harris, Charles Stuart and Son 573
Harrison, George 550, 552, 553
Harrison, James A. 65
Hart, Napthali 626
Hartkopf 31
Harvey, E.M. 514, 518
Haseler, H. 599
Hatchard, Anne 180
Hathways 404
Hatton, Joseph 218
Hattori 257
Haunted Man, The 67
Haven, Peter Nicolai von 628
Hawker Typhoon 20
Hawthorn R. & W., Leslie & Co. Ltd 490
Hayes, James 346
Hayne and Carter 615
Hayne, Jonathan 624
Hayne, Samuel 597
Hayworth, Rita 59
Heath & Middleton 623
Heath Robinson Gold Course, The 442
Heathen-Chinee 98
Heaton, J. Aldam 314
Hebden, Luke 634
Hebden, Thomas 601
Heeley, Benjn. 217
Heifetz, Jascha 570
Heigl, Martin 231
Heinrich & Co. 146
Heliostat 454
Helmets 36-39
Heming, Thomas 593
Hemingway, Ernest 54
Henderson, Ewen 150
Hendrix, Jimi 552, 553, 555
Henkels, Jan 218
Hennell, David 618
Hennell, Robert 605
Hennell, Robert and David 575
Hennell, Robert and Samuel 586
Hennell, Samuel 594, 595
Henning, John 529
Henry, A. 40
Henry, Paul & Prospère 526
Henry, S.S. 283
Hepburn, Audrey 262
Hepplewhite, George 289
Her Wedding Night 444
Herbert, S. & Co 599
Hessler, J.C.W.P. 626
Heubach 148
Heubach, Gebruder 252
Hick 270
Hicks, J. 63
Higashiyama 68
Hill, David Octavius 529
Hilton, H. and Smith G.G. 441
Hindmarsh, George 607
Hispana Moresque 151
Hispano-Suiza 496
History of Modern Wiltshire, The 66
Hitchcock, Alfred 59
Hitler, Adolf 568
Hld, Edward 415
HM Queen Victoria 567
HMS Cheerful 490
HMS Viper 490
HMV 484
Hoare, Sir Robert Colt 66
Höchst 151
Hoffmann, Dezo 553
Holden, William 265
Holland & Sons 310
Holland II, Thomas 618
Holland, Henry 606
Holloway, A.L. 494
Holloway, John 198
Holly, Buddy 554
Hollywood Poster 444-447
Hone, Horace 538
Hood 204
Hoogenstraaten & Voom 322
Hornby 492, 493
Höroldt, J.G. 169, 173
Hoskins, John 536
Hotado 187
Houghton, G.B. 495
Houghton, Solomon 575
House, E.M. 54
Howard, E. & Co. 231
Howard, J. & Co. 656, 657
Howard, Leslie 55, 59, 264
HRH Prince Edward 567
Hukin & Heath 412, 413, 421, 577, 579, 595, 599, 608, 609, 621, 627, 629
Hull, Charles 242
Hunt and Roskell 588, 623
Hunt, J.S. 585, 588, 607
Huntley and Palmer 16
Hussars 36
Hutchinson, H.G. 441
Hutchison, J. 480
Hutschenreuther Hohenburg 148
Hutton, Edward 584
Hutton, William & Sons 577, 584, 602, 623, 628
Hyatt, John 583
Hygrometer 452

Iacob, G. 296
IBH 614
Icart, Louis 540-543
Icons 448-449
IL 622, 634
Illustrated Book of Poultry, The 65
Imari China 152, 153
Imhof, Heinrich Maximillian 480
Inagaki, T. 542
Inagawa 450
Incredible Hulk, The 22
Inkinzan zi 186
Inkstand 241, 604
Inros 450-451
Instruments 452-457
Irish Open 441
Iron & Steel 458-461
Iron Man 22
Isles de France et de Bourbon 519
Isotta Fraschini 498
Italian China 154-157
Ivory 462-465
Iwami 472

J&T 588
JA 619
Jacquemart, Henri-Alfred-Marie 73
Jack, George 334
Jackets 243
Jackson Five, The 551
Jackson, Michael 552
Jackson, Thomas 590
Jacobs, Hendrik 508
Jacobs, John 619, 623
Jacot, Henri 210
Jade 466, 467
Jagger, Mick 554
Jaguar 496, 499-501
Jameson, J. 442
Janety, Etienne 577
Janse, Johannes 575
Jars 420
Jasper, Theodore 65
Jazz Singer, The 446
Jean, Phillip 539
Jenks, Wm. 44
Jenner, Edward 53
Jensen Georg 470, 577, 609, 629
Jewell, A.L. & Co. 656

Jewelry 468-471
Jiaquing 140
Jin Dynasty 115
JJ 125
Johnson, G. 204
Johnson, Herbert 504
Jolson Al. 58, 568
Jones, John 606
Jones, Paul 65
Jordain, William 217
Josef, Franz 50
Joyce, Richard 110
JP 238
JS 591, 592
JT 633
Jugs & Pitchers 421
Jugs 605, 606
Justice League of America 23

K & W 249
Kajikawa 450
Kakiemon China 158
Kalker, Jurriaan van 604
Kändler, J.J. 130, 170-173
Kangxi China 159
Kar, Ida 525
Karloff, Boris 262
Karsh, Yousef 529
Kauffer, E. McKnight 18
Keeler, Christine 571
Kéléty, A. 69
Kelly, Grace 570
Kent, William 121, 486
Kerr and Binns 206
Kerr and Philips 596
Kesborer, Samuel 597
Kestner, J.D. 253
Kettle 238, 241
Kettlewell, John 259
King George I 54
King George II 56
King George V 568
King James I 50
King, Peter 217
Kinkozan zo 186, 187
Kinryusai 510
Kiobenhavn, Rasmus Koch 452
Kirk, Jos. 209
Kizan 186
Klein, William 529
Kloss, Johann Georg 630
Kneehole Desks 324, 325
Knibb, Joseph 209
Knishott, Chas. 483
Kohlheim, Johann Gottlieb 581
Kohn, A.J. & J. 337
Koma Kansai 450
Koma Yasutada 451
Komo Kyoryu saku 450
Komoru 236
Konig & Wernicke 249
KPM 103, 104
KPP 104
Krügener, Dr. 85
Kutani China 160
KW 128
Kyoto school 510, 511

L & Co. 602
L&B 600
La Banque Royale 514
Lacquer 472, 473
Lakin & Poole 179
Lalique 92, 93, 224, 406-409, 414, 416, 422, 423, 425-428, 431-434
Lambert, George 580
Lamborghini 501
Lamerie, Paul le 573, 591
Lamps 474-477
Lanark Rifle Volunteers 47
Lancashire Fusiliers, The 39
Lancia 495
Lander, J. 206
Lane, Lois 23
Langdon, Harry 59
Langer, A. & Sohne 232
Langlands & Robertson 592
Lantern Clocks 215
Lanz, J.W. 147
Large Tables 366, 367
Larnhill, Abrm. 219
Laurel and Hardy 261, 264
Laurel, Stan 261, 264
Laurent, Claude 508
Laver, John 596
Lawley & Co. 216
Lawrence, C. 87
Lazzarini, Alessandro 481
LD 611
Le Coultre 235
Le Mille 24
Le Roy & Fils 223
Lea, Samuel 592
Leach, Bernard 161
Lebrun, Marc-Augustine 573
Lecomte-Vernet, C.E.H. 147
Leeds Creamware 162
Leigh, Vivien 59, 261, 263
Leitz, Ernst Canada Ltd. 513
Leleu Art Deco 273
Lelong, Rene 504
Lenci 162
Lenci 248, 250
Lennon, John 552-555
Leopold Ltd. 582
Lesturgeon, D. 215
Leuchars, William 632
Levinger, Heinrich 587
Lewis, Jerry Lee 550
Ley, Timothy 612
Lias, John and Henry 618
Lias, Messrs 595
Liberty & Co. 176, 177, 211, 220, 257, 523, 579, 600, 602, 631
Liberty Motors 411
Light, Edward 508
Ligurian 156
Like A Flash 25
Limbach 146
Lincoln, C. 76
Lincoln, Elizabeth Neave Lingenfelter 183
Lindbergh, Charles 21, 569
Lindean Mill 409
Linen Presses 326
Lines, G. & J. 644, 646
Linnaeus, Sir Charles 64
Linnit, John 636
Linossier, Claudius 238
Linthorpe 162
Linwood, Matthew 632
Lione & Co. 63
Liquid Lino 16
Live Aid 550
Liverpool Creamware 164
Livery Companies 114
Lloyd, Harold 264
Loetz 406, 430, 433
Loetz 476
Lofgren, Nils 551
Lofthouse, Mary 600
Log Cabin/Sarsaparilla 403
London Punch House, The 523
London Stereoscopic Co. 84, 512
London to Ladysmith via Pretoria 67
Longcase Clocks 216-219
Longfellow, Henry 54
Longton Hall China 165
Lord Nelson 64
Lorenzl 68, 477
Lorre, Peter 58
Loughlin, John 630
Lowboys 327
Lowestoft China 164
Loyal Suffolk Troop 36
LR 166
Lucie Rie China 166
Ludlow, Hal 441
Ludwigsburg 148
Lugosi, Bela 58
Lund, Benjamin 128
Lustre China 167
Lutyens, Sir Edwin 97, 299, 324
Lynn, F. 494
Lynn, Thos. Oldmeadon 208
Lyon, Danny 527
Lyon, Nogaret A. 297
Lytton, Lord Edward Bulwer 67

M & S 611
Macfarlane, Walter 461
Machin, Arnold 198
Macintyre, James & Co. 176, 177
Maggini, Giovanni Paolo 509
Magnani, Anna 58
Maker, Harvey 47
Makin, George & Sons 226
Manchester Amateur Photo Soc. 87
Mangie, Edward 601
Manhattan Melodrama 446
Mannheim 223
Manning, J. 455
Mansanari 462
Mansell, Nigel 505
Mansfield, Katherine 50
Mantel Clocks 220-227
Manton, John, Son & Co. 45
Maple & Co. 302
Mappin & Webb 576, 581, 602
Mappin Brothers 583
Mappin, John Newton 575
Marble & Alabaster 478-481
Marblehead Pottery 99, 100
Marc, Hy. 214
Marc, Hy. 227
Marchinville, M. 439
Marconi, Guglielmo 56
Marcus, Eugen 578
Marfia Kalap 17
Marie Sophie 490
Märklin 492-494
Marks, Gilbert 598
Marot, Clement 64
Marsh, Jacob 620
Marshall & Summers 624
Martin Brothers 167, 168
Martin, B. 452
Martin, F 645, 649
Martinware 167

Masaka 510
Masakatsu 511
Masatami 510
Maserati 499
Mason Factory 660
Massier, Clément 143, 144
Mathsson, Bruno 290
Mauter, Conrad 357
Maw & Co. 108
Maw, S. Son & Thompson 456
Mayer & Newbold 109
Mayer, T.J. & J. 16
Mayhew and Ince 313, 320
Mays, Raymond 17
Mazzega, A. 409
MB & C 633
MC 439
McCartney, Paul 550, 552, 555
McLeish, Minnie 107
Meccano 19
Mechanical Music 482-485
Mecklenburg-Schwerin Infantry 38
Meigh, Charles 109
Meiji 160, 186, 236, 237, 256, 285, 462, 464, 465, 473, 566, 662
Meir, John 179
Meissen 169-173
Melba, Nellie 570
Mêne, Pierre-Jules 70
Menpes, Mortimer 541
Mercedes-Benz 498, 499
Mercier & Fils 210
Mercier, E. 258
Mercier, S. 531
Merrythought 641
Metchless Metal Polish 17
Meure, Peter 596
Meure, Peter 629
MGM 444-447
Michael, George 554
Michigan Central Railroad, The 564
Mickey Mouse 93, 233, 246, 247
Microscopes 452, 453
Miers and Field 572
Miers, John 572
Mighty Thor, The 22
Miller, Arthur 260
Mills, Nathaniel 608, 632, 633
Ming 113-117
Ming Dynasty 466, 472
Mingozzi 502
Minnie Nouse 246
Minton 174, 175
Mirecourt, Antonie Aubry A. 507
Mirrors 486-489
Miscellaneous Glass 422-423
Miscellaneous Silver 607
Mitchison, John 625
Mitsuaki 463
MJJ 589
MM 439
Mobile & Alabama Grand Truck Railroad Co. 565
Model Ships 490, 491
Model Trains 492
Models 494, 495
Möhslinger, Franz 230
Moigniez, J. 68, 71
Moir, D.J. 495
Moller, Henrik 620
Monroe, Marilyn 260, 261
Montelupo 155, 157
Montgolfier Balloons 20
Montgomery, James 66
Moorcroft 106, 107
Moorcroft China 176, 177
Moore, John 620
Moore, Roger 215
Moore, Thomas 65
Moreau, Louis 69
Moreau, Mathurin 71
Morelli, P. 480
Morris & Co. 28, 291, 334, 423
Morris Cowley 497
Morris Mini 500
Morris, Tom 441
Morris, William 65
Morrison, Jim 551
Morrisware pottery 107
Morson & Stephenson 605
Morton, James Ltd 456
Moser 412
Motley, John 217
Motor Vehicles 496-501
Motoring Irems 502-505
Moulsen, William 599
Mount Washington Glass Co. 415, 421
Mtot MV Agusta Agenzia 503
Muddle, Tho. 215
Müeller, Alfred 255
Mugs 612, 613
Muirhead, Jas. 222
Muller, Berthold 604, 610, 631
Müller, Clemens 562
Muller, Martin Friedrich 593
Munro 442
Murdoch, T. 40
Murphy, H.G. 468
Murray, Keith 200
Musical Instruments 506-509
Mustards 614, 615
Muston & Garth 220
Muzio, Claudia 569
My Man Jeeves 65
Mysterious Dr. Fu Manchu, The 444
Mystery, Chinese Crystal Gazer 25

Nairne, J.G. 517
Nanbe Seizo 186
Nantgarw China 178
Naomitsu 510
Naoyuki 566
Nathan & Hayes 580
National Bank of New Zealand 514
Natural History of Spiders and Other Curious Insects 66
NB 593
Neal, John 228
Negretti & Zambra 513
Nelson, Horatio 52, 64
Neri, A. 64
Netsuke 510, 511
Neuber, Johann Christian 438
New Caledonia 514
New England Glassworks 417
New Frontier, The 444
Newcomb College Pottery 100
Newell, Steven 422
Newman and Guardia 84, 85, 87, 88
Newport pottery 106
Newton, Sir William John 536
NG 593
Nicholas, Jules 248
Nihon Satsuma 187
Nilson, J.E. 151
Nimroy, Leonard 261
Niven, David 262
Nixon, Harry 133
Nobusane 462
Nock, H. 33
Noke, Charles 133, 134, 136
Nolan, W. 622
Northern Bank Ltd. 516
Northern Song 115
Norton, J. & Co. 101
Nove 157
Nuvolari, Tazio 502
Nye, Bill 98
Nymphenburg 178

O'Neale, Jefferyes Hammett 112
O'Neill 252
Occasional Tables 368-371
Oeovres 64
Oertling, Aug. 452
Oettner, Andreas Philipp 151
Ogden, Thomas 216
Ogura 510
Ohneburg, M. 332
Ohr, George E. 98
Ohrström, Edvin 434
Oliver, Peter 536
Olivier, Laurence 260, 264
Olympia, The 490
Optical Instruments 512, 513
Oriental Bank Corporation 518
Osterspey, Jakob 148
Otto, F. 184
Our Boys Clothing Co., The 654
Oxo 19

Pack, E. & Sohne Siegfried Waffen 34
Packard 497
Paget, T.H. 465
Paillard, Victor 70
Palermo 157
Panon Camera Shoko Co. 84
Panormo, J. 508
Pantoscope 454
Paper Money 514-519
Paper Weights 424-425
Papier Mâché 520, 521
Paramount 444-447
Paramount-Artcraft 445
Pardoe, Thomas 178
Paris, Gaveau 531
Parker 270, 271
Parkinson, John 67
Parkinson, Norman 524
Parnell, Charles, S. 53
Parsons, John & Co. 583
Pauli, F. 197
Pavely, Ruth 180
Pavlova, Anna 54, 568, 569
Paxton, Peter 443
Payne, Humphrey 612
PC 600
Peake, Robert 603
Pearlware 178, 179
Pearson, John 238
Peaston, William 610
Peche, Dagobert 146
Pecs, Zsolnay 139
Pellat, Apsley 410
Pembroke Tables 372, 373
Penn, Irving 525
Pepfenhauser, Johann 580
Pepys, Samuel 51
Perchin, Michael 632
Pere Marquette Transportation Co., The 564

Périn-Salbreuz, Louis-Lié 539
Pero, John 593
Perriand, Charlotte 337
Perry, Son & Co 238
Petit, Jacob 143
Petit, N. 311
Petty, Tom 550
Peugeot, A. & Cie 255
Pewter 522, 523
Phalibois, J. 60
Philadelphia and Lancaster Turnpike Road 563
Philip, Hugo 443
Philips 254
Phillipe, P. 73
Phillippe, Patek & Co. 234, 235
Phillips's Tea 16
Philos 497
Photographs 524-529
Piaf, Edith 570
Pianos 530, 531
Piazza, A. 478
Pickard, Thornton 87
Pickering, A. 495
Picture Frames 532, 533
Pierrot and Harlequin 484
Pilar d'Algesiras 66
Pilgrim, The 447
Pilkington's Lancastrian 110
Pilot 548
Pipes 534, 535
Pistols 40, 41
Pistor and Martins 457
Pitchers & Ewers 616
Pitt, William, The Elder 52
Planché, Andrew 131
Planck, Ernst 512
Plank, Ernst 494
Platinum Blonde 446
Plê, Henri Honoré 68
Plentywin 24
Plummer, William 574
Pocket watch 247
Podio, Joseph Felix 574
Poertzel, Prof. Otto 464
Poiterin, G. 190
Poland Springs 405
Pomeroy, Frederick William 68
Poole Pottery 180
Popeye 247
Porringers 617
Portrait Miniatures 536-539
Posters 246, 247
Postnikov, A. 578
Pothier, I. 296
Pound, John 655
Powder Flasks 42, 43
Power, John 601
Power, Tyrone 265
Pradier, Jean-Jacques 70
Prangnell, Eileen 180
Prattware 182
Preiss, Johann Phillipp Ferdinand 75
Pressenda, Giovanni 506
Price, Chrles 615
Priess, F. 462-464
Priest, W. 368
Prince Charles and Princess Diana 53
Prince Philip 571
Prints 540-543
Prodigal Daughters 445
Provincial Bank 515
Pugin, A.W.N. 316, 343
Pugin, E.W. 290
Punjabis 35
Pye 548

Qianlong 114, 116, 117, 122, 132, 140, 237, 466, 467
Qing Dynasty 466, 467, 609
Queen Elizabeth II 52, 571
Queen Mary 52
Queen Victoria 53
Quilts 544-547

Rachmaninoff, Sergei 57
Radios 548
Rakuzan 510
Ramsden, Omar 469, 577, 579, 611, 627
Randall, John 182
Ranford, Samuel 207
Rathbone, Basil 262, 263
Rawlins and Sumner 613
Rawlins, Charles 637
RB 613
RC 581, 600
Read, A.B. 181
Reagan, Ronald 569
Red Headed Woman 444
Reed & Barton 598
Reeds/Bitters 401
Regina Corona 485
Reid, William Ker 629
Reimirol & Cie 233
Reiss 616
Renault 498
Renmiken zo 186
Renpet Nefret 27
Republic 444
Republic of China 564
Revere, Paul 98, 99
Reymond, Georges 439
Rhead, Charlotte 108
RI 600
Richard, Alfred 75
Richards, George John 574
Richards, James 41
Richards, Keith 552
Richmond, Thomas 539
Richter 104
Ridgway, John 109
Rie, Lucie 166
Rifles & Guns 44, 45
Rigaud, Pre. 227
RKO 444, 446
RN 614 ,617
Robbins, John 624
Robert, John & Co. 590
Robertson and Darling 625
Robertson, Allan 443
Robin, The Boy Wonder 23
Robins, T. 625
Robins, Thomas 619
Robinson, Edward G. 265
Robinson, William Heath 442
Robots 549
Rocca, Guiseppe 506
Rochard, Simon Jacques 536
Rochette, Laurent 316
Rock n Roll 550-555
Rockingham China 182
Roddenberry, Gene 261
Rodigue, M. 259
Roe, Ebenezer 622
Rohrers 405
Rolex 234
Rolling Stones, The 552
Rolls-Royce 496, 497, 500
Romanelli, Pasquale 479
Romanelli, R. 478
Rookwood 183
Rosse, Susan Penelope 537
Rough Notes on the Birds 66
Roullet & Decamps 61
Round Up, The 445
Roux Roman Bordier & Compre 232
Royal and Ancient Game of Golf, The 441
Royal Dux China 184
Royal West Kent Regt. 36
Rozenburg pottery 139
RS 624
RSFBJ 253
Ruffony 92
Rugs 556-559
Ruhlmann, Jacques-Emile 360
Rundell, Philip 586
Ruskin 185
Russell, Gordon 374, 388
Ruyckevelt, Ronald Van 205
Ryozan 187

Sadler 200
Sage, Augustin Le 605
Salla, A. 62
Salo, Gasparo da 509
Salter, Geo. & Co. 456
Salts & Peppers 618
Samovar 241
Samplers 560, 561
Sander, Peter 553
Sanderson Brothers 35
Sandison, L.G. 442
Sandoz, Gerard 587
Sandwich Glass Co. 410
Saratoga Mt. Glassworks 408
Satsuma 186, 187
Satsuma yaki cho Shuzan 187
Saturday Evenings Girls Pottery 98, 99
Sauce Boats 619
Savage, Lyman & Co. 214
Savona 155, 156
Savory, Adey Bellamy 607
Savory, Joseph & Albert 595
Sawyer, Richard 585
Saxon Electroral Guard 38
Sayer, Robert 540
Scarpa, Tobia 434
Scent Bottles 426, 427
Sch., H. 103
Scheid, Georg Adam 471
Scheier Pottery 100
Scheir Pottery 476
Scheurich, Paul 169
Schiapareli 243
Schlictig, J.G. 333
Schliepstein, Gerhard 147
Schmid, Johann Heinrich 147
Schmidt, Charles 183
Schmied, F.L. 64
Schoeller & Co. 255
Scholler, W. & Sons 138
Schuppe, John 594
Scott, Captain Robert F. 570
Scott, James 625
Screens 328, 329
Seaman, R.J. Beattie 503
Seaman, Richard 567
Secretaire Bookcases 330, 331
Secretaires 332, 333

Seguso, Archimede 416
Seikozan 187
Sekkosai Masayoshi 463
Selby's Illustrations of British Ornithology 65
Selby, Prideaux John 65
Semmes, Raphael 55
Sené, Jean-Baptiste-Claude 328
Serpoukhoff Regiment of Lancers 39
Seth Thomas Clock Co. 230
Settees & Couches 334-337
Settle, John 590
Sevin, Pierre 452
Sèvres 174, 188-190
Sewing Machines 562
Sex Pistols, The 550, 553
Seymour, Charles 583
Seyrig, Delphine 260
SH 252
Shades 428
Shall We Dance 444
Shand Mason 494
Shapland and Petter 309
Share Certificates 563-565
Sharp, C. 45
Sharp, Robert 593, 603, 616
Shaw, Richard Norman 314
She Done Him Wrong 447
Shell Oils 18
Shelley, Samuel 536
Shibayama 566
Shield 30
Shigemasa to 510
Shirayamadani, Kataro 183
Shoes 244, 245
Shounsai 511
Shu-Sin 26
Shutoho 450
Sibley, Richard 604, 605, 622
Sicardi, Louis-Marie 538
Side Tables 374, 375
Sideboards 338, 339
Siege of Khartoum 519
Siena 155
Signed Photographs 567-571
Silbermann, J.T. 454
Silhouettes 572
Silver 573-634
Simmance, Eliza 135
Simmons, R. 494
Simon & Halbig 248, 249
Simonnet, Lucien 530
Sinclair, R. 65
Sinding, Stephan 74
Sir Golly de Wogg 65
Sissons, W. and G. 588
Sitting Bull 57
Skeleton Clocks 228, 229
Sky Jump 25
SL 634
Sloane, Hans 67
Smart, John 539
Smart, Thos. 216
Smith & Sons 210
Smith, Beck and Beck 512
Smith, Benjamin 630
Smith, D. 603
Smith, Daniel 593, 616
Smith, Frederick 578
Smith, George 342, 343
Smith, George 600
Smith, Gordon Grant 443
Smith, Henry 509
Smith, Samuel 206
Smith, Stephen 588, 597, 616
Smith, Tate, Hoult and Tate 595
Smiths Celestial Globes 452
Snow White and the Seven Dwarfs 246
Snuff Bottles 635-637
Sofa Tables 376, 377
Somerville, John 553, 554
Somme, Théophile François 142
Son of the Golden West 445
Son the Shiek, The 446
Sondag, Rudolph 573
Song Dynasty 75, 114, 659
South Staffordshire 256, 257
Spangler, W.H. 303
Spencer 41
Spencer, Gervase 538
Spider-man 22
Spirit of Ectasy 92, 93
Spirit of the Wind 93
Spode 191
Sprimont, Nicholas 598
Springer, Col. Robert C. 56
Springsteen, Bruce 551
St. Louis 424, 425
Stabler, Harry 181
Stabler, Phoebe 108, 180
Staffordshire 192-195
Stamp, James 592
Stands 340-341
Stanley, Henry M. 55
Star Trek 261
Starkey, Michael 624
Starr, Ringo 552
Stasuma yaki Nangakurei 186
Steele, Edwin 182
Steiff 640, 641, 649
Steinbeck, John 57
Stephenson's Rocket 493
Stephenson, George 57
Stephenson, Robert 57
Stern, Bert 528
Stevens & Williams 406
Stevens, A.J. & E. 460
Stickley Bros. 361
Stickley, Gustav 302, 334, 338, 339, 368, 370, 382, 384, 391
Stickley, L. & J.G. 272, 300, 301, 337, 342, 358
Stinton, James 206
Stockwell, E.H. 588
Stoker, Bram 50
Stools 342-345
Storr, Paul 590, 593, 594, 603, 610, 624, 630, 634
Stowell, A. 221
Strachan, Alexander James 637
Stradivari, Antonio 507
Strand Bridge 563
Strauss, Richard 571
Stravinsky, Igor 50
Studer, Jacob Henry 65
Suffolk Bitters 405
Suites 346-349
Summers, Gerald 299, 325
Summers, William 637
Sunbeam 500
Sunbeam Record Car 494
Sunderland 167
Sundial 398
Super Shell 16
Super Steer-A-Ball 25
Superboy 22
Susse Frs Edts 75
Sutiro, The 445
SW 624
Swan 270, 271
Swan Hunter & Wigham Richardson Ltd. 491
Swanson, Gloria 264
Swift, John 591
Swords 46, 47
Sykes, Charles 92

Tabard, F. 508
Tadolini, Scipione 399
Talavera 156
Talbot 499
Tallent, Garry 551
Tang Dynasty 115
Tankards 429
Tankards 620
Tantalus 429
Tapestries 638, 639
Tarzan and his Mate 445
Tatham, H. 41
Tattersall's Ltd. 565
Taylor, L.D. 490
Taylor, Robert 265
Taylor, Samuel 622
Taylor, Taylor & Hobson 88
Tea & Coffee Sets 621
Tea Caddies 622
Tea Kettles 623
Teapot 247
Teapots 624-626
Teco pottery 99
Teddy Bears 640-641
Teenage Mutant Ninja Turtles 23
Teiko 566
Teimin 450
Telescope 240, 452-455
Temple, Shirley 262
Tenerani, Pietro 69
Tennyson, Lord Alfred 571
Terrey, J.E. 628
Tête Jumeau 252
Textiles 642, 643
The Art of Glass 64
Theatrum Botanincum 67
Theobalds, William 601
Theodolites 452, 453
Theroude, A. 251
Thieme, Carl 146
Thomason 242
Thompson, John 495
Thompson, Robert 'Mouseman' 273, 300, 301, 322, 361, 390
Thorn, Leonard 221
Thorsteinsson, Silvert 616
Three Gun Bomb Dropper 25
Three Stooges, The 263
TIC 592
Tiffany & Co. 90, 212, 213, 235, 259
Tiffany Studios 422, 428
Tilly, John 66
Tittecke, Abraham 597
TJ 632
TNT 555
Toast Racks 627
Tobacco box 239
Toikka 416
Tomlinson, William 218
Tomomasa 511
Tomoo 542
Tompion, Tho. 232
Tong balance 240

Tongue, John 601, 632
Tononi, Carlo 506
Toscanini, Arturo 54, 58
Toshosai Hozan 451
Toto Shugetsu 511
Toulouse-Lautrec, Henri de 541, 542
Townsend, Pete 550
Toyo saku 451
Toys 644-653
Tracy, Spencer 58
Trapp Family 568
Travel Requistes 654, 655
Travelling Wilburys, The 550
Trays & Salvers 628
Tregent, James 232
Triang 247
Troughton & Simms 453
Trunks & Coffers 386-389
Tsar Nicolas II 567
Tsubas 48, 49
Tsunekawa 450
Tunney, Gene 571
Tureens 629
Turpin, Ben 262
Tuscan 155
Twells, Louis B. 228
Typewriters 456, 457
Tyson, Mike 570

Ulanova, Galina 569
Ulster Bank 517
Union porcelain 98, 101
Union Special Machine Co. 562
Unior Gold Mining Co. 565
Unique Art Manufacturing Co. 646
Unite, George 611
United Artists 446
Universal System of Natural History 64
Unknown, The 445
Urbino 155, 157
Urns 396-399
Urns 630
Urquahart, Duncan 626

Vachette, Adrien-Jean-Maximilien 438
Valentino, Rudolph 260, 263
Vallotton, Felix 541
Valspar enamels 17
Valton 75
van Hoften, James D. 57
Vardon, Harry 441
Vases 430-434, 631
Vedar III 418
Venice China 196
Venini 410
Vesta Cases 632
Veyrat 610
Vienna China 197
Villanis, E. 68
Vinaigrettes 633
Vincent, Edward 591
Vincent, William 622
Virgin Records 550
Vitagraph 445
Vittoz, E. 222
Voller Brothers 506
Voltaire, François Marie Arouet de 64
Vonham, Frederick 80
Voyage to the Islands Madera, A 67
VR BP 295
Vuilliamy, Tho. 232
Vuitton, Louis 654, 655
Vyse, Charles 107, 108

Waagen, Arthur 70
Waals, Peter 390
Wadeheath 247
Wadere, H. 585
Wagner 197
Waistcoats 243-245
Wakefield Castrol 17
Wakefield, John 614
Wakelin, Edward 622
Wakelin, John 575
Walker Bros. 255
Walker, F. 62
Walker, John 583
Wall Clocks 230, 231
Wallace, John 442
Wallace, R. & Sons Mfg. Co. 578
Wallendorf 147
Waller, Fats 570
Walley Pottery 100
Wallis, Thomas 624
Waltham Clock Co. 231
Ward, Joseph 584, 626
Ward, Rowland 67
Wardrobes & Armoires 390, 391
Warhol, Andy 55, 540, 551
Warmers 634
Warneke, Wijnand 606
Warner Brothers 446
Warner's Patent 41
Warrington, Simcock 216
Washstands 392
Watches 232-233
Water, H.B. & Co. 411
Waterman 270,271
Watkins & Hill 454
Watners 401, 404
Watson, John 586
Watson, L. 217
Watson, Micael 505
Watson, W. & Sons 87, 452, 453
Watts, Jn. 209
Way Out West 447
WC/JL 617
Weathervanes 656-657
Webb 407, 426
Webbe, A.J. 579
Webber, Andrew Lloyd 568
Wedgwood 198-200
Weilandt, Nicholas 217
Weinberg, Max 551
Well at the World's End, The 65
Wellby, D. & J. 631
Wellings, Norah 251
Wemyss 201
Werum, Christopher 581
West, Mae 263
West, Matthew 573
Western Zhou Dynasty 26
Westerwald 202
Westley Richards 44
Weydinger, Joseph-Leopold 190
WF 613
WG 617
Whaley 229
Whatnots 393
Whatson, Sam 209
Whieldon 203
Whight & Mann 562
Whipham, Thomas 592
Whitaker, Robert 552
White, Ethelbert 540
White, J. & Sons 457
White, John & Co. 440
White, John 591
White, Samuel 624
Whitehead Aircraft Ltd. 563
Whitford, Samuel 586
Whiting, Riley 225
Wickes, George 619
Wien, J.S. 233
Wilde, Oscar 567
Wilding, Dorothy6 23
Wilkie, E.H. 513
Wilkinson Ltd. 107
Wilkinson, Henry & Co. 582
Willaume, David 574
Willems, Joseph 112
Willette, A. 259
Williams, David 218
Williams, Hank Snr. 57
Williams, Ralph Vaughan 51
Williamson, Henry 590
Williamson, John 219
Willmore, Joseph 633
Wilmott, Louis 608
Wilson & Co. 33
Wilson & Sons 455
Wilson, J. 442
Wilson, Woodrow 54
Wincarnis 18
Wine Coolers 394, 395, 634
Wine Funnels 634
Wine Glasses 435-437
Wisdome, John 620
Wizard of Oz, The 447
WJD 18
WMF 522, 523, 609
Wodehouse, P.G. 65
Wolfsohn, Helena 139
Wonder, Stevie 551
Wood 658-662
Wood China 203
Wood, Enoch 203
Wood, Ralph 124, 203
Wood, Samuel 584, 624
Worcester China 204-207
Worcestershire Regt. 37
Wordsworth, William 55
Work Box & Games Tables 378-381
World Before the Flood, The 66
Wright, John 66
Wright, Lewis 65
Wrist Watches 234, 235
Writing Tables & Desks 382-385
WS 590
Wustlich, Otto 104

Yasukyo saku 186
Yavno, Max 525
Yi Dynasty 27, 160
Yokohama Specie Bank 515
Yonge, Geor. 208
Yongzheng 140
Yosci tsukuru 451
Young Rajah, The 444
Young, Brigham 56
Young, Wm. 218
Ysart, Paul 424
Yuan 114

Zale, Tony 569
Zecchin, Vittorio 475
Zimmerman, A.J. Ltd. 583
Zincke, Christian Friedrich 439, 537
Zorer, Christoph 576